Praise for
COALESCENT

"Baxter is at the top of his form here: formally audacious, constantly surprising, clinically subversive of genre norms, cosmic irony always at hand to awe and undercut the reader."
—*Locus* magazine

"*Coalescent* is more than an introduction, and stands on its own as one of Baxter's best novels."
—*The Denver Post*

"A gripping read . . . Baxter continues to prove that he has phenomenal insight into humanity, giving us not only an inspired book, but more to think about in regards to our own evolution. *Coalescent* is a stand alone read but. like ~~all~~ ~~~~, leaves the reader wanting more."

Also by Stephen Baxter

MANIFOLD: TIME
MANIFOLD: SPACE
MANIFOLD: ORIGIN
EVOLUTION
COALESCENT

With Arthur C. Clarke
TIME'S EYE
SUNSTORM

COALESCENT

STEPHEN BAXTER

DEL
REY

BALLANTINE BOOKS • NEW YORK

Coalescent is a work of fiction. Names, places, and incidents either are products of the author's imagination or are used fictitiously.

A Del Rey® Book
Published by The Random House Publishing Group

Copyright © 2004 by Stephen Baxter

All rights reserved under International and Pan-American Copyright Conventions. Published in the United States by Del Rey Books, an imprint of The Random House Publishing Group, a division of Random House, Inc., New York, and simultaneously in Canada by Random House of Canada Limited, Toronto.

Del Rey is a registered trademark and the Del Rey colophon is a trademark of Random House, Inc.

www.delreydigital.com

ISBN 0-345-45786-2

Manufactured in the United States of America

First Edition: December 2003
First Mass Market Edition: December 2004

OPM 9 8 7 6 5 4 3 2 1

To Neil, Ann, Katherine, Anna, and Clare Baines

ONE

I have come to stay in Amalfi. I can't face going back to Britain—not yet—and to be here is a great relief after the swarming strangeness I encountered in Rome.

I've taken a room in a house on the Piazza Spirito Santo. There is a small bar downstairs, where I sit in the shade of vine leaves and drink Coke Light, or sometimes the local lemon liqueur, which tastes like the sherbet-lemon boiled sweets I used to buy as a kid in Manchester, ground up and mixed with vodka. The crusty old barman doesn't have a word of English. It's hard to tell his age. The flower bowls on the outdoor tables are filled with little bundles of twigs that look suspiciously like fasces to me, but I'm too polite to ask.

Amalfi is a small town nestling in a valley on the Sorrento Peninsula. This is a coast of limestone cliffs, into which the towns have been carved like seabird nesting grounds. People have adapted to living on a vertical surface: there are public staircases you can follow all the way to the next town. Nothing in Italy is new—Amalfi was a maritime power in the Middle Ages—but that sense of immense age, so oppressive in Rome, is absent here. And yet much of what shaped the horror in Rome is here, all around me.

The narrow cobbled streets are always crowded with traffic, with cars and buses, lorries and darting scooters. Italians don't drive as northern Europeans do. They just go for it: they *swarm*, as Peter McLachlan would have said, a mass of individuals relying on the unwritten rules of the mob to get them through.

And then there are the people. Just opposite my bar there is a school. When the kids are let out in the middle of the day— well, again, they swarm; there's really no other word for it.

They erupt into the piazza in their bright blue smocklike uniforms, all yelling at the tops of their voices. But it's soon over. Like water draining from a sieve, they disperse to their homes or to the cafés and bars, and the noise fades.

And, of course, there is family. You can't get away from that in Italy.

Amalfi used to be a center for making rag paper, a technique they learned from the Arabs. Once there were sixty mills here. That number has dwindled to one, but that one still supplies the Vatican, so that every papal pronouncement can be recorded forever on acid-free rag paper, now made fine enough for a computer printer to take. And that surviving Amalfi mill has been operated without a break by the same family for *nine hundred years*.

The swarming crowds, the thoughtless order of the mob, the cold grasp of ancient families: even I see visions of the Coalescents everywhere I look.

And I see again that extraordinary crater, collapsed in the middle of the Via Cristoforo Colombo, with the plume of gray-black tufa dust still hanging in the air above it. Workers from the offices and shops, clutching cell phones and coffees and cigarettes, peered into the hole that had suddenly opened up in their world. And the drones simply poured out of the crater, in baffling numbers, in hundreds, thousands. Obscured by the dust, they looked identical. Even now there was a kind of order to them—but nobody led. The women at the fringe would press forward a few paces, blinking at the staring office workers around them, and then turn and disappear back into the mass, to be replaced by others, who pushed forward in turn. When it reached the edge of the road, the flowing mob broke up, forming ropes and tendrils and lines of people that washed forward, breaking and recombining, probing into doorways and alleyways, swarming, exploring. In the dusty light they seemed to blur together into a single rippling mass, and even in the bright air of the Roman afternoon they gave off a musky, fetid odor.

I suppose I'm trying to compensate. I spend a lot of my time alone, in my room, or walking in the hills that loom over the towns. But a part of me still longs, above everything else, to *go back*, to immerse myself once more in the Coalescents' warm tactile orderliness. It is an unfulfilled longing that, I suspect, will stay with me until I die.

How strange that my quest to find my own family would lead me to such mysteries, and would begin and end in death.

chapter 2

It began at a strange time for everybody, in fact. The news had just emerged about the Kuiper Anomaly, the strange new light beyond the sky. London is the place to be when a story like that breaks, the kind of massive, life-changing news that you want to share with your friends, at the office watercoolers or in the pubs and coffee bars, and chew over the latest wrinkles.

But I had to go home, to Manchester. It was duty. I had lost my father. I was forty-five.

My father's house, the family home where I had grown up, was one of a short street of identical suburban properties: a neat little semidetached, with scraps of lawn at the front and back. Standing in the drive on a dazzling, bright September morning, I tried to keep control of my emotions, tried to think like a stranger.

When they were built in the fifties, not long before my birth, these little houses must have seemed desirable compared to the back-to-back terraces of the inner city, and a hell of a lot better than the tower blocks that would follow in a few years' time. But now, in the first decade of the new century, the brickwork looked hasty and cheap, the little flower beds were subsiding, and some of the exterior work, like the plaster-covered breeze blocks that lined the driveways, was crumbling. Not much of the street's original character remained. There were plastic-framed double-glazed windows, rebuilt roofs and chimney stacks, flat-roofed bedrooms built over the garages, even a couple of small conservatories tacked on the front of the houses opposite my father's, to catch the southern light. After nearly fifty years the houses had mutated, evolved, become divergent.

The people had changed, too. Once this had been a street of

young families, with us kids playing elaborate games that paused only when the occasional car came sweeping in off the main road. One car to a household then, Morris Minors, Triumphs, and Zephyrs that fit neatly into the small garages. Now there were cars everywhere, cluttering every drive and double-parked along the pavement. Some of the small gardens had been dug out and paved over, I saw, to make even more room for the cars. There wasn't a kid to be seen, only cars.

But my home, my old home, was different from the rest.

Our house still had the original wooden concertina-style garage doors, and the small wooden-framed windows, including the bay at the front of the house where I used to sit and read my comics. But I could see how the woodwork was chipped and cracked, perhaps even rotten. There had once been an ivy, an extravagant green scribble over the front of the house. The ivy was long gone, but I could see the scars on the brickwork where it had clung, palely weathered. Just as when my mother had been alive—she'd gone ten years earlier—my father would only do the most basic renovation. He did most of his work for the building trade, and he said he had enough of building and decorating during the week.

One of the few nods to modernity I could spot was the silver box of a burglar alarm stuck prominently on the front wall. Dad's last burglary had been a few years back. It had taken him days to notice it, before he had discovered the neatly broken lock on the garage door, and the smashed window in the car he rarely used, and the neatly coiled turd on the floor. Kids, the police had said. Panic reactions. My father had been defiant, but he had been troubled by the draining of his own strength, and his inability to fight back as he always had before against the cruel selfishness of others. I had paid for the alarm and arranged for it to be installed. But, I'm ashamed to say, this was the first day I'd actually seen it in place.

Alarm or not, a single windowpane in the front door gaped, broken and unrepaired.

"George Poole. It is George, isn't it?"

I turned, startled. The man standing before me was bulky, balding. He wore clothes that were vaguely out of joint, perhaps too young for him—bright yellow T-shirt, jeans, training shoes, a chunky-looking cell phone stuck in a chest pocket.

Despite his bearlike size you instantly got an impression of shyness, for his shoulders were hunched as if to mask his height, and his hands, folded together in front of his belly, plucked at each other.

And despite the graying hair, high forehead, and thickened neck and jaw, I recognized him straight away.

"Peter?"

His name was Peter McLachlan. We had been in the same year at school, for most of our careers in the same classes. At school he was always Peter, never Pete or Petey, and I guessed he was the same now.

He stuck out his hand. His grip was tentative, his palm cold and moist. "I saw you drive up. I bet you're surprised to find me standing here."

"Not really. My father used to mention you."

"Nice duffel coat," he said.

"What? . . . Oh, yeah."

"Takes me back to school days. Didn't know you could buy them anymore."

"I've a special supplier. Caters for the style-challenged." It was true.

We stood there awkwardly for a moment. I always did feel awkward with Peter, for he was one of those people who could never relax in company. And there was something different about his face, which took me a couple of seconds to cue in on: he wasn't wearing the thick glasses that had always been inflicted on him as a kid in the seventies. I couldn't see the telltale eye widening of contacts; maybe he'd had laser surgery.

"I'm sorry about breaking your window," he said now.

"That was you?"

"It was the night he died. Your father didn't come to the door when I brought him his evening paper. I thought it was best to check . . ."

"You found him? I didn't know."

"I would have had to go into the house to fix the window, and I thought I shouldn't until you—you know."

"Yes." Moved by his thoughtfulness, I gently slapped his shoulder. I could feel muscles under his sleeve.

But he flinched. He said, "I'm sorry about your father."

"I'm sorry you had to find him." I knew I had to say more. "And thanks for checking on him."

"Didn't do him much good, I'm afraid."

"But you tried. He told me how you used to look out for him. Mow the lawn—"

"It wasn't any trouble. After all, I got to know him when we were kids."

"Yes."

"You haven't been in there yet, have you?"

"You know I haven't if you saw me park," I said a bit sharply.

"Do you want me to come in with you?"

"I don't want to trouble you anymore. I should do this."

"It's no trouble. But I don't want to impose . . ."

We were circling around the issue, still awkward. In the end, of course, I accepted the offer.

We walked up the drive. Even the tarmac was rotten, I noted vaguely; it crackled softly under my weight. I produced a key, sent me by the hospital that had notified me of the death. I slid it into the Yale lock, and pushed the door open.

There was a noisy bleeping. Peter reached past me to punch a code into a control box set in an open cupboard in the porch. "He gave me the code," he said. "The burglar alarm. In case of false alarms, you know. That's how I was able to turn it off, when I broke the window to get in. In case you were wondering how . . . I was a key holder. But he had a deadbolt and a chain, which was why I had to break the window—"

"It's okay, Peter," I said, a little impatient. *Shut up.* He never had known when to do that.

He subsided.

I took a breath and stepped into the house.

Here it all was, my childhood home, just as it had always been.

In the hall, a hat stand laden with musty coats, a telephone table with a seventies-era handset and a heap of scribbled names, numbers, and notes piled up in a cardboard box, notes in Dad's handwriting. In an alcove Dad had carved out of the wall, a small, delicate statue of the Virgin Mary. Downstairs, the dining room with the scarred old table, the small kitchen with greasy-looking stove and Formica-topped table, the living room with bookshelves, battered sofa and armchairs, and a surprisingly new TV system, complete with VCR and DVD. The narrow staircase—exactly fifteen stairs, just as I'd counted as a child—up to the landing, where there was a bathroom, the master bedroom and three small rooms, and the little hatchway to the attic. The wallpaper was plain, but it didn't look as shabby as I'd expected, or feared. So Dad must have decorated since I'd last visited, five or six years ago—or had it done, perhaps by Peter, who stood on the doormat behind me, a great lumpen presence. I didn't want to ask him.

It all felt small, so damn small. I had a fantasy that I was a giant like Gulliver, trapped in the house, with my arms stuck in the living room and kitchen, my legs pinned in the bedrooms.

Peter was looking at the Virgin. "Still a Catholic household. Father Moore would be proud." The parish priest, kindly but formidable, when we were both kids; he had given us our First Communions. "Do you practice?"

I shrugged. "I'd go to Mass at Christmas and Easter with my dad, if we were together. Otherwise I guess you'd call me lapsed. You?"

He just laughed. "Since we know so little about the universe, religion seems a bit silly. I miss the ritual, though. It was comforting. And the community."

"Yes, the community." Peter was from Irish Catholic stock, my mother's family Italian American. Both clichés, in our way, I thought. I stared up at Mary's plaster face, frozen in an expression of pained kindness. "I suppose I was used to all this stuff as a kid. Faces staring down at me from the wall. Seems vaguely oppressive now."

Peter was studying me. "Are you okay? How do you feel?"

Irritation flared. "Fine," I snapped.

He flinched, and pressed his forefinger to the space between his eyes, and I realized he was straightening nonexistent glasses.

I was suddenly ashamed. "Peter, I'm sorry."

"Don't be. I'm not here to make you feel sorry. This is your time." He spread his big hands. "Everything you do now, you're going to remember for the rest of your life."

"Christ, you're right," I said, dismayed.

I walked the few paces to the kitchen door, which was open. There was a musty smell. A cup, saucer, and plate sat with bits of cutlery on the table. The plate was covered with cold grease and dried flecks of what looked like bacon. There was a little puddle of liquid in the bottom of the cup, on which green bacterial colonies floated; I recoiled.

"I found him in the hall," Peter said.

"I heard." Dad had suffered a series of massive strokes. I picked up the cup, saucer, and plate and carried them to the sink.

"I don't think the fall itself hurt him. He looked peaceful. He was lying just there." He pointed to the hall. "I used his phone to call the hospital. I didn't go into the rest of the house. Not even to clean up."

"That was thoughtful," I murmured.

I looked out of the kitchen window at the small back garden. The grass needed cutting, I noted absently, and the pale spires of ant colonies towered amid the green. In one corner of the garden, where they would get the most light, were the skeletal forms of the azaleas, my father's pride and joy, cherished for years—Christ, decades. But at this time of year they were as barren and stark as at midwinter.

I looked down at the sink. Clean dishes, looking dusty, were racked up, and there was a stink of staleness from the drain. I turned on the taps and tipped the mold out of the cup into the drainer. The cold tea poured away, and green bacterial spots slid silently, but there was still plenty of scum clinging to the cup. I looked for washing-up liquid, but couldn't see any, even in the small, crammed cupboard under the sink. I pulled the cup out of the water again and looked into it, feeling foolish, futile, ensnared.

Peter was standing in the kitchen door. "I'll bring over some Fairy Liquid if you like."

"Fuck it," I snarled. I stepped on the pedal of the bin in the cupboard and threw in the dirty cup. But the bin was half full and stank, too, of what might have been rotten fruit. I got to my knees and began to root in the cupboard, pulling aside cardboard boxes and yellowed plastic bags.

"What are you looking for?"

"Bin liners. The whole damn place is a mess." Everything

seemed *old*, even the cans and plastic dispensers of cleaning stuff in the cupboard, old and dirty and crusted and half used up but never thrown out. My searching was getting more violent; I was scattering stuff around the floor.

"Take it easy," Peter said. "Give yourself a minute."

He was right, of course. I forced myself to back up.

He had left this, my father had, this little set of dirty dishes. He'd never come back to finish the tea. He'd just stopped, his life cutting off at that moment, like a film breaking. Now I had to tidy this stuff away, a chore I used to loathe as a kid: He never would clean up after himself. But when it was done, *there would be no more,* no more dirty cups and greasy crockery, not ever. And as I worked my way through the house, room by room, I would be fixing messes that he would never make again.

I said, "It's as if he's dying, a little bit more. Just by me doing this."

"You had a sister. She was older than us, wasn't she?"

"Gina, yes. She came over for the funeral. But she went back to America. We're going to sell the house; we share it fifty-fifty, according to Dad's will—"

"America?"

"Florida." My maternal grandfather had been a GI, an Italian American, stationed briefly in Liverpool some time before the war. You might say my mother was a premature war baby, conceived during that stay. After the war the GI had not fulfilled his promise to come back to England. I told Peter all this. "But there was a happy ending," I said. "My grandfather got back in touch sometime in the fifties."

"Guilt?"

"I suppose. He was never a true father. But he sent money over, and took Mum and Gina over to the States a few times, when Gina was small. Then we inherited some property in Florida, left to my mother by a cousin she'd met over there. Gina went to work over there, took the house, raised a family. She works in PR—I'm sorry, it's a complicated story—"

"Family stories are like that."

"Episodic. No neat narrative structure."

"That makes you uncomfortable."

It was a perceptive remark I wouldn't have expected from

the Peter I'd known. "I suppose it does. It's all kind of a tangle. Like a spider's web. I felt as if I got myself out of it, by building a life in London. Now I have to get tangled up again." And I resented it, I realized, even as I tried to finish these few last chores for my father.

Peter asked, "Do you have kids of your own?"

I shook my head. It occurred to me I hadn't asked Peter a single question about himself, his life since school, his circumstances now. "How about you?"

"I never married," he said simply. "I was a policeman—did you know that?"

I grinned; I couldn't help it. Peter the school dork, a copper?

Evidently he was used to the reaction. "I did well. Became a detective constable. I retired early . . ."

"Why?"

He shrugged. "Other things to do." I would find out later what those "other things" were. "Look, let me help. Go see to the rest of the house. I'll sort this out—I can fill a bin liner for you."

"You don't have to."

"It's okay. I'd like to do it for Jack. If I find anything personal I'll just leave it."

"You're very thoughtful."

He shrugged. "You'd do the same for me."

I wasn't sure if that was remotely true, and I felt another layer of guilt pile up on already complicated strata. But I didn't say any more.

I started upstairs. Behind me I heard a dim bleeping, the baby-bird sound of Peter's cell phone calling for attention.

My father's bedroom.

The bed was unmade, the sheets crumpled, a dent in the pillow where his head had lain. There was a waist-high basket nearly full of dirty clothes. On the small bedside cupboard, where an electric lamp was alight, a paperback book lay facedown. It was a biography of Churchill. It was all as if my father had left it a moment ago, but that moment had somehow been frozen, and was now receding relentlessly into the past, a fading still image on a broken video.

I turned off the lamp, closed the book. I poked about the room listlessly, unsure what to do.

The dressing table before the window had always been my mother's domain. Even now the rows of family photographs—my graduation, smiling American grandkids—looked just as when I'd last seen them, perhaps as she'd left them. The dust was thicker behind the photographs, as if Dad had barely touched this corner since she'd gone. There was some mail scattered on the surface, a few bills, a postcard from Rome.

Cancer had taken my mother. She had always been a young mother, just nineteen when I was born. She still seemed young when she died, right to the end of her life.

On his last night my father had emptied his pockets here, never to fill them again. I threw a grimy handkerchief into the laundry basket. I found a little change and some bills, which I absently pocketed—the coins felt heavy and cold through the fabric of my pocket—and his wallet, slim and containing a single credit card, which I also took.

The dresser had two small drawers. In one was a bundle of mail in opened envelopes, from my sister, my mother, my younger self. I pushed the letters back into the drawer, a task for later. In the other drawer were a few checkbook stubs, a couple of bank account passbooks, and bank statements and credit card bills, held neatly together with treasury tags. I swept all this stuff up and crammed it into my jacket pocket. I knew I was being a coward in my priorities: closing down his financial affairs was something I could do on remote control, easily, without leaving my comfort zone.

Suits hung in the wardrobe. I riffled through them, evoking a smell of dust and camphor. They were cut to Dad's barrel-shaped frame and would never have fit me, even if they hadn't been old, worn at cuffs and shoulders, and indefinably old-mannish in their style. He had always folded his shirts and set them one on top of another in the shallow drawers of the wardrobe, and there they were now. Shoes, of patent leather and suede, lay jumbled up on top of each other in the bottom of the wardrobe: he had been wearing his slippers when they took him to the hospital. There were more drawers full of underwear, sweaters, ties, tiepins and cufflinks, even a few elastic armbands.

I explored all this, touching it hesitantly. There was little I would want to keep: a few cufflinks, maybe, something I would associate with him. I knew I should just sweep up all this stuff, cram it into bin bags, and take it to an Oxfam shop. But not today, not today.

Gina had already said she didn't want any of this old stuff. I resented her not being here, for running back to the Miami Beach sun and leaving me to this shit. But she always had kept herself out of the family fray. *Peter McLachlan was a better son than she was a daughter,* I thought bitterly.

I was far from finished, but enough for now. I got out of there.

On the landing walls were more Catholic ornaments, more Marys—even a Sacred Heart, a statue of Jesus with His chest exposed to show His burning heart, the realization of a particularly gruesome medieval "miracle." I wondered what I should do with all the Catholic tokens. It would seem disrespectful, if not sacrilegious, to just dump them. Perhaps I could take them to the parish church. I realized with a start that I had no idea who the priest was; no doubt he was decades younger than me.

I glanced up at the hatchway to the access to the attic space. It was just a little square panel cut out of the ceiling. If I wanted to go up there I ought to find a ladder.

The hell with that. Bracing against the wall of the stairwell, I managed to get one foot on top of the banister rail and lifted myself up. This was how I used to climb into the attic as a kid. I could see spiderwebs, and bits of unevenness in the ceiling paintwork that cast fine shadows from the landing window light. I pushed at the hatch. It was heavier than I remembered, and, evidently a long time undisturbed, had glued itself into place. But it came loose with a soft ripping noise.

I poked my head up into the attic. It smelled dusty but dry. I reached up to a switch mounted on a cross beam; the light, from a bulb dangling from a rafter, was bright but reluctant to spread far.

I set my hands on the edge of the frame. When I tried the last step—kicking off the banister rail and pushing up with my arms—I was suddenly aware of my greater bulk, and feebler muscles; I wasn't a kid anymore. Just for a second it felt as if

I wouldn't make it. But then my biceps took the strain. I hauled my belly up through the hatch, and sat heavily on a joist that ran across the roof, breathing hard.

Boxes and trunks receded into the shadows like the buildings of a gloomy miniature city. There was a sharp smell of burning, as the dust on the bulb was incinerated. Looking down into the brightness of the house was like a vision of an inverted heaven. I was rarely allowed up here when I was small, and even as a teenager never allowed to fulfill my ambitions of turning it into some kind of den. But I had always loved the sense of remoteness I got when I passed out through the skin of the house into this other world.

I swung up my legs. The roof was low; I had to crawl over the boards I had nailed down over the ceiling insulation in my twenties, when it had emerged that fiberglass insulation wasn't good for you. Soon my hands were filthy and my knees were starting to ache.

Most of the boxes contained Dad's stuff—he had been an accountant, his last few years working independently, and there were files from his various employers, even a few musty old accountancy training manuals. I doubted I would need to keep any of this stuff; it was more than eight years since he had retired. In one box I found a small red clothbound book, an ancient, battered, and much-used set of log tables: *Knott's Mathematical Tables (Four-Figured)*. The binding of the little volume was actually *fraying*. And here, too, was a slim cardboard box that contained a slide rule, wooden, with scales marked in pasted-on paper. I could barely see the tiny numerals, but the plastic of the slider was yellow and cracked. I put the rule back in the box and set it aside with the log tables, meaning to take them down later.

I moved deeper into the loft. I found one box marked XMAS DECORATIONS—WILMSLOW, 1958—WILMSLOW, 1959—MANCHESTER, 1960 . . . and so on, down through the years, right up until, I saw, the year of my mother's death. In a box of assorted junk I found a couple of stamp albums and a half-filled box of first-day covers, plastic board games in ugly seventies-era boxes—and a scrapbook of pictures, original sketches, photographs patiently clipped out of magazines and comics, all pasted onto thick gray paper. My sister's, from her own childhood years. It was a cobbled-together depiction of a family legend, a tale told by grandfathers and great-aunts: the story of a girl called Regina, who had supposedly grown up in Britain in the time of the Romans, and when Britain had fallen she had fled to Rome itself. And we were Regina's remote descendants, so the story went. I'd grown up believing it, until maybe the age of ten. I put the book aside; perhaps Gina would like to see it again.

Then I came to a box that caught my eye: TV21S, read the label. (GEORGE). With some eagerness I hauled the box back to the light and opened it up. Inside I found a pile of comics—"*TV Century 21*, Adventures in the 21st Century—Every Wednesday—7d." They were neatly stacked, from a very grubby and fragile issue number 1 downward. This was, of course, the comic that had been spun out of the Gerry Anderson science fiction puppet shows during the sixties, and a monumental part of my young life. I had thought my parents had burned this stack when I got to around twelve, with my uncertain adolescent acquiescence.

I opened one at random. The comic was a broadsheet. The much-thumbed paper was thin, delicate, and all but rubbed away along its spine. But the full-color strips within were as bright as they had been in 1965. I found myself in issue 19, in which the Kaplan, the leader of the Astrans—aliens oddly like huge jelly beans—is assassinated, JFK-style, and Colonel Steve Zodiac, commander of the mighty spacecraft Fireball XL5, is assigned to find the killers and avert a space war.

"Mike Noble." It was Peter; he had stuck his head through the hatch.

"Sorry, I was lost again."

He handed me a mug of tea. "My mug, my tea, my milk. I guessed you don't take sugar."

"Right. Mike who?"

"Noble. The artist who drew *Fireball* for *TV-Twenty-one*— and later *Zero X*, and *Captain Scarlet*. Always our favorite."

Our? . . . But, yes, I remembered that a shared interest in the Anderson shows, and later all things science-fictional and space-related, had been an early hook-up between me and Peter, links that had overcome my reluctance to be associated with the school weirdo. "I thought my parents burned this lot."

Peter shrugged. "If they'd told you they were up here they'd never have gotten you out of the attic. Anyhow, maybe they meant to give them back to you someday, and just forgot."

That sounded like Dad, I thought sourly.

"Do you have a complete run in there?"

"I think so," I said dubiously. "I think I kept buying it right until the end."

"Which end?"

"Huh?"

He clambered a little higher—I saw he had brought a stepladder—and perched on the rim of the open hatch, legs dangling. "*TV Twenty-one* went through a few changes as sales began to fall. In nineteen sixty-eight—issue one ninety-two— it merged with another title called *TV Tornado*, and began to run more non-Anderson material. Then, after issue two forty-two, it merged with a *Joe Ninety* comic and began a second series from number one . . ."

"The last issue I remember buying had George Best on the cover. How do you know all this?"

"I researched it." He shrugged. "You can reclaim the past, you know. Colonize it. There's always more you can find out. Structure your memories." He sighed. "But for *TV Twenty-one* it has gotten harder with time. There was a surge of interest in the eighties—"

"When our generation reached our thirties."

Peter grinned. "Old enough to be nostalgic, young enough to form irrational enthusiasms, rich enough to do something about it. But now we're passing through our forties, and . . ."

"And we're becoming decayed old fucks and nobody cares anymore." *And*, I thought, *we are being picked off one by one by the demographics, as if by a relentless sniper.* I flicked through the comics, looking at the brightly colored panels, the futuristic vehicles and shining uniforms. "The twenty-first century isn't turning out the way I expected, that's for sure."

Peter said hesitantly, "But there's still time. Have you seen this?" He held up his cell phone. It was a complex new toy from Nokia or Sony or Casio. I didn't recognize it; I've no interest in such gadgets. But the screen was glowing with a bright image, a kind of triangle. "Just came in. The latest on the Kuiper Belt. The Anomaly."

Two days after the discovery, everybody on Earth within reach of a TV probably knew that the Kuiper Belt is a loose cloud of comets and ice worlds that surrounds the solar system, stretching all the way from Pluto halfway out to the nearest star. And a bunch of astronomers, probing that chill region with radars or some such, had found something unusual.

Peter was explaining earnestly that the image on his screen wasn't a true image but had been reconstructed from complicated radar echoes. "It's the way you can reconstruct the structure of DNA from X-ray diffraction echoes—"

The little screen gleamed brightly in the dark of the loft. "It's a triangle."

"No, it's three-dimensional." He tapped a key and the image turned.

"A pyramid," I said. "No—four sides, all of them triangles. What do you call it?"

"A tetrahedron," Peter said. "But it's the size of a small moon."

I shivered in the cold gloom, feeling oddly superstitious. It was an awful enough time for me already, and now there were strange lights in the sky . . . "Something artificial?"

"What else could it be? The astronomers got excited just from their detection of straight-line edges. Now they're seeing *this*." His pale eyes were bright, reflecting the blue glow of the little screen. "Of course not everybody agrees; some say this is just an artifact of the signal processing, and there's nothing there but echoes . . . There's talk of sending a probe. Like the Pluto Express. But it might take decades to get there."

I looked down at the comics. "They should send Fireball," I said. "Steve Zodiac would be there in a couple of hours." Suddenly my vision misted, and a big heavy drop of liquid splashed from my nose onto a colored panel. I wiped it off hastily. "Shit. Sorry." But now my shoulders were shaking.

"It's okay," Peter said evenly.

I fought for control. "I hadn't expected to fucking cry. Not over a fucking *comic*."

He took my mug, still full, and headed down the stairs. "Take as long as you want."

"Oh, fuck off," I said, and so he did.

* * *

When I got over my spasm I clambered down out of the loft, bringing only the slide rule and log tables with me. I'd intended to head back to my city-center hotel, comforted that at least I'd pushed through the barrier, at least I'd been inside the house, and whatever else I turned up couldn't distress me as much as today.

But Peter had one more surprise for me. As I came down the stairs I saw he was hurrying out of the door carrying what looked like a cookie tin, a deep one.

"Hey," I snapped.

He stopped, looking comically guilty, and actually tried to hide the damn tin behind his back.

"Where are you going with that?"

"George, I'm sorry. I just—"

Instantly my innate suspicion of Peter the school weirdo was revived. Or maybe I just wanted to act tough after crying in front of him. "You said you wouldn't touch anything personal. What's this, theft?"

He seemed to be trembling. "George, for Christ's sake—"

I pushed past him and snatched the box out of his hands. He just watched as I pulled the lid off.

Inside was a stash of porn magazines. They were yellowed, and of the jolly skin-and-sunshine *Health and Efficiency* variety. I leafed through them quickly; some were twenty years old, but most of them postdated my mother's death.

"Oh, shit," I said.

"I wanted to spare you."

"He hid them in the *kitchen*?"

Peter shrugged. "Who would have thought to look there? He always was smart, your dad."

I dug deeper into the box. "Smart, but a randy old bugger. It's porn all the way down—wait."

Right at the bottom of the tin was a picture in a frame. It was a color photograph, very old, cheap enough for its colors to have faded. It showed two children, age three or four, standing side by side, grinning at the camera from out of a long-gone sunny day. The frame was a cheap wooden affair, the kind you can still pick up in Woolworth's.

Peter came to see. "That's the house. I mean, *this* house."

He was right. And the faces of the kids were unmistakable.

"That's me." The girl was a female version of me—the same features, the blond hair and smoky gray eyes, but more delicate, prettier.

Peter asked, "So who's that?"

"I don't know."

"How old did you say your sister was?"

"Ten years older than me. Whoever this is, it isn't Gina." I carried the photograph toward the daylight, and peered at it long and hard.

Peter's voice had an edge to it. Perhaps he was taking a subtle revenge for my accusation of theft. "Then I think your father was hiding more from you than your comics."

A click sounded from the living room. It was the video recorder. The machinery of my father's home continued to work, clocks and timers clicking and whirring mindlessly, an animated shell around the empty space where Dad had been.

chapter 3

Everything started to go wrong for Regina on the night the strange light flared in the sky. Looking back, she would often wonder at how the great events of the silent sky were so linked to the business of the Earth, the blood and the dirt of life. Her grandfather would have understood the meaning of such an omen, she thought. But she was too young to comprehend.

And the evening had started so well, so brightly.

Regina was just seven years old.

When she heard that her mother was getting dressed for her birthday party, Regina abandoned her dolls and ran whooping through the villa. She scampered all the way around three sides of the courtyard, from the little temple with the *lararium*—where her father, looking exasperated, was making his daily tribute of wine and food to the three *matres*, the family gods—and through the main building with the old burned-out bathhouse she was *forbidden* ever to enter, and then to her mother's bedroom.

When she got there Julia was already sitting on her couch, holding a silver mirror before her face. Julia brushed a lock of pale hair from her forehead and murmured irritably at Cartumandua, who stepped back from her mistress, combs and pins in her hands. The slave was fifteen years old, thin as a reed, with black hair, deep brown eyes, and broad, dark features. Today, though, her face was a sickly white and slick with sweat. There were two other slave women here, standing by with colored bottles of perfume and oils, but Regina didn't know their names and ignored them.

Regina ran forward. "Mother! Mother! Let me fix your hair!"

Cartumandua held back the comb, murmuring in her thick country accent, "No, child. You'll spoil it. And there is no time—"

It was just as she had spoken to Regina when she was a little girl, when Cartumandua had been given to her as her companion and guardian. But Regina didn't have to take orders like that from a slave. "No!" she snapped. "Give me the comb, Cartumandua. Give it to me!"

"Sh, sh." Julia turned and took her daughter's small hands in her delicate, manicured fingers. She was wearing a simple white tunic, soon to be replaced by the evening's elaborate garments. "What a noise you're making! Do you want to frighten all our guests away?"

Regina gazed into her mother's gray eyes, so much like her own—*the family eyes, eyes filled with smoke,* as her grandfather always said. "No. But I want to do it! And Cartumandua says—"

"Well, she's right." Julia pulled at Regina's own unruly mop of blond hair. "She's trying to fix my hair. I can't go into my birthday party looking as if I've been held upside down by my ankles all day, can I?" That made Regina laugh. "I'll tell you what," Julia said. "Let Carta finish my hair, and then you can help with my jewelry. How would that be? You're always so good at picking out the right rings and brooches—"

"Oh, yes, yes! Wear the dragon."

"All right." Julia smiled and kissed her daughter. "Just for you I'll wear the dragon. Now sit quietly over there . . ."

So Regina sat, and Julia turned back to her mirror, and Cartumandua resumed her work on her mistress's hair. It was an elaborate style: the center was braided, drawn back, and wrapped around, while another braided piece rose directly from Julia's forehead to be pulled back across the head. The silent attendant women anointed the hair with perfume and oils, and Cartumandua inserted jet pins, dark against Julia's bright golden hair, to keep it all in place.

Regina watched, rapt. It was a complicated style that took time and care to assemble, and needed the focused attention of a whole team of assistants—which was, as Regina had heard her mother say in one of those adult conversations she didn't really understand, why she wore it in the first place. *Other* people might be burying their money in the family mausoleum, but she was going to *wear* the family's wealth and let everybody know about it. And it was fashionable on the continent, at least according to the images on the most recent coins to reach Britain from the continental mints. Julia was determined to keep up with the latest styles, even if she was stuck out here in the southwestern corner of Britain, about as far from Rome as you could get without falling off the edge of the world.

Regina loved parties, of course. What seven-year-old didn't? And Julia gave plenty of them, lavish affairs that illuminated the villa here on the outskirts of Durnovaria. But even more than the parties themselves, Regina loved most of all these elaborate preparations: the subtle scents, the soft clinks of the bottles in the hands of the silent slaves, the hissing of the combs through her mother's hair, and Julia's instructions, soft or firm as required, as she expertly commanded her little team in their complex task.

As the styling continued Julia smiled at Regina and began to sing, softly—not in her native British tongue, but in Latin, an old, strange song taught her by her own father. Its words, about mysterious vanished gods, were still baffling to Regina, despite her own fitful attempts to learn the language at her grandfather's insistence.

At last Julia's hair was finished. Cartumandua allowed the attendants to approach with their bottles of perfume and cream. Some of these little bottles were carved in elaborate shapes; Regina's favorite was a *balsarium* in the shape of a bald-headed child. Julia selected a face cream of sandalwood and lavender on a base of animal fat, a little white lead for her cheeks, soot to make her eyebrows contrast strikingly with her blond hair, and one of her most precious perfumes, said to come from a faraway place called Egypt. Regina was under strict instructions never to play with any of this stuff, for it had become so hard to find; until things got back to normal, so her mother said, and the big trade routes that spanned the Empire opened up again, this was all the stock she had of these wonderful things, and they were *precious*.

Finally it was time to select the jewelry. As Julia slid a selection of rings onto each finger, most of them set with precious stones and intaglios, Regina demanded that she be allowed to bring her mother the dragon brooch herself. It was a very old British design, but rendered in the Roman style, a swirl of silver that was almost too big for Regina to hold in her small hands. She approached Julia with the marvelous brooch held out before her, and her mother smiled, the white lead on her cheeks shining like moonlight.

It was midsummer, and the afternoon was long. The sky was blue as a jackdaw's egg and free of cloud, and it stayed bright even when the sun had long disappeared.

By the slowly dimming light, the guests arrived, walking, riding, or in their chaises. Most of them came from Durnovaria, the nearest town. Some of them stood in the balmy summer air of the courtyard, around the fountain that had never worked in Regina's lifetime, while others sat in couches or basket chairs, talking, drinking, laughing. They began to pick at the food set out on the low slate tables. There were round loaves of fresh-baked bread, and bowls of British-grown fruit like raspberries, wood strawberries, and crab apples. In addition to salted meat, there were plenty of oysters, mussels, cockles, snails, and fish sauce—and, obtained at great expense, some figs and olive oil from the continent. The highlights were showy extravagances of culinary labor: dormice sprinkled with honey and poppy seeds, sausages with damsons and pomegranates, peahens' eggs in pastry.

The guests loudly admired Julia's latest decor. In the main hall the plaster walls were painted with blocks of purple or gray veined with blue, and the dado was an elegant design of small rectangles outlined in green. Regina had learned that the old design—nature-themed, with imitation marbling, garlands, and candelabra all adorned with ears of yellow barley—was now *seriously* out of fashion on the continent. Her father had complained loud and long about the expense of repainting the walls, and the difficulty of finding workmen these days. Her grandfather had just raised his thick eyebrows and said something about how absurd it was to paint one half of a villa when the other half had burned down and you couldn't afford to fix it . . .

But to Regina's young eyes, the new design looked much better than the old, and that was all that mattered.

The entertainment started soon after the first guests arrived. Julia had hired a storyteller, an old man—perhaps as old as fifty—with a great ferocious gray-black beard. He told a long and complicated story, entirely from memory, about how the hero Culhwch had sought the hand of the daughter of the giant Ysbadden. It was an ancestral tale of the olden days before the coming of the Caesars. Few people listened to him—even Regina was too excited to stay for long, though she knew it was a good story—but the old man would patiently tell and retell his stories all night, and as the party wore on, and as the drink had its effect, his deep voice would attract more attention. At the start of the evening, though, the musicians were more popular. They played a mixture of instruments from Britain and the Continent, bone flutes and panpipes, harps and citharas and tibias, and their bright music drifted like smoke on the still air.

Julia's father, Regina's grandfather, was here. Aetius was a towering soldier who, after adventures abroad, was now stationed at a mysterious, magic-sounding, faraway place called *the Wall*. And having traveled the length of the diocese of Britain for his only daughter's twenty-fifth birthday party, he stomped around the villa and grumbled loudly at all the expense—"It's as if the Rhine never froze over," he would say mysteriously.

Marcus, Regina's father, was a thin, clumsy man with severely cut dark hair and a drawn, anxious-looking face. He was dressed in his toga. This formal garment took skill to wear, for it was very heavy and you had to walk correctly to make the drapery fall easily, and Marcus wasn't used to it. So he walked about slowly and ponderously, as if he were wearing a great suit of lead. No matter how carefully he took each step—and he didn't *dare* sit down—the precious toga dragged on the floor, or folded and flapped awkwardly, or fell open to reveal his white tunic underneath.

But Marcus proudly wore his Phrygian cap, pointed forward at the front, which marked him out as an adherent of the cult of Cybele, old-fashioned but popular locally. Four hundred years after the birth of Jesus, Christianity was the religion of the empire. But in the provinces Christianity remained a cult of the cities and villas, with the countryside people—who comprised most of the population—still clinging to their ancient pagan ways. And even among the elite, older cults still lingered. Cybele herself was a mother goddess who had come from Anatolia, imported into Rome after a conquest.

If Marcus was always going to be awkward in polite company, Julia herself was every bit the hostess. She wore a long *stola* over a long-sleeved shift, tied at the waist. The thick material of the *stola*, brightly colored blue and red, fell in heavy folds, and she wore a mantle over her shoulder, pinned in place with the wonderful dragon brooch. Not a hair seemed out of place, and to Regina she lit up every room more brightly than any number of bronze lamps or candlesticks.

As for Regina herself, she flitted through the rooms and the courtyard, where the oil lamps and candles glimmered like fallen stars. She was shadowed by Cartumandua, who was under strict instructions about the foods Regina could eat and what she could drink (*especially* since the infamous incident of the barley ale). Everywhere Regina went people bent to greet her, the faces of the women thick with powder, the men greasy with sweat and the effects of wine or beer, but everyone smiling and complimenting her on her hair and her dress. She lapped up their attention as she recited her Latin verses or prayers to Christ, and danced to the bright music. One day, Regina knew, *she* would become a lady as grand and elegant as her mother, with her own retinue of slaves—none so clumsy and sallow as Cartumandua, she was determined about *that*—and she would be the center of attention at her own parties, every bit as lavish as her mother's, perhaps even at this very villa. And as the evening wore on, she just wished she could somehow drag the sun back up above the horizon, to put off the dread hour of bedtime a little longer.

But then her grandfather pulled her aside. He took her out through the folding doors at the end of the dining room and onto the terrace, amid the rows of apple trees and raspberry canes. The tiled floor was crumbling, but the view of the countryside was beautiful. The sky was darkling, and the first wan summer stars were poking through the blue; she could just see the pale river of stars that, at this time of year, ran across the roof of the sky. Regina had learned that the Latin word *villa* meant "farm": she could make out the silhouetted forms of the

barn and the granary and the other outbuildings, and the fields
where the cattle grazed during the day. In the rolling hills beyond the villa's boundary, a single cluster of lights twinkled. It
was a delightful night.

But Aetius's face was stern.

Aetius was a big man, a slab of strength and stillness, out of
place in this glittering setting. She had expected Aetius to
come to the party wearing his armor. But he had on a simple
tunic of unbleached wool, with strips of color at the hem and
sleeves. He wore a soldier's shoes, though, thick wooden soles
strapped to his immense feet with strips of leather. Though he
wore no weapon, Regina could see the scars cut deep into the
muscled flesh of his arm.

Marcus had told her that Aetius had served in the field army,
and had spent four years in Europe under the command of
Constantius, a British military commander who had taken his
army over the ocean so that he could make a play for the imperial purple itself. Constantius had been defeated. The field
army was dissipated or absorbed into other units, and never returned—save for isolated figures like Aetius, who now served
with the border forces. Marcus had muttered gloomily about
all this, and the weakened state of the army in Britain. But
Regina understood little, and had a sunnier outlook than her
grumpy old father anyway, and she thought the story of Constantius was rather exciting. An Emperor from Britain! But
when she asked about his adventures Aetius just looked at her,
his pale gray eyes sunken and dark.

Now he crouched down on his haunches to face Regina,
holding her small hand in one huge paw.

She stammered nervously, "What have I done wrong?"

"Where is Cartumandua?"

Regina glanced around, realizing for the first time that the
slave girl was not in her customary place, a few paces behind
her. "I don't know. I didn't get rid of her, Grandfather. It's not
my fault. I—"

"I'll tell you where she is," he said. "She's in her room.
Throwing up."

Regina began to panic. Being told off by Aetius was a *lot*
worse than any admonishment from her mother, and definitely

from her father; if Aetius caught you, it really did mean trouble. "I didn't do anything," she complained.

"Are you sure? I know what you *used* to do," he said. "You would make her run around in circles, until she was dizzy. Your mother told me about it."

It was shamefully true. "But that was a long time ago. It must be—oh, it must be *months*! I was just a *little* girl then!"

"Then why is Carta ill?"

"I don't know," Regina protested.

His eyes narrowed. "I wonder if I should believe you."

"Yes!"

"But you don't always tell the truth. Do you, Regina? I'm afraid you're becoming a spoiled and willful child."

Regina tried not to cry; she knew Aetius regarded that as a sign of weakness. "My mother says I'm a good girl."

Aetius sighed. "Your mother loves you very much. As I do. But Julia isn't always—sensible." His grip on her hands softened. "Listen, Regina. You just can't behave this way. Life won't be the same when you grow up. I don't know how things *will* be—but for sure they will be different. And Julia doesn't always understand that, I don't think. And so she doesn't teach *you*."

"Are you talking about Constantius?"

"That buffoon, among other things, yes—"

"Nobody tells me anything. I don't know what you mean. Anyway I don't care. I don't *want* things to be different."

"What we want makes very little difference in this world, child," he said levelly. "Now, as to Carta. You must remember she is a person. A slave, yes, but a person. Did you know she has the name of a queen? Yes, the name of a queen of the Brigantes, a queen who may have confronted the Emperor Claudius himself." The Brigantes were a tribe of the old days, as Regina had been taught, and it had been Claudius who had brought Britain into the Empire, long, long ago. "But now," said Aetius, "that family of royalty is so poor it has had to sell its children into slavery."

"My parents bought Carta for *me*."

"Yes, they did. But Carta is still the daughter of a princess. And you're lucky to have a slave attendant at all. Once there were slaves for everything. You would have a slave to call out the time for you—a human hourglass! But now, only your mother, and a few others, believe they can afford slaves. Anyhow you mustn't hurt Carta."

"But I didn't."

"And yet she is ill."

Regina thought back and remembered how pale Carta had looked during Julia's dressing. "But she was ill before the party. I *saw* her. Go ask her what's wrong."

"She was?" Still doubtful, Aetius released her hands. "All right. If you are lying, you know about it in your heart . . . *Oh.*" His eyes widened, his huge head tilted back, and he looked up into the sky.

Startled, she looked up, too. It took her a moment to spot the light in the sky. It was right in the middle of the great band of stars—*a new star,* brighter than any of the others, flickering like a guttering candle. People drifted out of the villa, drink and food in their hands, and their chatter faded as they gazed up at the strange light, their faces shining like coins in the last of the twilight.

Despite the warmth of the evening, Regina suddenly felt cold. "Grandfather, what does it mean?"

"Perhaps nothing, child." He folded her in his arms, and she pressed her slim warmth against his strength. She heard him mutter, "But it is a powerful omen, powerful."

During the night, after all the guests had gone home, Regina heard shouting. The raised voices, oddly like the cawing of crows, carried across the still air of the courtyard to Regina's room. It wasn't unusual for her mother and father to argue, especially after wine. But tonight it sounded particularly vicious.

With that going on, she found it impossible to sleep. She got out of bed, and crept along the corridor to Cartumandua's room. The night sky, glimpsed through the thick glass of the windows, seemed bright. But she avoided looking out; perhaps if she ignored that strange light, she thought, it would go away.

When Regina had been smaller she had often come into Carta's room to sleep, and though it had been some months since she had done so it still wasn't so unusual. But when

Regina appeared in the doorway Carta flinched, pulling her woolen blanket up over her chest. When she saw it was Regina she relaxed, and managed a smile, dimly visible in the summer twilight.

Regina crossed to the bed, the tiled floor cold under her bare feet, and crawled under the blanket with the slave. Vaguely she wondered whom Carta had thought had come to her room, whom she was afraid of.

Even here she could hear the drunken yelling of her parents. Though it wasn't cold, Carta and Regina clung to each other, and Regina nuzzled her face into the familiar scent of Carta's nightdress.

"Are you better now, Carta?"

"Yes. Much better."

"I'm sorry," she whispered.

"What for?"

"For making you sick."

Cartumandua sighed. "Hush. I've been ill, but it wasn't your fault."

"You've been stealing food again," said Regina, softly admonishing.

"Yes. Yes, that's it. I've been stealing food . . ."

Regina didn't notice the strained tone of her voice, for, cradled in Carta's arms, she was already falling asleep.

In the morning, there was no sign of her mother. Not that that was so unusual after a party. Servants and slaves moved to and fro, emptying lamps and cleaning away pots and sweeping floors. They looked tired; it had been a long night for them, too. The day was hot, much more sultry than yesterday, and Regina wondered if a storm was going to break.

Regina ate the breakfast of fruit and oats brought to her by Carta. There would be no schooling today, as a treat for her mother's birthday. Carta, who seemed just as pale as yesterday, tried to distract Regina with games. But today her terra-cotta dolls and little animals of carved jet seemed childish and failed to engage her attention. Carta found a wooden ball, but they could find no third to make up a game of *trigon*, and throwing the ball back and forth between the two of them was dull. Besides, it was too hot for such exercise.

Bored, restless, Regina roamed, trailed by a weary Cartumandua. She didn't find her mother, or Aetius, but at length she came across her father. He was in the living room, surrounded by his papyrus rolls and clay tablets. He was talking to a tenant, a thickset bearded man wearing a dun-colored tunic and breeches. Regina peered through an unglazed window; Marcus didn't notice her.

Marcus looked as pale as Carta, and, hunched over his columns of figures, more strained than ever. Midsummer was the end of the rent year, and it was time for Marcus to collect the rent he was due for his land, as well as the Emperor's taxes. But things weren't going well.

The farmer said in his thick brogue, "We haven't seen the Emperor's man for a year or more—probably two."

Marcus said doggedly, "I have kept the tax you paid me and will render it up duly at the next visit. Even if the system is sometimes—ah, inefficient—you must pay your taxes, Trwyth. As I must. You understand, don't you? If we don't pay our taxes, the Emperor can't pay his soldiers. And then where would we be? The barbarians—the *bacaudae*—the Saxons who raid the coasts—"

"I'm no callow boy, Marcus Apollinaris," the farmer growled, "and you show me no respect by treating me like one. And we haven't seen a soldier for nearly as long, either. None save that grizzle-haired father of your wife."

"You must not speak to me this way, Trwyth." Regina could see her father was shaking.

Trwyth laughed. "I can speak to you any way I want. Who's to stop me—you?" He had a small sack of coins in his hand; he hefted it and slipped it back into a pocket of his breeches. "I think I'll keep this, rather than let you add it to your hoard."

Marcus tried to regain control of the situation. "If you prefer to pay in kind—"

Trwyth shook his head. "I hand over half my yield to you. If I don't have to grow a surplus to pay you and the Emperor, I just have to feed myself, and what a relief *that* is going to be. And if you go hungry, Marcus Apollinaris, you can eat the painted corncobs on your walls. You let me know when the Emperor next comes calling, and I'll pay my respects. In the meantime, good riddance!"

Marcus stood unsteadily. "Trwyth!"

The farmer sneered, deliberately turned his back, and walked out of the room.

Marcus sat down. He tried to work through the lists of figures on his clay tablet, but quickly gave up, letting the tablet fall to the floor. He hunched over and plucked with his fingers at his face, chin and neck, as if for comfort.

Regina couldn't remember any tenant speaking to her father like that, *ever*. Deeply disturbed, she withdrew. Cartumandua followed her, just as silently, her broad face impassive.

They walked aimlessly around the courtyard. Still it was unbearably hot; still there was no sign of her mother. More than ever Regina wanted something to take her mind off her parents and their incomprehensible, endlessly disturbing problems. She almost missed her lessons: at least her thin, intense young tutor with his scrolls and slates and tablets would have been *company*.

After completing three futile circuits of the courtyard, still trailed by a passive Cartumandua, a strange impulse took hold of Regina. When she came to the doorway to the old bathhouse—instead of passing it as before—she just turned and walked through it.

Carta snapped, "Regina! You aren't supposed to be in there . . ."

And so she wasn't. But neither was her mother supposed to be in bed when the sun was so high, neither was a tenant like Trwyth supposed to withhold his taxes from the Emperor, neither were peculiar lights supposed to flare in the sky. So Regina stood her ground, her heart beating fast, looking around.

The roof of the bathhouse had burned off, but the surviving walls, though blackened and their windows unglazed, still stood. They surrounded a small rectangular patch of ground, thick with grass, weeds, and small blue wildflowers. This forbidden place, out of bounds for her whole life, was like a garden, she realized, a secret garden, hiding in the dark.

"Regina." There was Carta, in the doorway, beckoning her back. "Please. Come back. You're not supposed to be in there. It's not safe. I'll get in trouble."

Regina ignored her. She stepped forward gingerly. The soil and the grass were cool under her bare feet. Rubble, broken blocks of stone from the walls, cluttered the floor under the thin covering of soil, but she could see them easily, and if she avoided them she was surely in no danger. She came to a patch of daisies, buttercups, and bluebells. She crouched down in the soil, careless of how her knees were getting dirty, and began to pick at the little flowers. She had a vague notion of making a daisy chain for her mother; perhaps it would cheer her up when she eventually awoke.

But when she dug her fingers into the thin layer of earth, she quickly came to hard, textured stone beneath. It must be the floor of the bathhouse. She put her flowers aside and scraped away the soil with her hands. She exposed little tiles, bright colors—a man's face, picked out in bits of stone. She knew what this was; there was another in the living room. It was a mosaic, and these bits of stone, brick red and creamy white and yellow-gold and gray, were tesserae. She kept scraping, shuffling back on her knees, until she had exposed more of the picture. A young man rode a running horse—no, it was *flying*, for it had wings—and he chased a beast, a monster with the body of a big cat and the head of a goat. Eager to see more, she scraped at more of the soil. Some of the picture was damaged, with the little tiles missing or broken, but—

"I thought I'd find you here. The one place you aren't meant to be." The deep voice made her jump. Aetius had come into the bathhouse through a rent in the ruined wall at the back. He stood over her, hands on hips. He wore a grimy tunic; perhaps he had been riding.

Cartumandua said, "Oh, sir, thank the gods. Get her out of there. She won't listen to me."

He waved a hand, and she fell silent. "You'll be in no trouble, Cartumandua. I'll be responsible." He knelt down beside Regina and she peered into his face; to her relief she saw he wasn't being too stern. "What are you doing, child?"

"Grandfather! Look what I found! It's a picture. It was here all the time, under the soil."

"Yes, it was there all the time." He pointed to the young man in the picture. "Do you know who this is?"

"No . . ."

"He's called Bellerophon. He is riding Pegasus, the winged horse, and he is battling the Chimaera."

"Is there more of it? Will you help me uncover it?"

"I remember what was here," he said. "I saw it before the fire." He pointed to the four corners of the room. "There were dolphins—here, here, here, and here. And more faces, four of them, to represent the seasons. This was a bathhouse, you know."

"I know. It burned down."

"Yes. There was a sunken bath just over there, behind me. Now, don't you go that way; it's full of rubble now, but the bath's still there, and if you fell in you'd hurt yourself and we would all be in trouble. We used to have water piped in here—great pipes underground—our own supply from the spring up on the hill." He rapped at the mosaic. "And under the floor there is a hollow space, where they used to build fires under the ground, so the floor would be warm."

Regina thought about that. "Is that how it all caught fire?"

He laughed. "Yes, it is. They were lucky to save the villa, actually." He ran his finger over the lines of Bellerophon's face. "Do you know who made this picture?"

"No . . ."

"Your great-grandfather. Not my father—on your father's side." She dimly understood what he meant. "He made mosaics. Not just for himself. He would make them for rich people, all over the diocese of Britain and sometimes even on the continent, for their bathhouses and living rooms and halls. His father, and his father before *him*, had always done the same kind of work. It's in the family, you see. That was how they got rich, and could afford this grand villa. They were in the Durnovarian school of design, and . . . well, that doesn't matter."

"Why did they let it get all covered over?" She glanced around at the scorched walls. "If this bathhouse burned down all those years ago, why not rebuild it?"

"They couldn't afford to." He rested his chin on his hand, comfortably squatting. "I've told you, Regina. These are difficult times. It's a long time since anybody in Durnovaria or anywhere near here has wanted to buy a mosaic. In the good days your father's family bought land here and in the town, and they've been living off their tenants' rent ever since. But they really aren't rich anymore."

"My mother says we are."

He smiled. "Well, whatever your mother says, I'm afraid—"

There was a scream, high-pitched, like an animal's howl.

Regina cried out. "Mother!"

Aetius reacted immediately. He picked her up, stepped to the doorway over the scattered dirt, and thrust Regina at the slave girl. "Keep her here." Then he strode away, his hand reaching to his belt, as if seeking a weapon.

Regina struggled against Cartumandua's grip. Carta herself was trembling violently, and it was easy for Regina to wriggle out of her grasp and run away.

Still that dreadful screaming went on. Regina ran from room to room, past knots of agitated servants and slaves. She remembered that her father had been in the living room with his tenant and his figures. Perhaps he was still there now. She ran that way as fast as she could. Carta pursued her, ineffectually.

So it was that while Aetius was the first to reach Julia, his daughter, Regina found Marcus, her father.

Marcus was still in the living room, on his couch, with his tablets and scrolls around him. But now his hands were clamped over his groin. Red liquid poured out of him and over the couch and tiled floor, unbelievable quantities of it. *It was blood.* It looked like spilled wine.

Regina stepped into the room, but she couldn't reach her father, for that would have meant walking into the spreading lake of blood.

Marcus seemed to see her. "Oh, Regina, my little Regina, I'm so sorry . . . It was her, don't you see?"

"Mother?"

"No, no. *Her.* She tempted me, and I was weak, and now I am like Atys." He lifted his hands from his groin. His tunic was raised, exposing his bare legs, and a meaty, bloody mess above them that didn't look real. He was smiling, but his face was very pale. "I did it myself."

"You fool." Aetius stood in the other doorway now, with his strong arm around Julia. Julia was hiding her face in her hands, her head bowed against her father's shoulder. "What have you done?"

Marcus whispered, "I have atoned. And like Atys I will return . . ." His voice broke up as if there were liquid in his throat.

"Mother!" Regina ran forward. She was splashing in the blood, actually splashing in it, and now she could smell its iron stink, but she had to get to her mother. Still she kept on, running across the room, past the couch with the grisly, flopping thing that was her father.

But Julia twisted away and fled.

Aetius grabbed Regina and folded her in his arms, just as he had the night before, and no matter how she struggled and wept, he wouldn't release her to follow her mother.

chapter 4

I stayed in Manchester another seventy-two hours.

I retrieved my father's boxes of business material from the loft, and found a few more files downstairs. He'd actually carried on working after his nominal retirement, doing bits of bookkeeping for friends and close contacts. Much of this work concerned small projects in the building trade.

I spent the best part of a day checking through all this material, trying to close down any loose ends. There were actually some bits of work my father hadn't completed, a few fees he hadn't collected, but they were all for small amounts, and everything was resolved amicably. I came away with a short list of requests for the return of some material. Most of the contacts were his friends—I knew a couple of them myself—and most hadn't heard of the death. The round of calls was painful, and the friends' reactions brought back the immediacy of it all.

I checked through Dad's most recent bank statements. Most of the statement lines were unremarkable. But I did find a few orders for foreign checks. Some of these were for more than a thousand pounds, and they went out every month, usually in the first week. I had no idea what they were for. I considered calling the bank branch, and wondered if they would tell me what was going on.

But then I came to a month earlier in the year, without the regular foreign payment. It wasn't like Dad to be so untidy as to leave this gap. On an impulse I checked his check stubs. And sure enough, one stub showed how he'd bought a thousand pounds' worth of euros from a travel exchange desk in one of the Manchester stations—that transaction showed up in the statement. On the back of the stub he had written, in his neat hand, "March pmnt. To Mry Qn of Vgns, overdue." I imagined him parceling up the currency and pushing it into the post—an unwise way to handle money, but fast and effective.

"Mry Qn of Vgns." To the eye of a Catholic boy that cryptic note unraveled immediately: Mary Queen of Virgins. But I had no idea who this was—a church, a hospital, a charity?—nor why Dad had been handing over so much money to them for so long. I found nothing else in his correspondence to give me any clues. I put it to the back of my mind, with a vague resolution to follow up the lead and close down the contact.

The personal stuff was more difficult than the financial matters, of course.

There were photographs around the house: the framed family-portrait stuff on the dresser, the big old albums in their cupboard in the dining room. I flicked through the albums, moving back in time. Soon the big glossy colored rectangles gave way to much smaller black-and-white images, like something prewar rather than early sixties, and then they petered out altogether. There were surprisingly few of them—only one or two of me per year of my childhood, for instance, taken at such key moments as Christmas, and family summer holidays, and first days at new schools. It seemed an odd paucity of images compared to the screeds people produce now. But then, I realized, glimpsing through these portals into sunny sixties afternoons long gone, that my memories of great moments, like the day the training wheels came off my bike, were of my father's face, not of a magnifying lens.

I tried to be brisk. The Catholic tokens went to the parish. I gave most of Dad's personal stuff to the charity shops. I kept back the photographs, and a few books that had some resonance for me—an ancient AA road atlas mapping a vanished Britain, and some of his Churchill biographies—nothing I'd ever read or used, but artifacts that had lodged in my memory. I didn't *want* this stuff, but of course I couldn't bear to throw any of it out, and I knew Gina would take none of it.

I swept it all into a trunk and hauled it into the boot of my car. My boxed-up *TV21* collection went in there also, thus beginning a migration from one attic to another. I wondered what would happen to all this junk when I died in my turn.

I kept out the little picture of my "sister," though.

I had the phone disconnected, sorted out such details as the TV license, but left the utilities running, billed to my account, to keep the house dry and intact, the better to present it to prospective buyers. On the last morning I cut the grass, knocked over the anthills, and did a little brisk weeding. It seemed the right thing to do. I was going to miss those big old azaleas. I wondered about taking a cutting, but I didn't know how to. I didn't have a garden to grow it in anyhow.

I engaged a house clearance firm—"friendly and sympathetic service," according to the Yellow Pages. A surveyor with an undertaker's doggedly glum manner came, glanced efficiently over the furniture and utilities, and made an offer for the lot. It seemed ruinously low. Part of me, loyal to the notion of what my dad's reaction would have been, was inspired to fight back. But I just wanted shut of the business, as the surveyor surely calculated, and the deed was done.

The last step was to place the house with a real estate agent, where a kid with spiky gelled hair and a cheap suit lectured me about "market stress" and how long it would take to get an offer. We were, of course, negotiating over the sale of the home where I'd grown up; I suspected the Gelled Arsehole sensed my vulnerability. But fuck it. I signed the forms and walked away.

I left the keys with Peter. He promised to check over the place until it was sold. I felt uncomfortable with this—I didn't like the idea of becoming entangled in some kind of debt to him—but unless I was to house-sit myself I needed somebody to do what he was offering.

I didn't quite know why I was uncomfortable about Peter. There had always been something *needy* about him. And if Peter wanted to work his way back into my life, he had found an angle to do it. Perhaps, I thought, he imagined we would become Internet pen pals, swapping reminiscences about *TV21*. Perhaps, like the Gelled Arsehole, Peter had spotted my vulnerability and was exploiting it for his own ends.

Or maybe I was just being uncharitable. Whichever, as I set off back to London, I drove away watching him waving with a handful of keys.

* * *

When I got back to work, there was nothing for me to do, literally. Which tells you all you need to know about my career.

I worked for a smallish software development company called Hyf—a bit of Anglo-Saxon that is apparently the root of *hive*, for we were all supposed to be busy busy bees. We were based near Liverpool Street, in the upper floor of what used to be a small rail station, long disused. The office was open-plan, save for a small hardware section where minis hummed away in blue-lit air-conditioning. It was an environment of neck-high partitions, trendy curved desks that made it impossible to get close to your PC without stretching out your arms like a gibbon, and everywhere a flurry of polystyrene Starbucks containers, yellow stickies, postcards from skiing holidays, and the occasional bit of "comedy" Internet porn.

Walking down the central aisle under the pleasing architecture of the Victorian-era curved roof, I hurried along. I found I didn't want much to speak to anybody—and nor did they to me; most had probably already forgotten the reason I had been away. As usual there was a whole series of scents as I walked down that aisle. The combative mix of cigarette smoke and air-freshener sprays was overlaid with a strong coffee stink and the stale scents of yesterday's lunch. Sometimes, when I worked in there late at night, I could swear I picked up a subtle and unmistakable almond whiff.

I was privileged enough to have an office, one of a set arrayed along the side walls of the office, for I was a manager, in charge of "test coordination," as we called it. I hung up my jacket and dug a bottle of Evian water from the bottom drawer of the filing cabinet. I booted up my PC and waited for it to download my intranet mails. I riffled through the snail mail: just a few flyers from software utilities vendors.

Vivian Cave walked into the office next to mine. She was late thirties, perhaps forty, a midheight graying blonde. She spotted me through the glass walls that separated us, gave me a half smile, and raised an invisible glass to her lips. *Drink later?* I waved back. *Sure.*

The PC screen speckled with icons. I found a total of thirty-two mails, after four working days away. Just eight a day? And most of them were routine stuff about Internet viruses, an offer to sell an unused snorkel set, and a mighty eleven mails with soccer score updates sent to the rest of the office by one diligent observer working late during a European Champions League match. But nothing from my line manager, or the software development project managers whom I was supposed to work with.

No work for George today. I knew I should launch myself into the online reports, or storm around the office setting up meetings. With a role like mine, fighting for work was part of the job.

I kicked the door closed, sat down, and sipped slowly at my Evian.

I'd been here three years. It wasn't the first job of its kind I'd taken. I'd drifted into positions like this much as I'd drifted into my career in software development in the first place.

Leaving school, fairly bright but hopelessly unfit, I'd had vague *TV21* dreams of becoming a scientist—an astrophysicist maybe, probing the far reaches of the universe, or a space engineer, building and controlling rockets and spacecraft. I was bright enough for college, but a few "down-to-Earth" harangues from my dad the accountant had made me see the wisdom of keeping my options open.

I got a place at Warwick University, where I read math. It was a bright, friendly place, the math faculty at the time was sparky and innovative—the home of then-trendy catastrophe theory—and I soon found myself forgetting the ostensible reasons I'd gone there. Working my way tidily through the groves of axioms, postulates, and corollaries, I quickly hit my intellectual limits, but I discovered in myself a deep appreciation of logic and order.

In my last year I traipsed around the milk round of potential employers, trying to find something that would plug into that interest in mathematical logic. I found it in software development—which brings a wry smile to the lips of all my acquaintances who have ever found themselves staring at a blue screen with a baffling error message.

But software *ought* to be logical. The math underlying relational databases, for instance, accessed by virtually every Internet user every day, is pure and beautiful. There is a whole discipline called "formal methods" in which you set out what you want to achieve and write a program that is a *self-proof* that it will do exactly what it's supposed to do.

That was the dream, as I began my career—first in Manchester, and then, inevitably, in London, the center of everything in Britain. When I could afford it I took a small flat in Hackney, and started a gruesome daily traveling routine by bus and Tube. But as I started work, first in the software development departments of large corporations and then in independent development houses, I soon found that rigor was expensive—less so than the cost of fixing all the bugs later, but an upfront cost virtually nobody was willing to pay.

Eventually I drifted into testing, the one place where you are *supposed* to be rigorous. For a while I prospered. The fashion was for development methods that were, if not formal, at least structured and so open to inspection. I would draw up my test plans covering every conceivable condition the software could take, with predictions of how it should react. I turned up errors at every level from typos in the code to compilation into machine code to fundamental design flaws—but that was okay; that was the job, and it was *satisfying* to make things better.

But there was a constant pressure to cut costs on testing, which higher-level managers could never quite figure the benefit of, and endless turf wars between competing teams of developers and the testers come to rip to pieces "their" code. I started to be bypassed by development managers who could boast they were delivering something of direct benefit to the end user—and who, unlike me, had significant budgets and teams to run.

Not only that, they were all tall men. It's always tall men who get on in management hierarchies, no doubt some deep primate thing. I'm a man but was never that tall, so was stuffed from the start. My trace of a Manchester accent didn't help, either.

And then, in the nineties, a new wave of software development techniques came along. The new languages were much lower level than some of those in the past: that is, closer to the machine. As a developer you could deliver all sorts of fancy miracles. But your code would be dense and highly interconnected: difficult for an outsider to read, hard to test, all but impossible to maintain. In the wine bars and pubs of post-yuppie

London I would rage against this retreat from the mathematical high ground to a kind of medieval craftsmanship, and the lower standards it would bring. But the tide was against me, even as giant applications in the stock exchange and the health service crashed and burned, even as every user of PC software howled with rage at errors so fundamental they should never have gotten past the most elementary level of inspection.

Long before I was out of my thirties my career was stalling. I still had choices, even stable employment of a sort. Testing was never going to be fashionable, but you could hardly run a respectable software development shop with no testing effort at all.

And so here I was at Hyf. I was aware that I was really a kind of totem, a personalized embodiment of the company's illusory commitment to "high-quality deliverables." But I'd stayed there, for three years already. Whatever I thought of the job I had bills to pay and a pension to build up. And, just sometimes, I managed to get some work done that satisfied my need to carve order from chaos—a need, as I was going to find out, that went deep in me and my family, indeed.

If I sat up in my chair I could see the end wall of the office, a slab of Victorian brickwork capped by the curving roof of the old station structure. I was struck now by how good the brickwork was compared to my father's house. A station clock maybe six feet across was set into the wall, a translucent disc marked with big Roman numerals and two spearlike hands. The back was faced over with glass that revealed the works, which still operated. Sales types would use it to impress clients. I stared at the big minute hand long enough to see it wobble its way through two, three, four minutes. It was a relic of vanished days, I thought, days of heroic engineering. There have always been engineers in my family.

It struck me suddenly how *young* everybody was here—everybody but me, that is. None of them was interested in the brickwork.

The big station clock reached eleven-thirty, and I hadn't done a damn thing all morning. In the afternoon, I told myself, I would resume the good fight. For now, I shut down the computer, gathered my jacket, and walked out for an early and long lunch.

* * *

It was a gray day, unseasonably cold for mid-September. I bought a small orange juice and an avocado and bacon sandwich from a Pret A Manger. I walked as far as Saint Katherine's Dock before settling to a bench and eating.

Then, restless, cold, reluctant to go back to work, I walked toward Liverpool Street.

On impulse I stopped into a cybercafé. It was half empty, despite the time of day, and the customers were either eating or chatting rather than logging on. I bought my time credits and a tall latte, and sat at an empty terminal, placing myself as far from anybody else as possible.

I logged onto my home email account, got into a search engine, and typed "Mary Queen Virgins" into the query line.

Of course I could have done this at work; most people would, I suppose. But my strict but useless sense of what was right tripped me up. I had always felt uncomfortable purloining the firm's resources, from computer time to paper clips, always aware that in the end somebody somewhere would have to work a little harder to make up for my petty theft. Or perhaps it was just that I wanted to keep my private affairs out of the office.

Most of the results were dross: straightforward crank sites put up by religious nuts of one kind or another, a remarkably large number of churches with similar names, and the usual irritating clutter from the high schools and colleges that have developed the antisocial habit of placing the entire contents of their course materials on the public Internet, thus baffling every search engine yet devised. I skimmed past most of this stuff. I felt confident I could discard anything from outside Europe—in fact from outside the single-currency Euro zone, since I knew my father had once used euros.

At last I hit on a major-looking site. "THE PUISSANT ORDER OF HOLY MARY QUEEN OF VIRGINS—About Us—Information—Contact Us—Site Map—Genealogy Resources . . ." The URL showed it was based in Italy.

I dug into the link, and found myself facing a WELCOME screen. The wallpaper behind the lettering and icons was the face of the Madonna, taken from a medieval painting I didn't recognize, a beautiful, sad, impossibly young visage. Beside

her was a kind of corporate logo, a twist of chrome: it might
have been an extended infinity symbol, or an outline of two
fish face to face. The background colors were pale blue and
white, colors I had always associated with my mother's statues
of the Virgin, and, just looking at the screen I felt oddly rested,
oddly at home. As did, no doubt, every other Catholic boy logging on from around the world.

I poked around in the site. There were plenty of smiling female faces and beautiful old buildings. It was a busy design, I
thought with my software professional's eye, but it seemed to
be comprehensive, with language options in English (the default), Italian, Spanish, French, German, and even Japanese,
Chinese, and some Arabic tongues.

The order, it seemed, was an ancient Catholic grouping
based in Rome itself. They were making money by offering a
subscription genealogy service—something like the famous
Mormon site, to which they had links, but if anything more
comprehensive. Since I was calling from a UK address I was
offered a range of British-focused resources, including a deeds
database spanning from 1400 to 1900, five hundred maps of
the UK, Ireland, and Europe, a charter of baronial pedigrees
that went as deep as the thirteenth century, and information
from censuses up to the end of the twentieth century. There
was even a *Titanic* passenger list. They had 350 million names
indexed and cross-referenced over five hundred years, boasted
the pop-ups.

I skimmed through most of this stuff, wondering what it had
to do with my father. As far as I know he had never been much
interested in family trees—and certainly, if he had been paying a thousand quid a month for these services, he hadn't had
anything to show for it.

But then my eye was caught by a user ID in the contact line:
casella24. My mother's maiden name had been Casella.

I fired off a quick email, telling casella24 of my father's
death, and asking for details of his contacts with the order. Always assuming I had the right place.

I finished my coffee, logged off, and made my way back to
work.

* * *

At the end of the afternoon Vivian took me out for the drink she had promised.

We made our way to a bar just off Liverpool Street. Called the Sphinx, the place had been made over several times during my working life in London. Now it was done out in faux brick-work painted a dull yellow, and specialized in acrid Egyptian coffee. It actually had loose sand scattered on the floor. But somehow the atmosphere worked.

Over the long bar was a series of TV screens. Most of them were tuned to music and sports, and somewhere a tinkling pop song was playing. But one screen carried a news channel. The newsreader was a girl with an achingly beautiful face, and over her shoulder was an image I recognized: it was the glistening tetrahedron that had been found in the Kuiper Belt. Evidently the Anomaly was still news, even days after my conversation with Peter. I felt vaguely surprised to see it again. The association brought back unwelcome memories of Manchester.

Vivian ordered a glass of house white and sipped it slowly. She asked me about the funeral. I tried to tell her something of my feelings of dislocation.

"Midlife crisis," she said immediately. "Welcome to the twenty-first century."

"I always looked forward to the twenty-first century. I just didn't plan on being *old* in it. I mean, look at these arse-holes . . ."

The gathering in the bar was a typical London noncommunity. There were some small groups at the tables scattered over the sandy floor, but an awful lot of people were alone, at the tables or the bar or walking across the floor—alone, that is, save for their cell phones, which they worked persistently.

"So young, and so fucking arrogant, as if they own the place. They walk around as if London were built yesterday, a playground just for them. And look at the way they thumb away at those damn phones." I mimicked texting. "Another few years and kids will be born that are all giant thumbs and no brains, hopping around on knuckle joints."

"You're ranting, George," Vivian said with her usual even good humor. "Maybe you're right about the phones, though. It is an odd way to live, isn't it, to ignore the people physically with you while contacting friends who might be hundreds of miles away? You'd think the new technology would bring us together. Instead it seems to be pushing us apart."

That was why I'd always liked talking to Vivian. I didn't know anybody else who would make such observations.

She was a solid-framed woman who wore business suits that were crumpled enough to show she didn't take herself too seriously. She looked healthy; I knew she used a gym, and as a mother of two small daughters her home life must be active enough. Her hair was close-cropped over a broad face, with a small flattish nose and pale brown eyes. She had no cheeks, no chin, and would never have been called beautiful save by a lover, but in the frankness and humor of her gaze I had always known I was in the presence of a solid, grounded personality. To put it another way she was one of the few human beings to have slipped through Hyf's recruitment filter.

I said, "My father never had a cell phone. Didn't need one, he said, even though I tried to give him one for emergencies. You know, in case he fell . . . Didn't have a computer, either. Enjoyed his DVD, though."

"He wasn't a Luddite like you, then," she said.

"No. He was just selective."

She sloshed her wine around her glass. "My parents died a few years back. Ten years ago, actually."

"How?"

"Car accident. It was a mess to sort out, as they'd gone together. Their wills were out of date . . . Well. I think I know how your sister feels. I wanted to just run from the whole thing. But oddly, it wasn't such a bad time in the end. People come together, you know."

I tapped my thumbnail against the bottle's foil label. "You're not counseling me, are you, Viv?"

"No. Just telling you how I felt."

"But it was different. You were younger. I feel—shit, I suddenly feel old. It's as if now *he's* gone, the lid is off my generation, antiquity-wise. Do you know what I mean?"

She laughed. "So what do you want to do?"

I snorted. "What can I do? I'm trapped."

"By what?"

"By my routine. The choices I've made, good or bad, that

have landed me here. By the way I've slowed down." I slapped my belly. "By this. The way I get out of breath, and ache in the mornings. Even the way I get pissed on a couple of bottles of beer at lunchtime. I'm trapped by myself."

"There are always choices, George." She put her glass down on the table and leaned toward me, rumpled, kindly, earnest. "I wasn't counseling you before, but I am now. I think you need to reconnect. I went back to face what had happened to Mum and Dad."

"I did go back."

"Well, I think you need more. Take some time off. I bet you're owed some vacation. And you wouldn't be missed for a while," she said dryly. "Maybe you ought to talk to—uh—"

"Linda?" My ex-wife. We'd divorced before I'd come to work for Hyf; Vivian had never met her. "Don't think so."

"She's going to know you better than anybody else. Or go see your sister in Texas."

"Florida."

"Wherever. Spoil your nephews a little." She snapped her fingers. "Why don't you follow up this business of your missing sister?" I'd told her about that. "A little mystery to solve to occupy that analytical brain of yours—and nice deep family connections to soothe your heart . . ."

I felt uncomfortable. "There's probably nothing. Maybe she was adopted."

"Why would that have happened?"

"Or maybe she died," I said brutally. "And they wanted to spare me."

"Well, even if so," she said gently, "you surely want to know."

"I wouldn't know where to start."

"Ask your sister in Florida," she said. "She's, what, ten years older? She ought to know something. And if this kid was three or four in the photo, maybe she'll have been to school somewhere. A prep school maybe."

"But which one?"

"I'd start with the one your older sister went to. *Du-uh.*" She rattled her fingernails on the table. "Come on, George, snap out of it; get that brain working again."

"But it's all a mess, Viv. Christ, families. They all lied to me throughout my life. Even Gina!"

"Unresolved issues," she said. "So resolve them. Reconnect with the past." There was an edge to her voice now. *You've had as much sympathy from the world as you're going to get, George; stop whining.*

"You know, that's pretty much what Peter said. That I should 'reclaim the past.' "

She frowned. "Who's Peter?"

At that moment I found myself looking at the TV carrying the news channel. The pretty newsreader had gone, but the image of the Kuiper Anomaly remained. And there, beside it, was a chunky, high-browed face, talking rapidly. It was Peter McLachlan.

I pointed. "Him," I said.

chapter 5

Regina, her hand firmly clasped by Cartumandua, was allowed to attend the anointing of her father's body.

Jovian touched the dead man's eyes, formally closing them. Jovian was her uncle, her father's brother, from Durnovaria. He was a big, doleful man, a bronze worker, with big hands scarred by splashes of liquid metal, and he wore a Phrygian cap, just as her father had done. As the body was washed and anointed, Jovian stood over it, singing a soft Latin lament. The air was filled with powerful scents, like very strong perfume. But Regina knew that somebody had already cleaned up her father's body, for there was not a trace of all the blood she had seen before.

When the cleansing was done, Marcus was dressed in his toga. It took several men to lift him as the woolen sheet was draped over him, for his body was stiff, his limbs like bits of wood.

After that the funerary procession formed up. Eight men carried Marcus on a kind of litter. Musicians went before him. They played double pipes and a *cornu*, a kind of curved trumpet with a sweet, sad voice. Everybody else, including Regina, had to follow on behind. Lit up by candles and lanterns, the procession filed out of the grounds of the villa and over a hardened track through the fields.

As they walked, Regina glimpsed her mother for the first time that day. With her hair coiffed and her dress immaculate, Julia looked as elegant as ever, but she kept her face hidden behind scented cloth. Regina wanted to run to her, but Carta kept a firm hold of her hand.

They came to the mausoleum. This was a little stone building, like a temple. There were only three tombstones here, marking the deaths of Regina's grandfather and grandmother, her father's parents—and one small, poignant plate that marked the infant death of a little girl, born to Marcus and Julia some years before Regina's own birth, taken by a coughing sickness in her first month. She had been the "sweetest child," according to her stone. Regina wondered if any toys had been put in the ground for her to play with in the afterlife.

A coffin had already been placed in the ground, ready for Marcus. It was a lead box, its walls elaborately molded with scallops, an oceanic motif to symbolize the crossing to the afterlife.

Carta murmured soothing nonsense words. But Regina didn't feel distressed. This little scene, the lanterns and musicians and mourners gathered around a hole in the ground, was too strange to be upsetting. And besides, the awkward thing on the litter didn't seem to have any connection to her father.

Jovian placed a coin, a whole solidus, in his brother's mouth, payment for the ferryman. Then the body was lowered, a little clumsily, into the coffin. Marcus was wearing his best shoes, Regina noticed. Well, you couldn't go into the afterlife without shoes. Under Aetius's orders, Marcus was placed facedown.

One by one the mourners came up and dropped tokens into the coffin. There were remembrances of Marcus's life, like farming tools, and even a handful of tesserae from an unfinished mosaic; and there were objects to ease the passage to the afterlife, a vial of wine, a haunch of pork, some candles, a little bell to ward off evil.

Regina got a little upset now, for she had brought nothing to give her father. "Nobody *told* me!" she hissed to Carta, only to be admonished for making a noise.

She pulled away from Carta and looked around the mausoleum. In grassy corners she found some mayweed, poppy, and knapweed. The petals were closed and heavy with dew, for it was night. Still, she picked the wildflowers and dropped them into the grave. Perhaps they would open in the afterlife, where it was surely light all the time.

A load of chalk, pale in the starlight, was dumped into the coffin, to preserve the body. Finally the coffin lid was lowered and the heaps of earth beside the open grave briskly returned.

The soil smelled damp and rich. A simple tombstone was placed over the fresh earth—smaller than her grandfather's, for, as she had been told, such things were very expensive nowadays. She bent to read its inscription, but the writing was fine and in Latin, and it was too dark.

At the end of the burial, the mourners departed for the funerary banquet back at the villa. Regina looked for her mother. She couldn't see her.

But Aetius was here. He got to his haunches and faced Regina. He had something in his hand that he hid from her; she wondered if it was a toy, a present. But his broad face was dark.

"Little one, you have to understand what has happened here. Do you know why your father died?"

"I saw the blood."

"Yes. You saw the blood. Regina, Marcus followed a goddess called Cybele."

"Cybele and Atys. Yes."

"It's a strange business. On Cybele's birthday you drench yourself in the blood of sacrificed bulls, and dance yourself into a frenzy." His hard soldier's face told her what he thought of such foolishness. "But the most significant thing the priests of Cybele do is castration." He had to explain what that meant. "They do it to themselves. They have special forceps that stanch the blood flow. It is an act of remembrance of Atys, who castrated himself as punishment for a moment of unfaithfulness."

She tried to work all this out. "My father—"

"He castrated himself. Just like Atys. But he didn't have any priests' forceps," Aetius said grimly.

"Why did he do that? Was he unfaithful?"

"Yes, he was." Aetius kept his eyes on Regina's face.

Regina was aware of the stiffness of Cartumandua beside her, and she knew there was much she did not yet understand.

"But he didn't mean to kill himself."

Aetius cupped Regina's face. "No. He wouldn't have left you behind, little one. And anyhow he probably thought that even if he did die he would be resurrected, just like Atys . . . Well. Your father even now is finding out the truth of that. And I suspect he may not be sorry to be gone. At least he won't have to face recalcitrant farmers anymore. It was all getting a little difficult for him . . ."

"Grandfather?"

It was as if he had forgotten she was there. "Whether he meant it or not, he is gone. And you, little Regina, are the most important person in the family."

"I am?"

"Yes. Because you are the future. Here—you must take these." Now he opened his hand, and, to Regina's shock and surprise, he showed her the *matres*, the three little goddesses from the *lararium*, the family shrine. They were figures of women in heavy hooded cloaks, crudely carved, little bigger than Aetius's thumb. Aetius shook his head. "I remember when my own father brought these back—they are just trinkets, really, produced in their thousands by the artisans along the Rhine—but they became precious to us. The family is the center of everything for all good Romans, you know. And now you must take care of our gods, our family. Give me your hand now."

As she opened her palm to take the goddesses, Regina couldn't keep from flinching. She thought the *matres* might burn her flesh, or freeze it, or crumble her bones. But they were just like lumps of rock, like pebbles, warm from Aetius's grasp. She closed her fingers over them. "I'll keep them safe for my mother."

"Yes," Aetius said. He stood up. "Now you must go with Carta and pack up your things. Your clothes—everything you want to take. We're going on a journey, you and I."

"Is Mother coming?"

"It will be exciting," he said. "Fun." He forced a smile, but his face was hard.

"Should I take my toys?"

He rested his hand on her head. "Some. Yes. Of course."

"Grandfather—"

"Yes?"

"Why did you make those men put my father facedown in the coffin?"

But he wouldn't reply, saying only, "Be ready first thing tomorrow—both of you."

Excited, clutching the goddesses, Regina tugged at Carta's hand, and they began to make their way back to the villa.

It was only much later that Regina learned that laying a corpse facedown in a coffin was a way of ensuring that the dead would not return to the world of the living.

The next day, not long after dawn, Aetius sacrificed a small chicken. Seeking omens for the journey, he inspected its entrails briskly, muttered a prayer, then buried the carcass in the ground. He cleaned his hands of blood by rubbing them in the dirt.

A sturdy-looking cart drew up in the villa's courtyard.

Of course Regina was only half packed, even with Carta's help. When Aetius saw the number of boxes and trunks that lay open around her room, he growled and began to pull out clothes and toys. "Only take what you *need*, child! You are so spoiled—you would never make a soldier."

She ran around picking up precious garments and games and bits of cheap jewelry. "I don't want to be a soldier! And I *need* this and this—"

Aetius sighed and rolled his eyes. But he argued until he had reduced her to just four big wooden trunks, and, in the final heated stages, allowed her a few more luxuries. A beefy male slave called Macco hauled the boxes out to the cart.

Carta helped her dress in her best outdoor outfit. It was a smart woolen tunic, woven in one piece with long sleeves and a slit for her neck. She wore it over a fine wool undertunic, with a belt tied around her waist.

Aetius stood before her stiffly, clenching and unclenching a fist. Then he knelt to adjust her belt. "Beautiful, beautiful," he said gruffly. "You look like a princess."

"Look at the colors," Regina said, pointing. "The yellow is nettle dye, the orange is onion skins, and the red is madder. It's all fixed with salt so it will *never* fade."

"Not ever? Not in a thousand years?"

"Never."

He grunted. He straightened and glanced up. "Cartumandua! Are you ready?"

Carta was wearing a tunic of her own, of plain bleached wool, and she carried a small valise.

Regina asked, "Is Carta coming, too?"

"Yes, Carta is coming."

"And Mother—shall I go and find her?"

But Aetius grabbed her arm. "Your mother isn't coming with us today."

"She'll come later."

"Yes, she'll come later." He clapped his hands. "And the sun is already halfway across the sky and I hoped to be a speck on the horizon by now. Hurry, now, before the day fades altogether . . ."

Regina ran outside and clambered onto the carriage. It was a simple open frame, but it had big wooden wheels with iron rims and complicated hubs. She was going to ride in front, with Aetius, so she could see everywhere she went. Cartumandua would be in the back, with Macco, the burly slave, and the lashed-down boxes.

Regina noticed Macco strapping a knife to his waist, under his tunic. She snapped, "Put that down, Macco, right now. Nobody is allowed to carry weapons except the soldiers. The Emperor says so."

Macco had a heavy shaven head, and broad shoulders his loose tunic couldn't conceal. He was a silent, gloomy man—Julia had always called him "dull" and ignored him—and now he glanced up at Aetius.

"What's this? Wearing weapons? Quite right, Regina. But I am a commander in the army, and if I say it's all right for Macco to have a knife, the Emperor isn't going to mind."

Regina pulled a face. "But he's a *slave*."

"He's a slave who would lay down his life for yours, which is why I've chosen him to come with us. Now hush your prattling."

She flinched, but subsided.

So it was in a stiff silence that the little party finally set off. Aetius sat beside Regina, a mighty pillar of muscle, his face as rigid as an actor's mask. Regina looked back once, hoping to see her mother, but nobody came to wave them off.

That minor disappointment soon faded, as did her sulk over being ticked off in front of Macco, because the ride, at the beginning at least, was fun. It was another fine day. The sky was cloudless, a pale blue dome, and the horses trotted comfortably along, snorting and ducking their heads, the musky stink of their sweat wafting back to Regina.

Soon they reached the broad main road, heading east. The road cut as straight as an arrow across the green countryside. It was built by and for walking soldiers, and was uneven, and the ride was bumpy. But Regina didn't care; she was too excited. She bounced in her seat, until Aetius, horse switch in hand, told her to stop.

Aetius tried to explain that they would travel east, all the way to Londinium, and then cut north.

"When will we see Londinium?"

"Not for a few days. It's a long way."

Her eyes widened. "Will we ride through the night? Will we sleep in the cart?"

"Don't be silly. There are places to stay on the way."

"But where—"

"Never mind your prattle."

They encountered little traffic. There were a very few carriages, pulled by horses, donkeys, or bullocks, a few horse riders—but most of the traffic was people on foot. Many pedestrians carried heavy loads, bundled in boxes or cloth, on their heads or shoulders. Aetius pointed to one rider in a bright green uniform whose horse trotted at a bright clip, quickly overtaking the carriage. Aetius said he was from the Imperial Post, the *cursus publicus*. Along the roadside there were many small stations with stables and water troughs, places where a post rider could change his horse.

Sometimes the people walking along the road would peer at the carriage with an intensity that frightened Regina. At such times Macco was always alert, gazing back with his blank, hard face, the hilt of a weapon showing at his waist. Regina would stare into the faces of the people, hoping to glimpse her mother.

They passed one girl who couldn't have been much older than Regina herself. Walking with a group of adults, she was bowed down under a great bundle strapped to her back. She had heavy-looking black leather boots on her feet; they dwarfed her thin, dirty legs.

Regina said, "Why doesn't she get a carriage? She could put

her stuff in the back. I certainly wouldn't like to carry *my* luggage along the road like that . . ."

Aetius grimaced. "I doubt if anybody other than Hercules could carry *your* luggage, child. But I'm afraid she doesn't have a choice."

"Because she's poor."

"Or a slave. And look, over there." A group of people, shuffling behind a slow-moving carriage, were bound together by ankle chains. "Carriages and horses are faster, but not everybody can afford a horse."

She frowned. "Are slaves cheaper than horses?"

"Yes. Slaves are cheaper than horses. Look at the countryside. I bet you've never been so far from home before, have you?"

She had no idea if she had or not. She looked around at fields and hedgerows. There were a few buildings scattered here and there, small square huts and a few roundhouses with timber frames and thatched roofs; in the distance she saw the bright red roof tiles of something bigger, probably a villa.

It was farming country. Much of the Roman diocese of Britain was like this. Nobody knew for sure how many people lived in Britain south of the Wall, but there were thought to be at least four million. Only perhaps one in ten of the population lived in the villas and towns. The rest worked the land, where they cultivated wheat, barley, oats, peas, beans, vegetables, and herbs, and raised their cattle, sheep, and goats. Many of them had worked this land for generations, since long before the coming of the Romans: Regina might have been traveling through the landscape of five centuries earlier.

It was this way from end to end of the Empire, across two thousand miles, from Britain to the Middle East. The Empire was the most materially sophisticated civilization the western world had yet seen—but the overwhelming majority of people lived off the land, as they had always done.

Aetius spent a long time trying to explain some of this, but he got stuck on the meaning of the word *million*. Regina's attention drifted, distracted by the sway of the horses, the clatter of the wheels, the buzzing of flies.

"Oh, stop fidgeting," Aetius snapped. "If only I could just *order* you to sit still . . ." He pointed with his switch at a little cylindrical pillar set beside the road. "Well, what's that? Do you know?"

She knew very well. It was a waystone. "It tells you how far it is to the nearest town, and who the Emperor is."

He grunted. "Somehow I doubt that poor Honorius has gotten around to painting his name on the stones . . . But, yes, that's the idea. Now, the stones are set every thousand paces or so along each main road. And if you count them, you'll know how far we've come, won't you?"

"Yes!" She rubbed her nose. "But what if I fall asleep? Or what if it's dark?"

"If you fall asleep I'll count for you. And don't rub your nose. You have to start now. That's *one* . . ."

"One." Solemnly she folded a finger back as a marker, and peered along the road for the next pillar. But it seemed an awful long time coming, and by the time she saw it she had forgotten what she was supposed to be doing, and had let her finger fold out again.

Her grandfather seemed determined to keep up her schooling, and as they rattled along he told her the story of the road itself. The soldiers from the army of Emperor Claudius had first come this way, surveying the route. The road had been built by the soldiers themselves, and people drafted in from the countryside.

"How much did they get paid?"

"Paid? Hah! Everybody was a barbarian in those days, child. You didn't get *paid*. Look. You put down a gravel core, and lay on a surface of crushed limestone. You use stone slabs where you can find them. The water drains out into those side ditches—can you see? . . ."

She was good at pretending to listen, while being occupied with her own thoughts. But eventually she drifted asleep, slumped against Aetius's sturdy form, dreaming fitfully about the little girl in her hobnailed boots.

She dozed through the day, or listened to Aetius's complicated talk, or played word games with Cartumandua. They stopped only to water and feed the horses; the passengers ate on the move in the cart, bread with fish and meat.

The last time Regina woke up that day, the cart was pulling

into a courtyard. As Aetius and the others jumped down and began to unload, Regina stood up on her seat, stretched and massaged a sore rump, and looked around. The light was fading from the sky, and high, thin clouds had gathered. To her right she could see a wall, tall and formidable, a great curtain of slate gray two or three times her height that curved away across the ground.

She pointed. "There's a town! Is it Durnovaria?"

Aetius snorted. "We've come a little farther than that. Haven't you been counting the waystones? We passed twenty-three—not a bad pace after a slow start. That is Calleva Atrebatum."

"Aren't we going to stay there? . . . What's this place? Is it a villa?"

It was no villa but one of the *mansiones*, a way station designed to support the messengers of the Imperial Post. It was here, Aetius said, that they would spend the night, for it was safe enough, and he would "swim to Hades before I give over any more 'gate tax' to any more swindling landowners in any more towns."

The station turned out to be comfortable enough. It even had a small bathhouse, where Aetius retired with a pitcher of wine and a plate of oysters, bought for a price that made him groan out loud.

After a day spent largely sitting on a wooden board, Regina was too full of energy to sleep. And so, after she had eaten, despite the lateness of the hour, she, Macco, and Carta played *trigon*, a complicated three-person game of catch-the-ball. Regina ran and laughed, burning up her energy, and her voice echoed from the station's plaster walls. Macco stayed as silent as ever, but his smile was broad.

The next day Aetius was again up and ready to go not long after dawn. It didn't take long to reload the carriage, and soon the four of them were on the road again—though not before Aetius sniffed the air and inspected the clouds and the trees and the birds, seeking omens for their journey.

They continued to head steadily east. The road ran straight and true, unchanging, the way markers sliding past one by one. But the landscape changed slowly, becoming more hilly, and some of the plowed-up fields gleamed white with chalk.

Some of the villas looked abandoned, though, even burned out. On one farm, close to the road, Regina recognized a vineyard, rows of vines set out on a south-facing hillside. But though the vines were green and heavy they looked untended, and the nearby buildings were broken down. Aetius did not comment on the abandoned vineyard, and Regina thought nothing of it. If she had, she would have said that things must always have been this way. She did want to go see if there were any grapes, but Aetius ignored her pleas.

That night they again stayed in a way station.

And the next morning, soon after the start, when they passed over the crest of a hill, Regina glimpsed Londinium itself. The town was a marvelous gray-green sprawl of buildings contained within a far-flung wall. A shining river ran through it. Smoke rose everywhere, thin threads that spiraled to the sky. Regina thought she saw a ship on the river, a green-sailed boat that sparkled in the low morning sun, but she couldn't be sure.

"Are we going on a ship?"

"No—child, I told you already. We aren't stopping in Londinium. We're going on. Don't you listen?" Aetius seemed to be getting angry. But Carta put her hand on Regina's shoulder, and he subsided.

They turned their backs on Londinium, heading north. Regina looked back at the city as it receded. "I'll go there one day," she said. "I'll go far beyond it, too! I'll go all the way to Rome!"

Aetius grimaced, and hugged her with his massive arm.

For Regina, after the city, this third day turned out to be the most difficult so far. The sky lidded over with gray cloud, and although the sun was gone the temperature rose steadily. They were all soon sweating uncomfortably, and they had to stop frequently to allow the horses to drink.

Aetius, apparently trying to compensate for the absence of Regina's tutors, chose this difficult day to lecture her on the essentials of Roman Britain.

Britain was a diocese within the Praetorian Prefecture of Gaul. So the *vicarius*, the governor of Britain, reported to the prefect of Gaul, who reported to the Emperor. Similarly there was a hierarchy of towns, from the lesser market towns, up through the local and provincial capitals, to Londinium, the capital of the diocese.

The most important activity of the central administration was the collection of taxation and the spending of government funds. Most of the tax money came from the countryside, because that was where most people lived. Landlords, like Regina's father, collected the Emperor's taxes from his tenants, along with his own rent. The tax revenue paid the salaries of the army and the sailors of the British fleet, who kept Britain safe from the barbarians who would otherwise swarm from the north and across the sea.

People grumbled about the taxes they had to pay. But most of the money collected came back into circulation. And the fact was the vast volumes of foodstuffs, animals, clothing, metalwork, pottery, and other goods bought by the government to supply the army and its other agencies was central to the working of the economy . . .

Aetius struggled to explain: "It's like a wheel, Regina. It goes around and around, a great wheel of money and goods, taxing and spending, keeping everyone safe and wealthy. But if a wheel comes off its hub—"

"We'd fall over."

"Exactly. Everything would fall over. Now then, when my old chum Constantius took us soldiers away for his adventure in Europe, some people in the towns decided they didn't need to pay his taxes anymore, and threw out his collectors and officials, and said they would collect the money for themselves and keep it for their own towns, rather than give it all to some distant Emperor they never saw. But while people will pay up for an Emperor, especially if he has an army to collect for him, they're a lot less willing to pay some fat fool of a local landowner . . ."

Regina was a bright child, and capable of understanding a great deal. But at seven she was an experienced enough student to know that while Aetius might be a fine soldier he was no teacher. He was *boring*.

And as the day wore on and the heat continued to stifle, Regina got more and more uncomfortable. It had been days now since she had seen her mother. Aetius never mentioned Julia, and Regina was wary of asking. She missed her mother even so, and wondered where she was. She grew withdrawn, sullen.

Eventually Aetius relented and let Regina sit in the back with Carta. They tried to play *ludus latrunculorum*—"soldiers," a fast-moving game a little like chess played only with rooks—but the rattling of the carriage knocked the colored glass counters away from their squares. So they settled for *par impar*, a simple game of odds and evens, played with pebbles held in the hand.

That night they stayed at yet another way station. The next day they made another early start, but Regina found it increasingly hard to sit still.

Things came to a head when, about midday, the weather abruptly broke, and an immense storm lashed down from a gray lid of sky. Aetius insisted they kept going, but soon they were all soaked through. Regina was cold and frightened; she had never been exposed to such elemental rage before.

When the storm finally let up she pushed away from Aetius and jumped down from the carriage. "I won't go any farther! I want to go home, right now! Turn around and take me home! I *command* you!"

Aetius was angry, placating, demanding, but he got nowhere; and when his will broke against her seven-year-old stubbornness, he stomped around the road, fists bunched.

Cartumandua, with some courage, intervened. Soaked herself, she clambered down to the road surface and brushed at Regina's hair, calming her down. She said to Aetius, "Sir, you can't speak to her as if she's one of your legionaries. And you can't expect her to sit there day after day on that wooden bench and listen to you lecture about procurators and prefects."

"She needs discipline—"

"It's not *natural*. You need to give her time."

"But every heartbeat we stand here in the road is wasted time."

"The Wall has stood for three centuries, and I daresay it will still be there if we take a few days more. If you don't make allowances, I don't think we'll get there at all."

He walked back grudgingly. "Catuvellaunian princess or not, you are a feisty one for a slave."

She dropped her head submissively. "I'm just trying to help."

Aetius crouched down before Regina. "Little one, I think we have some negotiating to do . . ."

They continued the journey, but after that to a different pattern. They would ride a while, and break a while, generally long before Regina got too bored or uncomfortable—although Aetius retained the right to keep on if he was ill at ease with the countryside, or the company they kept on the road. Their pace dropped, from fifty or sixty waystones a day to less than forty.

But for Regina, though she lost count of the days, and had only the dimmest idea of where they actually were by now, the trip became much easier—even fun again, as the days settled into a new routine.

As they worked steadily north the countryside changed character.

Though the road still arrowed past farmsteads, there were far more roundhouses of the old British type, rather than the rectangular Roman-style buildings. The towns here were more like bristling forts, with tall walls and looming watchtowers. Here and there Regina saw plumes of dust and black smoke rising up. Aetius said they were mines. Once they passed a man driving muzzled wolves along the road; he was a trapper, hoping to sell these animals to a circus.

In the roadside dirt Aetius sketched a map of the island of Britain, and slashed a line from southeast to northeast, from the Severn to the Humber. "Southeast of this line there are plains and low hills. Here you'll find fields and citizens, with everything run from the towns—under the greatest town of all, Londinium, capital of the diocese. Northwest of this line there are mountains, and barbarians, and tribes and chiefs who run their own affairs and have barely heard of the Emperor, and pay his taxes with the utmost reluctance. To the southeast there are a thousand villas, but none at all in the northwest. That is why, to the northwest, the diocese belongs to the army." But Regina continued to have only a dim grasp of the country's geography, or indeed of where they were.

In the final days, as the endless northward journey continued and they rattled across high, bleak moorland, Aetius told her something of his family's past.

"We were all Durotriges. Your father's people were aristocrats—landowners—even before the Romans came," he said. "*My* people—and your mother's—were farmers, but they were warriors." He glanced back at Cartumandua. "The Catuvellaunians call themselves a great warrior people. But when Claudius came they rolled over and bared their arses to him . . ."

Regina gasped at this language, shocked and delighted, and Carta colored.

"But *we* fought back. While the Emperor Claudius was still in Britain, one of his generals, Vespasian, had to fight his way west, taking hill fort after hill fort, supported by the fleet tracking him along the coast. It was a mighty feat of generalship—and later Vespasian himself would become Emperor—but, by my eyes, we made him earn that throne. And that is why the men of the Durotriges became such good soldiers for the Empire."

"Like you, Grandfather."

He said gruffly, "You'd have to count my lumps. But, yes, I've been a soldier all my adult life. As was my father, and his before him. But things have changed. There have always been barbarians—"

"In the north, and beyond the sea."

"Yes. They aren't soldiers but professional savage fools, farmers, bound to the land. They could not even mount a genuine campaign. They were no match for the Empire—not until the *barbarica conspiratio.*"

It had come more than forty years earlier, a great barbarian conspiracy, a coordinated attack on Britain by the Picts across the Wall from the north, the Franks and Saxons from across the North Sea, and the Scotti from Ireland. Defenses designed to hold against an attack from any one of these enemies had been overwhelmed. There was much muttering of espionage, for the British military commanders on the northern frontier and the coasts were ambushed and killed.

"It was a terrible time," Aetius muttered. "I was not fifteen years old—no older than you, Cartumandua. For a time the countryside was full of roaming bands of barbarians—and, I have to say, of deserters from the army itself. Even Londinium was sacked. It took the Emperor two years to restore order. My own view is we're still trying to recover from that great shock."

Carta spoke up again. "Sir, she is only a child."

Aetius said grimly, "She needs to hear it even so, Cartumandua, and to hear it again until it sinks in. Let me say this. Six years ago I was on the Rhine—Gaul's great river frontier. In the middle of winter it froze over, and into Gaul swarmed the Vandals and the Alans and the Suebi and Jove knows who else. They just walked across the damn river, as cool as you please. We couldn't hold them—we fell back and fell back. *And they are still there now,* crawling around the prefecture, far inside the frontier. I was glad to get a posting back to Britain and away from all that, I can tell you . . . I suspect this poor child will spend much of her life seeking a place of safety."

Regina sniffed. "This poor child understands every word you say, you know."

Aetius looked at her, astonished. Then he laughed, and clapped her on the back. "So now I've got *you* to contend with, as well as the Vandals and the Picts and the Saxons . . ."

"Look." Behind Regina, Cartumandua stood up and pointed. "I can *see* it."

Aetius reined in the horses. Regina stood on her seat, shielded her eyes with her hands, and stared until she saw it, too.

A line of darkness stretched across the world, from one horizon to another, rising and falling over the contours of the moorland. Along that line, smoke rose up everywhere, and mud-colored buildings huddled. Suddenly she knew exactly where she was, exactly how far she had been brought: from one end of the country to the other.

She wailed, "*It's the Wall.* What are we doing here? Aren't we going to a villa, or a town?"

"No," said Aetius grimly. "This is where we will live now, here at the Wall. It won't be so bad—"

"This is a place for dirty, stinking soldiers. Not for *me!*"

"You'll just have to make the best of it," he growled warningly.

Carta hugged her. "Don't worry, Regina. We'll be fine here, you'll see."

Regina sniffed. "We won't be here *forever*, will we?"

Carta looked at Aetius. "Why, I—"

Regina asked, "Just until things get back to normal?"

Aetius looked away.

Carta said, "Yes. Until things get back to normal."

Regina looked about more brightly. "Where's my mother?" None of the adults would reply. "My mother isn't here, is she?"

Aetius sighed. "Now, Regina—"

"You *promised* me."

His mouth opened and closed. "Well, that's jolly unfair. I promised no such thing."

"Liar. *Liar.*"

Carta tried to subdue her. "Oh, Regina—"

"She doesn't want me. She's sent me away."

"It's not like that," Aetius said. "She loves you—she will always love you. Look—she asked me to give you this." From a fold of his tunic he produced the precious silver dragon brooch.

She dashed it from his hand; it fell to the coarse grass, where it gleamed. She turned on Cartumandua. "And don't you *dare* pick it up, Carta! I *never* want to see it again."

Cartumandua flinched from the command in her voice.

And that was when the tears came, in a sudden flood, sudden as a rainstorm. Aetius folded her in his arms, and she felt Carta's small hand on her shoulder. She wept for her mother and herself, as the carriage clattered its way the last few paces toward the Wall.

chapter 6

I took Vivian's advice and set off in search of my sister.

I booked some overdue leave. I had no trouble getting it through my line manager, or even through the Nazi killer robots who ran Human Resources. But I saw the way their gazes slid away from me as I handed over the forms and explained my vague plans. My days at Hyf were numbered. To hell with it.

I drove north, listening to news radio all the way. Along with the sports and the useless traffic bulletins, the main topic of the day was undoubtedly the Kuiper Anomaly. Absorbed with my own affairs, I just hadn't noticed the way this thing had continued to mushroom in the public consciousness.

Reaching Manchester at around ten that evening, I drove to the city center, to the hotel I'd stayed in before. I actually parked the car. But I didn't get out. I remembered what Vivian had said: *reconnect*. I shouldn't be here.

I turned the car around and drove out to the suburbs. I canceled my hotel reservation with my cell phone.

There was a real estate agent's sign outside my father's house. I hesitated to disturb Peter, but when I knocked on his door he was awake—I heard the hum of PC cooling fans; perhaps he was working—and he was happy enough to give me a key. I let myself into Dad's house. Inside it was warm and clean, but of course it was stripped of furniture; somehow I hadn't been able to imagine it this way. There were pale patches on the wallpaper where furniture had stood for years. Empty or not it still managed to smell musty.

To my chagrin I finished up knocking on Peter's door again. I borrowed a sleeping bag, pillow, and flask of tea. I spent the night on the thick carpet of my old bedroom. Lulled by the sound of distant trains passing in the night, immersed in a familiar ambience, I slept as well as I had in years.

In the morning, around eight, Peter showed up. It was a bright, fresh morning, the sky a deep blue. He brought soap, towels, a glass of orange juice, and an invitation to come over for breakfast. I accepted, but I promised myself I'd get to the shops and stock up as soon as I'd eaten.

Set on the other side of the road, Peter's house was a mirror image of my father's, the staircase and rooms eerily transposed from left to right. I went in there with some trepidation: this was the domain of Peter the solitary weirdo, after all. Well, it was plainly decorated, so far as I could see, with bland pastel paint hiding old wallpaper. The furniture looked a little old, and certainly wasn't modish, but it wasn't shabby. There were bookcases everywhere, even in the hall. The books seemed neatly ordered, but not obsessively so.

Peter wore a gray sweat suit of soft fabric, and thick mountaineer's socks—no shoes or slippers.

We consumed Alpen and coffee in the kitchen. I told him I'd seen him on TV, and we talked about the media frenzy over Kuiper. Peter said it was all to do with positive feedback.

"It's like that Mars story a few years back. You know, where they found fossil bacteria in a meteorite—"

"Thought they found."

"And Clinton zipped himself up long enough to pronounce that NASA had discovered life on Mars. Suddenly it was everywhere. The story itself became the story." It was the nature of the world's modern media, he told me. "The days when news was controlled by a few outlets, the big networks, are long gone. Now you have CNN, Sky, Internet news sites: thousands of sources of news at local, national, and international level. And they all watch each other. A story sparks into life somewhere. The other outlets watch the story and the reaction to it, and pick up on it . . ." He was overfamiliar with this stuff, and tended to talk too rapidly, using specialist jargon, words like *mediasphere*. He showed me an editorial he'd clipped from the *Guardian* decrying the bubble of hysteria over Kuiper. "There's even news about news, which itself becomes part of the story. It usually finishes with a spasm of self-loathing. 'What This Hysteria Says About Our Society.' Patho-logical, really. But it shows the kind of world we live in now. We're all densely interconnected, like it or not, and this kind of feedback loop happens all the time."

Densely interconnected. For some reason that phrase ap-pealed to me. "But the fuss about Kuiper has been good for you," I said.

"Oh, yes," he said. "It's been good for me."

Cradling our second mugs of coffee, Peter led me into his living room. Beyond a big double-glazed picture window, a garden glowed green in the soft light of the autumn morning. The room obviously served as an office. In addition to a music stack and wide-screen TV with various recorders and set-top boxes, there was a large table given over to computer technol-ogy: a big powerful-looking desktop, a laptop, various hand-helds, a scanner, a joystick, and other bits of gear I couldn't recognize. The desktop was booted up. There were books and stacks of printouts on the desk and on the floor.

All this looked like the environment of a freelancer working at home. But there was no sense of style, and a certain lack of ornamentation and decoration—no photographs, for in-stance—a lack of personality.

The only exception was in the little alcove over the fire-place. In my home my parents used to keep silly souvenirs in there—tiny wooden clogs from Amsterdam, a little Eiffel Tower, other family knickknacks. Peter had set up a little row of die-cast model toys. Intrigued, I asked, "May I?" Peter shrugged. I reached up and brought down a fat green aircraft. It was a Thunderbird Two, heavy and metallic-cold. I turned it upside down, trying to see a manufacturer's date. Something rattled in its pod. On the edges of the wings and along the base the paintwork was chipped and worn away.

"It's a Dinky original. Nineteen sixty-seven," Peter said.

I cradled it in my hands like a baby bird. "I never had one of these. My parents got me a plastic snap-together substitute."

"Without a detachable pod? I sympathize."

"They didn't understand. This must be worth something."

He took it back and restored it to its place. "No. Not without the original box, and it's hardly in mint condition."

"Much loved, though."

"Oh, yes."

I stepped toward the big gear-laden table. I could smell Johnson's Pledge, I realized, and it struck me that the Thunderbird toy had been free of dust. Up on the desktop screen was what looked like a prototype Web page. It was complex, crowded, and partly animated; it showed stanzas of music that cycled rapidly, along with a kind of binary code I didn't recognize. Peter stood awkwardly beside the table, big hands wrapped around his coffee cup.

"This is your work?—Peter, I hate to admit it, but I don't know a damn thing about what you do now you're retired from the cops."

He shrugged. "After the funeral you had other things on your mind." There was a note in his voice, a subtext. *I'm used to it.* "But you got interested when you saw me on TV. Well, that's okay. I make a living from Web design, mostly corporate sites, and game design."

"Games?"

"Web-based, multiuser. I was always good at computer games. It's something to do with a facility for spotting patterns in patchy and disparate information, I think. It made me a good copper, too. That and being out of control."

"Out of control?"

He grinned, self-deprecating. "You knew me, George. I was never much in control of anything about my life. I was always awkward socially—I could never figure out what was going on, stuff other people seemed able to read without thinking about it." He was right about that. In later years, we, his friends, even speculated he might be mildly autistic. He said, "You see, I'm used to being in situations where I don't know the rules, and yet making my way forward anyhow. Decoding a chaotic landscape."

"So is this one of your games?"

"It's a personal project."

I pointed at the screen. "I see music, but I don't recognize it. Some kind of encryption system?"

"Sort of, but that's not the purpose." He seemed briefly embarrassed, but he faced me, determined. "It's a SETI site."

"SETI?"

"Search for Extraterrestrial Intelligence."

"Oh, right."

He talked quickly. "We've spent forty years now listening for radio whispers from the sky. But that's twentieth-century thinking. If you were an ETI, and you wanted to learn something about the Earth, what would you study? What better than the Internet? It's by far the largest, most organized information source on the planet."

I said carefully, "You imagine aliens are logging on?"

"Well, why not? You'd learn a lot more about humankind than by sticking a probe up the rectum of a farmer from Kansas." He seemed to sense what I was thinking. He grimaced. "Let's just say I've been intrigued by the possibility of extraterrestrial life on Earth since the first showing of *Fireball XL-Five*. Haven't you?"

"I suppose so. But you've stayed interested. You've become—um, an expert on this stuff."

"As much as anybody is. I'm plugged into the right networks, I suppose. My name is known. Which is how I got on the TV."

"And your site is designed to catch their attention?" I peered at it. "It looks a little busy."

"Well, I doubt an ETI is going to be interested in snazzy Web page design. The site is information-rich, though— you're looking at the works of Chopin, here, rendered in compressed binary—and encoded in forms that ought to make it easy for the ETIs to pick up. Bait, you see. And if the ETIs do find my site—look, this is a long shot, but it's cheap to set up and maintain . . . and the payoff would be of incalculable value. Isn't it worth trying? I'm not alone in this," he said, a bit defensively. "There's a network of researchers, mostly in the States . . ."

He told me something of a bizarre-sounding online community of like minds. "We call ourselves the Slan(t)." He had to write that down for me. "*Slan* is an old science fiction reference—made up to date, you see . . . It sums up how we see ourselves. The Slan(t)ers are a new kind of community, a bunch of outsiders, the fringe united by new technology."

"I bet there are a lot of Californians."

He grinned. "As it happens, yeah. It was set up long before I joined." He said there was no hierarchy to Slan(t); it was all "bottom-up." "It's a self-organizing community. The hardest thing to model online is social interaction—the kind of unconscious feedback we humans give each other face to face, feedback that moderates behavior. So we devised a system where we would moderate each other's contributions to the clickstream. If you are uncivil, or just plain uninteresting, your scores go down, and everybody sees."

"A bit like eBay."

"Like that, yes."

"Plenty of scope for bullying."

"But that's antisocial, too, and there are always plenty of people who would mark the bully down accordingly. It works. It is homeostatic—actually another example of feedback. But this time it's *negative* feedback that tends to make a system stable, rather than drive it out of control." He talked on, describing the Slan(t)ers' projects.

I felt awkward. This was the kind of conversation we'd had as kids at school, or later as booze-fueled students: excitable, complex, full of ideas, the more outlandish the better. Peter had always been good at that, because he'd learned to be. Whereas other fat kids, it's said, get a break from bullying by being funny, Peter's defense was to have wilder ideas than anybody else. But now it wasn't the same. We weren't kids anymore.

And there was something else I couldn't quite read in the way he spoke, this big, clumsy man with folded hands and his habit of adjusting invisible spectacles, talking earnestly. I had the impression of shadows, ranked behind him in the electronic dark, as if Peter was just a front for a whole network of densely interconnected, like-minded obsessives, all working for ends I didn't understand.

Anyhow Slan(t) sounded like one giant computer game to me. "Interesting."

"You don't really think so," he said. "But that's okay."

"But now," I said, "perhaps we do see the aliens, in the Kuiper Anomaly. Isn't that what you've been saying on TV?"

"That's obviously a gross signature of something out there. Yes, it's exciting." His face was closed. "But I have a feeling that the origin of the Anomaly is going to turn out to be stranger than we think. And besides, it's not the only bit of evidence we have."

"It isn't?"

"Perhaps there *are* traces out there, if you know how to look. Traces of life, of other minds at work. But they're fragmentary, difficult for us to recognize and interpret. But I, well, as I told you I have this facility for pattern matching."

I looked into my coffee cup, wondering how I could get out of the conversation politely.

But he had rotated his chair until he faced the desktop, and was briskly working a mouse. Images flickered over the screen. He settled on a star field—obviously color-enhanced—the stars were yellow, crimson, blue, against a purple-black background. Around a central orange-white pin-point were two concentric rings, like smoke rings. The inner one was quite fine, but the outer, perhaps four times its diameter, was fatter, brighter. Both the rings were off-center, and ragged, lumpy, broken.

I searched for something to say. "It looks like a *Fireball XL-Five* end credit."

Sometimes he lacked humor. "*Fireball* was in black and white."

"Tell me what I'm seeing, Peter."

"It's the center of the Galaxy," he said. "Twenty-five thousand light-years away. A reconstruction, of course, from infrared, X-ray, gamma ray, radio images, and the like; the light from the center doesn't reach us because of dust clouds. The sun is one of four hundred billion stars, stuck out in a small spiral arm—you know the Galaxy is a spiral. At the core, everything is much more crowded. And everything is big and bright. It's Texas in there." He pointed at the image. "Some of these 'stars' are actually clusters. These rings are clouds of gas and dust; the outer one is maybe a hundred light-years across."

"And the bright object at the center—"

"Another star cluster. Very dense. It's thought there is a black hole in there, with the mass of a million suns."

"I don't see any aliens."

He traced out the rings. "These rings are expanding. Hundreds of miles a second. And the less structured clouds are hot, turbulent. It's thought that the big rings are debris from massive explosions in the core. There was a giant bang about a million years ago. The most recent eruption seems to have been twenty-seven thousand years ago. The light took twenty-five thousand years to get here—it arrived about two thousand years ago; the Romans might have seen something . . . If you look wider you can see the debris of more explosions, reaching much deeper back in time, some of them still more immense."

"Explosions?"

"Nobody knows what causes them. Stars are simple objects, George, physically speaking. So are galaxies, even. Much simpler than bacteria, say. There really shouldn't be such mysteries. I think it's possible we're seeing intelligence there—or rather stupidity."

I laughed, but it was a laugh of wonder at the audacity of the idea. "The Galaxy center as a war zone?"

He didn't laugh. "Why not?"

I felt chilled, but I had no clear idea why. "And how does Kuiper fit into this?"

"Well, I've no idea. Not yet." He pulled up an image of his own face on CNN. "I'm hoping that if I can tap into the interest in Kuiper, I'll get resources to push some of these questions farther. For instance, there may be links between the core explosions and Earth's past."

"Links?"

"Possibly the explosions tie in with extinction events, for instance."

"I thought an asteroid impact killed off the dinosaurs."

"That was a one-off. There have been eighteen other events. You can see it in the fossil record. Eighteen that we know of . . ."

I lifted my mug to my lips, but found it drained of coffee. I put the mug on the computer table and stood. "I ought to start my day."

He looked at me doubtfully. "I've gone on too long. I'm sorry; I don't get much chance to talk; most people wouldn't listen at all . . . You think I'm a crank."

"Not at all."

"Of course you do." He stood, looming over me, and grinned. Again there was that disarming self-deprecation, and

I sensed, uncomfortable again, that he really was glad to have renewed his connection with me, regardless of my reaction. "Maybe I am a crank. But that doesn't mean the questions aren't valid. Anyhow, you're the one with the abducted sister."

"That's true. I ought to go."

"Come back and tell me what you find."

chapter 7

Magnus sat cross-legged, hunched over the little wooden game board.

Magnus was a great bear of a man with a head the size of a pumpkin, it seemed to Regina, a head so big his helmet seemed to perch on top of it. But then, his helmet wasn't actually his but had been passed on to him from another soldier, just as had his sword and shield. Meanwhile his cowhide boots and his woolen tunic and his *cucullus*, his heavy hooded cloak, had all been made in the village behind the Wall, nothing to do with military issue at all. That awkward secondhand helmet had a dent in it, big enough to have held a goose's egg. Regina wondered sometimes if the mighty blow that had inflicted the hollow had been the cause of the original owner's "retirement."

For all his bulk Magnus was a patient man, which was why Aetius approved of him as a companion for Regina. After five years on the Wall she thought she knew her way around, but some of the rougher soldiers, she had been told in no uncertain terms, were *not* suitable companions for the prefect's twelve-year-old granddaughter.

Magnus was a good man, then. But he was so *slow*. His great ham of a hand hovered briefly over the board, but then he withdrew it.

"Oh, Magnus, come *on*," Regina pleaded. "What's so *difficult*? It's only a game of soldiers, and we've barely started. The position's *simple*."

"We haven't all got a prefect's blood in our veins, miss," he murmured laconically. He settled himself more comfortably, his spear cradled against his chest, and resumed his patient inspection of the board.

"Well, my backside is getting cold," she said. She jumped to her feet and began to pace up and down along the little tiled ridge behind the battlements.

It was a bright autumn day, and the northern British sky was a deep, rich blue. This was a sentry's lookout point, here on the wall of the fortress of Brocolitia—in fact, strictly speaking Magnus was on sentry duty right now—and she could see across the countryside, to the farthest horizon in every direction. The land here was rolling moorland, bleak even at the height of midsummer, and as autumn drew in it was bleaker still. There was no sign of life save for a single thread of black smoke that rose toward the sky, far to the north, so far away its source was lost in the mist that lingered even now, so close to noon.

And if she looked to left or right, to east and west, she could see the line of the Wall itself, striding away across a natural ridge of hard, black rock.

The Wall was a curtain of tiled brick and concrete, everywhere at least five times a man's height. A steep-sloped ditch ran along the north side. It was clogged with rubbish and weeds—and in some places the detritus of battles, broken sword blades and dented shields and smashed wheels; sometimes the hairy folk from the north would creep down to scavenge bits of iron. To the south, beyond the line of the road that ran parallel to the Wall, was another broad trench called the *vallum*. The *vallum* had been filled in here and there, to provide easier access between the fortresses on the Wall itself and the muddy little community of huts and roundhouses that had, over the generations, grown up to the south.

It was thrilling to think that the Wall's great line was drawn right across the neck of the country. On a clear day she could see the sentries walking back and forth along its length, all the way to the horizon, like ants on a bit of string. And while on the north side there was nothing but moorland, heather, and garbage, on the south side there was a whole string of communities, inhabited by the soldiers and their families, and those who lived off them. It was like a single town, some of the soldiers said, a Thin Town eighty miles long, a belt of drinking and whoring and cockfighting and gambling, and other vices she understood even less.

But much had changed during the Wall's long lifetime—so she had learned from Aetius's dogged teaching. The threat the Wall faced had evolved. Compared to the scattered, disunited tribes faced by Hadrian who'd built the Wall in the first place, today's great barbarian nations, like the Picts to the north of the Wall, were a much more formidable proposition.

Once, Aetius said, the Empire's military might had been like the snail of a shell: break through it and you were into the soft, defenseless core of the settled provinces. After the disastrous barbarian incursions of the recent past, that lesson had been learned well. For all its imposing presence, today the Wall was only part of a deep defensive system. Far behind the line of the Wall there were forts in the Pennines and farther south, from where any barbarian incursion could be countered. And north of the Wall itself there were more forts—though few of them manned these days. More effective were the *arcani* who worked among the northern tribes, spies spreading dissension and rumor and bringing back information about possible threats.

Regina had grown to love the Wall. Of course it showed its age. Much of this old fortress had been demolished or abandoned, for much smaller units were stationed here now. And time had inevitably ravaged the great structure. Some of the repair work was visibly cruder than the fine work of earlier generations—in places the old stonework had even been patched up with turf and rubble. But the barbarians had always been pushed back, the Wall reoccupied, the damage by friend or foe repaired, and so it would always be. In the five years since Aetius had brought her here, enclosed by its massive stones, she had come to feel safe, protected by the Wall and the power and continuity it represented.

Conversely, though, she was prone to anxiety over the future. Overall there were far fewer soldiers in Britain than in the past, Aetius said: perhaps ten thousand now, compared to fifty thousand before the disastrous imperial adventure of Constantius, which had stripped Britain of its field troops. Two nights ago a red glow had been easily visible in the night sky to the east, and in the morning there was a great pall of smoke, coming from the direction of the next fortress to the east, Cilurnum. Troops had been dispatched there to find out what had happened, and hadn't yet returned—or if they had, Aetius wasn't saying so to her. Well, there was nothing she could do about that.

Regina shivered, and rubbed her arms to warm up. The Wall might be a safe place, but it was uncomfortable. The great masses of stone retained the cold all through the day. After five years here, though, she had gotten used to the brisk climate and needed nothing more to keep her warm but her thick woolen tunic. And she had learned never to complain about the rigors of life here, so stripped-down compared to life in the villa, which she still remembered brightly. She had no wish to be called a spoiled child again, even though she knew that as the granddaughter of the prefect she was given special privileges.

". . . Ah," Magnus said.

She walked back to him. "Don't tell me you've moved at last, O Great General."

"No. But your grandfather's come out to play." He pointed.

On the southern side of the Wall, Aetius had led his cohort out of the fortress and was drawing them up on parade. Aetius stood straight and tall, an example to his troops. But Regina understood how much effort that cost him, for at sixty-five years old he was plagued by arthritic pains.

The soldiers' helmets and shields gleamed in the sun, and most of them wore the chill, expressionless bronze parade masks that had so terrified her when she first saw them. But their lines were ragged, with many gaps, and Aetius, waving his arms with exasperation, called out the names of the missing: "Marinus! Paternus! Andoc! Mavilodo! . . ."

Regina knew how infuriating Aetius found such ill discipline and lack of professionalism. Aetius had once served with the *comitatensis* forces, the highly mobile, well-equipped field army. Now he found himself the prefect of a cohort of the *limitaneus*, the static border army, and things were very different. These frontier troops had been on station here for *generations*. Indeed, nowadays most of them were drawn from the local people. According to Aetius, the *limitaneus* troops had become thoroughly indolent, even immoral. He raged at their habit of bringing actors, acrobats, and whores into the fortress itself, and their tendency to drink and even sleep when on watch.

All this was cause for concern, to say the least. Without a meaningful *comitatensis* in the country, these ragtag troops were all that stood between civilized Britain and the barbarians. And it was up to Aetius to hold them together.

Aetius consulted a clay tablet and called out a name. One unfortunate trooper stepped forward, a burly, harmless-looking man who didn't look as if he could run a thousand paces, let alone fight off a barbarian horde.

"I was only drinking wine to wash down horehound to get rid of my cough, Prefect."

"Do we not treat you well? Do you not enjoy medical attention even the citizens of Londinium would not be able to obtain? And is this how you repay us, by dereliction of duty?"

Regina knew that Aetius's scolding was harder for the miscreant troopers to bear than the lashings that would follow. But now the fat soldier lifted up his arm and shook it, so his bronze purse rattled. "And is this how the Emperor repays *me*? When was the last time *you* were paid, Prefect?"

Aetius drew himself up. "You are paid in kind. The temporary lack of coin—"

"I must still buy my clothes and my weapons, and bribe that old fool Percennius to give somebody else the latrine duty." There was laughter at that. "And all for the privilege of waiting for a poke up the arse from some Pict's wooden spear. Why do you think Paternus and the others have run off?"

Regina stared; she had never seen such defiance. She was uneasily reminded of how that farmer had stood up to her father.

But Aetius was not Marcus.

Aetius took a single step forward and slammed his gloved hand against the man's temple. To the clang of bone on metal, the man fell sideways into the dirt. Grunting, he rolled on his back—and, Regina saw, he actually touched the hilt of the short sword at his waist. But Aetius stood over him, fists bunched, until he dropped his hand and looked away.

The rest of the troop stood utterly silent.

Aetius pointed at two of them. "You and you. Take him. A

hundred strokes for drinking on guard, and a hundred more for what he has had to say today."

The men didn't move. Even from here Regina could feel the tension. If they were to disobey Aetius's order now . . . She felt a hot flush in her belly, and wondered if that was fear.

The two troopers, with every show of insolent reluctance, moved to their fallen colleague. But move they did. Aetius stepped back to let the man stand. His arms held behind his back, he was walked toward the whipping post. The tension bled out of the scene. But Regina still felt that odd warmth at her center.

One of the troopers, glancing up, pointed at her. "Look! Septimius—look at that! The red rain has begun . . ." The other troopers looked up at Regina, and began to point and laugh. Aetius railed at them, but their discipline was gone now.

She felt heat burn in her cheeks. She had no idea what she had done.

Magnus was at her side. He put an arm around her and tried to pull her away. "Come now. Put my cloak around you. It's all right."

"I don't understand," she said. And then she felt warmth on her legs. She looked down and saw blood, dripping out from beneath her tunic. She looked up in horror. "Magnus! What's happening to me? Am I dying?"

For all his strength he looked as uncertain and as weak as a child; he couldn't meet her eyes. *"Women's matters,"* he gasped.

Now the soldiers were catcalling. "I've waited all these years for you to blossom, little flower!" "Come sit on me, your old friend Septimius!" "No, me! Me first!" One of them had lifted his tunic to pull out his penis, like a floppy piece of rope that he shook at her.

Regina grabbed Magnus's heavy, musty-smelling woolen cloak and wrapped it around her. Then she clambered down the ladder to the ground and ran over the *vallum* toward the settlement, hiding her face.

For all Aetius raged at them, the soldiers kept up the baffling, terrifying barrage.

* * *

In their five years together at the Wall, Aetius had tried to tell Regina something of the world beyond the Wall. "There's been an awful lot of trouble for everybody. It all started the night the Rhine froze over, and the barbarians just walked into Gaul. But for Britain that wretch Constantius was the one who nailed down the coffin lid . . ."

The problems went Empire-wide, said Aetius. When the Empire had been expanding, new wealth had always been generated, from booty and taxation. But those days were long gone. And with the new, better-equipped, more powerful barbarian enemies, just as economic pressure increased, so did pressure on the borders, and more money had had to be found to pay for the defense of the realm. For a generation there had been problems and instability throughout the western provinces. Sometimes Aetius talked nostalgically about the great Stilicho, military commander in the western provinces, who had protected Britain. Aetius seemed to worship this Stilicho, even though, it turned out, he was a barbarian, Vandal-born. Barbarian or not, he had been the effective ruler of the west, under the ineffectual Emperor Honorius. But even the greatest generals grow feeble—and make lethal enemies at court.

And in Britain, since Constantius's adventure, the problems had been particularly acute.

After Constantius's subjects had thrown out his hierarchy of officials and tax collectors and inspectors, the cycle of taxation and state spending had broken down. Not only that, there was no mint in Britain, and after the expulsion of the moneymen there was no way to import coins from the rest of the Empire. Suddenly there weren't even any coins to circulate.

As everybody hoarded what they had left, people returned to barter. But with its lifeblood of coinage cut off, the economy was rapidly withering.

"There's just no money to pay the troops. You know, I heard that before I was posted here the soldiers even sent a deputation across the ocean to try to get the back pay they were owed. They never returned."

"They must have found some other place to live."

"Or had their throats slit by barbarians. We'll never know, will we? The people in the towns actually wrote to the Emperor himself and asked for help. This was only a few years ago. But by then, so it is said, Rome itself had been sacked by the barbarians. Honorius wrote back saying that the British must defend themselves as best they could . . ."

Aetius was worried about Regina's future. That was why he lectured her about politics and history and wars. He thought it was important to equip her for the challenges of her life.

And Aetius was obviously worried about his own future, too. If you completed twenty years' military service you could become one of the *honestiores*—the top folk in society. A career as a soldier was a way for a common man to retire to a nice house in the town or even a villa. But there was no obvious successor to Aetius, here in his station on the Wall, and he had no contact with the diocese's central command. If he stepped down, the troops would fall apart; he knew that. And besides there was nowhere for him to retire to. He had to hang on.

"Look," he would say, "this nonsense in Gaul has to stop. Rome is already back on its feet, and when he gets the chance the Emperor will reassert his authority here."

"And things will get back to normal."

"Britain has been lost to the Empire before—oh, yes, many times—and each time won back. So it will be this time, I'm sure." And when that happened, at last, when the tax collectors returned and the coins started to circulate once more—when the soldiers were properly paid and equipped and there was a secure place for him to retire—Aetius could allow his own career to end.

As it turned out, however, for Aetius it was all going to end much sooner than that. And far from everything returning to normal, Regina would have to suffer another great disruption.

After her humiliation before the soldiers, Regina fled to Cartumandua.

Carta was cooking a haunch of pork wrapped in straw. She had hung a big iron cauldron from a tripod and was using tongs to load in fire-hot rocks from the hearth; they sizzled as they hit the water. Her house was a wooden shack, built in the rectangular Roman way. The "kitchen" was just a space around a hearth built in a stone-lined pit, around which you would squat on the ground.

When Regina came bursting in, weeping, Carta dropped the tongs and ran to meet her.

"Carta, oh Carta, it was awful!"

Carta held Regina's face to her none-too-clean woolen smock, and let her weep. "Hush, hush, child." She stroked Regina's hair as she had when Regina was a pampered child of the villa, and Cartumandua a young girl slave.

Carta herself was still only twenty. Aetius had long made her a freedwoman, and allowed her to seek out her own destiny in this little below-the-Wall community, but she still had room in her life for Regina.

When Regina had calmed down enough to show her the blood, Carta clucked disapprovingly. "And nobody told you about this? Certainly not that old fool Aetius, I'll bet."

Regina gazed in renewed horror at the dried blood. "Carta—I'm afraid I'm dying. There must be something terribly wrong."

"No. There's nothing wrong—nothing save that you're twelve years old." And Carta patiently explained to her what had happened to her body, and helped her clean herself, and showed her how to pad herself with a loincloth tied with cords.

In the middle of this Severus came in, carrying a bundle of firewood. He was a soldier, a heavyset man, his stubble grimed with dirt. He glared at Regina. She had never seen him performing strictly military duties. He only ever worked around the little village, carrying food, repairing buildings, even working in the fields where oats were grown and cattle fed. In the shadow of the Wall the lines between the soldiers and the rest of the population had gotten very blurred, especially since marriage between the locals and the soldiers had been made legal.

Regina didn't like Severus. She had always hoped that Carta would take up with Macco, the stolid, silent slave who had accompanied them from the villa. But one night Macco had slipped away, apparently gone to seek his freedom in the countryside beyond the Emperor's laws. For Severus's part he seemed somehow jealous of Regina's relationship with Carta, which long predated his own attachment. Regina wasn't even sure what Severus's relationship with Carta was. They certainly weren't married. Regina thought he gave her some measure of protection, in return for companionship. It wasn't an uncommon arrangement.

But Carta was in control. Now she just waited until he dropped the wood and went away.

Carta made them both some nettle tea, and they sat on mats on the ground. Regina tried to describe how the soldiers had taunted her—now she was no longer afraid of dying, that seemed worst of all—and Carta comforted her, but told her such attention was something she was going to have to get used to. Slowly Regina calmed down.

Regina glanced around at the smoke-stained walls. The hut was wattle and daub, just mud and straw stuffed into the gaps in a wooden frame.

Carta said, "What are you thinking now?"

Regina smiled. "About my mother's kitchen. It was so different. I think I remember a big oven with a dome on it."

Carta nodded. "That's right. You could put charcoal in it and seal it up. It made perfect bread—that wonderful dry heat. And then there was a raised hearth."

"I could never see over the top of that. I wonder if it's still there."

"Yes," Carta said firmly. "I'm sure of it. You know your grandfather put the villa in the hands of a steward."

"But in these times you can't be sure of anything," said Regina.

Carta giggled girlishly. "Oh, my. You sound like an old woman! You can trust your grandfather to look after your family's property. He's a good man, and family is everything to him. *You* are everything . . . Won't he be worried about you? Maybe I should send a message—"

Regina shrugged. "Let him worry. He should have told me about the bleeding."

Carta snorted. "I think he'd rather face a thousand blue-faced Picts than that."

"Anyway he saw which way I came. If he's worried he'll come after me."

Carta sipped her tea. "He doesn't often come here, to the shadow of the Wall."

"Why not?"

"He doesn't fit. For one thing he's older than anybody here."

"What? That can't be true."

"Think about it," Carta said, eyeing her. "You know a good few people here. You're popular here, as you are everywhere! How many men over forty do you know? How many women over thirty-five?"

None, Regina thought, shocked—even though, she was sure, much older people had been commonplace in her parents' circle of friends, with wrinkles and white hair, the badges of age.

"Why is it like this?"

Carta laughed. "Because we don't live in villas. We don't have servants and slaves to clean our teeth. We have to work hard, all the time. It's the way it is, little Regina. Only the rich grow old."

Regina frowned. Even now, she resented being spoken to like that by a slave—even a former slave—even Carta. "There was no shame in the way we lived," she said hotly. "Our family was *civilized*, in the Roman way."

To her surprise Cartumandua gazed at Regina coldly. She said, " 'The allurements of degeneracy: assembly rooms, baths, and smart dinner parties. In their naïveté the British called it civilization, when it was really all part of their servitude.' "

"What's that?"

"Tacitus. You're not the only one who's learning to read, Regina." She got up and walked to her cauldron, and poked at the haunch of meat with a long iron skewer.

It was evening, a few days after Regina's humiliation on the Wall. By flickering candlelight, she was reading, in halting Latin, from the historian Tacitus. " 'Good fortune and discipline have gone hand in hand over the last eight hundred years to build the Roman state, which destroyed will bring down all together . . .' " She had asked for Tacitus after Carta's mild reprimand. This was a speech said to have been given three centuries earlier to rebelling tribes in Gaul by Petillius Cerialis, soon to be governor of Britain.

She was in Aetius's chalet, one of a row in this little community in the lee of the Wall. It wasn't grand, just a hut of four rooms built of wattle and daub to the rectangular Roman plan.

But it had a tiled floor and a deep hearth, and was cozy and warm. It had been erected when long-stay soldiers had first been allowed to marry and raise families. It was here, during an earlier tour of duty with the border troops, that Aetius had brought his bride Brica, and here that Julia, Regina's mother, had been born.

Its centerpiece was the *lararium*, the family shrine that Aetius and Regina had built together after their flight from the villa. The three crudely carved *matres* in their hooded cloaks sat at the center of a little circle of gifts of wine and food. But this was a soldier's shrine, and there were also tokens to such abstract entities as Roma, Victoria, and Disciplina, as well as a coin bearing the head of the latest Emperor anybody had heard of, Honorius.

And it was in his chalet that, at Aetius's insistence, Regina had continued her education. He expected her to become fluent in both her native language and in Latin—and to know the difference; Aetius despised what he called the "muddle," the patois of Latin-flavored British much favored by the ordinary people of the behind-the-Wall community. He had her read Tacitus and Caesar, historians and emperors and playwrights, from his store of fragile, ancient papyrus scrolls. She learned to write with styli on tablets of wax on wood, and with ink made of soot and a pen of metal. Later, he promised, he would train her in the art of rhetoric. But he believed in combining the best of the British and Roman traditions, and he also had her memorize long sagas of heroes and monsters in the old British style.

" 'At present, victor and vanquished enjoy peace and the imperial civilization under the same law on an equal footing. Let your experience of the alternatives prevent you from preferring the ruin that will follow on revolt to the safety that is conferred by obedience . . .' "

There was some disturbance outside. Shouting, what sounded like singing. No doubt the soldiers were getting drunk again. But Aetius didn't react, and Regina knew she was safe with him.

Aetius sat in his favorite basket chair, sipping beer. "Yes, yes . . . *the same law on an equal footing.* The law is above all of us—the landowners, the senators, even the Emperor him-

self, whoever that is right now. That is the genius of the old
system, you see. It doesn't matter who is in charge. It is the
system itself that has spread so far and sustained itself, even
though we have had soldiers and administrators and even emperors chosen from among those who would once have been
called barbarians. The system persists, while we come and go."

Standing there, holding the fragile papyrus in her hand, she
said, "Like an anthill. The Empire is like an anthill, and we are
all just ants, running around."

He slammed his wooden tankard down on the arm of his
chair. "Ants? Ants? What are you talking about, girl?"

"But an anthill organizes itself without anybody telling it
what to do. And even when one ant dies another takes her
place—even the queen. That's what the Greeks say, and they
studied such things. Isn't your Empire just like that?"

"Rome is not an anthill, you foolish child! . . ."

So they argued on, both aware of and enjoying their roles,
she mischievously provoking, he spluttering and snapping—

The door was thrown open with a crash.

In the doorway, framed by darkness, stood a soldier. He
staggered into the room, visibly drunk. When he saw Regina
he grinned.

Aetius seemed as shocked as Regina. But he took a step forward. *"Septimius,"* he said, his voice like thunder. "You're
drunk. And you should be on watch."

Septimius just laughed, a single bark. "Nobody's on watch,
you old fool. What does it matter? I haven't been paid. *You*
haven't been paid. Nobody cares anymore." He took a lurching step into the room. He was still staring at Regina, and she
could smell the drink on his breath. He was, she remembered,
the soldier who had exposed himself to her when she bled on
the Wall.

She backed away, but she found herself pressed against the
table and, in the confines of this little chalet, couldn't retreat
any farther.

Aetius took a measured step forward. "Septimius, get out of
here before you make things much worse for yourself."

"I don't think I will be taking any more floggings from you,
old man." He turned to Regina. "You know what I want, don't
you, miss? You're just ripe for the plucking—" He reached for

her. Regina flinched away, but Septimius grabbed her small breast and pinched it hard.

Aetius barreled into him, shoulder-first. Septimius was slammed against a wall, and the whole chalet shook with the impact. Aetius staggered upright. "You keep away from her, you piece of filth—" He hurled his fist, his mighty fist like a boulder.

But Septimius, drunk as he was, ducked underneath the punch. And as he rose, Regina saw a flash of steel.

"Grandfather—*no!*"

She actually heard the blade go in. It rasped on the coarse wool of Aetius's tunic. Aetius stood, staring at Septimius. Then dark blood gushed from his mouth. He shuddered and fell back, rigid, to the floor.

Septimius's mouth dropped open, as if he were aware for the first time of where he was, what he had done. He turned and ran into the night. Aetius lay on the floor, breathing in great liquid gurgles.

There was blood on the floor, blood pooling as it once had from her father's body. Regina forced herself to move. She ran to Aetius, and lifted his heavy head onto her lap. "Grandfather! Can you hear me? Oh, Grandfather!"

He tried to speak, coughed, and brought up a great gout of dark blood. "I'm sorry, little one. So sorry."

"No—"

"Fool. Been a fool, fooling myself. It's over. The Wall. They'll leave now, the last of them. No pay, you see, no pay. Cilurnum fell, you know. You saw the fire on the horizon. Cilurnum gone . . ." He coughed again. "Go with Carta."

"Cartumandua—"

"Go with her. Her people. No place for you here. Tell her I said . . ."

She asked the question that had burned in her young heart for five years. If he died, he could never answer it, she might never know. "Grandfather—*where is my mother?*"

"Rome," he gasped. "Her sister is there, Helena. So weak, that one. Wouldn't even wait for you . . ." He grabbed her shoulder. His palm was slick with blood. "Forget her. Julia doesn't matter. You're the family now. Take the *matres*."

"No! I won't go. I won't leave you."

He thrashed in his spreading pool of blood, and more crimson fluid gushed from the ripped wound in his chest. "Take them . . ."

She reached out and grabbed the little statues from their shelf in the *lararium*. At last he seemed to relax. She thought he wanted to say more, but his voice was a gurgle and she could make out no words.

Suddenly something broke in her. She pushed away his head, letting it fall to the floor, and ran to the broken doorway, clutching the statues. She looked back once. His eyes were still open, looking at her. She fled into the night.

chapter 8

Somewhat to my surprise, the head of Saint Bridget's, the school Gina had attended, was welcoming, initially anyhow. She listened to my tale of the photograph, though she was obviously skeptical about my story of a missing sister.

She had me sit in her office, on an armchair before her big polished desk. Ms. Gisborne was a slim, elegant woman of maybe fifty-five, with severely cut silver-gray hair. Over a business suit she wore a black academic gown lined with blue—the school colors, as I vaguely remembered from my sister's day. The office was well appointed, with a lush blue carpet, ornate plasterwork around the ceiling, a trophy cabinet, a large painting of the school on the wall opposite big windows, lots of expensive-looking desk furniture. It had the feel of a corporate boardroom; perhaps this sanctum was used to impress prospective parents and the local sponsors that seem essential to the running of any school these days. But an immense and disturbingly detailed Crucified Christ hung from one wall.

My chair, comically, was too low. I sat there sunk in the thing with my knees halfway up my chest, while the head loomed over me.

She didn't remember Gina—in fact, Ms. Gisborne was actually about the same age as my older sister—but she had taken the trouble to find some of her reports. "She came over well: a bright, pretty girl, natural leader . . ." The kind of thing people had always said of Gina. But she held out little hope of tracing any record of any younger sister, and clearly thought it odd that I should even be asking. "There was a preschool department here in those days—for the under-fives, you understand—but it has long since closed down. The school's gone through a lot of changes since then. I'll see if Milly can find the records, but I'm not optimistic. It's all so long ago—no offense!"

"None taken."

While we were waiting for the secretary to go down into the dungeons, Ms. Gisborne offered me the choice of a coffee, or a quick tour of the school. I felt restless, embarrassed, foolish, and I knew I would quickly run out of conversation with the headmistress of a Catholic school. I chose the tour. I had a little trouble hauling my bulk out of the tiny chair.

Out we walked.

The school was a place of layered history. A frame of two-story Victorian-era buildings enclosed a small grassy quadrangle. "We encourage the students to play croquet in the summer," said Ms. Gisborne lightly. "Impresses the Oxbridge interviewers." The corridors were narrow, the floor hardwood with dirt deeply ground in. There were immense, heroic radiators; huge heating pipes ran beneath the ceiling. We walked past classrooms. Behind thick windows rows of students, some in blue blazers, labored at unidentifiable tasks.

"It all reminds me of my own school," I said uncomfortably.

"I know how you feel; many parents of your generation feel the same. Narrow corridors. Oppressive ceilings." She sighed. "Doesn't create the right atmosphere, but not much we can do short of pulling it all down."

We passed out of the central block. The peripheral buildings were newer, dating from the fifties through to more recent times. I was shown a custom-built library constructed in the eighties, a bright and attractive building within which there seemed to be as many computer terminals as bookshelves. The students worked steadily enough, so far as I could see, though no doubt the presence of the head was an encouragement.

Ms. Gisborne kept up a kind of sales patter. Once the school had been run by a teaching order of nuns. During the comprehensivization of Britain's schools they had left, or been driven out, depending on your point of view. "Although we still have contacts with them," Ms. Gisborne said. "And with a number of other Catholic groupings. Since Gina's time, as I said, we have closed down our preschool section, and merged administratively with a large boys' school half a mile away. We now provide what would have been called sixth-form support in your day—sixteen- to eighteen-year-olds. Our academic record is good, and . . ."

I suspected she was as bored with me as I was of her, and that half her mind was elsewhere, engaged with the endless, complex task of running the place.

The most spectacular new building turned out to be a chapel. It had a concrete roof of elaborate curves. It turned out this was intended to model the tents within which Moses's flock lived while crossing the desert. Beneath that startling roof the interior space was bright, littered with fragments of red and gold from the long stained-glass windows, and there was a smell of incense.

I felt oddly uncomfortable. The school still retained its profoundly religious core, within a shell of reform and renovation, persisting through the decades, an old, dark thing surviving.

Ms. Gisborne seemed to sense my unease, and from that moment in the chapel she grew oddly hostile.

"Tell me—when was the last time you were in a church?"

"Two weeks ago, for my father's funeral," I said, a bit harshly.

"I'm sorry," she said evenly. "Was your parents' faith strong?"

"Yes. But I'm not my parents."

"Do you regret having had a Catholic education?"

"I don't know. It was such a huge part of my life—I can't imagine how I might have turned out if I hadn't."

"You will have left school with a strong moral sense, a sense of something *bigger* than you are. Even if you reject the answers, you keep the questions: *Where did I come from, where am I going? What does my life mean?*" She was smiling, her face strong and assured. "Whether you turn away from the faith or not, at least you have been exposed to its reality and potential. Isn't that a legacy worth taking away?"

"Do you think your secretary will have finished by now?"

"More than likely. You know, I'm surprised you came here, searching for this mysterious 'sister.' "

"Why? Where else would I go?"

"To your family, of course. To Gina. Perhaps you aren't very close. Pity." She led the way out of the chapel, back across the compound to the main block.

The secretary, Milly, had indeed come up with a stack of old preschool records. Forty years old, they were sheets of yellowed paper, some ruled into columns by hand, closely handwritten or typed, and kept in battered-looking box files. Somewhere there must be similarly dusty fossils of my own school career, I realized bleakly.

Ms. Gisborne riffled through the boxes briskly, running a manicured nail down rows of names. I could see she was getting nowhere. "There's nobody with the surname *Poole* in here," she said. "You can see I've looked a year or two to either side of—"

"Perhaps you could try another name. Casella."

She frowned at me. "What's that?"

"My mother's maiden name. Maybe that was how she registered the child."

She sighed and closed the box file. "I fear we are wasting our time, Mr. Poole."

"I have the photograph," I said plaintively.

"But that's all you have." She didn't sound sympathetic. "There are many possible explanations. Perhaps it was a cousin, a more distant relative. Or simply another child, a playmate, with a chance resemblance."

I struggled to say what I felt. "You must see this is important to me."

She stared at me, an intimidating headmistress faced by an awkward student. But she turned back to the first of her box files and began again.

It took her five more minutes to find it. "Ah," she said reluctantly. "*Casella*. Rosa Casella, first attended nineteen sixty-two . . ."

I found my breath was short. Perhaps on some level I hadn't quite believed in the reality of this lost sibling after all, even given the photograph. But now I had a kind of confirmation. Even a name—*Rosa*. "What happened to her?"

Ms. Gisborne riffled through a couple of pages. "When she reached primary school age she was transferred—ah, here we are—to an English-language school in Rome . . ." She read on.

I sat there feeling, of all things, jealous. Why should this mysterious Rosa have had the benefit of an education in some fancy Roman school? Why not me?

Abruptly Ms. Gisborne dropped the pages back in the box file and closed it with a snap. "I'm sorry. This is too irregular. I shouldn't be telling you this. The connection is only through what you claim was your mother's maiden name—"

I guessed at another connection. "This school in Rome. Was it run by a Catholic order?"

"Mr. Poole—"

"The Puissant Order of Holy Mary Queen of Virgins?"

"Mr. Poole." She stood up.

"It was the Order, wasn't it? That was the name you just read." It was a strange situation. I couldn't understand her sudden hostility when we had gotten to the records of the Order. It was as if she were defending it—but why I had no idea. Perhaps she had something to hide. I stabbed in the dark. "Does this school have links to the Order, too? Is that why you're suddenly so defensive?"

She walked to the door. "Good day to you now." As if by magic Milly opened the door, apparently waiting to throw me out.

I stood up. "Thanks for your time. And you know—you're right. I will go see Gina. I should have gone there first." I smiled, as coldly as I could. "And if I find out anything that embarrasses your school and its murky past you can be sure I'll broadcast it."

Ms. Gisborne's face was as expressionless as a statue's. "You are an unpleasant and flawed man, Mr. Poole. Good day to you."

And as the big school door was closed against me, *unpleasant and flawed* was just how I felt—along with a big dose of good old Catholic guilt.

Guilty or not, on the way home I used my cell phone to book a flight to Miami.

chapter 9

The journey south from the Wall, through a dismal, closed-in British autumn, was a blur, a bad dream. It was nothing like the adventure with Aetius, five years earlier. This time the three of them—Regina, Cartumandua, and Severus—weren't even riding in a proper carriage but in a crude, dirty, stinking cart used for carrying hay and cattle muck. In five years the road had decayed badly, with the roadside ditches clogged with weeds and rubbish, the waystones tumbled, smashed, or stolen, and potholes where the locals had prised cobbles out of the surface for building materials. The way stations and inns seemed a lot more run-down, too.

But Regina didn't care.

She sat in the back of the cart with Cartumandua, wrapped in her *cucullus*, hunched over on herself, with the three *matres* clutched to her belly. She didn't talk, wouldn't play games, and was reluctant to eat. She wasn't even afraid, despite Severus's constant, gloomy warnings of the danger they faced from *bacaudae*. These wanderers who plagued the countryside were refugees from failed towns and villas, or barbarian relics of beaten-back invasions, or even former soldiers who had abandoned their posts. The *bacaudae* were symptoms of the slow breakdown of the diocese's society, and all had to be assumed a threat.

She slept as much as she could, though her dozing was interrupted by the jolting of the cart. At night she lay on straw-stuffed pallets, or sometimes just on blankets and cloaks scattered on dirt floors, listening to Severus's drunken fumblings at Cartumandua. Sometimes she stayed awake all through the night, until the dawn came. At least she was alone in the dark. And if she stayed awake she had a better chance

of escaping into the oblivion of sleep during the misery of
the day.

But when she did sleep, each time she woke she was disappointed to be back in this uncomfortable reality, the endless,
meaningless, arrow-straight road surface, and to the fact that
she was *alone* now, alone save for the *matres*—and perhaps
her mother, who had abandoned her to go to Rome.

At last they approached a walled town. The town was set beside a river, on a plain studded with farmsteads. Beyond the
town a hillside rose steeply, with a scattering of buildings on
its flanks and at its summit.

The town's wall was at least twice Regina's height. It was
faced with square tiles of gray slate, but in places the slates
had decayed away or had been stripped off, exposing a core of
big rubble blocks set in concrete, interspersed with layers of
flat red bricks. It would have been dwarfed, of course, by the
great northern Wall.

They came to a gate, a massive structure with two cylindrical towers topped with battlements. There were two large entrances through which the road passed, and two smaller side
passages, evidently meant for people. But the side passages
were blocked with rubble, and one of the big archways had
collapsed.

A man stood before the gate, blocking their way. He wore
the remnants of a soldier's armor, strips of tarnished metal
held in place over his chest by much-patched leather bands.
He was armed—but only, comically, with what looked like a
farmer's iron scythe. Severus negotiated. As a former soldier
he had a basis of contact with the gatekeeper, and they shared
dull, incomprehensible details of assignments and ranks and
duties.

From the walls other men watched, men armed with swords
and bows. They peered down speculatively at Regina and
Carta. Regina stayed hunched inside her cloak, trying to make
herself shapeless and insignificant.

Old soldier or not, Severus had to pay a toll to be allowed
into the town, at which he grumbled loudly. The cart rattled
through the gateway, jolting over debris. The wall was thick

enough that the gateway was a kind of tunnel, and the clatter of the horses' hooves echoed briefly.

When they emerged into the light again, they were inside the town—but Regina's first impression was of green. Away from the road almost every bit of land was farmed, given over to orchards and vegetable gardens. Animals wandered: sheep, goats, chickens, even a pig rooting at a broken bit of the road-way. People bustled, adults and children walking or running everywhere, all of them dressed in simple woolen tunics and cloaks. There was a strong stink of animals, of cooking food, and a more powerful stench underlying it all, the stench of sewage.

It wasn't like a town at all. It was a slice of countryside, cut out by the wall. But here and there grander structures— arches, columns—loomed out of the green, and threads of smoke lifted to the sky.

Under Severus's direction the cart nudged forward cau- tiously through the crowd.

Carta murmured to Regina, "Well, we have arrived. Do you know where you are?" When Regina didn't answer, she said, "Do you even care?"

"Verulamium," Regina snapped. "I'm not *stupid*."

Carta smiled. "But I would call it *Verlamion*. This was the town of the Catuvellauni, my people. In the days when we bat- tled Caesar himself, under our great king Cymbeline . . ."

"I know all that. So you've come home."

"Yes." Carta leaned and faced her. "But it is *my* home," she said. "I am no slave now."

"Am I to be *your* slave, Cartumandua?"

"No. But you are a guest here. You will remember that."

Regina turned away, not wanting to be with Carta, not want- ing to be here in Verulamium, not wanting to be *anywhere*. But even she was impressed when the cart pulled up at a grand town house, set at the corner of two intersecting streets. A cen- tral courtyard was bordered by an open cloister lined by slim columns. In the courtyard itself was a small hut that might have been a porter's lodge, but it was boarded up. There were some signs of dilapidation, but the white-painted walls and the red-tiled roofs were mostly intact.

Three people came out of the buildings. An older man and a

woman were similarly dressed, in plain woolen tunics, but the younger man wore brighter colors. The woman, it turned out, was a servant, called Marina. She helped Severus remove the horses' harness, and led them away to a small stable outside the main compound.

"Marina is a servant, but not a slave," Carta murmured in Regina's ear. "Remember that."

The older man, beaming, embraced Carta. But he seemed to shun Severus. He turned to Regina and bowed politely. "Cartumandua wrote to tell me all about you. You're very welcome in our home. I am Carta's uncle—the brother of her mother. My name is Carausias . . ." He was a short, stocky man, shorter than Carta, with the big, callused hands of a farm laborer. He had Carta's dark coloring, deep brown eyes, and broad features, though his neatly cropped black hair was shot with gray, and his wide nose was flattened and crooked, as if it had been broken.

"And this is my son. His name is Amator."

The boy was about eighteen. His tunic was short and extravagantly colored, and he had it pinned over one shoulder by a silver brooch, leaving the other shoulder bare. He had the family coloring, and his features, as wide and blunt as Carta's or her uncle's, could not have been called handsome. But as he bowed to Regina, wordless, his gaze was intense.

She felt something stir inside her: something warm, even exciting—and yet tinged with the fear and disgust she had first known when confronted by Septimius's drunken lust. She turned away, confused. She was aware of the boy's gaze following her.

As Carta, Severus, and the others unloaded the cart, Carausias took her to the room where she would sleep. It had a plain tile floor and green-painted walls. To Regina's dismay there were two beds in here, along with small cupboards and trunks. "Will I share with Carta?"

"Well, no." Awkwardly he said, "Carta and, umm, Severus will want to be together. I've opened up another of the rooms for them, where the roof isn't too bad . . . You will share with Marina."

"With the *servant*?"

He stiffened. "Marina is a good woman, and she is clean and

quiet. I am sure you will be fine." He hesitated. "Look—Carta has told me what happened. I know things have been difficult."

"I am grateful for your hospitality—"

He waved a hand. "It doesn't matter. I will ask Marina to sleep elsewhere, just for a while, until you find your bearings. Even the kitchen, perhaps. She's a good soul; she won't mind . . . You can have the room to yourself for a bit. How would that be?"

She took a step into the room. "Thank you."

"Would you like to rest? If you need to bathe—"

"No."

"When it's time to eat—"

"Could I eat in here? In my room?"

Carausias seemed taken aback, but he spread his broad hands. "I don't see why not. I'll send Carta to talk to you later."

"Yes. That will be fine . . ." She shut the door on the kindly little man, and receded into the darkness and silence with relief.

She curled up on one of the couches—the one that smelled more fresh—and slept until Carta came, with a small bowl of water for her to wash and clean her clothes.

That first day she emerged only to use the latrine in the little bathhouse. Carta brought her food, mildly reminding her that she would be welcome to eat with the family. Regina stirred from the couch only to set up her *lararium*, just an improvised little shrine in an emptied-out cupboard, with the three *matres* standing sullen and silent at its center. She lit a candle beside them, and gave them bits of her food and the watered-down wine that came with it.

They wouldn't indulge her forever.

On the second day Carta forced Regina out of the room, and walked her in a slow circle around the courtyard, showing her the layout of the house.

"Here we have the *triclinium*—" It was the Latin word for a 'dining room,' deriving from the couch that ran around three sides of the room. The mosaic floor was intact, and the walls' painted designs, mock pillars, and glimpses of fabulous gardens, were clean and neat, though they looked faded. In one corner of the compound was a still grander room, but it was cluttered by low tables and cooking implements, pots, pans, and heaps of crockery and cutlery; a row of narrow-based amphorae leaned against one wall. "This was a reception room," Carta said a little wistfully. "Now it's a kitchen. It even had underfloor heating, but Carausias says you just can't get the workmen to maintain it. Anyhow the cooking keeps it warm enough. And the courtyard faces south, you know; in the summer it's quite a sun trap . . ."

There were private rooms along the two remaining sides of the courtyard, a small bathhouse, and a narrow staircase that led down to the family shrine. The house was a grand place, if not as grand as her parents' villa had been. But it had obviously seen better days. Many of the rooms were boarded up, and one showed signs of a fire.

As they walked she saw a flash of color, a lithe movement on the far side of the courtyard. It was the boy, Amator. He had been tracking them, watching her with that heavy, liquid gaze.

Regina repaired to her room as soon as she could get away from Carta.

On the third day there was a knock on the door. She opened it, expecting Carta again. It was Carausias. He smiled at her, his hands folded over his belly. "May I come in?"

"I—"

Before she could resist he had stepped through the doorway. He glanced around at the room, her little piles of clothes and effects, and nodded respectfully at her *lararium*. "I'm terribly sorry, my dear, but I'm afraid Marina needs her room back. She's hardly comfortable sleeping in the kitchen. And besides she's out of clean clothes."

"Fine," Regina snapped, and she sat on her bed, arms folded. "Let the servant back in. I'll sleep in the kitchen. Or in the stable with the horses."

"Now, that's absurd." He crouched before her, his features softened in the gloom. "We only want to make you feel welcome. Welcome and safe."

"I don't want to be here. I don't want to be with *you*."

He looked hurt. "Then where do you want to be?"

"In Rome," she said. "With my mother."

He sighed. "But Gaul is full of barbarians, my dear. I don't think anybody is going to be traveling to Rome for some time.

Not until things settle down. And in the meantime," a little more sharply, "perhaps it's time you made the best of it."

She laughed at him. "What *best*? There is no best. I'm stuck here in this *dump*. And—"

"But this dump is all that's available," he said, his voice steady but firm. "Listen to me now.

"Not long ago I and my wife and my son, all of us, were servants, like Marina. We worked on a villa, not far from the town walls. When the troubles began, things got difficult for the owners. They were extravagant, and they didn't want to stop their spending, even when their savings ran low. They tried to sell us—*sell us all,* to work as farm laborers—but we were not slaves. In the end the owners fled, taking everything of value from the villa—the money, the jewelry, the pottery, even much of the furniture. But they abandoned the buildings, and the land. And us.

"And so we took over. We began to work the land ourselves. We brought in our relatives and friends to live on the farmsteads. We soon had a surplus, which we brought into the town to buy goods for ourselves. This is only three harvests ago.

"After the second year we had accumulated enough to be able to buy this town house, from an owner desperate to flee to Londinium. Though stewards still run our villa, it is safer for us within the walls.

"We have done well. There are only ten houses like this left within the walls of the city, and of those, three are empty. No doubt things will settle down, when the Emperor overcomes his troubles. But in the meantime, we will do what we Catuvellaunians have always done. We will work hard, and we will support each other, and we will get by."

He stood up. "You are not even Catuvellaunian. But Carta has brought you here. I am inviting you to become part of this family, this community. You will have to work hard, for we all must work. If you do, you are welcome. If not—well, we can't even afford another servant. You must understand this." He stood over her, waiting.

At length she said, "The kitchen."

"What?"

"I'd like to go to the kitchen. Please."

He seemed nonplussed. But he said, "Very well." He held out his hand.

Marina was working in the kitchen, making lunch for the family. There was a rich smell of fish sauce, which Marina was mixing into a salad of legumes and fruit. She was a stolid, cheerful-looking woman of about thirty. She wore her brown hair pulled back in a simple bun. She smiled at Regina, apparently not offended at this stranger who had stolen her room for so long.

Regina looked around. Shelves had been fixed to the walls over grand, fading paintings; on them were stacked mortars, colanders, cheese presses, and beakers, flagons, platters, and bowls of metal, glass, and pottery. The amphorae leaning against the walls had once, according to their inscriptions, contained olive oil, dates, figs, fish sauce, and spices from the east. Now, much repaired, they contained nuts, wheat, barley, oats, and the flesh of animals and fish, salted, pickled, or smoked.

There was no oven, but a hearth had been set up in the middle of the mosaic floor, and a chimney cut crudely into the ceiling. No fire burned today, but soot stained the paintwork of the ceiling and upper walls. Many of the mosaic's tesserae had been cracked or charred by the heat. A gridiron was set over the charred patch, with a large cauldron suspended from a chain above it. Regina could see that the mosaic had featured a girl, slim and pale, surrounded by leaping dolphins.

Marina nodded to a quern stone, set up in the corner of the room. "We need flour. I'll bake some bread later. Do you know how to use the stone? . . ."

And so Regina, under Marina's instructions, sat on the floor and began to grind wheat. The familiar, eternal smells and sounds of the kitchen soon immersed her, and as she worked at the stone, her muscles tingling with the unaccustomed effort, she felt her obsessive thoughts dissolve.

She hardly noticed when the tears started.

Marina did, though. The servant came to embrace her, patting her back, making sure she didn't make a mess of the few gritty handfuls of flour she had managed to produce.

* * *

The next day Carausias took Regina for a walk through the town. They were to go shopping in the Forum.

They set off in bright midmorning—it was a cold, clear, crisp October day—but Carausias warned Regina she had to be alert. "You were protected in your villa, and even on the Wall. But in the town it's different. People don't behave very nicely. There are plenty who'll slit your purse—or slit your throat for their trouble . . ."

Regina listened. But she had found her way around the Thin Town, and had endured similar warnings from Aetius since the age of seven.

The town, surrounded by its walls, was shaped like a lozenge. It was crisscrossed by a grid pattern of streets, dominated by the road from the north that passed through the town toward Londinium in the south. A great arch spanned the Londinium road. Regina stared at this monument of carved marble, more ornate than any single structure she had seen in her young life. But ivy and lichen clung to its face, obliterating the inscription on the lintel, and a bored-looking crow hopped about on its guano-streaked carapace.

Near the arch the road passed close by a very strange building. It was an open space bounded by a semicircular wall several times her height, with steps leading up to its parapet. It was, said Carausias, the theater. When she asked if she could climb the steps, he agreed, smiling indulgently.

The steps were wooden, and were old and broken. At the parapet she found herself looking down into a bowl. Sloping terraces were covered by semicircular rows of wooden seats, now broken and stained. At the front was a stage like a little temple, fronted by four slim columns. The only performers on the stage right now were mice, a pair of which scuttled from pillar to pillar.

Carausias followed, wheezing a little with the exertion. "You could seat four hundred people in here. And the plays—some of them went over my head, but I liked the *fabula togata*, the comedies, like *The Accusation* and *What You Will*. And then there were the farces—my late wife was especially fond of *The Vine Gatherers*—how we laughed at that one, where the fellow with the grape basket falls over, and . . ."

None of this meant much to Regina. She only knew what a

play was through her readings with her grandfather. The theater was full of rubbish, a compost of rotting food waste and rubble and smashed pottery and even what looked like the bloated corpse of a donkey, all littered by the dead leaves of autumn. The garbage was rising like a slow tide up the bank of seats, and when the wind turned, a stench of rot hit her.

Carausias sighed, plucked her sleeve, and led her down the stairs.

They cut down a side street, heading for the Forum. This street was lined with shops. They were long, narrow buildings, set very close together, with workshops and dwellings in the rear sections. Peering inside, Regina recognized a butcher's store, a carpenter, and a metalworker; the butcher's was doing the briskest business. But several of the shops were closed up.

Carausias said regretfully, "Here, only a few years back, you could buy the finest pottery—imported if you want, even Samian, but the stuff from the west country and the north was just as good and a lot more affordable. Now you can't get new pots no matter what you pay; we just have to make do and mend, until the Emperor sorts himself out." He eyed her. "What about you, Regina? Have you thought how you'd like to occupy yourself when you're older? Perhaps you could learn pottery. I bet this shop could be bought for a song . . ."

Regina had no idea how pottery was made, but imagined it must involve sticky messes of clay and a lot of hard work. She said politely, "I don't think I'd be enough of an artist for that, Carausias."

They reached the Forum. It was an open square, crowded with stalls of canvas and wood. People thronged, buying and selling, immersed in a cloudy stink of spices, meat, vegetables, and animal dung. Chickens ran clucking, chased by grimy-faced children.

But around this melee the Forum was surrounded on three sides by small temples and colonnaded walkways. And on the fourth side was a great hall, constructed of brick, flint, and mortar, and roofed with red tile. It loomed over the rest of the town. Regina gaped. Aside from the Wall itself she had never seen anything built on such a scale.

Carausias gently tucked his finger under her chin and closed her mouth. "Now, you must be careful, for if the villains see you are distracted—"

"Is it a temple?"

"No—although the Basilica does host a shrine to the Aedes, the tribal god, as well as shrines to the Christ and the Emperor. Look—can you read the inscription up there?"

She squinted, trying to make out the chipped Latin markings: "TO THE EMPEROR TITUS CAESAR VESPASIAN, SON OF THE DEIFIED VESPASIAN . . ."

"This is the Basilica. It is here that the town council meets, that the court settles disputes, that offices of tax and census operate—there are schoolrooms, too."

Under the imperial administration, the towns had been the center of local government. Nowadays, though the tax system had pretty much imploded after the rebellion during Constantius's reign, the local landowners kept up the court system and were discussing ways to raise levies to keep up the town's amenities, like the sewers, the baths, and the Basilica itself, which were slowly falling into disrepair. These would all be temporary measures, of course, Carausias continued to insist, until the Emperor resolved his difficulties.

"But people ought to show a little more civic responsibility," he complained. "Nowadays people will sink endless amounts of money into their villas or town houses, while they let the sewers of Verulamium go to ruin. There has always been a tension in your Roman between civic responsibility and a veneration of the family, living and dead. In times of hardship he retreats to the family, you see. But how does he think the soldiers who protect him will be paid, if not for taxes, and how will taxes be collected, if not for the towns? Eh, eh? And that's why *I* pay for keeping up sewers and water pipes and all the rest. I know where my interests lie . . ."

Regina wasn't much interested in this.

Carausias and Regina moved through the Forum, checking the stalls. They were particularly seeking spices, olive oil, and above all pottery. But they found little but local produce. Much of the commerce was conducted in kind—meat for vegetables, a bit of secondhand pottery for some shoe nails—though some people, including Carausias, used handwritten scrips.

The fruits and vegetables on display looked poor to Regina. She fingered a bunch of spindly, discolored carrots. Carausias said dismissively, "You get folk from the town moving out into fields not tilled since their great-grandfathers were alive. They haven't the first idea. And this is the result . . ." Regina put down the carrots guiltily. They had come from a stall manned by a thin woman with sallow, dirty skin, and protruding teeth. A swollen-bellied child clung to her leg.

When they had done their shopping, mostly unsuccessfully, Carausias led her back to the Londinium road, and they walked away from the Forum, heading farther southeast.

They came to a temple. It was set in a place where the main road forked, and it had been shaped by its location into a V shape, a triangular courtyard before a purple-painted building.

There was a scent, like wood smoke. Regina sniffed. "That's lovely."

"Burned pinecones." Carausias watched her carefully. "Do you know what this place is? What about the inscription?" Set over the main entrance to the courtyard, it was a dedication to the *dendrophori* of the town. "That word means 'branch bearers' . . ."

"I don't understand."

Carausias touched her shoulder. "Child, Cartumandua told me what became of your father."

She felt her face close up.

"This is a temple to Cybele, who is popular here. I myself come here to worship . . . If you would like to come inside—"

"No," she snapped.

"You should make your peace with the gods—and with your father's memory—and with yourself."

"Not today."

"Well, perhaps that is wise. But the temple will always be here, waiting for you. Shall we go and see what Marina has prepared for supper? And we still have water to fetch . . ."

He took her hand and they walked together, back through the grubby bustle of Verulamium, toward home.

At Carta's insistence she had brought her scrolls and tablets with her from the Wall. Carta said that she should try to keep up her studies, for it was surely what Aetius would have wanted.

At first she tried. She would study in the courtyard of the house, or in her room when Marina was working. But she had to work alone. There was nobody here who could tutor her. For all his obvious business acumen and firm grasp of people, Carausias was no more educated than his niece, and beyond telling anecdotes of half-remembered plays from a decade before, he could not help her. He certainly couldn't afford to hire a tutor.

Gradually she got bored with her solitary studying. And as the weeks wore on, the days shortening as winter approached, the work came to seem less and less worthwhile. Who was ever going to care if she remembered lists of emperors and their accession dates or not? Nobody in Verulamium was sure who the *current* emperor was.

And then there was Amator to distract her.

One day, as she was trying to study in her room, Amator came wandering in. "Study, study, study," he teased her. "All you ever do. You're so *boring*."

"And you are a lazy clod with nothing better to do than annoy people," she shot back, repeating one of his father's taunts.

He strolled to Marina's bed. Grinning at her, he got to his knees and felt about in the space beneath the pallet. "Aha!" he proclaimed in triumph, and he pulled out a bit of bloody rag. It was one of the loincloths Marina used to pad herself during her periods. He sniffed the dried blood and rubbed it against his cheek. "Ah, the scent of a woman . . ."

Regina was laughing, and outraged. She put down her papyrus and came after him. "That's disgusting! Give it back—"

But he wouldn't, and they chased around the room for a while. They had developed a way of chasing without touching, of coming close but not quite into contact, a game with subtle, unspoken rules.

At length he yielded, threw himself down on Marina's bed, and tucked the bloody little relic back where it had come from.

"She'll know," said Regina.

"So what if she does? It's only Marina." He got up again and walked to her *lararium*, in one corner. "I've never taken a proper look at this before." He picked up one of the *matres*. "By Cybele's left nipple, how ugly."

"Put it down."

"And how *cheap*—"

"Put it down."

He looked up, startled at her tone. "All right, all right." He put down the little statuette—not in the right place; she promised herself she would fix it later. He said, "So every day you waste good food and wine on these bits of nonsense . . ." He eyed her. "But have you ever seen a *real* god?"

"What do you mean?"

For answer he beckoned her, and tiptoed out of the room. Of course, she followed.

Amator had his own chores to complete. Carausias was trying to train him to run the villa, the cause of much conflict between the two of them. But he always seemed to have plenty of spare time, and he seemed happy to spend a lot of it with Regina. When he discovered she liked "soldiers" he proclaimed himself an expert, dug out an old set from some corner of the house, and set it up in the courtyard where they would play. Or he would play ball-catching games with her, or simply chase her through the colonnades, or in the open spaces beyond the town walls. Gradually, almost tentatively, a relationship had built up between them.

But there was an edge to Amator. At eighteen he was so much older than she was. Perhaps she enjoyed the undercurrent of danger that she sensed about him, a boy who knew so much more than she did, had surely *done* so much more, and yet was so inexplicably interested in her. Amator was mysterious, disturbing, somehow enchanting—but above all he was fun, and he always seemed to dress with color and style, unlike the drab townsfolk.

Cartumandua maintained a frosty silence about all this.

They walked around the courtyard until they came to the head of the stone stairs that led to Carausias's shrine.

She stepped back. "No. I mustn't go down there. Carausias wouldn't like it."

"Well, Carausias doesn't like being bald and fat and old, but he's got to live with it. Come on—unless you're scared." He set foot on one step, then another, and was suddenly trotting down and out of sight.

After a heartbeat's hesitation, she followed.

The shrine was just a pit in the ground. She could hear Amator scratching, and then he held up a candle. His face seemed to hover in the dark.

In the uncertain light she could see that above the stonework of this little underground shrine there was a layer of darker earth. When she probed at it, it crumbled, and left black on her fingers, like soot. Later she would discover that twice during its short history Verulamium had been burned to the ground, and these burned ash layers were relics of those catastrophes.

An arched hollow had been cut into the wall. In it stood a little statuette, apparently bronze, of a man riding a horse. His outsized head bore a crested helmet. Small offerings had been laid out before him, perhaps fragments of food.

"Behold," said Amator mock-sepulchrally. "Mars Toutatis, the warrior god of the Catuvellauni. Held to be the Mars of Rome, while that was politically convenient. What now—do you think he will become the Christ? Will we have to carve a *chi-rho* above his head?"

"You shouldn't talk like that," she whispered.

"Or what? Is his horse going to piss down my leg?"

"We shouldn't be down here."

"I daresay you're right. But nobody is going to know." He bent forward and blew out the flame. The darkness was complete, save only for the faintest of diffuse daylight glows from the stairwell. She could sense his heavy warmth, less than a hand's breadth from her, and his breath was hot on her cheek.

He backed away, his tunic rustling softly. "Now we share a secret." He laughed, and his feet clattered on the stairs. She followed him into the daylight, but when she reached the ground, he had gone.

chapter 10

Miami Airport was a thoroughly unpleasant place. The queues of grimy adults and unhappy kids before the immigration barriers were as long and slow moving as I could remember in any American airport.

I'd taken many trips to the States over the years, for work, vacations—and in pursuit of my sister. After going to work in America some fifteen years before, Gina had come home only a handful of times, most recently, and even then grudgingly, for our father's funeral. Her two boys were the only kids in the family—that I knew of, I reminded myself, thinking of Rosa. They had quickly become precious to me, no doubt through some mixture of sentiment and genetic longing. But to get to see them, every time I had to endure these red-eye flights and the ferocity of U.S. immigration controllers.

Outside the terminal, the weather seemed unseasonably humid and hot for October. Nobody was there to greet me, of course. I took a cab from the airport to my hotel in Miami Beach. I was only maybe twenty miles from my sister. But taking a hotel room was my habit. I'd long learned not to put unnecessary pressure on Gina by actually having her put me up, despite my having flown around the world to see her.

I generally stayed at Best Westerns, but for this trip I'd decided to spend a little money, and had used the Internet to find a room at a big spa hotel on the coast. The hotel's air-conditioning was merciless, of course, and the temperature must have dropped twenty degrees as I stepped through the sliding doors to reception. But I was pleased with the plush, sweeping interior, the atrium done out in tiles of chrome and purple, the huge sunken bar, the glimpses of chlorine-blue pools beyond wide glass doors. Meeting rooms in bays clustered around the atrium; evidently the hotel relied a lot on corporate business, and I wondered if Gina got much work here.

My room was on the twelfth floor. I turned on the TV and briskly unpacked. The room was big, expansive, with a balcony that gave a view of the sea—at least it did if you crowded right up against the rail, and peered past the flank of the building and across a busy highway. It was late afternoon, but as always after a transatlantic flight it was eerie to see the sun still stranded so high above the horizon. I've always found flying tough.

I knew I should shower, have a drink, sleep as long as possible. But I felt restless, vaguely disturbed; right now my life seemed to be too complicated to let me relax.

I put on a fresh shirt, grabbed a handful of dollars, made sure I had pocketed my magnetic room card, and went out to the elevator.

I walked through the bar, through those big picture-window glass doors, and out to the pool area, a complex miniature landscape of white concrete. The heat was heavy, steamy, and my English trousers, shoes, and socks felt ridiculously heavy. For sure I wished I had brought a hat.

There were only a few people by the pool. A group of thirty-something women, bronzed, in bikinis, a little overweight, had gathered on sun loungers and were cooing over images in a digital camera—housewives attending the hotel's health club, perhaps.

There was an ungated gap in the rear wall of the pool area. I passed through and walked down a short path edged by long grass. I found myself on a boardwalk, a long wooden walkway standing over the sand and grass on low stilts. It stretched to my left and right, to north and south. Before me, beyond a broad stretch of pale gold sand, was the sea. There was a breeze in my face, hot but blustery. I could see nobody swimming, and a red flag fluttered over a small stilted structure, maybe a Coast Guard station. Hurricane Jonathan was rattling around the west Atlantic; it wasn't expected to touch down on land but was creating swell and wind.

I wasn't planning to swim anyhow.

I knew that if I walked south I would approach the town cen-

ter, so I turned that way and set off. I walked briskly past a series of gargantuan hotels, great art deco confections of concrete in shocking pink or electric blue, like spaceships parked
along the Atlantic coast. The boardwalk was easy on the feet,
but I seemed to be the only stroller. A few people passed
me, or overtook me, joggers or speed-walkers, mostly young
professional-looking types, dressed in Lycra or sweat suits,
tiny headphones clamped to their heads, their faces closed, un-
seeing. At regular intervals there were little open kiosks, with
big buttons you could press to call for police help.

This was my first time in Miami Beach. Gina had moved
here only nine months earlier. She ran a small company in
partnership with her husband of fifteen years, a New Yorker
called Dan Bazalget. They had met in New York during an
electronics product-launch event; they had both been working
in PR, for the same company on different sides of the Atlantic.
They had already been in their forties, with the complicated
pasts you acquire by that age; Gina had a childless divorce behind her, and Dan actually had a twenty-year-old daughter,
whom I'd never met. But once they had glommed onto each
other they had soon gone into business together, and then
sailed into parenthood, producing two fine boys as easily
as shelling peas, despite Gina's age. Now, based on Gina's
Florida inheritance, they sold something called "conference
visioning and management"—coordinating probably unnecessary conferences for senior business types.

My father the accountant had always mocked Gina's job
title. "I mean, can you take a degree in 'conference visioning'?" he would ask. Well, actually, yes, you could. I didn't
begrudge Gina her thoroughly modern choice of career or her
commercial success—not much, anyhow, given the usual
sibling-rivalry envy for a sister who in every aspect of her life
had always seemed to do better than I ever had.

When I had passed most of the big hotels I cut inland, passing through an alleyway. I crossed Ocean Drive, where even
the police officers wore skintight shorts, to reach a main street
called Collins Avenue. I bought a small tourist map for a few
dollars from a drugstore and briskly toured Miami Beach's
highlights. There was an art deco area, a small district pep-
pered with ornately decorated buildings—hotels, private

homes, banks, bars, some set behind heavy security gates. The most beautiful building of all seemed to be the town's main post office, a pointlessly grand edifice across whose magnificent floor queues snaked desolately.

I couldn't quite get the city into focus. There was a faint sense of sleaze about the place, of a past of dirty money and menace—and yet somebody had made a determined effort to clean it up, as witness the alarm buttons on the boardwalk. And I knew my sister well enough to know she wouldn't bring her kids to a place she couldn't make them safe. Still, I was relieved to get back to the boardwalk, and the huge physical presence of the sea.

I never watch American TV. Those constant ad breaks make me feel hyperactive, as if I've been taking too much sugar. I ordered up a movie, a comedy, and a room service "snack," bigger than most Sunday lunches back home, with a half bottle of Californian Chardonnay. I was asleep before the movie was over.

"George. Lovely to see you, et cetera." She took my shoulders and actually gave me an air-kiss, her left cheek brushing mine, her lips missing me by a good couple of inches. Automatically I shaped up for a second kiss on the right, but I'd forgotten that's the European way—in America you get just the one.

Well, that was about as much affection as I generally got from Gina.

She said, "As you can see I took time off work to see you, though Dan couldn't get away. The boys are on their way home from school. I secured them a half day off." Her accent was vaguely mid-Atlantic.

"I appreciate that . . ."

Her house was modern, the walls wooden, perhaps a little sun-bleached around the front door. The rooms were filled with light, lined with bookcases and TVs—it seemed there was a set in every room, and in most a computer—and there was a bright but slightly irritating smell, perhaps of pine-scented air freshener. This was a big, sprawling homestead set in an extensive acreage of finely cut lawn, over which sprinklers hissed, even at this hour, eleven in the morning. There is always so much space in America, so much room.

But the first thing I saw when I walked into her hallway was Dad's grandfather clock.

It was a big, moth-eaten, unmistakable relic, whose heavy, tarnished pendulum and time-stained clock face had made it a kind of focal point of our childhood. I hadn't noticed it missing in my clear-out visits to the house in Manchester. But now here it was—it looked as if it might even have been renovated—and I realized that Gina must have taken it from Dad, presumably with his consent, before he died.

She saw me looking at the damn clock. We both knew what it signified. It wasn't that I wanted the clock, or would have stopped her taking it, but I would have appreciated some discussion over this bit of our shared heritage. It wasn't a good start to the visit.

She took me to a breakfast room, sat me at a polished pine table, and loaded a coffee percolator. We sat and talked, inconsequentially, about the continuing fallout from our father's death: the sale of the house, his business affairs. She didn't ask me about my own life, but then she never did.

She looked her age, midfifties, but good with it. She looked physically relaxed, the way you do if you work out just enough. She'd let her thick blond hair fill with gray, and it was swept back from her temples and forehead, a little severely. I always thought of her face as a far more beautiful version of mine, her features more delicate, her chin smaller, her nose not quite so fleshy. Now wrinkles spread around her eyes and mouth, and her skin was a little weather-beaten, polished by the Florida sun. But she still had the family eyes, limpid and clear gray, what one of her boyfriends used to call *smoke-filled*.

We ran out of facts to swap, and the silence was briefly awkward.

She said, "It's good of you to come. It's important to be with family at a time like this. Et cetera."

"So it is," I said. It was true. For all the unending tension between us, as I looked into that face that was so like my own, I felt a certain peace I had lost since Dad's death.

But she broke the spell by saying sharply, "I know you think I should have stayed longer after the funeral."

"You've got your life to live here. It was easier for me to handle it."

"I suppose it was," she said. It was a coded put-down, of course. *You had the time because, by contrast with me, you don't have a life*. That's sibling rivalry for you.

I pulled her scrapbook about Regina out of my jacket pocket and put it on the table. "I found this at home. I don't remember you making it."

"Before your time, I suppose."

"I thought you might want it."

She pulled the dog-eared little book toward her. She didn't pick it up, but turned the pages with the tips of her thumb and forefinger. It was as if I had presented her with her afterbirth pickled in a jar. She said coldly, "Thanks."

I was irritated, with her and myself. "Shit, Gina. Why do we find it so hard to get on? Even at a time like this. I'm not here to fight—"

"Then why?" she said coldly.

"For Rosa," I said without hesitation. I was satisfied to see how her smoke-filled eyes, so similar to mine, widened.

That was when the boys burst in, to our mutual relief.

"George!" "Hey, Uncle George . . ."

Michael was ten, John twelve. They were wearing summer gear, T-shirts, shorts, and huge, expensive-looking trainers. Michael had some kind of complicated Frisbee under his arm. I actually got a hug from Michael, and a punch on the shoulder from his older brother, hard enough to hurt. From those two I took whatever I could get.

I could see their gazes wandering around the kitchen. "Go to my hire car and take a look in the boot."

"The *trunk*," they chorused.

"Whatever. Go, go."

I always enjoyed playing the indulgent uncle, if only because I had a knack of spotting presents that suited my nephews' tastes. John always seemed a little duller than his brother, and would be content with computer games and the like, passive entertainments. But little Michael was always a tinkerer. Once I found an old Meccano set—an antique from the sixties, from my own childhood, but in mint condition. Michael had loved it.

My gifts didn't work quite so well this time. I'd bought them both robot-making kits. You'd put together a motor and wheelbase with a processor you could command via a PC interface, so producing a little beetlelike creature that could scuttle around the room, avoiding chair legs. The beetles could even learn simple tasks, like how to push a table-tennis ball up a ramp. But in the better American schools they build critters like this for homework. The boys dutifully played with the kits for a while, though.

We ate lunch, a simple but typically delicious fish salad—my sister was annoyingly good at everything—and Gina sent us all outside the house.

Over the immense back lawn we chased Michael's Frisbee back and forth. He had modified it: it had a series of round holes carved neatly around its perimeter. It shot through the air like a spinning bullet. More engineering: later Michael showed me a whole collection of modified Frisbees, kept in a box under his bed.

He was actually working through a series of experiments in a systematic way, using a bunch of stuff from junk shops and friends' lofts, trying to design a better Frisbee. At first he had done what you'd expect a kid to do, cutting out smiley faces, building on cabins for model soldiers, installing gigantic fins. But he'd quickly progressed to experiments focused on improving the Frisbees' actual aerodynamic performance. He had cut out patterned holes, or notched their edges, or scratched spirals and loops into their surfaces. He was even keeping a little log on his computer, with a scanned-in photograph of each change, and results given as objectively as he could, such as records of greatest distance achieved. I was impressed, but I felt kind of wistful, for I would have loved to have been around to share this with him.

I found flying that damn Frisbee hard work, however. When the boys had been smaller it had been easy for me to keep ahead of them. But now John was nearly as tall as me, and both of them were a hell of a lot more athletic. I was soon puffing hard, and embarrassed at my lack of competence with the Frisbee. And tensions between the two of them soon emerged.

They made up a catching game with rules that quickly elaborated far beyond my comprehension, and when John infringed a rule—or anyhow Michael thought he did—the bickering started.

Anyhow, so it went. Running around that sandy lawn, with the Atlantic breakers rumbling in the background, I worked as hard as I could while the boys barely broke a sweat, and it was with relief that I welcomed the next milestone in the day, which was Dan's arrival home from work.

"Hey, boys." He left his briefcase at the back door of the house and came bounding out onto the lawn to join in the Frisbee game. "George! How's the mother ship?"

"England swings, Dan."

He asked about my flight and my hotel, and I was gratified that Michael started telling him about my robot kit. We played for a while. Then we took a walk along the beach—sandy and empty, a private stretch reserved for the estate of which this house was a part.

As the boys ran ahead, still impossibly full of energy, Dan and I walked together. Dan Bazalget was a big man, built like a rugby player. I knew he had played football at college, thirty years before, and his bulk seemed too large for his short-sleeved white shirt. His face was broad, his eyes small. He was bald, and had shaved the remnant fringe of his hair, so that his head gleamed like a cannonball.

Dan was good at conversation. He asked me about the aftermath of Dad's death, and unlike my sister drew me out a little about the state of my life, my work. But there was always an odd reserve about him, his deep brown eyes unreadable. He would look at me and smile, ostensibly generous, neither judging nor caring. To him I was surely just an appendage of his wife's past, neither welcome nor unwelcome in his life, just there.

As the sun began its journey down the western sky, we returned home for dinner, the boys running ahead, still whooping, hollering, and fighting.

The meal was strained. The kids picked up on the tension and were subdued. Gina was polite enough during the meal, and her gentle chiding of her children for lapses in manners and so

forth was as calm and efficient as ever. But her smiles were
steel and fooled nobody.

Before the dessert she went to the kitchen, and I joined her,
ostensibly to stack dishes and help make coffee.

"I'm sorry," I said.

"For what?"

"For springing that on you about Rosa. It wasn't fair."

"No, it wasn't." She loaded her dishwasher with as much
aggression as her expensive crockery would allow her.

"But I know she exists, Gina. Or at least existed." I told her
about the photograph.

She sighed and faced me. "And now you're asking me."

"*You must know.* You must have been—what, twelve, thirteen? You saw her born, growing up—"

"I don't want to think about this."

"I need you to tell me the truth," I said, my voice harder. "I
think you have a duty, Gina. You're my sister, for Christ's sake.
You're all I've got left. Et cetera. I even know where they sent
her—to some kind of school, run by a religious order in
Rome. The Puissant Order of—"

"Holy Mary Queen of Virgins." I knew she must have known,
but it was still a shock to me to hear those words from her lips.
"Yes, they sent her there. She was about four, I think."

"Why send her away—why to Italy, for God's sake?"

"Remember I was only a kid myself, George . . . Take a
guess. The simplest reason of all."

"Money?"

"Damn right. Remember, I was about ten when you were
born. It had been a long gap. Mum and Dad had taken a long
time trying to decide if they could raise another kid. You know
how cautious Dad was. Well, along you came, but they hadn't
banked on twins—you and Rosa."

"We were twins?" Shit, I hadn't known that. Another kick in
the head.

"And then, just after you two were born, they ran into trouble; Dad lost his job, I think. The timing of it all was one of
God's little jokes. They didn't tell me much, but it was going
to be a struggle: I remember they talked about selling the
house. They wrote to relatives, asking for help and advice.
And then this offer came in, from the Order. They'd take in

Rosa, school her, care for her. Suddenly, with just *you*, they were back to the position they'd bargained for when they decided to have a second kid."

I felt a complex melange of emotions—relief, envy. "Why her, not me?"

"The Order only takes girls."

"Why didn't she come back?"

She said, "Maybe the Order has rules. I don't know. I wasn't privy to the discussions."

I wondered briefly why, if my parents had always been as hard up as they claimed, my dad had continued to send money to the Order, long after Rosa must have completed her education.

"They never told me about Rosa," I said. "Not a word."

"What good would it have done? . . . I swore it would never happen to me," Gina said suddenly.

"What?"

"Being so poor you have to send your kid away. Et cetera." She was staring at the wall.

For once I thought I could read her. I'd only been seeing this from my point of view. But Gina had been old enough to understand what was happening, though of course she'd only been a helpless kid herself. When Rosa was sent away, she must have been afraid it would be her next.

Impulsively I put a hand on her arm. She flinched away.

She said, "Look, Mum and Dad believed they were doing the best for Rosa. I'm sure of that."

I shook my head. "I'm no parent. But I don't see how any mother could send her little kid away to a religious order full of strangers."

She frowned. "But they didn't. How much do you know about the Order?"

"The name. Rome." Apart from a request that I keep up Dad's payments, which I'd refused, the Order hadn't responded to my emailed requests for information. "Oh, the genealogy business."

"George, that's not even the half of it. The Order are family. *Our* family. That's how Uncle Lou made contact with them in the first place."

"Lou?" He was actually our mother's uncle, my great-uncle.

"He was in the forces—the American forces—during the war. He was in Italy at the end, and somehow found them. The Order. And he found out they saw us as a kind of long-lost branch of the family."

"How so?"

"Because of Regina."

"Who? . . . Not the Roman girl. That's just a family legend."

"Not a legend. History, George."

"It can't be. Nobody can trace their family tree that far back. Not even the queen, for God's sake."

She shrugged. "Suit yourself. Anyhow Lou always kept the contact to the Order, and later when Mum and Dad got into trouble—"

I eyed her. "Dad sent money to this damn Order. Do you?"

"Hell, no," she snapped back. "Look, George, don't cross-examine me. I don't even want to talk about this."

"No, you never did, did you?" I asked coldly. "You left it all behind, when you came here—"

"Yes, away from that cramped little island with its stifling history. And away from our murky family bullshit. I wanted my kids to grow up *here*, in the light and the space. Can you blame me? But now it's all chased me here . . ." She became aware she was raising her voice. Only a screen separated this part of the kitchen from the dining area.

"Gina, do you think all families are like ours?"

"One way or another," she said. "Like huge bombs, and we all spend the rest of our lives picking our way through the rubble."

"I'm going after her." I was making the decision as I spoke. "I'm going to find Rosa."

"Why?"

"Because she's my sister. My *twin*."

"If you think that will help you sort out your screwed-up head, be my guest. But whatever happens, whatever you find, don't tell me about it. I mean it." She actually shut her eyes and mouth, as if to exclude me.

"All right," I said gently. I thought fast. "What about Uncle Lou? Is he still alive? Where does he live?"

He was alive, and lived, it turned out, not far from Gina. "Florida is heaven for the elderly," she said dryly.

"You have his address? And you must have a contact for the Order. An address—maybe an intermediary . . . Dad gave you a damn grandfather clock. I can't believe he wouldn't have given you a contact for your sister. Come *on*, Gina."

"All right," she said dismissively. "Yes, there's a contact. A Jesuit priest in Rome."

"Have you checked it out?"

"What do you think?"

"But you'll give me the addresses."

"I'll give you the fucking addresses. Now," in flat, brutal Mancunian, "piss off out of my kitchen."

The boys hadn't heard what we said, but they had picked up the tone of our voices. We ate our summer puddings in awkward silence. Dan just looked at me, evaluating.

chapter 11

". . . The notion that man has been innately flawed since the Creation is nothing but an artifact of our own difficult times. Just as the wise farmer gathers his harvest and sets aside his store for the winter, so a just man will, through good works, love and the joy of Christ, earn his passage to God's eternal kingdom . . ."

The voice of the Christian philosopher was thin and high, and only fragments of what he had to say carried to Regina on the soft breeze that swept over the hilltop. The crowd pressing around her did their best to listen to what was said, and to the replies of the rival thinkers who rejected this "heresy of Pelagius," preferring the depressing notion that humans were born into the world with ugly, flawed souls.

She suppressed a sigh, her attention drifting. It had come to something, she thought, when the most exciting event in her life was a debate between two splinter sects of the followers of the Christ. She didn't actually like the Christians; she found their intensity, and their habit of praying with arms spread, hands raised, and faces lifted, disturbing and off-putting. But at least they knew how to put on a show.

And at least the little Christian community, here on the hill, was flourishing. It was outside Verulamium itself, close to the gaudy shrine that had been constructed over the presumed grave of Alban, the town's first martyr—indeed, it was said, the first Christian martyr in all of Britain. A group of wooden roundhouses, rectangular huts and even a little area set aside as a marketplace had gathered around the focal point of the shrine. You could see how marble from one of the old town's arches had been cut up and reused to build the shrine itself, the only stone building here; inscriptions in Latin, a language that few spoke anymore, had been sliced through unceremoniously and then scratched over with the *chi-rho*, the symbol of the Christians.

This hilltop village was still small and, in its rough un-planned clutter, hardly a Roman community. But pilgrims came from afar to visit Alban's *martyrium*, bringing their wealth with them. Even today, listening to this dry stuff about the nature of sin, there might have been forty people—a big gathering for Verulamium nowadays—and many of them were brightly dressed for the occasion, in jauntily dyed tunics and cloaks. People had brought their children, who played at their feet. There was even a seller of roast meat working the crowd, adding to the odd carnival atmosphere.

She looked back down the hill to the old town itself. From here she could easily trace the lines of its walls, the lozenge shape sketched on the plain by the river, and she could make out the neat gridwork of the street layout, connected up to the roads that marched away to north, south, and west. There was plenty of activity, carts and pedestrians passing along the main roads and through the gates, and a bustle of activity around the stalls in the Forum. But she could see how stretches of the wall had been broken down, and how, even in the six years she had been here, the green had risen like a tide, encroaching the cen-ter of the town and flooding the broken-down shells of aban-doned buildings.

Carausias complained of how the community around the shrine was drawing the last blood out of the old town. But Regina cared nothing for that. Why should she bother about the upkeep of public buildings, or the problems of paying sol-diers, or keeping *bacaudae* out of the town? She was seven-teen years old. All she wanted was to have fun. And the fact was, such excitement as there was to be had was up here on the Christians' hill.

". . . Who would ever have thought that my little Regina would grow up to be a student of theology?"

It was Amator. At the sound of his voice Regina whirled.

He stood close, not a hand's breadth away. He was dressed in a bright tunic of yellow and green, and he wore an elaborate scarf of what looked like silk, pinned at his throat by a small brooch. His thick black hair, brushed back from his tanned face, was heavy with powder and oil. At his side was a man she did not recognize: perhaps about the same age, he was a thickset fellow wearing a tunic in the barbarian style, made of leather and wool and studded with a big, crudely constructed silver brooch.

Regina had not seen Amator for three years, not since he had left for Gaul—to "make his fortune," as he had said. And yet his gaze had the same searching intensity it had always had, and she couldn't help but respond with a surge in her belly, a flush she could feel spreading to her cheeks. But at seventeen she wasn't a child anymore. And by now he wasn't the only man who had ever looked at her that way.

She lifted her head and looked him in the eye. "You made me jump."

"I bet I did. And have you missed me, little chicken?"

"Oh, have you been away?" Regina lifted her finger and drew it down Amator's cheek. His eyes widened; he almost flinched at her touch. "The sun has changed you."

"It shines more strongly on southern Gaul."

"It has turned your face to old leather. Shame—you were so much better looking in the old days."

Amator glowered.

The friend laughed. "She has the measure of you, Amator." His accent was thick, almost indecipherable. "You have run your sword through him, madam; every morning he spends an enormous time plastering his cheeks with cream and powder to restore his pale color." This other turned out to be called Athaulf; he bowed and kissed her hand, his gaudy barbarian jewelry glinting. "A pretty face *and* a sharp tongue," he said.

Amator said, "But you, Regina—you have become still more beautiful—but perhaps I shouldn't have left you alone so long, if this dry-as-dust theology is the highlight of your life."

She sighed. "Life has been a little duller since you left, Amator," she admitted. Duller, and lacking the edge, the sparkle, the frisson of *danger* that she had always associated with Amator.

"Well, now I'm back . . ."

"Back to work," Athaulf reminded him. "Hard though it is to drag myself away from this young lady, aren't we due to meet those landowners?"

"So we are, so we are. I'm a man of business now, Regina. Business, property, wealth, great concerns beyond the ocean. And so I must deal with old corpses like my father, when I would much rather be flirting with you."

"But your business won't take all day," she said, as coolly as she could.

"Indeed it won't." He glanced at Athaulf. "Tell you what. Why don't we have a party?"

She clapped her hands, though she was aware she must look childish. "Oh, wonderful! I will tell Carausias and Cartumandua and Marina—we will prepare the courtyard—"

"Oh, no, no," he said gently. "We don't want to be depressed by that gloomy lot. Let's make a party of our own. Come to the bathhouse. Shall we say a little after sunset?"

"The bathhouse—but nobody goes there anymore. There's no roof!"

"All the better, all the better; nothing like a little faded grandeur to make the blood flow. After sunset, then." He cocked an eyebrow. "Unless you need to catch up on your theology."

"I'll be there," she said evenly. "Have a good day, Amator. And you, sir." With that she turned and walked away, letting her hips sway, aware of their silence as they watched her.

But once out of their sight she ran down the hill, all the way home.

Even in the few years she had lived here it had gotten a lot harder to make her way through the streets of Verulamium.

Some of the abandoned houses, roofless and gutted by fire, had begun to crumble seriously. Serious looting for tiles and building stone had advanced that decay, although that had tapered off as most new buildings were wattle and daub, and nobody had much use for stone. There were plants sprouting on top of walls and ledges. What had once been gardens and orchards were choked with weeds: dandelions, daisies, rose bay willow herbs. On some, longer abandoned, the shrubs and saplings grew waist-high, or higher. As the population of the town had continued to fall, nobody even used these bits of wasteland for pasture. The few new buildings, just wattle and daub with crudely thatched roofs, had mostly been built on the surface of the old streets, where the risk of falling masonry was least. So you had to step off the road and dodge around the houses, clambering over piles of rubble, and passing by broken drains and clogged sewers that nobody ever got around to fixing, and trying to avoid the children and chickens and mice that ran everywhere.

In one place she walked past a grave, crudely dug into the raw earth and marked with a wooden slab. Strictly speaking burial inside the town walls was still against the law, just as under the rule of Rome. But the magistrates rarely met, or if they did nobody listened to their pronouncements.

Even the great Basilica was affected by the general decay. Its walls still stood, but after its final abandonment by the landowners and their councils, its roof had collapsed, and birds nested in the glass-free frames of its gaping windows. But the building still had its uses. Even without the roof, the great walls provided some shelter from the weather—and a miniature village had grown up in there, on the floor of the great hall itself, with roof posts and beams driven into the walls to support small wooden lean-to shacks. It was an extraordinary sight. If you wanted proof of the Emperor's gross dereliction of his duty to sort things out, Regina thought, it was in this single image of lean-tos huddling timidly in the lee of the mighty walls. When things got back to normal there would be an *awful* lot of work to do to put all this back together again.

Still, the Forum, the beating heart of the town, was as crowded as ever. Regina plunged into its noisy, smelly melee with a will.

Regina was popular with the Forum vendors, if only because she was younger than most of them. There were few young people to be seen in town nowadays, and fewer still with money. The town had never been able to sustain its own population numbers; infant mortality had always been too high for that. But because there was no work for them to do anymore, the flow of immigrants from the countryside had long dried up. Anyhow Regina played on her youth and energy for all it was worth, ruthlessly haggling with middle-age men who should have known better.

The stalls nowadays sold mostly fruits, vegetables, and meat from the local farmsteads, gardens, and orchards. There were very few manufactured goods for sale. But sometimes there were treasures to be found. A shipment of brooches or scents or fabrics from the continent might find its way here, or the contents of a town house or villa would be sold off by its owners, who had decamped in search of a better life elsewhere.

Today, in her rummage through the stalls, she was lucky. She found a shawl made of bright yellow wool that its vendor swore had come all the way from Carthage, and even a set of rings—only bronze, but one of them was set with an intaglio, a cut stone once used by some grand lady to seal documents. She was able to pay for all this in coin, though she had to pass up a pretty iron brooch in the shape of a hare, for its vendor insisted on payment only in kind.

After that, bursting with energy, she raced back to the town house. Everybody knew Amator was home, and Carausias was beaming that his son, so long away, had returned. Regina yelled for Cartumandua. On a day like today it was only Carta, trained by Julia herself at the villa, who could help Regina prepare for her party.

Regina ran to the room she still shared with Marina, and threw her purchases onto her bed. She rummaged through her cosmetics and jewelry. She was running out of space on the little wooden shelves she used to store her things, so she shoved the three little *matres* out of the way and spread out her newest brooches, trying to decide which was the brightest. Beside the jewelry the *matres* looked like what they were, just dull lumps of crudely carved stone.

Once she had finished her chores in the kitchen, Carta came to help Regina with her toilet. She brought hot water, towels, and a scraper to cleanse Regina's skin. She used tweezers, nail cleaners, and ear scoops to ensure that every part of her was perfect, and she patiently braided her hair. And she dripped perfume onto her skin, scooping it out of little bottles with a bronze spoon. Meanwhile Regina went through her growing collection of hairpins and enameled brooches, beads of glass and jet, and rings and earrings, trying to decide what to wear.

But as she prepared charcoal—she ground it up in one of her own most precious possessions, a tiny mortar and pestle small enough to be held between thumb and forefinger—

Carta let Regina know how much she disapproved. "To spend good money on brooches and hairpins and shawls! You *know* what Carausias is saving for . . ."

Things had gone from bad to worse in Britain. It was just as Aetius had tried to explain to her, long ago. There had been a great wheel of state taxation and spending, with the towns at the hub; but now that wheel was shattered. The towns had lost their key functions as centers of revenue collection, administration, state expenditure, distribution, and trade. And now that money was disappearing altogether, nobody could buy fancy pottery or ironware or clothing, and the towns' manufactories had all but collapsed, too. Carausias and the other landowners had a deepening dread that the towns were simply becoming irrelevant to the lives of the people in the countryside, on whom, in the end, everything depended.

Meanwhile, without pay—as Regina knew too well—even the standing armies of the north and the coasts had dispersed. It was said that some of their leaders were setting themselves up as kinglets in their own right. Seeking security, the Verulamium town council had even tried to contact the *civitates*, the tribes of the north and west who had always stayed somewhat independent of the Empire, content to pay the Emperor's taxes. But there wasn't much leadership to be had there, either, and there was much bloody conflict between factions and rival bands. It was as if Britain, amputated from the Empire, were withering like a detached limb. There was no obvious solution in sight, not until the Emperor returned to sort everything out.

In Verulamium things were peaceful for now, if a bit shabby, despite wild rumors from the countryside of roaming *bacaudae* and vicious barbarian hordes. But sometimes, even to Regina who tried not to think about all this, it felt like the calm before the storm.

Meanwhile Carausias was hoarding all the coinage he could get his hands on.

He hoped to secure passage for the family from Britain to Armorica. This was a British colony in western Gaul, where a cousin of Carausias's had a villa. There the imperial mandate still ran strong, and it was a refuge for many of the elite and wealthy from Britain. And there, as Carausias put it, the family could "ride it out until things get back to normal."

But Carausias needed coins. Whereas the economy of the
towns was mostly run by barter nowadays, the captains of
the few oceangoing ships that still called at Londinium or the
other main ports would accept payment only in the Emperor's
coin—and, it was said, at exorbitant rates at that.

That was why Carta was scolding Regina. "It would break
Uncle's heart if he knew—"

"Oh, Carta, don't nag me," Regina said, pouting into her
hand mirror to see if her black lip coloring was thick enough.
"You can't *get* this sort of stuff for a handful of beans. You
have to pay for it. And it is my money; I can do what I want
with it."

Carta stood before her, mixing the charcoal with oil on a little palette. "Your allowance is a gift from Carausias, Regina.
He means to teach you some responsibility with money. But it
isn't *yours*. You must remember that. You came here from the
Wall with nothing but the clothes on your back . . ."

Which was true, as she had learned over the years. Poor
Aetius had had nothing but his soldier's salary and a few mea-
ger savings. Even his chalet under the Wall had, it turned out,
belonged to the army. Nobody knew what had become of her
family's money. It wasn't a pleasant subject to be reminded of.
Sometimes Regina regretted throwing away that dragon
brooch of her mother's. She could never have borne to wear it,
but at least she could have sold it, and had a little of her
mother's wealth.

But all this was a bother. "I know all that," Regina said
crossly. "I just want to have a little fun, just for one night. Is
that so much to ask? . . ."

Carta sighed, put down her cosmetic palette, and sat with
Regina. "But, child, yesterday was *just one night*, too. As will
tomorrow be. And the next night, and the next . . . What about
the future? You don't keep up with your share of the chores, in
the kitchen, cleaning, in the stables."

Regina pulled a face. She found her future hard to imagine,
but she was sure it wasn't going to involve mucking out stables.

Carta said, "And what about your studies? Aetius would
be disappointed if he could know that you've all but given
them up."

"Aetius is *dead*," Regina said. But she said it brightly, as if it were a joke. "Dead, dead, dead. He died and left me all alone with *you*. Why should I care what he would have thought?" She got up and skipped lightly. "Oh, Carta, you've become such an old woman! I'll deal with the future when it comes. What else can I do?"

Carta glared at her. But she said, "Oh, come here and be still. We aren't done yet." She bade her lean down and carefully painted the charcoal around her eyes. "There," she said at last. She held up a hand mirror.

Even Regina herself was startled by the effect. The darkness of the charcoal paste made her eyes shine, while the pink of her light woolen tunic was perfect for bringing out their smoky gray. As she slipped on her new bronze rings Regina's mood of anticipation deepened. Briefly she thought of Aetius, and the responsibility he had tried to instill in her. *You are the family now, Regina . . .* But she was seventeen, and her blood was wine-rich; surrounded by her jewelry and clothes and cosmetics she felt light, airy, floating like a leaf on a breeze, far above the earthy stonelike concerns embodied by the *matres*.

She said, "Carta, I hear what you say." She took more steps around the room. "But I'm only dancing."

Carta forced a smile. "And maybe I don't dance enough. Dance, then. Dance for all you're worth! But—"

"Oh, Carta, always a *but*!"

"Be careful who you dance with."

"You mean Amator?" Her translucent mood turned to irritation. "You never did approve of him, did you?"

"He was too old, you too young, to be flirting the way you used to."

"But that's *years* ago. He's different, Carta." *And so am I,* she thought, in a dark warm secret core of herself, which contemplated possibilities she didn't dare broach even in her own mind. "Carta, Amator is your cousin. You should trust him."

"I know I should." Carta eyed her. "Just be careful, Regina."

"Carta—"

"Promise me."

"Yes. All right, I promise . . ."

Carta surprised Regina by hugging her, briefly. They stepped apart, both a little embarrassed.

"What was that for?"

"I'm sorry, child. It's just, made up like that, you look so beautiful. That fire in your eyes when you argue with me—you have spirit, and I can't blame you for that. And—well, sometimes you look so like your mother."

She couldn't have said anything that would have moved Regina more. Regina touched her cheek. "Dear Carta. You mustn't worry so. Now help me fix my hair; this bone pin just *won't* stay in place . . ."

But Carta's face, already lined though she was only in her midtwenties herself, remained creased with concern.

Amator and Athaulf met her at the old bathhouse, not long after sunset. Amator was carrying a great flagon of wine.

The bathhouse, like the Basilica, had long lost its roof. Domes, broken open like eggshells, gaped in the dark. Somebody had dug down through the fine mosaic floor of the main chamber, smashing the design and scattering the tesserae: perhaps it had been a Christian fanatic who had objected to some pagan image. Nobody knew; nobody cared.

With Amator and Athaulf was a girl called Curatia. Regina didn't know her, but she knew about her. About Regina's age, Curatia routinely went about dripping with as fine a collection of hairpins, jewelry, and cosmetics as you could find in Verulamium. But, so went the gossip, she lived alone, and had no obvious means to pay for such things—none save her popularity with a variety of men, some old enough to be her father . . . Regina felt faintly disturbed to find such a girl here; immediately the evening seemed soiled.

But Curatia had brought a lyre. When she played, with her black hair cascading over the strings, Regina had to admit her music was quite beautiful. And once she had begun to sip Amator's wine, Regina began to feel much more relaxed about the girl's presence. It was a balmy autumn evening, the fragments of mosaic and the wall paintings that had survived the weather were poignant and beautiful, and even the weeds and saplings that grew waist-high looked fresh and pretty. And when Amator and Athaulf had set out the candles they had brought, on the floor, on the walls and in the gaping windows, the shadows became deep, flickering, and complex.

Amator and Regina sat together on a stretch of broken wall. Amator sifted rubble with his hand and dug out a collection of oyster shells. "Once people ate well here," he said. He shrugged and let the shells drop.

"I've never eaten oysters," Regina said wistfully.

"Oh, I have."

Athaulf crawled around the half-ruined building, poking into crevices and cracks and feeling under the floor. "Did they really light fires under the floor? . . ."

"It's called a *hypocaust*, you pig chaser!" Amator shouted out in Latin, waving his wine. He said to Regina, "You must forgive Athaulf. He's still a ragged-arse barbarian at heart."

Regina leaned against Amator's legs. "I never heard a name like that. *Athaulf.*"

"Well, he's a Visigoth. And like all his kind his name sounds like you're hawking to bring up phlegm . . ."

Visigoth he might be, but Athaulf's family wielded power in Gaul. After the disastrous night on which the frozen Rhine had been crossed by the barbarians from Germany, Roman military commanders had managed to stabilize the province by giving the barbarians land inside the old border. Thus a Visigoth federation had been established in southwestern France, centered on Burdigala. Athaulf was a rich man, and a solid business partner for Amator.

Amator drank deeply of his wine. "Thus the Visigoths, who are barbarians, are employed on the Emperor's payroll to keep down the troublesome *bacaudae*, many of whom are Roman citizens. Makes you think."

"But I don't *want* to think," she said, and held up her cup for more wine.

"Quite right, too."

Athaulf stood up in the rubble of the hypocaust. "Look! I found an iron hook!"

"It's a *strigil*, you savage. It's supposed to keep your skin clean. Oh, throw it away. Cura! Enough of that funeral music. We want to dance!"

With a whoop, Curatia abandoned her gentle dirge and launched into a lively rhythmic tune, an ancient British piece.

Amator yelled, dragged Regina to her feet, and took her in his arms. They started with formal steps, but soon, as Athaulf joined in, they clambered in and out of the old hypocaust and ran laughingly along the sections of broken walls.

As she danced in the ruins, and the cool autumn air mixed with the heady wine and the scent of the candles—and as Amator's legs brushed hers, and his arm circled her waist—Regina could feel her intoxication growing, as if her blood were burning. This multileveled place, full of complicated light and Curatia's shimmering, oddly wistful music, came to seem as unreal and enchanted as if they had been transported to a cloud.

Later, she found herself lying on a thick woolen blanket, cast over the stones of the broken wall. She was panting hard, the blood in her head singing from the whirling dance. Amator was lying beside her, propped up on his elbow, looking down at her. She could sense his old intensity in the way he looked at her. But that frisson of fear she had once felt had gone now, leaving only warmth.

"I wish this night would last forever," she said, flushed and breathless. "This moment."

"Yes," he murmured. "So do I." He lay beside her, his arm over her stomach, and she felt his tongue flicker at her ear.

She stared up at the silent stars. "She had such parties," she whispered.

"Who?"

"My mother . . . Why did it all go wrong, do you think? The town. The way people lived. There are no barbarians *here*."

"None save capering oafs like Athaulf."

"But there aren't. The ocean didn't freeze over, like the Rhine, so the barbarians could walk in. And there was no plague, no great fire that burned everything up. It all just—stopped. And now Cartumandua can't buy a new vase, because nobody makes them anymore, and money is useless anyhow . . ."

"It was all a dream," he said softly. "A dream that lasted a thousand years. The money, the towns, everything. And when people stopped believing in the dream, it disappeared. Just like that."

"But they will believe again."

He snorted, and she could feel his hot breath on her neck. "Not here they won't. Here they are pursuing a different dream, of a man on a cross, a martyr's grave at the top of the hill."

"No, you're wrong. When things get back to normal—"

He leaned over her; his eyes were black pits, unreadable, deep, and welcoming. "Elsewhere the dream goes on."

"Where?"

"In the south and the east. Around the coasts of the central sea, in Barcino and Ravenna and Constantinople, even Rome itself . . . There are still towns and villas. There are still parties, and wine, and perfumes, and people dancing. That's where *I'm* going." He leaned closer. "Come with me, Regina." His hand moved beneath her tunic, and caressed her thigh.

Her blood was surging; his every touch was like fire. "I thought you didn't like me," she whispered. "I knew how you looked at me when I first arrived. But you never touched me. And then you went away."

"Ah, Regina—would I pluck an apple before it is ripe? But—"

"What is it?"

"There has been nobody else?"

"No," she said, averting her face. "Nobody else, dear Amator."

He took her chin and made her face him. "Come with me, then, little Regina, little chicken. Come to Rome. There we will dance for another thousand years . . ." His face descended toward hers, and she felt his tongue probe at her lips. She opened her mouth, and he flowed into her, like hot metal.

At first there was pain, sharp and deep, but that soon transmuted to pleasure.

Amator rolled away from her, turning his head. She felt oddly cold, and reached for him. He came back, and filled her cup with wine.

After that, her thoughts became fragmentary.

There were only bits of clarity, scattered like the tesserae of the smashed mosaic. The sharpness of the pain of the rubble that dug in her back when he lay on her. The sense of bruising in her legs and belly as he thrust. A glimpse of Athaulf standing on the broken walls with his tunic raised, pissing noisily on the ground beyond, while the girl Curatia massaged his legs and bare buttocks.

And then the last time, a different weight, a different scent, a different sensation between her slippery thighs. When he pulled away, belching, not looking at her, this time it was not Amator but Athaulf. But she felt too broken, too disconnected to grasp at that thought.

The last memory of all was of a painful stagger through the streets of Verulamium, where with every pace she seemed to trip over some bit of rubble, her arm draped over Curatia, for Amator and Athaulf had gone.

After that it seemed just a moment before she woke in her bed—and was immediately assailed by the stink of vomit—but Marina was here, wiping at her brow, while Cartumandua's face hovered beyond like a concerned, disapproving moon. Her head throbbed, her throat was sore with vomiting, her belly was filled with an empty ache, and between her legs was what felt like a single great bruise that spanned from one thigh to the other.

That first day she stayed in the dark, sipping the soup and water Marina brought her. Amator didn't call for her, to take her to Rome.

The second day she got up and dressed. She felt a lot better, save for a lingering sickness at the base of her stomach—and a sharp pain between her legs, a pain she clung to, trying to keep her memories of Amator strong, despite that disturbing final image of Athaulf.

She emerged into bright daylight, and, somewhat sheepishly, sought out Cartumandua. To her relief Carta didn't scold her, or remind her of her previous warnings, or of her promises. Carta gave her chores, cleaning tasks in the kitchen and the bedrooms. But she wouldn't meet Regina's eyes.

Regina tried to make a fuss of Marina. She made a special effort to clean out the room they shared, after the mess she had made of it. Oddly, though, she felt uncomfortable in the room in those first few days, and had trouble working out why—until she saw that the *matres* were still in the corner of their shelf, where she had so carelessly shoved them aside to make room for her jewelry. She restored the goddesses to their position. But they felt cold and heavy in her hands, and their small faces seemed to watch her.

She was not the same person as she was last time she had touched them, and never would be again. Somehow the *matres* knew it. And beyond their blank stone faces she saw Julia and Aetius and Marcus and everybody she had known staring at her in dismay.

She nursed the secret of Amator's promise to take her away to the southern cities, a secret promise that made everything she had gone through worthwhile. But still Amator didn't call. Still the pain in her belly lingered.

And as the days wore on, the bleeding didn't come. She knew what that must mean. Her anxiety and sense of dread deepened.

It all came to a head on the night of the fire.

It had been a difficult night from the beginning.

After dinner Carausias had made a terrible discovery. He had wailed and wept. Then he had given way to anger. He stormed around the house, smashing furniture and crockery and even some of Carta's irreplaceable pottery, despite the efforts of Carta and Severus to restrain him.

Regina had no idea what was troubling him. He had always seemed so strong, so solid. Frightened, she had retreated to her room where she lay on her bed.

She had dark troubles of her own. Her bleeding hadn't returned. She longed to talk to Carta, to throw herself in her arms and ask for her forgiveness and help. But she could not. Then there was another secret, the secret that was lodged deep in her mind, as the growing child must be lodged in her belly, a secret truth she had tried to keep even from herself: that Amator would not come back for her, that he would never come back, that he had already taken all he wanted from her.

As she lay brooding, at first she imagined that the stink of smoke, the sound of screaming, was part of her own fevered imagination. But when red light began to flicker beyond her window, she realized that something serious was happening. She got out of bed, pulled on her tunic quickly, and ran to the door.

Carta, Carausias, and the others were standing in the courtyard. Their faces shone red, as if they faced a sunset. But the sun was long gone, and the light came from a great bank of flames, visible over the silhouetted rooftops. There was a great crash, more screams, and sparks rose up like a flock of tiny, glowing birds.

Regina ran to Carta and took her hand. "What is it?"

"I think that was the Basilica," Carta said.

"It may have started there," Carausias growled. "But it's spreading fast. All those stalls in the Forum. The thatched roofs . . ."

"I think it's coming this way," said Carta.

Carausias's voice was bitter. "Once there were volunteers to put out such fires. We'd have run with our bowls of water and our soaked blankets, and everything would be saved—or if not saved, rebuilt until it was better than before—"

Carta snapped, *"Uncle!"*

He turned and looked at her, eyes wide. "Yes. Yes. The past doesn't matter anymore. We must leave. Even if the fire spares the house, the town is done after this. All of you, now, quickly . . ." He turned and ran into the house, followed by Severus and Marina.

Carta held Regina's shoulders. "Get your things. Nothing but what you can carry, nothing but what you need."

"Carta—"

"Are you listening, Regina?"

"Where will we go? Will we go to Londinium, and book the ship to Armorica? Perhaps we will meet Amator there—"

Carta shook her, sharply. "You must listen. Amator is gone. I don't know where. And he took Carausias's money."

It was hard for Regina to take this in. *"All* of it—"

"All of it. All the savings."

"The ship—"

"There will be no ship. Can you not listen, child? When the house is destroyed, we will have nothing."

There will be no dancing, Regina thought stupidly, no more dancing. And when she thought of the growing mass in her belly she felt panic rise. "How will we live, Carta?"

"I don't know!" Carta yelled, and Regina saw her own fear.

There was a fresh roar as another great section of building

collapsed. From the streets outside the courtyard there came yells, screams, and a strange, twisted laughter.

"Time is running out. Go, child!"

Regina ran to her room. She dragged out the largest bag she thought she could carry, and scooped into it clothes, her perfumes, her pins, her jewelry, everything she could grab in those few frantic heartbeats.

It was only at the very last moment that she thought of the *matres*. She unfolded a tunic, carefully wrapped the little stone goddesses, and tucked them into the bag. They were small, but they made the bag unaccountably heavier. She hoisted the bag onto her shoulder and ran out into the courtyard.

Soon all of them had gathered, Carausias, Carta, Marina, and Severus, all laden with bags and bundles of blanket. By now the glow of the fire was bright as day, and the billowing smoke made it hard to breathe.

Regina thought she saw moisture in Carausias's rheumy eyes. But he turned away from his house. "Enough. Let's go."

Half running, stumbling over the debris in the road, the four of them joined a ragged line of refugees who streamed out of the burning town through the northern gate and into the cold country beyond. Away from the town there were no lights, and the night was overcast. Soon they were fleeing into pitch darkness.

chapter 12

Despite all the tension with Gina, I wanted to trace Uncle Lou. I stayed on in Florida a few more days, through the weekend.

A day after that unsatisfactory conversation with my sister I got an unexpected call. It was Michael, asking me if I wanted to come over to watch the space shuttle launch.

"Sure. I mean, if that's okay with your mom. You'd better put her on . . ."

"Whatever," said Gina.

So I drove over. The launch was scheduled for eight P.M.

"I didn't know a launch was due," I said. "Do they show it on TV?"

Michael said, "On NASA TV, yes. But you can see it from the porch."

I felt a foolish prickle of wonder. "You can see a spaceship take off from your back door? . . ." I'd been to Florida many times, but that had never occurred to me.

The boy grinned. "Sure. Come on, I'll show you."

Gina said, "Don't go sitting in the damp. And don't stay out too long if it's delayed, and you get cold—"

"We won't," I said. "Come on, kid." I stood up and let Michael lead me by the hand, out through the darkened hall to the back door.

At the back of the house was a long covered porch. A couple of big swing benches hung from the roof, and big electric lamps were fixed to the wooden wall, banishing the night; beyond was just darkness.

"Shall we sit here?"

Michael said, "It's kind of hard on your butt. Mom puts the cushions indoors to keep them dry."

"Oh, okay."

"Anyhow it isn't the best view. Come on." Still holding my hand, the boy made his way along a gravel path, barely visible to me, that sloped down toward the coast. He stepped confidently, secure in his little domain. I tried to follow without hesitation.

Gradually, as the house receded, a little island of light, the night opened up around us. The sky was black and huge, and speckled with stars. Behind me, inland, the lights of the city stained the scattered clouds orange-yellow. But when I looked east, toward the sea, there was only darkness. I could hear the ocean now, a low, restless growling.

Michael led me off the path a little way. I found myself walking on fine sand that slid into my shoes, so that I walked with a rasp. After a few paces Michael flopped to the ground. I somewhat gingerly lowered myself down, and found myself sitting on soft sand matted with coarse grass. The grass was prickly and a little damp with dew, and I knew my back would soon get stiff. But for now I was comfortable enough.

"My mom won't let me go farther toward the sea at this time of night," Michael said solemnly. A soft ripping noise told me he was tugging at the grass.

"Well, that's sensible." I spotted a light, far out on the breast of the sea. I pointed it out to Michael. "I wonder if it's something to do with the launch. Don't they have ships to pick up those solid-rocket boosters that drop off when the shuttle flies?"

Michael snickered. "I don't *think* so. The recovery ships are a *long* way downrange."

"Oh, right."

Michael started talking briskly about shuttle launch operations, miming the assembly of the booster stack, and the liftoff from the Canaveral pads with his small hands. He parroted technical terms and acronyms, and when I gently tested him by asking about what lay behind the acronyms, he was always able to answer.

It was all of a piece with his work on the Frisbees. It hadn't been so long—Christ, just a few years—since we had watched the *Apollo 13* movie on TV, and we had chanted the countdown together, because that, said Michael, was the magic you needed to make a spaceship go. Later we had talked each other through the dreadful loss of the *Columbia*. Now his enthusiasm was still endearing, but his depth of knowledge was startling. To him, the shuttle was no longer a magical chariot, but a piece of engineering that you could pore over and take apart and *understand*—and maybe even make a better version of one day.

I suppressed a sigh. After all that he was only ten years old. Childhood is so long when you live it, but so brief when you look at it from outside. And my visits, the brief forays across the Atlantic at Christmas and in the summer, so precious to me, amounted to no more than a few days in total, spread over that evanescent decade.

Michael suddenly sat bolt upright. "Look! Look, there it is!"

And so it was, right on time. Looking to the north I saw a spark of light, supernova bright, climbing, it seemed, out of the sea. Its trajectory was already curving, a graceful arc, and I saw how the spark carved out a great pillar of smoke in the dense sea air, a pillar that itself was brightly lit from the inside. All this took place in utter silence, but the sense of power was astonishing—like something natural, a waterfall or a thunderstorm—it was startling to think that this mighty display was human-made.

We both erupted into cheers and applause, and hugged each other.

When we ran out of cheers I could hear more distant noise, a kind of crackle like very faraway thunder, or even gunfire. It might have been the sound of people cheering, strung out along this coast, or it might have been the sound of the shuttle's ascent. As the shuttle climbed farther its light spread over the ocean, and a hundred reflected sparks slid over the gently swelling surface, tracking the rising spacecraft.

In the pale rocket light the face of Michael Poole Bazalget was like an upturned coin, but his mouth was set with a kind of determination, his eyes shadowed. I felt unaccountably disturbed. I wondered what this child, and his own children after him, would do with the world.

chapter 13

The little party of refugees straggled up the hillside from the road.

The farmstead was just a huddle of buildings, lost on the hill's broad flank. There were no lights. Regina saw the gaping holes of unglazed windows, decayed roofs, fields sketched out by drystone walls but choked with weeds. Beyond the buildings a forest, dense and dark, coated the upper hillside.

The place was abandoned.

There were five of them—Regina, Cartumandua and Severus, Marina, Carausias—and they stood in a huddle. Already the night was falling, the cold descending. They had been on the road for nearly a month, since the burning of Verulamium, a month they had spent walking ever west. They must look as lost and helpless, Regina thought, as the buildings themselves.

"They said they would wait," Carausias said plaintively. "Arcadius was a friend of my brother—a close friend. They said they would wait for us."

Severus broke away, snarling his contempt. "I've heard nothing but your whining and excuses, old man, all the way from Verulamium."

Carta said wearily, "Severus, we're all exhausted."

"And because of this old fool's sentimental stupidity we are stranded on this hillside. I told you we should have gone to Londinium."

"We've been over this. There was nothing for us in Londinium."

"Arcadius said he would wait," Carausias repeated. He rummaged beneath his cloak. "I have the letters, the letters—"

Severus stalked off over the darkling hillside.

Marina said, frightened, "Severus, please."

Carta held her back. "Let him go. He'd do no good here."

"But what are we to do?"

Carta had no answer. Carausias walked purposelessly back and forth over the hillside, limping as he had done since the first day, despite the bandages that cradled his feet inside his leather shoes. It was as if they were all locked in their own heads.

Regina crouched down, hugging her knees to her belly. At least she was spared the cramps she had suffered almost continually since they had started their great trek from Verulamium.

Arcadius was a friend of the family who had a farmstead here, deep in the heart of the countryside to the west. It had always been the plan for Arcadius and Carausias to pool their resources and make for Armorica together. Because of Amator, Carausias had lost his money, and he admitted that it had been a year or more since he had been in contact with Arcadius, because of the unreliability of the post these days. But he was sure that Arcadius would wait for him, and would welcome them into his home.

That had been the promise that had sustained them through that first, terrifying night of flight from burning Verulamium—the first dismal hours when they had tried to sleep out in the open, keeping away from the stream of refugees, the crying children and limping invalids, the drunks—the promise that had kept them all going through the days and nights of their hike ever west, as Carausias and Severus had used the last of their money to buy a little food, water, and shelter from broken-down inns.

Then the countryside had been hostile. The collapse of the Roman province had affected most directly the one in ten who had lived in the villas and towns, many of whom were now trying to find a place in the countryside, like Regina and her party. But the farmers had been affected, too, however they had grumbled about tax. Without the need to produce a surplus to pay the Emperor's taxes the farmers had cut their workload back to what was necessary to maintain their families. But with the towns declining there was no market to sell or trade what surplus there was, and there was nowhere to buy manufactured goods like pottery or tools. Iron goods in particular were in very short supply, for people had forgotten the ancient craft of iron making. Many farms were being operated at a more basic level than the farmers' ancestors had achieved centuries before.

Anyhow there had been no place for Regina and her party: no hospitality, no offers of help from hungry, resentful, suspicious people, and they had used up the last of their money on overpriced inns. But it didn't matter. Once they got here, to this hill farm and Carausias's friends, everything would be all right.

But now here they were, and there was nobody after all. It was just another betrayal. As never before the future seemed a blank, black, terrifying emptiness. Regina wrapped her arms over her belly and the growing, hungry life it contained.

Carta sat beside her. "Are you all right?"

"None of us is *all right*," Regina said. "What a mess."

"Yes. What a mess," Cartumandua said. "This farm must have been abandoned at least a year. Poor, foolish Carausias."

"There's nothing for us here."

"But there is nowhere else to go, and we have no more money," said Carta grimly. "It doesn't seem such a bad location to me. There is water down there." She pointed to a marshy area at the foot of the grassy hill, the thread of a sluggish river beyond. "The fields are overgrown but they have been worked before; they should not be difficult to plow. This hillside is a little away from the road. Perhaps we will not be such a target for the *bacaudae*."

"What are you talking about? Who is going to plow the fields? How will we pay them?"

"Nobody will plow them for us," Carta said doggedly. "*We* will plow them."

Regina stared at her. "You are making up stories. We have nothing to eat *now*. We'll be lucky to live through the night. And, if you haven't noticed, it is the autumn. What crops will we grow in the winter? And besides—Carta, I don't *want* to be a farmer."

"And I didn't want to be a slave," Carta said. "I survived that, and I will survive this. As will you." She clambered to her feet and pulled Regina's arm. "Come on. Let's go and take a look at the buildings."

Reluctantly Regina followed.

The farm buildings were clustered around a square of churned-up mud. There were three barnlike structures, with neat rectangular plans of the Roman kind, and the remains of a roundhouse, a more primitive building with a great conical roof of blackened thatch, and walls of wattle and daub.

Regina drifted toward the square-built structures, the most familiar. Once they must have been smart, bright buildings; she could see traces of whitewash on the walls and a few bright red tiles still clinging to the wooden slats of the roofs. But one had been burned out altogether, and the roofs of the others, all but stripped of tiles, had rotted through. She stepped through a doorway. The floor was littered with rubble and cracked by a flourishing community of weeds. Something scuttled away in the gloom.

Carta pointed at the roundhouse. "We'd be better off in this."

Regina wrinkled her nose. "In that mud pie? I can smell it from here. And look at that rotting thatch—there are animals *living in it*!"

"But we have a better chance of repairing it," Carta said. "Face it, Regina—how are we to bake roof tiles?"

"We could get them replaced."

Carta laughed tiredly. "Oh, Regina—by whom? Where are the craftsmen? And how are we to pay them? . . . Regina, I know this is hard. But I don't see anybody standing around waiting to help us, do you? If we don't fix it ourselves—well, it won't get fixed."

Regina rested a hand on her belly. Carta's realism and doggedness somehow made things worse, not better.

There was a call from the lower slopes of the hillside. Severus was returning, with something heavy and limp slung over his shoulder. Regina soon made out the iron stink of blood, and a deeper stench of rot. Grunting, Severus let his burden fall to the muddy ground. It was the carcass of a young deer. Its head had almost been severed from its body, presumably by Severus's knife. Severus was sweating, and his tunic was stained deep with blood. "Got lucky," he said. "Leg stuck in a trap. Already dying, I think. See?"

The deer had been very young, Regina saw. Its horns were mere stubs, and its body small and lithe. But one of its legs dangled awkwardly, and a putrid smell rose from blackened flesh.

Severus leaned over the limp corpse. With inefficient but brutal thrusts he dug his knife into the hip joint above the deer's good hind leg. With some noisy sawing of cartilage and bone, he ripped the joint apart, and hung the limb over his shoulder. "We've got neighbors," he said, pointing with his bloody knife. "I saw lights. A farmstead over that way, over the ridge. I'm going to see if they'll trade."

"Yes," said Carausias urgently. "There are many things we need—"

"What *I* need is some wheat beer," said Severus. "I've had enough of this for one night."

Carausias called, "You can't be so selfish, man!"

But Carta only said, "Come back alive."

When he had gone, the others stood over the carcass. Blood slowly leaked out of its throat and into the mud.

Carausias whispered, as if he might wake the deer, "What do we do?"

At length Regina sighed. "I used to watch the butchers at the villa. We need rope . . ."

They dug through the garbage in the buildings until Marina found a mouse-chewed length of rope. To Regina's horror the deer's flesh was warm and soft; she had never touched anything so recently dead. But she got the rope tied around the deer's remaining hind leg. She slung the rope over the branch of a tree. With the three of them hauling, they managed to drag the carcass into the branches.

The deer dangled like a huge, gruesome fruit. Blood, and darker fluids, flowed sluggishly from its neck and pooled on the ground.

Carta watched dubiously. "We should collect that blood."

"Why?"

"You can cook it—mix it with herbs—stuff the intestines with it. I've seen it done. We shouldn't waste anything."

Regina felt her gorge rise. But she said, "We don't have a bowl to catch it. Next time."

"Yes."

Regina stepped forward with Carausias's knife. Calling on grisly memories from childhood, she reached up, plunged the knife into the deer's skin under its belly, and with all her strength hauled the blade down the length of the carcass. Intestines slipped out, tangles of dark rope. She flinched back, trembling. Her tunic and flesh were splashed with dark blood, and her hands were already crimson to the wrists. She stepped behind the carcass and began to tug at the flaps of skin. "Help me," she said. "After this we should cut off the other legs."

Carausias built a fire in the ruins of the roundhouse. The wood they gathered was young and damp with dew, and they had trouble getting it burning. But when it was fully alight, and bits of the meat were cooking on an improvised spit, they huddled together around the light and warmth. The meat was tough, lean, almost impossible to bite into, and its bloody, smoky stink was repellent. But Regina was always aware of the speck of life inside her, and so she forced the meat into her mouth, and chewed it until it was soft, and swallowed it down.

"We are like savages," Carausias said. "Barbarians. This is no way to live."

"But barbarians have their arts," Carta said. "Your butchery, Regina—"

"I was clumsy."

"You will do better. There are older skills we must try to recall. For instance, we should keep the hide, cure it if we can. And preserve the meat. We have been lucky, but we are not hunters; it may be a while before we have another windfall like this one. We could smoke it, dry it in the sun, perhaps pack it in salt . . ."

"How?"

"I don't know. But we will learn. And in future we should save the fat, too. Perhaps we could make tallow—candles—"

Carausias placed a hand on her shoulder. "Enough for tonight, niece."

When the eating was done, Regina shrank into the deepest shade of the roundhouse roof she could find. With a corner of her cloak she tried to wipe the animal blood from her hands and face. Soon her skin was sore, and the cloth was starting to shred, but still the blood wouldn't come off her skin.

Carausias came to her in the dark. He sat beside her and rested his hands on hers, stopping her obsessive scrubbing. "In the morning we will find water," he said. "And then we will all get clean."

"I don't want this," Regina hissed. "I don't want to live like a, like a *dog*. Carta is so strong."

"Yes. And that makes it worse, doesn't it? Because by accepting it, she makes it real. But you are strong, too, Regina. The way you handled the deer—"

"I don't want to be strong. Not like this." She looked up at his kindly face, blood-streaked and obscure in the dark. "Things will get back to normal, won't they, Carausias?"

He shrugged. "Even now, Rome spans a continent, a thousand-year-old imperium just a day's sailing away, over the ocean. This has been a dreadful interval for us all. But why should we believe we live in special times, the end times? How arrogant of us, how foolish."

"Yes. But in the meantime—"

"It will surely only be a few weeks before we see the post messengers clattering along the roads again. Until then, we must just get by."

"Just a few weeks. Yes."

The deer fed them for the first few days. They were able to supplement the meat with late-blooming berries. For water they had to trek several times a day to the marsh at the bottom of the hill; they carried the water home in a wooden bucket salvaged from the ruins of the farm.

But the first rains nearly doused their fire, and turned the floor of the roundhouse into a quagmire. Despite his attempts at bravery Carausias wept that night, bedraggled, cold, humiliated at how far he had let his family fall.

They had to repair the roof, Regina realized.

Severus said he could handle this. He clambered onto the roof, hauling branches of oak and hazel over the gaping hole. Regina felt optimistic: surely such a crude structure as this required only the crudest repairs. But when Severus shifted his weight unwisely, his heaping gave way, and he fell to the muddy floor in a shower of snapped branches. He got to his feet and kicked at the mess, swearing oaths to the gods of the Christians, the British, and the Romans, and stalked off in a sulk.

So Regina decided she would have to do it.

She walked around the little house, studying the roof's structure. Its conical shape was built on several main rafters that had been leaned together and then tied off at the top to a central pole. There was more complicated woodwork, the remains of a ring beam and crisscross rafters. But the main problem was that two or three of the big rafters had gone.

None of Severus's hasty gatherings would serve as new rafters, and they had no ax. But in the forest on the upper reaches of the hillside they were able to find long, fallen branches. It took Carausias, Regina, and Carta together to drag the branches down the hill. Then, together, they pushed their improvised rafters into place. Marina, reluctant but the lightest, was sent to climb up the thatch to the hut's apex, where she tied the new rafters to the old. The complicated cross structure was beyond Regina for now. But she did have Marina tie light hazel branches to her new rafters, and they began expeditions to the marsh to pile up river reeds as thatch, great layers of it.

It was crude, ugly, but it worked.

Once the roof was waterproof things got better quickly. There were still whole dynasties of mice inhabiting the old thatch, but a few days of intensive smoking saw to that. The ruined roof had allowed the rain to attack the wattle-and-daub walls, but their basic structure of thin, interwoven hazel branches was still sound. Regina and Carta plugged the holes in the walls with mud and straw, pushing the stuff in from either side and smoothing it off with their fingers.

When at last they shut out the last of the daylight, they had a small celebration. They sat in a circle around their fire, with smoke curling out through the chimney hole in their new roof, and their deer-fat candles burned smokily. They ate the last of the deer's liver, cooked with wild garlic Marina had found growing behind the huts. They felt they had done well; it was still only a few days since they had gotten here.

It was then that Regina felt ready to unwrap her precious

matres from the length of cloth in which they had been carried. She set them in a crude alcove, to watch over the heap of dried reeds on which she now slept.

Next time they caught a deer, in a simple trap Severus had set, they were more efficient in using it. They kept the hide intact to cover the roundhouse floor, and even boiled the bones to extract the marrow.

Most of their food came from traps—mostly smaller game, especially hares. But they established a tentative trading relationship with the farm Severus had found beyond the ridge. The farmer, a tall, ferociously bearded, suspicious man called Exsuperius, was prepared to exchange their meat for winter vegetables like cabbage, and even clothing, worn-out tunics, cloaks, and blankets. The clothing, old and lice-ridden as it might be, was hugely welcome. Regina began to experiment with ways to wash their clothes in the river—wood ash, being slightly caustic, made a good cleansing agent.

But no matter how Carausias or Carta pleaded, Exsuperius would spare them no pottery, no footwear, and no tools—no saws or hammers or knives—no iron at all, in fact, not so much as a nail for their shoes.

Severus did his share, if grudgingly. As the strongest of them by far he would haul the heaviest loads, and he experimented with bigger traps and slingshots to bring down more game. But he was unreliable and short-tempered. He would barely speak to the rest of them, and he even seemed to neglect Carta.

Regina felt she would never understand Carta's relationship with Severus. They never seemed happy together—there had never been any hint that Carta wished to have a child with Severus—and yet their relationship, now years old, somehow endured. It was as if neither of them hoped for anything better from life.

When she learned that Severus had kept trying to trade meat for beer from Exsuperius, Regina understood that he could not be depended on.

The days turned to weeks, and then to months. They watched every day for soldiers or post carriers to come along the road. But things did not get back to normal.

Little by little they made themselves comfortable. But every day she had to figure out something new: the business of survival was remarkably complicated. And life was relentlessly hard, every hour from dawn to dusk filled with hard physical labor. The frosts of winter came, and life grew harder yet.

Still, even though the new life in her belly grew relentlessly, Regina felt herself becoming stronger, the skin of her hands and feet and face hardening, the muscles in her legs and shoulders thickening. She ate ravenously, to feed her unborn baby and to keep out the cold. But she did not fall ill. Carausias suffered a good deal, though; his joints and back, already frail, never recovered from the long walk from Verulamium, and though he gamely tried to keep up his share of the work, his weakness was obvious.

And it was, to Regina's horror, Cartumandua who became the most seriously ill of all.

It started with a pain in her belly. It persisted no matter what she ate, and even when she didn't eat at all. When Regina touched Carta's belly she found a hard lump, below her rib cage, almost like another, malevolent child.

None of them had any idea what could be ailing Carta. There was, of course, no doctor to call on. Regina even tried begging medicines from the bearded farmer. Exsuperius offered nothing save advice about letting Carta chew on willow bark. When Carta tried that she found the gathering pain would, if only briefly, be lessened. But gradually, day by day, Carta grew weaker and more sallow, and Regina felt a growing dread.

When the days were shortest, much of the marshy land froze. The daily chore of fetching water could never be skipped, but they had to walk farther to find a place where the water wasn't frozen, or where the ice was thin enough to break. The water walks came to dominate their lives, the first thing Regina woke up thinking about each morning.

On one particularly bleak, gray midwinter morning, she and Marina made the first walk down to the marsh. They had dug a cesspit here. Regina squatted over the hole in the ground, her dress lifted up to expose her backside to the raw cold.

Suddenly she imagined how her younger self might have

felt if she could have seen her crouching in this muddy pond. In her mother's villa there had been a latrine close to the kitchen, so water from the kitchen could be used to flush. There were sponge sticks and vials of perfumed water to keep yourself clean, and the little room was always rich with cooking smells. And now, *this*. She had come to this pass step by step—and every step downward—she had been so busy staying alive that she had forgotten how far from home she had come.

But you had to shit. She squatted, strained, and finished her business as quickly as she could, cleaning herself with a handful of grass.

Today was misty but not as ferociously cold as it had been, and the marsh might be unfrozen at the center. So, carefully, she walked down to its rough shore and picked her way over frozen mud and puddles of sheer ice. She came to a patch of open, slushy water, where dead reeds, brown and lank, floated like hair. She bent and reached into the ice-cold water to pull the reeds aside. But she felt a sharp pain.

She pulled back her arm. Her palm had been gashed, and bright red blood, the brightest color in a landscape of gray and green-brown, dripped down her arm, mingling with the water that clung to her skin.

Marina came to her nervously. "What is it?"

"I think I've been bitten. Perhaps a pike—"

Marina inspected her hand. "That looks like no bite to me. You need to wash that off . . ."

"Yes." Regina bent to peer into the water. Through the layer of reeds she could see no fish. But she did make out a bright gleam, like a coin in a well. More cautiously, with her good hand, she reached down and explored. It was hard to judge the depth of the murky water. She quickly found something hard and flat—a blade. Carefully she took hold of it between thumb and forefinger, and pulled it out.

It was a knife. Its iron blade was heavily rusted, but its hilt, of bright yellow metal engraved with swooping circular designs, seemed unmarked. "I think this is gold," she said, wondering.

Marina was unimpressed. "Old Exsuperius would probably

give you a bag of beans for the iron, nothing for the gold," she said, businesslike.

"I wonder how it got here."

"An offering," said Marina unexpectedly. "To the river. When you die—you give it your armor, your weapons, your treasure. It's what they always did, away from the towns. Like they did before . . . We probably pulled it up when we tugged on the reeds."

A dead man's hoard. It was an eerie thought, and Regina glanced around uneasily at the mist-laden, murky landscape.

In many parts of the countryside the touch of Roman rule had always been light. As long as folk kept the peace and paid their taxes, the Emperor had never very much cared what they got up to in their private lives. Perhaps a community in this remote farmstead had kept up the rituals of their distant forebears, and thrown their personal goods into the marsh as propitiations to the goddesses of the water and the earth. The rational corner of her mind wondered if it might have been better for these vanished warriors to hold on to their weapons, to keep their money and spend it on trade or defenses, rather than hurl it into this marsh so extravagantly. Then they might have resisted the Romans better.

Probably there were bodies here, too, hurled into the water. They would be the dead, not of her time, but of the strange times of the deeper past, before the legionaries and census keepers and tax collectors: not *her* dead, but the dead of other, alien folk, whose spirits might, somehow, still linger in the mists of this ancient, endlessly reworked landscape.

She was shivering. She tucked the little weapon into her belt.

Back at the roundhouse Carta poured urine over Regina's hand to clean out her wound, and rubbed in honey, expensively bought from Exsuperius, to stop any infection. The next day it was brighter, and Regina's odd superstitious fears were banished. But the brightness brought a deeper cold, and the marsh was frozen over, hiding its strange trove.

As winter turned to spring, Regina's heavy belly slowed her down. But this was a community of three women, one old

man, and the unreliable, lazy Severus, and there was no room
for passengers.

Still, it wasn't so bad. One way or another they never ran
short of food, even during the worst of the winter. And as the
days grew longer and warmer, despite the load in her belly, she
felt stronger, oddly, than she ever had before.

And it seemed that as Carta had gradually weakened, the
others had come to look to Regina for leadership. So she was
the first off her pallet of reeds each morning, the first to take
her turns with the water fetching, the first to check the traps,
always setting an example with her own efforts.

She was poor at bending and lifting, and couldn't climb
onto the roof of the roundhouse. But she could work a foot
plow. One morning she set to hauling it across one of the fields
on the slope behind the farmstead. She had to dig its iron point
into the soil, push it in with her foot, and then haul back on the
handle, which was nearly as tall as she was, to break open the
soil.

The iron plow with its bowed wooden handle had been a
precious find, left under a heap of decaying sacking by the
vanished Arcadius and his workers. They had used more of
their hunted meat to buy seed stock for wheat, kale, and cabbages from Exsuperius. Now the time was coming—as she
dimly recalled from her memories of life in the villa—to plow
and plant.

With the foot plow, however, it was only possible to scratch
a shallow groove in the ground. It was galling to remember
how her father's tenants had used ox teams to break the soil
over vast areas, while she was reduced to this pitiful scraping.
But Exsuperius, in one of his bits of taciturn advice, had told
them to plow their fields twice, in a crisscross pattern, to break
up the ground better. And she found that when she came to the
second set of furrows the plow fairly slid into the already broken soil.

By midday, her muscles had thoroughly warmed up, and the
sun shed a little warmth on her face.

After so many months she no longer felt quite so obsessively bitter about Aetius, and Marcus and Julia, and Amator—especially Amator—all the people who had, one way or
another, abandoned her. As for her companions here on the

farm, they had been thrown together by chance, and they were none of them perfect: Carausias an overtrusting old fool, Severus lazy, selfish, and sullen, Marina timid and lacking initiative, and Carta—dear Carta, now terribly weakened. These were *not* the people with whom Regina would have chosen to be spending the eighteenth year of her life. But they were *her* people, she was coming to see: they were the people who had taken her in after her grandfather's death, who had sheltered her as best they could . . .

It was at that moment, just as she had reached the nearest thing to contentment she had enjoyed since that night with Amator, that the first contraction came. She fell to the ground, yelling for Carta, as waves of pain rippled over her belly.

What followed was a blur. Here were Marina and old Carausias, their faces looming over her like moons. They were too weak to carry her, so she had to get to her feet and, leaning heavily on their shoulders, limp to the house.

Carta's face was yellow and drawn. She looked as if she could barely stand herself. But she placed her hands on Regina's belly, and felt the pulsing muscles, the position of the baby.

Regina yelled, "It's too early! Oh, Carta, make it stop!"

Carta shook her head. "The baby has its own time . . . Get her on the bed, Marina, quickly." She lifted Regina's tunic, grubby with dirt from the fields, and placed a wooden plank, scavenged from one of the other buildings, under Regina's buttocks.

"Here. Take this." It was Carausias, looming over her. He had brought her one of her precious *matres*. They, at least, had never abandoned her; she clutched the lumpy little statue to her chest.

The contractions were coming in waves now.

Carta snapped, "Regina, pull back your knees." Regina reached down and, with a huge effort, hooked her fingers behind her knees and pulled her legs back and apart.

Carta forced a smile. "I knew I shouldn't have let you plow that wretched field."

"And who else was to do it? . . . *Ow-w!* Carta—"

"Yes?"

"You *have* done this before, haven't you?"

"What, delivered a baby? Have *you* plowed a field before?"

With the next contraction the pain became unbelievably intense, as if she were slowly being torn apart.

Carta leaned closer. Even through her own pain Regina saw how pale she was, her white face glistening with oily sweat. "Regina, listen to me. There's something I have to tell you."

"Can't it wait?"

"No, child," Carta said sadly. "No, I don't think it can. Your father . . . You remember how he died."

It was an awful image to come wafting through her clouds of pain. "I could hardly forget—"

"It was me."

"What?"

"I was the one he was unfaithful with. I was the reason he punished himself."

Regina gasped. "Carta, how could you? You betrayed my mother—"

Carta's bloodless mouth worked. "He gave me no choice."

Marina screamed, "I can see its head!"

Carta pulled back to see. "Marina, help me . . ." She reached down to support Regina's perineum, and cupped her hand around the baby's head. "The cord is around its neck . . . Uncle, give me that knife. *Now,* you old fool." Even through her own pain Regina could feel Carta's hands trembling as she worked.

When the cord was cut, the baby's body slid smoothly out, tumbling into Marina's waiting arms with a last gush of fluid. Marina picked mucus from the baby's button mouth. Carta stayed with Regina until the afterbirth had emerged, and then she packed her vagina with moss to stem the bleeding.

Regina, despite her weakness and exhaustion, had eyes only for her baby, which had begun to wail thinly. "Let me see . . ."

"It's a girl," Marina said, her eyes bright. She had wrapped the baby in a clean bit of blanket, and now she leaned down toward Regina so she could see the round pink face.

Carta said, "I think—I think . . ." And she fell back, slumping to the floor. Regina tried to see, but could not raise her head.

Carausias cried, "Cartumandua! Come, oh come, my little niece, we can't have this." He fumbled for a small flask;

Regina knew it contained an extract of deadly nightshade, a heart stimulant bought at great expense from Exsuperius. He tried to pour droplets between Carta's lips, but her face was like a wax mask.

Her goddess heavy on her chest, fear and rage flooded Regina. "No! No, you sow, you bitch, you cow, you whore, Cartumandua! You won't leave me, not you, too, you slave, not now!"

But Carta did not respond, not even to apologize. The baby's crying continued, thin and eerie.

That evening Severus returned from his hunting. He saw the baby, the mess in the hut, Carta's body.

Severus stayed that night and the next. He helped Carausias and Marina prepare the body, and he used the plow to dig a shallow grave in the rocky ground at the top of the hill. But when Carta's body was buried, he walked away, taking nothing but the clothes on his back. Regina knew they would never see him again.

chapter 14

"I followed General Clark as we climbed the steps of the *cor- donata* toward the Piazza del Campidoglio on the Capitoline Hill. And all around Rome the bells of the campanili rang out . . ."

Lou Casella, my mother's uncle, my great-uncle, was over eighty. He was a short, stocky man, bald save for a fringe of snow-white hair, with liver-spotted skin stretched over impressive muscles. His voice was soft, husky, and to my ears, mostly educated by movies and TV, he sounded like a classic New York Italian American, something like an old Danny De-Vito, maybe. He sat facing Lake Worth, sunset light glimmering in his rheumy familiar eyes—the family eyes, gray as smoke—as he told me how, in June 1944 at age twenty-two, he had entered Rome as an aide to General Mark Clark, commander of the victorious Fifth Army.

"In the place where I stood with Clark, Brutus, fresh from the murder of Caesar, once came to speak to the people. Augustus made sacrificial offerings to Jupiter. Greek monks prayed their way through the Dark Ages. Gibbon was inspired to write his great history. And now here *we* were, a bunch of ragged-ass GIs. But we'd made our own piece of history already. All I could see was faces, thousands upon thousands of Roman faces turned up toward us.

"And even then I knew that among those hopeful crowds I would find family . . ."

I had found Lou in a retirement home just off Seaspray Avenue in Palm Beach.

"What the hell kind of a coat is that?" he asked of my duffel. It was the first thing he said to me. "Where do you think you are, Alaska? Haven't seen a thing like that since the army."

It had taken me a while to trace him. The address Gina gave me was out of date. She wasn't apologetic. "I haven't seen him for ten years," she said. "And anyhow you don't think of people that age *changing address*, do you?"

Evidently Lou was an exception. His old address had been a rented apartment in Palm Beach. There was no forwarding contact, but Dan advised me to try the American Association of Retired Persons, which turned out to be a muscular lobby group. They were reluctant to give me his address, but acted as a third party to put us in touch. In all it took a couple of days before Lou finally called me at my hotel, and invited me over.

Lou showed me around his rest home. It was like a spacious hotel, every room sunlit, with dozens of white-coated staff and its own immense grounds. You could get permits for golf courses and private beaches. There was a daily program of exercise. As well as old-folk nostalgic social events like wartime picture shows and big-band dances, I saw notices for guest speakers from universities and other learned organizations on such topics as Florida history, coastal flora and fauna, art deco, even the history of Disney.

When I enthused about all this, Lou slapped me down. He called the place "the departure lounge." He walked me to a dayroom, where rows of citizens sat in elaborate armchairs, propped up before a gigantic, supremely loud wide-screen TV. "They like reality shows," he said. "Like having real live people here in the room with them. We do have a little community here. But every so often one of us just gets plucked out of here, and we all fight over his empty chair. So don't get all nostalgic about being old. You're fine so long as you keep fit, and you don't lose your marbles." He tapped his bare, sun-leathered cranium. "Which is why I walk three miles a day, and swim, and play golf, and do the *New York Times* crossword every day."

I was impressed. "You complete the crossword?"

"Did I say complete? . . . So you want to talk about your sister."

I'd told him the story on the phone. I'd brought a copy of the photograph, scanned and cleaned up by Peter McLachlan; Lou had glanced at it but didn't seem much interested. "I want to close the whole business off," I said.

"Or you're picking a scab," he said warningly. "I never met her, your sister. So if you want to know what she's *like*—"

"Just tell me the story," I said. I spread my hands, and tried to imitate his *Godfather* accent. "Picture the scene. Rome, nineteen forty-four. The liberating army is welcomed by a smiling populace—"

He laughed, and clapped me on the back. "Shithead. Christ, you are your father's boy; he made the same kind of dumb jokes. All right, I'll tell you the story. And I'll tell you what was told to *me* by Maria Ludovica."

"Who?"

"Your cousin," he said. "Or whatever."

Maria Ludovica. It was the first time I'd heard the name. It wouldn't be the last.

We sat in a bright dayroom, and began to talk.

"When we had operations established, and we got the electricity back to the hospitals on the second day, and the phones working on the third, and so forth, I had time to look around a little . . . I knew the family had roots in Rome. I knew where my grandparents had come from—near the Appian Way—and it wasn't hard to dig out some Casellas in the area. Whatever you say about those fascists, they kept good records."

So young Sergeant Casella had ventured nervously down the Appian Way, the ancient road that led south out of Rome. In that hot autumn of 1944 the area was crowded with refugees, and everything was shabby, poor, dirty, deprived, despite the liberators' best efforts.

He had found a "nest of Casellas," as he put it, an extended family living under the stern eye of a black-wrapped widow who turned out to be a cousin of his father. "It was a small house in a kind of down-at-the-heel suburb. I mean it had been down-at-the-heel even before the damn occupation. And now there were, hell, twenty people living in there, stacked up. Refugees, even a wounded soldier—"

"All relatives."

"Yep. And with no place to go. They made me welcome. I was a liberating hero, *and* family. They made me a vast meal, even though they had so little themselves. Aunt Cara produced this tub of risotto with mushrooms—dense and thick and buttery, though God knows where she got the butter from . . ." He closed his eyes. "I can taste it to this day. They asked me to help, of course. I couldn't bend the rules, but I did what I could. I had my own salary, my own rations; I diverted some of that.

"They had some sick kids in there. Two boys and a girl. They were pale, hollow-eyed, coughing . . . I couldn't tell what was wrong, but it looked bad. They had to wait in line for the civilian docs, and in those days medical supplies were scarcer than anything else, as you can imagine. I tried to get an army medic to come out, but of course he wouldn't."

"And so you turned to Maria Ludovica?"

"It was all I could think of."

By this time Maria Ludovica had come looking for *him*. In an inverse of the family search Lou had performed, Maria, or others from the Puissant Order of Holy Mary Queen of Virgins, had inspected the new invaders of Rome for any family connections, and they had found Lou.

"Maria was really your cousin?"

"No. Something farther away than that. Remember it was my grandparents—your, uh, great-*great*-grandparents, I guess—who left Rome for the States in the first place. Hell, I don't know what you'd call our relationship. But she was a Casella all right. Those gray eyes, you know—you have them," he said, looking at me. "But she had black hair tied up around her head, cheekbones you could have eaten a meal off, and an ass—well, I guess I shouldn't say stuff like that to a kid like you. But she was sexy like you wouldn't believe. No wonder Mussolini couldn't keep his hands off her."

"Mussolini?"

"She was never a fascist—that's what she told me, and of course she would say that to an American soldier in nineteen forty-four—but I believed her. It turns out she'd known the Duce since the thirties. She first saw him in October nineteen twenty-two, when he first came to power, and she joined in the March on Rome: four columns, twenty-six thousand strong, closing on the city. The army and the police just stood aside as all those blackshirts marched in. Maria was sort of swept up;

where she came from, in Ravenna to the north, it was politic just to go along with it."

"And she became—what, his mistress?"

"You might call it that. She met him face to face the first time on Christmas Eve in 'thirty-three, when she was brought to Rome as one of the ninety-three most prolific women in the country."

"You're kidding."

"Nope. Ninety-three women in black shawls, mothers of thirteen hundred little Italians, soldiers for fascism."

I did the math quickly. *"Thirteen each?"*

He grinned. "They were heroes. But we've always been a fecund family, George. Our women stay fertile late, too." That was true, I reflected, thinking of Gina. "The heroic mothers were taken on a tour of the city, and they saw the *Exhibition of the Fascist Revolution*, where Maria kissed a glass case that contained a bloodstained handkerchief—the Duce had held it to a bullet wound in his nose after he survived an assassination attempt." He winked at me. "But that wasn't all she kissed."

I spluttered.

"Come on, kid. I think we need a walk."

And walk we did, at an impressively brisk pace, trotting around town on what I took to be one of his regular three-mile routes.

Palm Beach is set on a narrow tongue of land between the Atlantic, to the east, and Lake Worth, to the west. The city itself is set out according to a classic American grid layout, a neat tracing no more than four blocks wide from coast to coast. We tramped south down the County Road, peering dutifully at landmarks like the town hall and the Memorial Park fountain, a water feature fringed by swaying palm trees under a powder-blue sky. Then we turned onto Worth Avenue, four blocks of overpriced shops: Cartier, Saks, Tiffany, Ungaro's, stocking everything from Armani clothes to antique Russian icons, anything you wanted, nothing with a price tag. One of the shops boasted the world's largest stock of antique Meissen porcelain. Outside the shops limousine engines idled.

Lou said, "So what do you think? A little different from Manchester?"

"Too bloody expensive."

"Yeah, but if you were rich enough your head would work differently. You don't spend to *get* stuff. You spend as a statement. But it hasn't always been this way. I started to come here in the early sixties. We had a beach house, farther up the coast."

"We?"

"Lisa, my wife. Two boys. Already growing up, even then." He didn't mention the wife and kids again; I inferred the usual story, the wife had died, the kids rarely visited. "It was a good place for the summer. But back then it was kind of different." The town had been founded in the nineteenth century as a winter playground for the well heeled. In the twenties had come further development. "It was a winter town. In the summer they used to dismantle the traffic lights! Now, though, it stays open all year. Some say it's the richest town in the Union."

"So you've done well to end up here," I said.

"*End up.* You're not around old people much, are you?"

"Shit. I—"

"Ah, forget it. Yes, I did okay. Stock options—" His talk drifted back to the Second World War. He had been a draftee. "I was lucky. Spared the fighting. I already had some business experience, helping my father run his machine shop as a kid. So I got staff positions. Logistics. Requisitions. The work was endless.

"The invasion of Italy was the biggest bureaucratic exercise in history. We were heroes of paperwork." I grinned dutifully. "But it was good experience. I learned a hell of a lot, about people, business, systems. Stuff you learn in the army you can apply anywhere.

"I went back home after the war, but my father's business felt too small, with all respect to the old man." Having grown up in New York—he was old enough to remember the Wall Street crash—Lou took some positions in the financial industry. "But I got impatient with being so far from the action. After Italy, moving funds around, buying and selling stocks, watching numbers on a ticker tape—it was all too remote. I'm not a miner or an engineer. But I wanted to work somewhere I could see things being built."

So, after taking some kind of business degree, he had moved to California to work for none other than North American Aviation in Downey, California.

"It was North American built Apollo. You know, the moon ship?" I nodded. Evidently he was used to younger people never having heard of the program. "Not all of it," he said. "Just the CSM—the command and service modules, the part that came back to Earth. I did well at North American. I was in the right place at the right time. We believed we could achieve anything, on any scale, if we worked hard enough, with our flow charts and schedules and critical paths. Why not? That was how we won the war, and how we managed Project Apollo. Four hundred thousand people, all across the country, all doing their tiny part—but all controlled from the center, all those resources pouring in, like building a mountain out of grains of sand, a huge mountain you could climb all the way to the moon."

He was a solid character, intense, engaged, vividly real. In his anecdotes I glimpsed a postwar America growing fast, confident and rich, a time of technological growth and economic expansion—and I liked the idea that a relative of mine had been there at the fall of Rome, and had worked on Apollo. But I wasn't enjoying the encounter. Beside him I felt pale, diminished, uncertain, maybe a bit intimidated. And *young*.

We turned off Worth onto Lake Drive South, which ran north along the coast of Lake Worth. Here the road was part of a bicycle trail, and in the low afternoon light there were people cycling, skateboarding, jogging.

"Here, you can buy me a Popsicle."

It turned out he meant an ice lolly; we had come to an ice cream stall. I stumped up for two great gaudy confections, so sugary I couldn't finish mine. But we sat on a stone bench and gazed out at the ducks paddling on Lake Worth. The flat western light made his face look like a bronze sculpture, all plains and grooves.

By 1943 the war was going badly for the Italians. Mussolini was removed and arrested, and an armistice signed. When the Allies landed at Salerno, the Germans found out about the deal. Rome quickly fell to the Nazis.

"The Order was involved in the resistance, in a quiet way,"

Lou said. "So Maria Ludovica told me. The Germans tried to call up all the young men for work on factories or farms or mines, or on the defense lines they were building to oppose the Allied advance. And the city was full of escaped POWs. Lots of people to hide. We estimated that at one time, of a city of a million and a half or so, about two hundred thousand were being hidden, in homes, churches, even the Vatican."

"And the Order—"

"They have a big complex there, big and old and deep. Not that I ever saw it." I wondered, *Deep?* "Yes, the Order did their share. And it was not without risk. Family, huh—I guess we should be proud."

Air raids began, even though Rome was supposed to be an open city, aiming at railway lines but hitting civilians in such customary friendly-fire targets as hospitals. "The gas and electricity went altogether," said Lou. "They cut up the benches and trees in the parks for wood. The Order started selling meals, hundreds a day, at a lira a head.

"But then the citizens started to hear the heavy guns.

"Maria Ludovica came out to the Lungotevere to watch the Germans go. Armed to the teeth but dejected, bedraggled. Everybody was silent. Makes you think," he said. "A Roman crowd, surrounded by all those ancient monuments, once again seeing the retreat of an occupying army."

"And then you arrived."

"Yep. I walked in after the tanks that came up the Porta San Giovanni. In the evening everybody lit a little candle in the window. It was, you know, magical." And he told me how, on June 5, 1944, the day before D-Day, he had climbed the steps of Michelangelo's *cordonata* with General Clark. "Not that the Romans were grateful," he said with a grin around his Popsicle stick.

He leaned closer. "Maria never told me all of it, about Mussolini. Far too delicate for that. But I figured it out. He was kind of a brisk lover. He'd just nail you, right there on the floor of his office. He wouldn't even take his shoes or trousers off. And when he was done he'd just send you right out of the room and get back to work."

"What a charmer."

"But he was Mussolini. Knew a lot of guys in the army who had similar habits, mind you . . ."

I half listened. I was trying to put this together, trying to figure out how old this Maria Ludovica must be. Say she was about twenty during the 1922 march. That would put her in her thirties when she'd become a "prolific woman," and in her *forties* during the war. Was it really credible that a forty-year-old mother of so many children would be the selection of Mussolini, who had, I supposed, the whole of Italy outside the convents to choose from? And could such a woman really have been the sex goddess glimpsed by the callow young Sergeant Casella in 1944? Was Lou somehow conflating the memories of more than one woman?—but his stories seemed detailed and sharp.

"You know, Mussolini was going to build a giant statue of Hercules, as tall as a *Saturn Five* rocket, with the face of Mussolini and its right hand raised in a fascist salute. All they made was a head and a foot." He laughed. "*Credere! Obbedire! Combattere!* What an asshole. But still, if he made a pass at you, you didn't turn him away. I'm pretty sure that by letting the Duce poke her, Maria Ludovica earned a lot of protection for the Order in those years."

"What was Maria's connection to the Order? Did she start it?"

"Hell, no. Boy, don't you know any of the family history?"

I frowned. "The story of the Roman girl—"

"Roman British, yes. Regina."

"Just a legend. Has to be. The records don't go back that far."

He sucked on his Popsicle. "If you say so. Anyhow, for sure the Order was a lot older than Maria Ludovica."

"And when you found the Casellas you turned to Maria."

"She, the Order, knew about the Casellas. The Order itself was based not far away. But they hadn't known about the sickness. When I got in touch, they came—Maria, and three other women. Medically trained, apparently. They wore these simple white robes. I remember cradling one of the boys while they crowded around with their stethoscopes and such. They were all three about the same age. And all similar, all like Maria, like sisters. And the family eyes, smoky gray. It was strange looking from one face to the other. They kind of blurred together, until you couldn't be sure who was who."

"And they helped the children."

"They were short of resources, like everybody else. They treated one boy. He recovered. The other boy died. They took the little girl away."

"What?"

He turned to me. "They took her away. Into the Order."

"But they brought her back to her parents."

"No." He seemed puzzled by that. "They just took her in, and that was that."

"And the parents didn't mind? These people they'd never seen before, relatives or not, just turn up and take their kid away—"

"Hey." He put a broad, heavy hand on my arm. "You're raising your voice . . . You're thinking about your sister."

"There does seem an obvious parallel. Gina said you brokered that deal, too."

"I wouldn't put it like that. Your sister wasn't sick. But she was in need—your whole family was. Your parents just couldn't afford the two of you. They put out feelers in the family for help—" I could imagine how my father would have felt about that. "It got to me, by a roundabout route. And I thought of the Order."

"How could any parent give up a child to a bunch of strangers?"

Lou's gaze slid away from mine. "You don't get it. The Order aren't strangers. They're *family*." Again that heavy hand on my arm. "I knew I could trust them, and so did the Casellas in Rome, and so did your parents."

I said nothing, but he could read my expression.

"Look, kid, you're obviously mixed up about this. If you've come to me for some kind of absolution, you're not going to get it."

"I'm sorry?"

"Or is blame the game? Your father isn't around anymore, so you're looking to come take a shot at me. Is that it?"

"I'm not here to blame you."

"Nor should you. Or your parents, God rest them." He jabbed a nicotine-stained forefinger at my chest and glared up at me. "We all did the best we could, according to the circumstances, and our judgment at the time. If you're a decent person, that's exactly what you do. We're human. We try."

"I accept that. I just want to know."

He shook his head. "I suppose I'd be the same if I was in your shoes. But I warn you, you might be disappointed."

I watched him, baffled. I was reminded of the headmistress. What was it about the Order that made people thousands of miles away want to defend it like this?

I gazed toward the setting sun. Anyhow, I knew now that this Order had taken my sister, as it had the little girl in 1944, and no doubt many other girls and maybe boys, relatives, over the decades—or centuries, I wondered coldly. But what I needed to know now was what they took them *for*. Lou was wrong. Trust wasn't enough. Even being family wasn't enough. I needed to know.

I asked him, "Do you send the Order money?"

"Of course I do." He eyed me. "I guess your father did, but that must have stopped now. I guess it's your turn. Do you want some bank account details? . . ." He searched for numbers in his billfold.

chapter 15

In the dense, moist heat of noon, Brica's gentle, lilting voice carried easily through the trees. ". . . The sidhe live in hollow hills," Brica was saying. "They are invisible. They can be seen when they choose, but even then they are hard to spot, for they always wear green. They are harmless if you are friendly to them, which is why we drop bits of bread in the furrow when plowing, and pour wine on the ground at harvesttime . . ."

Not wishing to disturb her daughter, Regina approached as silently as she could. Not that that was so easy now she was forty-one years old, and already an old woman, and anyhow her forest skills would never match those of the younger folk.

". . . But you must never eat sidhe food, for they will lead you into their hollow hills, which are entrances to the Other-world, and you may never find your way out—or if you do, you might find a hundred years have passed, and all your family, even your brothers and sisters, have grown old and died, while you have aged only a day. But if a sidhe frightens you, you can always chase her away with the sound of a bell—but it must be made of iron, for the sidhe fear iron above all . . ."

Her daughter sat at the center of a ring of children, their faces raised intently. Nearby a fire flickered. Brica saw Regina, and held up a hand in apology. She had been due to meet her mother at the farmstead.

Regina was content to wait in the cool of the shade and let her heart stop thumping from the climb up the hillside from the farmstead. The sun was almost overhead now, and its light, scattered into green dapples by the tall canopy of trees, lit up the curl of white smoke that rose from the fire. Regina recognized the rich, strong scent of burning oak, stronger than beech or ash. She sometimes wondered what Julia would have

thought if she could have known that one day her daughter
would become an expert on the scents of burning firewood.
But they had all had to adapt.

Brica, given an old British name after Regina's own grandmother, shared Regina's features—the pale, freckled skin, the
somewhat broad nose, lips bright as cherries, the eyes of
smoke gray. But at twenty-one years old she was more beautiful than Regina had ever been. Her face had a symmetry that
Regina's lacked, and there was a kind of exquisite perfection
in the oyster-shell curl of her ears, the fine lines of her eyebrows. Even her one undeniable gift from her never-seen-
again father Amator, her black hair, was thick and lustrous.

And she was very good at holding the children's attention.
This morning she had shown them how to start a fire, with a
bit of flint and a scrap of char-cloth. It was their most essential
skill of all, and one that the children were shown over and over
again, just as Brica had been taught as she had grown up.
And buried in the fables Brica told the children were warnings
that might ensure their safety: even this tale of the sidhe, the
fairies.

Few adults believed in supernatural beings moving among
them. But you would sometimes glimpse strangers: a very odd
kind of stranger, moving over the sparely populated hills,
often wearing green—just as in the stories. These were humans, no doubt about that, and they carried tools of stone or
bronze. And they were robbers. Rather like foxes, they would
take chickens and the odd sheep, or even—if they could get
it—bread or cake. It was said they were dangerous when cor-
nered, but they would flee when challenged. And it was true
that they were terrified of iron—especially iron weapons,
Regina thought dryly, against which their flimsy bronze was
little protection.

Nobody was sure where they came from. Her own theory
was that the sidhe came from the west, perhaps the southwestern peninsula or Wales, or even the far north beyond the Wall.
Perhaps in those distant valleys an old sort of folk had persisted—older even than the barbarian culture that had pre-
ceded the arrival of the Romans—so old they didn't even have
the skills to make iron. Now that the legions were gone, and

the land was emptying, they were, perhaps, slowly creeping back.

If they seemed to Regina's folk as furtive, creeping, uncanny spirits, she wondered how her folk must seem to them. *And after all,* she thought wistfully, *nowadays we can't make iron, either.*

The children all wore simple shifts of colorless wool. Some of them wore daisy chains around their heads or necks, and one small boy had a broad black stripe of birch-bark oil on his cheek, a lotion applied by Marina to a deep graze. Sitting there they looked like creatures of the forest, Regina thought suddenly, quite alien from the little girl she had once been.

At length Brica's fable was done. The children scattered through the woods in twos and threes, to find mushrooms and other fruits of the forest for that evening's meal, and then to make their way home.

Brica approached her mother and kissed her lightly on the cheek. "I'm sorry, I'm sorry."

Regina tried to be stern. But she cupped her daughter's cheek and smiled. "Let's just get on."

Brica briskly stamped out the little fire, and the two of them walked out of the belt of forest and into the sunshine. They looked down the broad breast of hillside at the farmstead's three roundhouses, and beyond that to the valley where the silver-gray thread of the river glistened like a dropped necklace. But they turned away and began to walk along the crest of the hill, making for the ruined villa. Brica was always busy, always alert. She would run away to inspect a trap, or pick a handful of berries from a cane, or dig mushroom flesh from a fallen tree trunk. She was like fire, Regina thought, filled with a blazing energy Regina herself couldn't even envy anymore.

"So," she said carefully, "have you seen Bran again?"

"Not for a few days." But Brica turned away, her smoky eyes dancing. Bran was a boy, a little younger than Brica herself, from a farmstead a couple of hills away. He was the grandson of old Exsuperius, in fact, their first grumpy, grudging neighbor, now long dead. Brica said, "He isn't a bad sort, you know, Mother."

"Not a bad sort behind a plow, no, but he can read no better than you could at the age of five. And as for his Latin—"

Brica sighed. "Oh, Mother—nobody *reads*. What use is it? A papyrus scroll won't plow a field, or tend the birth of a calf—"

"Maybe not now. But when things—"

"—get back to normal, yes, yes. You know, there are girls *five years younger* than me who have husbands and children."

"You aren't those girls," Regina snapped.

"You don't think Bran is good enough for me."

"I never said that."

Brica slipped her hand into her mother's. "The only reason he's learning to read at all is to please you."

Regina was surprised. "It is?"

"Doesn't that show how he cares about me—even about you?"

"Perhaps." Regina shook her head. "You must make your own decisions, I suppose. *I* made many foolish choices—but if I had not, I wouldn't have *you*. I just want you to be sure what you want. And in the meantime be careful."

Brica snorted. "Mother, I go to Marina every month."

Regina knew that Brica was talking about the herbal teas Marina made up as a contraceptive treatment. Marina had, over the years, become something of an expert on remedies gathered from the forests and fields; in the absence of a doctor such wisdom was the best anybody could do.

"Well, you know what I think of potions like *that*," Regina snapped. "If Bran really did care about you he would use a condom. There's no tea that's as effective as a pig's bladder."

Brica flushed red, but she was suppressing a laugh. "Mother, *please*!"

"And another thing . . ."

Bickering, laughing, gossiping, they made their way along the broken ridge.

There were more than twenty people at the farm now, a community grown from the seed of that panicky flight from Verulamium. Around the old core of Regina and her daughter, Marina and Carausias, others had gathered: refugees from an old town to the south, the second eldest son of an overcrowded farmstead to the west and his family.

In the beginning, in this dismal ruin on its breast of green hillside, Regina had felt utterly lost. The sense of isolation was the worst. The richer parts of the countryside were inhabited and cultivated as they had always been, but scattered farmsteads like this one on more marginal land, farmed only when it had been necessary to pay Roman taxes, now lay abandoned. Their neighbors were few and far between—there were few lights to be seen on the hills at night. The crown of forest at the top of the hill became a source of almost superstitious dread for Regina, a thick green-black tangle within which lurked boar, wolves, and even a bear, a shambling, massive form she had glimpsed once. She suspected that as the years went by the forest was gradually creeping down the hillside, and wild animals of all kinds were becoming more numerous, as if nature were seeking to reclaim the land it had once ruled.

The endless labor had been hard on them all. Regina counted herself lucky that she hadn't been afflicted by the chronic back problems many had suffered, or the worms and other parasites. But it broke her heart that a third of all the children born here had died before their first birthdays.

Still, she and the others had persisted. They would not be driven from this place—after all, they had nowhere else to go. And slowly, they had managed to improve things.

After a time, as their numbers had grown, they had plucked up the courage to try to build another roundhouse—but its roof had blown off in the winter's first storm. There was a trick to the angle of the thatch, it turned out; a perfect one-in-one slope would wash away the rain and resist the wind, and if you didn't allow the lip to dangle too close to the ground it remained safe from the mice.

And now, by Jupiter's beard, there were *three* roundhouses. It was a little village, a busy place. They had dug pits in the ground for surplus grain, and every day you could hear the steady grinding of quern stones.

In the spring and autumn there was the plowing to be done—twice a year, for in the autumn they would seed the fields with winter wheat and other seasonal crops. They cultivated emmer wheat, spelt wheat, hulled six-row barley, kale, and beans. Wild garlic and parsnips could often be found, and in summer blackberries, elderberries, and crab apples. They kept a few chickens, sheep for their wool and milk, and pigs, useful creatures that could be turned out into the fields to root in the stubble, or driven into the forest for forage in the winter. Only old animals were butchered. Most of their meat came from hunted deer and occasionally boar, and they still used the simple traps for hares they had made from their very earliest days.

And then there were all the other essentials of life. It still startled Regina sometimes that you really couldn't *buy* anything anymore. Anything you couldn't barter for, from shoes to clothes to tools to new roofing for your house, you had to *make*.

Take clothing, for instance. As their few garments had quickly worn out, Regina had had to find out how to pluck wool off their sheep with combs of wood or bone, and to spin it into yarn, and even to weave it with simple looms. The clothes they made were simple—just tubes of cloth, made into tunics and undershirts and *braecci*, trousers for the men, and a *peplum*, a sleeveless dress for the women—but they did the job.

Shoes were more of a challenge. When their old town-bought shoes had worn out, their first attempts at making leather replacements had been disasters, ill-fitting lash-ups that had rubbed and burned and caused blisters. Even now they were only beginning to learn the knack of cobbling a good serviceable boot. It amazed her how much time she spent thinking about her feet.

They had even tried their hand at pottery, to replace their cups and bowls of carved wood. They experimented with pit clamps. You would line a shallow pit with hot embers overlaid with green wood. The pots would be carefully placed on top, and the whole thing covered with dry wood, damp straw, and soil to make an airtight mound. If you left it for a full day, making sure the covering of soil was intact, you might be lucky to have a quarter or a third of your pots come out whole—blackened, coarse, but intact.

Carausias and Marina seemed to find great satisfaction in making such things, while Brica and the children were used to nothing better. But Regina remembered her mother's precious Samian ware, and she wondered how long it would be before the trade routes were restored and the markets opened again, and she would once again be able to buy such treasures as easily as breathing.

But all that was lazy thinking, she told herself sternly, pointless longing, a distraction from the business of simply staying alive that occupied nearly all their time, from dawn to dusk. After all she had an example to set.

As the years had gone by, somebody had to lead. It would never be Marina, who, despite her own two children and three grandchildren, had never thrown off her self-denigrating cast of mind as a servant. As he aged, poor Carausias, who after all had led them all here in the first place, became less and less effectual, often sinking into the state of unhappy confusion from which he had never really recovered since his betrayal by Arcadius.

And so it had become Regina who led, more or less by default. It was Regina who welcomed newcomers or turned them away, Regina who took the floor at their regular meetings, Regina who sat in judgment like a Verulamium magistrate to resolve disputes over share-outs of chickens' eggs, Regina who traveled the area to keep up their tentative contacts with their neighbors—Regina who had discovered in herself the leadership without which, all seemed to agree, the farmstead would long since have failed and they would all have become *bacaudae*, if they had survived at all.

It wasn't a situation she liked. She always promised herself that the whole thing was just temporary. But in the meantime there was nobody better to do it.

To her frustration they were out of touch with the great events of the world here. There was still no news of the Emperor's return. The old road still bore some traffic, and the travelers or refugees sometimes brought news of kings: there was one Cunedda in Wales, for instance, and a Coel in the north, rumored to be the last of the Roman commanders there, now styling himself the Old King. From the east came rumors of one Vitalinus, who called himself Vortigern—a name that meant "high king"—who, it was said, had taken on the job of uniting the old province and keeping it safe from the marauding Saxons and Picts and Irish. The farmsteaders heard nothing from these grand men. "We'll know they mean business," Carausias would say, "when the taxman comes to call."

Nobody ever did call. And, almost unnoticed, while Regina built her farmstead into a place of prosperity and safety, more than twenty years passed by.

When they reached the villa Regina and Brica separated and began a systematic search through the ruined buildings.

The villa had been sited in a natural bowl of green landscape, with a fine view of the western hills. Once it must have been grand indeed, Regina thought—grander even than her parents' villa—a complex of seven or eight stone buildings set around a courtyard, with barns and other smaller wooden buildings nearby.

But it had been abandoned long before she had first discovered it. Its tile-stripped roofs had already decayed, and weeds had choked the courtyard and had started pushing their way up through the floors. Since then things had only gotten worse, as nature had followed its inexorable cycle. The floor of what must once have been the bathhouse had been broken open from below by the spreading roots of an ash, and the rooms were strewn with dead leaves. Since her last visit, last autumn, fire had burned out one of the stone buildings, removing the last vestiges of the roof and leaving its interior a shattered and smoky mess.

Despite all the damage, though, she could still see the grand plan of the villa in the great rectangular pattern of its walls, and the stumps of the broken columns that had once formed a colonnade around the courtyard. But she wondered how long it would be before the mortar crumbled and the stones rotted, and nothing was left but hummocks in the green. It was as if the world itself were a constant foe, with its million fingers of plants and insects, frost, sunlight, and fire, a relentless destroyer of all human ambition.

Regina made for the largest building in the complex. Probably it had once been a reception room. The roof was long gone, save for a few stumps of rotting beams. The floor was covered by a litter of soil and leaves, and after years of exposure to the weather the painted plasterwork had crumbled off the wall in great sheets. The walls themselves were intact, and still the room impressed by its sheer size. But the room had long since been stripped of furniture, and even the little sockets on the walls were empty of the oil lanterns they had once held.

Regina got down on her hands and knees and started to comb through the dirt. After so long, anything large enough to be seen easily had long since been smashed or carried off, and the only hope of finding anything was a fingertip search, bit by bit. But in a time when even a shoe nail was precious, it was worth the effort. Last time she had been here, in fact, she had found a small perfume bottle. As she had raised it into the light she had been stunned by its symmetry and perfection compared to the crude bowls and wooden pots she was forced to use at home, as if it had leaked into this world from some better place. She kept the bottle in the little alcove she had built for the *matres*, and every so often she would hold it, and take it out into the light.

Through the ruined walls she could see Brica. She had settled to a heap of dirt in one corner of what might once have been a kitchen and was exploring it carefully. It was a disconcerting juxtaposition of images, her daughter in her grubby shift rooting under a wall that still bore the marks of shelving, and even a hint of flower-design fresco work. She knew Brica felt uncomfortable in such places as these ruins, as if she believed they were ghost-haunted relics built by giants of the past, as the children's tittle-tattle had it. Sometimes Regina worried about what would happen if this unsatisfactory situation went on so long that the last of those who remembered died off, leaving only ruins, secondhand memories, and legends.

She thought about Bran. He was a little dull, but he really wasn't a bad young man, Regina thought. And it wasn't as if Brica had much choice.

There was no civic structure here; there was no nearby town or functioning villas. But as time had passed Regina and her people had settled into a loose community of neighboring farmsteads. They were somewhat wary—some of these hill-folk were very long established and were suspicious of new-comers—but they would help each other out with harvests or medical emergencies. And they would trade, vegetables for meat, a wooden bowl for a blanket of woven wool. If not for such contacts, Regina mused, it was probable none of them would have survived.

But the population was sparse. The land had drained as people fled south, dreaming of Armorica, abandoning even farms on the best land, driven away by the rumored advances of the Saxon raiders in the east and the Picts and Irish in the west and north. And in this empty landscape of ghost towns and abandoned farms, there was a paucity of suitable mates for Brica, that was for sure.

Regina's opposition to Bran didn't make much sense, then. But she was opposed even so. It seemed there was some deep instinct inside her about the destiny of her daughter. Yet when she thought hard about this her mind seemed to skitter away, like a pebble over a frozen pond. No doubt she would eventually figure it out.

Absently Regina brushed at the debris, she exposed a bit of floor, revealing scarlet, a patch of color picked out in tesserae. It was part of a mosaic.

With sudden eagerness she brushed aside the dirt with her forearm, exposing more of the mosaic. It showed a man's face, large-eyed, bearded. The head was surrounded by colors, gold, yellow, orange, bright red, in a sunburst pattern. It might have been Apollo, or perhaps it was some Christian symbol. Though some of the gold-leaf tiles had been prized out by hopeful robbers, most of the colors still shone as bright as the day they had been laid down. With obsessive motions she began to clear more of the floor. It seemed wrong that such beauty should be wasted under dead leaves and crawling worms, as if the young man in the picture had been buried alive. Suddenly it struck her how the farmstead, much as she was proud of it, was a place of drab gray-green and brown, as if everything had been molded from mud. How she missed color! She had forgotten how bright the world used to be. She was carried back to another time, impossibly warm, bright, and safe, when she had crept into the ruined rooms of her parents' villa and discovered another mosaic . . .

A single scream pierced the air. It was cut off suddenly.
Brica.

Regina's thoughts evaporated, replaced by hard, cold fear. She got to her feet and ran out of the room.

* * *

Brica was standing in the kitchen. Her gray eyes were wide with terror.

The man behind her was taller than Brica by a head. He held Brica easily with one hand clamped over her face, and in the other he held a short iron sword with an elaborately cast handle. He wore a cloak of dyed wool. His blond hair was long and tied back from his head, and his drooping mustache was clogged with bits of food. When he saw Regina he smiled, showing yellowed teeth. He said something in a language she did not understand.

He reached down, dug the heft of his sword into the neck of Brica's tunic, and let the corner of the blade cut through the soft wool. When he had exposed her chest he massaged her breast with the fingers of his sword hand. He seemed to enjoy the way she flinched when his cold metal touched her bare flesh. Again he spoke softly to Regina, as if inviting.

He was a Saxon, of course. She had seen his like before—scattered parties of them, riding west along the old Roman road. They had always kept on past the poor farms of this hillside. But now this Saxon had her daughter; now he cupped her whole life in his hands. It was as if the room expanded around her, as if time itself stretched, so that past and future were banished. There was nothing in the universe, no time or space, nothing but this moment and the three of them, locked in fear and calculation.

She forced herself to smile. It was the hardest thing she had ever done.

Looking at the Saxon, not at Brica, she walked up to him. He eyed her expectantly, as if trying to see her figure through her shapeless, leaf-strewn shift. She pulled at the fabric over her thigh, and parted her lips. She reached out to her daughter, and touched Brica's breast as coarsely as had the Saxon.

He laughed out loud. She could smell barley ale in his breath. His huge hand still clamped over Brica's mouth, he dragged the girl sideways, so his body was exposed; he was wearing a torc of tarnished silver around his neck. Regina stepped closer to him, touched his chest, then ran her hand down over his crotch. She could feel the bulge there. She smelled urine, semen, the stink of horseshit and the road. He grinned and spoke again, and she pressed her body against his.

The knife slid easily out of her sleeve. Using all her strength she rammed it through layers of coarse cloth into his crotch, above the root of his stiff penis.

His eyes bulged. The Saxon brought down his sword arm. But Regina was standing inside the arc of the stroke and he could do her no harm, not in that first crucial heartbeat. She got both hands on the hilt of the knife and dragged it upward, cutting into flesh and gristle.

And now Brica was at his back, her cut-open tunic flapping. She thrust her own knife into his back and twisted it, seeking his heart. Still the Saxon stood, flailing with his sword arm, as the women ripped and tore with their knives. It was like a dance, Regina thought, a gruesome dance of the three of them, in wordless silence.

Then the Saxon clutched Regina against his torso, and blood dark as birch-bark oil spilled from his mouth into her face. He shuddered and toppled like a felled tree, pulling both women down with him.

With disgust, Regina slithered backward across the dirt-strewn floor. She wiped the blood off her face with her hands. Brica fell on her mother, burying her face in Regina's chest. Regina tried to comfort her daughter, to stroke her hair and soothe her.

Their return to the farmstead created panic. Marina insisted on treating the bloody scrapes on Brica's chest with her poultices.

Regina longed to get the Saxon's blood off her. But first she instructed the younger men to round up the children and animals, while others checked over their simple weapons—a few iron swords and knives, mostly spears and arrows tipped with wood or stone. Meanwhile, led by limping, ancient Carausias himself, now more than sixty years old, others were to go back to the villa, take what they could from the Saxon's body, and dispose of it. The rest of his raiding party might yet ignore the farmstead, as had others in the past—but they surely would not ignore the murder of one of their own.

When everything was in hand, all Regina wanted was to get

to her pallet. In the gloom of her house she curled over on herself, as if trying to escape the world.

She had done many things over the years in order to survive. But she had never killed a human being before. She remembered the little girl who had once run to her mother as she dressed for her birthday party. *That child is long dead,* she thought, *the last vestige of her now gone; and I am like her ghost, or her corpse, kept alive but steadily decaying.*

Not without purpose, though. Poor or not, she knew that what they had built here—what *she* had built—was something to be proud of, something worth saving.

But now the Saxons were here. And Regina must decide what to do.

With the dawn she was awake.

After a brief toilet she pulled on an old tunic and cloak. She slipped out of the compound and walked down the hillside to the marshy land at the side of the river.

On some level she had always known this day would come. She had put it out of her mind, hoping, she supposed, that things would return to normal before she had to face it. But now the day of trial was here, and she had woken with shame that in her denial she had left her people, her own daughter, woefully undefended. They hadn't even built a palisade around the compound.

She waded out into the water and began to rummage in the black, reed-choked mud. The weather had been dry since spring and the water level was low. She had not forgotten the rusted iron dagger she had once found here, and she had always wondered if any more of that long-dead warrior's hoard might have survived. If so, it might provide better weaponry than their own poor wooden sticks and stone-tipped arrows. It was a poor idea, but she could think of none better.

She had found nothing but a shield, so corroded it was no more protection than a papyrus toy, when Brica came running down the hillside.

"Regina! Oh, Regina! Mother, why are you here? You must come!"

Regina straightened up, startled. There was smoke in the air.

It came from the west. "Exsuperius's farm," she said grimly. "The Saxons—"

Brica reached her and grabbed her arm. "We have visitors," she said.

"Who?"

"I don't know—you'll see—you have to come—" She grabbed her mother's hand and dragged her from the marsh. Together they hurried up the hillside to the farmstead.

A group of soldiers stood before the largest roundhouse, their hands resting casually on the hilts of their swords. They wore leather body armor, short tunics, and woolen trousers. The people of the farmstead stood in a sullen row before the soldiers. With them was the boy Bran, grandson of Exsuperius. His face was blackened by soot, perhaps from the burning of his home, and he stood in subdued silence, a mute testament to the power of these new arrivals.

"There are more of them down on the road," Brica whispered. "A few carts, too, and a sort of trail of people behind them. Their leader came up and demanded to be let in—we didn't know what to do—you weren't here—"

"It's all right," Regina said.

"Are they Saxons?"

"I don't think so."

One of the soldiers was taller than the rest, obviously the commander. He wore a red cloak and an elaborate leather cuirass, inset with metal buckles. He was perhaps thirty, but his face was lined with the dirt of the road. Regina's first impression was of strength, competence, but fatigue. And his short brown hair was brushed forward, in the Roman style— even his garb was almost Roman. For a brief moment her heart beat a little faster. Was it possible that the *comitatensis* had returned?

She stood between her people and the interlopers. She drew herself to her full height, disregarding the dirt on her face and legs, her disheveled clothes, the people in their mud-colored clothes behind her.

The leader hadn't even noticed her. *"Riothamus—"* One of the soldiers tapped his shoulder, indicating Regina. He seemed surprised to find himself facing a woman. He asked, "Are you the leader here?"

"If you wish it. And what rank are you, *riothamus*?" She pronounced the word mockingly, masking disappointment. It was Latin, but a version of a British word—'high king.' This was no soldier, no officer of the imperial army, but a mere warlord.

He nodded. "That is the only rank I have, and not one I wished for."

"Oh, really?"

He spread his hands. "I am not here to harm you."

"Oh," she said. "And you did not harm this boy, Bran, by burning down his home."

"I did him the least harm that way."

"Your definition of *harm* is interesting."

He grinned, his eyebrows raised. "Defiance! We have found a new Boudicca, boys." He won a ripple of laughter from his troops.

She drew herself up. "You will not mock us. We are living poorly here; I can't deny that. But if you think we are illiterate Saxons—"

"Oh, I can see you are no Saxons." He waved a hand. "Your grain pit, for instance . . . I have seen some Saxon farmers. There are many in this country already, you know, off to the east. The way they do things is sometimes better, sometimes worse than what you have worked out here. But they do not do things quite like this. And it is the threat of the Saxons that has brought me here. Listen to me," he said, raising his voice to address the rest of the people. "Things have changed. *The Saxons are coming.*"

"We know that," Regina said.

He growled, "Perhaps you have heard of Vortigern. That foolish kinglet was much troubled by Pict raiders from the north. So he invited in the Saxons, to help keep the Picts at bay." It had been an old trick of the Romans, Regina knew, to allow in one set of enemies as allies to oppose another lot. "I will not deny that the Saxons did a good job. They are sea pirates after all, and fared well against the Picts in their clumsy coracles.

"But," said the *riothamus*, "the Saxons, under their brute of a leader Hengest, who is already notorious on the continent, betrayed Vortigern. They brought in more and more of their cousins, and demanded more and more in tribute from Vortigern. But the more they took from him, the less he could pay them, and the weaker he became.

"Now Vortigern is dead, his council slain. And now that they have a foothold in the east, the Saxons are becoming greedy.

"You may have heard of their cruelty. They are not the Romans! They hate towns and villas and roads, all things of the Empire. And they hate the British. They are spreading across the countryside like a plague. They will burn these flimsy huts, they will drive you out of here, and if you resist they will kill you."

"The Emperor will help us," somebody called.

The *riothamus* laughed, but it was a grim sound. "There have been pleas. No help comes. We must help ourselves. *I* will help you," he said boldly. "I am building a new kingdom in the west—I have a capital there. It is a place the Romans themselves struggled to defeat, and it will see off a few hairy Saxons." There was a little laughter at that, and Regina saw the skill in his mixture of fear and humor. "But I need you with me. The land is emptying. Everybody flees, fearing the raiders. And if you come with me—" He drew his sword, and flashed its polished surfaces in the air above his head. "—I swear before the gods that I and Chalybs will protect you to my own death!" *Chalybs,* which he pronounced *Calib,* was the Latin for "steel."

He was met by uncertain silence.

Regina stepped forward to face him. "We don't need you, or your shining Chalybs. For all your posturing and speeches you are just another thug, another warlord, as bad as the Saxons or the Picts."

The *riothamus* eyed her. "You have done well to survive here, Boudicca. Few have prospered so well. I can see you are a strong woman."

She glared. "Strong enough not to be patronized by a popinjay like you."

He seemed to want to convince her. "I am earnest in what I say. I am not a Saxon or a Pict. *I am like you.* I am your kind. I grew up in Eburacum, where my father was one of the landowners . . ."

"Earnest or not—son of a citizen or not—you are still a war-

lord. And if I submit to you it will only be because I have no
choice, because of your force, not because of your rhetoric."

He laughed. "Are you bargaining with me? I offer you survival, with me, in my compound. But you want more than
survival, don't you?"

She glared at him. "I am old now—"

"Not so old."

"—and I may not live to see the day when the emperors return. When we don't have to scratch at the land like animals,
and live in fear of barbarians. *I* may not see it. But my daughter will, and her daughters. And that is what I want for my
family. For them to be ready . . ." She fell silent, suddenly
aware of how wistful she sounded, before this silent tower of
muscle in his scuffed cuirass.

"I have met Romans," he said softly. "I have dealt with them
in southern Gaul and elsewhere. You know what the Romans
call us? Celtae. It means 'barbarians.' Their Empire is a thousand years old. We were barbarians before our assimilation,
and we are barbarians now. *That* is how they think of us."

She shook her head tightly. "My daughter is no barbarian.
And when things get back to normal—"

He held up his hand. "You are determined that the light of
civilization will not go out. Very well. But until that day of
blessed recovery comes, until the Emperor rides in to tell us
what to do, we must fend for ourselves. Do you see that? Well,
of course you do, for I can see what you have built here. You
must come with me—you and your family, and the others who
depend on you. I can protect you in the dangerous times to
come . . . You can't do it all yourself, Boudicca," he said more
gently.

"And if we refuse?"

He shrugged. "I can't let you stay here, for what you have
built will give succor to the Saxons."

"What will you do—burn us out, as the Saxons have our
neighbors?"

"I hope not," he said. But he was still and silent as a statue,
and she could see his determination.

Once again she faced an upheaval in her life—the abandonment of all she had built, the security she had made. But it
could not be helped.

"Do you make iron?" she asked suddenly.

"Yes," he said. "Not well. But we have begun." He seemed amused. "Are you assessing me?"

"I would not throw my lot in with a fool," she snapped. "I have lived too long, and seen too many fools die. If we come with you, it will not be as captives, or slaves, or even servants. We will live with you as equals. And we will live inside your fort—we will not grub in the fields beyond, exposed to the blades of the Saxons."

The moment stretched, and she wondered if she had pushed him too far. And she was aware, too, of the crusted mud that clung to her legs and stiffened her hair. But she held her nerve, and returned his startled gaze.

At last he laughed out loud. "I would not dare challenge you, my Boudicca. Very well. As equals."

She nodded, her heart pounding. "Tell me one more thing, *riothamus*. What is your name?"

"My name is Artorius." It was a Roman name, but his *t* was soft, and he spoke in the Welsh style: *ar-thur-ius*. He smiled at her, and turned away to issue crisp commands to his soldiers.

chapter 16

When I got back to my hotel room after my visit with Lou, I used the room's clunky pay-for-use plug-in keyboard to check my email. There were two significant notes.

The first was a long missive from Peter McLachlan.

"Most of the universe is dark," Peter wrote. "*Dark matter.* An invisible, mysterious substance that makes up some ninety percent of all the mass of the universe. You can tell it's there from gravitational effects—the whole Galaxy is embedded in a big pond of it, and turns like a lily leaf in a pail of scummy water. But otherwise it passes through our planet like a vast ghost. How marvelous, how scary, that so much of the universe—most of it, in fact—is quite invisible to us. Who knows what lurks out there in the glassy dark? . . . I'm inspired, George. Something about my contact with you, this little mystery in your life, has sparked me off. That and Kuiper. I've been in touch with the Slan(t)ers again . . ." He was an unusual email correspondent. There was no *BTW* or *abt* or *lol*, no smiley faces for Peter. His mails were clearly thought through, composed, even spellchecked, like old-fashioned letters: they were genuine correspondence. ". . . Of course we do have a handful of human-built space probes that have reached almost as far as the Kuiper Belt. They aren't capable of studying the Anomaly, sadly. But they are running into strangeness . . ."

My finger hovered over the DELETE button. Part of me responded to all this stuff. But the adult part of me was beginning to regret letting this strange obsessive into my life.

I read on.

He told me about the Pioneers: two deep-space probes launched in the seventies by NASA. They had been the first probes to fly past Jupiter and Saturn. And after that, they had just kept on going. By now, more than three decades after their launch, they had passed far beyond the orbit of Pluto—and there was nothing to stop them, it seemed, until they swam among the stars a few hundred thousand years from now.

But something was slowing them down. More anomalous information he and his pals the Slan(t)ers had dug up.

"The two Pioneers are decelerating. Not by much, a mere ten-billionth of an Earth gravity, but it's real. Right now the first Pioneer is off-course by the distance between the Earth and the moon. And nobody knows what's causing it." But perhaps it was dark matter. "Maybe for something as isolated and fragile as a Pioneer, dark matter effects start to dominate. It's interesting to speculate what will happen if we ever try to drive a starship out there—"

Or it might be a fuel leak, I thought. Or just paint, sublimating in the vacuum. Oddly, I felt reluctant to discourage him.

"I'm coming to think dark matter is the key to everything . . ."

I pressed a key to store the file.

The second notable mail was from my ex-wife.

Linda had heard about my dad's death from our mutual friends, and wanted to see me. We had always gotten together regularly. I suppose we both accepted that after a decade of marriage, now buried in the irrevocable past, we had too much in common to ever cut the ties completely. Over an exchange of mails, we agreed to meet on neutral territory.

I flew back to London the next day. I left Florida without regrets.

It was my idea to meet Linda at the Museum of London. I was starting to become intrigued by what I'd heard of the Roman British girl Regina, who according to our dubious family legend was supposed to have traveled from the collapsed province of Britain, across Europe, all the way to the fading glory of Rome itself. Somehow she, or at least her legend, seemed to be central to what had happened to my family. And if any of it was true, perhaps she once traveled through London itself—Londinium, as the Romans had called it. But like most of London's peripatetic population, even though I'd spent much of my working life in the City, I'd paid no attention whatsoever to its history. I'd never so much as been inside the Tower, though it had only been a quarter hour's walk away from the offices where I once worked. Anyhow, now was a chance to put some of that right.

A check on the Internet showed me that the Roman city had been confined by a wall that contained much of the modern City of London—the financial center—excluding the West End, and points farther east than the Tower. The Museum of London was itself set on a corner of the old wall, or rather, on the line it had once traced out. It might give me a few clues about Regina.

And two thousand years of history might distract Linda and me sufficiently to keep us from bickering for a couple of hours.

The museum turned out to be just outside the Barbican, that concrete wilderness that seems to have been designed for cars, not humans. The museum itself is set on a traffic island cut off by a moat of roaring traffic. I seemed to walk a mile before I found a staircase that took me up to an elevated walkway that crossed the traffic stream and led into the museum complex itself. I was early—I'm always early rather than late, while Linda is the opposite—and I spent the spare time poking around the museum's show-and-tell displays and scale models, showing Londinium's rise and fall.

After Caesar's first foray, the Emperor Claudius, equipped with war elephants, had begun the true conquest of Britain. By sixty years after the death of Christ, Londinium had grown into a city big enough to be worth being burned down by Boudicca. But in the fifth century, after Britain became detached from the Empire, Londinium collapsed. The Roman area would not be reoccupied for four hundred years, the time of Alfred the Great. I picked through the little models and maps, trying to figure out what date Regina must have come through here, if she ever did. I didn't know enough to be able to tell.

I dug around in the gift shop. I felt like the only adult in there; the museum's only other visitors were some Scandinavian tourists, all long legs, backpacks, and blond hair, and a batch of young-teenager schoolkids who seemed to swarm everywhere, their behavior scarcely modified by the yells and yips of their teachers. Eventually I found a slim guidebook to the "Wall Walk," a tour around the line of the Roman wall. I queued up to pay behind a line of the schoolkids, each of them buying a sweet or a sparkly pencil sharpener or an AMO LON-DINIUM mouse pad. An old fart in a duffel coat, I gritted my teeth and stayed patient, reminding myself that all this junk was helping keep the museums free to enter.

Linda found me in the coffee shop. She had come from work; she was an office manager in a solicitor's office, based on the edge of Soho. She was a little shorter than me, with her hair cut sensibly short, a bit flyaway where it was going to gray. She wore a slightly rumpled blue-black suit. Her face was small, symmetrical, with neat features set off by a petite nose. She had always been beautiful in a gentle, easy-on-the-eye way. But I thought I saw more lines and shadows, and she looked a little stressed, her eyes hollow. She always programmed herself right up to the last minute, as no doubt she had today; she'd have had to make room for me in her schedule.

I bought her a coffee and explained my scheme to do the Wall Walk.

"In shoes like these?"

She was wearing plain-looking flat-soled black leather shoes, the kind I used to call "matron's shoes," when I dared. "They'll do."

"Not mine. *Yours.*" I was wearing a pair of my old Hush Puppy slip-ons. "When the hell are you going to get yourself some trainers?"

"The day they go out of fashion."

She grunted. "You always were perverse. But still—two hours of London roads on a muggy day like this. Why? . . . Oh. This is family stuff again, isn't it?"

She had always been suspicious of my family, ever since it had become clear that my mother had never really approved of her. "Too dull for your personality," Mum would say to me. I think Linda had been quietly pleased that I was always remote from them at the best of times, and had drifted even farther from my dad after Mother's death. We had had enough fights over family issues even so, however. But then we had fights about everything.

"Yes," I said. "Family stuff. Come on, Linda. Let's be tourists for once."

"I suppose we can always go to the pub when it doesn't work out," she said.

"There's always that."

She stood, briskly gathered up her belongings, checked her cell phone, and led the way out.

The London wall was a great semicircle arcing north from the river at Blackfriars, east along Moorgate and then back south to the river at the Tower. Not much of the wall itself has survived, but even after all this time the Romans' layout is still preserved in the pattern of London's streets.

The walk didn't follow the whole line of the wall, just the section that cut east of the museum at the Barbican, passing north of the City and then down to the river by the Tower. There were supposed to be little numbered ceramic plaques you could follow, with the first few in the area of the museum itself, which had been built on the site of one of the Romans' forts. Number one plaque was at the Tower and number twenty-one near the museum, so we were going to have to follow the line counting down, which bothered my sense of neatness, and earned me the day's first bit of mockery from Linda.

The first few plaques were hard to find in the Barbican's three-dimensional concrete maze of roads and highwalks—"Like an inside-out prison," as Linda put it. The first plaque was glued to the wall of a modern bank building; it showed the site of a late Roman city gate, now long demolished. By the time we got there Linda was already sweating. "Is this going to be the story of the afternoon? Crappy little plaques showing where things *used* to be?"

"What did you expect, *Gladiator*? . . ."

The next few plaques led us around the perimeter of the old Roman fort. Stretches of the wall were visible in scraps of garden below the level of the roadway. Much of the wall had been built over in medieval times, then uncovered by the archaeologists. The ground level had risen steadily over time; we walked on a great layer of debris centuries thick, a measure of the depth of time itself.

Plaques seventeen to fifteen caused us some arguments, be-

cause they were scattered around the ruins of a round medieval tower set in a garden in the shadow of the museum itself. We traipsed over the grass-covered ground, to the water
and back, trying to figure out the peculiar little maps that supposedly showed us how to get from one plaque to the next in
line.

Plaque fourteen was in a churchyard that turned out to be a
little oasis of peace, set away from the steady roar of the traffic. We sat on a bench facing a rectangular pond, bordered by
concrete. The wall, with its complex layers of medieval building and rebuilding, stretched its way along the bank opposite
us, passing the remains of a round fort tower. I'd brought a
couple of bottles of Evian, one of which I now passed to
Linda. She had been right about the shoes. My arches were already aching.

"You know, I used to have a toy like this," I said. "A castle,
I mean. It was all plastic, a base with cylindrical towers and
bits of walls you snapped into place, and a drawbridge for little knights to ride in and out . . ."

She leafed through the walk guidebook. "I can't believe
you're actually *ticking off* the plaques as we find them. You're
so anal."

"Oh, lay off, Linda," I snapped back. "If you want to pack
it in—"

"No, no. I know how you'll fret if we do." Which was code
for her saying she was vaguely enjoying the little expedition.
"Oh, come on."

We walked on.

As we counted down the plaques, we passed the sites of
vanished city gates and found more sunken gardens set away
from the road, like islands of the past. But as we headed down
Moorgate the plaques were less interesting, spaced farther
apart and set on office walls. Moorgate itself was a bustling
mixture of shops and offices, with, as ever, immense redevelopment projects going on. We had to squeeze our way on temporary walkways around blue-painted screens, scarily close
to the unrelenting traffic, while intimidating cranes towered
overhead.

One of the prettier sites was another little garden area close
to the entrance of All Hallows Church: office workers sat

around, jackets off, smoking, their cell phones glistening on the grass beside them like tame insects. But the plaque—number ten—was missing from its plinth, probably long ago vandalized and never replaced. Number nine was gone, too, and number eight seemed to have been swallowed up by redevelopment. My little book was acquiring frustratingly few ticks. The walk itself dated back to 1985, long enough for time and entropy to have started their patient work, even on the plaques.

I asked, "So why did you want to see me?"

Her eyes hidden by her Ray-Bans, she shrugged. "I just thought I should. Jack's death . . . I wanted to see if you're coping."

"That's good of you." I meant it. "And what do you conclude?"

"I guess you're healthy. You still have that damn duffel coat, and your sphincter is as tight as ever . . ." She turned to me. I could see her eyes, flickering in the shadows of her glasses. "I'm worried about this quest to find your mythical sister."

"Who told you about that?"

"Does it matter?"

"I suppose you think it's anal again . . ."

As we approached Aldgate, we were entering the financial district of the City, the area where I had spent so much of my working life. At this time of day, late afternoon, the pavement was crowded with people, mostly young and bright, many with cell phones clamped to their ears or masking their faces. It felt genuinely odd to be tracing the wall, this layered relic of the past, through a place that was so bound up with my own prehistory.

She asked me, "So what will you do? Will you go to Rome?"

Lou had suggested that, but I still wasn't sure. "I don't know. It seems like a big commitment—"

"—to a project that might be completely wacko. But it might be the only way you're going to be able to clear this up, if you're serious about it."

"I'm serious. I think. I don't know."

"Same old same old. George, you're a good man. But you're so fucking indecisive. You blow with every breeze."

"Then you were right to kick me out," I said.

We walked in silence for a while.

Plaque four was at the back of an office building—we had to be bold enough to walk into private grounds—where we found a sloping glass frame, like a low greenhouse, set over a trench in the tarmac. A section of the wall was exposed, twenty feet deep under the glass, through which we peered. We couldn't see the lower section, the Roman bit, because the office workers in their dungeon below had stacked boxes and files against it.

I was the first to say it. "Okay, I'm sorry. But I'm really not sure I need advice right now. My family may have been something of a screwup, but there's nothing I can do to change the past. And now it's gone—Gina's fled about as far as she can go—and all I'm left with is . . ."

"This loose end. Which you can't resist tugging. Well, I think you should go. Let's face it, the death of a parent is as big a loss as either of us is ever likely to face. I think you should take some time to get through it. And if this sister thing is an excuse to do that, fine. Go to Rome. Spend some lira."

"Euros."

"Whatever."

"I was sure you'd try to stop me."

She sighed. "Listening is just one of the skills you never acquired, George." She touched my hand; her skin was warm and comfortable. "Go. If you need anything just call."

"Thanks."

"Now let's finish this stupid walk." She marched on.

We passed out of the City area and came down Cooper's Row, passing under the rail line into the tourist-oriented area close to the river, and the Tower. We passed through the Tower Hill underpass by the Tube station entrance, peered at the ruin of a robust-looking medieval gate, and then walked back through the subway to where a sunken garden at the northeast corner of the underpass contained the statue of an emperor—and, ironically, right at the end of the walk, the best-preserved section of wall we'd seen all day.

We sat on a bench and sipped our water.

"One more tick for your little book," Linda said, not too unkindly.

"Yep." It was all of thirty feet high, and the Roman section itself maybe ten feet. The Roman brickwork was neat rows interspersed with red tiles that might have come from my father's house. The medieval structure above it was much rougher. "If I didn't know better I'd have said that the Roman stuff was Victorian, or later," I said. "It's as if the whole wall has been turned upside down."

Linda asked, "Civilization really did fall here, didn't it?"

"It really did."

"I wonder if she came here. That great-grandmother of yours. Regina."

". . . And I wonder if she knew that it would all disappear, as if a small nuclear bomb had been dropped on the city."

The third voice made us both jump. I turned to see a bulky, somewhat shambling figure dressed in a coat that looked even heavier than my duffel. Linda flinched away from him, and I felt the tentative mood between us evaporate.

"Peter. What are you doing here?"

Peter McLachlan came around the bench and sat down, with me between him and Linda. "You mentioned doing the walk." So I had, in an email. "I thought you'd end up here. I waited."

"How long?"

He checked his watch. "Only about three hours."

"Three hours?"

I could see Linda's expression. "Listen, George, it's been good, but I think—"

"No. Wait, I'm sorry." I introduced them quickly. "Peter, why did you want to see me?"

"To thank you. And tell you I'm going to be away for a while. I'm off to the States."

"Visiting the Slan(t)ers?" Linda caught my eye again; I pursed my lips. *Don't ask.*

"I feel the need to catch up. Be refreshed."

"Refreshed with what?"

He shrugged. "The energy. The *belief.* That's why I want to thank you. Somehow you have shaken me out of my rut. Your bit of mystery with your sister. Layers upon layers . . . That and Kuiper, of course." He leaned past me and thrust his face toward Linda. "Of course you know about the Kuiper Anomaly. Have you seen the latest developments?" He produced his handheld and started thumbing at its tiny controls, and Web pages flashed over its jewel-like screen.

Linda plucked my sleeve. "This guy is seriously weird," she whispered.

"He's an old school friend. He helped my dad. And—"

"Oh, come on. Your dad's buried. He's followed you *to London*. And all this spooky stuff—what does it have to do with you and your sister?"

"I don't know."

"Look, George, I changed my mind. It's as if the people around you are parts of your personality. Your family was the clingy, oppressive, Catholic part, and you need to get away from all that, not indulge it. And this guy, he's like your—"

"My anus."

That brought a stifled laugh. "George—go back to work. Or paint your house. Get away from memories, George. And get away from this guy, or you'll end up on a park bench muttering about conspiracies, too . . ."

"Here." Peter thrust his handheld before my face; data and diagrams chattered across it. "The Kuiper Belt is a relic of the formation of the solar system. We see similar belts around other stars, like Vega. The outer planets, like Uranus and Neptune, formed from collisions of Kuiper Belt objects. But according to the best theories there should have been many more objects out there—a *hundred times* the mass we can see now, enough to make another Neptune. And we know that such a swarm should coalesce quickly into a planet."

"I don't understand. Peter, I think—"

"*Something disturbed the Kuiper Belt.* Something whipped up those ice balls, about the time of the formation of Pluto—so preventing the formation of another Neptune. Since then the Kuiper objects have been broken up by collisions, or have drifted out of the belt."

"When was this disturbance?"

"It must have been around the time the planets were forming. Maybe four and a half billion years ago." He peered at me, eyes bright. "You see? Layers of interference. The Anomaly, the Galaxy core explosions, now this tinkering with the very formation of the solar system. *This* is what we're going to investigate."

"We?"

"The Slan(t)ers, in the States. You read my emails."

"Yes . . ." I turned. Linda had gone. I stood up, trying to see her, but as the rush hour approached the crowds pouring into the Tube station were already dense.

Peter was still in midflow, sitting on the bench, talking compulsively, bringing up page after page of data. He was hunched forward, his posture intense.

Standing there, I could either go after Linda, or stay with Peter. I felt that somehow I was making a choice that might shape the whole of the rest of my life.

I sat down. "Show me again," I said.

TWO

For Lucia it had begun eleven months before the death of George Poole's father. And it began, not with death, but with stirrings of life.

It came at night, only a few days after her fifteenth birthday. She was woken by a spasm of pain in her belly, and then an ache in her thighs. When she reached down and touched her legs she felt wetness.

At first she felt only hideous embarrassment. She imagined she had wet her bed, as if she were a silly child. She got out of bed and padded down the length of the dormitory, past the bunk beds stacked three high, the hundred girls sleeping in this great room alone, to the bathroom.

And there, in the bathroom's harsh fluorescent light, she discovered the truth: that the fluid between her legs, and on her fingers and her nightclothes, wasn't urine at all, but blood—strange blood, bright, thin. She knew what this meant, of course. Her body was changing. But the shame didn't go away, it only intensified, and was supplemented now by a deep and abiding fear.

Why me? she thought. Why *me*?

She cleaned herself up and went back to bed, past the stirring ranks of the girls, many of them turning and muttering, perhaps disturbed by her scent.

Lucia was able to conceal that first bleeding from the other girls, from Idina and Angela and Rosaria and Rosetta, her crowding, chattering sisters with their pale gray eyes, all so alike. You weren't supposed to keep secrets, of course. Everybody knew that. There were supposed to be no secrets in the Crypt. But now Lucia had a secret.

And then her second period came, during a working day.

The stab of pain warned her in time for her to rush to the bathroom again. The cubicles had no doors, of course—though before her menarche it had never occurred to Lucia to notice the
lack—but she was lucky to find the room empty, and was able
again to conceal what had happened, even though she vomited,
and this time the pain lasted for days.

But now she had compounded her secret.

She hated the situation. More than anything she cared what
the people around her thought of her. The other girls were her
whole world. She was immersed in them night and day, surrounded by their scent and touch and kisses, their conversation
and their glances, their judgments and opinions; she was
shaped by them, as they, she knew, were shaped in turn by her.
But ever since she had started growing taller than the average,
at the age of ten or so, barriers between her and her old friends
had subtly grown up. That got worse at age twelve or thirteen,
when her hips and breasts started to develop, and she had
started to look like a young woman among children. And now
this.

She didn't want any of it. She wanted to be the same as
everybody else; she didn't want to be *different*. She wanted to
be immersed in the games, and the gossip of what Anna said
to Wanda, and how Rita and Rosetta had fallen out, and Angela would have to choose between them . . . She didn't want
to be talking about blood between her legs, pain in her belly.

She had to tell somebody. So she told Pina.

It was during a coffee break at work.

This was November, and Lucia's regular schooling was in
recess. For the second year she had come to work in the big office called the *scrinium*. This was an ancient Latin word meaning "archive." Despite the antique name, it was a modern,
bright, open-plan area with cubicles and partitions, PCs and
laptops, adorned with potted plants and calendars, and with
light wells admitting daylight from the world above. This
bright, anonymous place might have been an office in any
bank or government ministry. Even the ubiquitous symbol of
the Order, two schematic face-to-face kissing fish, was rendered on the wall in bronze and chrome, like a corporate logo.
Quite often you would even see a *contadino* or two in here—

literally "countryman" or "peasant," this word meant "out-sider; not of the Order."

But beyond the office was a computer center, a big climate-controlled room where high-capacity mainframes hummed and whirred in bluish light. And beyond that were libraries, great echoing corridors, softly lit and laced with fire-preventive equipment. Lucia didn't know—nobody in her circle knew—how far such corridors extended, off into the darkness, tunneled out of the soft tufa rock; it didn't even occur to her to ask the question. But it was said that if you walked far enough, the books gave way to scrolls of animal skin and papyrus, and tablets with Latin or Greek letters scratched in clay surfaces, and even a few pieces of carved stone.

In these vaulted, interconnected rooms the Order had stored its records ever since its first founding, sixteen centuries be-fore. Nowadays the archive was more valuable than it had ever been, for it had become a key source of income for the Order. Information was sold, much of it nowadays via the Internet, to historians, to academic institutions and governments, and to amateur genealogists trying to trace family roots.

Lucia worked here as a lowly clerk—or, in the sometimes archaic language of the Order, as one of the *scrinarii*, under a supervising *bibliotecharius*. She spent some of her time doing computer work, transcribing and cross-correlating records from different sources. But mainly she worked on transcrip-tion. She would copy records, by hand, from computer screens and printouts onto rag paper sheets.

The Order made its own rag paper, once manufactured by breaking up cloth in great pounding animal-driven pestles, but now directly from cotton in a room humming with high-speed electrical equipment. It was medieval technology. But the rag paper, acid-free, marked by special noncorrosive inks, would last far longer than any wood-pulp paper. The Order had little faith in digital archives; already there were difficulties access-ing records from older, obsolescent generations of computers and storage media. If you were serious about challenging time, rag paper was the way to do it.

Hence Lucia's paradoxically old-fashioned assignment. But she rather liked the work, although it was routine. The paper always felt soft and oddly warm to her touch, compared to the coarse stuff you got from wood pulp.

Her tasks had taught her the importance of accuracy; the archive's main selling point, aside from its historical depth, was its unrivaled reliability. And Lucia's calligraphy was careful, neat—and accurate, as proven by the triple layers of checks all her work was put through. It seemed likely, said the supervisors, that the *scrinium* would be her career path in the future, when she finished her schooling.

But that, of course, was thrown into uncertainty, like everything else in her life, by the unwelcome arrival of womanhood.

Pina sat on Lucia's desk, her hands clasped together over her knees as if in prayer. They had no privacy, here as anywhere else, of course; there must have been fifty people in the office that morning, working or chatting, and the waist-high partitions hid nothing. Lucia spoke so softly that Pina had to lean closely to hear.

Pina was ten years older than Lucia. She had a small, pretty face, Lucia thought, lacking cheekbones but with a pleasing smoothness. Her eyes were a little darker than most, a kind of graphite gray, and her hair was tied neatly back. Her mouth was small and not very expressive when she talked, which gave her an aura of seriousness compared to other girls—that, and her ten years' age difference, of course. Still, though, her features were quite similar to those of everybody else, including Lucia's, the typical oval face, the gray eyes well within the range of variation.

And, though she was twenty-five, she was small, smaller than Lucia, with a slim figure, her breasts only the slightest swellings under the white blouse she wore.

She had been friendly to Lucia since her first day here in the *scrinium*, showing her the basics of her work and such essentials as how to work the coffee machine. Now Pina looked uncomfortable, Lucia thought, but she was listening.

"Don't worry," she said. "Anyhow, now you've drawn me into your secret."

"I'm sorry. If it's one it's a secret, if it's two—"

"It's a conspiracy," Pina said, completing the crèche singalong phrase. "Well, I'll forgive you. Especially as it can't remain a secret for long."

Lucia pulled a face. "I don't *want* any of this. I never wanted to be taller—I don't want this bleeding."

"It isn't unnatural."

"Yes, but why me? I feel—"

"Betrayed? Betrayed by your own body?" Pina touched her arm, a gesture of support. "If it's any consolation I don't think you're the only one ... I suppose my memory is that bit deeper than yours. Things have been different the last few years. People have been—" She waved her hands vaguely. "—agitated. Every summer the new cadres come up from the downbelow schools, all fresh faces and bright smiles, like fields of flowers. Always charming. There are always one or two who stand out from the crowd."

"Like me."

"But in the last few years there have been more." Pina shrugged. "There are some who say there is trouble with the *matres*. Perhaps that's somehow disturbing us all."

Lucia had only ever heard the word *matres* a few times in her life. Some called those mysterious figures the *mamme-nonne*—the mother-grandmothers. She had only the dimmest idea about them. *Ignorance is strength*—another crèche slogan. You weren't even supposed to talk about subjects like the *matres* ...

She pulled back from Pina. Suddenly it was too much; she was crashing through too many taboo barriers. "I should get back to work," she said.

"Why don't you talk to somebody?"

"Who? Nobody would want to know."

"I don't mean the girls in your dormitory." Pina thought briefly. "How about Rosa Poole?"

Lucia knew Rosa, a woman in her forties who had a job in the remoter layers of the Order's administration. Rosa had lectured Lucia's classes a few times on aspects of information technology—database design, programming theory.

"Rosa is approachable," said Pina earnestly. "She would know what you have to do."

"Do?"

Pina sighed. "Well, to begin with, you're going to need towels, aren't you? You have to be practical, dear. And after that ... Well, I'm not sure—"

"Because it never happened to *you*."

Pina kept her face blank, but Lucia, her nerves taut, nevertheless thought she detected a little smugness in her friend's face. "No, it never did. Which means I'm not much use to you. Rosa might be, though. She's approachable, for a member of the *cupola*." The Order had no hierarchy in theory, but in practice, at any time there was a rough-and-ready chain of command among the senior women, known informally by everybody as the *cupola*.

"I don't know, Pina."

Pina said a little harshly, "You think if you keep it secret it might all go away. You think if you were to talk to someone like Rosa it will make it real." She looked closely at Lucia. "You think even talking to *me* about it makes it real, don't you?"

"Something like that," Lucia said reluctantly. "This is very difficult."

Pina said softly, "We can sort this out, Lucia. Don't be afraid. You're not alone."

Lucia smiled, but it was forced. She longed only to put the clock back a few weeks, back to the time before the bleeding had afflicted her—or better still back two or three or four years to when she had just been another little girl, just one of the crowd, invisible.

As it turned out her secret didn't last another twenty-four hours. She didn't approach Rosa Poole of the *cupola*. Pina did it for her.

chapter 18

For days Artorius marched them along the old roads, far to the west. At night they slept in the open, perhaps sheltered by a hastily constructed lean-to, their only bedding the spare clothing they carried with them. Every day Regina woke to a rough breakfast of salted meat. She was always stiff and cold despite the mildness of the midsummer nights.

Eventually, though, Regina found herself recognizing the countryside. It was a land crowded with hills, green and rounded—a human-scale landscape, very unlike the wastes of the border country around the Wall.

Her geography remained sketchy, little better informed than by Aetius's map drawn in the dirt. But this was, she realized slowly, *home*. Blown by the winds of fate, she had sailed in a great circle, and come back to where she had started. Still, she had no idea exactly where the site of the family villa was: she had left at age seven, after all, and there was nobody left alive, Carta or Aetius, who might know. Perhaps it was best not to know; she could not bear to see it a ruin.

And there were changes. Even here the country seemed far from friendly: on every hilltop, walls loomed and the smoke of fires curled into the air. It had become a land that bristled with defenses, like a hedgehog's quills.

Artorius's proposed new capital was a fort built on a brooding hill—what he called, in the old language, a "dunon." Artorius had already assembled a community of a few hundred people, scraped together from across the country, and the place was alive with activity. Regina did not know what the hill might have been called in the days of the Romans; it seemed to have no Latin name. But some of the locals called it by the name of a nearby stream. It was the Caml hill, or the Caml fort.

On their first full day at the dunon Regina's people were assigned to fetching stone from what was called a "quarry." Artorius told Regina he would spare her this toil. She had made a good impression on him with her defiance, and she could stay here with him in his capital; perhaps he could find her a different role.

Brica encouraged her to accept. "He seems to like you, Mother, Jove knows why. You need to play on that for all it's worth."

"Oh, I will," Regina said. And she would. From the moment of Brica's birth she had been determined to do whatever it took to ensure the survival of her family. But she refused Artorius's offer; she was not yet ready to be separated from those with whom she had spent two decades on the hillside farm.

So they marched out in a group of about thirty, under the command of one of Artorius's lieutenants. It would be a two-day walk south, and they spent another night in the open.

About midday on the second day, she found herself approaching the wall of a town. It sparked more memories of her childhood: this must be Durnovaria, the center of local civic society. To her childish eyes it had seemed a magical place, clean and bright, surrounded by mighty walls, and full of tremendous buildings fit for giants. But now the town had been abandoned for more than twenty years. The wall had been stripped of its tiles, exposing a core of mortared rubble and red binding bricks. The gate where the road passed through the wall had once been a complex multiple archway, but now the arches had collapsed.

Inside the wall everything was covered in a blanket of green. Most of the buildings had vanished into rubble and vegetation. There was much evidence of fire—perhaps the chance result of lightning strikes on long-abandoned buildings choked by dead leaves. Their plots were covered with a layer of dark, weed-choked earth, the residue of collapsed wattle-and-daub walls, now heavily overgrown. A few of the monumental stone structures survived, still immensely strong, but they were ruined giants, burned out, roofless, overrun with creepers and with shrubs and ivy growing out of cracks in the walls. Even the hard road surface was coated by a mulch of weed debris and dead leaves, and trees were sprouting, ash and alder, their roots cracking open the cobbled surface and exposing the earth once more to the sun. She glimpsed creatures from the forest—voles, field mice—and even the animals that lived off those small colonists, like foxes and kestrels. It was as if, after years of abandonment, the original owners of the land were moving back in. But the place was eerily silent—there wasn't even birdsong.

As they passed through the town some of the younger people in the party averted their eyes from the monumental ruins and muttered prayers to the god of the Christians and other deities. But Regina quietly mourned. These ivy-covered stones spoke to her about the depth of the generation-long holocaust that was assailing Britain more eloquently than any historian, even Tacitus, could ever have. And how strange it was, she thought, that none of this had been inflicted by the Picts or the Saxons—none of the raiders had yet come this far west, in numbers sufficient to do this kind of damage. The town had collapsed all by itself. It was all as Aetius and Carausias had once foreseen, that once people stopped paying their taxes, the towns had no purpose, and had fallen in on themselves. Or perhaps Amator had been right, that the town was simply a relic of a thousand-year-old dream, from which humankind was now coldly waking.

Their destination proved not to be the town itself but a graveyard that sprawled over a hillside nearby.

It was vast, so densely packed with tombs it was like a pavement of tile, sandstone, and marble; there must be thousands buried here. People were already working: they were prizing up gravestones, slabs of sandstone or marble, with picks of wood and iron. The work was under the direction of a couple of Artorius's soldiers. They did not hang back from the labor but joined in themselves, stripped to the waist in the summer heat.

"So this is our 'quarry,' " Regina said. "A graveyard, which we are desecrating for bits of stone."

Brica shrugged. "What does it matter? The dead are dead. We need the stones."

Regina felt a sense of shock. If at age seven, or even age seventeen, she could have seen herself now and learned what she must do to stay alive, she would have been horrified. And she felt a pang of sadness that Brica, still so young, saw nothing difficult about it. *How we are fallen,* she thought.

Strangely, a small farmstead had been established at the center of the graveyard, complete with a barn and a couple of granary pits. A woman was selling food to the workers in return for nails and other bits of iron. Perhaps the bones of the dead had made the ground rich for vegetables, Regina thought morbidly.

Neither Regina nor Brica had the muscle for digging up gravestones, so they were put to work fetching pails of water from a stream for the workers to drink and wash off their dust. They moved among the opened graves, stepping over smashed-up stones.

Regina stopped by one grave whose stone was intact enough for its Latin inscription to be read. "DIS MANIBUS LUCIUS MATELLUS ROMULUS . . . 'May the underworld spirits take Lucius, born in Spain, served in the Vettones cavalry regiment, became a citizen, and died here aged forty-six.' And here is the grave of his daughter—Simplicia—died aged ten months, 'a most innocent soul.' I wonder what poor Lucius would think if he could see what we are doing today."

Brica shrugged, hot, dirty, not much caring. "Who are all these people? Were they to do with the town?"

"Of course they were. These were the citizens—there are the dead of centuries here, perhaps."

"Why weren't they buried inside the town?"

"Because it wasn't allowed. Unless you were a very young baby, in which case you didn't count as a person anyhow . . . That was the law."

"The Emperor's law. Now we make up our own laws," Brica said.

"Or some thug like Artorius makes them up for us."

"He isn't so bad," Brica said.

Regina read another gravestone. " 'A sweetest child, torn away no less suddenly than the partner of Dis.' "

"What does that mean?"

Regina frowned, trying to remember her lessons with Aetius.

"I think it's a quotation from Virgil." But the poet's name meant nothing to Brica, and Regina let it pass.

Some of the graves had evidently once held wooden coffins, now long rotted away, and these graves were filled only with a scatter of bones. But in some of the grander tombs coffins of lead-lined stone had been used. These were prized out of the ground, roughly opened, and the grisly contents dumped back into the yawning ground so that the lead could be salvaged. Occasionally there were grave goods: bits of jewelry, perfume bottles, even tools—and, in one small and pathetic grave, a wooden doll. The workers would snatch these up, inspect them briefly, and pocket them if they looked like they were worth anything. There was no great stench, save for the scent of moist open earth. These bodies were decades old at least, and—except for those corpses tipped out of the more robust lead coffins—the worms had done their work.

Toward the end of the day the broken gravestones were loaded into carts, or set on people's backs, for the haul back to Artorius's capital.

On their return to the dunon, Artorius again came to seek out Regina. He insisted that she not spend another day at the gruesome cemetery-quarry, but come with him to inspect his developing capital.

"I value your opinion," he said, his grin confident and disarming. "Intellect and spirit are all too rare these sorry days. You are wasted digging up bones."

"I am no soldier."

"I have plenty of soldiers, who are all trained to tell me what I want to hear. But you, as I know very well, have no fear of me. I know, above all, that you are a survivor. And survival is what I am intent on: the first priority."

So she agreed. After all, she had no real choice.

They walked around the dunon. The hill was flat-topped, a plug of landscape. To the east was a ridge of high ground, but from the hill's upper slopes there was a long view to be had of the plains to the west.

The plateau itself rose up to a summit, where a beacon bonfire had been built. Some of the flatter ground had been given over to cultivation, but there would be little farmland up here.

Artorius's capital would be fed by farmsteads on the plain outside the fort. Part of the bargain behind this was that the farmers would be able to huddle inside the walls in times of danger.
In a lower part of the plateau a wooden hall was being built to
house Artorius himself. The burned-out remains of a much
older building had been cleared—perhaps the home of some
chieftain of pre-Roman times.

They walked around the edge of the plateau. A perimeter
wall was being constructed—or rather reconstructed, she saw,
based on the foundations of some ancient predecessor. It
would be five paces thick, a framework of wooden beams
filled with stones, most of them coming from the Durnovaria
cemetery. Already the framework skirted most of the plateau,
and work had begun on a large, complex gate in the southwest
corner. Regina was impressed with the scale of all this, and the
efficiency of Artorius's organization.

"You are able to command the work of hundreds."

Artorius shrugged. "They tell me that the emperors once
commanded a hundred *million*. But one must start somewhere."

There had been rain, and the grass-coated slopes of the hill
were intensely green. The slopes were surrounded by lines of
banks and ditches. Men were working their way over the
forested banks, cutting down trees with their iron axes and
saws and hauling the trunks to the summit of the hill.

They were making the rings of ditches into a defense system. Artorius pointed. "There are four lines. See how we look
down on the earthworks? The Saxons will have to run up that
slope, arriving exhausted, and then down this face below us,
where they will offer an easy target to our arrows or spears.
The banks are overgrown with trees—three or four centuries'
growth, I suppose, quite mature—and the slopes need to be
cleared to avoid giving cover to any assailants, but we can deal
with that."

"It is a lucky arrangement of ditches and ridges to be so
useful."

He looked at her quizzically. "Luck has nothing to do with
it. I thought you understood—Regina, there is nothing natural
about those ditches. Everything you see was dug out by

hand—by our ancestors, in fact, in the days before the Caesars."

She could scarcely believe it. "This is a *made* place?"

"It certainly is. It looks crude, but is well thought out. The fort is a machine, a killing machine made of earth and rock." He scratched his chin. "The work required to assemble even our paltry new wall is enormous. To have sculpted the hill itself—to have built those banks and ditches—defies the imagination. But, once built, it lasts forever."

"And yet the Caesars cleared out this place, as mice are cleared from a nest."

He eyed her. "I have had little opportunity to study history."

She told him what she remembered of her grandfather's stories: of how the Durotriges had resisted the Roman occupation long after more wealthy kingdoms had fallen or capitulated, and how the general Vespasian, destined to become Emperor himself, had had to fight his way west, dunon to dunon.

"Dunon to dunon," he mused. "I like that. Although one must admire the achievements of Vespasian, who won a huge victory, far from home, indeed having crossed the ocean itself . . ."

"But now the Caesars have gone," she said.

"Yes. But we endure."

Only one new structure had been built on the hill in the Roman days, a small temple. It had been a neat rectangular building with a tiled roof, surrounded by a colonnaded walkway. Artorius and Regina stood and inspected what was left.

"Now the temple is destroyed, the columns mere stumps, the tiles stolen, even the god's statue looted," said Artorius. "But at least that god was here. So in successive ages this was a place of defense, and of worship. Perhaps I have selected an auspicious place for my capital."

She let her face reflect her scorn.

He pursed his lips. "You mock me again. Well, you are entitled to. I have little to show, in the present. But I have past and future on my side."

"Past?"

"My family were kings, based in Eburacum. When the Romans came, yes, they became clients of the Empire. They were *equites*." These were the class from whom, in the early days of the Roman occupation, the town council had been elected. "My ancestors ruled their lands well, and contributed to the wealth and order of the province. I myself would have been a soldier—an officer in the cavalry, that was my destiny— but . . ."

"But by the time you grew up there was no cavalry."

He laughed ruefully. "There was only the *limitaneus* left, the border army. And in some places it was so long since they had been paid they had eaten all their horses!"

She smiled. "And the future?"

"I have three goals, Regina. The first is to make this place safe." He waved an arm. "Not just the dunon, but the area it will rule. Safe from the Saxons and Picts and *bacaudae* and whoever else might wish to harm us. I am confident I can achieve that. Next I must restore order—not for just this generation but the next, and the next. We need a civic structure, invisible, yet as strong as these walls of wood and stone. For example, I will tie the farmsteads to the central authority by renting them cattle. Perhaps other taxes can be levied."

"The central authority. You mean yourself."

He shook his head. "As soon as I can I will submit myself for election as a magistrate." He used the Latin word, *duumvirs.* She guffawed, but he insisted, "I am serious. I tell you I am no warlord, Regina—or if I am it will not be forever.

"With order will come prosperity. We must make pottery— a decent kiln or two. And coins. I will start a mint. I have already begun the process of establishing an ironworks here. It is under the direction of my good friend Myrddin—you must meet him—a crusty old buffoon, but he knows the ancient wisdom that survived beyond the reach of the Romans, to the west of here. A marvelous man—so knowledgeable is he, some call him a wizard—my aim is to empty his head before he dies."

"And your third priority—"

"To return the diocese of Britain, or as much of it as I command, to the Emperor. Only that way can the farthest future be assured. Even if I have to go to Gaul, I will do it."

"How laudable," she said dryly. "But you have chosen to come here, to reoccupy this centuries-old fort, rather than to go back to Durnovaria, say."

"The town is dead. Its walls, even if restored, are feeble, its drains and water pipes clogged—and the system on which it relied has vanished. I mean the money, the flow of goods. We cannot buy metalwork from Germany or pottery from Spain anymore, Regina. We must live as our ancestors did."

"And so we are abandoning the Romans' towns and villas, and are creeping back to the old ways, the earthworks of our ancestors. How strange. How—wistful. You know, ever since I was a little girl, bit by bit, I have fallen away from the light, and into the darkness of this new, bleak time, where I recognize nothing."

He studied her seriously, his dark eyes grave. "I do understand, you know," he said gently. "I am no illiterate savage. I want what you want. Order, prosperity, peace. But I accept the times as they are; I accept what I must do to achieve those ends. I have told you my dreams, and my ambitions. Now tell me what you are thinking, Regina—tell me what you think of *me*."

She considered carefully. If anybody could restore order in this confused, collapsed landscape it was surely Artorius—a man full of dreams, but a man with the power and realism, it seemed, to make those dreams come true. For a moment, there on the busy plateau, it seemed to her that in this man, this Artorius, she had found a rock on which she might at last build a safe future for herself and her family—that there might come a time when she could rest.

"I am—hopeful." And so she was, tentatively.

He seemed moved; apparently her good opinion really was of value to him. He grabbed her hand; his palm was dry and warm. "Work with me, Regina. I need your strength."

But then there was a cry from the bottom of the slope, where the men had been digging out the clogged-up defense ditches. "*Riothamus!* You might want to see this, sir . . ."

Artorius clambered quickly down the zigzag path to the base of the ditch.

The men had found a jumble of bones. Many were broken, some charred. The men picked through this unwelcome trove carefully. There were many skulls—surely more than a hundred.

When Artorius clambered out, his face had a hardness she had not seen before. In one hand he cradled the skull of a child, in the other a handful of coins, just slivers of metal, stuck together from their immersion in the soil. "You see, Regina—from the bones it's hard to tell men from women, young from old. But you can always tell if it's a child. And at least this one did not suffer in the fire. See the crater in the back of the skull—inflicted by a legionary's sword hilt, perhaps . . ."

"The fire?"

"There was some kind of building down there." He pointed. "We've found the stumps of posts. The people were gathered up and crammed inside, and then it was torched."

"Who would do such a thing?"

"Who do you imagine?" He held out his handful of coins. One of them bore the name of the Emperor Nero. "Was it not during the reign of Nero that Boudicca led her rebellion against Roman rule? It seems that reprisals were fierce." He hefted the child's skull. "This little warrior must truly have terrified the mighty Roman army."

"Artorius—"

"Enough." Holding the skull, he walked back down the hill and began issuing commands.

For the rest of that day and most of the next, a large proportion of Artorius's scarce resource was devoted to digging out a new mass grave and transporting the broken and burned bones to it. The burial was done in the style of the Celtae. Three pigs were slaughtered and their carcasses thrown on the bones, to provide sustenance for the journey to the Otherworld. For each skull a beaker or cup was placed in the grave, so that the dead could drink from the great cauldrons in the Otherworld's banqueting halls.

As the grave was filled in, Artorius's iron-making genius Myrddin led prayers. He was a small, wild-eyed man with a mass of gray-black beard, and his arms were covered with puckered smelting scars. His voice was thin, his western accent heavy: "Death comes at last and lays cold hands upon me . . ."

*   *   *

For the rest of that year the fields around the dunon were to be prepared for sowing the following spring, and provisions like dried and salted meat were laid up for the winter.

Life continued to be harsh, with hard labor for all but the very smallest children. But Artorius had insisted they make time for such measures as the digging of proper latrines as one of the first priorities—and so they were spared the plague of fever that swept the countryside in late summer. And long before the season turned it was clear to all that they had amassed enough food to see them through the winter, even if some of it had been taken by force by Artorius's soldiers. Regina could not deny the energy Artorius brought to his task, the great sense of loyalty and industry he instilled in others—including herself, she admitted—nor the great strides the new community had made by the autumn.

But Artorius was changing.

Artorius announced that from henceforth they would follow the old calendar of the Celtae, rather than that of the Romans. This was marked out by four main feasts: Imbolc at the end of the winter, when the ewes lactated for their lambs; Beltane in early summer, when the cattle would be driven between purifying fires to open grazing; Lughnasa at the start of harvesting; and Samhain in early autumn—the start of the new year for the Celtae, a time when the old gave way to the new, and the world could be overrun by the forces of magic. The next full year, beginning that Samhain, would be the first in which Artorius's new kingdom would begin to find its feet, and Artorius announced that the Samhain would be marked by a mighty feast.

Regina listened to all this with some disquiet. But she kept her counsel.

Similarly she said nothing when Artorius began to abandon his old, much-repaired Roman armor and dress for a more traditional costume. He wore brightly colored *braccae* and cloaks, and when the weather turned colder a *birrus*, the hooded cloak that had always been associated with Britain. The effect was completed when he began to wear a handsome golden torc around his neck, looted by one of his officers from a Saxon raiding party. Though Regina spent much time in his company discussing practical matters, she never heard him refer back to his talk of starting a mint, or styling himself a magistrate.

Later, when Regina thought back, it seemed to her that the incident of the mass grave had been a turning point for Artorius: after that something hard and cold and old emerged in him, slowly becoming dominant. Or perhaps it was just the ambience of the ancient place they had come to reinhabit, their return to this old place of earth and blood, as if the age of the Roman peace had been nothing but a glittering dream.

Certainly, after that day, there had been no more talk of turning his country over to the emperors.

But none of it mattered, she told herself, so long as she and Brica were safe. The family: that was her only priority. Every night, as she lay down to sleep in the corner of the hilltop roundhouse she shared with Brica and several other senior women, she stared at her *matres*, carefully preserved across all these years, the three worn little statues perhaps older than this piled-up fortress itself, and said a kind of prayer to them—not to preserve her life, for she knew that was her own responsibility—but to grant her guidance.

On the evening of the Samhain, it felt like autumn for the first time, Regina thought. There was a hint of frost in the air, and her head was filled with the smoky scent of dying leaves. As she prepared to enter Artorius's hall, she lingered in the open, oddly regretful to leave the last of the daylight behind—the last of another summer, now her forty-first. But it was Artorius's feast, and she had no time for such reflections. With a sigh she entered his great hall.

The hall was already crowded, the torches of hay and sheep fat burned brightly on the walls, and she was bombarded by heat and light, smoke and noise.

Though even now there was much work to be done on it, she had to admit the hall's magnificence. The centerpiece was a hearth, a great circle of scavenged Roman stone, on which a huge fire was blazing. The fire cast light and heat around the hall's single vast room, and filled the noisy air with smoke. From an iron tripod twice the height of a man, a cauldron had been suspended, and she could smell the rich scents of stew— pork and mutton flavored with wild garlic, from the smell of it.

Already Artorius's men were lining up to take their share of the meat. Artorius himself served it up, yanking joints out of the simmering broth with iron hooks. There was a constant jockeying for position among the subordinates, and there was nothing subtle about the way Artorius fished for the best cuts of meat to reward his favorites. He fumbled one serving, dropping the meat on the floor, and two of his soldiers began to fight over the honor of whom it had been intended for. The others didn't try to separate them, but gathered around and roared them on.

Old Carausias was beside Regina.

She said, "What a display—grown men, squabbling over bits of meat."

He shook his head. "But with such contests his lieutenants are working out their status—who is closer to the sun."

"How savage."

Carausias shrugged. "It's a shame your grandfather isn't here. I'm sure the legionaries in their barracks behaved much the same way. Anyway it's their night, not ours."

When the soldiers had had their share of the food, the other men and the women were allowed to approach the cauldron. Regina herself took only a little of the broth, and drank sparingly of her cup of wheat beer.

When Artorius took his place on the floor at the center of a circle of his men, the storytelling began. One soldier after another got to his feet, generally unsteadily, to boast how he—or perhaps a dead comrade—had bested two or three or five savage Saxons, each taller than a normal human being and equipped with three swords apiece. They all drank steadily, at first from a communal cup carried by a servant who moved to the right around the circle, and then, as the evening got rowdier, from their own vessels. It had been a heroic labor for the little community to produce the vast vats of wheat beer that would be consumed this night.

Then the iron maker Myrddin got to his feet and began a long and complex tale about giants who lived in magical islands across the ocean, far to the west of Britain: *"There are thrice fifty distant isles / In the ocean to the west of us / Larger than Ireland twice / Is each of them, or thrice . . ."*

"All true, all true," murmured Carausias. He belched, and

Regina realized that he was getting as drunk as any of Artorius's soldiers.

As the beer continued to flow, the talk and horseplay became more raucous, and some of the soldiers and younger
men started mock-fighting and wrestling. Regina sat stoically
in her corner beside a dozing Carausias, wondering how much
of this she could endure.

There was a touch on her shoulder. Startled, she looked up.

Artorius was beside her. She could smell the beer on his
breath, but unlike his men he was not drunk. "You are quiet,"
he said.

"You should go back to your men."

He smiled, glancing back. "I don't think they need me anymore tonight. But you . . . I know what you are thinking."

"You do?"

"You are remembering your mother. The parties she gave, in
the villa. The glittering folk who would come, the expensive
preparations she would make. You've told me as much. And
now you must put up with *this*."

"I don't mean to judge."

He shook his head. "We are all prisoners of our past. But the
present is all we have. Those men wrestling over their beer are
as rough as sand—but they will give their lives for me, and for
you. We must make the best of the times we live in, what we
have, the people around us."

"You're wise."

He laughed. "No. Just a survivor, like you." He took her
hand with an odd gentleness. "Listen to me," he said intensely.
"That old fool Myrddin is full of legends . . . He says I must
become Dagda for these people."

"Dagda?"

"The Good God—but the most humble of gods. *All that you
promise to do, I will do myself alone* . . . But Dagda needs a
Morrigan, his great queen. And at Samhain," he whispered,
"the time of reconciliation, the god of the tribe and the goddess of the earth come together, so that the opposing forces, of
life and death, dark and light, good and evil, are balanced once
more."

"What are you suggesting, Artorius? . . . We fight, you and
I. We are in constant conflict."

"But life itself results from the interplay of opposing forces. That's the point."

"You foolish man. I am old, and no goddess. Find yourself a younger woman."

"But none of them has your strength—not even your daughter, beautiful though she is. *You,* you are my Morrigan, my Regina, my queen." He cupped her cheek and leaned close to her, his breath flavored with the meat and the beer, his eyes bright.

She looked into her heart. There was no affection there, not even lust. There was only calculation: *If I do this, will it increase my chances of keeping Brica alive another day?* Only calculation—but that was enough.

She stood, and let him lead her out of the hall. She looked back once to see Carausias's eyes on her, rheumy, but a mirror of her own coldness.

chapter 19

The elevator, having risen up through the nested levels of the Crypt, delivered Lucia and Rosa Poole to a small front office. Rosa nodded to the staff. They walked out to the street, emerging into thin November sunlight. They both squinted at the brightness. Rosa donned small fashionable-looking sunglasses, while Lucia pulled on her heavy blue-tinted spectacles, of the kind issued to every member of the Order.

This was a modern district of residences, shops, and businesses, just off the Via Cristoforo Colombo, a broad, traffic-heavy avenue that snaked south from the center of Rome, running roughly parallel to the ancient Appian Way. Rosa led Lucia to a small taxi rank; they had to wait a couple of minutes for a cab to arrive. The air was clear, crisp, not very cold.

Lucia wasn't sure where Rosa was taking her. The older woman had barely spoken two sentences to her since calling for her in the *scrinium*. But there was no escape, any more than from her periods.

Lucia suppressed a sigh. She had forgiven Pina for what had felt like another betrayal. Pina had only done what would have had to be done eventually; in her way she had tried her best to help. Lucia just had to endure whatever was to come.

The cab took them north toward the city center. They passed a breach in the massive, ugly old Aurelian Wall and headed northeast, driving through the areas dominated by the old imperial ruins, to the Piazza Venezia.

The Venezia was the heart of the Roman traffic system. It was just a broad field of tarmac sprawling before the *Vittoriano*, the grandiose Vittorio Emanuele monument erected to celebrate Italy's national unity, a mound of pillars and marble that loomed over the skyline, even dominating the imperial relics. The Venezia was crowded with traffic that seemed to be flying in every direction, and Lucia quailed when the cab-driver launched his vehicle into the mob, horn honking briskly. Gradually, as cars edged this way and that, nobody apparently giving way to anybody else, a route forward opened up, bit by bit, and the driver made his way to the exit he wanted, for the west-running Via del Plebiscito.

To Lucia's surprise, Rosa took her hand in her own. Rosa smiled, her eyes hidden. "Listen, I know how you feel. I know how difficult this is for you."

Sitting in the cab, apparently unperturbed by its jolts as it lurched forward through the traffic, Rosa was elegant, cool, and her narrow face with its strong nose seemed kind, though Lucia could not make out her eyes. She was tall, taller than Lucia, certainly taller and more slender than most Order members, who tended to be short and somewhat squat. But then, as everybody knew, Rosa was one of the few at the heart of the Order who hadn't been born in the Crypt. Though she had come to the Order as a child, her fluent Italian still bore traces of England, short vowels and harsh consonants.

"At school we come up here every week," Lucia said. "To the city, I mean. Even so I can never get used to it."

"What, exactly? The crowds, the noise—the light?"

"Not that," Lucia said, thinking. "The *chaos*. Everybody going every which way, all the time."

Rosa nodded. "Yes. You know that I'm something of an out-sider. Well, I always will be, and it's not to be helped. But it does give me a certain perspective. There are some things about the Crypt that we all take for granted, and we notice only when they are taken away. In the Crypt everything is orderly, calm, and everybody knows what she is doing, where she is going. Even the temperature is controlled, the air clean and fresh. But out here it's quite the opposite. Out here is anarchy, everything out of control. And now you, Lucia, feel that even your own body is out of your control. And you fear—"

"I fear I don't belong anymore," Lucia blurted.

The driver had a broad head, all but hairless, with a band of greasy pores above his collar. He looked about fifty. At her slightly raised voice, he turned, glancing in his mirror. His speculative gaze was heavy on her; she looked away.

Rosa said, "You won't be turned out—out into this messy chaos—if that's what you fear. In fact, quite the opposite. You're more likely to be drawn into the center."

"The center?"

"You'll see. You have nothing to be ashamed of, Lucia. The Order needs you." Rosa smiled. "It's just that you may be needed for something other than record keeping or calligraphy . . . Ah. Here we are."

Lucia was, of course, full of questions. But the cab was drawing to a halt, and there was no time to ask.

She got out of the cab to find herself in the Piazza di Rotonda. The square was thronged with tourists bustling between ice cream stalls and cafés. She stood before the blocky walls of a great building that loomed over them like a fortress—and indeed, said Rosa, it had been used as a fortress in the Middle Ages, as had been most of Rome's ancient buildings; the brick walls were, after all, six yards thick. This was the Pantheon.

Rosa pointed to a ditch around the walls. "See that? The road level is higher than the base of the building. Since this place was built the rubble and dirt has risen like a tide . . . Come." She took Lucia's hand.

They walked under the great colonnaded portico at the front of the building. Though the height of the tourist season had been the summer, the space among the great gray columns was crowded by people, many in shorts, T-shirts, and baseball caps and with tiny cameras in their hands. In the Crypt everybody was trim, neat, and would get out of each other's way without having to be shoved. Not here. The people all seemed grossly overfed and clumsy to Lucia. It was like being in a herd of cattle—slow-moving and aggressive cattle at that.

And then there were the boys, and even some of the men, who looked at her, stared in fact, with a calculating intensity, a greed that made her shudder.

But there was one boy whose gaze seemed clearer. He looked perhaps eighteen, with a pale face, high forehead, and red hair in which sunglasses nestled. He stared, too—he seemed fascinated by her—but there was an innocence in his gaze. He actually smiled at her. She flushed and looked away.

Rosa didn't seem troubled by the tourists. She was stroking the cool marble of one of the columns. "My father is an ac-

countant, but he did a lot of work with the building trade,"
Rosa said. "I know what he would say if he was here." She
switched to English. *"Imagine shifting one of these buggers."*

"You were only small when you came here, to the Crypt."

"Yes. But I still remember him. I remember his hands." She
spread her own fingers. "Big, scarred hands, great slabs of
muscle, like a farmer's hands. He always had strong hands,
even though most of his life was spent behind a desk."

Lucia didn't know what to say, how to join in a conversation
about fathers. Lucia had seen her own father only once or
twice. He was a *contadino* who did occasional work in the
Crypt. He was a slightly overweight man, characterless, given
to smiling a little weakly. She'd never even spoken to him. To
Lucia, even to think about your father seemed unnatural.

"Do you miss your father?"

Rosa smiled, her eyes hidden. "No, I don't miss him. I lost
him, or he lost me, too long ago for that." She touched Lucia's
shoulder. "And anyhow, the Order is my family now. Isn't that
true?"

Lucia was uncertain how to respond. "Of course." That
didn't need saying. It shouldn't *be* said.

"Come on. Let's go inside."

Lucia looked back once. The redheaded boy had gone.

The Pantheon enclosed a broad, airy volume. There was an
altar, the walls were decorated with paintings and holy figures,
and the floor was a cool sheet of marble across which tourists
wandered.

But it was the roof that drew Lucia's gaze. It was a dome,
decorated with a cool geometric design, quite unlike the clutter on the walls. The structure seemed to float above her. The
only illumination in this immense space came from a hole in
the domed ceiling, the oculus. The light it cast showed as a
broad beam in the dusty air, and splashed a distorted circle on
one wall.

Rosa murmured, "The dome is bigger than that of Saint
Peter's in the Vatican. Did you know that? But the building
was started before the birth of Christ. The Pantheon was built
as a temple to all the pagan gods, but was turned into a Christian church in the seventh century, which saved it from being
torn down. Now it's the most complete of the buildings of an-

tiquity left. Of course it has suffered even so. Once the dome was clad, inside and out, by bronze, but that was stripped away by the Barberini popes to make cannons. *What the barbarians didn't do, the Barberini did,* as they say."

Lucia gazed up at the disc of blue sky. "We used to get taken to the Forum area all the time, as kids. But you get used to the imperial-era stuff as just a heap of ruins. You forget that it was once all intact—that it was once all like this."

"Yes." In the subdued light of the Pantheon, Rosa had taken her dark glasses off, to reveal slate-gray eyes, just like Lucia's own.

Lucia said, "I think you should tell me why you brought me here."

"All right. Look at this building, Lucia. It was rebuilt by the Emperor Hadrian, but the Renaissance artist Raphael is buried here, as are the first kings of Italy. The same building, you see, serving many purposes over time. But at root it is the same Pantheon, the same expression of its architect's vision."

"I don't understand."

Rosa laughed. "I'm starting to think I'm becoming heavy-handed in my old age. I'm being metaphorical, Lucia."

"Oh." Lucia made a stab in the dark. "The Pantheon is like the Order?"

"Well, yes, I suppose so, though that isn't what I meant. After all, this church is even older than the Order itself. Yes, the Order has survived for sixteen centuries by adapting, by changing what we do to suit the needs and pressures of the times. But *we,* who we are and why we gather together, that at heart hasn't changed.

"And just as the Pantheon has survived, though it changes—just as the Order survives, though *it* changes—so you, too, will survive the changes your body is taking you through, now and in the future. That's what I wanted to show you. Why, if you hadn't grown up in the Order your menarche would seem *normal* for a girl your age. Whatever becomes of you—*whatever is asked of you*—you will still be yourself. Remember that."

Whatever is asked of you: now Lucia felt scared.

Rosa raised her face to the great halo of light in the ceiling. "You should take some time for yourself, Lucia. Come out again—immerse yourself in Rome. One of the most remarkable cities in the world is on our doorstep, and yet down in the Crypt we often behave as if it doesn't exist! And I don't mean with your classes. Come by yourself—or with a friend or two, if you like. That girl Pina seems sensible. Immerse yourself in humanity for a while."

It will prepare me, Lucia thought. *That's what she's telling me. I must broaden my experience, to prepare for—what?*

"You're talking in riddles, Rosa," she flared. "What is to be asked of me?"

"A great deal, if you are lucky. You'll see. I'll do what I can for you—but always remember, I envy you! It isn't duty, but privilege." Rosa glanced at her watch. "Now we must go back. There's somebody I want you to meet."

"Who?"

"Maria Ludovica."

Lucia felt as if her heart had stopped, there in the dusty air of the Pantheon. Ludovica was one of the *matres*.

Rosa smiled, watching her reaction.

The elevator was steel-walled, and it slid into the ground smoothly, all but silently. All very modern, as was much of the equipment in the Crypt. Rosa stood in patient silence watching the elevator's LED display, hands calmly folded before her. Lucia envied her composure.

Lucia vaguely imagined the Crypt as a great drum shape, sunk deep into the ground beneath the old Appian Way. There were at least three levels—everybody knew that much. On the first story, nearest the surface, there were schools, offices, libraries, and the computer center where she herself worked on the *scrinium*'s endless projects. On the story beneath that—downbelow, as the Crypt jargon had it—there were living accommodations, the dormitories and rest rooms and dining rooms, food stores, kitchens, a hospital, all of them crammed, day and night, with people. Few of the day girls who attended the Order's famous schools would ever descend this far, and the light shafts didn't reach; there was only the pale glow of electric lights, and in the old days, it was said, candles and torches.

And there was at least one more level downbelow.

The elevator whispered to a halt. The doors slid open to a mundane white-walled corridor: the third story. Rosa led the way out with a reassuring smile. Lucia followed reluctantly. The corridor was narrow. Some of the doors leading off the corridor were heavy, as if designed to keep an airtight seal. There was a faint smell of antiseptic here, heavily overlaid with a more pleasant scent, like lavender.

Lucia's heart pounded. She didn't know anybody who had visited the third level. Lucia herself hadn't, not since she was a very small child. From what little she knew, this was a place of nurseries and crèches. She herself had been born here, and had spent her first couple of years here. She remembered nothing but a blur of smiling faces, of pale gray eyes, all alike, none special, all loving.

And, so went the whispers in the dark, this was a place of mortuaries. You were born downbelow, here on the third story, and you died downbelow. So it was said. Lucia didn't want to know.

The corridor was crowded, of course. In the Crypt, everywhere was crowded. People smiled, nodded, and ducked out of the way as Rosa forged ahead. Almost everybody was female. Most people wore everyday clothing, but some wore simple cotton smocks that looked like nurses' uniforms. Though most shared the usual lozenge-shaped features and smoky gray eyes—and even though everybody seemed young, not much older than she was—there wasn't a single face here that Lucia recognized.

Lucia had heard bits of dormitory gossip that the Crypt might hold as many as *ten thousand* people in its great halls and corridors. That scarcely seemed credible—but then, wherever you looked, there were always more corridors, more chambers, stretching on into the electric-lit dimness: who was to say how far it stretched? She would never know, for she would never need to know. *Ignorance is strength . . .*

And it was possible, she thought now, that *nobody* knew the whole picture—nobody at all.

Here on the third level people stared at her openly. Their manner wasn't hostile—some of them even smiled at her—but Lucia felt herself cringe. This wasn't her place; they knew it, and she knew it. The pressure of those accusing glares made

her long to flee back to where she belonged. She felt breathless, almost panicking, as if the air in these deep chambers
were foul.

If only she could be like Rosa, who seemed to be accustomed to flitting between the stories with the ease of a dust
mote in the Pantheon.

At last Rosa paused by a door. Lucia felt a vast relief. Whatever lay ahead, at least she was done with the ordeal of the corridor. Rosa opened the door, and let Lucia go through first.

She was immediately struck by a sense of richness. It was
like a drawing room, she thought, with dark oak panels on the
walls, and marble inlays in the floor, and furniture, tables and
chairs and couches. The furniture looked as if it had come
from a number of periods, perhaps as far back as the eighteenth century, but there was a wide-screen television, set in a
large walnut cabinet. The furniture was heavily used: worn
patches on the seat covers, scuffs on the table surfaces, even
wear in the marble tiles on the floor. Clocks ticked patiently,
their faces darkened by a patina of time. There was more of a
sense of *age* here than in any room she had ever visited in the
Crypt.

And there was a unique smell—sour, strong, quite unlike
the antiseptic hospital smell of the corridor—something hot,
animal, oddly disturbing.

At the center there was a bed, or a couch, the single largest
piece of furniture in the room. There was somebody lying on
the couch, still, frail looking, reading a book. There was one
other person in the room, a young woman who sat patiently in
a big, worn armchair, quietly watching the woman in the bed.
Rosa nodded at the attendant, smiling.

Rosa led Lucia forward. Their footsteps seemed loud on the
marble, but as they neared the bed they reached a thick rug
that deadened the noise.

There was one large painting on the rear wall, Lucia saw
now. It showed a melodramatic scene of a line of women, their
clothing rent, standing before a mob of marauding men. The
women were wounded and defenseless, and the intent of
the men was obvious. But the women would not give way. The
picture was captioned: 1527—SACCO DI ROMA, the Sack of
Rome.

The woman on the bed did not look up from her book. She was very old, Lucia saw. Her face looked as if it had dried out and imploded, like a sun-dried tomato, her skin leathery and marked with liver spots. Wisps of gray hair lay scattered on the cushion behind her head. On a metal stand beside her bed a plastic bag fed some pale fluid into her arm. A blanket lay over her legs, and she wore a heavy, warm-looking bed jacket, although the room seemed hot to Lucia.

This was Maria Ludovica, then, one of the legendary *matres*. She looked terribly old, tired, ill—*and yet she was pregnant;* the swelling in her belly, under the blanket, was unmistakable.

The stink was powerful here, a stink like urine. Lucia felt drawn, repelled at the same time.

Rosa leaned forward and said softly, "Mamma—Mamma—"

Maria looked up blearily, her eyes rheumy gray pebbles. "What, what? Who's that? Oh, it's you, Rosa Poole." She glanced down at her book irritably, tried to focus, then closed the book with a sigh. "Oh, never mind. I always thought old age would at least give me time to read. But by the time I've got to the bottom of the page I've forgotten what was at the top . . ." She leered at Lucia, showing a toothless mouth. "What an irony—eh? So, Rosa Poole, who is this you've brought to see me? One of mine?"

"One of yours, Mamma. She is Lucia. Fifteen years old."

"And you've reached your menarche." Maria reached out with one clawlike hand; she compressed Lucia's breast, not unkindly. Lucia forced herself not to flinch. "Well, perhaps she'll do. Is she to be your champion, Rosa?"

"Mamma, you shouldn't talk that way—"

Maria winked, hideously, at Lucia. "I'm too old not to speak the truth. Too old and sick and tired. And Rosa doesn't like it. Well, I've stirred you all up—haven't I? At least I can still do that. It's just as when I'm ready to pup. I can see how it agitates them, all these slim breastless sisters. Their little nipples ache, and their dry bellies cramp—isn't that true, Cecilia?" She snapped the question at her patient nurse, who merely smiled. "Well, I'm pregnant again—*and* I'm dying, and that's stirred them up even more. Hasn't it, Rosa Poole?" Maria cackled. "I feel like the pope, by God. White smoke, white smoke . . ."

Lucia remembered what Pina had said, about a disturbance in the Crypt going back years, of more girls like her—*more freaks,* she thought gloomily—coming into their menarche, instead of staying young, like everybody else, everybody normal. Perhaps the illness of this strange old woman really was having some kind of effect—perhaps it had somehow affected *her.*

If so, she resented it.

Maria Ludovica saw that in her eyes. "By Coventina's dugs, there is steel in this one, Rosa. If she is your choice she is a good one." That claw hand shot out again to grab Lucia's arm. She whispered, "You know, child, I'm old, and shut up in here, but I'm no fool, and I'm not out of touch. Things are changing in the world, faster than ever, faster than I can remember. The new technology—phones and computers, wires and cables and radio waves everywhere—everybody joined up . . . We have many new opportunities to do business—don't we, Rosa? You see, Rosa and her rivals know this. But they know that if it is to prosper in a time of change the Order must be based on the firmest of foundations. And I, a foundation stone, am crumbling. And so the rivals maneuver, through looks and glances, visits of their candidates and inquiries after my health, testing their strength against each other as against me—"

Lucia said, "Rosa, what does she mean?"

Rosa shook her head. "Nothing. She means nothing. Mamma, you should not say these things. There are no rivalries, no candidates. There is only the Order. That's all there ever has been."

Maria held her gaze for a few seconds, and then subsided. "Very well, Rosa Poole. If you say so."

Rosa said, "I think the mamma is tiring, Lucia. I wanted you to meet her before—"

"Before I die, Rosa Poole?"

"Not at all, *Mamma-nonna,*" Rosa said, gently scolding. "You'll be giving us all trouble for a long time to come yet. Say good-bye, Lucia . . . Give Maria a kiss."

Lucia could think of few things she would less rather do. Maria watched with her wet, birdlike eyes as Lucia took a step forward, leaned over, and brushed her lips against Maria's imploded cheek. But despite its off-putting appearance it was just skin, after all, human skin, soft and warm.

"Good, good," Rosa murmured. "After all, she is your mother."

When the interview was over, Rosa took Lucia to one side. "You know, you are honored, the way she spoke to you. But you still don't understand, do you? Let me ask you something. When you were a child, here in the Order—were you happy?"

"Yes," Lucia said honestly. "Immensely happy."

"Why?"

She thought about that. "Because I always knew I was safe. Nothing I needed was denied me. I was surrounded by people who protected me."

"What would they have done for you?"

"They would have given their lives for me," she said firmly. "Any one of them. There was nobody near me who would have harmed me."

Rosa nodded. "Yes. They would have sacrificed themselves for you; they really would. I was brought up in a family—a nuclear family—a family with difficulties. My parents loved me, but they were remote . . . That is how it is for most people, how it has been for all of human history—how it was for me. But you are one of the lucky few for whom it was different. And that was why you were happy." Rosa stepped closer to Lucia, her face intent. "But, you must realize, one day you will have to pay for your happiness, your safety. That is the way of things. You have to pay it back. And that time is coming, Lucia."

Lucia quailed, baffled, trying not to show her fear.

chapter 20

There was a nervousness about the hill fort today. Artorius was due to return from his latest campaign against the Saxons, and nobody knew how their loved ones had fared.

But Regina set this aside. After six years in the hill fort she had learned it was best to stick to orderly habits. So, first thing that morning, she went to her small room at the back of Artorius's roundhouse. With a mug of bark tea at her side, she settled on a wooden stool and spread out her calendar.

The calendar was a bronze sheet, divided into columns, carefully inscribed by Myrddin with Latin lettering—she had insisted on Latin, despite the barbarian origin of the calendar itself. It had sixteen columns, each representing four months. This sheet covered a five-year cycle. In fact the sheet was one of a set that made up a complete nineteen-year calendar, and it was said that the Druids, who had devised this mighty tabulation, worked on much longer cycles still.

It was a calendar for farmers and warriors. Each year was divided into two halves, with a "good" half—*mat*—stretching from Beltane in the spring to Samhain in the autumn, and the "bad" half—*anm*—spanning the winter months. And then each month, of twenty-nine or thirty days, was itself split into good and bad halves. The *mat* months corresponded not just to the growing season but also to the annual campaigning season: for Celtae a good day was a day for war. But Samhain was approaching once again, and another campaigning season was almost done, to her relief. Regina understood the necessity for war, but hated the waste of life it represented, and every year longed for it to be over.

Anyhow the calendar was very intricate. But it worked—once she had gotten used to *thinking* like one of the Celtae rather than trying to translate back to the Roman equivalent; that had been the key. The point of the calendar was that each day, right through the complete nineteen-year cycle, had a different divine flavor, which subtly determined the decisions to be taken, the combination of gods to be placated. In a way it was even comforting to believe that the shape of the universe, down to the day and the hour, had been shaped by ancient cosmic decisions. It reminded her of old Aetius, her grandfather, whom she had thought the most superstitious man she had ever met, until coming to Artorius's capital; when it came to the old gods there had been nothing particularly rational about the Romans.

She would think like the Celtae, then. She could hardly have refused to use the calendar at all, for it had been the idea of Artorius himself. But she wouldn't give up her bronze sheets and her Latin. The Druids maintained their centuries-spanning calendar entirely in their heads, but it took a Druid novice *twenty years* to memorize the oral law that lay at the heart of the old religions. Well, she was already in her late forties, and if she was granted twenty more years she could think of better things to do with her time than *that*.

With her scrutiny of the calendar done, her head full of properly regulated auguries and omens, she picked up her wax tablet and stylus and left her office for her daily inspection.

It was midmorning. The sunlit air was clear of mist, though it had a nip that foretold the winter to come.

The colony on the hilltop plateau had grown: nearly five hundred people lived up here now, and many thousands more in the farmed countryside nearby. This morning fires still burned in the huts and roundhouses, and the air was full of the rich scent of wood smoke, and the greasier scents of cooking. There was a great deal of bustle. People moved among the houses, and a steady column marched out of the compound's open gate, or returned with such staples as wood, pails of water, and bales of hay. Children ran underfoot as they always did, cheerful, healthy, and muddy from head to toe.

As well as the great hall of Artorius there were now granaries and storage pits, seven large roundhouses, and simple rectangular buildings used by the craftsmen. Great capital this place may one day be, but there were always chickens and even a few pigs wandering the lanes, and there were still a few areas of green. At the back of Artorius's own hall a small kitchen garden grew garlic, mint, and other herbs; the *riothamus* had started a fashion among his nobles for highly spiced food.

In the manufactories the day's work had started.

Regina approached the carpenter's. On the walls were arrayed hammers, saws, axes, adzes, billhooks, files, awls, and gouges, and wooden boxes of nails were stacked on the floor. Today Oswald—the head of the little manufactory, a great bear of a man with huge scarred hands—was working his new toy, a pole lathe. A rope ran from a beam above to a foot pedal, and when he worked the pedal the central spindle ran smoothly. He was still getting the hang of the device, but already the stool legs and wooden bowls he was turning out had a pleasing symmetry.

Meanwhile, in the pottery, the kiln had been fired up. One worker mixed clay with the crushed flint that helped avoid shrinkage and cracking, another shaped a pot by hand, a third prepared the kiln itself. The kiln was an updraft design, far advanced over the simple pit clamps Regina had used on the farmstead. Firing took a whole day, with the temperature raised and lowered in careful stages. Maybe one in ten of the pots still failed, but the rest was solid red earthenware. The potters were even learning how they could control the color of their product, from black through gray or red, by changing the amount of air available in the kiln. It was still coarse stuff—they had yet to master the technique of using a wheel—but it was solid and useful.

Regina's old friend Marina ran the largest of the cloth works, from a big roundhouse she ruled as firmly as Artorius did his kingdom. The looms themselves, three sturdy frames taller than Artorius himself, were set just inside the entrance to the house, so the weavers could get the best light.

Regina liked to watch the weavers. The most skillful of them was another Marina—a docile sixteen-year-old, one of the old woman's own grandchildren. Young Marina worked steadily. A warp, threads of spun wool, was suspended from a top bar and kept under tension by small triangular stones. Marina pulled the horizontal heddle bar toward her, opening up a gap between alternating warp threads. She pulled the weft, a horizontal thread, through the shed, and then released the heddle to pull the alternate threads backward, and then passed the weft back through the gaps. Every few passes Marina would pause to push her weaving sword, a flat wooden board, into the gap between the warp threads, and thus compacted the weft. All this was done fluidly and without pause, and her speed of working was remarkable; just standing here, Regina was able to see how the cloth's crisscross pattern was emerging, row by row.

Regina had been proud of the success they had had with her own weaving experiments back on her farmstead, but all they had been able to produce was coarse cloth. This loom design had come from another of the experts Artorius had gathered up in his sweeps across the countryside, and the results were far better.

She passed a little time with old Marina. Marina liked to talk of old times in Verulamium, and Regina knew that the skill and loyalty of her granddaughter had been a great comfort to Marina since the death of poor Carausias a few winters before. But Regina escaped before Marina produced her foul-smelling buckets and asked her to contribute. Marina's vegetable dyes needed a fixing agent, and the best fixer of all was stale urine: a vintage half a month old was generally thought to be just right.

Regina made more marks on her wax tablet, and moved on.

Of all the industries that had sprouted here on the dunon's plateau, the most significant was iron: fully half the manufactory area of the plateau was given over to its complex production. Myrddin ruled his little empire of iron and fire and charcoal as if he were king of the underworld. As she approached the forges, two of Myrddin's helpers—unfree, recent arrivals both of them—were working on a charcoal clamp. Myrddin insisted on training up his clamp workers personally, and from the look of the hollow, sleepless eyes of these two men, his training regime had been as brutal and unrelenting as ever.

This clamp was a few days old and several paces across. A mound of timber had been covered with a thick layer of damp leaves and bracken, turf, and soil. Fire had been started inside with embers poured into a hole in the top, and then the mound was capped off, so that the wood within could only consume itself. Running the clamp was a skilled job. A constant watch had to be kept on it by day and night, for as the wood turned to charcoal it would shrink, and the clamp could collapse on itself—and if air got in the whole thing would go up in an unproductive blaze. When the burning was done the mound had to be dismantled carefully, and the charcoal doused with water, for while hot it had a tendency to erupt into flames spontaneously. There were many such clamps, some much larger, in operation day and night beyond the hill fort, for Myrddin's works demanded a constant and heavy supply of charcoal. You could smelt some metal ores with wood fires, but only charcoal could provide the high temperatures needed for iron.

Myrddin himself ran the next stage in his process. His shaft furnace was just a tube of wattle and daub, vitrified by repeated firings. By the time Regina arrived the furnace had been running since early morning, and two more unfree were laboring mightily at their animal-skin bellows. They were naked save for loincloths, and their bodies were slick with sweat and soot. Myrddin was supervising the day's first charge of charcoal and ore.

He preferred charcoal made from alder, which he said burned hotter than any other sort, and ocher, a relatively easy ore to smelt. The furnace would be worked all day, and then allowed to cool; by tomorrow Myrddin would be able to pull out a bloom, a dense, irregular mass of metal and impurities. This would be subject to repeated hammering and heating until the last of the slag was gone. It took several blooms for Myrddin to produce one of his ingots, a flat bar about the size of a sword blade, ready for further work. All this had baffled Regina—it seemed an awful lot of work for a small piece of iron—until Artorius had gently explained that even charcoal ovens were not hot enough actually to melt iron, and Myrddin's elaborate practices were necessary to coax the iron out of its ore.

Though she despised the way Myrddin used his secret knowledge as a source of power, she could not deny the reality of that knowledge. Watching his careful, almost delicate work as he constantly inspected and assessed his furnaces and clamps, she thought she could see something of the centuries, or millennia, of trial and error and constant study that had led to the development of such techniques.

And the end product was iron, the most precious resource of all, pieces of iron that, remarkably, had not existed before. Piled up in Myrddin's workshops were some of the final products of all this industry: carpenters' tools like adzes and saws, tools for the farmers like harness buckles and sickles and reaping knives, weapons for warriors like swords and knives—and even tools for Myrddin's own use, like tongs and an anvil. It was Myrddin's proudest boast that he was the only craftsman who produced all his own tools.

But Myrddin was Regina's enemy.

When he spotted her, he greeted her with a kind of snarling smile. "Here to check up again, Regina? Tap, tap, tap with your stylus . . . a shame we can't eat your words, or nail our soles to our shoes with your letters, eh? But at least we can wipe our arses on your scrolls . . ." And so on. She endured it, as always, and walked on.

A young apprentice called Galba was working at a forge, and Regina paused.

He wore a sleeveless tunic, and his bare arms were pocked with hot-metal scars, already a little like Myrddin's. He was working a piece of iron—a short blade, perhaps for a knife—in the forge, while an unfree toiled at the bellows. Galba would thrust the blade into the furnace until it became red hot, beat it into shape while still heated, and then quench it quickly with water. It seemed that the fire didn't just make the iron soft enough to work; something about the charcoal in the furnace made the iron stronger. And sometimes the iron, beaten flat, would be folded over and beaten again, the invisible layers adding strength. There were many subtleties to Myrddin's art, which Galba and other apprentices were learning slowly.

The blade appeared to be done. Galba quenched it once more and set it aside. Then he noticed Regina. "Madam—good day—would you like me to call your daughter?"

"If you please," she said stiffly.

He went into the back of the workshop, calling Brica's name. Regina sat on a low wooden bench and waited.

* * *

As Artorius's kingdom had grown, so it had become necessary to find efficient ways to shape it, and to run it.

Despite Regina's own inclinations the order that was emerging had little to do with imperial forms, but was based on older Celtae structures. The center of it all was the dunon itself. The hill fort provided facilities for trade and exchange, a religious center, a resident population of craftsmen with growing expertise—and, most importantly, administrative control.

Artorius's nation was divided into three classes. The nobles included the soldiers, but also jurists, doctors, carpenters, bards and priests, and metalworkers like Myrddin. Artorius's rule was moderated by a meeting on every feast day of the *oenach*, an assembly of the nobles. Below the nobles were the free commoners, the lesser craftsmen and the farmers, who were actually the productive level of society. It was their rents, taxes, and tithes that sustained Artorius's nascent government, and paid for his army and their campaigns. Finally, the lowest level were the unfree: former criminals, slaves, and late-arriving refugees who found no free land to farm. Their fate was simply to serve, and they provided the bulk of the labor.

The basis of society was the family. According to the old tradition the property and other rights of a man extended to his *derbfine*, his descendants as far as his great-grandchildren, through four generations. Basic rights were assured by each person having an "honor price," a level of compensation to be paid in case of injury, insult, or death. But the system extended only to the free; the unfree had no rights, and no views that were listened to at higher levels.

It was a crude system, of course, a barbaric structure to regulate the relationships of a warrior people, with nothing like the sophistication of Roman law. But any attempts Regina made to reform the ancient code were resisted, especially by Myrddin, who seemed to have appointed himself a kind of keeper of the truth here in Artorius's kingdom. Perhaps more civilized forms would emerge with time.

Still, in this great project, Regina had found a place.

She had never forgotten the lessons Aetius had taught her. Aetius would say that it was information as much as sword blades that had enabled the emperors to take and hold such a vast territory: not just military knowledge, but records of

wealth and taxes, payments and savings, gathered by the officials in the towns and transmitted by the *cursus publicus* along
the great network of roads, which had been built as much to
carry facts as soldiers' feet.

It had not been hard for her to convince Artorius of the truth
of this. Her very first attempts at record keeping rapidly bore
fruit in exposing unpaid tithes and unjust levies. He had since
granted her all the time and resources she needed.

She had pupils in her work—she, at least, was not jealous of
her knowledge. She taught her pupils to read and write, and
to argue and analyze in the forensic tradition of the Roman
system. Literacy was very important to her. It was a peculiar
horror to her that most Saxons couldn't read. Records and literature were the memory of humanity: if the Saxons were ever
to overrun this place her past would truly be lost, lost forever.

Aside from her moments of solitude with the calendar, this
brief tour of inventory compiling was the most pleasurable
part of her daily routine. She never forgot that all the dunon's
busywork was primitive compared to what had been available
in the poorest of the towns in the old days, when the old continentwide trading routes had still worked, and there was little
here that hadn't been made on the spot. But they had come a
long way since the time, only a few years ago, when she had
scoured the rubble of abandoned villas in search of iron nails
for her shoes. She felt she was in an island, a haven where civilization was slowly recovering, in the midst of the country's
devastation and collapse.

Brica came running out to her mother and kissed her on the
cheek. They sat together on the bench.

"I heard you talk to Myrddin," Brica said. "That old monster
gives you a roasting every day."

Regina shrugged. "I can't take him seriously, not with a
beard like that."

Brica snorted laughter. "But he does know his craft. I think
he just resents being watched over."

To Regina, Brica showed an alarming lack of interest in the
subtleties of human interaction. "It isn't that," Regina said
slowly, massaging her daughter's hands. "Not really. Myrddin
is no fool, whatever else he is. He knows the value of record

keeping as well as I do. His problem is not the record keeping but who's keeping the records."

"You?"

"Myrddin sees me as a rival for Artorius's attention. He whispers in one ear about the glory of the Celtae and the magic of the old ways; I whisper in the other about record keeping and tax revenues. We are like two poles, like past and future."

Brica grinned. "But you are the one who sleeps with the *riothamus.*"

"Yes. Though I think that if Myrddin thought he could lure Artorius to his bed he would cut himself a new hole—"

Brica's mouth gaped. "Mother!"

Regina patted her hand. "Reassuring to know I can still shock you, dear. Anyhow, I think the *riothamus* likes having us both around, even having us fight, so he can take in contrasting opinions. The mark of a wise leader . . ."

Artorius still called her his queen, his Morrigan. But their relationship nowadays had little to do with the fierce love of gods—little to do with passion, in fact, for he rarely visited her bed, even in the rare intervals he broke off from his campaigning and alliance building to return to the fort by the Caml.

Artorius's bold early notions of stepping down and submitting himself to election had long been quietly dropped. But he and Regina had privately spoken of his own eventual succession, and the need for him to find male descendants. It was unspoken between them, but it was obvious that she would not be the source of his children and the *derbfine* that would follow. She suspected he was also talking to other advisers, such as Myrddin—and perhaps he was already taking other women to his bed. But she cared nothing for that; her liaison with Artorius, in ensuring her own survival and Brica's, was serving her purposes.

As Regina mused, Brica's attention was drifting. Galba was moving about at the back of the manufactory, wiping his hands on a rag and joking with another worker.

Galba was short, stocky, with broad heavyset features; he had a pale complexion and thick red hair, which betrayed his people's probable origin among the Picts north of the Wall. He was young—younger than Brica, who was now a venerable twenty-eight. He had come down from the north with his family, en route to Armorica. They had fallen afoul of Saxons, but a chance encounter with a party of Artorius's soldiers had saved their lives. Galba's family had taken over an abandoned farm only half a day's ride from here, and had become commoners in the new kingdom. Brica had met Galba at a feast on one of the farmsteads. She had prevailed upon Regina to bring the man into the dunon for a trial at the forge. Galba had acquitted himself so well that Myrddin had taken him on at the manufactory permanently.

And Galba's move into the dunon had made Brica more than happy, too, to Regina's chagrin. Galba was cheerful, sturdy, competent, and obviously attractive—but, to Regina, crushingly dull. In that way he was astonishingly like Bran, Brica's farmboy first love, a relationship Regina had crushed long ago.

Now Galba came out of the workshop, softly calling Brica. Somehow he had managed to scorch a lank of soot-filled red hair at the side of his head. Brica took a knife and carefully began to saw at the blackened ends. Galba crouched a little so she could reach, and as she worked her body moved closer to his, her cheek resting on the side of his head.

They belonged together. It was a sudden, unwelcome truth, and yet it could not be denied. But Regina found jealousy gathering inside her. *I can't allow this,* she thought suddenly.

Not for the first time, she found she had come to a decision intuitively, and had to unravel it retrospectively. She felt as hostile to Galba as she had once to Bran. Why?

Galba was now a larger part of Brica's life than Regina was. So he should be. There were women younger than Brica who were already *grandmothers*. It was the way of things. A daughter matters more to a mother than a mother can ever matter to the daughter, for the daughter represents the future, and the future must predominate over the past. Regina should simply— let go.

And yet the past contained everything Regina valued in her life: the villa, her own mother, the towns, the fine things. Peace and order, richness and beauty. If she were to let Brica go into the arms of this cloddish boy, this apprentice smith who thought better with his muscles than with his head, then

Brica's future would count for everything, and Regina's past for nothing. It was a tension between past and future—and it was a tension that resolved in her head, as suddenly as clouds might clear from the face of the sun, and a warm determination filled her.

I will stop this liaison, she thought, *just as I got rid of Bran. I don't know how yet, but I will find a way. I have to, for the sake of the past, which is more precious than the future, and which must therefore be preserved.*

A braying of trumpets drifted from the west: it was a peal that announced the return of the *riothamus* and his army. All over the dunon work was abandoned, and everybody ran to the gate.

In the six years since Regina and Brica had been brought here, the predations of the rebellious Saxons from their fastnesses on the east coast had become a severe problem across southern Britain.

In her long conversations with Artorius about his diffuse foe, she had learned much about the Saxons. For a start they weren't really "Saxons," even though that was what everybody called them. After they had erupted from their homeland in the north of Germany, the Saxons had become sea pirates, traversing the Mare Germanicus, which facilitated links among Jutland, Frisia, and Francia. Now nobody could precisely say who or what they were—they were all kinds of Germanics—not that that mattered if you were on the receiving end of a Saxon blade.

The Saxons were not savages. Some of the booty Artorius had brought home from his wars, particularly the fine metalwork, was as beautiful and complex as anything she had ever seen. But they were not remotely civilized in the Roman sense. They were not even like the Vandals and Goths and Franks who were moving through Gaul. Those barbarians often tried to ape the rulers they displaced, and even tried to maintain the forms of society that had prevailed there, with more or less degrees of incompetence.

But the Saxons were adventurers, wanderers, marauders, pirates. They were certainly not capable of running anything like the old imperial administration—and besides, Regina thought ruefully, in Britain there really wasn't much left of the old system to run anyhow, for it had all collapsed even before the Saxons got here. The Saxons actually seemed to hate the towns and other relics of the Empire. They were intent not just on plunder but also on massacre, conquest, and destruction.

The only choices for the natives were to serve the new rulers, to flee—or to die. Many people had indeed fled, it was said, either to the west and north, the harsher mountainous lands beyond the effective reach of the old diocese, or else they had gone overseas to the growing British colonies in Armorica. Great stretches of the countryside were depopulated altogether.

But Artorius and his growing armies had formed one of the few foci of resistance to the marauding Saxons.

With a mixture of Roman discipline and Celtae ferocity, even before the present campaigning season Artorius had scored nine significant victories. People had come flocking to his hill fort capital, and the petty warlords and rulers who had emerged from the collapse of the old diocese had been keen to vow their allegiance to him—Vortimer, for instance, son of Vortigern, who had tried to avenge his father's destruction by Hengest. As Artorius's power, influence, and reputation grew, he was slowly earning his self-anointed title of *riothamus*, king of kings. Not that Regina trusted many of the bandits he dealt with, many of whom she suspected of making equally vivid declarations of loyalty to the Saxon warlords.

Despite such doubts, she had no choice but to cling to Artorius, for he was a beacon of hope in a terrible time. And despite all his efforts the Saxon advance was a wall of slow-burning fire that left nothing but a cleansed emptiness behind it: Roman Britain was suffering a slow, terminal catastrophe.

The army came in a great column of thousands of men and as many horses. The foot soldiers yelled and struck their shields, the cavalry raised their slashing swords so they glinted in the low autumn sun, and the trumpeters blew their great *carynx* trumpets, slender tubes as tall as a man and adorned with dragons' mouths.

As the first of the booty wagons was hauled up the steep path toward the gate, Regina saw that it was piled high with

heads—the severed heads of Saxons, complete with long tied-
back hair and heavy mustaches, heads piled up like cabbages
on a stall, their rolled-up eyes white and their skin yellow-
white or even green. Behind the cart a prisoner walked, attached by a length of rope wrapped around his hands. He was
a big man with a golden torc around his neck. The skin of his
face was broken and caked with blood and dust. He had evidently been dragged all the way from the site of his defeat, for
he was staggering.

Women and children ran down the slope from the dunon,
anxious for news of their husbands, brothers, fathers. Regina
held her place, just outside the gate. It was like something out
of the past, she thought wonderingly, an army from four or five
or six centuries ago, the kind of force that must once have met
the Caesars.

And yet Artorius had made great changes. To those old
Celtae forces, fighting had been ritualistic. Armies would
draw up to face each other, would make a racket and an elaborate display, and only small teams of champions would be
sent to do battle together. And they couldn't sustain a long
campaign: Celtae armies, recruited from local farmers, had
been forced to disperse when the crops needed harvesting. All
that had had to change when the Romans had come with their
propensity for pitched battles with decisive outcomes: The
Celtae had quickly learned the techniques of long campaigns
and massed slaughter.

Now the Romans were gone, but their lessons lingered. Artorius had been assiduous. He had even picked Regina's brains
over what she could remember of Aetius's reminiscences of
the *comitatenses*. Now Artorius's warriors were an effective
and mobile fighting force, just as capable as the Romans of
waging a pitched battle—and of mounting a summer-long
campaign.

But Artorius's practices were increasingly laced with a
primitive darkness.

Regina knew the old beliefs, spouted by Myrddin and others. To take the head of your enemy was to possess his soul, so
when these Saxon heads were mounted on stakes around the
walls of the hill fort their souls would keep out danger. Regina
wasn't sure how much of this Artorius believed, but she could

see how he used its symbolism, working on both friend and foe, to cement his victories.

Regina lived with barbarians, and was the mistress of a warlord. But she could live with that until, as she always promised herself, things got back to normal, and the Emperor returned with his legions to sweep out the Saxon marauders, dissolve the petty native kingdoms—including Artorius's—and restore Roman dignity and order, so that this brief and bloody interval would come to seem no more than a bad dream.

Now here came the *riothamus* himself, at the head of his army.

At the gate, Artorius embraced Regina. He was hot, his armour scuffed, and she could smell the stink of his horse. "We have won great victories, my Morrigan. Everywhere the Saxons lie slain, or they run away at the sound of our trumpets. They are falling back to their fastnesses in the east, but perhaps next season—"

"Your deeds will live on for a thousand years, *riothamus*."

He cocked an eyebrow. "You sound like Myrddin. However I hear a 'but' in your voice . . ."

"But your collection of severed heads would have appalled Vespasian."

His face clouded. "The Caesars aren't here. They abandoned us to the Saxons. I do what I have to do. In fact—" Artorius turned speculatively, looking east, the direction of Europe and the rump of the Empire. "Perhaps, in fact, now that we are strong, we should be planning what to do about the Caesars and their betrayal of Britain."

She studied his face, alarmed, uncertain; she had never heard him talk of such plans before. But he was lost in his proliferating thoughts of future battlefields.

One of his lieutenants came to him. "We are ready for the show, *riothamus*."

The "show" was the execution of the Saxon chieftain. It was a triple murder, a sacrifice to the ancient Celtae veneration of the number three.

Artorius himself raised his axe, and slammed its blade into the back of the Saxon's head. But the man was not killed, and Artorius gave his limp form to his soldiers. Next a cord was tied around the Saxon's neck and tightened, by the twisting of a piece of wood, until the bones snapped. And finally, and most ignominiously, his face was pushed into a vat of water, so that he drowned. Regina couldn't tell how long the Saxon stayed alive, for the crowd of soldiers around him bayed and yelled.

Artorius grinned at Regina. "I wonder what your Caesars would have made of *this* . . ."

chapter 21

A week after her encounter with the mother-grandmother, Rosa sent Lucia out for a study day in a library in the Centro Storico area—not far from the Pantheon, in fact. Pina accompanied her.

The two of them had finished their day's work by three. They decided to take a walk toward the Tiber, and perhaps make for the gardens of the Villa Borghese, across the river. They set off along the Corso Vittorio Emanuele, heading west. It was a bright December afternoon, and they were walking into the sun.

The Centro Storico was the medieval heart of the city. It was enclosed by a great eastward bend of the Tiber. Rome's ancient core had always been the seven hills, where the great forums and palaces had been built. But after the collapse of the Empire, the ancient aqueducts had broken down, and the dwindling population of Rome had gravitated toward the river, seeking drinking water. The ruins in the area had provided building materials for houses, churches, and papal complexes. Later, as Renaissance families competed for power and prestige, the area had become cluttered with grandiose monuments, and it grew into a center for craft guilds, filled with *botteghe*, workshops. To some extent that was still true, Lucia saw as they walked down the Via dei Cestari, filled with shops selling clothes and equipment for the Catholic priesthood.

In the low, dazzling light, the streets swarmed with cars and the pavement was crowded with chattering schoolchildren, slow-strolling tourists, and office workers yelling into their cell phones. The crowd was purposeful, agitated, and continually noisy, and Lucia felt out of place.

"You aren't saying much." Pina walked beside her, bag

swinging at her shoulder, phone in her hand, sunglasses on her nose.

"I'm sorry. It's just all these *people*. It's the way they talk. Everybody is so intense—see the way their muscles are rigid—as if they are on the point of shouting the whole time. But what is it they are shouting about?"

Pina laughed. "You know, we're spoiled in the Crypt. We emerge as helpless as nuns evicted from their convents."

"I don't know." Lucia pointed to a group of three nuns in simple pale gray vestments. Chatting brightly in a small pavement café, they all wore sunglasses and expensive-looking trainers, their cell phones set among the cappuccinos before them. One wore a baseball cap over her wimple. Rome always seemed full of nuns, here to visit the Vatican, and perhaps to catch a glimpse of the pope, *El Papa*. *"They* seem all right."

Pina linked her arm through Lucia's. "Come on. When we get to the Villa Borghese I'll buy you an ice cream."

Lucia remained unhappy. As usual when out of the Crypt, she longed for its calm and order, where every direction she looked she would see a face like her own. But she knew that even back in the Crypt, even in her dormitory, she would have trouble finding peace. She was layered with secrets now—the painful mystery of her menstruation, Rosa's peculiar pursuit of her with her hints of an assignment to come—*secrets,* huge painful bewildering secrets, in a place where you weren't supposed to hold any secrets from those around you, not even the smallest.

Still, she was relieved when they reached the river, and the crowd thinned a little.

They crossed over the Vittorio Emanuele bridge and walked northeast, following the great curve of the Tiber. There were houseboats moored to the banks; Lucia saw people sunbathing, laid out over the boats' decks like drying fish.

The Villa Borghese was in an area where wealthy Romans had built their country estates since imperial times. It had been saved from the twentieth-century property developers when the state had bought it, and preserved it as a park. Lucia had always liked these gardens, with their winding paths and half-hidden flower beds; she and her sisters had been brought here when they were small. It was best to avoid the weekends, when

the population of Rome moved in here en masse, overwhelming the place with yelling children, chatting mothers, fathers
with radios clamped to their ears for soccer scores. Today,
though there were plenty of children, brought here by their
mothers after school, their shouting seemed remote and scattered.

Lucia and Pina found their way down to a little circular lake,
bounded by a path. On the edge of the water stood a small
temple, dedicated to the Greek god Aesculapius. They sat on a
wooden bench that had seen better days. People were rowing
on the lake, sending shimmering bow waves across the dense
green water and disturbing the reflection of the god's statue. It
was always a calming place, Lucia thought; she had been disappointed to find that the temple was only a reproduction. Pina
fulfilled her promise by buying an ice cream cone from a
cart—not very reputable looking, but drawn by a patient
horse, irresistible in his battered straw hat.

While they ate their ice cream, they watched a young woman
in Lycra jogging gear sitting near them, earnestly peering into
the tiny screen of her cell phone. She had a dog with her, a big,
aged, slow-moving Labrador. He meandered happily through
the dappled shade. But when he walked behind a set of rail-
ings he couldn't figure out his way back, and peered through
the bars at his owner, whining theatrically. His owner retrieved
him, comforting him with strokes and tugging at his collar.
But then, as she returned to her earnest texting, the dog would
wander off into his conceptual prison and begin his whining
once more, making Lucia and Pina laugh.

Lucia renewed the sunblock cream on her face, hands, and
arms. It had been less than an hour since her last application,
but even in the weak December afternoon sunlight her skin
prickled. Pina, however—cradling her phone in one hand—
took off her sunglasses, closed her eyes, and lifted her face
to the dipping sun. It was unusual for a woman of the Order to
have a skin able to tan. Lucia wondered how it would feel to
relax, to enjoy the sunlight on her face, without the need to
block it out.

Pina's face showed no signs of aging, no wrinkles or lines.
Her skin might have belonged to a seventeen-year-old. This
would baffle the *contadino* males, she knew; she had heard

young men whistle, or mutter, *"Ciao, bella,"* or *"Bella figura,"* after sisters of the Order old enough to be their mothers, and yet looking younger than they were. It was strange, Lucia supposed. But she had never thought about it before. There was much about life in the Order she hadn't questioned, hadn't even *noticed*, until the last few disruptive weeks. Perhaps it wasn't the outsiders who were strange, but the Order. After all, she thought, there are very many more of them than *us*. Perhaps she had become a kind of outsider herself, and was learning to look back at the Order through the eyes of a *contadino—*

"Excuse me."

She turned, peering into the sun. Pina snapped her sunglasses into place like a mask.

A man was standing before them—a young man, half silhouetted in the sun. He wore a blue Italy soccer shirt and jeans that looked as if they had been faded by time, not design. He carried a bundle of books under his arm. He was slim, and not tall, no taller than Lucia was. He had red hair, and his face had a weakish chin and a rounded profile, a smooth curve that proceeded from his long nose to his brow—which was high, she saw, and covered in freckles. He was young, perhaps not yet eighteen . . .

She was staring. She recognized him, of course. She dropped her gaze, hot.

"I'm sorry," he said. "I didn't mean to startle you. I just—"

Pina snapped, "Who are you?"

"My name is Daniel Stannard. I'm a student. I attend an expat college in the Trastevere. I'm studying for my bachelor's degree. My father is American . . ." He had an accent, a slightly singsong American intonation to his Italian.

Pina smiled. "Why should we care, Daniel Stannard? Have you a habit of bothering girls in the park?"

"No—no. It's just—" He turned to Lucia. "Haven't I seen you before?"

Pina laughed. "That's your best line?"

Lucia said, "Hush, Pina."

Daniel said, "I mean it. At the Pantheon—about a week ago, I think. I remember seeing you—I'm sure it was you—in the colonnade . . ."

"I was there," Lucia said.

Daniel hesitated. "I kept wondering if I'd see you again." He turned to Pina defiantly. "Yes, I know it's corny, but it's the truth."

Pina tried to stay stern, but she laughed. She muffled it with her hand.

Tentatively Daniel sat on the bench, next to Lucia. "So—you're sisters, right?"

"We're related, yes," said Pina.

"The lady you were with last week—who was that, your mother?"

"An aunt," said Pina.

"Kind of," Lucia said, and she was rewarded with a glare from Pina.

Pina said, "And you say you're a student?"

"Of politics, yes. My father's a diplomat here, with the American embassy. He's been stationed here for six years. He brought over the family to continue our schooling. I arrived age eleven . . ."

And so you are seventeen, Lucia thought. "Your language is good," she said.

"Thank you . . . My school was international, but most of the classes were in Italian. What do you do?"

"She's still at school," Pina snapped. "After that, the family business."

He shrugged. "Which is?"

"Genealogy. Record keeping. It's complicated."

Complicated, yes, thought Lucia. *Complicated like a web in which I'm tangled. And even the little you have just been told about me isn't true. For I am lined up for a new destiny—not genealogy or record keeping—something dark and heavy.*

She looked at Daniel. He had large, slightly watery blue eyes and a small upturned mouth that looked full of laughter. *He has already become at ease in two separate countries,* she thought, *while I have spent my life in a hole in the ground.* She had never thought of it that way before, but it was true. Suddenly she longed to have this boy's freedom.

In a silent moment of communication, she felt her inchoate emotions, of confusion and frustration, pulse through her body, and surely into her face, her eyes. *Help me,* she thought. *Help me.*

His blue eyes widened with surprise and dismay.

"We have to go," Pina said hurriedly. She got to her feet and grabbed Lucia's arm, pulling her upright. Before she knew what was happening Lucia was marched off along the circular path around the lake, toward one of the roads that cut through the park. As she walked Pina started texting urgently.

Daniel, startled, grabbed his books and clambered to his feet. "Your sister is kind of ferocious," he said, stumbling after Lucia.

"She's not my sister."

"Let me see you again."

"Why?"

"I don't know. Just to talk."

"I can't."

"The Piazza Navona," he said. "Tomorrow at three." Pina's pace had picked up almost to a run, and Daniel stopped chasing them.

Lucia looked back.

"I'll be there every day," he called. "At three, every day. Come when you can."

When they reached the Piazza le Flaminio, outside the park, a car was waiting for them.

Pina bundled Lucia inside. "Lucia, what were you thinking? He's a *contadino.* What did you want with him?"

"Something. Nothing," said Lucia defiantly. "I just wanted to talk to him. Aren't I supposed to be learning about outsiders?"

Pina leaned toward her. "You aren't," she said heavily, "supposed to be inviting them into your knickers."

"But I wasn't—I didn't mean—"

"Then what did you mean?"

"I don't know." Lucia buried her face in her hands. "Oh, Pina, I'm confused. Don't tell, Pina. Don't tell!"

chapter 22

Early the next spring Artorius traveled to Londinium. He asked Regina to travel with him. She in turn insisted that Brica accompany her.

At first Brica resisted the trip, even daring to refuse bluntly, for Regina's opposition to her liaison with Galba was now obvious. With patience and pressure Regina won her over. But the journey to the east along the old roads, with the two of them riding side by side in an open chariot just behind Artorius and his party, was silent and sullen.

The party approached a gateway, near a fort in the northwestern corner of the city's wall. The wall remained intact, though here and there it had undergone hasty repairs with great blocks of stone, no doubt scavenged from abandoned buildings. The fortress itself was manned, though not by troops answerable to the Emperor. Remarkably, many of the soldiers were Saxon mercenaries. According to Artorius, Saxon defectors from the Londinium garrison had played a big part in sparking the unrest and revolt among the wider Saxon population, once Vortigern had allowed them their toeholds in the east.

With the payment of a nominal toll, the party passed through the gate, and they were granted their first views of the city itself.

North of the dock area by the river, the center was a place of monumental buildings, many of which would have put Verulamium's best to shame. There were temples, bathhouses, triumphal arches, and great statues of copper and bronze set on columns. Once, it was said, the center had been dominated by a basilica greater than any of these survivors, but that had been long demolished. Regina's eye was drawn by stranger buildings, like nothing in Verulamium: blocks of tenements, some three or four stories high, in which the less splendid inhabitants of the city had once lived, each in a small cubicle. They looked oddly like ships, stranded on the hillsides of Londinium.

Brica, child of a hillside farm to whom the dunon of Caml was a metropolis, was subdued to wide-eyed silence.

But as they made their way through the city, Regina saw that most of the public buildings showed signs of neglect. The amphitheater, a bowl of rubble, had been turned into a market. One bathhouse had been systematically demolished, robbed of its stone: a child in a colorless smock clambered over the rubble, and Regina wondered if she had any idea what this strange, alien ruin had once been for. Most of the big tenement blocks had been abandoned, too. Evidently only a fraction of the number of people who had once dwelled in the city remained, and there was no need for them to cram themselves into the little cubicles anymore. Away from the central area, indeed, the city seemed depopulated. The buildings had been demolished or collapsed, and large areas were given over to pasture, even within the walls.

Still, Regina heard the muttering of Artorius's men as they peered up at the great buildings, and compared them with the huddled farmers who now raised their cattle in their shade. The city was the work of giants, they said, who must have passed away a hundred generations ago.

And there was still prosperity here. Among the ruins were town houses of recent construction, well maintained and brightly painted, their red-tiled roofs gleaming in the sunlight. Perhaps these belonged to *negotiatores*—traders and brokers. The more crowded streets close to the Forum were full of men and women in Roman garb, tunics and cloaks, and Regina stared at these reminders of her own vanished past. But most wore the trousers and woolen cloaks of the Celtae, or had the flowing hair and long mustaches of Germans.

As the imperial writ had declined over the rest of the diocese, Londinium had drawn in on itself, sheltering like a hedgehog behind its defensive walls. So far it had weathered the Saxon catastrophe that was overwhelming the rest of the country. Even now wealth still flowed through its harbors from trade with the continent; even now you could get rich here. Decayed it may be from its greatest days, but Londinium was still busy, prosperous, bustling, powerful—an arena for the ambitious. And that was why Artorius was here.

They had come to Londinium because the development of Artorius's ambitions had continued, despite all Regina's subtle discouragement. He seemed determined to mount an assault on Gaul, and then, perhaps, to march on Rome itself, to try for the purple as had Constantius and so many other British leaders before him.

It was a challenging ambition. Britain was far from united, the Saxons far from subdued. And for all his successes Artorius commanded only a fraction of the number of troops he would need for such an adventure, and would have to rely on allies. But, fired by a dozen victories over the Saxons, Artorius was determined. And so he was coming to Londinium for a council of British chiefs, magistrates, kings, and warlords, to see if he could shape a common intent. Regina was disturbed by this. The disaster that had followed Constantius's withdrawal of Britain's forces, she thought, should be obvious to everybody, and not an adventure to be emulated. But she was here, ostensibly supporting Artorius, in fact wary, uncertain of her own future.

The party reached the river, close to the site of another fort at the eastern corner of the wall. Londinium had once sprawled across both north and south banks of this great east-flowing river. In latter days, though, the settlement on the south side had declined. Today, to the south of the river there was nothing to be seen but farmsteads, low buildings, meandering cattle, threads of smoke. But a bridge still spanned the river, from north to south. It was an impressive sight, a series of broad semicircular arches, its roadway high enough to allow the passage of oceangoing ships.

Brica stared at the bridge openmouthed. She was muttering, "Lud, Lud . . ."

Regina touched her shoulder. "Are you all right?"

Brica turned, her pretty eyes blank. "It's the bridge. It's as if the river has been tamed, the mighty river itself. But this is the dun of Lud, the god of the water . . ."

"The Romans took to calling the city Augusta," said Regina

dryly. "It never caught on. But if there are such legends buried in a mere name, perhaps they were wise to try . . ."

She was disturbed. She didn't want her daughter's soul to be so primitive that she was astonished at the sight of a mere bridge. At least Regina remembered the villas and the towns as they had been. What next—would Brica's daughter in turn cower from thunderstorms, fearing the anger of the sky gods?

I must get her away from that place, the dunon, Regina thought with renewed determination. *And I must save her from Galba, and his mind like a sink of stupidity and superstition.*

Artorius had negotiated the use of a town house for himself, Regina and her daughter, and others of his party. The town house was the home of a particularly wealthy *negotiatore* called Ceawlin. A grossly fat man of about fifty, Ceawlin was of Welsh origin, but he spoke fluent Latin and Greek. Having risen to the top of Londinium society, such as it was, he seemed determined to expand his business interests on the continent, and had become one of Artorius's most significant backers.

But he troubled Regina. He clearly dismissed her as unimportant, a mere woman. In her presence he would let slip the mask of smiling beneficence he kept up before Artorius—and Regina saw the greed and calculation in his fat-choked eyes. His motivation was his own wealth and power, she saw immediately, and Artorius, this barbarian soldier-king, was no more than a means to an end.

While Regina was to be admitted to Artorius's councils, Brica was expected to stay with Ceawlin and his household. But she was unhappy—and loathed Ceawlin on sight. "They laugh at me," she groused. "These pretty children and their vapid mother. They laugh at the way I speak, and the clothes I wear, and the way I do my hair. But I bet not one of them could strangle a chicken or gut a pig. And that Ceawlin makes my skin crawl; he stinks of piss, and he stands so *close* . . ."

Once Regina herself had been like Ceawlin's spoiled daughters, she thought, and would have laughed just as much at a girl from an old hill fort. She embraced her sturdy, bronzed daughter. "I'm proud of you," she said. "And anyhow it won't be for long." She was sure that was true—she was becoming

convinced she was nearing an end game with Artorius—
though she didn't yet know how that end game would play out.

And at the same time she faced another problem.

It had become obvious to both Brica and Galba that Regina
opposed their union. Regina was so powerful that Galba and
his family did not dare stand up to her, and Brica herself had
so far stopped short of open rebellion. But Regina knew that
could not last forever. Just as Artorius's ambitions were over-
weening, so Brica's frustration, as the years flowed steadily by,
was becoming overpowering.

In both areas of Regina's life a crisis was approaching, then.
She had no clear idea how she would handle these twin is-
sues—not yet. But this Londinium trip would surely be useful.
It would let her gauge the seriousness of Artorius's ambitions;
and it would buy her a little time by taking Brica away from
Galba for a while.

And perhaps, in Britain's greatest city, other opportunities
would open up. Before setting out, with no clear intention in
mind, she had taken the three *matres*, her deepest symbol of
family, carefully wrapped them in her softest cloth, and
lodged them in her luggage.

Artorius held his war council in Ceawlin's reception room. It
was a large, well-appointed chamber, but it was crowded, for it
held no less than ten petty kings and their advisers.

Regina quickly got to know a few of these ambitious warlords. Aside from Ceawlin, two struck her as significant.

One was a very young man, barely twenty it seemed, who
called himself Ambrosius Aurelianus. In his shining body
armor he was a slab of muscle and determination, and it
seemed to Regina that he would follow Artorius wherever he
asked—and perhaps, on Artorius's inevitable death, take up
Chalybs and wield that mighty sword himself against the
Saxon hordes.

The other was a thin, intense man called Arvandus. He was
actually an official of the Roman Empire, a prefect in the troubled, half-dislocated province of Gaul. But his ambition was
clearly to rule not in the Emperor's name but in his own right.
Regina fretted that because he had already betrayed one ruler,

in the Emperor, he would likely have few qualms in betraying another.

Artorius, in his zeal and passion, seemed to have no idea that such complexities might be brewing among his nominal followers, that these men were not like the loyal soldiers with whom he had fought side by side, but men with their own goals and ambitions, even their own dreams: In Artorius's blindness Regina felt she saw his destiny clearly shaped.

They spent much time discussing the tactical situation across the country. Information was patchy, the situation complex. Though the Saxons were unified in their hostility to the British and the Roman legacy, they were not a politically coordinated force, and their advances were opportunistic and scattered. Meanwhile the British response was equally fragmentary.

"But what is sure," said Artorius grimly, "is that there isn't a blade of grass east of Londinium that isn't now in Saxon hands. And time is short . . ."

He described the Saxons' destruction of the town of Calleva Atrebatum. They had not just slaughtered or driven off the population, not just plundered and burned down the remaining buildings; the Saxons had also hurled blocks of building stone down the wells, so the site of the town could never be reoccupied. It was an erasure, systematic and deliberate.

"And by such acts they are erasing our will as well as our towns," Artorius said. "We still far outnumber the Saxon settlers. But in some parts you feel as if the Saxons have won already. While the old elite flee to Armorica, I've seen farmers give up their lands to the Saxons without a fight. But if they think the Saxons will welcome them, they've another think coming. For the Saxons don't want *us*, we British! Oh, no. The Saxons just want our country. And if we don't oppose them now—it may take them decades, but in the end they will kill us or push us out, bit by bit, until we are banished from the land that was once ours, our only refuge in the rough lands to the west and north. And the worst of it is, nobody will even realize it's happening . . ."

Now Arvandus said, his heavily accented voice as thick as oil, "Perhaps we should wait for the response to our plea to the *magister militum.*"

Regina had seen a copy of this letter to the Roman military commander in Gaul. "To the thrice consul, the groans of the British . . . The barbarians drive us to the sea and the sea drives us back to the barbarians. Between these two types of death we are either slaughtered or drowned . . ." It had given her hope that such a missive had been sent to the Roman authorities, even if it was stated in such ludicrous terms.

"If the *magister* were going to reply," Ceawlin said, "he would have done so by now. There will be no help from Rome. Besides, they are too busy facing the Huns."

"Then we should try again," Regina said.

Every head swiveled. She was the only woman here, save for the servants.

She said, "We will not defeat barbarians by acting like barbarians. We must ensure we maintain our alliance with the civilized world. That is the only way things will ever return to normal."

Ceawlin laughed. "*Normal!* Woman, what is *normal*? It is a generation since Constantius. There are children—adults—all across Britain now who have never heard a word of Latin . . ."

"The Empire has lasted a thousand years," she said calmly. "We can wait a thousand days for the *magister* to reply."

Artorius shook his head angrily. "I will crawl to no *magister*, in Gaul or Rome or anywhere else. This is our island. We will defend it, and we will build it anew—not the Roman way, not the Saxon way, but *our* way."

There was a silence; none of them seemed sure how to respond.

Artorius stood. "We will break. Eat, bathe, sleep—with your kindness, Ceawlin." The fat *negotiatore* nodded his head. "We will talk later."

After the meeting broke up Artorius came to Regina and led her to a quiet corner of Ceawlin's colonnaded courtyard, away from the others. "Why do you betray me?" he demanded in a sharp whisper. "I found you in your wretched scraping on the hillside and made you what you are. I brought you into this council. Why will you not support me before the others?"

"Because I don't agree with you," she said. "The adventure you are planning in Gaul. Your drive for the purple—"

His eyes narrowed. "Are you worried that I will make the mistake of Constantius, and drain the island of its strength?"

She tried to explain how she felt. "Yes, there is that. But there is more. I think you are being—seduced. Your war against the Saxons is justified, because it is clear that given the chance they would kill every one of us, and fill our island with their own bawling, blond-haired brats.

"But now you are talking of fighting for its own sake. I think to you war as an adventure, a great game. But this is no game of 'soldiers,' Artorius. The tokens you spend are not stones or beads of glass. They are men—humans, each with a soul, an awareness, as bright and vivid as yours or mine."

He looked at her blankly. "Regina—"

"Your soldiers believe there were better people in the past," she said, "who built the great ruins at which they gawp. I wonder if people will be better in the future. Perhaps our remote grandchildren will understand the sanctity of life, and to them using the lives of others, as if they were of no more consequence than bits of stone, will be as unthinkable as for me to pluck out my own heart."

"But until that happy day, we flawed mortals must get along as best we can," said Artorius dryly. "How do you think the Empire itself was built, save through war? How do you think its peace was kept for so long, save through endless war?" He grinned. "And—Regina, if it is a game it is a marvelous game. The world is an arena for the ambitious, and the prize for victory is no petty favor from a stadium crowd. What else is life for?"

"Once you prized my strength of character," she said. "My defiance."

"But now you are starting to irritate me, my Morrigan." He stepped closer to her, his face even. "Do not oppose me tomorrow."

When he had gone she stood for a time, in the cool shade of the colonnade, thinking through her problems. Artorius was determined on this course, a course that must lead him to disaster. And then there was Brica with her moon-faced barbarian boy.

Both her problems had a single solution.

It is time, she told herself. She must not go back to the

dunon. Perhaps she had anticipated this decision, for she had after all packed the *matres*, the heart of her home. The decision made, all that remained was to work out how to achieve her new goal.

And yet, standing here, she felt suddenly old, and weak, and tired. Must she do this? Must she uproot herself again, build yet another life? And would she have to fight even her own daughter to do it? But she knew there was no choice, not anymore.

As it happened, an opportunity to get what she wanted showed itself before the next council.

Ceawlin sought her out in her small chamber. Standing in the doorway, his bulk seemed to fill the room.

"I saw the tension between you and the *riothamus*," he said evenly. "If I can help—"

She eyed him, calculating, wondering what motives had brought him here. "Perhaps you can. I need passage."

"Passage? Where?"

She took a breath. "Rome."

"Why do you want to go to Rome?"

"To find my mother."

He gazed at her, his eyes invisible behind layers of fat. "You fear Artorius. You think he is leading us all to disaster. You, specifically."

"My relationship with Artorius isn't your concern. Can you get me a passage?"

He shrugged massively. "I am a *negotiatore*. I can provide anything—for a price." He considered. "Come with me."

He walked with her out of the house and along the line of the wall beside the river, heading west toward the bridge.

After a short time they came to the docks. A massive series of timber quays and waterfronts had been constructed in the shadow of the bridge. Behind the quayside was a row of warehouses, and behind them, as Ceawlin pointed out to her, was a district of workshops. There was a handful of boats in the quays. Most of them were small, but one was larger, with bright green sails furled against its masts.

"Here is the heart of Londinium. Goods from the heart of the Empire flow into these wharfs and warehouses, and our goods flow out. The workshops house crafstmen—shipwrights, carpenters, metalworkers, leatherworkers—to service the ships, and to process the trade goods. Once British wheat fed half the western Empire, and our metal clad the mighty armies that held Gaul. Now the port is much declined, of course. But there is still a profit to be made," he said, patting his belly complacently.

"Why have you brought me here, Ceawlin?"

He leaned close, so she could feel his breath on her ear; there was a stink of urine about him. "To see that green-sailed ship. It belongs to the Empire. It is bound for the coast of Spain—and from there, my note of credit will buy you passage to Rome itself. Once you are out of British waters, away from the raiding Germans, the sailing is safe."

"How much?"

"More than you can pay," he said lightly, as if it were a joke. "I know that you are a creature of Artorius, with no wealth of your own. There is nothing you own that I could want—your pathetic bits of jewelry are of little value . . ."

"Then why are we talking?"

"I do have other—ah, needs. Call it an appetite, perhaps." He lifted his hand to her breast. He pinched her through the layers of her clothes, hard; his hands felt strong despite their pudginess.

She closed her eyes. "So that's it. You disgust me."

"That hardly concerns me," he said.

"How do I know you won't betray me? Take what you want and—"

"—and leave you stranded here? Because I would be stranded, too. And you would no doubt go to Artorius, who would no doubt have me killed." He winked at her. "Of course you could do that now. Oh, you see, you already have the upper hand in our negotiation. I am a poor businessman!"

She nodded. "What now?"

He eyed her with an intensity she hadn't experienced since Amator. "Perhaps you could grant me a little on account." He began to pull up his tunic.

So there, in the shadow of the river wall, she knelt before him. His crotch stank of stale urine. As he grew excited he began to thrust, threatening to choke her.

"But it is not you I want," he said, gasping. "Not a fat old sow like you. *Your daughter.* That is the bargain, lady Regina. Send me Brica. If not I will risk the wrath of Artorius himself . . ." He grabbed her head and pushed her face into his crotch. *"Aah."*

Artorius faced his council. He was naked, save only for an iron torc around his neck, made for him by Myrddin. He had shaved his body, and the hair on his head was thickened with limewash so it stood up in great spikes from his head. This was how his ancestors had met Julius Caesar, he believed, and how he would challenge the latest holder of the purple.

His council gazed at him, frozen in shock. In the stony expressions of men like Ceawlin, Regina saw veiled amusement, even contempt. Only young Ambrosius Aurelianus stared at this savage, antique figure with something like awe.

You fool, Artorius, she thought.

Artorius said, "Many centuries ago—so the bards say—a great host of those the Romans call barbarians, the Celtae, thrust across Europe and burned down Rome itself. There were British among them—so it is said. What can be done once will be done again . . ."

He was calling for a great rising of the Celtae—for their culture had been swept aside, he argued, first by the Caesars and now by the Christian popes. It would be a campaign to free Britain and Europe once and for all from the yoke of Rome. And he would do that by taking Rome for himself.

"Some accuse me of seeking the purple," Artorius said now. "The mantle of the Emperor. But I seek the mantle, not of the Caesars, but of Brutus and Lear and Cymbeline, the forefathers of Britain. And the gods who will protect me are not the Christ and His father, but the older gods, the true gods, Lud and Coventina and Sulis and the triple mothers . . ."

Ceawlin maneuvered himself close to Regina. There was a faint stink of urine even now.

Regina closed her eyes. His stink made her gorge rise, as it had done that day by the river wall. And yet she must put that aside, and think with the clarity for which she prayed daily to the *matres.*

Brica would be harmed by her contact with this fat pig. But

the family would be harmed more badly if she sat by while Artorius submitted himself to his suicidal venture, and all he had built was cast to the winds, all the protection she had carefully accrued dissipated. Brica was the most precious person in the world to her. But together they were family. And the family, its continuity into the future, was of more importance than any individual.

There was only one choice.

She whispered to Ceawlin, "One condition. Don't make her pregnant."

Ceawlin sat back, and the stink of him receded a little.

Artorius had done talking now. His colleagues—those who would follow him across Europe, and those who would betray him before he walked out of this room—cheered and yelled alike.

chapter 23

Lucia took a bus to the Venezia. From there it was a short walk to the Piazza Navona. She took a seat at an open-air café and sipped an iced tea. It was a bright January day.

The Piazza was a long, rectangular space surrounded by three- and four-story buildings. The square was crammed with street painters and vendors selling bags and hats and bits of jewelry from suitcases. There were no less than three fountains here. The one at the center was the *Fountain of the Four Rivers*, four great statues to represent the Ganges, the Danube, the Plate, and the Nile. When she was small Lucia had wondered why the Nile statue was blindfolded; it was because when the statue was created the source of the Nile had still been a mystery.

This pretty piazza was one of her favorite places in Rome. She wondered how Daniel could have guessed that. Then she decided she was being foolish; it was just coincidence. She glanced at her watch: a quarter past three. She sipped her tea and, masked by her blue glasses, flinched from the speculative stares of the passing boys and men.

Of course she had no right to expect him to be here. It had been three weeks since that chance meeting by the lake, and even that, contaminated by Pina's hostility, had only lasted a few minutes.

She was pretty sure Pina hadn't told any of the *cupola* what had happened before the Temple of Aesculapius. But since then Pina had found a reason to accompany Lucia every time she left the Crypt. For the first few days she had even followed Lucia to the bathroom. On her last trip out, though, Pina, busy with other chores, had let her go alone. Perhaps Pina had relaxed a little. Lucia hadn't dared do anything that day. Today, however, she had again managed to leave the Crypt's above-ground offices without Pina seeing her, as far as she could tell. And so Lucia had taken the chance.

But she had wasted her time. Twenty past three. This was stupid. She began to collect together her bag, the magazine she had spread on the table for cover. Maybe it was for the best, she thought. After all, if this boy had turned up, what could she possibly have said to him? And besides—

"Hi." He was standing before her, no sunglasses this time, that high forehead glistening with sweat. "I'm sorry I'm late. The damn bus broke down and I had to run."

She was sitting there, foolishly clutching her bag.

He sat down. "But you know what? I wasn't worried. I told myself that the Law of Sod wouldn't let me down. Today was the one day in three weeks I am late, so today is the day you would come . . ." He grinned. "Sorry."

She put her bag down under her seat, and in doing so nearly knocked over her iced tea. Daniel had to grab it. "Don't apologize," she said. Even her voice sounded awkward. "I'm the one who should be sorry. It's me who hasn't turned up for three weeks."

"You had no reason to. You don't know me." He looked more serious. "Anyhow, I know you have difficulties. That bulldog of a sister of yours is very protective."

"It's not as simple as that," she said defensively.

He studied her, his blue eyes wide.

A waiter in white shirt and bow tie slid past their table with menus. Daniel quickly ordered more iced tea for them both. The waiter smiled at them, and moved a little bowl of dried flowers from a neighboring table.

"How about that. He thinks we're on a date."

"We can't be on a date," she said clumsily.

He raised his eyebrows. "We can't?"

"For one thing I'm only fifteen."

"Okay," he said, nodding. She thought he was masking disappointment, repositioning. "We can still be friends, can't we? Even if you're just fifteen."

"I guess so."

He glanced around the square, breaking the slight tension. "Look at that. It's January, and they're still stocking Befana dolls." There was a stall stocked with them next to an old painted wooden merry-go-round, around which small children clustered.

Befana was the sister of Santa Claus. She wore a kerchief and glasses, and carried a broom. She had missed the Three Wise Men on their way to visit the baby Jesus. In recompense she brought presents for good Italian children on the twelfth day of Christmas—and for the bad ones, bits of coal.

"To me she looks kind of like a witch," Daniel said.

"You don't have Befana in America?"

"No. I grew up with the Coca-Cola Santa Claus. But that was okay."

"We always had Befana, without Santa." It was true. Christmas was celebrated in the Crypt; there were great mass parties in the theaters and meeting halls where the age groups would mingle, and games and competitions would be played. And there were presents, toys and games and clothes, even bits of jewelry, cosmetics, and clothes, commercially bought, for the older ones. But Befana, a woman, was the central figure, not Christ or Santa, and the great celebration was always on Twelfth Night, the Feast of the Epiphany.

The waiter delivered their tea.

Daniel said, "You mentioned *we*? You mean your family? Let's see. There's you, and Pina, and your aunt from the Pantheon . . ."

"More than that." She managed a smile. "We're a *big* family."

He smiled back. "It's nice to see you look a little less worried. So, your family. What do your parents do?"

How could she answer that? *I've never spoken to my father. My mother is a hundred years old . . .* There was so much she could tell him; there was nothing she could tell him. He was, after all, a *contadino*.

He saw her hesitating, and began, smoothly, to tell her of his own upbringing. His father, as he'd told her, was a diplomat who had had a series of postings with NATO and the American diplomatic corps, culminating in his nine years in Italy. Daniel had seen a lot of the world, especially in his early years, and had decided he wanted to study politics himself.

"I always liked this square," he said.

"Me, too."

"It's got the kind of depth of history I like about Europe. I know that's an obvious thing for an American to say."

"Well, I never met an American before."

Reassured, he said, "It's built on a stadium, put up by the Emperor Domitian. Did you know that? The stadium fell into ruin, and the stones were hauled off to make houses and churches and whatnot. But the foundations were still here, and the houses were built on top of them, so the square keeps the original shape of the racetrack." He shook his head. "I love that. People living for two thousand years in the ruins of a sports stadium. It gives you a sense of continuity—of depth. Do you know what I mean?"

"I think so," she said seriously. She felt baffled by his rapid-fire speech. How could she match such perceptions? She felt stupid, malformed, a child; she was afraid to open her mouth for fear of making a fool of herself.

He rambled to a halt, and looked at her shyly. "Hey, I'm sorry."

That made her laugh. "You are always apologizing. What are you sorry for now?"

"Because I'm boring you. I'm a seventeen-year-old bore. My brother says this is why I'll never get a girl. I always lecture them. I'm full of *bullshit*." He used the English word. "But it's just that I think about this stuff so hard. It just comes out . . . You know, you're beautiful when you laugh. And you're also beautiful when you are serious. It's true. I think we should always say what's true, don't you? That's what I noticed about you in the Pantheon. Your skin is pale, but there is a kind of translucence about it . . ."

She could feel her cheeks burn, something warm move inside her. "I like your seriousness. We should be serious about the world."

"So we should." He was watching her. The light was fading a little now, and his face seemed to float in the glow of the lights from the café's interior. "But not serious all the time. Something's troubling you, isn't it?"

She looked away sharply. "I can't say."

"Okay. But it's something to do with your sister, and your aunt . . . Your mysterious family."

She folded and unfolded her fingers. "It's a matter of duty."

"Are they trying to get you to do something you don't want to do? What—an arranged marriage of some kind? I've heard of that in southern Italian families." He was fishing.

"I can't say anything." She didn't even know herself.

Suddenly he covered her hand with his. "Don't be upset."

His skin was hot, his grip firm; she felt the touch of his palm on the back of her fingers. "I'm not upset."

"I don't know what to say to you." He withdrew his hand; the air felt cold. "Look, you may or may not believe it, but I've no designs on you. You're a beautiful girl," he said hastily. "I don't mean that. Anybody would find you beautiful. But—there's something about you that draws me in. That's all. And now I'm a little closer to you, I can see there's something hurting in there. I want to help you."

Suddenly the intensity of the moment overwhelmed her. "You can't." She stood up.

"Where are you going?"

"To the bathroom."

He was crestfallen. "You won't come back."

"I will." But, she found, she wasn't sure if she would.

"Here." He produced a business card from a pocket. "This is my cell number. Call me if you need anything, anything at all."

She held the card between thumb and forefinger. "I'm only going to the bathroom."

He smiled weakly. "Well, in case you get lost on the way. Put it in your bag. Please."

She smiled, slipped it into her bag, and moved into the shop. When she glanced back she could see his face, his blue eyes following her.

In the event, she didn't even make it as far as the bathroom.

They converged on her, Pina on one side, Rosa on the other. They grabbed her arms. Rosa's face was set and furious, but Pina seemed more regretful. They immediately began to march her out toward an open door at the back of the shop. There was absolutely nothing Lucia could do about it.

Lucia said to Pina, "You promised you wouldn't tell."

"I didn't promise anything. You made me think you were over this stupid crush."

"You followed me."

"Yes, I followed you."

They passed into the street, and Lucia found herself bundled into a car. Lucia couldn't even see if Daniel was still watching. She would never know, she thought, if she would have gone back to him.

"Pina was right to call me," Rosa said. "I'm glad somebody has some sense."

Lucia shouted, "Can't you leave me alone?"

"No," Rosa said simply.

"I just wanted to see him. I was curious."

"Really? Curious about what, Lucia? Where did you think this little liaison would lead? Do you really have a crush on this boy, this Daniel? But you've only just met him. Do you want to fall in love? Do you want romance so badly that you'll approach a perfect stranger——"

"Stop it," Lucia said. She tried to hide her face in her hands.

But Rosa wouldn't let up. "Listen to me. You are part of the Order. In the Order, there is no room for love or romance. In the Order, efficiency is everything."

Lucia, forced to look at her, tried to understand what she was saying. "Efficiency in what?"

"In relationships. In reproduction. I'm talking about the demands of survival, Lucia. Do you think the Order would have lasted so long if it had allowed its members to follow the random dictates of *love*?"

Lucia didn't understand any of this, but she felt a deep horror creep over her.

Pina, too, looked shocked. "You shouldn't be saying this, Rosa," she said in a small voice.

Rosa sat back. "It's the last time I will allow you out of the Crypt. The last time, do you hear? If I have to bell you like a cat . . ."

Lucia, released, turned away.

If she tried hard she could imagine the warmth of his hand on hers. When she thought about that she could feel heat in her lips and eyes, and a hot tautness across her breasts, and her skin tingled under her clothes, and there was a deep burning at the pit of her belly. In the dismal, silent interior of this car, despite the cold severity of Rosa beside her, she had never felt more alive. Rosa hadn't won.

And she still had Daniel's card in her bag.

chapter 24

As their long sea journey drew to a close, despite the tension between them, Regina and Brica crowded together at the prow of the small ship, hungry for their first glimpse of Italy.

The early-morning air was already hot and dense, and the salt smell of the sea was exotic. The crew called coarsely to each other as they pursued their bewildering tasks, adjusting the ship's green sails as it approached the shore. This was just a small cargo craft dedicated to transporting jewelry, fine pottery, and other expensive and low-bulk wares, and the ship creaked as it rolled. But to the women, now veterans of an ocean crossing from Britain, the tideless rolling of the Mediterranean was as nothing.

It was Brica who saw the lighthouse first. "Ah, look . . ." It loomed over the horizon long before the land itself was visible, a fist of concrete and masonry thrusting defiantly into the misty air. Soon afterward a great concrete barrier came into view, cutting across the horizon. This was the wall of the harbor, one of two huge jutting moles. The ship was steered easily toward the break between the moles, and sailed past the lighthouse.

The lighthouse was centuries old. It had been constructed, like the port itself, by the Emperor Claudius, who had conquered Britain. But though its concrete fascia was weathered and cracked, it surely stood as solid and intimidating as the day it was constructed. As she passed, Regina could see how it was founded on a sunken ship, whose outlines were dimly visible through the murky, litter-strewn water. The story was that this great vessel had been built to transport an obelisk from Egypt, and then filled with concrete and deliberately sunk. The huge old lighthouse loomed over the ship, utterly dwarf-

ing it. But the crew seemed oblivious to its presence, and
Regina tried not to cower.

Inside the harbor, the water was a little calmer—but this
harbor was so vast it was itself like an enclosed sea. Ships of
all sizes cut across its surface. Most of them were wallowing
cargo ships, decorated with the dark green of the imperial
navy: grain transporters, scores arriving here every day from
Italy and Africa. The seamanship required to maneuver these
huge ships in such cramped and crowded conditions impressed Regina, and there was much mocking rivalry between
the crews as they hailed each other across the narrow strips of
water between their vessels.

Regina's ship passed through this crowd and approached another concrete-walled entrance at the far end of the harbor.
When they passed through, Regina found herself in yet another harbor, much smaller, a landlocked inner basin. It was
octagonal in form and was lined with wharves and jetties,
where ships nuzzled to unload their cargo. This harbor within
a harbor had been constructed by the emperors to provide a
port close to Rome capable of taking large oceangoing ships
in all conditions. A canal had been cut from here to the Tiber,
and grain and other goods were carried on smaller freshwater
vessels to Rome itself. The engineering was mighty. This inner
harbor alone could have swallowed the whole of Verulamium
or Durnovaria, and the port complex would probably have
drowned Londinium. But it was necessary; the flow of grain
into the city could not be allowed to fail, no matter what the
weather.

As the ship nuzzled toward a jetty, Regina tried to ignore the
fluttering in her stomach. Already, long before reaching Rome
itself, she was beginning to feel overwhelmed by the sheer
scale of it all. Here in this bright, liquid Italian air, Britain
seemed a remote, murky, underpopulated, undeveloped place,
and everything she knew, all she had built, seemed petty indeed.

But she did not have time to be overwhelmed. She had a
tablet on which was scrawled an address: that of Amator, the
rogue son of Carausias, the last legacy of that stubborn old
man. That address was where she would begin her Roman ad-

venture—and where, she thought coldly, Amator would begin to pay back the debt he owed her.

Standing at the prow of the ship she raised herself to a fuller height. As Artorius had said, once this great city had been overwhelmed by the Celtae, her people. And indeed, only decades before, it had suffered its first sacking at barbarian hands in eight centuries. *I have nothing to fear of Rome,* she thought. *Let Rome fear me.*

They landed safely, and their few scraps of luggage were briskly off-loaded. Regina's first steps were unsteady. After so many days at sea, it felt odd to walk on a surface that did not swell under her. The land behind the wharves was crowded with warehouses and manufactories. Great machines, powered by slave muscles, were used to off-load the grain into giant granaries. Spanish oil, Campanian wine, and many other goods came in amphorae, carried by dockworkers who filed back and forth from ship to shore like laboring ants. The bustle, noise, and sense of industry was overwhelming.

There were plenty of *negotiatores* to be found at the quaysides. It did not take Regina long to secure a carriage that would take them to Rome itself.

The road to Rome cut across marshy farmland, studded with olive groves and red-tiled roofs of villas. The road was crowded with pedestrians: great files of people plodded to and from the port, their heads and shoulders and backs laden with crates and sacks. Carriages, chariots, and horseback riders picked their way through the crowds. They passed strings of way stations, and vendors competed to sell food, water, footwear, and clothing to the passing traffic.

Regina checked the contents of her purse. "That's nearly the last of Ceawlin's money."

Brica peered down glumly at the throng. "I hope you thought it was worth it," she said coldly.

"Yes, it was worth it," Regina said. "It was worth it because we had no choice. Listen to me, Brica. I'm not sure what waits for us in Rome. It will surely be another challenge—as great as I faced on the hill farm when you were born, or when we were taken to Artorius's dunon. We will overcome it. But we must support each other. And we must lance this festering sore between us. Remember how I saved you from the Saxon. I risked my life—"

"Yes, you saved me from the Saxon. But that was long ago, far away. I don't know what's happened to you since then, Mother. I don't know what you have become."

"Brica—"

"I am your daughter, your only child," Brica said tonelessly. "I am the future, for you. I am everything. That's how it should be. Perhaps that was once true. But *you*, you have destroyed my life, bit by bit. You took me away from Bran, and then from Galba, who made me happy, and with whom I wanted to have children of my own. And then you sold me to that pig of a *negotiatore*."

Regina grimaced. She had never told her daughter how she, too, had been used by Ceawlin. "I had no choice."

"There is always a choice. I think your mind has died, or your heart—"

Regina grabbed her by the chin and forced her head around. "Enough. *Look at me.*"

Brica resisted, but she had never had her mother's physical strength. Her head turned, and her eyes, smoky gray like Regina's, met her mother's.

Regina said, "Do you think you are the only one who has made sacrifices? You *are* precious to me—so precious. If I could save you from harm I would. But there is something more precious still, and that is the family. If we had stayed in Britain while Artorius got himself killed posturing on the battlefields of Europe, we would not have survived him for long. And if you had married Galba, your children would have been farmers, their minds dissolving in the dirt, and within two generations, three, they would have remembered nothing of what they once were—"

"But they would exist," Brica snapped. "*My* children. Mother, it was my choice, not yours." She pulled her face away. "And now you're looking for your own mother, who abandoned you all those years ago. Whether or not she lives, you are selfish and morbid. Your relationship with your mother no longer matters. *You do not matter.* All that matters is me, for my womb is not yet dry, like yours. The future is mine—"

"No. The future is the family." *And even you, my beautiful child,* Regina thought sadly, *are only a conduit to that future.*

Regina's determination was strong, clear, untroubled. She was dismayed, she admitted to herself, by the iron coldness she saw in Brica. It was as if the recent events had crushed the life and warmth out of her—and thoroughly wrecked her relationship with her mother. Well, a lifelong battle with Brica would be hard, but Regina was used to hardships, and to overcoming them.

And it wasn't as if Brica could get away. Ironically the narrowness of her upbringing on the farmstead and the dunon, against which Regina had always railed, now left her stranded and baffled away from her home ground; Brica couldn't leave Regina's side no matter how much she wanted to.

Now they were both distracted, for they approached the city itself.

Ahead, the air was striped with a thick layer of orange-yellow: the cumulative smoke from thousands of fires and lanterns, not yet dispersed in the morning light. On the horizon Regina glimpsed aqueducts, immense structures that strode across the landscape, imposing straight-line geometries of astonishing lengths. There were ten of them, she knew, ten artificial rivers to water a city of more than a million souls. As they neared the city, gaudy mausoleums sprouted beside the roadway. Citizens were allowed to inter bodies only outside the city walls, so routes out of the city became lined with sarcophagi. And around the cemeteries of the rich crowded the remains of the poor, the ashes of cremations stored in amphorae stuck in the ground, only their necks protruding into the air.

"The scale of it, even of their dead, is astounding," Regina murmured.

Their driver turned to grin at her. He must have been more than sixty years old, and a single tooth stood like a stump in his mouth. He spoke a coarse country Latin she found it hard to make out.

Brica said, "What was that?"

"He welcomed us to the *caput mundi*. To the head of the world . . ."

They fell silent, each locked into her own thoughts, as the carriage wound its way along the crowded road.

Rome was dominated by mud brick and red tiles. But at its heart were the Capitoline and Palatine Hills with their great palaces and temples, like a floating island of gleaming marble. Regina thought she glimpsed the curving wall of the Flavian Amphitheater, astoundingly huge, like a house for giants.

But as the carriage approached the center of the city it entered a maze of streets, and the wider view was lost. The closer they got to the center the more crowded the buildings were, and the taller they seemed to grow; they were rickety heaps of wattle, daub, and crimson-red tiles, two, three, four stories high, like unhealthy plants competing for light. In some places these *insulae*, islands, were so closely packed together that their balconies touched, shutting out the sky altogether. The stink was overwhelming, of rotting sewage, cooking food. And the noise of the city seemed to engulf Regina, a constant clamorous racket. It was the noise of a million people, she thought, a million voices joining into one great unending roar, and as they penetrated deeper into this crowded, unplanned maze, Regina felt as if she were becoming lost in a great formless sea of people.

Brica grew even quieter, receding into herself. Probably, Regina thought, in the last hour her daughter had seen more strangers' faces than she had seen before in her entire life.

On the driver's recommendation they were brought to a restaurant. The owner, who happened to be the driver's brother-in-law, also owned some of the apartments in the block above the restaurant, and the driver had promised he would rent the women a room.

Set on a street crowded with shops, the restaurant occupied the block's ground floor. It was a low-roofed, well-lit place: people sat on benches at the front, eating snacks and drinking wine as they watched the bustle of the street. Regina glimpsed marble counters on which samples of dishes were displayed, and behind them was a green-lit central atrium, set with more tables.

From the outside the *insula* actually had an attractive appearance, with its roof of terra-cotta tiles, its stucco facade

decorated with tiles and small mosaic images. Balconies of
wood and brick projected from each story, and potted plants
were set on each one. But the apartments were small and
cramped, and got steadily worse as you climbed the stairs. And
Regina's and Brica's, on the topmost floor, must have been the
worst of all.

The windows were covered with sheets of bark. The only
furniture was two beds fixed to the wall, some shelving and
cupboards, and a few stools and low tables. There was a brazier for heating and an open stove for cooking, appliances
Regina immediately vowed she would use sparingly, for she
was convinced that they would set the *insula* and the whole
district on fire, and would be the death of them both. Even in
this cramped setting their few belongings, homemade at the
dunon, looked pathetic and provincial. But Regina unpacked
the three *matres* and set up an improvised *lararium* in one corner of the room.

Even up here the smells from the restaurant reached them,
and soon they were both very hungry. Regina ventured back
down the stairs. The menu food was predominantly cooked
meat, highly spiced with pepper and fish sauce and garlic—
but she didn't have the money to spare. She went out to the
street stalls and bought a little bread and salted meat, and a
small pitcher of wine.

While she was gone Brica waited for her, curled up on her
couch with her knees tucked into her chest. When Regina returned, Brica didn't seem to have moved at all.

In their cramped room they ate their bread, trying to ignore
the enticing smells from below. Regina left a little of their
poor bread and wine for the goddesses of the family, who sat
squat in their corner of this strange, unpleasant little room.

In the days that followed, they tried to settle in.

The restaurant had connections to the water supply from the
aquifers and to the main sewers. The apartments above did
not. Every day you had to fetch your water from a fountain a
couple of streets away, where there was always a queue. And
every morning you had to carry down your buckets to a
cesspit in the *insula*'s basement—that was, if you could be
troubled to. Some of the *insula*'s less sociable inhabitants
would store up their waste for days without removing it, until

protests from their neighbors about the smell forced them to. And others, lazier still, just threw it out the window, with a cry to warn any hapless passersby below.

As an alternative to the pots in their room, there was a public latrine a block away. The latrine turned out to be a long, dark building with two walls lined with scores of people squatting over holes that fed directly into the sewer system. The stink was astonishing. Though she had scarcely been used to privacy—there was no separate latrine in a roundhouse— Regina found it difficult to let her bowels move in front of so many strangers, all talking and laughing, walking and shouting, and the children, who ran around half naked at the feet of the adults, were even more off-putting. But it was an oddly jolly place, she thought, full of gossip and laughter: obviously a center of the community, a palace of shit and piss.

Rome, Regina quickly learned, was all about divisions. There were rigid barriers among social classes, from the ancient senatorial families down to the slaves. And the gulf between rich and poor was vast.

There were rich and poor everywhere, of course; even in Artorius's dunon that had been true. But here in Rome there were families that had spent a *thousand years* accruing wealth. It was said that at one time just two thousand individuals had owned almost all the cultivated land in the western Empire, from Italy to Britain. Though Rome sprawled over a vast area within its curtain of walls, there were so many public basilicas, circuses, temples, gardens, baths and theaters, and so many privately owned estates from the Emperor's palaces and gardens on down, that it was really no wonder that most people were forced to live in these tottering apartment blocks, crammed into whatever space was available.

Rome was never quiet, even during the darkest hours. There were always the shouts of drovers and wagoners, the uproarious noise of the taverns, some of which never closed, and the gull-like cries of the night watchmen. And too soon would come the morning, when her neighbors would start their days with clattering and banging, laughter and shouts and even noisy lovemaking that carried easily through the thin walls. One man in the apartment below had a particularly stentorian way of calling into the street, calling up water carriers first thing in the morning.

The Romans had a saying—*It costs money to sleep here.* They were right.

On their first afternoon, Regina sent a boy to take a message to Amator's home. There was no reply to her note that day, or the second, and Regina began to fret. She had never forgotten how she had waited for Amator's call after that night in the Veru- lamium baths, a message that had never come; and she hated to be put in the same position again. Besides, it had taken all but a few bronze scraps of coin from Ceawlin's money to buy them the room for a few nights. They couldn't afford to wait long.

But on the third day a retainer called, and said that Amator was prepared to meet her.

And so that afternoon she and Brica walked across the city. Regina stepped out boldly, but Brica walked with eyes down- cast and a fine cloth mask over her face.

It was a long and difficult trek. The streets were so crowded they could barely pass. The lower sections of the apartment blocks were given over to shops, taverns, and warehouses, and from stalls set up in the street itself everything from clothing to wine to cooked meats was on sale. Then there were the street entertainers—jugglers, snake charmers, acrobats. In one place a barber stoically shaved the jowls of a large, prosperous-looking gentleman; he held a spiderweb soaked in vinegar to stanch the bleeding from the frequent cuts he made. All this enterprise made the ways even narrower, and they were crowded with carriages, carts, baggage animals, sedan chairs borne by slaves, horseback riders. The road surface was filthy, littered with garbage and sewage. In the larger streets open trenches bore away the sewage toward deep-buried con- duits, ultimately feeding the patient Tiber. And meanwhile dirty children ran around the wheels of the passing carriages, and dogs sniffed at the debris that piled up in any convenient corner.

But people pressed cheerfully through the crush, babbling away in their fluent, rapid Latin—although there was a sur- prising peppering of other tongues. Regina had thought these must be barbarian languages, but she learned that amid this torrent she could hear the tongues of some of the founding peoples of Rome, the Etruscans and the Sabines, relics of days long past.

Amator's home turned out to be located in a grand complex called Trajan's Forum.

They entered the complex through a triumphal arch that towered over them, surmounted by an immense bronze sculpture of a six-horse chariot. A central piazza was dominated by a huge gilded statue of the Emperor Trajan himself, mounted on horseback. At one end of the piazza was an immense basilica, a monstrous marble cliff of offices and courts, fronted by tall columns of gray granite. It could surely have swallowed up the basilica of Verulamium whole. And looming beyond the basilica roof Regina could see a statue mounted on a great column—yet another representation of Trajan, who had evidently been a powerful emperor indeed, still peering loftily down at the citizens of the city he had built, centuries after the trivial detail of his death. The whole complex was too huge, out of scale, as if constructed for gods and set here in the middle of this human city.

But the roof of the great basilica showed signs of fire damage, and the marble floor of the piazza was crowded with shabby market stalls. Many of the shoppers wore the bold jewelry, skin cloaks, and brightly patterned tunics and trousers of barbarians, of Germans and Vandals, Huns and Goths. Few of them noticed the carved figures of defeated barbarians who peered down from the tops of the columns that ringed the piazza, images of the ancestors of these confident shoppers, symbols of an arrogant past.

To either side of the piazza were *exedrae*, huge semicircular courtyards, and Regina led Brica into one of these. They entered a warren of brick-faced concrete built into the terraced slopes of a hill. Regina felt her own nervousness increase. There were offices, shops, and courts here on many levels, all linked by stairs and streets and vaulted corridors. It was bewildering. But again there were signs that this place had seen better days, for there were comparatively few people here, and many boarded-up and even burned-out shops.

Amator seemed to be doing better than the average, though.

His home, set in an upper level of the complex, turned out to be a grand apartment fronted by a bakery. The shop was a busy place, and enticing smells issued from its big stone ovens.

A retainer came through the shop and led them into the house behind. The retainer was a boy of sixteen or seventeen, with plump, effeminate features. When he walked ahead of them there was a faint whiff of perfume.

At the heart of the home, a series of rooms crowded around a small tiled atrium, illuminated by a light well cut into the roof above. At the far side of the atrium a narrow passageway led them between larger rooms—an office, and a large, sumptuous-looking dining room—and out to a garden, surrounded on three sides by slender columns, and with a view to the south overlooking the city. The house itself was not large by the standards of Regina's villa—but then this was Rome, and she understood how much more expensive space was here.

The garden, called a *peristylium*, despite a small fountain with a statue of some aquatic goddess, was not terribly impressive in itself. But what made it remarkable was that it had been entirely built on the *roof* of the apartment below. Brica poked at the grass with one sandaled toe, trying to find the concrete base beneath.

Amator met them in the little garden. "Welcome, Regina . . ." His voice was as deep and rich as she remembered, and she felt a deep and unwelcome flush work through her belly, as if her body kept its own memories. But she was shocked at the sight of him.

A few years older than her, he was now in his middle fifties. His thin frame was swathed in a purple-edged toga, no doubt worn to impress her, she thought. But he had grown gaunt. His face had lost its fullness, and his cheeks and chin showed sharp bones. And his head was now completely bald—in fact, she saw with surprise, his eyebrows were gone, too, though two lines of livid flesh showed where they had been.

His retainer, the perfumed boy, hovered at his elbow, looking uncertain and nervous.

Regina gave Amator her hand, and he buffed his lips against it. "I am glad to see you are prospering," she said. "But you have changed."

He pursed his lips, and she saw that his eyes were as black and deep as ever. "You're talking about my hair? I can tell you've only just arrived," he said dryly. "You sound so provincial! Whole-body depilation is quite the fashion now. Of course you can't find a barber to do the job well these days. But Sulla here is an expert with his poultices of wax, if a little heavy-handed with the tweezers."

"And perhaps you enjoy the little pains, do you?"

He arched his head, and a smile tugged at the corners of his small mouth. "You've lost none of your sharpness, little chicken."

The retainer's reaction to this exchange was complex. He had flushed when Amator referred to him personally, but now he was watching Regina with alarmed calculation.

They are lovers, Regina realized suddenly. *And this wretched boy of Amator's is trying to work out if I am any threat to his position.* She eyed the boy without pity. The boy wore a gold *bulla* around his neck. Like a little pouch, this was a symbol of his free birth, and would normally be worn from infancy to manhood. He looked too old to be wearing such a childish token, and she wondered if Amator preferred to keep his companion young.

If Amator had chosen men over women, something of his old hunger showed in his eyes as he turned his intense gaze on Brica. Regina felt proud as Brica returned his lascivious stare with contempt.

"Your companion is lovely," said Amator smoothly. "Her paleness gives her an exotic look in these warmer climes—"

"Her name is Brica," said Regina. "She is my daughter. *And yours,* Amator." She heard a gasp from Brica; Regina had not warned her about this. "Although truthfully I cannot be sure if it was you or Athaulf whose restless cock impregnated me that night."

Amator's gaze clouded. But he smiled again at Brica, though with more levels of complexity than before. "Wine, Sulla," he murmured.

The boy now stared with open hostility at Regina and Brica, these relics of his master's complicated past. But he went to get the wine.

Amator waved his guests to the low couches set out around

the fountain. Sulla returned with jugs of wine and water, three fine blue glasses, and plates of figs, olives, and apples. Despite her hunger Regina only sipped a little wine. But Brica, without inhibition and despite the news she had just received, wolfed down the apples; Amator seemed startled by her animal directness.

Wary, calculating, clearly wondering what she wanted from him, Amator told Regina a little about himself. He had come to Rome in partnership with Athaulf. The German had long since vanished from his life; Regina wondered if their relationship had been deeper than she had suspected on that night when they had used her. Still, they had stayed together long enough to found a successful grain-shipping business.

"Rome is a relentlessly hungry city, Regina," he said. "It has been unable to feed itself since the days of Julius Caesar, and it was Augustus who introduced the *annona*." This was a dole of free grain, distributed to poorer citizens.

"We saw the port—the grain fleet."

"Yes. And with such mighty flows of goods, there are plenty of opportunities for a man of intelligence and charm to make a living for himself, even in these complicated times."

"And you always had those attributes in plenty."

"I've done well for the son of a servant from the provinces—don't you think? I've come a long way from there, to *this*."

Brica leaned forward, and spoke around a mouthful of fruit. "Why do you have a purple stripe on your cloak? It looks ridiculous." It was the first thing she had said to him.

"I belong to the equestrian order," he said smoothly. He displayed a big, gaudy gold ring. "It is an ancient order, dating from the times before the wars with Carthage, when the richest citizens were required to fund the cavalry in defense of the Republic. Today it is open to all adult citizens—provided you have enough money, of course—do you know, the Emperor provides me with a horse! But I don't ride; I keep the beast in a stable in my house in the country. I have various civic responsibilities, and—"

"You are also a member of three guilds," said Regina. "You have several patrons, including a senator called Titus Nerva."

"You seem to know a great deal about me," Amator cut in, eyeing her.

"Before he died, your father Carausias was very informative. Even though you rarely wrote to him unless you needed money or some other favor, he told me enough to follow your career."

Amator leaned forward. "So you know me, as one old lover knows another."

"Or as a hunter knows her quarry."

"Well, you have me at a disadvantage," he said. "You know my biography, but I have heard nothing of you since that longago night of exuberance and foolishness, which I had all but forgotten."

"*I* haven't forgotten. After that 'night of exuberance,' you left me pregnant. You or your German boyfriend. Verulamium fell. Because of the money you stole from your father we couldn't escape to Armorica. I was forced to trek, pregnant, across the country. I gave birth in an abandoned roundhouse of the Celtae. I was seventeen years old.

"I spent twenty years trying to make a farmstead work, scraping my food from the ground. But I raised your daughter, as you can see. Later we were overrun by the forces of a warlord called Artorius. Perhaps you have heard of him; he is ambitious. I saved my life and your daughter's by sleeping with him. Again I survived."

He glared at her. "Yes, you survived, little chicken," he said coldly. "And here you are with your demanding eyes and nagging voice. Why have you abandoned your barbarian warlord to come to Rome?"

"I want to find my mother."

He nodded. "I remember the stories you used to tell of her. She must be old—probably dead by now. Why do you want to find the woman who abandoned you?"

"Because she is my family. Because she owes me a debt. *As you also owe me,* Amator."

He smirked. "And what is it you want from me?"

"Only a little," she said evenly. "I will need time to find Julia. You will give us that time. Provide us somewhere to live—not here; the stink of your boy is too strong. And a little money."

"I am not as rich as you may think I am, Regina."

"And no doubt your tastes are expensive. Then give us work.

Brica can serve in your shop, perhaps." She ignored Brica's bemused reaction; she would deal with her later. "My demands will be reasonable—only what I need. I'm sure we can work something out."

"So that's why you've trekked across Europe, with your doe-eyed daughter in tow. Extortion! How delicious. And if I refuse?"

She shrugged. "I am persistent and dogged. I will explore all facets of your character and your past with your patrons, and other *equites*, and your business contacts in your guilds. Oh, and your boy—was his name Sulla?"

"I have nothing to be ashamed of," he flared. "This is not Britain. This is Rome. Things are done differently here."

"Then," she said mildly, "no one will be disturbed when I tell them how you groomed me for your pleasure from the time of my menarche, and the way you used me on that night in Verulamium. I wonder now if that had something to do with your preference for boys. Perhaps on some level women disgust you, Amator? Perhaps you set out *deliberately* to hurt me? Oh, and of course I will tell them how you abandoned your obligations to your child all those years ago, and how you destroyed your father's life with your theft—"

He leaned toward her, his depilated eyebrows flaring red. "You can't harm me, little chicken."

"Perhaps not. But it will be interesting to try."

He held her gaze for long heartbeats. She kept still, refusing to show how her heart was hammering—for if he called her bluff she had no alternative plan.

But then he laughed. "I always did like you, Regina. You had a spark. It wasn't just your boyish little body, you know." He clapped his hands and ordered his perfumed boy to bring more wine.

chapter 25

Pina was no support.

"You got what you wanted, didn't you? You wanted your *contadino*. You wanted something nobody else has."

"No, I—"

"Now you're *different*. Congratulations."

Lucia thought she saw something in Pina's face as she said this, just a flicker of remorse or pity. But Pina turned her back, just like the rest.

Nobody would speak to her. No, it was worse than that. Nobody would even *look* at her. It was as if waves of disapproval spread out from Rosa and Pina, eventually engulfing everybody Lucia knew.

She was never physically isolated—that was impossible in the Crypt—but everywhere she went she was alone in a crowd. At work in the *scrinium*, her work assignments were left on her desk or as impersonal email messages. They were instructions that might have been sent to a robot, she thought, a thing without identity. In the dormitory, little knots of conversation would unravel as she approached. In the refectories people would turn away and talk as if she weren't there. Cut out of the endless babble of gossip, it was as if a great story were moving on without her.

Listen to your sisters. That was another of the three great slogans of the Order's short catechism, incised on every nursery wall, repeated endlessly. But how were you supposed to listen when nobody would speak to you?

Now she was excluded, it had never been so apparent how closely everybody in the Order lived. People walked together, talking endlessly, arms linked, hips bumping together, heads bowed closely, lips brushing in platonic kisses. Sometimes, in the refectories, you would see groups of ten or fifteen or even twenty girls, joined one to the next by linked arms or hands on shoulders, or bodies pressed together. At intense moments people would grab each other's arms and shoulders, even kiss. At night, too, it wasn't uncommon for two, three, or four to cluster together in a few pushed-together beds, whispering, kissing, at last sleeping in each other's arms. There was nothing sexual in any of this, for there was nothing sexual about the sisters. As slim as seven-year-olds, they huddled together innocently for companionship and warmth.

But not Lucia, not anymore. Nobody came *near* Lucia, no nearer than a yard or two, never near enough to touch. It was as if she were trapped inside a big bubble of glass, around which people walked without even noticing what they were doing.

Or it was as if she *smelled* bad. And perhaps she did, she came to wonder. Sometimes, when she walked into a crowded room, she would detect a subtle scent, a kind of milky sweetness, gentle and welcoming. It was the smell of the sisters. By comparison *her* smell must be of blood and sweat, of a rutting animal, as if she was a beast in the field, not a human being like the others at all.

Once she was aware of it the scent of rut seemed to fill her head, day and night. She took to showering, two, three, four times a day, scrubbing at her skin until it was raw, and changing her clothes all the time. But still that stink gushed out of her body, a foulness that she couldn't escape—for it was the essence of *her*.

It went on and on. Food seemed to lose its flavor; it was like trying to eat cardboard or grass. It got to the point where she couldn't sleep. She would lie there alone in her bed, listening to the whispers and giggles and gentle snores that drifted around her. The lack of sleep and her poor diet soon wore her out. She dragged herself to work. But the work seemed as pointless as the rest of her weary days. In her spare time she would simply sit alone, silently loathing herself, aware of every pore in her skin oozing blood and dirt.

After a month of ostracism, she suffered violent stomach cramps. She staggered to a bathroom and endured half an hour of dry retching, bringing up nothing but acidic bile that burned her throat.

Rosa came to sit opposite her in the refectory. "I saw you in the bathroom." Her tone was analytical, not sympathetic.

Lucia had been sitting alone, without touching the cooling plate of food before her. She tucked her hands between her thighs, head down. Over her head an elaborate mosaic design showed the Order's kissing-fish logo.

"You know why you're ill, don't you? You've hardly eaten for a month. Or slept, by the look of you. The weight is falling off you."

"I don't care." Lucia's voice was scratchy. She couldn't remember the last time she had spoken to anybody, exchanged a single word. It must have been days, she thought.

"You feel like you don't exist. As if you're not really here. As if this is a dream."

"A nightmare."

"We aren't meant to be alone, Lucia. We're social creatures. Our minds evolved in the first place so we could figure out what is going on inside *other* people's heads—so we could get to know them, help them, even manipulate them. Did you know that? We need other people to make us fully conscious. So if you're alone, if nobody is looking at you or talking to you, it really is as if you don't exist."

"Everybody hates me."

Rosa leaned forward. "Can you blame them? You let us down, Lucia. The Crypt is a calm pond. You threw a great big rock into that pond, making a huge splash, sending ripples back and forth. You upset *everybody*."

Lucia dropped her head.

Rosa asked, "Do you remember what happened to Francesca?"

Lucia frowned. She had forgotten about Francesca.

Francesca had been a sister from Lucia's dormitory, neither more or less popular than anybody else, never standing out from the crowd—but then nobody did. Then, one day, suddenly Francesca hadn't been part of the group anymore. Everybody else, including Lucia, had simply stopped talking to her.

It was just as was happening to Lucia herself.

"Francesca was a thief," Rosa said sternly. "She had an ob-session for jewelry and accessories—sparkly, glittery things. She would steal from her sisters. She built up a cache under her bed. Of course she kept it all secret. When it was discovered—well, naturally, nobody wanted to talk to her again."

Lucia had never known about the thefts, about *why* Francesca's exclusion had come about. But then, you never asked questions like *why*. It had been easy, she thought wonderingly, easy just to ignore Francesca, to behave as if she didn't exist—for in a way she didn't anymore. As for Lucia, she had just gone along with what everybody else had been doing, as she always did, as she had been encouraged to do since she was a toddler, never questioning. She had scarcely noticed when Francesca had literally disappeared, when the pale solitary ghost in the refectory or the dorm had evaporated, never to return.

"What happened to her?"

"She's dead," Rosa said. "She killed herself."

Despite her own turmoil, Lucia was shocked. Dead, for a handful of cheap jewelry? How could that be *right*? . . . She should not think such thoughts. Yet she couldn't help it.

And she became afraid.

"I can't change," she said desolately. "Look at me. I'm a big stupid animal. My head is full of rocks. I stink. I know you can smell it. I can't help it, I wash and wash . . ." Though her eyes prickled, no tears came. "Maybe it's better if I die, too."

"No." Rosa reached forward, pulled Lucia's arm out from under the table, and took her hand. It was the first time any-body had touched Lucia for weeks. It was as if an electric current ran through her. Rosa said, "You're too important to lose, Lucia. Yes, you're different. But the Order needs girls like you."

Lucia said weakly, "Why? What for?"

But Rosa drew back, subtly, breaking the touch.

You weren't supposed to ask. *Ignorance is strength*. It said so, in big letters on the wall before her. Lucia said quickly, "I'm sorry."

Rosa said, "It's okay." She stood up. "Everything's going to be okay, Lucia. You'll see."

Lucia, weak, starved, sleep-deprived, clung to that. In her

dazed, hurting state, all she cared about was that her isolation should end. And she did her best to ignore the small voices in her head that even now asked persistent, impertinent questions: *How can it ever be made okay again, how, how? And what do they want of me?*

Rosa booked Lucia into the downbelow hospital.

The doctors said her condition wasn't too serious, though she had lost more weight than was healthy for a girl her age. She was given some light medication and put on a special diet.

Rosa encouraged Lucia's friends to come visit her. They came slowly and shyly: Pina the first day, Idina and Angela the second, Rosaria and Rosetta the next. At first they stared at Lucia with wide, curious eyes, as if she hadn't been among them for weeks—and, in a sense, she hadn't. They talked to her, feeding her little dribbles of gossip about what had been going on during her "absence."

It took three days before any of them could touch her without flinching.

But gradually Lucia felt old connections mending, as if she were a bit of broken bone being knitted back into the whole. The change in her mood was astonishing. It was as if the sun had come out from behind clouds.

After a week in the hospital the doctors discharged her. She was sent back to her dormitory, and her work in the *scrinium*, though the doctors insisted she call back every few days for checks.

She knew she should not reflect on any of this, nor analyze it, but simply accept it. She had to learn again to live in the moment.

chapter 26

Brica went to work in her father's bakery.

When she was with Regina, Brica remained withdrawn, sullen, somehow defeated. But away from Regina, Amator reported, she was more open, lively, willing, and she would socialize with the younger workers when the day was done. Amator was no doubt embellishing the truth; Regina was sure he would not miss an opportunity to slide a knife blade of difference between mother and daughter. But she didn't begrudge her daughter her bit of happiness.

As soon as the money from Amator started to come through, Regina began to search for her mother.

What made that hard was that so much of Rome was so obviously *unplanned*. The historic core of the city had always been the seven hills, easily defended in the days when Rome had been just one of a number of squabbling communities. The first Forum had been built in the marshy valley that nestled between the hills' bluff protective shoulders.

But since then, away from the monumental heart, the city had simply grown as it needed to. The streets wandered haphazardly, following the meandering tracks of animals across fields that now lay far beneath the strata of rubbish under her feet, nothing like the arrow-straight highways laid out in the provinces. The only orderly development that had ever been possible was when fire or some other disaster had laid waste to part of the city, giving a rare chance to rebuild. It was whispered that once the Emperor Nero had deliberately started a fire in the central districts to make room for the House of Gold he planned to build for himself.

And yet in this sprawling chaos there were, oddly, patterns. She could see it in the shops, for instance. There were distinctive artists' quarters, jewelers' quarters, fashion quarters. You could see how it happened. Where a successful bakery business opened, like Amator's, other food stores were attracted, selling fish oil or olives, lamb or fruit. Soon you had a district that became renowned for the quality of its food, and subsidiary businesses like restaurants might be drawn in. Or you might find folk of a similar inclination drawn together by common interests: thus Amator's house on the fringe of the Trajan complex was one of several in the area owned by grain and water magnates. Then there were more subtle, short-lived changes, as one area became more fashionable for some uncanny reason; or as another became more prone to crime and disorder, thus attracting more criminals and driving out the law abiding.

The way the city somehow organized itself struck her deeply. The growth of the city, street by street, building by building, had been driven not by any conscious intent, not even by the will of the emperors, but by individual decisions, motivated by the greed or nobility, farsightedness or purblindness that afflicted every human being. And out of the millions of small decisions made every day, patterns formed and dissipated, like ripples on a turbulent stream; and somehow, out of these patterns, the soul of the city itself emerged.

Remarkable it may be, but she feared it might take her years to get to know this mighty nest of a million people. She decided that the best thing to do to shorten the search was to let Julia come to her.

Using Amator's money, she began to make her name known wherever the better-heeled people gathered, in the more prominent baths and restaurants and theaters. She went to the temples, too—not just the new Christian churches that had been sprouting throughout Rome since the days of Constantine, including his mighty basilica over the tomb of Saint Peter, but also the older temples to the pagan cults. She hoped that if her name got to her mother one way or another, Julia might be drawn—by curiosity, shame, even the remnants of love?—to come seek out her daughter. Regina knew the odds were long, but she had no better idea. She got no quick result, however.

And as their weeks in Rome turned into months, Regina was

not surprised by a further development: Brica fell in love again. He was a boy called Castor, a customer of the store, a young freedman of good bearing and intelligence who had quickly risen to a position of some responsibility, working for one of the grander senatorial families.

Brica obviously expected Regina to oppose the match. But Regina kept her counsel. Even when Brica defiantly said she wished to marry the boy, Regina gave her blessing. She paid for a betrothal ceremony and banquet, and even provided a small dowry to Castor's family. This would normally be paid by the bride's father—and it had actually come out of Amator's money, if unwillingly extracted.

Brica had to live; Regina accepted that. She had no desire to control her daughter's every movement. It was enough that her own longer-term goals should be fulfilled. Even a wedding would not hamper that. After all, somebody would eventually have to be the father of Brica's children, Regina's grandchildren, and better a Roman boy with prospects than a doltish apprentice of Myrddin.

Besides, anything that encouraged Brica to learn better Latin must be a good thing.

It was more than three months after their arrival in Rome, as the leaves of summer had already begun to brown, that the mysterious package arrived for Regina. It was brought by a slim young girl with startling gray eyes, who would not leave her name.

The package contained a single brass token, which turned out to be for a seat in the amphitheater. There was no other label or note. Regina's pulse hammered.

As she counted down the days before the show, her sleep was even more disturbed than usual.

On the appointed day, Regina set out early in the morning. As she walked through the dense streets, she felt as nervous as if she were seven years old again and approaching her mother's bedroom, where Julia would be putting on her jewelry, and Carta would be fixing her hair.

And then she came upon the amphitheater itself. It was a tremendous wall of marble broken by four stories of colonnades, from which statues peered down at the thronging crowd. Her heart surged at its magnificence.

Her little token directed her to a numbered entrance. She had to walk a long way around the perimeter before she found the right one. Vendors worked the milling crowds, selling drinks, sweetmeats, hats, and favors for star performers. There were, she learned, a total of *seventy-six* entrances through which the crowd could be processed. There were also six un-numbered entrances, four for the Emperor's party, and two for the use of the gladiators—one through which they would walk back to their barracks if they survived, and the other through which their corpses would be dragged out if not. But no glad-iators fought to the death these days; the emperors had banned lethal contests some thirty years before, when a Christian mar-tyr, righteously interposing himself between two warriors, had been killed by a mob eager for its ration of blood.

Her entrance was an arch with detailed stucco paintwork, though much of the paint had faded and cracked away. She passed through and found herself inside the hollowed-out belly of the great building, a maze in three dimensions of cor-ridors and staircases up and down which people trooped—the big radial staircases were graphically called *vomitoria*. But Regina's ticket kept her on the ground level, and led her along a short corridor, deeper into the guts of the complex.

She emerged into daylight, and a wash of color and noise.

She found herself in a small concrete box lined with wooden benches. There was nobody else here; she sat down tentatively, on the end of a bench. She was surprised to find herself here, for she knew that these boxes were reserved for the Emperor's family, and for senators, magistrates, priests, and other notables.

She was in one of a series of boxes set just above the level of the wooden floor itself. Around her, the arena was a tremen-dous elliptical bowl. Behind her, rows of wooden seats rose up in four great terraces. The seats were quickly filling up, and the faces of the people receded to mere dots in the shadows of the upper tiers.

She saw workmen on the perimeter of the stadium's huge open roof. They hauled huge sheets of cloth over a spiderweb of ropes suspended over the gaping roof itself: this awning would shelter the spectators from the sun. It was said that the workers were sailors from the docks, a thousand of them brought here for their skills in working rigging and sails.

And when she looked across the floor to the far side of the arena, the people in those distant seats merged into a sea of movement, color, and flesh, a mob ordered by the amphitheater's vast geometry. In one glance she could take in twenty thousand people—perhaps four times the population of old Verulamium, as if whole cities had been picked up and shaken until their human inhabitants had tumbled out into this gigantic dish of marble and brick.

On the arena floor the spectacle had already started. To the blaring music of trumpets and an immense hydraulic organ, a parade of chariots raced around the floor, each bearing a gladiator dressed in a purple or gold cloak. They were chased by slaves carrying shields, helmets, and weapons. The crowd began to roar for their favorites. Though the arena was not yet full the noise was already powerful—exhilarating, terrifying—and the air was full of the scent of wood chips, blood, and sweat, making Regina shiver.

More performers appeared in the middle of the arena floor. They rose from trapdoors, but so cunning was the effect that it looked as if they had erupted from nowhere. They put on boxing matches, women fencers, and a series of clownish acts—like a race between two enormously fat slaves, driven by the spear tips of soldiers, which finished with both slaves left flat out and panting on the ground. The crowd appeared to enjoy it all.

Then the acrobats, jugglers, and clowns were cleared away, and a squadron of workers emerged to litter the arena floor with shrubbery and rocks. The traps sprung open again, and out poured a host of animals: leopards, bears, lions, giraffes, ostriches, even an elephant. These animals, startling and strange to Regina's eyes, wandered aimlessly, suddenly thrust into this great bowl of noise and sunlight, clearly terrified. Even the great predator cats were unable to take advantage of the confusion and closeness of their prey. Warriors ran on armed with spears, swords, nets, and shields, and they began to goad the bewildered beasts.

As the creatures began to die the noise of the crowd rose to a crescendo.

"So I am in time for the animal show." Regina could feel a warm breath on her cheek, smell a subtle scent of incense. The sudden voice, speaking a stilted Latin, was a woman's, soft in Regina's ear, with the husky growl of age. Regina couldn't see the arena anymore. "Once, you know, these games had religious significance. They were called offerings. But now we live in coarsened times, and the games are merely spectacles to placate the crowds of Rome, whom even the emperors fear. That is why the morning show, which still delivers authentic deaths, even if only of animals and criminals, is so popular . . ."

She had planned for this moment, tried to anticipate it. But now that it was here she felt frozen solid, like one of the hapless statues on the arena walls.

She turned.

The woman beside her wore a simple white *stola* and a cloak of fine wool. She was upright, slim, gray-haired, her face still handsome despite the wrinkles at her eyes and mouth, and the tightening of her skin by years of Italian light. But the smoke-gray eyes were clear and unchanged, and, in her sixties, she was still beautiful.

"Mother."

"Yes, child."

They embraced. But it was almost formal. Her mother's muscles were stiff, as stiff as her own. It was always going to be like this, Regina thought. For Julia to have survived in Rome she must have found a core of steel. It was a meeting of two strong women; it was not a gushing reunion.

Before them, disregarded, the professional beast slayers continued their taunting of the animals, whipping the beasts to a fury to satisfy the passions of the baying, jostling crowd.

They exchanged information. Facts, not feelings.

Julia seemed uninterested in Regina's brief account of her life since the night her father had died. To Julia, it seemed, Britain was a cold and dismal place far away and best forgotten. Or perhaps there was some morsel of guilt, Regina thought, even now uncomfortably lodged in her heart, trivial but irritating, like a seed between her teeth.

Julia was scarcely more animated as she quietly told her own story. "I came to Rome to be with my sister. Your aunt—"

Regina rummaged in her memory. "Helena."

"Helena, yes . . ." Helena, some ten years older than Julia herself, was, it turned out, still alive—one of the few seventy-year-olds in all of Rome. "But then," Julia said dryly, "we have always been a long-lived family."

Julia had needed help from her sister. Contrary to what Regina had always believed, Julia had left Britain with little in the way of the family fortune. Before his death Marcus—always nervous, always overcautious—had taken to burying his money in hoards, in and around the villa. "And there, so far as I know, the family's money lies still, rotting in the earth. Unless it has been purloined by Saxons, *bacaudae,* or other undesirables." She seemed not to care very much.

Sister Helena, it turned out, had maneuvered herself into a very influential position in Rome, for she had been one of the chief attendants to the Vestal Virgins.

The Virgins were a relic of Rome's earliest days. It was said the order had been founded by Numa Pompilius, the first king to follow Romulus himself, who had designated acolytes to attend to the sacred flame of Vesta, goddess of hearth and fireside. Novices were handed over between the ages of six and ten to the Pontifex Maximus, Rome's chief priest, and were required to remain pure for thirty years. The order had become central to the purity and strength of Rome, and the sacred fire had not been extinguished for centuries.

"But the flame burns no more," murmured Julia. "When Constantine began to build his Christian churches, everything changed."

There were many who believed that the extinguishing of the flame symbolized the decline of Rome itself, for the city had been sacked just sixteen years later. But some of the Virgins and their attendants, including a younger Helena, had not been without worldly wisdom as well as divine. Plenty of money had been salted away for just such a catastrophe.

"A faction of the Virgins found a way to survive," Julia said. "We still serve a god, still dedicate the purity of our young to her service. But she is a different god. We call ourselves the Puissant Order of Holy Mary Queen of Virgins. And we still report to the Pontifex Maximus—but now he is the pope of the Christians."

Regina gaped. "Mary—the mother of the Christ? Mother, have you become a Christian?"

"One must adapt." Julia smiled, and for a moment Regina saw something of Aetius's strength and resilience in his daughter's eyes. "And as you can see, we can still afford one of the amphitheater's best boxes. Your aunt Helena has two daughters, Leda and Messalina—I suppose Messalina is about your age. Messalina, too, has children, daughters." All daughters, Regina noted absently, no sons. Julia went on, "And I have one daughter—"

Regina closed her eyes. "Mother, you have *two* daughters."

Briefly Julia reached out to touch her hand, but she pulled back. "Two daughters, then. Your sister is called Leda."

"Half sister—"

"Yes. Her father is dead. He was uninteresting." This dismissal was chilling. "And now," Julia said softly, "*you* are here. What do you want, Regina?"

Regina spread her hands. "I am here to build a better life than I could have found in Britain." She told her mother something of the extirpating advance of the Saxons, and the foolishness of the British leaders like Artorius, still dreaming of empires. "And," she said, "I have come here for repayment of certain debts."

"Debts owed by this Amator. And, no doubt, by me."

Regina said evenly, "You had a duty to protect me—a duty doubled by my father's death. You didn't fulfill that duty. If it hadn't been for Aetius—"

Julia nodded, considering. "We are not rich, my Order. But we can take you in—you and your daughter—if that is acceptable. We are family: Leda, and Helena and her daughters, myself, we all live in the same community."

The proposal sounded acceptable to Regina. After all the family would be together, a network of mothers and daughters, aunts and nieces, sisters and cousins.

"I'll consider it."

"Good. We can discuss terms later."

Terms? . . . We are bargaining, Regina thought, *bargaining with duty and guilt. How cold we are—and how like me this woman is—or how like her I have become.*

The crowd bayed again, and Regina glanced back at the sun-drenched arena.

The beast slayers had almost done their work. The last animals were released—but they were not beasts but humans, Regina thought at first. Very tall, very naked, they ran like the wind, faster than anybody she had ever seen. And, she saw, their heads above their very human faces were flat, their brows reaching back from great ridges set over eye sockets, within which terror and bafflement was easy to discern.

No, not human; they were a kind of ape, her mother told her. These ape-folk's proximity to humanity made them a favorite of the crowds. They were brought to Rome along lengthy trade routes from China, far to the east, where isolated pockets of these creatures survived in the mountains. In this age, which seemed so crowded here in Rome, the world was still an empty and largely unexplored place, and its corners contained many relics of a deeper antiquity. The ape-folk would not fight, but they were lithe and very fast, and the beast slayers had to run them down with chariots before they could be killed.

"Next there will be executions," Julia said. "Bandits, rapists, heretics, and embezzling shopkeepers tied to posts so that beasts may maul them. It is a pitiable spectacle, but the crowd loves it."

"Mother, I brought the *matres*. From our *lararium*. I always took care of them."

Julia's face was composed, but there was something in her eyes, Regina thought, something a little warmer.

chapter 27

Once again Lucia journeyed with Rosa into the deep heart of the Crypt.

This time they took a different route, using older elevator shafts and stairs. They passed down from the bright upper level with its classrooms, libraries, offices, and computer centers, down through the vast, sprawling, comfortable layer of hospitals and dormitories, recreation rooms, sports halls and food centers, and then down into the deepest level, the complex of narrow interconnected corridors and small chambers, the level where the *matres* lived.

Lucia wanted to close her eyes, to shut out the detail that crammed into her mind: if you didn't need to know it, you shouldn't know it.

It was two weeks after the end of Lucia's ostracism. Rosa had come to find her, at the end of Lucia's working day.

Rosa had smiled. "I'm glad you look so well."

Lucia returned the smile. But she felt uncomfortable. She didn't want to think about the recent past.

Rosa seemed to perceive this. "I understand how you feel." She brushed Lucia's cheek with her fingers. "There's somebody I want you to meet."

"Somebody? . . ."

"He's waiting for you now."

Lucia had followed her—but once more her head buzzed with unwelcome questions. *He?* There were very few boys or men here in the Crypt, and she was close to none of them. *He* . . . She couldn't help but think of Daniel. She remembered his face, his oddly high forehead, his pale blue eyes, so different from everybody in the Crypt. But now that face was a dissolving memory, and she knew she must put him aside.

On the third story, Rosa led her down a long, gloomy corridor. They came to a nursery. This was a large, bright room with smoothly rounded walls and tiny pieces of furniture in glaring red or yellow plastic. The walls were brightly painted with huge smiling faces, and from hidden speakers tinkling music played.

And the floor was covered with infants. "The current crop of one- to two-year-olds," Rosa murmured.

There were about two hundred babies here, in this one great room. Adults dressed in pale gray uniforms walked among them. The children were dressed in identical blue-and-white romper suits, though some of them had worked free an arm or leg. The children played with each other and the toys that littered the floor, exploring, gnawing. The babies were a carpet of wriggling forms—like worms, Lucia thought oddly, or like stranded fish. She could smell them, a dense, pale smell of milk and piss and poops, and the noise they made was a shrill roar. And when they chanced to look toward her, they all had the same oval face, pale hair, smoke-gray eyes.

The attendants looked young themselves—some of them surely younger than Lucia herself. It occurred to Lucia that there was a pattern of age in the Crypt. She had seen it for herself. In these deep levels most people were young, children and young adults helping in the nursery, and doing basic maintenance. Older women, like Pina, tended to work at the higher levels, the schools and libraries, and in the surface offices. It wasn't an exclusive pattern; a few people, like Rosa, seemed comfortable everywhere. But still, she thought, the Crypt was like a great onion, layers divided by age, the oldest outside, getting younger as you penetrated deeper—until at the center were the youngest of all, the babies, and, paradoxically, the very oldest, the *matres*.

But this was another heretical analysis that she must try to block from her mind.

"I know what you're thinking," Rosa murmured.

"You do?"

"You've mixed with outsiders. I was brought up as a *contadino*, remember. You're seeing this through the eyes of an outsider—and you're thinking how strange this would seem to them."

Perhaps I was, Lucia thought.

"You don't have to deny it," Rosa murmured. "Well, so it would be strange to anybody who grew up in a little nuclear family. It seemed strange to me, until I understood how *right* it all was . . . Once you were a child like this, Lucia. Once you played in this room, as these children do now."

"I know."

"And then, with your year group, you moved through the stages of your life, the crèches and nursery schools, and then your formal schooling on the top story . . . And more children took your place here."

Lucia shrugged. "Everybody knows about that. It's the way the Order is renewed."

"Yes, of course it is. Now come." She walked on, and Lucia followed.

They went through a door, and passed down another corridor. It was colder here, and darker, lit only by a string of dangling bulbs.

Rosa said as they walked, "Ten thousand people live here, in the Crypt. Every year, about one percent of us die—some accidents and illnesses, mostly old age. That's *a hundred a year*. That's how many have to be replaced. You said it yourself: the Order must be renewed. Has it occurred to you to wonder how?"

Lucia frowned. "There must be a hundred babies a year, then. To maintain the numbers."

"That's right. Just as we saw in the nursery. The future of the Order: every year a hundred warm bodies are passed into the great processing machine of the Crypt at one end, and a hundred cold ones carried out the other. Eh?"

Lucia shuddered. "That's a horrible thing to say."

"But accurate enough. All right. But where do the babies come from, Lucia?"

Lucia, uncomfortable, said, "The *matres*."

"That's right. The *matres*, the mothers of us all. Lucia, you know that the Order is very old. Once the Order was small, and there were only three *matres*—like the three ancient goddesses in this alcove. But the Order grew, and we needed more babies, and the *matres* had to become nine, three times three. And then the Order grew again, and the nine became twenty-seven, three by three by three . . ."

It didn't seem at all strange to Lucia that to keep up an output of a hundred babies each of those twenty-seven must produce three or four babies each, every year.

They came to a little alcove, carved into the wall. In the alcove, behind a thick slab of glass, stood three tiny statues, grimy with age, worn with much handling. They looked like women, but they all wore hooded cloaks. Perhaps they were figures of Befana, Lucia thought.

Rosa touched the glass. "This is bulletproof . . . These are the first *matres*, the symbolic heart of the Order—just as the twenty-seven flesh-and-blood *matres* are its wombs.

"But soon, the twenty-seven will become twenty-six. Maria Ludovica is not, in fact, the oldest of the *matres*, but she is the frailest. And Maria is dying, Lucia." Rosa's eyes seemed huge in the dark. "The last decade, as Maria has weakened, has been a time of turmoil, and more girls like you have emerged—who have become mature, I mean. It is the way of things. Soon somebody must replace Maria. The twenty-seven must be restored."

"You're talking about me," Lucia whispered.

"It has taken me some time to convince certain others that *you* are the right candidate." Rosa seemed proud, as if she had won some victory.

Lucia felt only numb. She couldn't imagine the consequences of what Rosa was saying. She could see nothing to connect her fifteen-year-old self to the wizened, pregnant old woman she had met. "But I am nothing," she said. "A month ago I was starving to death because nobody would talk to me."

"In a way it was your—ah—breakout that helped me establish you as the right candidate. You have strength of mind, Lucia, strength of character. Not many of your contemporaries could have endured so much. And we need strength to face the future. The world changes, and the Order must change with it. We need a certain independence of thinking in our children, a will to accept the unfamiliar—even though there is a paradox, for to get by we all must accept our place in the Order, and not think *too* hard, as you know to your cost."

"It's impossible," Lucia whispered.

"No." Rosa took her arm. "Just a little hard to imagine, that's all. And now, here is the man I want you to meet . . ."

Lucia turned. The man was right behind them. She hadn't heard him approach.

He was perhaps thirty. He was taller than Lucia, and bulkier; his body looked a little soft, flabby, and his skin was pale. He wore casual clothes, a pale blue shirt and jeans. His hair was dark and neatly combed, but he had something of the features of the sisters, of Lucia and Rosa themselves.

He smiled at her. And as he glanced over Lucia's figure his gray eyes were alive with something of the intensity of the *contadino* boys.

Rosa touched Lucia's lips with one fingertip. "Don't say anything. You mustn't speak to each other. Lucia, this is Giuliano Andreoli. He's a *contadino*, strictly speaking. But he's actually your distant cousin—you can tell from the coloring—you can look him up in the *scrinium* if you like. He lives in Venice. He's a bricklayer . . . I think that's enough. Come now."

She took Lucia's arm and led her away. Lucia looked back, but Giuliano was already out of sight, around the bend of the corridor.

"I don't understand," whispered Lucia.

"Reproductive biology, Lucia. To produce babies you don't need just mothers, but fathers, too. Oh, of course, nowadays the new biotechnologies could make anything possible, but the ancient ways are the best, I think . . . Ninety-five percent of the babies born here are girls. Most of the boys leave after their schooling, and those who stay are mostly either homosexual or neuter." *Neuter:* it seemed a strange, cold, clinical term. Rosa went on, "So where are the fathers to come from? From outside, of course—though we like to keep it in the family if we can."

Lucia stopped. "Rosa, please—*who is Giuliano?*"

Rosa smiled, but there was a wistful sadness in her expression. "Why, he's your lover."

chapter 28

It would be a multiple ceremony, Regina decided, an overlapping celebration of life, motherhood, and complicated relationships.

First there was the birth of Aemilia, daughter of Leda, Regina's half sister, and niece to Regina herself. Then the girl Venus had reached her menarche. Venus was the daughter of Messalina, granddaughter of Regina's aunt Helena. And at the center of it all would be the marriage of Regina's own daughter Brica to the young, clear-eyed freedman Castor.

It would all be held, she had decided, on the spring feast of Beltane when, according to the tradition of the Celtae, the warmth of the returning sun and the fertility of the earth were celebrated. Regina and Brica had been here in Rome for two years already, and it would be a nice reminder of her days with Artorius.

Of course her elaborate plans immediately threw everybody into a state of confusion. For days the Order's big communal house on the Appian Way was filled with the smells of cooking, with the din of clumsily practiced musical instruments, and with the hammering of nails as decorations were put up everywhere.

Which was all, of course, according to Regina's design. For they all needed a distraction from the looming presence of the Vandals, the dreadful horde of black-painted barbarians who were even now, so it was said, camping on the plains north of Rome.

On the day before the ceremony, Amator came to visit her, at the Order's house.

He walked into her small office and prowled around its

shelves and cupboards, fingering the heaps of scrolls and wax tablets. His face was caked with cosmetics, with white powder on his cheeks and black lining to emphasise his eyes. Despite these expensive efforts he looked his age, or older, and, she knew now, he was plagued by ulcers and gout, the sicknesses of an indulgent old man. Today he seemed oddly nervous.

"I see you have found yourself some gainful employment," he said. "How long have you been here—two years? You have been busy. Busy, busy, busy."

She spread her hands over her scrolls and tablets, her seals with the Order's kissing-fish symbol. "I deal in information. That is how things work, Amator. Businesses, cities, empires. You should know that."

"I had no idea you had developed such talents."

"There is much you don't know about me."

"Perhaps I should have hired you, rather than Brica."

She shook her head. "I don't think so, Amator. My ambitions have nothing to do with you."

He faced her. "You're cool now that you don't need my money anymore, aren't you? And are these records of your Order's work?"

"Yes. But there is some history of the Order here—reaching back to the days of Vesta, in fact. I like to maintain such things. And—" She hesitated.

"Yes?"

"There is something of myself as well." She had begun to write out a kind of biography, the story of her own complicated life and the great events that had shaped it. "I want my granddaughters to know where I came from—how they got here. You have a starring role, Amator."

He laughed. "You should make it into a play. Your petty self-justification and trivial complaints would be a great favorite in the Theater of Nero." He turned around, arms spread, almost elegantly, like a dancer. "But none of this scraping and scribbling will do you a grain of good when the barbarians come. All *they* will want is your money. That and the bodies of your beautiful nieces."

"I have prepared for that contingency."

"You are a foolish and complacent old woman. The Vandals will slit your throat."

"We'll see."

He gazed at her, curious, clearly trying to be dismissive, not quite succeeding.

From her first days here she had, in fact, been preparing for the eventuality of breakdown. She had, after all, lived through it all before. Her life had been devoted to finding a safe haven for herself and her family. Rome itself, with its mighty walls and monuments of marble and eight hundred years of arrogant domination, would surely be more shelter than poor Verulamium had been. But still she had prepared what she thought of as a bolt-hole.

For all his bragging, she saw that Amator was not nearly so well prepared. Good, she thought; the more vulnerable he was the better, for she was not done with him yet. Toward that end, in fact, she had made sure to invite him to the wedding of her daughter and the other celebrations. The more he was close to her, the more opportunity she would have to deal with him.

"The ceremonies are not until tomorrow. Why are you here, Amator? Are you so sorry to lose a worker from your bread shop?"

"Brica is a flat, dull girl. She has looks, but none of your spark, little chicken." But his fencing was unconvincing. "I am more concerned about Sulla."

"Ah. Honesty at last. Your pretty boy."

Amator said tensely, "I was not aware until this morning that he is to attend your ceremonies. I had not intended to bring him."

"We gave him his own invitation."

"Yes," he said. "And I know why. *Venus.*"

The boy, whose true inclinations evidently did not match Amator's own, had become besotted with Venus, granddaughter of Helena, and he had been invited to the girl's coming-of-age ceremony.

"I have no problem with that. The boy has a good heart."

Amator jabbed a finger at Regina. "I know you engineered this, you witch. You made sure they met, and encouraged their relationship thereafter. And I know why."

She smiled. "To hurt you? Amator, how could you think such a thing?"

"Your revenge is petty, Regina." But his face, under its mask of cosmetics, was contorted.

"Sulla is just your bed warmer," she said. "And evidently a reluctant one at that."

"Oh, perhaps it started like that. But now . . ." He paced. "Can you understand, Regina? Have *you* ever loved?"

"I understand that you are a foolish and selfish old man," she said coldly. "Your heart has been kept beating, and your cock hardened, by the soft body of this boy. But now he is growing away from you. And when he is gone, you will have nothing left."

"My life is not complete," he said, sighing. "Of course I have a daughter—Brica—but she is not *mine* and never can be. I understand that; I accept it. And I have no son . . . I have named Sulla as my sole legatee. Do you see? The boy is no longer a servant, but my lover, my heir. He is the best part of me. And now, yes, now I fear I am losing him."

She shrugged, careful not to show any reaction to this news about his legacy. "I don't know why you're bringing this to me."

He hung his head. "Whether or not you have brought this cow-eyed niece of yours between us deliberately, I ask you to give him back to me. There—I submit myself to you. You have beaten me, Regina. Are you happy?"

She made no reply.

When he had gone, she summoned Amator's boy, Sulla, to her office.

Regina told him carefully that Amator was jealous and angry. That after tomorrow's feast Sulla would not be allowed near Venus again. That Amator had been lying about his intentions regarding his legacy. That he saw the boy as useful for one thing only, his supple body, and that in future he planned not just to use Sulla himself but also to hire him out to some of his friends, for the sport of it. That Sulla would not be released from this servitude until he was too old to be attractive, or his body too damaged to be useful.

She told Sulla all this briskly, and turned away to her work, as if uncaring of his reaction.

* * *

Regina had quickly become central to the working of the Order. The skills she had acquired as an administrator for Artorius for all those years were essential here.

After she had met her mother at the Flavian Amphitheater, she and Brica had moved without regret out of their cramped apartment over the restaurant and into this grand house. Situated in an outer suburb beyond the ancient Aurelian Wall, it was a large complex of buildings in the traditional style, centered on an atrium and *peristylium*.

But it was obvious that the estate had seen better days. It had once been the home of a senatorial family that, having backed the wrong candidate in one of Rome's many fratricidal contests over the imperial purple, had fallen on hard times and had been forced to sell up. The water supply from the aqueduct system had failed and the bathhouse had been closed down. With many roofs leaking, and the paving in the atrium and *peristylium* cracked and weed-ridden, some of the other buildings had been abandoned, too.

The Order itself hadn't been much healthier than the estate. The numbers in the little community had been dwindling for some time, and when Regina arrived they were down to twenty-five. Those who remained were crammed into the surviving buildings, where they slept on bunks, stacked up like amphorae on shelves.

Still, Regina and Brica had made themselves at home here. Regina had introduced her three sullen little goddesses into the estate's small temple: once the *lararium* of a senator, and now the shrine of a new and more complex family. But she was careful not to provoke Christian wrath. It had long been a tradition for Romans to identify their own deities with those of the barbarian folk they encountered in the provinces. So the *matres*, she said, were manifestations of the virgin mother of Christ, their three faces representing the three Christian virtues of faith, hope, and love.

Regina had not been shy in forcing her opinions and suggestions on Julia and Helena, even from her first days.

Money was the basic problem, as always. The Order was still essentially funded by savings from the last days of the Vestal Virgins, but that was a finite resource that was quickly running down. And as much of it was held in the form of gold coins and jewelry in underground caches, it was, Regina realized quickly, uncomfortably vulnerable to robbery. The only income came from the sporadic earnings of the Order's younger members, in such jobs as Brica's in Amator's bakery. But that was too little and too uneven: few women had ever earned high wages in Rome. And the group was top-heavy with older members like Julia and Helena who had no earnings at all.

Regina had immediately set about establishing a new stream of income.

She decided that the Order should build on its core strengths. It was, after all, a community run by women, and now firmly founded on respectable Christian principles. And yet it was an open secret, which she saw no harm in leaking, that they could trace their heritage back to the Vestal Virgins, and to the pagan goddess who had kept Rome inviolate for eight hundred years. There were plenty of traditionalists, even among practicing Christians, who were attracted to such a combination. To reinforce the image she requested that all the members of the Order wear a simple costume she designed, a long and modest white *stola* marked with a stripe of purple— she had observed how the simple addition of the color purple to a garment reassured these Romans.

It didn't trouble Regina at all that such a sales pitch, based on Christian morality *and* pagan purity, required the holding of two contradictory beliefs at once.

As to what they could sell to their traditionalist market, Regina, after some thought, settled on schooling. The education of the Empire's young had always been a somewhat haphazard process. Only the sons of the rich could expect to enjoy a full education at all three of the traditional levels, primary, grammar, and rhetoric. Girls and lower-class boys often received only the most basic primary education, at which they were taught reading and arithmetic. But in difficult times parents wanted their daughters to be as well equipped as possible to cope with an uncertain future—and that meant giving them an education as good as any boy's.

And that was what Regina determined the Order would provide. Teachers of rhetoric and grammar would be hired, and an education for female students up to a level equivalent to a boy's would be provided. During their teaching the students would be housed on the estate, and raised in a properly moral atmosphere. A fee would be charged, of course, but because teachers were shared among many pupils it would be at a much lower cost than if private tutors had to be hired by a single family.

Regina managed to set all this up within three months. After six the first classes were being held. Among the anxious Roman population it had been a great success. By now, the numbers of girls and young women resident here had risen to a hundred, with many more on waiting lists. This had led to a frantic growth in the estate, with buildings being renovated and hastily extended to cope with the new arrivals. And the money was rolling in. She had even begun a scheme whereby through legacies to the Order a family could ensure the education and upbringing not just of daughters but even of granddaughters, in the next generation.

Julia, Helena, and the other elders were more than happy to leave the running of it all to Regina, but it was trivial compared to the challenge of running Artorius's dunon and his haphazard kingdom. She introduced her own subtle innovations. She stuck to her Celtae calendar, for instance; though she had once protested at its barbarian obscurity, she had grown used to its way of thinking.

And in her new work, she was happy her own objectives were being fulfilled. She had never found a situation over which she had had so much control—never such an opportunity to achieve safety and security for Brica and herself. Indeed, in a sense the Order, dominated by her own relatives, was itself like an extension of her family.

She had little interest in Julia, though.

After that first meeting with her mother, and after she and Brica had moved into the estate, it seemed that some tension within her had been relieved. This introverted old woman had little to do with Regina's own vibrant memories of childhood. Sometimes, though, she caught Julia watching her, as if her arrival had stirred up guilt or remorse that she had thought was long buried. If so, Regina would shed no tears.

And anyhow, Julia was not the center of the family. *She*

was—she and the *matres*, who were with her now as they had always been.

In the morning—the day of the ceremonies—the news was not good.

The last barbarian assault on Rome had come a mere three years before, in the shape of the Huns under their squat and brutal leader Attila, "the Scourge of God." Pope Leo had met Attila in his headquarters, and had persuaded him to spare the city. But now even the pope, it seemed, could not find a way to persuade the Vandals to turn back.

Despite the ominous news, Regina was determined that her day of celebration would go ahead.

It had begun, in fact, the evening before, when Brica had come to Regina's room. It was a tradition for a bride to surrender the relics of her childhood, her toys and childish clothes, to the gods of the *lararium*. But nothing of Brica's childhood had come with them to Rome. So they cut a lock of her hair, tied it up, and burned it before the *matres*. Mother and daughter spent the evening quietly, and retired early, with barely a word passing between them, as they had spent so many evenings before.

In the morning Regina and her mother helped Brica prepare for the wedding ceremony. Brica's hair was dressed in an old Roman way, with six strands separated by a bent iron spear tip. She wore a simple tuniclike dress without a hem, tied around the waist by a woolen girdle. Over her dress she wore a cloak colored a gentle saffron, and on her head she donned an orange veil. Briefly she recaptured the brightness and beauty of the girl of the British forests, and Regina's tough old heart ached at what she had had to do to her daughter.

The morning was still young when the groom and his family arrived.

Castor had been born a slave, the son of slaves. It had only been recently that he himself had been freed, and with his earnings had been able to purchase the manumission of his mother and father. But both parents still wore around their necks the tags of beaten tin that had once marked out their servitude, evidently an act of perverse pride. They kept themselves to themselves, saying little to Regina, or the other elders of the community.

The ceremony itself was conducted immediately. Helena, Regina's aunt, acted as the matron of honor. She took the couple's right hands in her own frail fingers. There was a sacrifice—the killing of a small piglet, carried out in the *peristylium*—and then came the signing and sealing of contracts, which cemented the transfer of the dowry. All this was witnessed by as many of the community's students as could cram into the atrium. Some as young as five, they were a giggling, breathless mass of curiosity and eagerness, and Regina thought they loaned the ceremony happiness and light, like bright flowers.

Little Aemilia's birth ceremony was simple and traditional. It was the eighth day after her birth, so the baby was formally given her names: Aemilia as her family name, and the second taken from the name of her mother. The formal registration of the baby at the Temple of Saturn was to take place the next day.

The father, a stolid man involved in money lending, held the little bundle in his arms and raised her in the air. It was a vital moment for the child, Regina had learned. In Rome, despite its centuries of prosperity, fathers retained the right to reject their children, and the exposure of babies, especially in times of turmoil like the present, was not uncommon.

The coming-of-age ceremony for Venus was more complicated. There was no real Roman tradition to celebrate a girl's passage from childhood—unlike a boy, who, during the festival of Liber and Libera in March, would dedicate his childish clothes to the household gods, don his toga of manhood for the first time, and then march with his family to the Tabularium for registration. Regina had decided, however, that some such tradition should be instigated for the girls of the Order. So now Venus dressed in a simple *stola* to mark her adulthood, like that worn by the women who had taught her, though without the purple stripe of the seniors. She was asked to dedicate a scrap of cloth bearing a trace of her first bleeding, carefully wrapped up in white.

Through all this Regina observed Sulla hovering in the background, his doleful eyes on the girl, and Amator lurked behind *him*, flushed and already drunk, a cup of wine in his hand.

After the ceremonies, the festivities began. The atrium, *peristylium*, and big reception rooms had been set up for food, music, and dancing. When the party started Sulla made straight for Venus. He lavished on her food, wine, and attention, and danced with her as much as he could. Regina relished the deepening anguish on Amator's whitened face.

As the day drew to a close, with the banqueting done and the youngest children already falling asleep, the wedding procession formed up. Tradition had it that the bride should be accompanied by three small boys, one to hold her left hand, one her right, and the third to carry a torch lit from the hearth of her mother's home. Regina had decided that this tradition should be modified a little, and she had three of her younger students take the place of the boys. The procession, of bride, groom, attendants, and wedding guests, would now walk through the streets to the groom's home. There Brica would throw away the torch, and whoever caught it would be assured a long life. She would smear the doorposts with oil and fat, and wreath them with wool. Then she would let her husband carry her across the threshold. Once inside she would touch fire and water symbolically, and then she would be led to the bedchamber . . .

But none of this came to pass.

They had not yet left the compound when the first cries came up from the city. *"The Vandals! The Vandals are here!"*

Regina heard the first screams, saw the first glimmering redness of fires.

Brica clutched her groom's arm. The wedding procession broke up and the guests milled, carrying their torches, confused. Some of them were too drunk to be truly frightened, and some too drunk to care either way.

Julia came to Regina, wringing her hands. "The Vandals attack by night. Everybody knows that. They blacken their faces and their shields, and—"

Regina took her hands and pressed them between her own. Julia's fingers were thin, the bones as fragile as a baby bird's. "Mother," she said. "Don't be afraid. *I have prepared.* Follow my lead. If you support me, nobody need be harmed. Do you understand?"

Through her obvious fear Julia forced a small grin. "You always were the strong one, Regina."

"I'll show you the way. There won't be room for everybody. Family first, of course. Hurry, Mother!"

As Julia bustled away through the confused crowd in search of Helena and the other elders, Regina pulled Brica away from her groom and her attendants. Castor drifted after them, uncertain. They ran first to the small shrine, where Regina swept up the three *matres*, and then to the *peristylium*.

Regina had had a small trapdoor installed here. She peeled back a flap of turf and took a key she wore beneath her dress. The complicated lock was stiff, perhaps rusted, but by using two hands she managed to work its heavy mechanism. Then, with Brica's help, she lifted the trap to expose a blacked-out shaft, with iron rungs set into the wall.

Brica peered down uncertainly. "What is it?"

"A place of safety." Castor had a torch, she saw; she grabbed this from his hands. "Castor. Stay here. Guard this place. Don't let anybody down here. Not yet."

"But—"

"Your wife will be safe here. Will you do as I say?"

"Yes, mistress."

"Brica, follow me."

With the torch held high, Regina made her way down the iron rungs. It was a difficult journey to make with one free hand, and she felt stiff, heavy, clumsy; she was getting too old for such adventures. But Brica was following.

At the bottom of the shaft Regina found herself standing in an arched tunnel, lined with concrete and brick. The walls were pocked with chambers, shelves, and alcoves, as if she had entered a vast cupboard. The roof was only a little higher than her own head, and if she had reached out she could have touched both walls. This tunnel was only part of a great warren of passageways and chambers that had been dug into this soft rock. Everything was blackened by the smoke of torches and candles, and there was a smell of damp and rot.

Brica was fingering her dress, which was streaked with black mud. "I am filthy," she murmured.

Regina could hear a hint of humor in her daughter's voice. She hugged her briefly. "I doubt if your wedding procession is likely to take place today. Not unless you want a few black-painted barbarians to join it . . ."

Brica walked slowly down the narrow passageway. The walls were painted with symbols, lamb, fish, shepherd, Christian symbols, and the alcoves contained objects like lamps and glass vessels—and many, many wrapped-up shrouds. These were bodies, some already centuries old, wrapped in lime-coated cloth. "What is this place?"

"A Catacomb. A Christian cemetery, from the days of persecution. They dug out such cellars to bury their dead without interference. The owner of the estate in those days must have been sympathetic. There are many such holes in the ground, here along the Appian Way."

"And here you think we will be safe."

"The barbarians are not Romans," Regina said dryly. "They will not even know such places exist. And if they did they would ignore them for the easier pickings of the mansions and churches above the ground. As soon as I learned this place was here I realized its usefulness, and had passageways sunk to it from the house. I used workmen from outside the city—I doubt we will be betrayed."

"You always did think ahead, Mother," Brica said dryly. "We must fetch the others."

"I'll do that," Regina said sharply. "You stay here. When they come they will be confused, frightened. Drunk! Organize them. Reassure them. I am counting on you, Brica. Look—there is food *here*, a little water to be had from *this* spigot, torches to be lit *here*."

Brica nodded. "I understand."

"Good." Regina hurried up to the surface.

Julia and the elders had already organized a queue, reasonably orderly, before the gaping hole in the ground, where Castor still stood patiently.

Regina clambered up on a low wall and clapped her hands for attention. "We can take only the children, and some women. Julia, you go first, and help Brica. Then the children, the smallest first. If we can take mothers, we will do so. Husbands, fathers, please go to your homes. I know you will all understand your duty."

She was greeted by somber, blanched faces. There were grave nods of acquiescence.

The children started to file nervously into the shaft, many of them weeping to be separated from their mothers. Regina saw Venus pass into the ground, and the baby Aemilia in the arms of her mother, Regina's half sister Leda.

Sulla came to her. His broad, slightly bloated face was streaked with tears. But Amator was just behind him. Sulla said, "Regina, let me come. The Vandals—someone like me—" There had been rumors of how the Vandals treated those they saw as decadent, of pretty boys being murdered by impalement.

Amator pulled at his arm. "No, Come away, my love, come away with me. I will make you safe—you don't need this witch and her hole in the ground—"

Regina felt a cold satisfaction. She had not planned the arrival of the barbarians that day, but by keeping Sulla and Amator close to her, she had set up this opportunity. And now it was unfolding perfectly.

She stepped close to Sulla and whispered, "You can join us." *You and Amator's legacy,* she thought. "But first you must free yourself." Sulla looked confused. She let a knife fall from her sleeve—a knife she always carried in these difficult times—and slipped it into his hand. *"Free yourself."*

His eyes widened. He nodded and pulled away.

Castor approached Regina. "Is Brica—"

"She is safe."

He nodded. "Soon I will be with her."

"No. I have an assignment for you. When the last of us has descended, close the hatch and cover it over with turf. Move the furniture—a table, a couch—conceal the entrance. Do you understand? I know it means you will be kept apart from Brica. But it is the only way she can be safe. She is counting on you, Castor."

His eyes narrowed, and she wondered briefly if he read her calculation: that despite the marriage only that morning, already she was separating him from Brica, drawing her back into the family. But he nodded, and he hurried to help the elders usher the children to the shaft.

Regina stayed by the trapdoor, helping the students descend into the dark, until she saw Sulla embrace Amator—and Amator fell to the ground, unnoticed in the chaotic confusion in the garden—and then, as the smoke of the fires grew thick in the air, she clambered down into the ground herself.

The Vandals remained in the city for two weeks. They invaded the homes of the rich, broke into the Christian churches, stripped the gilded tiles from the ancient Temple of Capitoline Jupiter. And they murdered, maimed, and raped Romans both high and low.

Regina had prepared for a siege. She had installed a lead-pipe feed from the main water supply, and there were caches of food—dried fruit, meat, nuts. Even if the trapdoor entrance in the *peristylium* was discovered and broken open, the Catacombs were a warren that extended far underground, and there were many places where the tunnels could be blocked off and defended. There was even another tunnel that led out of here altogether to one of the main city sewers, out of which they could find a way to the daylight. It wouldn't be a pleasant journey, but it would lead them to safety.

Stuck in these soot-stained tunnels, it wasn't a happy time for anybody. But despite their protests at deprivation, fear for their families, and plain discomfort in this place of corpses, Regina knew that her charges accepted that she had delivered them to safety, out of sight of the black-painted monsters rampaging above.

Brica pined for Castor, but Regina was unconcerned. In the final crisis Brica had shown her true loyalties—to the family buried in the ground, not to the boy on the surface—and she sensed that their marriage, even children, would not change that. Brica, after all, carried Regina's own blood, and the blood of Julia, and it was no surprise that her instincts had in the end proven similar.

At last the Vandals marched back to their camps, with thousands of captives and wagons piled high with plunder. Regina kept her charges safe until she was certain the last of them had gone.

chapter 29

It was only two days after her meeting with Giuliano that Rosa came for Lucia. Maria Ludovica had, peacefully, died. And Lucia must be prepared.

It took a month. Then the day of her final induction arrived.

In a small chamber, deep on the third level, Lucia was asked to strip. She was examined quickly by a female doctor. In the last few days she had already endured a whole battery of medical tests.

Then she was dressed in a simple smocklike dress called a *stola*. It was white, but with a little purple fabric sewn in. The cloth was very soft, and she wondered how old it was. Her watch and bits of jewelry were taken from her. She wasn't allowed any underwear; she would be naked, save for the *stola*. But she was given leather sandals to protect her feet from the cold rock. Murmuring wordlessly, Pina braided Lucia's hair and tied it up into a bun.

Nothing had been explained to Lucia in advance. She did not know what to expect today. Since Pina had woken her that morning she had felt detached—as if she were a mere observer of what her body was going through, or as if she were fading back into the ghostlike, invisible, unreal figure she had become during her ostracism. She only wanted to be part of the Order, a sister again. She didn't want her head cluttered up with more questions. She simply accepted each event as it happened, trying not to think any further.

But she was glad Pina was here. Lucia had asked for her. At this strange time it would be comforting to have somebody who knew her so deeply close by.

Pina led her from the brightly lit changing room, out into the dark.

They followed a narrow, dank passage. Arches supported the roof—small red bricks embedded in thick mortar, just as you would see in Rome's imperial ruins. This was a very old place, she thought, very old indeed.

They came to a small, poky chamber. It was a kind of theater, Lucia realized. It had a raised stage, rooms for actors and scenery, and curved rows of seats, all carved from the tufa. It was very primitive, more or less cut out of the raw rock, and could hold no more than fifty people or so, but an elaborate chrome kissing-fish logo adorned one wall. There was a couch on the stage, which was otherwise bare.

The lighting was dim and smoky, coming from lamps in alcoves carved into the walls: Lucia could smell burning oil. And it was cold. She felt goose bumps on her arms, and her nipples hardened with the cold and pushed against the fine cloth of her shift. She longed to cover herself with her hands, but she knew she must not.

Rosa was here, waiting for her, and Rosetta, one of Lucia's sisters from her age group, and a couple of older women she didn't recognize. All of them were dressed in simple garments, like her own *stola*. Rosetta's shift had no purple inlay, though, and the round-eyed girl was wearing training shoes and socks.

The older women—*older* meaning perhaps Rosa's age— looked at her intently. She sensed hostility in their steady glare, as if they didn't really want her to be here, as if they would have preferred it to be somebody else. Rosa by comparison seemed triumphant, glowing. Lucia remembered how Rosa had said she had had to fight to ensure Lucia's acceptance as a new *mamma*. Perhaps these two women had fought for other candidates. Lucia knew nothing of these battles. But she was still fragile from her ostracism, and she quailed from their glares; she didn't want anybody to dislike her.

And finally, two very old-looking ladies sat in wheelchairs. They were swathed in silvery high-tech heat-retaining blankets that looked very modern and out of place here. They were *matres*, *mamme-nonne*—perhaps even older than Maria Ludovica. Their eyes were like bits of granite, sparkling in the lamplight as they stared at Lucia.

Rosa walked toward her, smiling. She was holding three little statues; they were the tiny, crudely carved figures from the alcove. "Lucia, welcome to your new life."

She turned away and began to talk softly in an unfamiliar language—it was Latin, Lucia realized after a time. Occasionally the *mamme-nonne* mumbled responses. Their voices were as dry as dead leaves.

Rosa beckoned Pina forward. Pina produced a small, folded white towel. She unfolded this, to reveal a scrap of linen, stained brown.

Lucia recoiled.

Rosa said, "A little of your first bleeding. You tried to destroy it all, didn't you? It took poor Pina a long time to find it. Well, now we can finish the job . . ."

Rosetta carried over a lamp. It was just a wick floating in a pot of oil, small enough to hold in cupped hands. Rosa fed the bit of cloth to the lamp's flame. It scorched, curled up, and vanished.

All through this the *matres* were chanting bits of Latin—the same phrases, it seemed, over and over.

Lucia whispered to Pina, "I don't understand what they are saying."

"That your blood is precious," Pina whispered back. "And they are saying, *Sisters matter more than daughters. Sisters matter more than daughters . . .*"

"It's just like kindergarten," Lucia whispered, trying to make her voice light.

Pina forced a smile. But her eyes were wide, scared.

"Now," Rosa said, "it's time." She looked past Lucia's shoulder.

Giuliano stood on the stage, beside the couch. He was wearing a shift like Lucia's, and he was barefoot. He was looking at her with an intensity that burned through his smile. And an erection pushed out the front of his smock.

Rosa and Pina took her hands and led her toward the couch on the stage. The others were watching, wide-eyed Rosetta, the *matres* with their eyes like hawks. They chanted Latin, and Pina softly translated: "Your blood is the blood of the Order itself. It must not be mixed with water. I think that means, diluted by the blood of an outsider, a *contadino*. Your blood is precious . . ."

It was like a dream—the rhythmic chanting, the uncertain light, the ancient, rounded walls of the theater—everything was unreal save the prickle of cold on her arms. Yet she submitted, as she had at each step.

On the stage, Rosa bade her lift her arms. With a swift motion Pina and Rosa peeled her shift up and over her body. She was left truly naked now, and the little warmth that the cloth had given her was gone.

When she met Giuliano's eyes, she thought she saw uncertainty. She wondered what he was thinking, how he was truly feeling. But then his gaze strayed to her neck, her breasts, and she was alone again.

Submitting to Rosa's gentle prompting, she lay down on the couch. It was covered by a thin mattress and a rich crimson cloth, but the couch felt hard under her back, and the cloth prickled her skin.

"Lift up your arms," Rosa whispered. "Welcome him."

Lucia did as she was told.

She was looking up at the ceiling, grimed by centuries of smoke, through the frame of her white arms, her limp fingers. In this frame appeared Giuliano. She felt his hands on her thighs. She opened her legs. He lifted up his shift, and placed his arms to either side of her body, to support his weight. His face descended toward hers like a falling moon. She folded her arms over his back; she felt a mat of thick hair there.

Unbidden, a memory of Daniel's face floated into her mind.

"This is the end of my life," she whispered to Giuliano.

He frowned. "We mustn't talk."

"The end of all choices—"

"I will be gentle." He leaned down and kissed her on the lips. She smelled garlic and fish on his hot breath.

She still had Daniel's business card, hidden in a corner of her bag.

When Giuliano entered her it hurt, terribly.

Once the ceremony was over, Rosa told Lucia that she would never see Giuliano Andreoli again. Love, it seemed, was over for her.

And it was only a few days after the ceremony that she found out she was pregnant.

chapter 30

In the morning of every seventh day, the Order's governing Council would meet in the Crypt's *peristylium*. Such meetings dated back to the difficult times after the Vandal incursion, already fifteen years ago, when the seniors, Julia, Helena, and Regina, had gathered with selected others to thrash out the priorities for the week.

Regina, now sixty-five years old and, since her mother's death, the most senior survivor of the Order's founding days, had deliberately developed a habit of being late for these meetings. This morning, instead of making for the *peristylium*, she began her day with a walk to the Crypt's farthest reaches, where the tunnels were steadily being extended into the soft tufa rock.

These days the Order employed experienced miners for this work. They used socketed picks and axes, and carried out rubble in framed leather sacks. To crack harder rock faces they would set fires; water would be thrown on the heated rock, and the sudden cooling would shatter the face. All this used a lot of wood, and more wood was required for lumber to prop up the shafts they dug; there were generally more lumbermen at work, in fact, than miners.

The miners were working under much the same conditions as in mines of coal and metal ore across Europe. Their working lives in these dark, sulfurous, smoke-choked conditions were short—not that that mattered, as most were slaves. But here, of course, their legacy would not be what they extracted from the ground but the holes they left behind.

When the miners had roughly shaped out the new chambers and corridors, engineers followed to line and reinforce the walls with concrete, which they would later face with brick.

The concrete was made from an aggregate of stone and tile set in mortar made with water, lime, and a particular volcanic sand called pozzolana. Making concrete like this took a toll on the slave labor used to ram it in place. But the use of that labor made it immensely durable.

The work was going ahead satisfactorily. After a curt talk with the foremen, Regina made her way back to the core of the Crypt, and, reluctantly, the Council meeting.

When she arrived, the meeting was well in progress—as it ought to have been, for Regina would fly into a fury if the sessions were held up for her absence.

Leda, Regina's half sister, was in the chair. Leda at sixty was a thickset, competent-looking woman. Brica was here, heavily pregnant once again, with her first daughter Agrippina at her side. Brica looked tired, her face drawn, and Agrippina held her hand in silent support.

The business in progress was a matter of reallocation. Leda said, "Three days ago the air in domain seven was notably foul, but when we moved cohort thirteen up from the second level, we discovered that the cold there became uncomfortable. I suggest we restore thirteen to the second and reallocate fifteen to the first . . ."

It was complicated but routine business, and Regina was happy to sit back and allow the discussion to continue. She noted approvingly that Aemilia, daughter of Leda and now fifteen years old, was painstakingly recording the meeting's deliberations on a series of wax tablets. Regina had always insisted on good record keeping. Records were the Order's memory, she said, and she who forgets her past is doomed to a short future.

And on the specific issue of quarters allocation—or "huddling," as some of the younger members called it—analysis of several years' allocation records, and the movement of the air through the corridors in response to the shifting of warm human bodies, had yielded some valuable lessons in the endless quest to keep the Crypt's air fresh.

Of course this place was not really a *peristylium*, for it was buried deep underground. But in a moment of fancy on Regina's part the plastered walls had been painted with vines and flowers, and the little chamber had been equipped with marble paving stones, trellises, and stone benches and low tables, just like a real garden. There was even a flower bed here, of sorts, in a stone tray; but all that grew were mushrooms, prettily arranged, buttons and folds and parasols of gray, brown, and black. Regina was fond of the place. Something about it reminded her of the ruined bathhouse in Julia's villa, where she had once discovered a secret garden of wildflowers. There was even a small, somewhat amateurish mosaic pavement, inset with the symbol some of the younger members of the Order had taken to favoring: two fish, like the old Christian symbol, but face to face, mouth to mouth, like sisters sharing a secret.

As the Council members talked on, two young girls were washing down the walls, a regular chore necessary throughout the Crypt to keep the walls and ceilings from blackening with soot and lichen.

All the women at the meeting wore simple tunics and dresses with a woven-in purple stripe: all the same design. There were no uniforms here, no status; this was not the army, or the Senate, and Regina had always been determined to keep it that way. She had even resisted attempts to formalize the religious aspects of the Order's life. There would be no hierarchy of clergy here, no *pontifices*, for that was just another way for power to accumulate in the hands of the few. The Order itself was more significant than any individual.

Even, as she reminded herself every day, Regina.

She returned her attention to the meeting, which had moved on.

Agrippina read from a tablet in her clear voice. ". . . This correspondent is called Ambrosius Aurelianus," she said. "He claims to be a general on the staff of Artorius, the *riothamus* of Britain." She looked expectantly at Regina.

Regina said, "I remember him." Ambrosius the bright boy, fierce and strong and handsome, willing to give his life for the dreams of the *riothamus*—a man in his forties now, she supposed, and yet still, it seemed, willing to follow the old dream. She was a little surprised to hear that Artorius was still alive, still battling on foreign fields.

The Council had fallen silent. They were looking at her.

"What? What did you say?"

"This Aurelianus is coming to Rome," Agrippina repeated patiently. "He wants to meet you, Grandmother. He has sent this note—"

"No doubt after money to waste on soldiering," Regina growled.

"It would do no harm for you to meet him," Leda suggested. "As you always tell us, you never know what might come of it."

"Yes, yes. Don't nag me, Leda. All right, I'll meet him. Next?"

Next, Messalina got carefully to her feet. Daughter of the long-dead Helena, she was about the same age as Regina, but time had not been kind; she was plagued with arthritis. She said, "I have decided I should stand down from the Council." She spent some time apologizing for this, blaming her health, and emphasizing what an honor it was to have served. "I suggest that Livia take my place." It had become the custom for outgoing Council members to nominate their successors. Livia was her sister, another cousin of Regina's. "Livia is five years younger than I am, and her health has remained strong, and—"

"No," said Regina flatly.

The others looked around at her, shocked. Messalina stood at a slight lean, her fingertips resting on the marble tabletop, watching her warily.

Regina said, "I'm sorry, Messalina. Livia is a fine woman. But I think she would be a poor choice." Regina pointed boldly at Venus—daughter of Messalina, here to assist her mother, and, save for Aemilia and Agrippina, at thirty the youngest person present. "Venus has contributed many times to the business of this group. She will fill her mother's place well."

Venus, once the object of Sulla's adolescent lust, had matured into a capable woman. She looked pleased, but a little frightened. But Messalina stayed on her feet some time, quietly arguing; she did not want to criticize her daughter before this group, but obviously thought her sister would be a better choice.

Leda pressed Regina to give a reason for her recommendation. Regina was not sure she could have articulated it. She had always made her decisions by instinct, and then had to rationalize them later. But it was best for the Order; she was sure of that.

A precedent had to be set. She knew in her heart that the Order could not be entrusted forever to its most senior members. She herself was in her sixties now, and while she had not slowed down as much as poor Messalina, she knew she would not last forever. She did not want the Order to be dependent on her. On the contrary, she wanted assurance that the Order would long survive her. She would like to arrange things so that *anybody* of healthy mind could serve on the Council and the business of the Order would still be done.

In fact, if she could have found a way, she would have abolished the Council altogether. The Order's systems, operating independently, should sustain it—just as once the great systems of taxation and spending, of law and class, had sustained the Empire itself far beyond the life of any one person, even the greatest of emperors.

Even though no individual human was immortal, there was no reason why the *Order* should not live forever. But to do that it had to shake off its reliance on people.

Of course, as the talking ran down, Regina's decision was upheld. Venus was welcomed to the select group of twelve Council members with a ripple of applause.

Messalina resumed her seat with ill grace. There was personal tension here, for Messalina had been a member of the Order long before her cousin Regina had arrived from Britain, with her rough accent and brisk ways: Regina was still a newcomer here, even after seventeen years. But Regina brushed that aside. Such things mattered nothing to her, as long as she achieved what she set out to achieve.

After a little more business the meeting wound up.

Brica approached her mother. Deep in her sixth pregnancy, she walked almost as cautiously as old Messalina, and she propped her hands on her back for support. Beside her, her eldest daughter Agrippina walked with eyes shyly downcast.

Regina smiled, and put her hand on Brica's bulge. "I can feel her, or him," Regina said. "Restless little soul."

"She longs to be out in the world—as I long for her to be out, too."

Brica truly did look exhausted. She was in her forties now, and this child, her third by her second husband, had proven especially trying. Besides, that new husband was not so supportive as dull but good-hearted Castor—who had eventually fallen in love with a woman from beyond the Order, and now lived in contentment with a young second family in a jostling suburb, safe from the subterranean strangeness of the Crypt. But still, Agrippina had proven a strong support as she had grown, as had Brica's second daughter, eleven years old, named Julia for her long-dead great-grandmother.

It was Agrippina, as it happened, that Brica wanted to talk about.

"Her bleeding has begun," Brica said softly, and Agrippina's face purpled. "It is time for her celebration—the first of my children to become a woman." Brica hugged her daughter. "Already the boys watch her—I've seen their eyes—and soon she will be having babies of her own."

"Oh, *Mother*," muttered the wretched Agrippina.

"I'll be a grandmother," said Brica. "And you, Mother, a *great*-grandmother. With Agrippina fertile I won't be having any more children of my own . . . I hope this will be the last before my change . . . As for the ceremony—"

"No," said Regina sharply.

Agrippina looked at her in shock.

Brica said, "But every girl since Venus—on my own wedding day, as you remember well, Mother—has been celebrated." Anger flared briefly. "What are you saying—that my daughter, your own blood, isn't good enough for such an honor?"

"No, of course not." Regina thought fast, but inconclusively. It had been another impulsive decision, whose basis she didn't yet understand herself. "I didn't mean that. Of course you must plan the ceremony," she said, seeking time to think.

But she and Brica were of course long-established combatants, and Brica had caught that note of sharpness. She glared at her mother, but her face was a hollow-eyed mask of fatigue, and she clearly did not want to argue.

Brica took her daughter's arm. "Fine. Come, Agrippina." And they left the *peristylium* without looking back.

Since that dreadful day when the Vandals had ravaged Rome, things had changed greatly for the Order.

As the Order's wealth had increased, a great deal had been invested in the estate on the Appian Way, which today served primarily as a school. But even more money had been sunk underground.

The use of the Catacombs had proven so obviously valuable that nobody had objected when Regina had suggested extending and modifying them. The old cemetery directly beneath the house remained, almost unmodified; for a Christian order it would have been disrespectful to have disturbed such a shrine. But the tunnels had been greatly extended, and new rooms and passageways had been dug into the soft rock.

After fifteen years of steady burrowing the Order's underground warren, buried deep in the Roman ground, had spread over two levels. It housed three hundred people, almost all of them women and children. It was comfortable, once you got used to the dim light and cramped corridors. Of course the Crypt would always be dependent on the surface world, for an inflow of food and water, an outflow of sewage, and for money and building materials and labor: the complex could never cut adrift of the world, like a ship sailing away into an underground sea. But the Council had done all they could to maintain a wide range of links and relationships with suppliers and customers and allies in the outside world, making their sources as diverse as possible, so they were dependent on no one group or person.

As the depth of the Crypt had increased, incidences of flooding or collapse had been dealt with by brute force, with the application of plenty of Roman concrete and brick. Problems with ventilation and heating had been more insidious. Air shafts had been dug out, to be concealed aboveground as artfully as possible. Great fires were lit at the base of some of these shafts, so that the rising air would draw fresh breezes through the tunnels—a practice adopted from deep mines, many of whose engineers Regina had hired to supervise the extension of the Crypt.

But the air shafts alone weren't enough. There had been a near disaster when a group of five students had been found unconscious, the air in their room foul, a stagnant puddle at the end of a corridor. It had been fortunate for all concerned, Regina thought, that only one student had died—and that her parents, a stoical equestrian family, had been happy to accept the death of their elder daughter as a price to be paid for the safety of their two younger children, both also with the Order. After that incident an elaborate air-monitoring system had been evolved. In every passageway and room there were candles burning, bits of reed dangled from the walls to show the air currents, and caged birds sang in most of the main chambers and corridors.

And it had been found that the simplest way to adjust the environment was by moving people.

A person blocked the flow of air, consumed its vital goodness, and pumped a lot of heat into it besides. So you could improve the flow of air into a problematic region by simply evacuating the passageways around it and moving the people somewhere else. You could likewise cool an area by taking out its people—or warm it up, by crowding more people in. It was impossible to solve every problem by "huddling." The kitchens, and the nursery and crèche where the Order's babies were cared for en masse, were a constant difficulty. But on the whole, with careful monitoring and analysis, the system worked well, and was becoming increasingly effective as they learned.

Of course there were many grumbles at this regime of constant shifting, but people had adapted. Space had been at a premium from the beginning, so you weren't allowed to bring a great deal of personal baggage into the Crypt in the first place. And furniture in each dormitory room was becoming uniform, so it made no real difference where you were.

As far as Regina was concerned, this constant uprooting was an unexpected side benefit. Regina wanted every sister to think of the whole Crypt as her home, not just her own little corner of it.

Meanwhile Order members began to spend an increasing amount of time underground.

In the Crypt there was no summer or winter, and no threats

from barbarians or bandits, and no disease, as all the food and water was clean. And it was *safe* in here, safe and orderly in a world that was becoming increasingly threatening. To the children who had been born here, in fact, it was the aboveground world that seemed strange—a disorderly place where the wind blew without control and water just fell from the sky . . .

One day, Regina mused, somebody would be born in the Crypt, would live out her whole life underground, and then die here, her body being fed to the great ventilation furnaces, a last contribution to the Order. Regina would not live to see it happen, but she was sure that grand dream would soon be fulfilled.

Regina met Ambrosius Aurelianus seven days later. He stood in the Forum, listening to an orator who declaimed the ruin of the world to a cheerful crowd. He wore the leather armor of a Celtae warrior, even here in the heart of Rome. Ambrosius had aged, but he was much as Regina remembered—the stocky frame, the sturdy, determined face. His startling blond hair was receding, and a deep scar disfigured one side of his face. But his blue eyes held the same warm zeal she remembered from Artorius's war councils, all those years ago in Londinium.

He greeted her with clumsy gallantry, insisting she hadn't changed.

She snorted at that. "You are a fool, Ambrosius Aurelianus, and from what I remember you always were. But you are a brave fool to try such endearments on a vicious old hag like me."

He laughed. "I have the diplomatic skills of most soldiers, madam. But I am glad to see you." It was strange to hear the British language spoken so fluently; even Brica rarely spoke more than the odd phrase nowadays.

They walked to a tavern she knew, a respectable *popina*, not far from the Forum; it was built in a cellar, and its dark, sweet-smelling interior, reminding her of the Crypt, made her feel at home. Ambrosius bought a pitcher of wine, which she drank with water and flavored with herbs and resin. He seemed hungry, and ordered olives, bread, and roasted meat cut into cubes; he said he relished the richly flavored Roman cuisine.

He described his visit. He was staying with a rich sponsor who entertained him with lavish Roman hospitality. "They say that everybody should see Rome before they die, and I am glad I have done as much." Regina was sure he was sincere. Despite times of trouble and uncertainty, the crowds in the markets were as busy and affable as ever, there were still wrestling matches and the slaughter of beasts in the amphitheater, and chariots still raced around the Circus Maximus. "But there are so many empty spaces. It seems to me that Rome's statues must outnumber the living."

"Perhaps. But it is not statues you have come to visit, Ambrosius Aurelianus, for statues have no purses."

He grinned ruefully. "And you never were a fool . . . No wonder Artorius always relied on you. And he needs you again, Regina."

He gave her a brief account of Artorius's career since her departure. His kingdom, based on the dunon, still thrived. But the Saxons continued their relentless advance. One leader called Aelle was proving particularly troublesome; he was said to have ambitions of founding yet another new Saxon kingdom on the south coast. Only Artorius, it seemed, offered any resistance to the Saxons' expanse, and their terrible cleansing; Regina listened somewhat impatiently to tales of his glorious exploits.

But his grander dreams remained. Each time the Saxons were driven back, Artorius would take his troops away to Gaul, where he continued to campaign season after season against the troops of the new kingdoms that were coalescing there, and even against the remnant Roman forces—all part of his long-standing ambition to march on Rome itself and claim the purple.

And, of course, Ambrosius was here to request money to support Artorius's campaigning, money from the Order's already fabled coffers.

"How ironic," Regina said, "that you have come to Rome to seek funds, so you can return with soldiers!"

Ambrosius spread his hands. "One must do one's duty, no matter how ironic."

Artorius must have been desperate even to have considered such an approach, she thought; and that made her decision not to waste any of the Order's funds even easier to make. "Here we celebrate life, not death," she said. "Here each life is to be cherished, not spent like a token in some military adventure. That is our fundamental philosophy—it has always been *my* philosophy. I have said as much to Artorius, not that I imagine he listened."

Ambrosius was a man of sense, who didn't believe in wasting time. He didn't try to change her mind. "I suspect Artorius already knows your answer," he said wryly.

"Yes, I suspect he does. Wish him my blessing . . ."

She urged Ambrosius to stay for another day, for tomorrow there would be the coming-of-age ceremony, which she invited him to attend. "I would like you to leave with positive memories," she said.

He agreed to stay.

He told her something of the fate of Durnovaria, the town closest to Artorius's dunon. Its decline had never been reversed, and now it had been abandoned for perhaps forty years. "In places you can see where the buildings used to be, from courses of stone, rectangles and lines across the ground. But otherwise it is like a patch of young forest, where oak trees are spreading and foxes lurk, with only a few hummocks to show that once a whole town existed . . ."

It was only after their conversation was over that Regina remembered the ceremony she had invited him to would be the awkward affair of Agrippina, her granddaughter.

Fifteen years after the first of these ceremonies, for Venus daughter of Messalina, the coming-of-age celebrations had evolved their own rituals, as had so many of the practices of the Order. But this time, Regina felt instinctively, a new precedent must be set.

At first Regina let events follow the time-honored pattern. Agrippina's sisters, aunts, cousins, and mother formed a circle around her on the stage of the Crypt's tiny theater. They were in a pool of light cast by an array of lanterns and candles, and they were surrounded by as many of the Order as could squeeze in.

The only male, apart from some small boys with their mothers and sisters, was Ambrosius. Standing tall in his dark brown armor, amid women and girls in their costumes of white and purple, he was like a pillar of male strangeness, utterly out of place.

As the final preparations were made, Regina approached him, amused. "You don't look terribly comfortable."

"I can't deny that," he said, and he mopped his neck. "It is the low ceilings. The dense air. The *smell*." He eyed her uneasily. "I don't wish to give offense—perhaps you have become used to it. It is a smell of people—or of animals, perhaps—almost like the amphitheater, during the hunting shows."

"And this makes you uncomfortable. You, a veteran of a hundred battlefields!"

"Then there's the *sameness*. Everywhere I look I see the same corridors, the chambers, the decorations—even the same faces, it seems. Though beautiful faces—those haunting eyes, like slate—I feel buried in this pit of yours—turned around, dizzy. It isn't for me!"

"It isn't meant for you," she said sharply.

The little ceremony began at last, Agrippina blushed prettily, and her gravid mother held her hand. Agrippina dedicated her childish clothes to the *matres* by feeding them into a brazier, and was given her first adult *stola*, simple white with a fine purple line woven in.

But when it came to the point where Agrippina was to burn a scrap of linen stained with a little of her first bleeding, Regina stepped forward.

"No," she said loudly, into a shocked silence. She had had time to think through her first instinctive refusal of this event, and she thought she understood what must be done. She took the scrap of linen from Brica, and held it up. "This is to be destroyed, but not celebrated." She fed it into the brazier, and as the little flames licked she heard the shocked gasps of those who watched. She took Agrippina's hand and placed it over Brica's swollen belly. "*This* is what is important. This, your unborn sister.

"Agrippina, your bleeding is no shame. But you are to hide it from others, and you will not remark on it. Your life belongs, not to your daughters, *but to your sisters*—the one here in Brica's belly, and those born thereafter. When Brica's blood dries—well, perhaps then your turn will come to serve. But until then, if you choose to bear a child, then you will bear it beyond these walls."

Agrippina looked terrified. "You would exile me for becoming pregnant?"

"It is your choice," said Regina. Though her tone was gentle, she knew the menace in her words was unmistakable. She turned and faced the watching group. "Do not question this. It must always be so—not because I say it, but because it is best for the Order. *Sisters matter more than daughters.*"

For a moment Brica faced her, and Regina thought she saw a spark of defiance in her daughter's eyes. But Brica was heavily pregnant, worn out by fifteen years of pregnancies—and besides, she had been defeated by Regina long ago. Her shoulders slumped, she led a weeping Agrippina away.

Regina felt a twinge of guilt. Why did it have to be like this? Why did she have to inflict so much pain on her children? . . . "Because it is for the best," she muttered. "Even if they cannot see it."

The group broke up, avoiding Regina. Only Ambrosius was left watching her, his eyes wide.

Later, in her office, they drank watered wine. Ambrosius was cautious, watchful.

She smiled, tired. "You think I am a mad old woman."

"I understand nothing of what I have seen here," he said honestly. "Would you really turn her out if she got pregnant?"

"Agrippina has spent almost all her life in the Crypt. What lies outside, the disorder, the chaos—even the *weather*— rightly terrifies her. But it would be for the best."

"She is your granddaughter," he said hotly. "How can you say such an exile would be the best for her?"

"Not for *her*," Regina said. "The best for those who follow. The best for the Order . . . It is hard for me to understand, too," she said bluntly. "I follow my instincts—make my decisions— and then try to understand *why* I do what I do, where is the rightness.

"But consider this." She poured a glass of wine. "We are safe in here, and we are bound by family ties. In fact we are so crammed in that it is only family ties that keep us from murdering each other. But with time family ties weaken. How can I keep that from happening?

"Imagine this wine is the blood of my daughter—blood that is mine, mixed with that of a buffoon called Amator—he does not matter. Brica gives birth." She poured some of the wine into a second glass, and mixed it with water. "Here is Agrippina—half the blood of Brica, half of her father—and so only a *quarter* mine. But if Agrippina were to have a child—" She poured the mixture into another glass, diluting it further. "Agrippina's blood is mixed with the father's, and so is only an *eighth* mine." She sat back and sighed. "My granddaughter's blood is closer to mine than is my great-granddaughter's. And so I want more granddaughters. Do you see?"

"Yes, but I don't—"

"We can't leave this Crypt," she snapped. "We have no arms, no warriors to protect us. And though we are expanding our space, our numbers expand faster. We can't support too many babies at once—we don't have the room. Now—" She pushed forward the glasses. "Suppose I have to choose between a baby of Agrippina's, or another baby of Brica's. Brica's baby would be closer to my blood, which would bind us more tightly together—and, if Agrippina were to support her mother, might actually have a better chance of living to adulthood. Which should I choose?"

He nodded slowly. "Yes, I see your logic—*sisters matter more than daughters*—it is better for Agrippina to support more sisters than to have her own children. But it is an insane logic, Regina."

"Insane?"

"It is better for you, perhaps, if you accept this hot logic of the blood, even better for your Order—*but not for Agrippina.*"

She shrugged. "If Agrippina doesn't accept it, she can leave."

He said gently, "You are like no woman I ever encountered. Like no mother, certainly. And yet you endure; I can't deny that." He strode and began pacing around the room, fingering the hilt of the dagger at his belt. "But I must get out of here," he said. "The airlessness—the closeness—forgive me, madam."

She smiled, and rose to show him out.

chapter 31

The changes in her body seemed to come terribly quickly. She passed water almost hourly. Her breasts swelled and became sensitive. She tried to maintain her normal life—her classes, her after-hours work in the *scrinium*—but if she had stuck out from the crowd before, now it was by a mile.

She sat with Pina in a refectory. "Before they ignored me. Now they stare the whole time."

Pina grinned. "They're just responding to you. A very basic human reaction. You glow, Lucia. You can't help it."

"Do you think they envy me?" She looked at her friend. "Do you?"

Pina's expression became complex. "I don't know. I will never have what you have. I can't imagine how it feels."

"A part of you wants it, though," Lucia said bluntly. "A part of you wants to be a mother, as all women were mothers, in primitive times."

"But what we have here is better. *Sisters matter more than daughters.*"

"Of course," Lucia said mechanically. "But I'll tell you what, if anybody does envy me, they can watch me throwing up in the mornings."

Pina laughed. "Well, you can't go on working in the *scrinium*."

"No. I distract everybody."

"Shall I speak to Rosa? You ought to continue your schooling. But perhaps they will find you an apartment down with the *matres*."

"Wonderful. Order my false teeth and smelly cardigan now . . ."

* * *

The day after that, her morning nausea was worse than ever. Soon she felt so exhausted that she had to give up her classes as well as her work.

By the sixth week, as Pina had suggested, she was moved to a small room on the third story, in the deep downbelow.

It was dark, the walls coated with rich flocked wallpaper and the floor thickly carpeted, and it was cluttered with ancient-looking furniture. It was an old lady's room, she thought miserably. But she had it to herself, and though she often missed the presence of others, the susurrus of hundreds of girls breathing all around her in the night, it was a haven of peace.

Her body's changes proceeded at their own frightening pace, and the weight in her belly grew daily. From the eighth week a doctor attended her twice a day. She was called Patrizia; she might have been forty, but she was slim, composed, ageless.

Patrizia pressed Lucia's gums, which had become spongy. "Good," she said. "That's normal. The effect of pregnancy hormones."

"My heart is rattling," Lucia said. "Though I feel sleepy all the time, it keeps me awake."

"It's having to work twice as hard. Your uterus needs twice as much blood as usual, your kidneys a quarter more—"

"I am always breathless. I pant—puff, puff, puff."

"The fetus is pressing on your diaphragm. You are breathing more rapidly and more deeply to increase your supply of oxygen."

"I can feel my ribs spreading. My hips are so sore I can barely walk. I get pins and needles in my hands and cramps in my feet. I either have constipation or diarrhea. I am a martyr to piles. My veins make my legs look like blue cheese—"

Patrizia laughed. "All this is normal!"

"Yesterday I felt the baby kick."

Patrizia, for once, hesitated. "Perhaps you did."

"But this is my *eighth week*. I am still in my first trimester!"

Patrizia looked down on her. "Somebody has been reading too much."

"Actually, I have been looking up the Internet from my cell phone." And from that she had learned the startling fact that among *contadino* women a pregnancy would last nine months, and you would not expect to have more than one child a year . . .

"There is nothing for you to learn on the Internet. Child, we have been delivering babies here for the best part of two thousand years—*our* way, and successfully." She placed her hand on Lucia's forehead. "You must trust us."

But after that conversation Patrizia took her cell phone away.

In the weeks that followed, the changes in her body only seemed to accelerate. She was subject to many more tests, some of them conducted with very modern equipment. She had a chorion biopsy, and a fetoscopy, and an alpha-fetoprotein test, and amniocentesis. Her baby was imaged with ultrasound. She was astonished at its size and development.

And then—just thirteen weeks after her sole intercourse with Giuliano—she went into labor.

Everything was a blur. She found herself squatting, naked, in a darkened room. Pina was behind her, supporting her under her armpits. Pina spoke to her, but she couldn't hear what she said. There was little pain, for electrodes taped to her flesh were passing currents through her back.

Patrizia was here, working competently, calmly, and quickly. And she was surrounded by women—Rosa, other doctors and nurses, even some of the *matres*, a great huddle of femaleness, touching her, stroking her belly and shoulders, kissing her softly, their lips tasting sweet, somehow reassuring.

In the last moments there was a sense of calm, she thought. It was oddly like a church. People spoke softly, if they spoke at all, and every eye was on her. She was the center of everything, for once in her life, the whole Order following the rhythms of her own body.

But it is only thirteen weeks, she thought, deep in her mind. *Thirteen weeks!*

The labor was as rapid as the rest of the pregnancy. When the baby crowned, she felt a burning sensation around her vagina, and then only numbness.

They showed her the baby briefly. It was a girl, a little crimson mass, but, Patrizia assured her, strong and healthy. Lucia held her, just for a moment.

Then Patrizia gently took the baby back. The nurses wrapped the child in blankets, and receded out of sight. Patrizia pressed an infuser at Lucia's neck, and the world slipped away.

chapter 32

As she grew older, in the smoky, unchanging warmth of the Crypt, time flowed smoothly for Regina, despite her careful calendar keeping and record making. Still, she often thought back to the day of her last meeting with Ambrosius Aurelianus, and of her treatment of Agrippina. Her actions that day had had significant consequences—that day, at least, had become memorable.

Three years after that day, Julia, the younger sister of Agrippina, reached the time for her own menarche—and yet no blood flowed. It was not until her eighteenth year, in fact, four years older than her sister, that her bleeding finally began, and even then it was fitful. Julia was a cheerful, competent girl, more confident in fact than her older sister, but it had been as if her body itself had been frightened by the treatment Agrippina had received from Regina, and had wished to postpone the same as long as possible.

Regina welcomed this strange development—even though it scared her a little to think that such strange powers might exist in the world, in *her*.

Some time after that, she heard of another consequence of that fateful day.

Artorius had mounted his last campaign. Thanks to the treachery of his "ally" the imperial prefect Arvandus, he had finally been defeated, by the Visigoth king Euric. He retreated to the kingdom of the Burgundians, after which nothing more was heard of him. He certainly never returned to Britain; he was probably dead.

Perhaps if she had stayed at his side, Regina wondered, her cunning might have kept him alive a little longer. But any money she had given Artorius, any support, would merely have been frittered away on one more campaign, one more battle, until death finally caught up with him.

Ambrosius Aurelianus went on to greater glories, though. After Artorius, his own leadership qualities emerged, and his defeat of the Saxons at the battle of Mount Badon granted the British a respite. It was a feat that won Ambrosius the nickname *last of the Romans*.

But more Saxons arrived to reinforce their petty coastal kingdoms. They pushed farther west and north, and the British, expelled from their homes, succumbed or fled, just as Artorius had long foreseen. And in the wake of the Saxons, Roman Britain was erased, down to the foundations. The despairing British were left with nothing but legends of how Artorius was not dead, but sleeping, his mighty sword Chalybs at his side.

There came a day when Brica's womb dried.

"But I am content," Regina said to Leda, her half sister. They were sitting in the *peristylium*, the strange underground garden of the Crypt, where the mushrooms seemed to glow like lanterns. The three most senior women of the inner family were here: Regina herself, Leda, and Venus, granddaughter of Regina's aunt Helena. "Brica has given me eight grandchildren—three boys, who have already started their apprenticeships in the world beyond, and five fine and beautiful workers for the Order. Nobody could do more."

"Yes, Regina."

"We are healthy stock—and our lives are long, in the shelter of the Crypt."

It was true. It was six years after the visit of Ambrosius Aurelianus. Regina was now in her seventies, and Brica herself was over fifty. Even at Rome's height, few people had lived beyond forty, fewer still past fifty; and in the current times of turmoil, with rampant disease, poor supplies of food and water, and assaults from barbarians, that average was dropping steadily. But not in the Crypt.

"And, as we live long, we stay fertile. But I am concerned for Brica herself." Now that she was barren, Brica seemed exhausted, worn out by the relentless demands of childbirth; she drifted around the Crypt purposelessly. "We must make her comfortable, reassure her . . ."

"But," Venus said delicately, "there is the question of the nursery."

Regina said vaguely, "The nursery?"

"The youngest child is already three," said Leda. "We need more babies. We must maintain—" She gestured.

"A flow." Regina opened her gummy mouth and cackled. "Like the great sewers. We need to push babies in at one end of the system, to ensure a nice smooth flow of effluent at the other."

"Not quite the way I would have put it," said Venus. Since being elected to the Council she had grown in confidence, and had developed a dry wit. "But, yes, you're right." She added delicately, "We need to decide on a—replacement—for Brica."

Leda nodded.

Of course they were right; this was the logic of how they had been running the Order, already for more than twenty years.

It was the slow unfolding of the instinctive vision Regina had always held in her head. Space would always be limited here. If all the female members of the family proved as fecund as Brica, there would soon be no room left. So, just as Regina had ordered with Agrippina, only a handful of women were encouraged to have children at any one time. Their siblings and growing daughters were expected to assist these central mothers to bear more young, to raise more sisters, even at the expense of families of their own. They should stay childless through the use of contraceptives, or abstinence—or best of all by simply delaying their menarche through the mysterious workings of their bodies, as had happened to Brica's second daughter Julia, and a number of other girls since.

Rationing births in this way kept the numbers down, *and* ensured that the blood was not diluted, that the family bonds stayed as tight as possible. It *worked*. And if this kept up, Regina saw clearly, then in a few generations there would be nobody here but family, a great mesh of sisters, mothers and daughters, aunts and nieces, a core locked together by insoluble bonds of blood and ancestry, able to cope with the inevitably cramped conditions of the Crypt.

But the system threw up dilemmas, such as now. Brica's fecund days were over, and a new mother must be found.

"I suggest Agrippina," Leda said. "Brica's first daughter," she went on to note, in case Regina needed reminding. "She has been patient since—"

"Since the day I ruined her life?" Regina cackled again. "I hear the mutterings."

"Six years," Venus said, "of coping with one little sister after another. Perhaps it is her turn."

"No," said Regina thoughtfully. "Let it be Julia." Agrippina's younger sister.

Leda frowned. "Agrippina will be disappointed."

Regina shrugged. "That's not the point. Think about it. Let Agrippina be the first of the Order to go through an entire life devoted not to the selfish demands of her own body, not to her own daughters, but selflessly to her sisters. *An entire life.* She will be a model for others, an inspiration for generations to come. She will be honored."

Leda and Venus exchanged a glance. Regina knew they didn't always understand her edicts. But then Regina didn't always understand them herself.

"All right." Venus stood up. She was heavily pregnant herself, again, and she winced as she hauled herself to her feet. "But, Regina, *you* can tell Agrippina—"

A messenger ran into the *peristylium*, flushed and excited, interrupting the women. Regina had been summoned to the imperial palace.

When she took herself out of Council meetings and the like and just walked around the growing Crypt, it sometimes startled Regina to realize there were already thousands of people involved in the Order, in one way or another.

She thought of the Order as like the bulb of a fine fat spring onion. At its heart was the family: the descendants of the sisters Julia and Helena, now both long dead, and their descendants, including Leda, Venus, Regina herself, and Brica and her children. Aside from them, at any one time there were hundreds of students living either in the Crypt itself, or in the buildings the Order maintained overground. Beyond that there were workers with peripheral connections to the Order: for example, the peripatetic teachers and orators, the miners who tunneled steadily underground, even bankers and lawyers who managed the Order's income and investments. And then there was a more diffuse outer circle of those who simply contributed to the Order, in cash or in kind: the families of students paying their fees, former students gratefully contributing through gifts or legacies to the establishment that had educated them so well.

But in all this, the safety of the central family was paramount. That had been Regina's goal when she had sacrificed her relationship with Brica to get her out of Britain and bring her here, and that was her goal now.

She was satisfied with what she had done so far. But of course everything was temporary. The Order didn't have to last forever—just long enough to shelter the family until things got back to normal. And she was becoming convinced that, yes, she had stumbled on a system that would work to achieve that goal.

Her own end could not be far away. She knew that from the dreadful weakness she felt in the morning, her unfortunate habit of coughing up blood—and the disturbing sensation of a hard, immovable mass in her belly, like a giant turd that would not pass out of her system. It was just like the illness that had taken Cartumandua, she remembered. She did not fear her own death. All she feared was that the system might not be completed before she was gone. What had she missed? That was the question she asked herself every day. What had she missed? . . .

She had no idea why the Emperor wanted to see her, but she could scarcely refuse him. So, on the appointed day, she walked alone across the city.

Rome had decayed visibly, even in the time she had lived here.

Many of the aqueducts and sewers were in urgent need of repair. The public granaries were closed. Many monuments and statues had been looted and violated—indeed, people stole stone from them either for building projects of their own, or simply to burn the marble for lime. The drainage of some of the fields beyond the city walls had failed, and they were de-

generating into swamps. Sometimes you would see dead cattle
drifting down the swollen waters of the Tiber, and starvation
and disease routinely stalked the poorer parts of the city. Many
of the rich had fled to the comparative comfort of Constantinople; many of the poor had died.

Regina was dismayed, but she had seen it all before. It was
Verulamium or Durnovaria writ large. But still the Forum and
the markets swarmed; even now it was a great city. And this
was Rome; even now she was sure its mighty lungs of concrete and marble still swelled, and the city would recover.

And as Regina approached the imperial palace on the Palatine Hill, even seventeen years after arriving in the city, she
was awed.

Itself three centuries old, the palace had been the residence
of emperors since Domitian. It sprawled across the whole central portion of the Palatine, a complex of buildings several stories high, roofed by red tiles and coated in decorative stones of
many colors. The imperial residence itself was said to be the
size of a large villa, with baths, libraries, and several temples—even a private sports stadium—and yet it was lost in the
greater maze of buildings. The palace was like a small town in
itself, a sink toward which the resources of a continentwide
Empire had once flowed.

She was met by a retainer in the Via Sacra, to the northeast-
ern side of the complex. She held her head up, ignoring the
nagging pain inside, determined to show no weakness. She
was led through two great arches, dedicated to the memories
of the emperors Titus and Domitian, and found herself in a
large paved area. It was the Domus Flavia that was her destination, the wing of the palace where official work was done.

The Domus Flavia was built onto a large platform set on top
of the hill. It consisted of several rooms set around a huge
peristylium. The walls and floors were decorated with mosaics
and imported stones; the colors were bright yellow, crimson,
and blue, the lines of the rectangular patterns sharp. There was
much business being done here, she saw; men walked this way
and that, arguing earnestly, bearing heaps of papyrus scrolls or
wax tablets. Despite the bustle, as with much of Rome there
was a sense of shrinkage, of emptiness, as if these busy men
were smaller than their ancestors. She wondered how it must

have been two or three hundred years ago when this building really had been the hub of the whole world.

A fountain set in the center of the *peristylium* was dry, its bowl mildewed, evidently long out of action. It made her think of her own long-lost childhood home; the fountain had never worked there, either.

"Madam. I am Gratian." The man who greeted her was tall, his hair white as British snow, with a thin, strong-nosed, elegant face. He was actually wearing a toga, a sight rarely seen nowadays. Gratian walked her toward one of the great buildings. It was a throne room; he called it the Aula Regia. "We will sit in the shade, over wine . . ."

Gratian was a senator, a close adviser to the Emperor—and a close relation. He was one of the cabal of rich and powerful men who actually controlled the imperial administration: though the Emperor Romulus Augustus bore two of the mightiest names in all Rome's long history, he was but a boy.

If the complex as a whole was impressive, the throne room was startling. The walls and floor were covered with a veneer of patterned marble, gray, orange, brown, green. The walls were fronted by columns, and in twelve niches stood colossal statues carved of night-black basalt. The room was covered by a vaulted concrete roof, and was oddly chill even in the heat of the day. The floor was warm, though, evidently heated by a hypocaust. At one end of the room was an apse where the Emperor received embassies and gave audiences. Today it was empty.

Gratian led her to a series of couches set in a semicircle, where they sat.

"If I am meant to be impressed," she said, "I am."

Gratian actually winked at her. "It's an old trick and not a subtle one. Rome herself has always been the emperors' most potent weapon. Do you know the history of the palace? The Emperor Domitian made his great platform on top of the Palatine by leveling earlier buildings, or filling them in with concrete. It is as if this mighty complex has used whole palaces as mere foundations! . . ." His talk was smooth and practiced.

"Perhaps," she said. "But this is power projected from the past, not the present."

He was apparently surprised at this sally. "But power even so."

A girl brought them wine—from Africa, Gratian said—and olives, bread, and fruit. She took a little of the wine, but watered it heavily; wine seemed to go to her head these days, perhaps because her blood was drawn by the thing in her belly.

"I take it," she said dryly, "that Romulus Augustus will not be receiving me today."

"He is the Emperor, and a god, but also a boy," Gratian said gently. "And today he is with his teacher of rhetoric. Are you disappointed?"

She smiled. "Is he?"

That made him laugh. "Madam, you have a spirit rarely seen in these difficult times. You have made a success of your life—and you have made your Order rather wealthy in the process." He waved a hand. "Our records are almost as good as yours are reputed to be," he said dryly. "Your Order contributes a great deal to the city—far more than most, in these times of declining civic sentiment. The Emperor understands, and he wants me to transmit his gratitude.

"But, madam," he went on, "we face a grave problem. The Germans are in Italy again. Their leader is a man called Odoacer: not a brute as some of these fellows are, but resourceful and uncompromising."

"Where are your legions?"

"We are overcommitted elsewhere. And tax revenues have been declining—well, for decades. It is not so easy to raise, equip, and pay an army as it once was . . ." He began a dismal litany of military commitments, triumphs, and setbacks, and the complexities and difficulties of the taxation system. What it amounted to was that Gratian was trying to raise a ransom from Rome's richer citizens and foundations: a bribe to make Odoacer go away, with minimal loss of blood.

And suddenly she saw what this thin, elegant man wanted of her. Sitting in this grand, ancient room, surrounded by the trappings of imperial power, she felt as if the whole world were swiveling around her.

So it has come to this, she thought with gathering dismay. *That an emperor should come to* me *for help: me, helpless little Regina.*

She had always believed that one day things would *get back to normal*—that the security she had perceived in her childhood would return. In the Order she had found a place of safety, even if they were "huddling in a hole in the ground," in the unkind words of Ambrosius, a place where they could wait out the storm, until it was safe to emerge into the light again. But Rome wasn't going to recover—she saw this clearly for the first time in her life. The fall had gone too far. "Normal" times would *never* come back.

She felt angry. The Emperor himself and his incompetent predecessors had betrayed her—as had her mother, Amator, Artorius in turn. And she felt afraid, as she hadn't even when the Vandals were raging within the walls of Rome. The future held only darkness. And all she had was the Order, which would have to preserve her family, her blood, not just through an uncertain hiatus, but—perhaps—*forever*.

I must go home, she thought. *I have much work to do, and little time left.*

She stood up, interrupting Gratian's monologue.

He seemed bewildered by her abruptness. "Madam, you haven't given me an answer."

"Bring him here," she said.

"Who?"

"Your German. Odoacer. Bring him here to the palace. Show him the marbles and tapestries, the statues and mosaics. Impress him with Rome's past as you have me, and perhaps he will spare the present. You're good at it—the *act*."

He looked at her angrily. "You're unnecessarily cruel, madam. I have my job to do. And that job is to preserve Rome from bloodshed, perhaps ruin. Is that ignoble?"

She felt a stabbing pain in her stomach—as if the thing in her belly had rolled and kicked, like a monstrous fetus. But by a monumental effort of self-discipline, she kept her posture upright, her face clear. She would not show weakness before this creature of a boy-Emperor.

She walked out of the palace without regret, and hurried home. But the pain followed her, a shadow in the brightness of the day.

chapter 33

After the birth, Lucia recovered quickly.

She understood what she was going through. She worked through her postnatal exercises for her abdomen and waist and pelvis. Her uterus was returning to its normal size. Her postpartum discharges did not trouble her and were soon dwindling. Like everything about the pregnancy, her recovery seemed remarkably rapid.

But she was not allowed to see the baby again.

Lucia tried to immerse herself in the workings of the Order once more, to *forget* as she was supposed to. But her anger grew, as did an indefinable ache in her belly, a sense of loss.

Rosa worked in a small office on the Crypt's top story. She had a role in the management of the larger corporate clients of the *scrinium*.

Lucia stood before her desk, and waited until Rosa looked up and acknowledged her.

"Why can't I see my baby?"

Rosa sighed. She stood, came around her desk and had Lucia sit with her in two upright chairs before a low coffee table. "Lucia, must we go through all this again? You have to trust those around you. It is a basic principle of how we live. You know that."

Perhaps, Lucia thought. But it was also a basic principle that they should not have conversations like *this*. You weren't supposed to talk *about* the Order at all; ideally you wouldn't even be aware of it. Rosa had her own flaws, she saw. Perhaps it was inevitable that Rosa, who was once a *contadino*, had a broader perspective than the rest, whether she liked it or not. She said none of this aloud.

She insisted, "I want to see my baby. *I don't even know what name you have given her.*"

"So? . . . I think we're talking about your needs, not the baby's. Aren't we, Lucia? You grew up in nurseries and crèches. Did you know *your* mother?"

"No—"

"And did that harm you?"

Lucia said defiantly, "Perhaps it did. How can I know?"

"Can you be so selfish as to blight your baby's life?"

Rosa's calm composure enraged Lucia. "Why didn't you *tell* me that my pregnancy would only last thirteen weeks instead of thirty-eight?"

"Is that what the Internet says a pregnancy ought to be? Lucia, there are twenty-seven *mamme-nonne*, who must among them produce a hundred babies a year—three or four each and every year . . . If you hadn't filled your head with nonsense from the outside, you would have *expected* a thirteen-week pregnancy, because that's the way we do things here. And whether you knew what was going on or not—Lucia, there was nothing to fear. It is what your body is designed for, you know." Rosa leaned closer and touched her hand. "Let her go, Lucia. You are one of the *mamme* now. In a sense you are already the mother of us all."

Lucia tried not to draw back. We always touch, she thought with a faint sense of distaste, we are always so close we can smell each other. "And *this* will be my life? Morning sickness and labor rooms forever?"

Rosa laughed. "It needn't be so bad. Here." She went to her desk, opened a drawer, and produced a cell phone.

Lucia studied the phone. It had gone dead. "It is my cell. Patrizia took it."

"Have it back. Use it as you like. Look at the Internet, if you want. Would you like to go outside again? There's no reason why not. I can talk to Pina—"

"I thought you didn't trust me."

"You mustn't turn this into some personal conflict between the two of us, Lucia. I am not your monitor. I am merely reacting to how you behave, in the best interests of the Order, which is all any of us do.

"Lucia, things are different now, for girls like you. You saw the pictures in Maria Ludovica's apartment—scenes like the Sack of Rome. Once a girl growing up in the Crypt had no realistic choice but to stay here. The world outside, chaotic and uncontrolled, was simply too dangerous. Now things have changed." She pointed to Lucia's phone. "Outside is a bright and superficially attractive world. Technology has liberated people in a way that could not have been imagined a couple of centuries ago. People are free to travel wherever they want, to speak to whoever they want, at any time, to call up any information they like.

"And all this penetrates even the Crypt. It is all shallow, of course." She snapped her fingers. "The great information highways could break down tomorrow, just as the Roman aqueducts once fell into ruin. But the world outside *looks* attractive. That's my point. You feel you have a choice, about whether to stay on in the Crypt, or seek some new life outside. But the truth is, you have no choice. Perhaps you must see that for yourself."

No choice because I'm different, Lucia thought. *I would never find a place outside the Crypt. And besides, there is something that will hold me here forever.* "I can't leave, because of my child. That's why you're letting me go outside, isn't it? Because you know I'll have to come back. Because you have my baby."

A look of uncertainty crossed Rosa's face. "There is no *you* and *we*—this conversation has been inappropriate. We should forget it."

"Yes," said Lucia.

"Take your phone. Go out, have a good time while you can. I don't think we'll need to talk again." Rosa stood; the meeting was evidently over.

As it turned out, Rosa was right, unsurprisingly. Despite her new freedom Lucia felt very reluctant to leave the Crypt. It would have felt like an abandonment of the baby that was even now yelling its lungs out in one of the Crypt's huge nurseries, even if she never saw it again. She returned to her studies, and considered going back to work in the *scrinium*. She would go back outside sometime in the future, she decided. Not yet.

Two months after the birth, though, she detected yet more

changes in her body. Changes unexpected, and unwelcome. She went to Patrizia again. The strange truth was quickly confirmed.

She knew the time had come to go out. If not now, then never. She still had Daniel's business card. It wasn't that she'd consciously kept it, not exactly, but it was there nonetheless. It took her only a moment to find it.

chapter 34

In the last days they gathered around her bed, faces drifting in the candlelit gloom.

Here were Leda, Venus, Julia, pretty Aemilia, even Agrippina. Oval faces, strong noses, eyes like cool stone, eyes so like hers, as if she were surrounded by fragments of herself. And there beyond them, silent witnesses to her death as her life, were the three *matres*, her lifelong companions, the last relic of her childhood home.

She was still concerned about the Crypt, the Order. Even as the illness rose around her like a bloody tide, she thought and calculated, worrying obsessively that there might be something she had overlooked, some flaw she had failed to spot. If the Order was to survive indefinitely, it had to be perfect—for, like a tiny crack in a marble fascia, enough time would inevitably expose the slightest defect.

When a coherent thought coalesced in her mind, she would summon one of the women, and insist she record her sayings.

Thus: "Three," she whispered.

"Three, Regina?" Venus murmured. "Three what?"

"Three mothers. Like the *matres*. At any time, three mothers, three wombs. Or if the Order grows, three times three, or . . . Three mothers. That is all. For the rest, *sisters matter more than daughters*—that is the rule."

"Yes—"

"When a womb dries, another must come forward." ·

"We need rules. A procedure for the succession."

"No." Regina grasped Venus's arm with bony fingers. "No rules, save the rule of three. Let them come forward, and make their own rules, their own contest."

"There will be conflict. Every woman wants daughters."

"Then let them fight. The strongest will prevail. The Order will be stronger for it . . ."

The blood must be preserved, kept pure, for the blood was the past, and the past was better than the future. *Sisters matter more than daughters.* Let them remember that; let them obey it, and the rest would follow.

And: *"Ignorance is strength."*

This time Leda was with her. "I don't understand, dear."

"*We* cannot survive. We old ones cannot run the Order forever. But the Order must be immortal. This is not a little empire and it never must be so. There must be no leader to fall, no traitor to betray us. The seniors must step back into the shadows, the Council must abdicate whatever powers it can. *The Order itself must sustain its own existence.* Let no one question. Let no one know more than she needs to perform her tasks. That way, if one fails, another can replace her, and the Order will go on. The Order, emerging from us all, will prevail. *Ignorance is strength.*"

Leda still didn't understand. But in the corridors of her failing mind, Regina saw it clearly.

To survive into the future you needed a system: that was the one indisputable lesson she had learned since arriving in Rome. The Romans had had a genius for organizations that functioned effectively for generations, despite political instability and corruption and all the other failings of humanity. Though the army was shamelessly used by pretenders to the throne and other adventurers for their own ends, it had always remained a military force of unparalleled effectiveness; and even though senators and others would misuse the legal system for their own ends, throughout the Empire, normal and competent processes of justice had served enormous numbers of people in every aspect of their daily lives. Even the city itself had sustained its own identity, its own organization, across a thousand years of unplanned growth, forty or fifty generations of people, for the city, too, was a system.

Systems, yes. And it was a system that she had been trying to establish here, following her instincts, bit by bit, as the years wore away. A system that would endure. A system that would work, *even when the people it sustained had forgotten it existed.*

The Order would be like a mosaic, she thought—but not of the kind her father used to make. Imagine a mosaic assembled not by a single master designer but by a hundred workers. Let each of them place her tesserae in harmony with those of her sisters. Then from these small acts of sympathy, from sisters simply listening to each other, a greater and enduring harmony would emerge. And it was a harmony that would survive the death of any one artisan—for the group was the artist, and the group survived the individuals . . .

You didn't need a mind to create order. In fact, the last thing you wanted was a mind in control, if that mind belonged to an ambitious idiot like Artorius.

"Listen to your sisters," she said.

"Regina?"

"That's all you need to do. And the mosaic will emerge . . ."

She slept.

chapter 35

Lucia arranged to meet Daniel at the Diocletian Baths. This was a monument just to the northwest of the Termini, Rome's central station. She arrived early. It was a hot, humid August day, and the sky, laden with clouds, threatened rain.

She walked around the walls. These baths had been built in the fourth century, and like many of Rome's later monuments they actually presented an ugly face to the world, great cliffs of red brickwork. Over the centuries such monuments had been steadily stripped of their marble, so that all that was left was a kind of skeleton of what had been.

But the monument was still massive, still enduring. Walls that had once been interior were now exterior, and she could make out the shapes of domes, broken open like eggs. The *exedra*, once an enclosed space surrounded by porticoes and seats where citizens would gather to talk, had been given over to a traffic-choked square.

The rain began to fall. She paid a few euros to enter the museum that had been built into the baths.

There were only a few tourists here. Bored attendants sat on plastic upright chairs, as still as robots switched off at the mains. The exhibits were sparse, cluttered together, and poorly labeled, for, she learned, the museum was in the middle of a long, slow process of being rehoused. Lucia wasn't very interested.

At the center of the museum she found a kind of cloister, a colonnaded covered walkway surrounding a patch of green. More antique detritus had been gathered here, all unlabeled. There were fragments of statues, bits of fallen pillars, broken inscriptions whose huge lettering told of the size of the monuments they had once graced. Some of the monuments had been set in the garden, where they protruded from the untidy green.

There were no seats, but she found she could perch on the low wall that fenced off the garden. She put her feet up on the wall's cool surface, rested her neck against a pillar, and cradled her hands on her belly. Her back was hurting, and to sit was a relief. The rain fell steadily, though not hard. It hissed on the grass, and turned the streaked marble of the fragments a golden brown. There was no wind. Some of the drops reached her, here at the edge of the cover of the roof, but the rain was warm, and she didn't mind. It was a peaceful place, away from the city's roar, just her and the dozing attendant, the antiquities, the rain hissing on the grass.

The time she had been due to meet Daniel came and went. She waited half an hour, and still he didn't come.

The rain stopped. A murky sunlight broke through smog the rain had failed to clear. By this time the attendant was watching her suspiciously—or perhaps it was just that he wanted to close up early.

She swiveled her legs off the wall and got to her feet. Her back still hurt, and the cool marble had made her piles itch, maddeningly, comically. Feeling very old, she made her way out of the museum.

She went back to the Crypt, for she had nowhere else to go.

That night, and the next day, whenever she found a little privacy, she made more covert calls to Daniel's cell. But the phone was switched off, and he didn't reply to the messages she left on his answering service.

The second day she tried to resist making any more calls. She was wary of scaring him off. She seemed to be aware constantly of the phone's mass in her pocket or her bag, though, as she waited for it to ring.

By lunchtime she lost her nerve. She went to a corner of the *scrinium* offices, shielded by filing cabinets, and made another call.

This time he picked up. ". . . Hello?"

"I—" She stopped, took deep breaths, tried to be calm. "It's Lucia." She sensed hesitation. "You remember—"

"The girl in the Pantheon. Oh, *shoot*." He used the English word. "We were going to meet, weren't we?"

"Yes. At the baths."

"Was it yesterday? I'm sorry—"

"No," she said, forcing herself to keep an even tone. "Not yesterday. Two days ago."

"You turned up and I didn't. Look, I'm really sorry. That's me all over." His voice sounded calm, faraway, untroubled save for a little embarrassment. A voice from another world, she thought. "Let me make it up to you. I'll buy you lunch. Tomorrow?"

"No," she snapped.

"No?"

"It doesn't matter about lunch . . . Let's just meet," she said.

"Okay. Whatever you want. I owe you. I don't want you to think badly of me. Where, at the baths?"

"Yes."

"I'll find you."

"Today," she gasped. "It has to be today."

Again she heard him hesitate, and she cursed herself for her lack of control.

"Okay," he said slowly. "I have a study break this afternoon. I can get away. I'll see you there. What, about three?"

"That will be fine."

"Okay. *Ciao* . . ."

She put away the phone. Her heart was hammering, her breath short.

She made an excuse and got out of the office. She changed into a shapeless patterned smock, loosely tied by a belt at the waist.

She caught a taxi back to the baths.

This time she walked around the complex until she came to the church of Santa Maria degli Angeli. In the sixteenth century this had been built into the ruins of the baths, to designs by Michelangelo. The church's name proudly adorned one of those broken-open domes.

Inside, the church was bright, spacious, and open, nearly a hundred yards across, richly decorated. There was an elaborate sundial inscribed on the floor, a great bronze gash that cut across one nave. She followed it to a complex design at its termination, where a spot of sunlight would map the solstices of years far into her own future. Here and there she made out relics of the building's origin, like seashell motifs on the walls. Michelangelo and the architects had used this great vaulting space well, but once this had been nothing more than the *tepidarium* of the tremendous complex of the baths.

She had chosen this place for Daniel's sake. She had been nervous about how he would react to her, especially in her changed condition. She thought the baths would pique his interest in the deep history of Rome, and how its buildings had been used and reused. Maybe he would come for the buildings, if not for her.

". . . Lucia."

She turned, and there he was. He wore what looked like the same faded jeans, a T-shirt labeled ROSWELL U RUNNING TEAM, and he clutched a baseball cap in his hand. The light behind him caught the unruly hair around his face, making it glow red.

He grinned. "You've changed. You're still beautiful, of course. What's different? . . ."

At the sight of him, the sound of his voice, the tears seemed to explode from her, fueled by longing, unhappiness, grief. She dropped her head and covered her face with her hands. How she would have reacted if he had come to her and taken her in his arms, she didn't know.

But he didn't. When she was able to look up, she saw that he had actually backed away a couple of steps. He was holding his baseball cap up before him, like a shield to fend her off, and his mouth was round with shock. "Hey," he said uncertainly. He laughed, but it was a brittle sound. "Take it easy. People are *staring*."

She struggled to get herself under control. Her face felt like a soggy mass. "Well, fuck them. Even if it is a church."

He was staring at her, eyes wide, mouth still agape.

She said, "Let's sit down."

"Okay. Okay. Sitting down is good—"

She grabbed his hand to stop him talking. She marched him to a pew in the nave where the sundial glistened on the marble floor.

They sat side by side, far from anybody else. He wasn't looking at her, she realized; his gaze wandered around the paintings on the wall, the marble floor. At last he said, "Look, if you're in some kind of trouble—"

She hissed, *"Why didn't you turn up?"*

"What?"

"Here, at the baths. On Tuesday. You didn't come."

"Hey," he said defensively. "So what? It wasn't important. It was just—" He leaned forward, so he was facing away from her. "Look. You have to be realistic. I'm seventeen years old. You're a pretty kid. And, well, that's pretty much it." He ticked off the points on his fingers. "I saw you in the Pantheon, and I spotted you in the park that day, and I thought, what the hell, and I said I'd meet you in the Piazza Navona, and there you were, and then—"

"And then?"

"And then you told me you were fifteen." He shrugged. "It was just a few moments, months and months ago. It wasn't even a date."

"It was important to me."

"Well, I'm sorry. How could I know?"

"Because you met me. We talked."

"Only for a few minutes."

But in that time, she thought, *we made a connection. Or did we?* She looked at him again, in his nerdish T-shirt, with his baseball cap on the wooden seat beside him. He was so young himself, she realized. He was just playing at relationships, playing at flirting. That was all he had been doing, all the time; even his supposed seriousness was just part of the game. Hope started to die.

He said, "I didn't mean to hurt you. Really. And anyhow, I did like you, you know."

She sighed. "Look, I don't blame you. The irony of it is, with almost anybody you met it would have made no difference."

"But it does with you." He turned around and looked back at her. In the church's soft light his skin seemed very smooth, very young. "Look, I was, am, and always will be an asshole. And I'm sorry." His face clouded. "I remember now. You said something about problems at home. Your family? If there's something serious, maybe my dad can help—"

"I've had a baby," she said simply.

That took him aback. His mouth opened and closed. Then he nodded. "Okay. A baby. When? How old were you? Fourteen, thirteen—"

"It was two months ago."

He laughed, but his face quickly drained of humor. "That's ridiculous. Impossible, in fact." He frowned, trying to remember. "You sure didn't look pregnant when I last saw you."

"That's because I wasn't. I was a virgin," she said. "I became pregnant in March."

That, absurdly, made him blush; he briefly looked away. "So," he whispered, "you had sex with some guy. You got pregnant. Then, what, you had a miscarriage—"

"I had a baby," she said rapidly. "A live, full-term baby, after thirteen weeks. I don't care whether you think that's impossible or not. It happened."

He sat silently for a moment, mouth gaping. Then he shook his head. "Okay. Suppose I concede you had a baby, *six months premature,* as if . . . Who's the father?"

"His name is Giuliano . . . I have forgotten the rest."

"You've *forgotten* his name? Did you know him?"

"No. Not really."

He hesitated. "Was it rape?"

"No. It's complicated."

"You're telling me."

"It's a family matter. There's a lot you don't know."

"Sounds like there's a lot I don't want to know . . . This guy who knocked you up. Was he older than you?"

"Oh, yes. About thirty, I think."

"Is that *legal* here? . . . Oh. He wasn't a family member, was he?"

"No. Well, a distant cousin."

"Murkier and murkier. Did your parents set you up somehow? Did they *sell* you?"

She shook her head. "It wasn't like that. I can't explain it. And you probably wouldn't believe me anyhow."

He gazed back at her, exasperated.

She studied him, trying to understand his mood. He wasn't scared anymore—or at least that wasn't his only emotion. He was genuinely listening, genuinely trying to understand, and his face showed a kind of determination.

He was constructing a new model of their relationship in his head, she thought. First he had believed he was a kind of romantic hero, the traveler in Rome. Then when he found out she was too young for a relationship, he decided he was playing a flirting, slightly edgy game with a precocious kid. Her news that she had given birth, and in a manner he couldn't understand, had broken all that apart. But now he was trying to construct a new vision. Now he was the knight who could ride in to save her, solve all her problems at a single blow—or anyhow a single phone call to his father.

He really was just a kid, Lucia thought almost fondly, and he saw the world in simplified, childlike ways. What he imagined was going on here had very little to do with the truth. But, kid or not, he was all she had. And, she thought coldly, if she had to use him to ensure her own survival, she would.

Lucia forced a smile. "You are an American," she said. "You made deserts bloom. You put people on the moon. Surely you can help me—"

But he was staring past her.

Pina was standing silently at the end of the pew.

Daniel stood up and confronted Pina. "Oh, it's you. The ugly sister."

"This is a church," Pina said levelly. "Let's not make a scene." She turned to Lucia. "Rosa is waiting outside, with a car."

Daniel said, a little wildly, "Are you going to drag her out of here, the way you dragged her out of that coffee shop?" He was guessing, Lucia saw, but he was hitting the mark.

Pina glared at him, calculating. Then she said, "I'll sit down if you will."

Daniel hesitated, then nodded curtly. They both sat.

Pina touched Lucia's arm, but Lucia flinched away. "Oh, Lucia. What are we going to do with you?"

"How did you find me this time?"

"This boy can't do anything for—"

"How did you find me?"

"There's a tracer chip in your cell phone. It wasn't hard."

Lucia glared at her. "You *bugged* me?"

"For your own good." Lucia still wouldn't let Pina touch

her, but she leaned forward, and Lucia could smell a milky Crypt scent on her clothes. "Come home, sister."

"I don't know what's going on here," Daniel said. "But she isn't going anywhere, except with me."

Pina laughed, softly, but in his face. "I believe sex with minors is known as statutory rape in your country. Do you want to find out about the Italian equivalent?"

It was an obvious ploy, but it made him hesitate. "I haven't touched her."

"Do you think that will matter?"

Lucia said, "Daniel, she won't go to the police."

"How do you know?"

"Because it's not the way the Order does things." She took a deep breath. "And besides, she would have to explain to them how come I'm pregnant."

Daniel was puzzled. "You mean you were pregnant."

". . . No. I *am* pregnant. Again."

There, she thought. *I've said it.*

Pina's mouth tightened. "What have you told him, Lucia?"

Daniel was staring at her, a mix of horror and incredulity on his face. "Was it him again? This guy Giuliano?"

"No. Or rather . . ."

Lucia remembered her bafflement when her menstruation had stopped, her growing puzzlement at the strange sensations in her belly—strange, yet familiar. She had gone to Patrizia innocently, wondering if she was suffering some kind of postnatal symptom.

She hadn't been able to believe what Patrizia had told her. But Patrizia seemed to have expected it. Patrizia called in others—Rosa, one of the younger *matres*, assistants from the delivery rooms and the crèches. They had clustered around Lucia, their smiles glistening wetly, touching her shoulders and back, kissing her brow and cheeks and lips, overwhelming her with their scent and taste of sweetness and milk. "It's a miracle," one of them had whispered in Lucia's ear. "A miracle . . ."

"A miracle," Lucia said hotly to a baffled Daniel. "That's what they called it. A miracle. But it isn't really, is it, Pina? Because in the Crypt it happens every week, two or three or four times."

Daniel asked, "What miracle?"

"I hadn't had sex," Lucia said. "Not since the birth. Not since Giuliano—and then, only that once, before my first pregnancy. *I hadn't had sex, but I'm pregnant anyway.* And it's Giuliano's baby again, isn't it, Pina? Conception without sex," she said bitterly. "Have you ever heard of such a thing, Daniel? Do they have such things in America? No, of course not. There are wonders happening in that Crypt to be found nowhere else in the world, I'm sure. Wonders in my own body." She turned on Pina. "But it isn't my body anymore. Is it, Pina? My body, my womb and loins, belong to the Order. My future is babies—more and more of them. My body is just a tool to be used as efficiently as possible for the Order's purposes. And *I*, I don't count for anything—my wants, my needs, my desires—"

"You never did," said Pina gently.

Daniel was staring at one, then the other, obviously baffled, scared. "I don't have idea one about what's going on here. But, hey, Grizelda, if you think I'm going to stand by—"

"Lucia!" The voice was high, evoking echoes from the high marble walls. Rosa was walking across the great marble floor toward them. She wore a business suit; she looked powerful, competent, unstoppable. She would be here in seconds.

"Hide me," Lucia said to Daniel.

"What?"

She stood. "Hide me now, or walk away."

Rosa broke into a run. Pina reached up to hold Lucia.

Lucia said, "Pina, please—"

Pina hesitated, for a second. Then she dropped her hands, a look of utter dismay on her face.

Daniel used that second to grab Lucia's hand. They ran together, out of the nave and across the floor. Daniel dragged her into a knot of visitors led by a woman who held an umbrella up in the air. They worked their way through the tightly packed group, toward the door.

When they had made it out into the open air, Rosa and Pina were nowhere to be seen.

They stared at each other—laughed, briefly hysterical—then fell silent. Lucia touched his cheek; it was hot. "Well, Daniel—now what?"

chapter 36

Brica came to her.

She stood over her mother, sullen, worn out, her face slack. There was little left of the bright, beautiful girl who had sat in the forest with the children and told them stories of the sidhe, and Regina's heart broke a little more.

But she said huskily, "Have you forgiven me yet for saving your life?"

"When you die I will be free," Brica said. "But it is too late for me. You should have let me go, Mother." It was a reprise of a conversation they had had many times since their days in Londinium, and the incident of the fat *negotiatore*.

"Your problem was you kept falling in love. But in these times there is no room for love."

"I couldn't help it."

"No, I suppose not. No more than I could help loving you."

Brica eventually went away. There would be no farewells, no final forgiveness. Regina knew that did not matter.

Sometimes Regina wondered if she really was mad, as Brica had sometimes accused her, if she was an unnatural mother. Yes, Brica was family. Yes, in normal times a mother must protect her children. Yes, she should release them to live their own lives when they come of age.

But Regina had not lived through normal times.

When Regina was born, Roman civilization was intact. It dominated the Mediterranean and much of Europe, just as it had for five hundred years. Britain, though rebellious and troubled, was still embedded in the imperial system, its economy and society and aspirations and vision of its future fashioned by Roman culture and values. Now, as the light faded for Regina, the Empire in the west had disappeared and its possessions were in the hands of barbarians.

In her lifetime of turmoil and destruction, as the Saxons had burned across Britain like a forest fire, as even Rome itself crumbled and shuddered, Regina had come to see her family—not as something to release to freedom—but as something to *preserve*: a burden that had to be saved. Even if it meant burying it in a hole in the ground. It was as if she had not allowed Brica to be born at all, but had kept her in the safety of her own womb, a dark thing, bloody, resentful—but safe.

In the last days the women were distracted. They talked excitedly about a new light in the sky, like a burning boat that sailed the great river of stars, and what such a remarkable omen might portend.

But Regina felt no apprehension. Perhaps it was the fire ship that had lit up her childhood, returned to warm her now that she was growing cold.

And then there was no more talk. The lights seemed to dim, one by one, in the corridors of her thinking.

But then she thought she heard someone calling her.

She ran through passageways. She was light and small, laughing, free of the thing in her belly. She ran until she found her mother, who sat in her chamber with a silver mirror held before her face, while Cartumandua braided her golden hair. When she heard Regina coming, Julia turned and smiled.

In that same year—the year 476 after Christ, the year of Regina's death—the boy-Emperor Romulus Augustus was deposed by the German warrior Odoacer. There wasn't even a nominal attempt to find a replacement. At last the system of the emperors broke down. Odoacer proclaimed himself king of Italy.

Odoacer was no Saxon. Odoacer and his successor, Theodoric, were advocates of harmony and a reverence for the past, and they tried to ensure continuity and preservation. Theodoric imposed a tax on wine, and used the revenue to restore the imperial palaces. He repaired the amphitheater after earthquake damage, and he instructed watchmen to listen for the subtle ringing sound that would betray a thief trying to steal an arm or leg or head from one of the city's thousands of statues.

In the time of these first barbarian kings of Rome, there were many rumors of hoards and treasures to be found underground, and even of rich convents full of beautiful women, perhaps nuns, laden with gold and jewelry. The lieutenants of Theodoric searched for the truth behind these legends, even going so far as to break open some of the old Catacombs along the Appian Way and elsewhere. But nothing of importance was ever found.

THREE

The da Vinci Airport is a few miles southwest of Rome. I got a cab to the city center. The driver might have been fifty. His face was like brown, crumpled leather. He seemed cheerful enough. He had a little wooden puppet hanging from his rearview mirror, like a red-painted Pinocchio.

We drove through rings of development. The outermost belt was the most modern, as you'd expect, a string of deeply ugly modern residential suburbs—tower blocks that would have shamed Manchester at its worst—and industrial sites, power plants, and other necessary but unattractive infrastructure. There were posters for British and American movies and pop stars, and an awful lot of kids in MANCHESTER UNITED soccer shirts and Yankees baseball caps. I could have been anywhere.

But within that concrete girdle there was a more attractive zone, of apartment blocks laid out around narrow roads and small greened squares. It looked like a nineteenth-century development. Here the traffic knotted up. My driver edged forward, honking, muttering, and gesturing.

We were close to the people now, pedestrians who squeezed their way along the narrow roads, mopeds that buzzed around us. Romans looked small, dark, round, a bit careworn. There was dirt and litter everywhere. Evidently the Romans had cleaned up their city in a great burst of enthusiasm to greet the year 2000. If that was so, I'd have hated to visit in 1999. The apartment blocks had rows of shuttered windows, and they were painted startlingly bright colors, yellow, orange, purple, even pink. It didn't look British—colors like that don't work well in the rain of London or Birmingham—still, I could have been in any great European city, I thought, in Paris or Brussels.

But then we reached the Aurelian Wall. *"Mura, mura,"* said the cabdriver, pointing. It was a great shoulder of brick, looming high above the road, dark, brooding, powerful, and the cars crept around its base like tinfoil toys. Even this first great slab could have absorbed *all* the scraps and fragments of wall I had seen in London, I thought, awed.

There was graffiti on the *mura*, though, in among the ads for trashy pop music and the political posters. I had no Italian, but I could recognize that the slogans were about immigrants and crime. The graffiti was everywhere, on every wall and doorway, every lamppost and bus shelter. Not the sign of a contented society.

I had twenty-four hours free before I was to meet Claudio Nervi, the tame Jesuit whose name I had extracted from Gina, and the resumption of my search for my sister. Twenty-four hours to decompress.

I had booked a hotel close to the Forum area, just like a regular tourist. The receptionist was a thin, neat young man in a black suit. His English was broken but serviceable: he was actually the first Italian I'd encountered since landing who had any English at all beyond a couple of words.

My room was small, and had a view of what looked like a back alley. But the Roman Forum was in sight from my room, just as the hotel's brochure promised, although you had to peer through alleyways of brickwork to make out the fallen pillars and strolling tourists. But that brickwork, I found out later, was itself a ruin of a development called Trajan's Market, a kind of giant shopping mall of antiquity. Anyhow the restricted view kept the price of my room down.

I unpacked, and searched unsuccessfully for a tea maker. The only English-language TV channel was CNN. But the room had an Internet connection, workable through the TV for the hire of a portable keyboard for a charge of a few euros, or a few thousand lira, according to the yellowing, outdated note on the TV cabinet.

I found a series of emails from Peter, sent from wherever he was ensconced with his Slan(t)ers in America. I paged through most of it, filing it in my mental category of "Peter's spooky stuff"—and enduring the occasional heart-stopping moment as the connection, always slow, threatened to freeze altogether. Some of it was kind of interesting, though.

One of the Slan(t)ers' principal activities was to search the world's media for "anomalies"—any peculiar patterns, inexplicable events, that might show the fraying of the fringe of our worldview. It's a hobby that's been enjoyed by the UFOlogists since the fifties, I understand. And of course the rise of the Internet has turned this into an industry: the Slan(t)ers had search and pattern-recognition software, more powerful than the fastest commercial search engine, Peter boasted, capable of picking through the vast slurry of information, rumor, hoax, and plain garbage that pours onto our information superhighway every day.

And, Peter said, while he had been in the States this endless searching had turned up something about his mysterious dark matter.

"If a chunk of dark matter were to pass through the Earth, we wouldn't see it. It would just pass through the planet's substance. But its gravitation would trigger seismic events: shock waves in the Earth's structure radiating away from its path. And, happily, we monitor seismic activity quite comprehensively . . ."

There is a global network of some five thousand government-sponsored seismic survey sites. They listen for the songs of the Earth, the great low-frequency waves that travel through the planet's crust. What the government monitors specifically look for are waves emanating from a single point source, which could be the location of an earthquake, say, or an illegal underground nuclear test. "Clean" signals of that kind are extracted from the data and published. The rest of the information is written off as meaningless noise. "And much of it probably is," said Peter. "You can get a seismic signature if a heavy truck passes by your station."

But *all* the data was put online nowadays by the U.S. Geological Survey and the Australian Seismological Network, and the Slan(t)ers had been able to get their hands on it. And in the disregarded "noise," they had seen "linear signals," as Peter put it—signals that emanated not from a point, but from a straight line. "What you have is a track through the Earth's layers," said Peter, "as if you'd fired a bullet through a wedding cake."

There had been occasional observations of linear signals for years. The Slan(t)ers, though, seeking patterns ignored by the seismologists, had found three such events in the last year.

Peter said, "Knowing the timing of the events, you can unwind the turning of the Earth to trace the path back beyond the planet to its origin, or destination. We can't find a unique destination for our three tracks—but they do seem to have a common origin. *The sun.* Somehow the sun is firing out dark matter nuggets, and some of them are passing through the Earth. What does this mean? Damned if I know. But there's more . . . I'm attaching a graphic file." Which I wouldn't be able to download here.

I skimmed Peter's verbose description, trying to get to the meat. Apparently, this particular "linear track," actually the second observed by the Slan(t)ers, wasn't so linear after all. "A little while after penetrating the upper mantle," said Peter, "this nugget's track diverged through about forty degrees. Then it skimmed the core and shot out of the Earth, in the vague direction of Mars. George, you see the significance? Dark matter passes through the Earth's core like a hot knife through butter. Earth's gravity field isn't intense enough to impose a deflection like that. This nugget *changed course* . . ."

Well, it was intriguing. But throughout my relationship with him, much of the information Peter tried to give me was simply too much for me—the ideas too big, too dislocated from the everyday, the stretching of my worldview too much to take. This was just such an example.

I sent him a note about how extraordinary claims require extraordinary proof. Then I shut down the system.

I ate that night in a little open-air tourist-trap restaurant, a complicated walk of a few blocks from the hotel. Most of the menu was seafood, served with or without pasta.

The next morning I walked around Rome. It was a voyage of discovery; I knew nothing about the city. My geographical research before setting off had been restricted to renting *The Italian Job*, which, it turned out, was set in Turin.

In the ancient area of the forums, embellished by all the

Caesars and ruined by time, herds of tourists grazed. I passed a couple of old ladies, American, who were debating whether to go with their guide into yet another site, the Forum of Augustus. "I'm getting a little tired," said one. "I think I'll go back to the bus. Will you do this one for me, dear?" She handed her tiny digital camera to the other. *So,* I thought unkindly, *it's the camera that is actually taking the tour.*

The area was cut through by a wide, attractive road called the Via dei Fori Imperiali, which led from the Colosseum to the National Monument. The Monument had been erected in the nineteenth century to celebrate Italian national unity. The locals called it the *Vittoriano,* after the king Victor Emmanuel—or, less respectfully, the *Typewriter.* And meanwhile that great via had been built by Mussolini, who had bulldozed his way over the ruins of the forums with barely a squeak from compliant archaeologists, in order to build a route for his fascist processions.

The National Monument dominated the broad, open square of the Piazza Venezia, the hub of the Roman traffic system: if all roads lead to Rome, they said, so all Roman roads led to the Venezia. And in the piazza the Roman drivers just drove at each other, neither giving nor expecting mercy. In Rome, the cars were clearly fueled by testosterone as much as petrol. And yet, I thought, watching for a few minutes from a pavement café, the crowding traffic actually cleared its way through quite efficiently. Somehow amid the apparent chaos, things sorted themselves out—just not the way I was used to.

I spent the morning poking around shopping streets. As the sun climbed so did the temperature, and I was soon sweating through my heavy English shirt; I stopped frequently at cafés or grocery stores for bottled water.

I quickly formed an impression of the Romans. Small and dark they were, and they all talked constantly. And they were intense: I decided that the characteristic Roman tone of voice was aggrieved exposition, just this side of exploding. They all seemed to have cell phones clamped to their ears, almost all the time—even quite small children—their eyes glazed, their free hands gesturing eloquently, futilely. The cell phone might have been invented for Italians.

But I did wonder what they had to talk about. The monuments all seemed to close for siesta periods in the middle of the day, the post offices all shut at one, the banks would open for maybe an hour in the afternoons if you were lucky, and *everything* closed on Mondays. The xenophobe in me wondered how I would feel if I were German or French, a fellow traveler on the great adventure of the single European currency. And yet, I knew, the Italian economy was actually large and healthy.

Somehow, like the traffic, the work got done, things sorted themselves out.

The Jesuit mother church is called the Gesu, just a block from the Venezia. Claudio Nervi was waiting for me on the pavement outside. "Call me Claudio," he said, shaking my hand, after I greeted him as "Father."

He was perhaps fifty and his hair was neatly combed silvergray. His eyes were blue, but his thin face was deeply tanned—he was handsome, in an aging-patrician way. He wore a black suit with the regulation priest's white collar, but the suit was suspiciously well cut, and I wondered if it came from a design house. He seemed poised, confident, intelligent.

"Well now—" He stretched his long arms. "—welcome to Rome. It's good to meet you, and I hope I can help you with your difficulty."

I thanked him. "Your English is good." It was, with the kind of upper-crust accent so familiar from Noël Coward films that nobody in England dares use in public nowadays.

He smiled. "I spent some years studying in a seminary near Oxford. Look, are you in a rush? Would you like to see the church? . . ."

I followed him into the gloom of the Gesu.

A handful of worshipers, old folk, sat patiently in the pews. The church was sumptuously decorated, as many Roman churches are, with a lush Baroque painting on one wall.

But on one high side altar, a human arm was on display.

At first I couldn't quite believe my eyes. I stepped closer. On top of that altar was a reliquary, an elaborate oval casket in gold and crystal, with an angel floating beside it. And inside the casket there was indeed a human arm, intact from the elbow socket down. There were even bits of flesh, black and withered, clinging to the bones.

Claudio was murmuring softly, "Many visitors are struck by the wealth of Roman churches. One looks at every surface, and the eye is greeted by treasure, and dazzled. But they are after all the result of two millennia of dedicated wealth accretion—one can't put it any other way—although today the Vatican is not stupendously rich; it is less wealthy than many of the larger American dioceses, for instance . . . Oh. I see you have met our hero."

The arm turned out to be a relic of Saint Francis Xavier, who in the sixteenth century had been a Jesuit missionary to India and Japan. He had died of a fever on an island off the coast of China, and had been buried there. The Jesuit general in Rome had ordered the body exhumed and reburied on Goa—and that the right arm be cut off at the elbow, to be enshrined back in Rome.

I shuddered. "The Catholic Church always did major on relics."

"It's all rather primitive, of course. But such things do actualize religion in the popular mind. And besides—" He waved at the gruesome body part. "—aren't we all fascinated by relics, of one kind or another, by physical traces of what went before—even in our own lives? What is your quest now, if not driven by relics of your own past?"

I said, a bit ruefully, "You know, I can tell you're a priest. When I was a kid, the parish priest spun every last sermon out of an analogy like that."

He smiled. "Then on his and my behalf, I apologize."

"And besides, I'm just looking for my sister. I never thought of it as a quest."

"What else could it be?"

I glanced around the church. I felt self-conscious with the worshipers present. "You have, um, an office here?"

"No. I'm conducting a project for the Pontifical Institute for Christian Archaeology. The Vatican, you know. I work out of an office there. Perhaps you'd be interested in seeing where I actually archaeologize. It's not far from here." He rubbed his hands together. "But first, lunch."

He wouldn't listen to my protests that I had eaten a sand-

wich in the hotel, and wasn't swayed by the fact that it was already past three. He took me to a small restaurant a few minutes' walk away from the main road, where, he said, we would
find the best *cucina romanesca*, what the Romans themselves
ate.

The waiter was round and smiling, dressed in an implausi-
bly white shirt and bow tie. Although the cooking smells made
me salivate, I knew I really wasn't very hungry, so we both settled on soup. It was *tagliolini alla baccorola*, which is little
tubes of pasta stuffed with bacon and cheese and drowned in a
hot chicken broth. That and a few bread sticks and a glass of
fruity white wine went down very well, but I knew it was
going to make me sleepy later.

The real reason Claudio wanted to buy me lunch soon began
to emerge: so he could mess with my head.

"So," Claudio said around his soup, "you seek your sister.
But it isn't a quest."

"It's a loose end," I said.

"But if you pull on loose ends your sweater can unravel." He
smirked at this sally. "I'm just interested in why you need to
find her."

"My father's death. I feel as if the whole thing won't be over
until I find Rosa."

"But what will you say to her?"

"Hell, I don't know—"

"Will you talk about your father?"

"Probably. What else?"

He put down his spoon. He said gently, "You see, I think
you're *curious*. Perhaps even envious. You want to understand
why *she* was sent away, to this opportunity—or to this prison,
depending on how it's turned out for her—and why not *you*.
Isn't that true? But it's really your father you should have spoken to."

"It's a little late for that," I snapped. I had spent too many
years breathing Catholic air. I felt deep responses kick in to
the gentle prying, the effortless assumption of moral superiority. "Look—Claudio—why are we having this conversation?"

He steepled his fingers over his soup bowl. "The encounter
you are planning could be very painful. I've seen such meetings before—for instance, among long-separated refugees—

and, believe me, I know. And the information I am providing for you is setting up that encounter. I feel I would be avoiding my responsibilities as a human being if I didn't raise that."

"Are you saying you won't give me the contact for the Order?"

"Oh, I've said no such thing." But on the other hand, he wouldn't give me the details, not yet; it seemed I had more intangible barriers to hurdle yet. "What do you know about the Order?"

"Hardly anything. It runs schools, and sells information for family trees."

"What do you *think* it is?"

I hesitated. "I think it's some kind of cult. That's why it's so secretive, why Rosa just—disappeared."

"A cult." He thought about the word. "You mean that pejoratively, don't you? What kind of cult, do you suppose?"

I shrugged. "A cult of Mary. That's what the name says."

"You are right, and you are wrong," he said. "The group does have the form of a religious order, but it is an unusual one. The Vatican has had contacts with the Order since its inception. At times of crisis in Rome's long history the Order and the Vatican have even worked together . . .

"It's certainly not a convent: children are born within its confines. Its focus isn't on Mary, in a sense—not just on the mother, you see—but on the *family*. And in that sense it's very Italian, of course. Italians aren't like north Europeans, George. We're a very—umm, *local* people. In England, young people leave home as soon as they can, for college, or work. Here, people stay at home. The family remains intact. It's common to have several generations of adults under one roof, or at least living close by. There is a word—*campanilismo*—the sense of one's loyalty to one's campanile, the bell tower."

"You can't generalize like that about a whole nation."

"Of course not," he said easily. "But I believe you will need to think this way if you wish to understand your sister's situation."

"This is what I'll find in the Order?"

"I'm telling you that the Order is like a family, but a family sixteen centuries deep. These are very close bonds, George.

You will find your sister has exchanged one family for another—and she may not want to reverse that exchange."

"I'll take the risk."

He spread those long pianist's fingers on the table. "It's your
choice. But first let me show you my archaeological project.
No, I insist." He snapped his fingers; the waiter responded immediately.

It turned out his project concerned a small church called
San Clemente, some minutes' walk away, on the other side of
the Colosseum. As a guest of Claudio's I didn't have to pay
any entrance fee. Inside and out the church looked unprepos-
sessing.

"But," said Claudio enthusiastically, "it is one of Rome's
best examples of a 'layered' church." By which he meant one
building laid down on top of another. He took me down
through the layers. It was a fascinating, eerie experience.

"You have an eighteenth-century facade, behind which is
this twelfth-century basilica. Here is a rather remarkable mosaic of that period, showing the triumph of the Cross . . . But
below all that we have a still earlier church, from the fourth
century. I am working with some Dominican monks on the ex-
cavation of this layer." Not that anybody was working here
today. "And below *that* is a mithraeum." This had probably
originally been a town house of the imperial days, dedicated in
the first century for use as a temple to the god Mithras, a secretive cult for men only. There was a faded fresco on one
wall. It had been of the wife of an emperor, said Claudio, but
retouched later to make it a portrait of the Madonna and Child.
"And we believe there are layers yet to be unturned under that
as well . . ."

He smiled in the gloom. "Look around you, George. Consider the deep layers of history, the extended and changing
usage, of this one small church alone; and consider how little
we understand even of this patch of ground. Then remember
you are in Rome, where everything is drenched in history, in
continuity through change. And then think of the Order.
Rather like the Vatican, the Order is woven into this fabric of
history and humanity . . ."

I was beginning to form an impression that this smooth

clergyman was a lot less forthcoming than his appearance suggested. He was good at eating up time, at deflecting my questions, at probing into my personality, uttering vague forebodings and generating doubt: better at all that bullshit than putting himself on the line and taking responsibility to *do* anything. *Maybe that's a quality you need to get along in the Vatican,* I thought; *the Church hasn't survived two thousand years by being proactive.* But it wasn't helping me.

And it was more than that. It was a feeling I'd had when meeting the headmistress, even Gina, even Lou. Every time I tried to take a step closer to Rosa I felt as if I were pressing against an invisible, intangible barrier, a force field of words and looks and subtle body language. It was as if all these people had been trying to put me off the search—perhaps without even realizing they were doing it.

But I'm a stubborn bugger if nothing else, and having come so far I wasn't about to give up. And maybe the wine was making me snappy. I decided to challenge him. "You work for the Order, don't you?"

"I've had some dealings with it."

"You find it recruits," I said rudely. I was guessing, but I hit a mark.

He lost his smile. "If I perceive a person in need, and if through the Order I can meet that need—"

"Will you get me that contact or not?"

He nodded curtly. "Tomorrow," he said. "I'll send it to your hotel."

When I got back to my room I booted up the Internet connection again. I found two more emails from Peter. In the first mail, to my surprise, he said he had booked a flight to Rome. He said he thought I needed help.

"I think we're up against a cult here, George. Some kind of weirdo mother-fixated Marian cult. And it's nearly as old as the church itself. If the Vatican is siphoning funds they're going to stonewall . . . Go back to your tame Jesuit," he wrote. "Maybe he can get me into the Vatican Secret Archives. All Slan(t)ers know that the answers to most of the universe's mysteries are to be found in there . . ." Well, maybe. I knew that Peter was of course following his own agenda—mine was just incidental to him—and I wondered if there was more to this sudden change of plan.

The second of his emails was more thoughtful.

"We're so short-lived, George. The Empire is buried a long way down, so far down it defeats the capacity of life to measure it. The oldest recorded human lived about one hundred twenty years. So if you go just a little more than a century deep you would find no human who's alive today—and yet you're still just a twentieth of the way back to the emperors.

"No mammal lives longer than humans, no elephant, no dog or horse. Your grandmother's parrot might beat a century. The oldest insects are jewel beetles that die at thirty; the crocodiles might last to sixty. The oldest land animals of any kind are tortoises—Captain Cook gave one to the king of Tonga that supposedly lived one hundred eighty-eight years—and some mollusks, like the ocean quahog, a thick-shelled clam, can last a couple of hundred years. But that's all. So if you go just *two* centuries deep into the abyss you leave behind *all* the living animals.

"Deeper than that and there are only the plants. In the gardens of the villa of the Emperor Hadrian there is said to be a cypress tree that has lived a thousand years, but even that is only halfway back to Hadrian himself. Oh, there is a great redwood that is said to be seven thousand years old, and living bacteria found in the gut of a frozen mastodon were more than eleven thousand years old—but such wrinklies are rare. Everything else has since died as we do, George, the grass, the fungi, the bugs; we may as well all be mayflies . . .

"Nothing living survives from the time of the emperors—not even vegetable memories. You are delving in deep time indeed, George. But you mustn't let it frighten you."

A new message came in. From Claudio, it was a telephone number for the Order. In fact, said Claudio's note, it was a direct line for my sister, for Rosa. My heart beat faster.

chapter 38

It was in the year 667 that Totila came to Rome. He wore an iron collar around his neck, for he was a criminal who undertook this pilgrimage as expiation.

Totila was a simple man, a farmer from southern Gaul. He had not denied the charge against him, of stealing a little bread to feed his daughters' swollen bellies. His crops had been ruined by floods and banditry, and he had had no choice. That didn't make it any less of a sin, of course. But the bishop had been lenient; his mouthfuls of bread had won him only a flogging, which would probably leave no scars, and the great chore of this journey to the capital of the world.

But in his whole life Totila had never walked more than half a day's journey from the place he had been born. Across Europe, the calm of empire had been replaced by turbulence, and this was not an age for traveling. The journey was itself overwhelming, a jaunt into endless strangeness.

And as he neared Rome itself, when he joined the flood of pilgrims who trampled along the weed-choked road that led to the city, and when he walked through the great arched gateway into the city itself, Totila felt as if his soul would spin out of his body in bewilderment.

Rome was a city of hills, on which great buildings sprawled—palaces and temples, arches and columns. But even at the center, two centuries after the last of the western emperors, white marble was scorched by fire, many of the buildings lacked roofs, and he could see grass and weeds thrusting through the pavement, and ivy and vines clinging to crumbling stone. Away from the central area much of the city within the walls was demolished altogether, flattened and burned out, and given over to green. Cattle and goats wandered amid bits of masonry that poked through the grass.

The many new churches, though, were fine and bright.

He wandered to the Forum area. It was dense with stalls selling food and drink, and many, many Christian tokens and relics. And people were buying. Some must be pilgrims like himself—he saw iron rings around necks and arms, marking out fellow criminals—but others were well dressed and evidently wealthy.

There was a blare of trumpets.

Suddenly he found himself being shoved along by a great swarm of bodies. Confused, scared, he kept his hand over his chest where, inside his tunic, his leather purse dangled on its bit of rope, for he had heard of the criminality of the Romans. He strained to see over the heads of the crowd.

A procession passed: a series of swarthy slaves, soldiers stripped to the waist with shield and trumpets, and a gilded sedan chair. In the dense Italian sunlight it was a dazzling, glittering vision, and Totila cast down his eyes.

"You're blessed," a voice whispered in his ear.

He turned, startled, to see a small dark man smiling at him. "Blessed?"

"It's not every pilgrim who gets to see the Emperor himself. After all," the man said dryly, "the great Constans does not grace us with his presence very often, preferring the comforts of Constantinople, where there are no goats nibbling your legs, so I'm told . . ."

These days Rome was once again under the sway of Constantinople, capital of the Empire in the east—much good it did anybody. Constans was staying in one of the old palace buildings on the Palatine, crumbled and roofless though he found it. But the Emperor had brought nothing to the city. On the contrary, he seemed intent on stripping it of such treasures as statues and marbles, and even the gilded bronze tiles on the roof of the Pantheon.

There was a scattering of boos as the Emperor passed.

"My name is Felix," the strange man said to Totila. "And you look lost."

"Well . . ."

As the crowd broke up, Felix took Totila's arm. Totila let the man lead him away, lacking any better idea; he had to speak to somebody.

Felix was about forty, simply dressed, but he seemed well fed, calm, composed. He spoke a basic Latin, heavily accented but easy to understand. It was hard to resist his air of command. Totila let Felix buy him a cup of wine and some bread.

Felix eyed Totila's collar. "You are here for a holy purpose," he said solemnly.

"Yes. I—"

Felix held up his hand. "I'm no bishop to hear your sins. I'm your friend, Totila, a friend of all pilgrims. I want to help you find what you want, here in Rome, for it is a big and confusing place—and full of crooks if you don't know what you're doing!"

"I'm sure it is."

From somewhere Felix produced a scroll. "This is a guide to the most holy sites. It tells you what routes to follow, what to see . . ." The scroll looked expensively produced, and when Felix told him the price Totila demurred; it would empty his purse in a stroke.

Felix's eyes narrowed. "Very well. Then I will be your guide, sir pilgrim!"

So, the rest of that day, Felix led Totila through Rome.

Everywhere they went there were reassuring crowds of pilgrims. Totila peered at the arrows that had pierced the body of Saint Sebastian, and the chains that had bound Saint Peter, and the grill on which Saint Laurence had been burned.

It had been the initiative of Pope Gregory some decades before to send appeals throughout Europe to call pilgrims to Rome, the mother of the church; and they had come. The city had quickly organized itself to cater for the new industry, which had brought much-needed revenue.

Totila shook his head when Felix brought him to a stall where he could have bought "martyrs' bones," a grisly collection of finger joints and toe bones. But he dropped a few coins in the bowls of half-starved mendicants, and made offerings at various shrines. He noticed that some of the worse-off mendicants were tended to by women—all young, all with pale gray eyes, dressed in distinctive white robes—who gave them food, and cleaned their wounds.

Felix watched all this, and eyed Totila's purse.

At last, as the evening began to fall, Felix led Totila to the Greek quarter of the city where, he said, Totila would be able to find cheap lodgings.

And in a dark alleyway, between two impossibly tall and crumbling tenement buildings, Felix produced a fine blade with which he slit open Totila's purse, and pierced Totila's belly for good measure.

As Totila slumped to the filth-strewn ground, Felix counted the coins in his palm and snorted. "Hardly worth my trouble."

Totila gasped, "I'm sorry."

Felix looked down, surprised, and laughed. "Don't be silly. It's not your fault." And he walked away, into the gathering gloom.

Totila lay in the stench of ordure and urine, unable to move. He kept his hands clamped over his belly, but he could feel the blood seeping through his fingers.

Somebody was here, standing before him. It was a woman in a white, purple-edged robe. She was one of those who tended the poor. She knelt in the dirt, pulled his hands away from his side, and inspected his wound. "Don't try to move," she said.

"This is a holy place to die, here in Rome."

"There is no good place to die," she murmured. "Not like this." She had pale gray eyes, he saw, the gray of cloud.

Having bound him up, she managed to get him to his feet and took him to an inn. She left him money, in a new leather purse.

He stayed two nights.

When he was able to walk, he approached the innkeeper with some trepidation, for he wasn't sure he had the funds to pay for his lodging. But he found that the account had already been settled.

Before he left Rome, Totila tried to find the woman who had helped him. But though everybody knew of the women in white, and of their charitable work for the helpless poor and victims of accident and crime—some called them angels, others virgins—nobody knew where they could be found. They seemed to melt out of the rubble of Rome by day, and disappear by night, like ghosts of a different past.

chapter 39

On the day I was due to meet Rosa I woke early, having passed a nervous, restless night.

Before breakfast I crept downstairs, tiptoed past the concierges, and walked along the Via dei Fori Imperiali. The dawn wasn't far advanced, and the traffic was light. Around me was the old Roman Forum, nestling in the timeless safety of its valley, and the Palatine and Capitoline Hills bristled with the imperial palaces and other mighty buildings of later antiquity.

In my week in Rome, I'd walked and walked, from the Vatican in the west to the Appian Way in the south, along the banks of the Tiber, and around great stretches of the Aurelian Wall. Like Edinburgh or San Francisco, Rome was a city of hills—that was the first thing that struck you—you really couldn't walk far without heading either uphill or down, and after a few days my thighs and calves felt as hard as a soccer player's.

But what was unlike any city I'd visited before was the sense of time here.

This place had been in continuous occupation since the Iron Age. It was as if time were untethered here, and great reefs of history kept sticking up into modern times, mounds of past as enduring as the ancient hills themselves.

Rome was starting to intimidate me, just as Peter had warned. It wasn't the right frame of mind to be in when meeting my long-lost sister.

I'd arranged to meet Rosa in a little coffee bar off the Appian Way, which was where, in our brief, terse phone call, she'd said she worked. The Way is an ancient road that leads south from a gateway on the Aurelian Wall. It was a fine morning and I decided to walk, to clear my head and get my blood pumping.

But I soon regretted the decision. The road was narrow, in long stretches without pavement at all, and the traffic was as disrespectful here as in the rest of the city. But perhaps it had been so for two thousand years, I thought; I shouldn't complain.

I survived a terrifying jog through a narrow tunnel beneath a road and rail bridge, and arrived at a junction close to a little church called Domine Quo Vadis. Across the street was a coffee bar.

And there, sitting at a pavement table, was an elegant woman in her forties. She wore a cream trouser suit. She sat easily, with her legs folded, a coffee cup before her, a cell phone in one hand. As I crossed the road she turned off the phone. She left it on the table, though, where it sat throughout our meeting, a mute reminder of her connections to another world.

When I reached the table she smiled—bright, white teeth—and stood up. She had expensive-looking sunglasses pushed up onto her brushed-back mouse-blond hair, not a streak of gray, and her eyes were as pale and smoky as my mother's had been. "George, George . . ." It turned out I was a little taller than her, so I had to lean to let her kiss me. She buffed my cheeks, as if we were two London PRs on a routine business meeting.

But this close to her, there was something in her smell—a sweet milkiness under the cosmetics, the smell of home perhaps—that made me, briefly, want to melt. Yes, suddenly I remembered her, a little girl in bright, blurry kid-memory images I'd long lost. I found myself struggling for composure.

She pulled back and regarded me, her face so like my own, her expression cool. "Please." She waved me to a seat. With effortless ease she called the waiter, and I ordered a cappuccino.

"So, after all this time," I said gruffly.

She shrugged. "The situation is not of our making."

"I know. But it's still damn odd."

She began talking, brightly, of the church over the road.

"Have you had time to see it? *Domine quo vadis*—'Lord, where are you going?' Peter had escaped from prison in Rome, and he met Jesus here and asked Him that question. Jesus replied, 'To let myself be crucified a second time.' He left His footprints in the road. You can see them inside the church. But if they are genuine, Christ had big feet . . ." She laughed.

She talked easily, fluently, her voice well modulated: neutrally accented English, perhaps the slightest Italian singsong. She looked at ease here. She looked *Italian*. Whereas I felt shabby and out of place.

The coffee arrived, which gave me a little cover.

"I don't know what to say. What do we do, swap life stories?"

She leaned forward and put her hand on mine. "Just relax. I'm sure we will work it out."

The sudden, unexpected touch oddly shocked me. "I don't think I have much more to tell you anyhow," I said. As a preliminary to our meeting I had sent her a long email from my hotel room.

"You told me about your past," she said. "But not your future."

"That's a little more cloudy. I've come to a fork in the road, I think."

"Because of Father's death?"

Not *Dad* but *Father*. "I think things had been building up anyhow. I need a change."

"I understand."

"Do you?"

With that slight sharpness, she looked at me, her smile more empty. "And in return for your biography, you expect mine?"

"You're my sister. I came all this way to meet you. Yes, I want to know what's become of you. You sell family trees," I said. "That's pretty much all I know about you."

She smiled. "That and the fact that I belong to a weirdo woo-woo cult . . . Don't worry; I know what people think of us. All right." In brisk, almost rehearsed phrases, she sketched her career for me, her life.

She seemed to be a kind of account manager, dealing with services and products for major clients—not individuals, but companies, universities, even churches and governments.

After being sent over here by our father, she had been put through schooling good enough to get her to a baccalaureate. She hadn't gone away to university, but, staying within the Order, had studied history and business administration to degree level. Then she had gone to work for the family firm, so to speak.

Even after this smooth patter she stayed out of focus. Thinking over what she had said, I found I couldn't visualize her school, or even the kind of social conditions she had been brought up in—not a family, that was for sure.

She began to talk about the Order's business. "Yes, we sell genealogy information. I brought some stuff for you to see . . ." She dug some promotional literature out of her bag: glossy, well produced. Tracing ancestry was one of the biggest growth areas on the Internet, she told me. "We're even offering a DNA matching service," she said. "If you're of British ancestry, say, you'll soon be able to tell whether you are of ancient stock, or came over with the Romans, or the Saxons, or the Vikings.

"There is a finite genealogical universe out there. Only a finite number of human beings have ever existed, and each of them had a mother and father, links to the great chain of descent. We see no limit in principle as to the information we may one day retrieve . . ." She was quite evangelical as she described all this. It was more than just a product to her, I saw.

But I felt as if she were pitching a sale. I didn't know how brother and sister were *supposed* to behave, after a forty-year separation. It isn't a situation you come across every day. But for sure it wasn't talking about DNA databases and high-speed Internet access options.

Actually, as she talked, she reminded me of Gina. Something about her cold competence, her distance from me.

I put aside the brochures. "You're telling me about genealogy," I said. "Not *you*."

She sat back. "Then what do you want to know?"

"You never came home."

She nodded. "But this *is* home, George. This is family, for me."

"It may feel like that, but—"

"No." Again she covered my hand, shockingly casual. "You

don't understand. *The Order is family—our family.* That's why Father was happy to send me here." And she reminded me of our story of the ancient past, of Regina, who had survived the collapse of Britain, and who had eventually come to Rome— where she had helped found the Order.

I was tired of this story. "That's just a family legend," I said. "Nobody can trace back to the Romans . . ."

"*We* can." She grinned, almost playfully. "We keep records, George. That's the one thing we do better than anything else. Our huge bank of historical data is the spine on which we have built our genealogy business. George, it's true about Regina. There has been a continuous thread of descent, from Regina's day to this, as the Order has survived. But that central line of family persists. And it's *our* family.

"Maybe now you can see why I stayed here." Again she touched me, unexpectedly. She slid one hand under my palm, and let the other rest on top, massaging the webbing between my thumb and forefinger with the ball of her thumb. It was extraordinarily intimate—not sexual—compelling, oddly confining. She said, "So that's why you don't need to rescue me."

"What do you mean?"

She laughed. "Come on, George. Isn't that why you're really here? To save me from my miserable exile. Perhaps on some level you were expecting to find the little girl you last saw, all those years ago. And I've somehow disappointed you by turning out to be a grown woman, with a life of her own, and capable of making her own choices. I don't need saving, as you can see."

I said angrily, "Okay. Maybe I'm a patronizing dope with no imagination. But I'm here, Rosa."

She surprised me by standing up. "But we each have our own lives, George. Well, that's that." She began extracting money from a small billfold. "Let me treat you," she said. "I insist."

I stood uncertainly. I hadn't been in control of any of this conversation, I realized, from first to last. "Is that it?"

"We must stay in touch. Isn't email marvelous? How long are you in Rome?—"

"Rosa, for Christ's sake." I struggled briefly for control.

"Don't we have any more to say to each other? After all this time?"

She hesitated. "You know, some said I shouldn't see you."

"Some who?"

"People in the Order."

"You told them about me?"

"We tell each other everything."

"Why shouldn't you have met me?"

"Because you might be a threat," she said simply. Her gaze was fixed on me. "But now I've met you I'm not so sure."

I had the impression she was recalculating.

She had felt impelled to go through with the meeting with me, to give me the minimum contact required to send me away, and keep me away. But now something—my persistence, maybe my distress—was making her rethink that plan. I know that's a cold analysis of her thinking. But I really didn't believe, even then, that whatever new plans she was drawing up had anything to do with compassion.

She made an abrupt about-face. "Maybe you're right. It shouldn't end here. As you said, you came all this way, did all that detective work, for *me*." Her eyes narrowed, and I thought she was making a decision. "Tell you what. Perhaps you'd like to see where I work, and live. What do you think?" She dropped her sunglasses onto her nose, businesslike.

She was following her own peculiar agenda, I saw. I really didn't know what she wanted of me. But it was a chance to spend a little more time with her. What else could I do but accept?

And so she took me to the Catacombs.

The entrance wasn't far away. Aboveground there was little to see: a very small chapel, a couple of souvenir and refreshment stalls, a ticket booth, all set in a little scruffy parkland. It was lunchtime and the public areas were locked up, the ticket booth windows covered with CHIUSO notices: this was Rome, after all. But a few bewildered-looking tourists lingered by the refreshment stalls, buying overpriced hot dogs and bottled water.

They watched enviously as Rosa led me to a small stone block, the size and shape of *Doctor Who*'s TARDIS. It had a heavy green door, which she opened with a swipe card. This was the public entrance to the Catacombs of Agrippina, Rosa told me. She palmed a switch, and electric light flooded down from strip lights set in the ceiling.

Steps cut down into the dark. Rosa led the way, her heeled shoes clattering on the worn stone steps. When I pulled the door closed after me, it locked automatically. It immediately felt colder. It was a creepy experience, even in the electric light.

At the bottom of the steps I found myself in a gallery. It was narrow enough for me to reach out and touch both walls, and it was tall, perhaps twenty-five feet high, with an arched roof. The walls were notched, with box-shaped cavities cut deep into them. The light was dim, the electric lamps sparsely scattered. There was more light, in fact, coming from the skylight trenches cut down from the surface.

Rosa gave me the guided tour. "People say they've never heard of a Saint Agrippina. There never was one, so far as we know. She was probably just a well-off local matron, sympathetic to the Christians' cause, who gave them the use of her land . . ."

Burials had given the early Christian community here a problem. Space was always at a premium in Rome. Because of their beliefs the Christians were reluctant to cremate, but land was expensive, even this far out of town. So they began to dig.

"The rock here is tufa," Rosa said. "Soft, volcanic. It's easy to work, and it hardens when exposed to the air. And the Romans were used to working underground anyhow. They would dig sewers, waterworks, underground passages for servants to cross from one side of a great villa to another. Many houses would even have a *cryptoporticus*, an underground recreation area. So when they needed a place to bury their dead the Christians dug, and dug . . ."

We descended another steep staircase and found ourselves in yet another gallery that stretched on out of sight. The corridors branched, one after another, and the walls were all cut with those deep notches.

I was already thoroughly lost, disoriented. We were alone, and the only sounds were our footsteps and Rosa's gentle voice, softly echoing. The temperature had settled to a mild chill. Around me those open notches gaped like black mouths—and I had no doubt what they had once held. It was an eerie experience.

"The oldest levels are the highest," she said. "Which makes sense if you think about it. They just kept digging, down and down. They would cut out family vaults, called *cubicula*, and these niches are called *loculi*."

"Niches for the bodies," I said, my throat hoarse.

"Yes. Wrapped in linen, or perhaps embalmed. Even popes were buried in the Catacombs. But many of the tombs were pillaged in later centuries. Bones were taken away by desecrators, or by seekers of holy relics, or for reburial. Still, some undisturbed tombs were rediscovered over the last few centuries—perhaps there are more still to find. George, this Catacomb alone encompasses fifteen miles, over four levels. And it is estimated that in all the Catacombs some *half a million* people were buried, over the centuries."

Like so many numbers associated with ancient Rome, it was a stunning, impossible figure.

"Look." She pointed to symbols, painted faintly on the walls. The light was kept low to protect the paintwork, it turned out. "Covert Christian symbols, from the days of repression and persecution. The fish you will recognize. The dove, and here the olive branch, symbolizes peace. The anchor implies resurrection. Oh, here is the famous *chi-rho*, formed of the first two Greek letters of Christ's name." It looked like the letters *P* and *X* superimposed. "And here—" Carved above one of the *loculi*, it was like the simple fish symbol, but two fish touched, mouth to mouth, so that it was almost like an infinity.

"What's that?"

"The symbol of the Order." I recognized it from my Internet search. She was studying me. "How do you feel?"

"I'm in a two-thousand-year-old graveyard. A little freaked out."

"You aren't worried by the enclosure? The narrow walls, the depth—you don't feel claustrophobic?"

I thought about that. "No."

"And if I told you I have more to show you yet—that we will go much deeper . . ."

"Are you setting me some kind of test, Rosa?"

"Yes, I suppose I am. Something about the way we talked in the café . . . You've reacted well so far, and I think you're ready to see more." She held out her hand. "Will you come? You're free to go, whenever you like."

By now I had come to distrust her obviously calculated touching, the overwhelming feelings it evoked in me. But I took her hand again. "What next—open sesame?"

"Something like that."

We were standing before an innocent-looking niche, empty as the others. It had a two-fish symbol carved over it. Now, to my surprise, Rosa dug out a swipe card and passed it into a slot hidden inside the stone, up behind the fish. I glimpsed a red light, heard the unexpected humming of electronic gear.

And then, with a stony grind, a kind of trapdoor opened up beneath me—and bright light flooded up into the dusty air. I leaned forward to see. There was another staircase, but this was of polished metal, and it led down to a floor of gleaming tiles.

There was a *whole room* down there—a modern office, I saw. I glimpsed a desk, a girl behind it in a simple white smock, peering up at us. Fluorescent light glared up gray-white but dazzling bright after the gloom of the Catacomb. I was amazed—even stunned. It was the last thing I'd have expected to see; it was hard to believe it was real.

Rosa was grinning. "Welcome to my underground lair, Austin Powers."

"Not funny," I snapped.

"Oh, lighten up." She turned and descended. I followed.

And so I entered the Crypt for the first time.

The receptionist sat behind her wide marble desk, smiling at us. I glimpsed a winking rack of small TV monitors behind the surface of the desk, and one red-eyed camera peered directly at me from a wall. It was all quite normal, electric bright, certainly not as chill as the Catacombs. But there was no daylight, of course, not a scrap; it reminded me how far I was underground.

"We don't use this entrance much," said Rosa. "There are many ways in, from our shops and offices on the surface—

most of them in the suburbs to the west of the Appian Way—
though we have a couple of routes that lead to the center of the
city. But I wanted to bring you this way. It is the oldest." She
smiled, almost mischievously. "I suppose I wanted to put on a
show . . . Are you okay?"

I simply had no idea what to expect. "I've never been in a
convent before," I said.

"You aren't in one now. Come on."

We walked toward the wall of the anteroom. Automatic
doors slid out of sight. We stepped into a corridor, just as
brightly lit as the anteroom.

The corridor curved out of sight. It was my first impression
of the true size of the place. For sure it was a hell of a lot bigger than the anteroom.

And the corridor was full of people: a great murmuring
crowd, deep underground.

There must have been hundreds, just in that first glimpse.
The human traffic in that corridor was as dense as Oxford Circus on a summer Saturday, or Times Square at New Year. Most
of them were women. Many were in street clothes, but some
wore a kind of uniform, a simple white dress or trouser suit
with sewn-in threads of purple. They walked in neat files,
passing in and out of the rooms that branched off the corridor.

Then there was the *smell*: not an unpleasant smell, not a
locker-room stink, but there was something animal in the air,
something potent. The air was hot, humid, and noisy; I found
myself breathing hard, dragging for breath.

All this concealed far underground, under that sleepy
tourist-trap park.

Nobody seemed aware of anything strange, nobody but me.
It was all I could do to keep from staggering back, into the relative calm of the anteroom.

Rosa was leaning toward me. "Don't let it get to you. I know
how you feel. But it's always like this here. Come on . . ."
Holding my hand, she pulled me forward, and we waded into
the streams of people.

Suddenly I was surrounded by faces, all young, many smiling, few showing curiosity at this big sweating Englishman
who had been thrust in among them. They all seemed to be

talking, and the hubbub battered me, like a wind. But they parted around us, accepted us into the flow.

We passed offices with desks and partitioned cubicles, potted plants and coffee machines. They all seemed very mundane, if crowded and noisy compared to most offices I'd seen, almost as crowded as the corridors. In some places there were copies of the kissing-fish infinity symbol of the Order, done out in chrome strips and fixed to marble walls. All very corporate.

On many of the walls slogans had been incised—in places crudely, by hand, and in others more professionally. They were in Latin, which I can't read. I tried to memorize them, meaning to ask Peter about them later; there seemed to be three key phrases.

Rosa said that the varying sizes of rooms had names, in the Order's peculiar internal language—basically modern Italian, I would learn, but laced with terms derived from Latin, and other sources I didn't recognize. The room names seemed to be a macabre joke, a remembrance of the Crypt's origin. The largest vaults of all were called *cubicula*, like the family tombs in the Catacombs, the next largest *arcosolia*, like the large tombs of the wealthy and the popes—and the smallest of all *loculi*, like the lonely niche-graves of the poor.

But there were few *loculi*, I would learn, because members of the Order were never alone: the bigger the room, the bigger the crowd, the better.

The deeper in we penetrated, the more powerful that animal smell became. It was like walking into a lion's cage.

I tried to keep a clear head. "The workers here seem young," I said. "Nobody much over twenty-five or thirty?"

"Actually, most people here are *older* than that."

"They don't look it . . ."

"There are some youngsters, of course. Everybody has to learn. But most of the Order's younger members work downbelow."

"Downbelow?"

"On the lower levels."

"There are *lower levels*?"

We passed through a domain of libraries. The books were densely packed, and, as you see in some academic archives, the shelf units ran on rails: in a whole room there would be only enough space for a single passageway between a pair of shelves, and you would have to turn a little handle to make the shelves roll back and forth until you got the access you wanted. There was a *lot* of material. Farther on there were rooms more like museum departments, which contained what looked like extremely ancient manuscripts, scrolls and clay tablets, all held in air-conditioned isolation and low light, many of them in the drawers of glass-topped cabinets.

This area was the *scrinium*, said Rosa, the Order's term for the monumental internal record center that had now been turned outward to fuel the Internet genealogy business. Rosa showed me cabinets full of somewhat dog-eared index cards. There was so much material, she said, that even the indices had an index. We passed a computer center, where great main-frames hummed behind sealed windows. I got a fresh sense of the power and wealth of this place.

Before we left the *scrinium* Rosa gave me a small hardback book. It turned out to be the story of Regina, our Roman British ancestress—"A more complete biography than of any-one else in the ancient world, even the Caesars," Rosa said. "Bedtime reading."

A little farther on, to my surprise, we came to classrooms, where children, mostly girls, sat in neat rows, or worked in groups at desks, or labored over baffling-looking experiments in a science.

Rosa told me that few of these pupils belonged to the Or-der. Offering quality education to outsiders had been the Order's earliest significant money earner—*earliest* in the Order's terms, I learned, meaning 'fifth century after Christ.' She said they even had accounting records that went back that far, though the earliest entries were of limited use: they pre-dated the invention of the double-entry bookkeeping system by the best part of a millennium.

"How inconvenient," I murmured.

In one place there was even a small theater, where a group of young teenagers was rehearsing a play.

Schools. A theater. A *play*. And all of this, remember, dug deep into the ground below four levels of Catacombs.

Again we walked on.

* * *

In that first visit I didn't even come close to figuring out the geography of the Crypt. The place isn't designed to give you long vistas and perspectives anyhow; it's designed to disorient, to make you forget where you are.

I would discover later that the Crypt was organized on three great levels. But each of those levels was subdivided by intermediate floors and mezzanines. The layout was functional, and changed all the time according to need, the arbitrary divisions between compartments blurring. All that helped mix up the geography in everybody's heads, of course. I certainly didn't figure out, that first time, how far those branching corridors and mushrooming chambers led; I never came to anything that could have been an outside wall, a layer of tufa like that I had seen carved out in the Catacombs above. Even so, I could see that the Crypt was immense.

And it was *full* of people. That was the one thing that struck me every second.

They were all around me, all the time, everywhere we walked. They all seemed similar, all smooth-faced and ageless, all of a compact, rounded build—and not tall; I was one of the tallest there, so I was seeing over the heads of the crowd. I was immersed in touch constantly: they would brush against me, and sometimes one would rest a hand on my shoulder as she squeezed past. There was that smell, the overall leonine stink of the compound, but something subtler when one of them came close, the milky sweetness I had noticed about Rosa.

And then there were the faces. It took me some minutes, after entering that first corridor, to recognize how *similar* they all were. They were all like Rosa, and therefore like me, almost all of them with oval faces, broad, flat noses—and the slate-gray eyes that have been a family trait for generations. They were all around me, faces like mirrors of mine—if younger, smoother, *happier*. There was a constant racket, but nobody seemed to be shouting, arguing, barging past anybody else; everybody was busy, but nobody was rushing or stressed out. Despite the hubbub, there was a great sense of *order* about the place.

I felt confused, baffled, battered by astounding impressions.

But, odd though it seems, I didn't feel uncomfortable. I've always been drawn to order, regularity—not control, necessarily, but calm. And this place, for all its unfamiliarity and surface strangeness, was at heart a deep well of calm; I could sense that immediately.

What I felt was: *I belong here.*

Rosa brought me to a kind of balcony. It was a rare viewpoint offering a cutaway view of at least some of the Crypt, like looking down into a shopping mall from a top level. Rosa pointed out a row of open-roofed chambers lined with bunk beds: dormitories. Farther away was a blocky structure that was a hospital, she said. People were everywhere I looked, moving, working, interacting with each other in little knots.

"There must be—" I waved a hand at the teeming masses below. "—a control center. Some kind of management structure."

"No control center. No bridge on this great underground submarine." Rosa was watching my face. "How do you feel now? Are you thinking about all the rock over your head? Do you feel shut in, lost?"

"I'm in an underground city, by God," I said. "I have to keep reminding myself that all this is dug into the ground under a Roman suburb . . . You know, I still haven't got you in focus, Rosa."

She wasn't fazed. "But the Order *is* me. I told you, it's my family—and yours. If you can't see that, you can't see anything about me." She waved her hand. "George, do you blame our parents, Father, for my being sent away—for this peculiar gap in your life?"

I frowned. "I'm not sure."

"*I* don't blame them," she said definitely. "They did what they had to do to enable the family to survive. I understand that now, and I think I understood it even as a child." I wondered if that could be true. "And besides, look around you. I've hardly suffered by being sent here."

Suddenly I felt resentful. I hadn't come here to see this vast subterranean city, after all, but *her*. And she seemed barely perturbed by my presence. This wasn't enough of a reaction for me, emotionally. I wanted to break down her complacency—to make her see *me*.

Harm may not have come to her. But harm has come to me, I thought.

I had no idea how long I had been down there. At last, something prompted me to get out of there.

Rosa didn't protest. She escorted me back along that long corridor, back to the anteroom, and then up to the Catacombs. We climbed alone, in the perpetual darkness, up the levels, before ascending that last staircase and emerging from the Catacomb's gloomy entrance.

It was dark, I saw, shocked. I must have been in the great pit in the ground for six, seven, eight hours. The place was deserted, the refreshment stalls shut up for the night. But the air was fresh, and smelled of the lemon trees in the scrubby parkland. I breathed deep, trying to clear my head of that leonine underground tang.

But standing there alone, out of the Crypt, I felt bereft.

I walked out of the Catacomb compound and began searching for a cab. When I found one, a couple of blocks away, I recoiled from the driver's face—dark, eyes deep brown—a perfectly normal, even handsome human face, but not like *mine*.

Rosa had let me go gracefully enough when I asked to leave. It was only later, thinking over the day, that I understood that she had decided—during our very first meeting at that coffee bar, as I tried to come to terms with suddenly meeting my sister again for the first time since childhood—to try to recruit me into the Order. Her first instinct had been to exclude me; after meeting me she had decided I should somehow be inducted. And everything she had shown me, everything she had done and said from that moment on, had been designed with that intent in mind. It had nothing to do with *me* at all.

chapter 40

Francesca walked with her companion through the *civitas Leonina*.

Leo Frangipani wanted to tell Francesca about the Pope's plans for a Holy Year, to be held in the forthcoming year 1300. "It's going to be a marvel," he said. "They are planning how to display the holy relics to maximize the revenue. It's said that the priests are already practicing with the rakes they will use to drag in the money thrown by the crowds onto their altars . . ." He was watching her. "Ah, you disapprove! These fishers of the endless river of the gullible and faithful that washes through Rome—"

"Not at all," she said. "Anybody would disapprove of thievery. But the pilgrims believe their money is well spent, and if it goes to preserve Rome, mother of the world, then surely they are right."

"Perhaps so. I do know that you ladies in white prefer to *give* your money away . . . I'll never understand how you survive."

But survive the Order did, after more than eight centuries.

The *civitas Leonina* was a city within a city, centered on the Vatican Hill, where stood Constantine's vast and crumbling basilica, the wheel hub of Christianity. The area was a huddle of monasteries, lodging houses, churches, oratories, taverns, cells for hermits, even an orphanage and a poorhouse, thé latter of which was funded, discreetly, by the Order.

There were many services here for the pilgrims—or, depending which way you looked at it, plenty of people with ambitions to separate pilgrims from their money. The cobblers would repair soles worn out from walking, butchers, fishmongers, and fruiterers would feed your body, and farmers would sell you straw for your bedding, some of it still caked with dung. And then there were the vendors of linen strips that had been in contact with the tomb of one martyr, and dried flowers said to have grown over the grave of another, and you could buy candles, relics, rosaries, icons, and vials of holy water and oil. Guides and beggars wandered everywhere, looking for the gullible. Even under the walls of Constantine's basilica itself moneylenders thronged and called, ringing coins on the tops of their tables.

But it was a thriving place; for every vendor there must have been ten potential purchasers—and probably as many criminals, Francesca thought uneasily.

She knew she stood out from the crowd. Though she had eschewed the Order's habitual white robes for a simple dress of brown-dyed wool, she wore a thick layer of cream and unguent on her face to protect her skin from the unaccustomed sun, and spectacles made of blue glass protected eyes used to candlelight and oil lamps. She looked *different*, and therefore was no doubt a target for beggars and thieves alike.

She had no fear, for with her was a Frangipani: a tall, imposing, well-dressed young man with a very visible sword at his waist, a scion of one of the city's wealthier families. But to Francesca, used to the calm of the Crypt's underground cloisters, this was a crowded, dirty, disturbing place.

And it was a place of madness, she thought suddenly, of a great plague of the mind: all these people drawn from across Europe to see shabby relics and to part with their wealth, all for the sake of an idea, the great rampaging mind-sickness of Christianity. Just as in ages past they had no doubt been drawn to the Colosseum, or the triumphs of the Caesars—other contagious ideas, all now vanished like the dew.

But she was pious, and the Order itself was of course deeply Christian; she felt dismayed to be formulating such doubts, and did her best to put them out of her mind.

As they climbed up out of the residential area toward the higher ground of the ancient hills, Francesca got a broader view of the city. She could see how small and cramped the densely populated area was, set within the area called the *disabitato*, the great expanse of scrubland and farms that occupied the rest of the space within the old walls. Here and there monuments of the imperial age loomed out of the green, but many of them had been badly damaged by time, demolished by siege weapons, or the marble broken up and burned for lime.

There had been centuries of conflict, with Rome a battleground between popes and antipopes, and between the popes and the Holy Roman Emperors. Rome had paid a terrible price. But now the papacy had thrown off the yoke of the German emperors, and Rome had begun slowly to recover. On the higher ground, the mansions and palaces of the rich loomed with their towers of burnt red brick. The Frangipani family, in fact, had built a series of towers all the way around the old Circus Maximus, the emperors' racetrack.

Leo was watching her.

She could read what he was thinking. He was trying to make out her body through her ground-length dress, its hem and sleeves now stained by Roman dirt. He was a good-looking boy, and he was scarcely older than she was, at twenty-four.

She felt a welcome flush. She was, after all, a woman. Which was, indirectly, the reason she was here.

"We're here to talk business," she reminded Leo gently.

"That's so." He stepped back, his smile apologetic, and averted his eyes.

"You have secured your interests in the land in Venice?"

"In principle." He smiled. "All I need is the deposit . . ."

Times were changing—and it was Francesca's instinct that the Order must change to suit.

Over the centuries the Order had continued to develop its charitable work. But it was a business, after a fashion. For every hundred of the poor or unfortunate whom the Order helped—so had been learned—there was always one who became rich enough later to make a significant donation to the Order's coffers, wishing to show his gratitude to those who had saved him when he was at his lowest. It was a long game, but the amounts doled out to the poor were actually so small that the gamble was more than worth taking. It was a business, like Rome's pilgrim-fleecing industry—but if it served a pious end it was surely a business worth carrying out.

But now there were new opportunities. After the death of

the last Emperor in Rome, the cities and towns across western Europe had shrunk back, to be replaced by small hamlets and migrants, with few communities numbering more than a thousand. Now agricultural innovations were seeping across Europe from Germany. Major communities were developing again—Venice, it was said, had more than a hundred thousand inhabitants—and with this revival had come new opportunities for profit.

Young Leo's scheme was simple: to buy marshland close to Venice, drain it, and then farm it until such time as he could sell it off in the face of the expected expansion of the city. Francesca could see the sense of it. For a small initial outlay he could multiply his holdings many times within a few years, and thus make his name within his family.

Francesca was prepared to make the loan to enable him to do this. But she had asked something in return. Now she outlined her latest plans: she needed soldiers.

As it spread out relentlessly, deep beneath the old Appian Way, the Order had broken through into another set of underground chambers, occupied by a group of Aryan Christians with a way of life strangely similar to the Order's: run by a small group of women with massive extended families, served by a network of childless nieces and daughters . . . It seemed that similar pressures, surrounding the collapse of Rome, had induced similar solutions. It said a great deal for the secrecy of the Crypt and its dark twin that the two groups had remained unaware of each other for so long.

But they could not coexist, of course. Francesca had seen that straight away, felt it on a deep gut level. The other "Crypt" had to be broken up, assimilated.

If you uncovered a problem you were expected to fix it yourself: that was the Order's central mode of working. So Francesca had made a quick decision. Leo would find soldiers to cleanse the parallel crypt, and the Order would break through and occupy the abandoned chambers. At a stroke the Crypt's effective size would be increased by more than half, and the Order would gain many servants.

If Francesca succeeded in her scheme she would gain great prestige within the Order—and, she hoped, get close to the *matres*. She had realized a year ago that Livilla, oldest of the *matres*, was dying. And it had been only a few months later that her own blood had started to flow—at the age of twenty-three, for the first time in her life. Then had come the realization that *she*, through skill, cunning and luck, might take Livilla's place.

The next time a bachelor was brought in from the city, it would be *her* body that would bewitch him, *her* loins that would bear his child. When she thought about that prospect she felt a dull ache in the pit of her belly, and a soreness in her breasts.

Conversely, if Leo's Venice adventure succeeded he would gain great influence in his family. They were both the same, really, she thought. The pursuit of individual ambitions, tied into the goals of the group: it was the way things were. As she studied his face, she saw that Leo understood this.

Leo still wasn't sure, though. He rubbed his nose. "I'm no soldier, Francesca. I've no idea if this plan, of sending mercenaries into the Catacombs like field mice into a sewer, will work."

She smiled. "Then hire a general who will know."

He laughed. "I don't think we need a general. But I do know somebody who might be able to help, as it happens . . ."

"Then bring him to me."

They concluded their business. When they parted he made playfully to kiss her cheek, despite its thick plastering of cream, but she would not allow it.

chapter 41

Peter turned up at my hotel a couple of days after my first descent into the Crypt. He stood there in the lobby, as big as Fred Flintstone, crumpled, faintly smelling of sweat, and yet untroubled. He arrived oddly short of luggage, bringing not much more than a carry-on bag, and he was out of money.

The first thing he said was, "Did you bring your duffel coat?"

"What? . . . No, I didn't bring my duffel coat. What's that got to do with anything?"

He grinned. "In Roman times the British used to export duffel coats. A duffel was a modish item for a while. It was called the *byrrus Britannicus*. George, you could have been fashionable for once in your life."

"Peter, forget duffel coats. What the hell are you doing here?"

"Cash-flow problems," he said.

"What are you talking about? You own a house, for God's sake. You must have savings—"

"My accounts have been frozen," he said. "Long story. Look, obviously I'll pay you back . . ."

Maybe I'm naive. It was a time in my life in which various people, including a Jesuit and my long-lost sister, seemed to have little difficulty keeping me away from awkward truths with simple deflections and guile. But that day I was distracted, as I had been since coming out of the Crypt. I couldn't get the memory out of my head; it was as if the milky air of the place were a drug, and I had been addicted in one quick hit.

So that was why I went with the flow concerning Peter, why I found it hard to focus on his evasions about what he'd been doing, why he'd turned up in this state. It just didn't seem to matter.

I didn't want to stump up for a separate room; the hotel was cheap but not that cheap. I upgraded to a twin, in my name. We moved into the room that afternoon.

It didn't take Peter long to unpack. That carry-on contained nothing much but his laptop and a couple of changes of clothes, some of which still had shop labels on them, as if he had purchased them in a hurry. He didn't even have a razor; he borrowed mine until he bought a pack of disposables.

He showered, shaved, sent his traveling clothes down to the hotel laundry. Then he spent the rest of the afternoon voraciously reading the little book Rosa had given me on my alleged ancestress Regina.

That evening, he let me buy him a meal at my favorite of the little roadside restaurants. I told Peter as much as I could about my sister Rosa, and the Order, and the Crypt. He just listened.

On a napkin I wrote down the three Latin slogans I had tried to memorize in the Crypt. He used online dictionaries, accessed through his handheld, to translate them:

Sisters matter more than daughters.

Ignorance is strength.

Listen to your sisters.

"What do you think they mean?"

"Damned if I know," he said. He filed them away, intending to research them later.

I tried to explain the appeal of the place.

Once I had a friend who had grown up in a series of military camps. They were rather bland fifties-flavor estates, dotted around the country. But they were secure, behind their barriers of wire and men with guns, and inside there were only service personnel and their families. There was no crime, no disorder, no graffiti or vandalism. Once he had grown up and completed his own service in the air force, my friend was finally expelled from his barbed-wire utopia. It seemed to me he spent his whole life after that looking back from our chaotic world at the little islands of order behind the wire. I had always known how he had felt.

And that was how I felt about the Crypt now. But there were

conflicting emotions—yes, a desire to return, but at the same time a dread of being dragged back into that pit of faces, the scents, the endless touching.

I tried to express all this. Peter made Halloween gestures. "They'll eat your soul!"

It wasn't funny.

After we'd eaten, we strolled back toward the hotel. But it was a fine night, dusty and warm, and we were in Rome, for God's sake. So we stopped at an *alimentari*, a grocery store, where I bought a bottle of *limoncello*. Close to the hotel there was a little square of greenery, with water fountains and cigarette butts and dog turds. We found a relatively clean bench and sat down. The *limoncello* was a lemon liqueur they manufactured down the coast near Sorrento. It was bright yellow and so sweet it stuck to your teeth. But it wasn't so bad after the insides of our mouths were coated by the first couple of slugs, and it topped off the wine we had drunk.

The sky was smoggy that night, and glowed faintly grayorange. There was plenty of light from the lamps that played on the monuments in the Forum and on the great gaudy *Vittoriano*. We were cupped by the great shoulders of Trajan's Market, which loomed all around us.

I had taken a couple of walks around Trajan's Market, which I found astonishing. You couldn't say the ruins were attractive: the market was just a mound of brickwork, of streets and broken-open domes and little doorways. But it had been a shopping mall, for God's sake. The little units—all neatly numbered and set on multiple levels along colonnaded passageways, or in great curving facades that would have graced the Georgians—had been planned and leased out, just like a modern development.

"That's what strikes you," I said to Peter. "There's nothing medieval about this area—not like the center of British cities. Everything is planned, laid out in neat curves and straight lines. The Forum looks antique, if you know what I mean. Columns and temples, very ancient Greek. But the big palaces look like the ruins of the White House. And this market looks like the ruins of Milton Keynes."

"Except Milton Keynes won't last so well as Roman brickwork. They didn't have slaves to mix the concrete so well."

"You know, in the Dark Ages they used this place as a fortress. From shopping mall to barricade."

He nodded thoughtfully. "Decline and fall, eh? But there were a few junctions in Rome's history where things might have turned out different."

"Such as?"

"Such as the loss of Britain. Needn't have happened. Britain wasn't just some kind of border outpost. Britain was protected by the ocean—mostly anyhow—from the pressures of the barbarians, and internally it was mostly at peace. For centuries it was a key source of wheat and weapons for the troops in Gaul and Germany, and it had a reserve of troops that could have been used to reverse the setbacks in western Europe. Even after the calamities of the early fifth century—if the emperors had won Britain back, they might have stabilized the whole of the western Empire. Maybe your grannie understood some of this."

"If she ever existed."

"If she existed. Well, she was the daughter of a citizen, the granddaughter of a soldier. If you're living in great times, decisive times, you know about it, even if you only glimpse a small part of it."

"Do you think this story of Regina can be true?"

"Well, I read the book. It's plausible. The place-names are authentic. Durnovaria is modern Dorchester, Verulamium Saint Albans, Eburacum York. Some of the detail makes sense, too. The old Celtic festival of Samhain eventually mutated into Halloween . . . Trouble is, nobody really knows much about how Roman Britain fell apart anyhow. For sure it wasn't like the continent, where the barbarian warlords tried to keep up the old imperial structures, though with themselves on the top. In Britain we got the Saxons—it was an apocalypse, like living through a nuclear war. The history and archaeology are scratchy, ironically, precisely because of that."

I nodded, and sipped a little more *limoncello*. The bottle was already getting low. "And if the Empire *had* survived—"

He shrugged. "Rome would have had to fight off the expansion of Islam in the seventh century, and the Mongols in the thirteenth. But its armies would have handled the Golden

Horde better than its medieval successors. It could have endured. Its eastern half did."

"No Dark Ages—"

"The one thing you get with an empire is stability. A solemn
calm. Instead of which we got a noisy clash of infant nations."

"No feudalism," I said. "No barons. No chivalry. And no
English language. We'd all have ended up speaking some de-
scendant of Latin, like French, Spanish—"

"No Renaissance. There would have been no need for it. But
there would have been none of the famous Anglo-Saxon tradition of individual liberty and self-determination. No Magna
Carta, no parliaments. If the Romans had gone to the Ameri-
cas they wouldn't have practiced genocide against the natives,
as we did. That wasn't the Roman way. They'd have assimilated, acculturated, built their aqueducts and bathhouses and
roads, the apparatus of their civilizing system. The indigenous
nations, in North and South America, would have survived as
new Roman provinces. It would have been a richer world,
maybe more advanced in some ways."

"But no Declaration of Independence. And no abolition of
slavery, either."

There would have been losses, then. But the fall of Rome—
all that bloodshed, the loss of learning—*the collapse of order:*
no, I realized, I didn't think that was a good thing. The order of
empires appealed to me—even if, for example, the Soviet
Union had been just such an empire by any reasonable definition. But that was my inner longing for order and regularity
expressing itself.

We sat for a while, listening to the cicadas chirp in the trees,
whose green leaves looked black as oil in the smoggy orange
light. One of the other drunks was watching us; he raised his
brown paper bag in ironic salute, and we toasted him back.

"So. My sister," I said. "What do you think of *her*?"

He shrugged. "Sounds inhuman. I don't know how you
ought to behave when your long-lost brother turns up out of
the blue, but surely it's not like that."

I nodded. "What do you think we're dealing with?"

"A cult. A creepy fringe-Catholic cult. I think your sister has
been indoctrinated. No wonder she reacted like a robot."

I forced a smile. "If you're thinking of deprogramming her, forget it. She says she doesn't need saving."

"Well, she would say that." More gently he said, "And after forty years, and after being taken at such a young age, there's probably very little left of your sister anyhow." He sighed. "Your dad was a good friend of mine. But he had a lot to answer for."

"What about the Order?"

"You know, Jesus Himself never meant to found a church. As far as He was concerned, He was living in the end times. He had come to proclaim the kingdom of God. The early church was scattered, chaotic, splintered; it was a suppressed movement, after all."

"And women—"

"When the persecutions began, women had it particularly tough. Women martyrs were made available for prostitution. Women would need a place to hide, a way to gather strength, to endure . . ."

"So the story of the Order makes sense."

"Once it became the religion of the Empire, the church quickly tightened up. Heresy wasn't to be tolerated: for the first time you had Christians cheerfully persecuting other Christians. In the centuries that followed, as the popes got a grip, the church became centralized, legalized, politicized, militarized. The Order would have had no place in the world-view of the popes."

"Yet it survived."

He rubbed his chin. "The Order is obviously secretive, but it's been sitting there an awfully long time, an hour's walk from the Vatican itself. The church has to know about it. There have to be some kind of links." He smiled. "I told you I always wanted to go have a root around in the Vatican's Secret Archives. Maybe now's the time."

I said dubiously, "I'll have to ask Claudio."

I wasn't happy with his response. On some level he might be right. But he hadn't taken on board what I'd tried to tell him about what I thought of as the *earthy* aspects of the Crypt: the faces, the smells, that deep pull I felt to remain there, to go back. Or maybe I hadn't wanted to expose all this spooky biological stuff to him.

Anyhow, though I couldn't shape the thought, I was sure there was more to the Order than just a cult. But maybe Peter was going to have to see it for himself.

As if on cue, an opportunity to do just that offered itself.

Peter had booted up his laptop—he was never without it—and every so often he checked his email. Now he discovered a note from some American kid called Daniel Stannard, who had somehow found his way through the Internet jungle to us. Daniel had concerns about a girl called Lucia, who sounded like she was some kind of refugee from the Order. Daniel wanted to meet us.

Peter smiled, a bit glassily. "I think the door of our secretive subterranean sisterhood has opened, just a crack."

Right then I was drunk enough not to care. "I wonder if my great-grannie really did shag King Arthur."

He snorted. "She'd have had a job, as he never existed . . ."

There were traces of history about Arthur. He cropped up in sources of Celtic mythology, like the Mabinogion from Wales, and you could trace Arthur in the genealogies of the Welsh kings. An inscription bearing the name ARTORIUS had even been found at one of Arthur's supposed strongholds. But by the ninth century, the myth was spreading. What Welsh prince wouldn't want his name linked with Arthur? And that ARTORIUS inscription, on closer inspection, looked more like ARTOGNUS . . .

Peter said, "The Roman British elite only managed to score a few victories against the Saxons. It was a desperate time. They must have looked for hope—and what is Arthur, not dead but sleeping, if not an embodiment of hope? It's a lovely story. But it's got nothing to do with the truth."

Perhaps, I thought. But unlike Peter, I had seen the Crypt, and its ancient, meticulous records. Perhaps I would be able to believe in Arthur—and it would be delicious if I could believe my remote great-grandmother had once kissed him, and in her way bested him.

We swapped the *limoncello* again, and I changed the subject.

"So," I said, "what became of that invisible spaceship that took a right in the center of the Earth?"

He glanced at me, a bit wearily. "You still don't take it seriously. George, something happened. It came from the sun. It made straight for the Earth, and it changed course. If it had been visible it would have been the story of the century."

"I don't see why you're so fascinated by dark matter in the first place."

He slapped the brick wall behind him. "Because for every ton of good solid brick, there are ten of dark matter, out there, *doing something*. Most of the universe is invisible to us, and we don't even know what it's made of. There are mysteries out there we can't even guess at . . ." He lifted his hand and flexed his fingers. "Baryonic matter, normal matter, is infested with life. Why not dark matter, too? Why shouldn't there be intelligence? And if so, *what is it doing in our sun?*"

I shook my head. I was drunk, and starting to feel sour. "I don't understand."

"Well, neither do I. But I'm trying to join the dots." He leaned forward and lowered his voice again. "I'll tell you what I think. *I think there's a war going on out there.* Some kind of struggle. It's going on above our heads, and we can't even see it."

I grunted. "War in Heaven? The dark against the light? I'll tell you what this sounds like to me. Peter, your background's showing. You've just somehow sublimated your Catholic upbringing into this great space-opera story of war in the sky."

His mouth opened and closed. "I have to admit I never thought of *that*. Well, you might be right. But my psychological state doesn't change the reality of the data—or the consequences. Just suppose you are a field mouse stuck in a World War I trench. What do you do?"

"You keep your head down."

"Right. Because one misdirected shell could wipe out your whole damn species. That's why some of us," he whispered, "believe that it would be a mistake to announce our presence to the stars."

I frowned. "I thought we'd already done that. We've been blasting TV signals to the skies since the days of Hitler."

"Yes, but we're getting more efficient about our use of electromagnetic radiation—tight beams, cables, optic fibers. We're already a lot quieter, cosmically speaking, than we were a few decades ago. We can't bring back our radio noise, but it is a thin shell of clamor, heading out from the Earth, getting weaker and weaker . . . Blink and you miss it. And besides, radio is primitive. The more advanced folk are surely listening out for more interesting signals. And there are some people out there who think we should start sending out just those kinds of signals."

"I take it you aren't one of these people."

"Not anymore." He was gazing into his hands as he said this, and his voice was unusually somber.

I remembered how he had fled to Rome, with no money, not much more than the clothes he stood up in. Suddenly I was suspicious. "Peter—what have you done?"

But he just smiled and reached for the bottle.

chapter 42

It was in the year 1527 that Clement came to Rome. He was in the service of Charles V, Emperor of Germany, who also happened to be king of Spain and Naples and ruler of the Netherlands.

A huge army of German *Landsknecht*, mainly Lutherans, had been raised by the king's brother, a mighty force to wreak vengeance on the Antichrist in Rome. They battled through torrential rain and snowstorms to cross the Alps. They advanced on Lombardy and joined the Emperor's main force of Spaniards, Italians, and others.

And then they converged on Rome.

Clement, after his travels, had seen much of the world. But Rome was extraordinary.

A great circuit of wall, it was said raised by the Caesars, was still in use today, much repaired. But within its wide boundaries there were farms, vineyards and gardens, even areas of scrub and thicket where deer and wild boar roamed. Here and there you could see broken columns and shapeless ruins poking out of the greenery, draped with ivy and eglantine and populated by pigeons and other birds. The inhabited area was small and cramped, a place of narrow streets and houses hanging over the muddy waters of the patient, enduring Tiber, with the spires of the rich looming over all.

There were many fine churches and palaces. But Rome was a city trapped in the past, Clement thought, a city that would have been humbled if set aside Milan or Venice or Trieste.

And now it was to be humbled further.

The pope offered an indemnity, which tempted the army's leaders. But the *Landsknecht* wanted pillage. And so it was that an undisciplined, heterogeneous, half-starved, and ragged army finally marched on Rome, dreaming of plunder. There were more than thirty thousand of them.

The attack began before dawn.

The first assault on the wall was repulsed, but the defenders, hugely outnumbered and lacking ammunition, were soon reduced to throwing rocks at those they called "half-castes" and "Lutherans." Up went the scaling ladders, and soon Germans and Spaniards were swarming over the wall. Some of the defenders fought bravely, including the pope's Swiss Guards, but they were quickly overwhelmed.

By the time Clement had crossed the wall the fighting was all but done. It was still dawn; still mist from the Tiber choked the city streets. Afterward, Rome was at the mercy of the Emperor's troops. Later, Clement would remember little of the days that followed, little save bloodstained glimpses of unbelievable savagery.

The Romans were cut to pieces, even if unarmed, even if unable to defend themselves. Even invalids in hospitals were slaughtered.

The doors of churches, convents, palaces, and monasteries were broken down and their contents hurled into the streets. When people tried to shelter in the churches they were massacred; five hundred died even in Saint Peter's. Priests were forced to take part in obscene travesties of the Mass, and if they did not they were eviscerated, or crucified, or dragged through the streets, naked and in chains. Nuns were violated, and used as tokens in games of chance, and convents were turned into brothels where the women of the upper classes were forced into prostitution. Holy relics were abused; the skull of the Apostle Andrew was kicked around the streets, the handkerchief of Saint Veronica was sold in an inn, the spear said to have pierced Christ's side was displayed like a battle trophy by a German.

Clement took part in the torment of one wealthy man who was made to rape his own daughter, and another, a very fat man, who was forced to eat his own roasted testicles. Afterward he would not be able to credit what he had done.

The Sack of Rome was the end product of decades of suspicion, jealousy, and hostility. The Renaissance popes had been great patrons of the arts, but they had acted like ambitious princelings and made many enemies. Meanwhile the great wealth of Rome had made the city a prize that the European powers, especially France and Spain, had eyed with jealousy. French, Spaniards, and landless German Lutherans had at last made common cause under Charles's imperial banner. But none of this could have justified the Sack.

It went on for months. It was said that twelve thousand were killed. Two-thirds of the housing stock was burned to the ground. On the resulting wasteland lay putrefying corpses, gnawed by dogs. Even on Sundays not a church bell sounded, across the whole of Rome.

One hot night Clement found himself with a party of a dozen or so that ventured outside the city walls. They were drunk. There might be nothing to find out here, but at least it would be a break from the stink of the city itself, where, it was said, by now you couldn't find a purse worth emptying or a virgin over twelve.

The Emperor's soldiers followed an old road the locals called the Appian Way. It was overgrown and rutted, but you could still trace its line, arrow straight. They drank, sang bawdily, and as they walked they probed with sticks and spears at the ground. There were tales of Catacombs out here, and where there were Catacombs you might find treasure.

It was Clement, as it happened, who found the door. His broken stick, in fact a smashed-off crucifix, hit wood—he thought—something solid, anyhow.

He called the others over, and soon they were scrabbling at the turf and dirt, pulling it away in great handfuls. Gradually they exposed a great square door in the ground. They tried to haul it open, but it would not budge.

So Philip, a great slab of a man from southern Spain, got to his hands and knees and began to hammer on the door. If it was not opened it would be smashed in or burned, he shouted, and it would be the worse for whoever was inside. None of this provoked a response, so the men began to gather wood for a fire, to burn their way through.

Then, without warning, the door pushed open. Philip scrambled off, and soon all the men were gathered around, hauling at the door.

A chamber in the ground was exposed. It was walled with white-painted plaster, Clement saw, and lamps flickered in the breeze. And there were women here—six of them—none younger than sixteen or older than twenty-five, he judged, and they were wearing white dresses. They stood in a row, peering up, like nuns praying. They were very pale, like ghosts, yet beautiful, and all of them full-figured.

When the men roared and reached for them, the women's nerve broke. They clung to each other and huddled back in their pit. But they could not escape the men's eager hands. They were hauled out of the pit, stripped, and taken, there and then, on the surface of the ancient imperial road. When the men realized the women were all virgins they fought among themselves to be first to have them. But in the end all the women were used, over and again.

As their pale bodies writhed Clement was reminded oddly of maggots, or larvae, wriggling when exposed to the light.

Once Philip and two others set on one woman at the same time. When they were done, they found they had crushed the breath out of their victim. She was left where they had finished her, for the dogs and birds to take. The other women were taken back into the city, where four of them were sold to a group of Germans, and the other gambled away.

Sated, occupied with the women, the men didn't try to penetrate the Catacomb further, and left the pit in the ground gaping open.

A few nights after that Clement and some others went back along the Appian Way, searching for the door once more. Clement's memory was good, and he had not been terribly drunk that night. But search as he might he could find no trace of a doorway in the ground, or of the debauchery that had been committed here, or of the woman killed. When he thought back, to that vision of the pale women writhing on the ground like uncovered worms, it seemed like a dream.

chapter 43

We agreed to meet Daniel and Lucia inside the Colosseum. Peter and I grinned at each other when Daniel, through his emails, suggested this cloak-and-dagger rendezvous. But anyhow we went along, one bright early-November morning.

The Colosseum was only a short walk down Mussolini's majestic boulevard from our hotel, and its ruined grandeur loomed ahead of us as we approached. In fact the Colosseum had been a key motivation for Mussolini to build his imperial way where he did, for he wanted a clear view of it from his palace off the Piazza Venezia. Its size was deceptive; it seemed to take us a long time to reach the foot of that mighty wall, even longer to walk around the tarmac apron at its base.

By the time we got to the public entrance, Peter was puffing and sweating profusely. He seemed agitated today, his untroubled demeanor gone, but he wouldn't say what was on his mind.

We joined a glacier-pace queue of more or less patient visitors before the glass-fronted ticket office. Hucksters worked the crowd: water sellers, tropical-shirted vendors of bangles and felt hats and fake-leather handbags, and a few plausible-sounding American-accented girls who offered "official" guided tours. Groups of blokes in fake legionary uniforms, all scarlet and gold and plastic swords, volunteered to have their photos taken with tourists. With my British sensibility I vaguely imagined these were "official," somehow sanctioned by the city or whichever authority controlled the Colosseum, until I saw them cluster around one hapless American tourist demanding twenty euros for each photograph they'd just taken.

But above all this indignity loomed the antique walls, to which marble still clung, despite fifteen hundred years of neglect and despoliation.

Peter wasn't comfortable in the gathering heat. "Fucking Italians," he said. "Once, you know, they could get fifty thousand people inside this stadium in ten minutes. Now *this*."

At length we inched our way to the head of the queue, bought our tickets, and passed through a turnstile and into the body of the stadium.

The huge structure was a hollow shell. Inside, cavernous corridors curved out of sight to either side. Peter looked a little lost, but all this was startlingly familiar to me, a veteran of the architecture of English soccer stadiums. Still, the corridors and alcoves were littered with rubble, stupendous fragments of fallen brickwork and columns and marble carvings. The place had long been neglected; even in the seventies the Romans had used these immense corridors as a car park.

We emerged at last into bright sunlight.

The interior of the stadium was oval. Walkways curved around its perimeter at a couple of levels. Because we were early, like dutiful tourists we completed circuits of the walls, and crossed a wooden walkway that passed along the axis of the stadium floor. The original floor, made of wood, had long since rotted away, exposing brick cells where humans and animals had once been kept, waiting to fight for their lives on the stage above.

After perhaps half an hour, it was time. We made our way to the small book stall, which had been built into an alcove close to the main spectator entrance. There was quite a crowd here, for this was where you congregated for your "official" guided tours.

I had no problem recognizing Lucia.

She had exactly the look that had characterized the women and girls of the Order: not tall, stockily built, with the oval face and pale gray eyes of that huge subterranean family. I had had a lot of trouble figuring out ages in the Crypt, but Lucia looked genuinely young—perhaps sixteen, or even younger. She had blue-tinged sunglasses pushed up on her head. But her simple blue dress was grimy, the hem ripped; it looked as if she had been wearing it for days.

She was heavily pregnant, I saw, startled.

When she saw me standing before her—and she recognized my similar features—her eyes widened, and she clutched the hand of the boy with her.

He was quite different: perhaps a couple of years older, taller, slim, with reddish hair that was already receding from a pale, rounded brow. His eyes were clear blue, and he peered at us suspiciously.

"So here we are," Peter said. "I take it you're Lucia—you speak English?"

"Not well," she said. Her voice was husky, her English heavily accented.

"But I do," said the boy, Daniel. "I'm an American."

"Good for you," said Peter dryly.

I tried to reduce the tension. "My name is George Poole. Lucia, it seems we are distant cousins." I smiled, and she nervously smiled back. "And this is Peter McLachlan. My friend."

Daniel wasn't reassured. He looked defiant, but scared. He was already out of his depth. His Internet contact with us, conducted from the safety of his home or some cybercafé, was one thing, but maybe he was having second thoughts when confronted by the reality of two hefty, sweating middle-age men. "How do we know we can trust you?"

Peter snorted, sweating. "You contacted us, remember?"

I held up a hand and gave Peter a look: *Go easy on them.* I said, "I'm family, and Peter is an old friend. He's here to help. I've known him all my life, and I trust him. Let's just talk. We can stay in public places all the time. Anytime you like you can just walk away. How's that?"

Daniel, still uncertain, glanced at Lucia. She just nodded weakly.

So we walked around the curving walkway. Lucia, gravid, walked heavily and painfully, her hand on her back. Daniel supported her, holding her arm.

I whispered to Peter, "What do you think?"

He shrugged. "That poor kid looks as if she's going to pup any minute . . . You think Daniel's the father?"

"I have no idea," I said truthfully. But somehow I thought it wouldn't be as simple as that.

Peter chewed a nail, a habit I hadn't noticed before. "I wasn't expecting this. This is supposed to be about your sister, and her cult. What are we getting into here?" He had seemed oddly jumpy all day, and his nervousness was getting worse. I had no idea why—but then I knew there was a lot about Peter, not least why he was in Rome in the first place, he wasn't telling me.

The Colosseum is a big place, and we soon found an out-of-the-way alcove where it looked as if we would be undisturbed. Lucia found a place to sit, on a worn row of steps in the shade. Daniel stood over her protectively. Peter had a couple of bottles of water in his day bag. He gave one to Lucia, and she sipped it gratefully. She was breathing hard, I saw, and sweating heavily.

"So," said Peter. "Tell me how you got in touch with us."

Daniel shrugged. "It wasn't hard . . . I thought I needed to find somebody outside the Order, and yet with a connection. You see what I mean?"

"Yes," I said. "Somebody else asking awkward questions."

And so, he said, he had hacked into the Order's email streams looking for likely candidates. "It was difficult—the Order's traffic is heavily encrypted—but—"

"But you're a smart little hacker," said Peter unsympathetically.

Daniel's eyes flashed. "I did what I had to do."

Peter said, "Let's cut to the chase. She's your girlfriend, and you got her pregnant. Is that the story?"

"No!" Daniel's denial was surprisingly hot. "I wouldn't be so stupid."

I studied Daniel. "How old are you, son?"

He was just seventeen; he looked older. No wonder he was out of his depth.

"If you aren't the father, how did you get involved with Lucia?"

For the next couple of minutes he gabbled out something of his life story—how he was the son of a diplomat, a student at an expat school in the city—and how his harmless flirtation with a pretty girl he spotted at the Pantheon had led him into deep waters. When he had gotten all this out, he seemed drained, some of his nerve gone. "I was only fooling. I didn't expect it to turn out like this. But when she asked me for help, I couldn't refuse, could I?"

"No," I said. "I'm sure you did the right thing."

Since she'd come to him he had been hiding her away, though he wouldn't say where. From her look, I doubted it was in much comfort. He hadn't told his parents what he was doing. He had done his best, I thought, and I wondered how well I would have coped with such a situation when I was seventeen.

I asked Lucia her age. I was shocked to find she was only fifteen. She looked too worn out for that.

"All right," said Peter. "Let's start at the beginning. Lucia— you're trying to get away from something. From the Order?"

That took a little translating. "Yes," she said, "from the Order."

"And that's why you contacted Daniel here."

"There was nobody else," she said miserably. "I didn't want to get him into trouble, but I didn't know what else to do, and—"

"It's okay," I said. "Just tell us. Why do you want to leave the Order?"

"Because they took my baby away," she said.

I did a double take. "Your first baby. You're now pregnant with your second."

"Yes." Lucia's eyes were downcast, and she rested her hands on her belly.

"Who was the father?"

"His name was Giuliano . . . something. His name doesn't matter. He was brought in."

"Who by?"

"By the *cupola*." I didn't understand that, and she said, "By Rosa Poole. Your sister."

Peter and I exchanged glances.

Hesitantly I touched her hand. "You can tell us. Were you raped?"

"No." She closed her eyes, shaking her head, almost irritably. "You don't understand. Daniel asked the same questions. People never *listen*."

I backed off. "I'm sorry. Just tell us."

"Giuliano was brought in, and he made me pregnant, and I had my baby, and they took her away. And now *this*." She patted her bulge. "I don't want to lose this one, too. And I don't want baby after baby. I don't want *this*." Suddenly she was crying, a flood of tears.

We three males all scrambled in our pockets; the comedy routine concluded when Daniel was the first to produce a tissue.

Peter sat back and blew out his cheeks. "Deeper and deeper. So who was the father of this second kid?"

"The same guy," said Daniel. "The same asshole. This Giuliano, whatever."

Peter frowned. "Then how come she doesn't know his name?"

Daniel took a breath. "Because he only slept with her once."

Peter thought that over, and laughed out loud.

Daniel, hotly embarrassed, said, "You don't know the half of it, man."

Lucia said desolately, "I told you they wouldn't believe me." With a tissue clutched to her nose, she looked up at me through water-filled eyes heartbreakingly like my own.

"Let's all take it easy," I said. "Lucia, you say you don't want to have baby after baby . . . Is that what they asked you to do? The Order—umm, my sister?"

"Yes. But they never *asked*," she said, with a trace of sulky petulance.

"And why you?" Peter asked.

She looked away. "Because I had grown up."

It took a little probing to establish that she meant that she had begun her periods.

Peter asked, "So it's some kind of baby factory down there?"

"Peter—"

"George, if you are unscrupulous about it a healthy white kid can bring in a lot of money. The big adoption services in the States—"

"It's not like that," Lucia said.

"But," Peter said, "every time a girl begins her periods she is made pregnant. Right?"

"No." She was finding this difficult, but there was determination in her face, I saw, a strength. "You just aren't listening. Not all girls. Just some. Just *me*. The other girls can't have babies."

The rule of three mothers, I thought absently, thinking of Regina's biography. "You mean they aren't allowed to?"

"No," she said. "They *can't*."

Peter thought that over. "They're neuters?" Again he laughed.

Daniel glared at him. "It's true, man. I've met one of them. A woman called Pina—about twenty-five, I think. Calls herself Lucia's friend, but she's no friend; she betrayed her to the other creeps. You should have seen her—no tits, hips like a ten-year-old boy's. She's twenty-five, *but she's prepubescent*."

It was impossible, of course. Absurd. But now I thought back to my own incursion into the Crypt, and I remembered those ageless people who had clustered around me in the corridors and mezzanines—mostly women and girls, few men, not slim, but with no figures, no busts or hips . . . Rosa, I realized, had been the only woman I saw there who had looked mature. It hadn't struck me at the time—I suppose I was simply overwhelmed by that dense, dizzying environment, by too much strangeness to notice such a simple thing—and yet, now that I thought back, it was startling.

I looked at Peter. "How could this happen?"

"And why? . . . I've no idea," he said uneasily. "But if any of it's true, I think this means we're facing more than just some money-grabbing cult here, George."

Lucia cried out, clutched her belly, bent over, and vomited.

Peter and I responded reflexively, jumping back out of the way of that stinking splash. But Daniel had better instincts. He leaned forward to grab her shoulders. "It's okay. It's okay . . ."

Peter dug in his pocket for his cell phone.

I said to Daniel, "I don't know what the hell's going on here. But she's going to the hospital. *Now*."

"No," he said. "The Order—"

"The hell with the Order." One-handed, Peter had punched in 113, the code to call an ambulance. "They aren't the fucking Illuminati—hey!"

Daniel had snatched the phone out of his hand and terminated the call. "Okay. But at least let's take her somewhere *they* might not expect."

Peter made a grab for his phone, but I pushed him back. "Where, Daniel?"

"There's an American hospital on the Via Emilio Longoni. Thirty minutes out of town."

"Too far," Peter growled.

I held him back. "Let him follow his instincts," I said. "He's done okay for her so far, hasn't he?"

Peter was unhappy, but subsided.

By the time Daniel had completed the call, Lucia had done vomiting. We had to help her stand. Peter and I walked at either side of the girl. She draped her arms over our shoulders, and we held her around her waist. When I brushed against her skin, she felt oddly cold, I thought, clammy.

We emerged from the Colosseum entrance into the bright light of midmorning, where the fake gladiators continued to milk the lengthening queues. People stared at us as we limped past. It struck me how helpless we were. We were essentially strangers. Poor Lucia was trapped in the travails of an evidently unwanted pregnancy, and all she had to protect her was a confused, headstrong kid and two screwed-up middle-age blokes—and we weren't even sure if we should be getting involved in the first place.

Daniel gave Peter his phone back, and he produced a floppy disc from his waist pack. "Here. I knew you wouldn't believe me." He handed it to Peter.

Peter slipped it into his pocket. "What's this?"

"About Pina no-tits. I hacked into hospital records. Lucia told me Pina was in a traffic accident a couple of years ago. Not serious, but she busted her leg, and she ended up in a city hospital for a few hours—long enough for the doctors to notice her, umm, peculiarities. And they ran some tests. The results were weird. But by the time they turned around to figure out more, she'd already gone. Whisked away by the witches from the Crypt." He glared at Peter. "Take a look at the disc. It's all there."

"Oh, I will."

Daniel walked jerkily, his shoulders set. He was angry and scared. He said, "And if you don't believe *that*, wait until we get to the hospital. Wait until the American doctors see her. Then explain to me how Lucia can have gone through a full-term pregnancy in *three months.* Explain how she can have got pregnant again *without having sex.*"

Lucia bowed her head, biting her lip.

Peter and I exchanged a glance. I murmured, *"Three months?"*

"One thing at a time," Peter said, and he rolled his eyes.

We all rode in the ambulance.

The Rome American Hospital turned out to be bright, modern, efficient, the reception area full of light cast from big picture windows. Lucia was taken out of our hands as soon as the ambulance doors opened, and she disappeared into the maw of the hospital.

We were quizzed about our relationship to Lucia. Peter lied with surprising smoothness. I was her uncle, he said, visiting from England—hence the family resemblance. Daniel and Peter were friends of the family. He had already contacted the direct family, who were on their way . . . I thought the nurse looked skeptically at us, and perhaps she was remembering Lucia's torn and dirty dress. But there was nothing to be done about that now.

I had to produce a credit card to guarantee payment for whatever treatment Lucia was going to need. "Ulp," I said to Peter. "I wonder if my travel insurance will cover this."

"I kind of doubt it. Are you concerned?"

I said, "That my bank account is about to be flattened?" I watched Daniel roaming around the reception area, restless, helpless, frustrated. "I don't think I am, no, given the circumstances."

"Conception without sex. The kid actually said that, didn't he? And three-month pregnancies. Jesus. What have we gotten into here?"

I studied him. "What's wrong with you, Peter? I've never seen you so—aggressive."

He snorted, and fixed his invisible glasses. "We came here looking for your sister, remember. Not for *this.*"

"Do you want to back out?"

"Rosa isn't my sister. Do *you*?"

I thought about it. I sensed that this murky mystery of poor Lucia tied in on some deep level with what I'd glimpsed of the Crypt—the biological strangeness I'd experienced, but which I'd not been able to express to Peter. If I wanted to unravel all that, I was going to have to deal with Lucia. And besides—I pictured Lucia's face: so pale, such deep shadows around her eyes. She was just a kid, and she really was in deep trouble, I realized, and I felt a sharp instinct to help. Peter's peculiar behavior—the furtiveness he'd shown since he'd arrived here in Rome, the half secrets he'd dropped about dark matter and the rest—was just complicating things. But it didn't change the essentials.

"No. I'm not backing out," I said firmly. "Simple humanity, Peter."

He laughed without humor. "I don't think there's anything simple about this situation." He cast about. "I need to get on the Internet. I'll see if there's a dataport in here, or maybe a phone socket. And I could use a coffee," he called over his shoulder, pulling his laptop out of his bag.

I walked up to Daniel. "You're pacing like an expectant father."

He looked at me sourly. "Bad joke."

"Yes. Sorry. Look, do you have any change? . . ."

Down the hall we found a machine that would dispense Starbucks-sized polystyrene beakers of coffee in return for euro coins and notes. We walked back to Peter, who had tucked himself into a corner seat and was pulling Daniel's hacked medical file off the floppy. He accepted the coffee without looking up, flipped open the little drinking flap in the plastic lid, and took a sip, all without ceasing to work at his keyboard.

"The man's a professional," I said to Daniel.

"Yeah."

We sat down. Daniel was full of nervous energy. He tapped the arm of his chair, and his legs pumped up and down in tiny, violent movements, as if he were ready to flee.

"I guess you haven't had much experience of hospitals," I said.

"No. Have you?"

"Well—"

"You have kids of your own?"

"No, I haven't," I admitted.

He turned away. "Look, it's not the hospital that bothers me. In fact, I enjoy being surrounded by people speaking English, or at least Italian with an American accent."

"The Order? That's what you're scared of?"

"Damn right."

"They can't harm anybody here." I pointed to a beefy security guard, who stood by the door, hands folded behind his back. "Lucia will be fine. We're in the best place she could be . . ." And so on.

"Yeah." He didn't sound convinced.

A typical adult–kid response came to my mind: *Yes, everything will be fine, she will be okay, we can all go home.* But I thought I should respect him more than that. "I really don't understand what's going on here, Daniel. You know more than I do. And I have no idea if she's going to be okay." I felt a stab of anger. "I don't even know what *okay* means, for a fifteen-year-old girl who will have had two kids by some guy whose name she doesn't even know."

"They had no right," he said.

"No. Whoever *they* are."

"I should be at school." He spread his hands. "What am I *doing* here?"

"Look—you did the right thing," I said awkwardly. "I've lived a quiet life. What do I know about how to deal with situations like this? You saw a kid in trouble—a human being—and you responded on a human level. Your parents will be proud."

He grimaced. "You don't know my parents. When they find out about this I am *toast*."

A junior doctor approached us. About thirty, she was short, brisk, competent, with severely cut hair. She had a yellow notepad in her hand.

Lucia was fine, the doctor said, in accented English. The girl was in the late stages of pregnancy, and it was possible she would soon go into labor. But the doctor looked a little puzzled as she said this, and I realized that she was keeping stuff back from us. Well, they had had only a few minutes to exam-

ine Lucia, and if even a fraction of what Lucia and Daniel had
told us was true, they had a right to be baffled.

Peter hit the doctor with questions. "What about her breathing? Her metabolism, pulse rate? . . ." She was startled enough
to try to answer him, referring to her pad a couple of times, before her customary doctor's mask of nondisclosure slid back
into place. "We'll let you know as soon as there is more news."
And she turned and walked briskly away.

Daniel said, "What use was that? She doesn't know what
she's dealing with." He returned to his seat, fuming, pent up.

I murmured to Peter, "Wish I hadn't encouraged him to
drink caffeine. What about those questions you were firing at
the doctor?"

He looked at me. "When we were helping her to the ambulance—didn't you feel her pulse? *Boom . . . boom . . . boom.*
Given the state she's in, and given that she'd just thrown up her
breakfast, it was bloody slow—I estimated less than fifty a
minute—slower than a top athlete's resting rate. And she was
cold. The quack's first test results confirm it, I think. George,
it kind of fits with what you told me of the Crypt. The air down
there must be dense, with high humidity, high on carbon dioxide, low on oxygen."

I nodded. "Which is why I felt breathless."

"With low oxygen levels, you get a low metabolic rate, low
body temperatures. A slow pulse, cold skin." He rubbed his
nose. "I'd like to get a look at any urine tests they do."

"Why?"

"Because in animals, one way of getting rid of excess cee-
oh-two is through your piss, in the form of flushed-out car-
bonates and bicarbonates. I wouldn't be surprised if they've
come up with some such adaptive mechanism."

"*Adaptive.* You're saying she's adapted to the Crypt." I
thought it over. "Like her pale skin. Her eyes. Those thick sunglasses."

"It does all fit together, sort of. And there's more. With a low
metabolic rate, you'd grow more slowly, mature later. Live
longer, too."

"Could that explain the sterility?"

"I don't know. You know, those people must have been down
that hole for a very, very long time."

"Peter—what are we dealing with here?"

He glanced at Daniel, and beckoned. We moved a few seats away from the boy.

Peter unfolded his laptop and showed me some images, which I could barely make out for the glare from the big windows. "What do you know about orangutans?"

As far as Peter could tell the file Daniel had given him on Pina was genuine. When Pina went into hospital for her broken leg, the doctors who examined her had been concerned enough by her appearance to insist on giving her more extensive tests.

"George, I think the kid was right. Pina had an imperforate hymen, and quiescent ovaries."

"Quiescent?"

He shrugged. "Not producing eggs. Never *had* produced eggs. There's a brief note here, where one doctor speculates about the mechanism—"

I waved a hand. "I'm not going to understand any of that."

"Anyhow they never did the conclusive tests before she was sprung. I've been onto the search engines and looked wider. The biologists call this 'arrested development.' It can happen for genetic reasons—for instance, a mutation in the receptor for a certain growth factor can cause a form of dwarfism. Or if food is short—say if you're an anorexic—puberty can be delayed. It makes a certain evolutionary sense, because if you can't feed yourself it makes no sense to waste calories on bone mass and fatty tissue for sexual characteristics until your body can be sure it will survive. It's actually quite common among the animals. Sometimes subordinate males don't develop sexual characteristics. Tree shrews. Mandrill monkeys. Elephants."

"And orangutans—"

"Even orangutans, even apes."

"Get back to Pina. You're saying she has this 'arrested development,' too."

"It looks that way. The tests weren't conclusive." He sighed, closed up his laptop, and massaged the bridge of his nose. "But suppose it's true, George. Suppose that poor kid really has gone through a pregnancy that mushroomed in three

months. Suppose there are neuter women down that hole in
the ground, a horde of them. Suppose Lucia's other peculiarities—her paleness, her slow metabolism—are adaptations to
living underground. And suppose it's true—it seems fantastic,
but just suppose—that Lucia had sex with this guy Giuliano
just once, but she's going to continue to get pregnant, over and
over . . ."

I sat on that plastic-coated seat, in the bright efficiency of
the thoroughly modern hospital, gazing through the big windows at the gardens with their cypress trees. "*Evolution.* They
are evolving differently. Is that what you're saying?"

Peter said, "If the story of Regina is true, the Order have cut
themselves off, more or less, from the rest of humanity for
sixteen centuries. That's, say, sixty, seventy, eighty generations . . . I'm no biologist. I don't know if that's enough time.
But it sounds like it to me." He shook his head. "You know,
twenty-four hours ago I'd never have believed we'd be having
this conversation. But here we are.

". . . I still don't see the big picture, though. Evolutionary
changes happen for a reason." Peter leaned close. "You'll have
to go back, George. Back into the Crypt. Call your sister
again."

"Why?"

"We need more information. We still have more questions
than answers, nothing but a lot of guesswork. If we could get
Pina or one of the other neuters into the hands of the doctors—"

"Daniel."

He looked around. "What?"

"Where's Daniel?" While we'd been talking, the boy had
disappeared from his seat.

We ran down the corridor, the way he must have gone. We
heard the receptionist call us back, a sharper yell from the security guy.

We hadn't gone fifty yards before we met a party coming the
other way. Daniel's arms were pinned by his escorts, a burly
male nurse on one side, a security guy on the other. The nice
young lady doctor was talking to him, steadily, calmly, about
how they had been unsure about our credentials, and it was

only proper that they should ask the girl herself about her family . . .

When he saw us Daniel struggled harder. "They took her back," he said, despairing. "The Order. They came, and *they took her back*!"

chapter 44

It was in the year 1778 that Edmund found Minerva, and lost her.

He was twenty-three years old. He had come to Rome as part of his "Grand Tour," in the traditional style, funded by his father's money and his own youth and energy. He stayed in an apartment in the Piazza di Spagna, which had become known as the English Ghetto. The apartment, a decent first floor and two bedchambers on the second, was small but well furnished, and cost no more than a scudo per day.

Edmund fell into the company of one James Macpherson, a forty-year-old Jacobite refugee and hardened rake, who proved a willing guide to the various delights of Rome—as long, of course, as Edmund continued to be a source of cash. Edmund understood this relationship very well, and was careful not to let James take advantage. But Edmund was catholic in his tastes, and soon learned to relish the *vitella mongana*, which he thought the most delicate veal he had ever tasted, and drank great quantities of Orvieto, a decent white wine.

Rome proved to be great fun. Night and day the piazzas were crowded with acrobats and astrologers, jugglers and tooth drawers. In the cramped, garlic-stinking alleys where grand mansions loomed over tiny houses, shop signs hung everywhere, of barbers, tailors, surgeons, and tobacconists. But the alleys were always clogged with noise and filth, since the Romans had the rude habit of relieving themselves against any convenient doorway or wall, and left their garbage heaped in every corner, waiting for the irregular call of the waste collectors.

But amid the noise, filth, and debauchery, there were true wonders.

Edmund found Saint Peter's and its piazza quite stunning—
he had James bring him back to it day after day, for there always seemed something new to see in it—and he was
enchanted by the area around the great cathedral, where elegant domes and cupolas rose from the morning mist. And then
there were the older monuments, sticking out of the past. Edmund often had James escort him to the top of the Palatine,
where mature cypress trees waved gently among the ruined
palaces.

Edmund found the Romans themselves pleasant and civil—
as well they might be, he thought, for they were surely the
most indolent people in Europe. There was no industry here,
no commerce, no manufacturing. The people relied for their
income on the steady flow of money from all over Christian
Europe, which continued as it had for centuries.

And religion dominated everything about the city. At any
one time there were as many pilgrims and other visitors, it was
said, as residents. There were three *thousand* priests and five
thousand monks and nuns serving three hundred monasteries
and convents and four hundred churches. It was fashionable to
dress like a cleric even if you had not taken holy orders. A
greater contrast to the dynamic industrial bustle of England
could scarcely be imagined; sometimes the cleric-choked city
struck Edmund as being in the grip of a great madness.

Edmund was not struck by the women of Rome, whose
beauty, he thought, did not match their city's. He remembered
a remark of Boswell's that only a few Roman women were
pretty, and most of the pretty ones were nuns. But he was not
above letting James introduce him to courtesans, of whom he
seemed to know a great number. Edmund had not come here
for debauchery, but he was no monk, and he had to admit it
was a peculiar thrill to indulge his carnal appetites here in the
home of the mother church—where, he learned, some of the
prostitutes actually carried licences issued by the pope himself!

But all that changed when he met Minerva.

One night he took in an *operette* at the Capranica. It was hard
to make out the performance for the drinking and gambling
going on in the private box James had hired. James introduced

him to the raucous company of the singers and actors, and in the course of a very long evening Edmund was astonished to learn that some of the beautiful "girls" who mingled with the company were in fact *castrati*. Happily he avoided making a fool of himself.

The next morning, his head more than usually cloudy, Edmund walked alone to the Forum.

He found a fallen column to sit on. The Forum was a meadow littered with ruins. He watched the hay carts lumbering across the open space, and animals grazing among the lichen-coated ruins. As the rising sun banished the last of the morning mist, despite his mildly aching head, he felt tranquility settle on him. It was a scene of ruin, yes, and there was poignancy in seeing the shabby huts of carpenters erected on the rostrum where once Cicero had stood. But there was great peace here, as if the present had somehow made a settlement with the past.

In one corner of the ancient space a bank of charcoal stoves had been set up, and he could smell the sour stink of cabbage and tripe. Idly he stood, brushed lichen from his trousers, and wandered that way. There were many places in Rome where you could find food being cooked in the open. Some of these open-air establishments were grand, and Edmund had enjoyed adequate lunches of salad, poached fish, cheese and fruits, rounded off with the ice cream with which the Romans seemed obsessed. But he could see that these cabbage cookers had humbler culinary ambitions than that, and that the wretched folk who clustered around the stoves were the poorest of the poor.

At first he thought the women working at the stoves must be nuns, for they wore simple white robes laced with purple thread. But they wore no wimples or hoods, and he saw that they were all young, all rather similar, almost like sisters—and all pale, as if they wore cosmetics of theatrical thickness.

That was when he saw Minerva.

She was one of the serving women. She had a beauty that made him gasp, as simple as that. Her face, small and lozenge-shaped, was symmetrical, her nose straight and neat, her mouth full and as red as cherries, and her eyes were gray, like windows on a cloudy sky. She was like her companions, but in her the combination of features had worked to stunning effect, like a perfect deal in a card game, he thought.

He felt he could have watched her all day, so enchanted was he by her simple elegance. And when she moved around the stove the sunlight, by chance, lit up her robes from behind, and he caught a glimpse of her figure, which—

Somebody was speaking to him. Startled, he came back to himself.

One of the workers was facing him—like the beauteous one, yes, not unattractive, but older, and with a sterner face. But her mouth twitched with humor.

He stammered, in English, "I'm sorry?"

She replied in careful Italian, "I asked you if you are hungry. You are evidently drawn to the scent of tripe."

"I—ah. No. I mean, no thank you. I just—"

"Sir, we have work to do here," she said, reasonably gently. "Important work—vital for those we serve. I fear you will distract us."

And, he saw, *she* had indeed noticed him. She responded to his stares with hooded, nervous glances, but looked away.

The older woman said dryly, "Yes, she is beautiful. She can't help it."

"What is her name?"

"Minerva. But she is not on the menu, I'm afraid. Now if you will excuse me—" She turned, with a last, not unkind glance, and went back to her work at the stoves.

Edmund couldn't simply stand there. Besides, some of the hapless poor were beginning to notice him, and were sniggering. He walked away, to find a place where he could sit and watch the women at work. Perhaps later he could engineer some opportunity to talk to the girl.

But to his shock, when he turned back, he saw they had gone, stoves and all, as if they had never existed. The poor, some still devouring their plates of cabbage and tripe, were dispersing.

He ran back and grabbed the shoulder of one man, though he quickly let go when he felt greasy filth under his palm. "Sir, please—the women here—"

The man could have been any age, so crusted was his face

with dirt. Bits of cabbage clung to his ragged beard. He would
say nothing until Edmund produced a few coins.

"The Virgins, yes."

"Where do they come from? Where did they go? How can I
find them?"

"Who cares? I'm here for cabbage, not questions." But he
said: "Tomorrow. They'll come to the Colosseum. That's what
they told us."

That evening Edmund felt restless in James's company. Their
usual circuit of the piazzas and taverns did not distract him. It
did not help when he heard one rotund innkeeper mutter that
English gentlemen on the Grand Tour were famously *"milordi
pelabili clienti"*—a soft touch as customers.

For Edmund, the night was only an interval until he could
find Minerva again among her stoves and cabbages.

A part of him warned him of his foolishness. But, though he
had been in love before, he had never felt anything like the
drowning desire he had experienced when he had gazed on
Minerva's perfect face, and the pale shadow of her slim body.

The next day he hurried to the Colosseum long before
midday.

Edmund had to pass through a hermitage as he entered the
great crater of marble and stone, with its mute circles of seats.
Squalid huts of mud and scavenged brick sheltered in the great
archways where senators had once passed; on the arena floor
trees had grown tall and animals grazed.

There was no little row of charcoal stoves, no women in
their white robes, no moist smell of cooked cabbage rising to
compete with the stink of dung. There were beggars, though,
milling about listlessly. They looked as disappointed as he felt,
though it was hard to tell through their masks of grimy misery.
None of them could answer his questions about Minerva or the
Virgins.

He spent a week combing the city. But he found no sign of
the Virgins, nor anybody who knew anything about them. It
was as if they had just disappeared, as evanescent as the mist
off the Tiber.

chapter 45

Trying to track down what had become of Lucia at the hospital, Peter and I got nowhere fast.

We established that a woman called Pina Natalini had come in a small private ambulance to sign her out and take her away, showing valid signed certificates from a family doctor. Lucia herself, it seemed, had wanted to check out, claiming Pina as a cousin. It was all aboveboard, and I had no reason to believe the staff of the American Hospital were telling any lies about what had happened.

Surely it wasn't the whole truth. I had no idea how much control this Pina and whoever else had come along—perhaps even Rosa—might have had over Lucia's vulnerable mental state.

But what could we do? To the hospital staff—and indeed in my eyes—Peter, Daniel, and I had no claim over the girl. We barely knew her.

Daniel found all this hard to accept. He hung around, agitating for us to *do something*. Maybe you have to be that way when you're young—you have to believe you can change the shitty state of the world, or else we'd all slit our wrists before reaching majority. But he became a pain in the arse. In the end I winkled his father's number out of him and had him picked up and sent back to school. It was a lousy trick, but I believed it was for the best for him.

That just left Peter, who likewise, in fact, wouldn't accept that we could go no farther. But his motives—and I still wasn't sure what they were—were, unlike Daniel's, murky, complexifying, entangling. I even had the feeling he was beginning to fit the mysteries of the Order into his wider worldview. I actu-

ally resented that. This was *my* issue—my sister—and I didn't
want to become just another sideshow in his paranoia.

Still, I thought he was right that I should go back into the
Crypt again. I had unfinished business with Rosa, after all, regardless of Lucia.

But I felt frightened. Not of the Crypt, or Rosa, or even of
the business surrounding Lucia. I was frightened of myself. I
found the memory of how I had responded to the Crypt more
disturbing the more I thought about it. So I put off the visit,
hoping to gather a little mental strength.

While I was stalling, Peter initiated a new inquiry of his
own. He tried to get access to the Vatican Secret Archives, to
try to trace some of the Order's complicated history between
the days of Regina and the present.

At first he drew blanks. When he applied for a pass to the
archives, the Vatican clerks trawled through his and my recent
contacts concerning the Order, including the head of Rosa's
old school, and even my sister in the States. The testimonials
were hardly ringing, and no passes were forthcoming.

"It's a fucking *conspiracy*," Peter groused. "I'm not exag-
gerating—*I* wouldn't use that word lightly. And it's all connected to the Order. These bastards are working together to
keep us out. We've hit an outer ring of defense, and we've
barely started . . ."

After a few days of that he leaned on me to go see my "tame
Jesuit" again. A couple of days after *that*, Claudio called me
up and offered me a tourist trip around the Archivio Segreto
Vaticano, the secret archives themselves.

"I hate to disappoint you," Claudio said, grinning. "But in this
context *secret* just means 'private' . . ." He met me at the Vatican's Porta Sant' Anna entrance. We had to pick up visitor
passes at the Vigilanza office; there was an awful lot of form
filling.

The entrance to the archives themselves was off a courtyard
called the Cortile del Belvedere, within the Vatican complex.

Claudio, it turned out, regularly researched here, and he
briskly showed me the areas to which visiting scholars were
allowed access: a ground-floor room called the *sala di studio*,

and the Index Room, which actually contained a *thousand* indices, many themselves very old.

Claudio walked me across to a rattling elevator, which took us down to what he called the bunker. This was the Manuscript Depository, built in the seventies to cope with the great inward flood of material that the Archives had had to cope with in the postwar period. It was an underground library, a basic, unadorned, ugly place, with shelving spread over two stories, and mesh flooring and steel stairs connecting everything. Some of the shelves were locked, holding sensitive material, and others were empty, waiting for more material yet to come.

We went through into the Parchment Room, where some of the more famous documents were stored for display. They were held in chests of drawers, each waist-high, with ten glass-topped drawers in each. These pieces could be stunning—often in Latin, some illuminated, others covered by wax seals.

Claudio kept up an engaging and practiced patter. From its very earliest days, even in the days of persecution, the church in Rome had adopted the imperial habit of record keeping. The first archives had been called the *scrinium sanctum*, a bit of language that startled me with recognition. But the archives were far from complete. The first collections had been burned around A.D. 300 by the Emperor Diocletian. When Christianity had become the religion of the Empire, the accretion of records had begun again. Little had survived, however, from the bloody turbulence of the first millennium.

In the fourteenth century the popes had, for a time, been exiled to France, and in the fifteenth a period of infighting had peaked with *three* rival popes rampaging around Europe—"A bibliographer's nightmare," said Claudio laconically. The later popes had started trying to unify the archives in the sixteenth century. But when Napoléon had taken Italy, he hauled the whole lot away to France for a few years, doing still more damage in the process . . .

"But all we have is here," Claudio said. "There are letters from popes as far back as Leo the First, from the fifth century, who faced down Attila the Hun. We have diplomas from Byzantine emperors. The correspondence of Joan of Arc. Reports of papal enclaves, accusations of witchcraft and other skulduggery in high places, sexual secrets of kings, queens, bishops, *and* a few popes. The records of the Spanish Inquisition, details of the trial of Galileo . . . Even the letter from England asking for the dissolution of the first marriage of Henry the Eighth."

"And somewhere in all this," I said, "is the true story of the Order. Or at least as the Vatican saw it."

He waved a hand. "What I'm trying to tell you is that the archives are overwhelming. There are scholars who have spent most of their lives in here. It isn't even all cataloged, and our only search engine is shoe leather. The idea that someone like your friend can just come in here—"

"Peter said you would be like this," I said bluntly.

He looked aristocratically bemused. "I'm sorry? *Like* what?"

"Obstructive. It's true, isn't it? It's just as when you stalled over giving me a contact with the Order in the first place. You don't want to come right out and refuse to help. Instead you're trying to put me off."

He pursed his lips, his eyes cloudy. I felt a stab of guilt; perhaps he hadn't even been aware of what he was doing. "Perhaps I'm not sure if I *should* help you."

Something in the way he said that triggered an idea in my head. I said at random, "But you could help us, if you wanted to. *Because you've done searches here on the Order yourself.*"

He wouldn't concede that, but his aristocratic nostrils flared. "You are making big inductive leaps."

"If you have, you could help Peter find what he wants very quickly."

"You haven't told me why I should."

"Because of Lucia." I knew Peter had told him about the girl. "Here's the bottom line. Peter and I think she is coming to harm, because of the Order. I certainly don't know for sure that she isn't. You're a priest; you wear the collar. Can you really turn away from a child in trouble? . . . You can't, can you?" I said slowly, thinking as I spoke. "And that's why you've done your own researches. You've had your own suspicions about the Order—"

He said nothing. He was right that I was making big inductive leaps in the dark, but sometimes my nose is good. Still, I could see he was in conflict, pulled by two opposing loyalties.

"Look," I said, "help us. I give you my word that we will do you no harm."

"*I* don't matter," he said, with a priest's steely moral authority.

"Very well—no harm to anything you hold dear. My word, Claudio. And perhaps we will do a lot of good."

He said little more that day. He showed me out, his remaining conversation brief and stiff. I suspected I had compromised whatever friendship I had with him.

But a day later, perhaps after sleeping on it, he got in touch.

Under Claudio's guidance, Peter immersed himself in the archives for days on end. And he surfaced with a string of tales: the diaries of pilgrims and nobles, records of wars and sackings, the account of a thwarted love affair—and even a mention of one of my own ancestors, a different George Poole . . .

George Poole had first come to Rome in 1863, in the company of the British government's chief commissioner of works, Lord John Manners. Poole was a surveyor. It had been a time when the Modern Age, in the form of hydraulics, telegraphs, steam power, and railways, was just beginning to touch the old city, and British engineers, the best in the world, were at the forefront.

Poole had even been in the presence of the pope himself, for a time. He had seen the papal train, with its white-and-gold-painted coaches, and even a chapel on bogie wheels. The pope had come to the opening of a steel drawbridge, built by the British, across the Tiber at Porta Portese. The pontiff took a great interest in the new developments, and had asked to meet Manners and have the bridge mechanism explained to him—much to his lordship's embarrassment, for in the middle of his working day he was carrying an umbrella and wearing an old straw hat.

When Poole came back to Rome twelve years later, it was in his own capacity as a consulting engineer. He returned at the invitation of a rather shadowy business concern fronted by one Luigi Frangipani, a member of what was said to be one of Rome's great ancient families.

Poole expected that much would have changed. During his

first visit it had been just three years since the great triumph of the Risorgimento had seen Italy unified under Victor Emanuele II. Now Rome was the capital of the new Italy. Among Poole's circle of old friends, there had been great excitement at these developments, and much envy over his visit, for he was coming to a Rome free of the dominance of the popes for the first time in fourteen centuries.

But Poole was disappointed with what he found.

Even now the great political and technological changes seemed to have left no mark on Rome itself. Within its ancient walls, the city was still like a vast walled farm. He was startled to see cattle and goats being driven through the city streets, and pigs snuffling for acorns near the Flaminian Gate. The source of wealth was still agriculture and visitors, pilgrims and tourists; there was still no industry, no stock exchange.

But there were changes. He saw a regiment of *bersaglieri*, trotting through the streets in their elaborate operetta-extras' uniforms. The clerics were much less in evidence, though you would see the cardinals' coaches, painted black as if in mourning. He even glimpsed the king, a spectacularly ugly man, passing in his own carriage. He gathered that the king was a far more popular figure than the pope had ever been, if only for his family; after all, no pope since the Middle Ages had been in a position to display a grandson!

After a day of wandering, Poole met Luigi Frangipani. They went for a walk through the cork woods on Monte Mario.

Frangipani sketched in something of the background to his approach to Poole. "There is much tension in Rome," Frangipani said, in lightly accented English. "It is a question of time, you see, of history. Rome is a place of great families."

"Like your own," Poole said politely.

"Some are prepared to accept the king as their sovereign. Others are prevented from doing so by loyalty to the pope. You must understand that some of the families are descended from popes themselves! Still others have made their fortunes more recently, such as from banking, and have yet a different outlook on developments . . ."

Poole thought all this talk of families and tradition sounded medieval—very un-British—and he felt oddly claustrophobic. "And what is it you want of me?"

They stopped at a wooden bench, and Frangipani produced a small map of Rome.

"We Frangipani, lacking the great wealth of some other families, are not so conservative; we must look to the future. Rome has been invaded many times. But now that it is the capital, a new invasion is under way, an invasion by an army of bureaucrats. The municipality was first asked for forty thousand rooms for all those teeming officials, but could provide only five hundred. To house its ministries the government has already requisitioned several convents and palaces. But much more housing is needed.

"So there is an opportunity. There is sure to be a building boom—and there is plenty of room for it in Rome. We believe the earliest developments are likely to be *here*—" He pointed at his map. "—between the Termini station and the Quirinal, and perhaps later *here*, beyond the Colosseum."

Poole nodded. "You are buying the land in anticipation. And you want me to work on its development."

Frangipani shrugged. "You are a surveyor. You know what is required." He said that Poole would be asked to survey the prospective purchases, and then lead any construction projects to follow. "There is much to be done. During their thousand years of control, the popes, while they ensured their own personal comfort, did little to maintain the fabric of the city concerning such mundane matters as drainage. Every time the Tiber floods the old city is immersed, and the fields beyond the walls are a malarial wasteland—why, the Etruscans managed such affairs better. We know your reputation and your experience," Frangipani concluded smoothly. "We have every faith that you will be able to deliver what we require."

Poole asked for time to think the proposal over. He went back to his hotel room, his mind racing. He was sure from his own reading that Frangipani's analysis of the housing shortage was correct—and that this was a great opportunity for Poole personally. He could look ahead to an attachment here for years, he thought; he would have to bring the family out.

But he was a cautious man—he wouldn't have become a surveyor otherwise—and he asked for reassurances about Frangipani's funding before committing himself further.

Two days later he met Frangipani again, in a café near the Castel Sant'Angelo.

Frangipani brought a colleague this time, a silent slate-eyed woman of about forty. She introduced herself simply as Julia. She wore a plain white robe of a vaguely clerical aspect. Frangipani said she was an elder of a religious group called the Puissant Order of Holy Mary Queen of Virgins—"Very ancient, very wealthy," Frangipani said with disarming frankness. The Order was the source of much of Frangipani's funding.

Julia said, "The Order has a mutually beneficial relationship with the Frangipani reaching back many centuries, Mr. Poole."

Poole nodded ruefully. "Everything in Rome has roots centuries deep, it seems."

"But we must grasp the opportunities offered by the times."

They talked for a while about the dynamic of the age. Julia seemed to Poole to have an extraordinarily deep perspective. "The harnessing of oil and coal is propelling a surge in the growth of cities not paralleled since the great agricultural developments of the early medieval days," she would say.

Clearly the Order was not run by fools; they intended to profit from the latest developments, just as, no doubt, they had profited in one way or another from previous changes throughout their long history.

Poole had more immediate concerns, however. He began to talk of his tentative plans to bring his family to Rome, and asked about schooling. Julia smiled and said that the Order provided education of a very high standard, including classes in English for the children of expatriates. It would not be difficult to find places for Poole's children, if he so desired.

After some days of further negotiation, the decision was made, the deal done.

George Poole would stay in Rome for twenty years, in which time he played his part in the advance of a great tide of brick, stone, and mortar over the ancient gardens and parks. His two daughters completed their education with the Order. But Poole found himself spending a good proportion of his income on relieving the conditions of his laborers and their families, part of a great throng of three hundred thousand in the growing city by the end of the century, who found themselves sleeping under ancient arches or on the steps of churches, or in the shantytowns that sprouted in many open spaces.

Even so he went back to England wealthy enough to retire. But one of his daughters, somewhat to her parents' disquiet, elected to join the Order herself when her tuition was complete.

"And that's how a Poole came to Rome," Peter said. "George, you have roots in the Order on *both* your mother's side and your father's . . .

"This stuff is incredible. And I believe I still haven't seen the half of it. I think there has been a relationship between the Vatican and the Order that goes back to the founding of them both. Surely the Order has provided funds to the popes over the centuries. Surely it has provided refuge or support in turbulent times—perhaps it has sponsored one candidate for holy offices over another.

"And in that great *scrinium* you describe, which unlike the Vatican Archive *hasn't* been burned by emperors or chewed by rats or plundered by Napoléon, there are secrets that no pope could bear to have revealed, even in these enlightened times. George, no wonder your tame Jesuit hovered over me all day. This stuff is explosive—your Order has got the pope by the balls! . . . George, you have to go back down there."

chapter 46

"Show me Lucia," I said to my sister.

She shook her head. "George, George—"

"Never mind the bullshit. *Show me Lucia.*"

But she just sat back in her chair and sipped her coffee.

I tried to keep up the pressure, tried to maintain my angry front. But it was hard. For one thing we weren't alone. Inside the Crypt, you were never alone.

I had finally succumbed to Peter's pressure, confronted my own complicated fears, and returned to the Crypt.

This time Rosa brought me to a place she called the *peristylium*. It was a small chamber, crudely cut out of the rock—but it contained a kind of garden, stone benches, trellises, a small fountain. There were even growing things here, exotic mushrooms sprouting in trays of dark soil, their colors bright and unreal. The garden was obviously very old, its walls polished smooth by centuries of soft contacts. A small stand supplied coffee, sweets, and cakes. Anywhere else this would have been a Starbucks concession, but not here; there were no logos on Crypt coffee cups.

Like everywhere else, the little garden was full of the ageless women of the Crypt. It was like an open-air café in a crowded shopping street, maybe, or a crowded airport concourse, with a dense, fluid, constantly changing, never thinning crowd. But the grammar of this crowd was different, the way they squeezed past each other, smiled, touched—for all these people were family. They talked brightly, loudly, and continually, sitting in circles cradling their coffees, close enough that their knees or shoulders touched. They would even kiss each other on the lips, softly, but not sexually; it was as if they were tasting each other.

And, sitting with Rosa with our own coffees, I was stuck right in the middle of it, in a bubble of unending conversation, constantly touched—an apologetic hand would rest briefly on my shoulder, a smiling gray-eyed face float before me—and my head was full of the powerful animal musk of the Crypt. It was like being immersed in a great warm bath. It wasn't intimidating. But it was damn hard to think straight.

As Rosa surely knew, which was why she had brought me here.

And on top of that I had to deal with my own complicated emotional situation. I still found Rosa's face extraordinarily disturbing. She was, after all, my sister. She was so *familiar*, and something warm in me responded every second I spent with her. But at the same time it was a face I hadn't grown up with, and there would always be a glass wall between us. It was quietly heart wrenching.

I tried to focus. "Rosa, if there's nothing wrong, why not show Lucia to me?"

"There's nothing that the doctors can't handle. You'd only disturb her."

"She came to me for help."

She leaned forward and put her hand on my wrist—more of her endless touching. "No," she said. "*She* didn't come to you. That hacker boyfriend found you."

"Daniel isn't her boyfriend."

She sat back. "Well, there you go. Anyhow, I don't think all this really has anything to do with Lucia."

"All what?"

"Your insistence on coming back to the Crypt. This isn't about Lucia. It's not really about *me*. It's about you." Her eyes were fixed on me. "Let's cut through all this. The truth is, you're jealous. Jealous of me."

"Rubbish," I said weakly.

"You know I got the better deal, don't you? Our family failed, as so many little families do." She said that, *little families,* with utter contempt. "It wasn't just the money problems . . . Mother and Father saw a way to give one of us a better chance. They knew that this opportunity was sitting here. It had to be me—this is mostly a community of women. If anybody should be envious, maybe it should be Gina, my sister, not you."

And perhaps Gina was envious, I reflected. Perhaps that was what underlay her sourness, and her decision to get about as far away from Manchester and her past as she could.

But I protested, "I don't envy you. That's ridiculous. I just think the Order keeps getting in the way."

"Of what?" Again she touched my wrist, and her fingers moved in that circular motion, a brief, tender massage. "Look, George—I can't be separated from the Order. Can't you see that yet? We come as a package. And if you want to 'connect' with me you have to deal with that." She stood up and brushed down her skirt. "You came all the way to Rome to save me, didn't you? What a hero. And now you've found out I don't want to be saved, you've decided to rescue poor Lucia instead. But don't you think you have a duty to figure out what it is you're saving us all from?" She held out her hand to me. "What, are you stuck in that chair? Come on."

Her tone of command, the outstretched hand, were compelling. And we had, oddly, become a center of attention, her standing, me sitting, a kind of eddy in the endless stream of people. I was surrounded by faces, all turned on me with a kind of half smile. I felt the most intense pressure to go with Rosa.

I drained my coffee, reached up, took her hand, and stood.

She was, of course, still working on my recruitment into the Order, or at least on neutralizing me as a threat. I knew that. She was following her own agenda. But by now, so was I.

We were brother and sister. What damaged goods we were.

Walking still deeper into the Crypt, we took the stairs.

That wasn't as simple as it sounds. The structure of the place internally was very complicated, with floors and partition walls and bits of mezzanines all over the place, and we had to walk sometimes hundreds of yards from one staircase to the next. Everything was bathed in a pearly, sourceless fluorescent glow, and looked the same in every direction. As I got turned this way and that I was soon lost. But that was probably

intentional; inside the Crypt you weren't *supposed* to know
where you were.

Still, it soon became clear that we had passed below what I
had roughly labeled as Level 1, the uppermost, most modern-
looking area of the Crypt, where schoolchildren studied purposefully and the *scrinarii* worked amid their computers and
card indices and steel library shelves. It was a big place; Level
1 was actually several stories and mezzanines. Now we clambered down steel staircases into the heart of the level below,
Level 2, which I had only glimpsed before from the mezzanine
levels above.

The furniture, partitions, ceiling tiles, lighting, and other
equipment were modern, just as above. Nevertheless there was
a different atmosphere down here. The corridors seemed narrower, lower, more confining, darker, while most of the chambers were big—if not huge—mighty, open *cubicula* each of
which could have held hundreds of people. The businesses of
the Order, like the genealogy service, were run from Level 1,
but most of the rooms down here were given over to functions
that served more basic needs. I was shown an immense hospital, equipped with modern gear but oddly open-plan, a refectory the size of an aircraft hangar, and dormitories in which
rows of bunk beds, jammed close in together, marched into the
distance.

I never saw a room empty, anywhere in the Crypt, and so it
was here. The hospital seemed to have few patients, but
swarmed with activity. People were sleeping in some of the
dormitories, even in midmorning, perhaps night-shift workers
tucked into their bunk beds like rows of insect pupae in their
cocoons. The corridors, too, were always packed with people,
squeezing to and fro on their endless chores.

Crowding around me, they would touch, squeeze past, smile
just as politely as above, and I saw the same faces, *the family
face,* as I thought of it now, with low cheekbones, pale gray
eyes. But the denizens of Level 2 had a slightly different look
about them. Many were very pale, and they seemed to have
exaggerated features—large, flaring nostrils, big eyes, even
prominent ears. They were all a similar size, smaller than either Rosa or me. *Compact, to fit into a compact space,* I
thought idly. They weren't freaks. None of them would have

looked out of place in one of Rome's ancient piazzas. But cumulatively, there was an impression of subtle difference, even from the level above.

And few of them talked. Oddly, it took me a while to notice that. But there was little of the incessant chatter of Level 1. Here, there were words exchanged, brief conversations, but no hubbub. It was, I thought, as if words weren't really needed here.

It struck me that I had already come deeper than most members of the public, like the schoolchildren in their classrooms above, would ever reach. Nobody would see this—nobody but another member of the Order—and to her, who had grown up with it, none of this would seem strange at all.

And the air was thicker, warmer, and more redolent with that earthy animal musk. I soon felt breathless; my chest strained as I breathed, my lungs ached. After a time I began to feel sleepy, and I had a vague sense of the Crypt and its inhabitants swimming past me, as if I were in a waking dream.

I struggled to think.

"Most people born in the Crypt stay here. Is that true?"

"Not all," Rosa said. She talked about how people would be sent "outside," for a day, a month, even years, during their education, or as part of their work. "Like Lucia. And some leave for good, like our own grandmother—"

"Grannie?"

"She was born here, but died in Manchester. You didn't know that, did you? How do you think families like ours, branches of Regina's ancient clan, end up in England, or America, or elsewhere? Of course people leave—they always have—sometimes for good. But they retain a loyalty to the Order." She smiled. "It's our shared heritage, after all."

There was a lot I never learned about the Order—how they allocated their children surnames, for instance. I wondered vaguely how babies born here were formally registered, whether the Order had some tame functionary in Rome's registry of births and deaths. Perhaps some of them grew up here without any official record at all, never leaving the Crypt, living and dying invisible to the state.

Rosa brought me to a kind of open oven, a brick-lined niche in the wall taller than I was. I lingered, curious. A wide chimney snaked up out of sight, caked with soot. There was no fire burning. This was very old—I recognized narrow Empire-era red bricks, the thick-packed mortar between them.

"So what's this, a barbecue?"

Rosa smiled. "Part of our ventilation system. Or it was. Nowadays we have modern air-conditioning equipment— ducts, pumps, fans, dehumidifiers, even carbon dioxide scrubbers. But that kind of gear has only become available in the last few decades or so. In the eighteenth century we did buy one of James Watt's first steam engines, but that was deinstalled and sold off to a museum long ago . . . The very first builders, digging down from the Catacombs, adapted techniques used in the deep mines. You'd light a fire under here and keep it burning, all day." She pointed upward. "The smoke and heat would rise up the chimney—and, rising, would draw air through the Crypt. Elsewhere there are vents to allow more air in. Sometimes they would work bellows."

"So you'd get a circulation. Ingenious."

"In case of problems with the airflow, the Order members would have to block a corridor or passageway."

"With what?"

"With their bodies, of course. They'd just run to where the problem was. It sounds crude, but it worked very well."

"Who told them what to do?"

She seemed puzzled by the question. "Why, nobody. You'd look around, see there was a problem, follow your neighbors, do what they were doing. Just as if you were putting out a fire. You don't *need* to be told to do that, do you? You just do it . . ."

I had no reason to disbelieve her. I had still seen no senior management floor, no corner offices for the Big Cheeses, no evidence of a chain of command. Evidently things just worked, the way Rosa had described.

She was still talking about the ventilation system. She slapped the solid brick wall. "The old infrastructure is still there. Always will be. Even now—though we have our own generators, like a hospital, independent of the public supply— we prepare for power outages. The youngsters are still taught about the old ways, given simple drills. If the very worst happened, we could always revert to the old methods."

I peered at the ancient brickwork. "The very worst? . . ."

"If everything fell apart. If there was no more power at all."

That took me aback. "You're planning for how to keep the air supply functioning, *even if civilization falls.*"

"Not planning, exactly. There are few *plans* here, George. But—well, we're here for the long term. And you read Regina's story. Civilizations do sometimes inconveniently fall . . ."

We walked on, down the crowded corridor. She led me away from the ancient hearth, down further staircases—some of them metal, some of them older, cut from the stone itself—staircases that led ever deeper into the core of the Crypt.

We reached Level 3, the deepest downbelow of all.

Many of the walls here were bare rock, polished so smooth by the passage of bodies they gleamed. It was clearly very old—and yet this level, the deepest, was paradoxically the youngest of this great inverted city.

The corridors here were still narrower than those above. They branched as we walked, until once again I had completely lost my bearings. The air was hot, moist, and thick, and was at first suffocatingly hard to breathe. Carbon dioxide is heavy, I remembered dimly, and it must pool, here at the bottom of the great chamber of the Crypt. But as my body became accustomed to the conditions the viselike pain that gripped my chest eased.

And everywhere we walked we had to push through the endless crowds, the smoky gray eyes huge in the gloom. Nobody spoke, here on Level 3. They just moved wordlessly around each other, on their way through the endlessly branching corridors. The only sounds were the rustle of their soft-soled shoes on the rocky floor, and the steady flow of their breathing—and even that, it seemed to me, was synchronized, coming in overlapping waves of whispers, like the lapping of an invisible ocean. I had the sense of these soft, rounded little creatures all around me, in the corridors that stretched off into the darkness every direction I looked, and of thousands more in the tremendous airy superstructure of galleries and corridors and chambers above me.

As I describe it now it sounds oppressive, claustrophobic. But it did not feel like that at the time.

Rosa seemed to sense that. "You belong here, George," she said softly. "I'm your sister, remember. If it's good enough for me . . . Can't you feel the *calm* in here? . . ."

I felt the need to cut through this odd seduction. "What about sex?"

"What about it?"

"You've a lot of young people here, cooped up together. There must be love affairs—casual flings—" I felt awkward; trying to discuss such issues with my long-lost sister, I was reaching for fifties euphemisms. "Do you let people screw?"

She stared at me in icy disapproval. "First of all," she said, "it isn't a question of 'letting' people do anything. There is nobody to 'let' you, or to stop you come to that. People just know how to behave."

"How? Who teaches them?"

"Who teaches you to breathe? . . . And anyhow it tends not to be an issue. Most of the men here are gay. Or don't have an inclination either way. Others usually leave." She said this as if it were the most usual setup in the world.

It might fit in. Peter, in his long, rambling analyses of what we had learned about the Order, had speculated it might be some kind of heredity cult. Like neuter women, like Pina, gay men could help out with the raising of the fecund ones, the Lucias. But neither class would be any threat to the precious gene pool, because they didn't contribute to it.

"Okay, but—Rosa, how come most of the people here are women?"

She looked uncomfortable. "Because most people born here are female."

"Yes, but how? Some kind of genetic engineering? . . . But you were around a long time before anybody even conceived of the notion of a gene. So how do you manage it? What do you do with the excess boys? Do you do what the Spartans did with their baby girls?—"

She stopped and glared at me, suddenly as angry as I had seen her. "We don't murder here, George. This is a place that gives life, not death." It was as if I had insulted somebody she loved—as, perhaps, I had.

"Then how?"

"There are more girls than boys. It just happens. You ask a

lot of questions, George. But in the Crypt we don't like questions."

"Ignorance is strength."

She glared at me. "If you really understood that, you would understand everything." She walked on, but her gait was stiff, her shoulders hunched.

We came to an alcove, cut into the rock. Before it a little shrine had been set up, a kind of altar carved of pale marble. Slender pillars no more than three feet tall supported a roof of finely shaped stone. A glass plate had been fixed before it. Rosa paused here, and looked on reverently.

"What's this?"

"A most precious place," she said. "George, Regina herself built this, fifteen centuries ago. It has been rebuilt several times since—this level didn't even exist for centuries after Regina's death—but always exactly as she had intended it. And what it contains, she brought from home . . . Take a look inside."

I crouched and peered. I saw three little statues, standing in a row. They looked like grumpy old women wearing duffel coats. The statues were poorly made, lumpy and with grotesque faces; they weren't even identical. But they were very ancient, I saw, worn by much handling.

Rosa said, "The Romans used to believe that each household had its own gods. And these were Regina's family gods—*our* gods. She preserved them through the fall of Britain, and her own extraordinary troubles, and brought them all the way to Rome. And here the *matres* have stayed ever since, as have Regina's descendants. So you see, *this is our home,* mine and yours. Not Manchester, not even Britain. *This* is why we belong here, because this is where our deepest roots go down into the earth. This is where our family gods are . . ."

All part of the sales pitch, I told myself. And yet I was impressed, even touched. Rosa made a kind of genuflection before moving on.

A way farther on, we came to a doorway.

It was a big room—I strained to see—but it had the atmosphere of an old people's rest home. A series of large chairs had been set out in the musty dark. The chairs looked elaborate, as if packed with medical equipment. Figures reclined in the chairs. Attendants moved silently back and forth, nurses perhaps, but wearing the bland smock uniforms of the Order. Most of the "patients" wore blankets over their legs, or over their whole bodies, and drips had been set up beside two of them. The faces of the women in the chairs looked caved in, old. But I could see bulges over the bellies of several of them, bulges that looked like nothing so much as pregnancy.

In one of the chairs, far from the door, a woman was sitting up. She looked younger, and her hair looked blond, not gray. Something about the shape of her face reminded me of Lucia. But she was too far away for me to see clearly, and an attendant came to her and pressed something to her neck, and the woman subsided back into silence.

"A hundred years old, and still fertile . . ." Rosa murmured.

It was all just as Peter and I had put together from the garbled accounts of Lucia and Daniel. But even so, standing here, confronted by the almost absurd reality of it, it was all but impossible to believe.

She squeezed my hand, hard enough to hurt. She led me farther on; her fingers were strong and dry.

We approached another doorway, cut into the rock. Light poured out, comparatively bright, and I heard a noise, chattering, high-pitched, and continuous, like seagulls on a rock.

There were babies in here. They were all very young, no more than a few months old. The walls were painted bright primary colors, and the rock floor was covered by a soft rubber matting, on which lay the babies—all pale, all wispy-haired, all with blank gray eyes—so many I couldn't even count them. The air in the room was hot, dense, moist, laden with sweet infant smells of milk and baby shit. As I gazed in at this the women of the Order pressed around me as they always did, warm and oddly sweet-scented themselves; a part of me wanted to struggle, as if I were drowning.

"From our oldest inhabitants," said Rosa dryly, "to our youngest."

"It's all true, isn't it, Rosa?" I asked her with cold dread. "Just as Lucia said. You turn young girls into old witches and keep them alive, keep them pumping out clutches of kids every year, until they're a hundred . . ."

She just ignored me. "You never had children, George. Well,

neither did I. We have our nephews, I suppose, out in Miami
Beach. I've never even seen them . . ." Her hand tightened on
mine, and her voice was insistent, compelling. It was almost
as if I were talking to myself. "You never meant to be childless, did you? But you never found the right woman—not even
the girl you married—never managed to create the right *environment* around yourself, never found a place you felt comfortable. And the years went by . . . *No kids*. How does that
make you feel? Our little lives are brief and futile. Nothing we
build lasts—not in the long run—not stone temples or statues,
not even empires. But our genes endure—our genes are a billion years old already—and they will live forever, *if* we pass
them on."

"It's too late for you," I said brutally.

She flinched. But she said, "No, it isn't. It's never too late for
any of us—not here."

"Look at these children, George. None of them are my own.
But they are all—cousins. Nieces, nephews. And *that's* the
reason I will always stay here. Because this is my family. My
way of beating death." Her face seemed to float before me in
the gloom, intense, like a distorted reflection of my own in
smoky glass. *"And it can be yours."*

At first I didn't understand. "Through nieces and nephews?"

She smiled. "For you, there might be more than that.
George, every child needs a father—even here. But you want
the father of your nieces to be strong, smart, capable: you
want the best blood you can find. It's best if the fathers come
from the family, as long as they are remote enough genetically—and the family is so big now that's no problem . . ."

She was finally getting to the point, I realized uneasily.

"George, you're one of us. And you've shown yourself to be
smart—resilient—decent, too, in your impulse to find me—
even in your attempt to help Lucia, misguided though it was."

I tried to think through what she was saying. "What are you
offering me? Sex?"

Rosa laughed. "Well, yes. But more. *Family,* George. That's
what I'm offering you. Immortality. You came looking for me,
looking for family. Well, you found both. A true family—not
that flawed, sad little bunch we were in Manchester."

I could stay here, that was what Rosa was telling me. I could become part of this. Like Lucia's Giuliano, I thought. And by submitting myself as a stud—it seems laughable, but what else could you call it?—I would find a way for my heritage to live on.

For a moment I didn't trust myself to speak. But none of this seemed strange or disturbing. On the contrary, it seemed the most attractive offer in the world.

My cell phone trilled. It was a bright, clean, modern sound that seemed to cut through the murk of blood and milk that filled the air.

I pulled my hand away from Rosa. I dug out the phone, and raised it to my face. The screen was a tiny scrap of plastic, backlit with green, that glowed bright as a star in that enclosing gloom. A text showed: GRT DNGER GET ARSE OUT PTR

I turned off the phone. The screen went blank.

Rosa was watching me. Around her the steady stream of white-robed women pushed past her, as they always did.

"Get arse out," I said.

"What?"

"He's right." I shook my head, trying to clear it. "I need to get out of here."

Rosa's eyes narrowed.

The others, the women nearest me, reacted, too. Some of them turned to me, even breaking their stride, looking at me in a kind of mild dismay. Their reaction spread out farther, as each woman responded to what her neighbor was doing. It was as if I had detonated an invisible bomb down there, and ripples of dismay were spreading out around me.

At the focus of all that, I felt ashamed. "I'm sorry," I said helplessly.

Rosa moved closer to me and put a hand on my shoulder. At that touch the posture of the strangers around us relaxed a little. There were even smiles. I felt a kind of relief, a forgiveness. I wanted to be accepted here, I realized; I couldn't bear the thought of exclusion from this close, touching group.

"It's okay," said Rosa. "You don't have to go. I can sort everything out. Tell me where your hotel is—did you say it was near the Forum? I'll call them—"

But I stuck to my thought of Peter. "Get arse out, get arse

out." I repeated it over and over, an absurd mantra. "Let me go,
Rosa."

"All right," she said, forcing a smile. "You need a little time.
That's okay." She led me down the corridor. A part of me was
glad to get away from the little knot of bystanders who had
seen what I had done, who *knew* how I had betrayed them; I
was glad to walk away from my shame. "Take all the time you
want," Rosa said soothingly. "We'll always be here. *I'll* be
here. You know that."

"Get arse out," I mumbled.

We came at last to the steel door of a modern high-speed
lift. We rode up in silence, Rosa still watching me; in her eyes
there was something of the pressure of the gaze of those deep
Crypt dwellers, their mute disappointment.

As we rose I'll swear my ears popped.

I emerged into a sunlit modern office on the Via Cristoforo
Colombo. I was nearly blinded by the light, and the dry
oxygen-rich air seared into my lungs, making me giddy.

Peter had hired a car. It was waiting for me on the Cristoforo
Colombo, outside the Order's office. Now, to my utter dismay,
he insisted on taking me for a drive.

chapter 47

"I was full of theories. Basically I thought the Order was just a wacko religious cult. Then, when we met Lucia, and found out about this girl Pina, I started to wonder if it was some kind of bizarre psychosexual organization, perhaps with a religious framework to give it some justification. But now, with what you described about what you found down there, George—and after I discussed it with some of the Slan(t)ers—I think I've put it together at last.

"The Order isn't about religion, or sex, or family. It isn't about *anything* its members think it's about—they don't know, any more than any one ant knows what an ant colony is for. The Order *exists for itself*."

"I have no idea what you're talking about," I said.

"I know you don't. So listen."

We headed straight out of town until we hit the outer ring road, the GRA. Soon we were stationary, one in a long line of cars, whose roofs and windscreens gleamed in the sun like the carapaces of metaled insects. Even at the best of times this road is a linear parking lot, and now it was the end of the working day, the rush hour. We inched forward, Peter thrusting the car into the smallest gaps with the best of them, blaring his horn and edging through the crowds. I'd have been scared for my safety if not for the fact that our speed was so slow.

The car was a battered old Punto. With a head still full of the Crypt, I felt utterly disoriented. I said, "This car belongs to the Pakistani ambassador."

He looked at me oddly. "Oh. Michael Caine. I saw that movie, too . . ."

"You're making some kind of point, aren't you?"

"Damn right," he said. "You won't understand, not at first. And when you *do* understand you probably won't believe me." His knuckles were white where he gripped the wheel, and he was sweating. "So I'll have to make you see. This might be more important than you can imagine."

I smiled. "*Important.* This from a man who thinks that alien ships are making three-point turns in the core of the Earth. What could be important compared to that?"

"More than you know," he said. "George, what causes traffic jams?"

I shrugged. "Well, you need a crowded road. Roadworks. Breakdowns."

"What roadworks?"

There were no works ahead, no obvious breakdowns or crash sites. And yet we were stationary.

Peter said, "George, to make a traffic jam all you need is traffic. The jams just occur. Look around. All that makes up the traffic is individual drivers—right? And each of us makes individual decisions, based, minute to minute, on what our neighbors are doing. There's not a one of us who *intends* to cause a jam, that's for sure. And there's not one of us who has a global view of the traffic, like you'd get from a police chopper, say. There are only the drivers.

"And yet, from our individual decisions made in ignorance, the traffic jam emerges, a giant organized structure involving maybe thousands of cars. So where does the jam come from?"

We were moving forward by now, in fits and starts, but, scarily, he took his eyes off the road to look at me, testing my understanding.

"I don't know," I admitted.

"This is what they call *emergence*, George," he said. "From simple rules, applied at a low level, like the decisions made by the drivers on this damn road—and with feedback to amplify the effects, like a slowing car forcing a slowdown behind it—large-scale structures can emerge. It's called self-organized criticality. The traffic always tries to organize itself to get as many cars through as possible, but it's constantly on the point of breakdown. The jams are like waves, or ripples, passing back and forth along the lines of cars."

It was hard for me to concentrate on this. Too much had

happened today. Sitting in that lurching car, I felt as if I were in a dream. I groped for the point he was trying to make. "So the Order is like a traffic jam," I said. "The Order is a kind of feedback effect."

"We'll get to the Order. One step at a time." He wrenched the wheel, and we plunged out of the traffic toward a junction that would lead us back toward the center of the city.

We roared up Mussolini's great avenue, hared through the Venezia, lurched left onto the Plebiscito. Peter rammed the long-suffering Punto into a few feet of parking space. I wouldn't have believed it if I hadn't seen it.

We got out of the car, locked it up, and made for a bar. I wanted coffee. Peter went to order while I found a table.

Peter returned with a bottle of beer. "You need this more than coffee, believe me."

And oddly, he was right. Something about the heft of the bottle in my hand, the cool tang of the beer, that first subtle softening of perception as the alcohol kicked in, brought me back to reality, or anyhow my version of it. I raised the bottle to Peter. "Here's to me," I said. "And what I truly am. An appendage clamped to the mouth of a beer bottle."

He had a Coke Light; he raised it ironically. "As a destiny, that will do," he said seriously. "Just don't lose yourself down in that hole in the ground . . ."

"Emergence," I said. "Traffic jams."

"Yes. And think about cities."

"Cities?"

"Sure. Who plans cities? Oh, I know we try to now, but in the past—say, in Rome—it wasn't even attempted. But cities have patterns nevertheless, stable patterns that persist far beyond any human time horizon: neighborhoods that are devoted to fashion, or upscale shops, or artists; poor, crime-ridden districts, upmarket rich areas. Bright lights attract more bright lights, and clusters start.

"This is what emergence is: agents working at one scale unconsciously producing patterns at one level above them. Drivers rushing to work create traffic jams; urbanites keeping up with the Joneses create neighborhoods."

"Unconsciously. They create these patterns without meaning to."

"*Yes.* That's the point. Local decision making, coupled with feedback, does it for them. We humans think we're in control. In fact we're enmeshed in emergent structures—jams, cities, even economies—working on scales of space and time far beyond our ability to map. Now let's talk about ants."

That had come out of left field. "From cities to ants?"

"What do you know about ants?"

"Nothing," I said. "Except that they are persistent buggers when they get into your garden."

"Ants are social insects—like termites, bees, wasps. And you can't get them out of your garden because social insects are so bloody successful," he said. "There are more species of ant in a square mile of Brazilian rain forest than there are species of primate across the planet. And there are more workers in one ant colony than there are elephants in all the world . . ."

"You've been on the Internet again."

He grinned. "All human wisdom is there. Everybody knows about ant colonies. But most of what everybody knows is wrong. Only the queen lays eggs, only the queen passes on her genes to the next generation. That much is true. But you probably think that an anthill is like a little city, with the queen as a dictator in control of everything."

"Well—"

"*Wrong.* George, the queen is important. But in the colony, nobody knows what's going on globally—not even the queen. There's no one ant making any decisions in there about the destiny of the colony. Each one is just following the crowd, to build a tunnel, shift more eggs, bring back food. But out of all those decisions, the global structure of the colony emerges. That social scaling-up, by the way, is the secret of the social insects' success. If a solitary animal misses out a task, it doesn't get done. But with the ants, if one worker misses a task somebody else is sure to come along and do it for her. Even the death of an individual worker is irrelevant, because there is always somebody to take her place. Ant colonies are *efficient.*

"But it is the colony that counts, not the queen. *That* is the organism, a diffuse organism with maybe a million tiny mouths and bodies . . . Bodies that organize themselves so that their tiny actions and interactions add up, globally, to the operation of the colony itself."

"So an anthill is like a traffic jam," I guessed. "Emergent."

"Yes. Emergence is *how* an anthill works. Now we have to talk about genes, which is *why* it works." He was off again, and I struggled to keep focused.

"Social insects have three basic characteristics." He ticked the points off on his fingers. "You get many individuals cooperating in caring for the young—not just parents, as among most mammals, say. Second, there is an overlap of generations. Children stay at home to live with their parents and grandparents. Third, you have a reproductive division of labor—"

"Neuters," I said.

"Yes. Workers, who may remain sterile throughout their lives, serving the breeders . . ."

I started to get a sense of where he was going. I didn't want to hear it. Dread gathered in the pit of my stomach. I pulled on the beer, drinking too fast. When I came back to George, he was talking about Darwin.

". . . Darwin himself thought ants were a great challenge to his theory of evolution. How could sterile worker castes evolve if they leave no offspring? I mean, the whole point of life is to pass on your genes—isn't it? How can that happen if you're neuter? Well, in fact, natural selection works *at the level of the gene*, not the individual.

"If you're a neuter, you give up your chance of having daughters, but by doing so you help Mom produce more sisters. Why do you do it? Because it's in your genetic interests. Look, your sisters share half your genes, because you were born from the same parents. So your nieces are less closely related to you than your own daughters. But if, by remaining celibate, you can *double* the numbers of your nieces, you gain more in terms of genes passed on. In the long term you've won the genetic lottery.

"The numbers are different for ants. The way they pass on their genes is different from mammals—if you're an ant your sister is actually closer to you genetically than your own daughter!—so they have a predisposition to this kind of group living, which is no doubt why it rose so early and so often among the insects. But the principle's the same.

"George, an ant colony isn't a dictatorship, or a communist utopia. *It is a family.* It's a logical outcome of high population densities and a hostile external environment. Sometimes it pays to stay home with Mom, because it's safer that way—but you need a social order to cope with the crowding. So you help Mom bring up your sisters. It's harsh, but it's a stable system; emergence makes the colony as a whole work, and there is a genetic payoff for everybody, and they all get along just fine . . . The biologists call this way of living 'eusociality'—*eu* like in *utopia*, meaning 'perfect.' "

"A perfect family? Now that's scary."

"But it's not like a human family. This genetic calculus doesn't have much to do with traditional human morality . . . Not until now," he said mysteriously. "And it's not just ants." He played his trump card. "Consider naked mole rats."

I had finished the beer. I let Peter call for another one.

Naked mole rats turned out to be spectacularly ugly little rodents—Peter showed me pictures on his handheld—that live in great underground colonies beneath the African deserts. They have bare, unweathered skin, and their bodies are little fat cylinders, to fit into their dark tunnels.

The mole rats' favorite food is tuber roots, which they have to go dig for. But the roots are widely scattered. So although they are stuck in cramped conditions underground, it is better to produce a lot of little mole rats than a few big ones, because many little helpers tunneling off to find the roots are more likely to succeed than a few.

"Exactly the conditions where you might expect eusociality to develop," Peter said. "A situation where you're forced to live with high population density, limited resources . . ."

Mole rats live in great swarms—and in each colony, of maybe forty individuals, at any one time there is only one breeding pair. The other males simply keep zipped up, but the other females are functionally sterile. They are kept that way by behavior, by bullying from the "queen."

The workers even have specialized roles—nest building, digging, transporting food. A mole rat will go through several roles as she ages, gradually moving outward from the center.

"Some of the ants are like that," Peter said. "The young serve inside the nest, where they do such chores as nest cleaning. When they get older they serve outside, maybe constructing or repairing the nest, or foraging for food . . ."

For the mole rats, everything works fine until the queen shows signs of falling from her throne. The sterile workers suddenly start to develop sexual characteristics, and there is a bloody succession battle—and the prize for the victor is nothing less than the chance to pass on her genes.

"And that's why the old fogies are pushed out to the perimeter of the colony," Peter said coldly. "They are the ones in the front line when a jackal digs up a tunnel—but they are dispensable. You want your young at the center, where they can be quickly deployed to replace the reproductive. But the old ones sacrifice themselves for the sake of the group readily enough. That's another eusocial trait—suicide to protect others.

"You see what I'm saying. The mole rats are eusocial," he said. "There is absolutely no doubt about that. As eusocial as any ant or termite or bee—*but they are mammals*."

He talked on about mole rats, and other mammals with traces of eusociality—hunting dogs in the desert, for instance. One detail startled me. In the mole rat warrens, the rodents would swarm and huddle to control the flow of air through their passageways. It was just like the Crypt, though I hadn't told him about Rosa's antique ventilation system.

By now I knew exactly where he was going. I felt cold.

"Mammals but not human," I said heavily. "And humans make choices about how they live their lives, Peter. Rational and moral choices. We're in control of ourselves, in a way no animal can be."

"*Are we?* How about that traffic jam?"

"Peter—get to the point. Forget the mole rats. Talk about the Order."

He nodded. "Then we have to talk about Regina, your great-great-greatest-grandmother. Because it all started with her."

In those first few turbulent decades, for the band of women huddling in their pit under the Appian Way, it had been just as it was for a band of naked mole rats out on the savanna—or so

Peter's analysis went. With imperial Rome crumbling around them, it became a lot safer for daughters to stay home with their mothers, to extend the Crypt rather than to migrate.

"So you have just the same kind of resource and population pressures as in a mole rat colony."

I frowned. "But Regina would never have made a choice about eusociality. In the fifth century she couldn't even have formulated it."

"But she had the right instinct. It's all there, in her own words. Remember those three slogans, carved on the walls?"

"Sisters matter more than daughters. Ignorance is strength. Listen to your sisters."

"Yes." He called up another file on his handheld. ". . . Here we are."

It was an extract from Regina's biography. I read: "Regina asked her followers to consider the blood of Brica, her daughter, and that of Agrippina, her granddaughter. Agrippina's blood is half the blood of Brica, half of her father, and so a quarter mine, said Regina. But if Agrippina were to have a baby her blood would mix with the father's, and so the baby would be only an eighth mine. Suppose I have to choose between a baby of Agrippina's, or another baby of Brica's. I can only choose one, for there is no room for both. Which should I choose? And they said, You would choose for Brica to have another child. For sisters matter more than daughters . . ."

Peter looked at me. *"Sisters matter more than daughters.* Regina thought in terms of keeping her blood from being diluted. It doesn't matter that the mechanics actually works with genes—her instinct was right. And once that is established, much else follows. The breeding rights of a few mothers, your *mamme-nonne,* are favored over everybody else's rights, even over their own children's. The drones' only chance of passing on their own genes is to help their mothers, and their sisters . . ."

It was the first time he had used the word *drones*.

"Slogan two: *Ignorance is strength.* Regina understood systems. And she wanted the Order's system, the whole, to dominate over the parts. She didn't want some charismatic fool taking over and ruining everything in the pursuit of some foolish dream. So she ordered that everybody should know as little as possible, and should follow the people close to them. The Order drones are agents who work locally, with only local knowledge, and no insight into the bigger picture.

"Three: *Listen to your sisters.* That slogan encourages feedback. Inside the Crypt there's a relentless pressure to conform. You told me you felt it, when you were in the Crypt, the endless social weight. Poor Lucia, who wouldn't conform, suffered exclusion. The social pressure is a homeostasis—like the temperature regulator of an air-conditioning system, a negative feedback that keeps everybody in their place."

"It was all just looks," I said uncomfortably. "Nothing was said."

He fixed nonexistent glasses, intense, determined, anxious. "You think when you were in the Crypt people communicated with you just with speech?" Again he tapped at his handheld, seeking the right reference. "George, we have many channels of communication. Look at this." He pushed the handheld at me; its tiny screen showed a dense technical paper. "We have a paralanguage—vocal stuff but nonverbal, groans and laughs and sighs, and body posture, touch, motion—going on *in parallel* to everything we say. The anthropologists have identified hundreds of these signals—more than the chimps, more than the monkeys. *Even without speech,* we would have a richer way to communicate even than the chimps, and *they* manage to run pretty complex societies. And all this is going on under the surface of our spoken interaction." He was staring at me now. "Tell me I'm wrong. Tell me you didn't feel a pressure from the way people in there behaved toward you, regardless of what they actually *said.*"

I imagined those circles of pale, disapproving faces. I shook my head to dispel the vision.

Peter said, "And then there are other ways to communicate. Touch, even scent . . . The smells, all that kissing you describe. *Tasting each other,* you said."

"That's ridiculous."

"Is it? George, weaver ants communicate with pheromones. And chemical communication is a very old system. Single-celled creatures have to rely on simple chemical messages to tell them about their environment, because only multicelled creatures—like ants, like humans—are complex enough to organize clusters of cells into eyes and ears . . . I admit I'm speculating about this.

"But, George, put it all together and you've got a classic recipe for an emergent system: local decision making by ignorant agents responding to local stimuli, and powerful feedback mechanisms. And then you have a genetic mandate for eusociality. All in those three slogans."

"All right. And then what happened? How did we get from there to here—from Regina to Lucia?"

He sighed and massaged his temples. "Look, George, if you haven't believed me up to now, you won't believe what comes next. In the wild—among the ants or the mole rats—once you get a reproductive advantage like that, of mothers over daughters, no matter how slight, you get a positive feedback.

"People started to change. To adapt. If the daughters aren't going to get a chance to reproduce, it's better for their bodies to stay subadult. Why waste all those resources on a pointless puberty? Of course you retain the potential to become mature, in case a queen drops dead, and you have the chance to replace her. Meanwhile, it pays for the mothers to pump out the kids as long and as often as possible . . ."

I felt a deep, sickening dread as his logic drew me in, step by step. "So in the Crypt they have kids every three months. And they stay fertile for decades past any outsider's menopause age."

"It's simple Darwinian logic. It *pays*."

"What about the men?"

"I don't know. Perhaps in the early days they just let the male infants die. Again, given enough time, selection would work; if the only way to pass on your genes is through female children, you have more daughters. Of course you still need fathers. So they bring in males from outside—wild DNA to keep the gene pool healthy—but preferably somebody from the extended family outside. And a candidate has to prove his fitness."

"Fitness?" In a way this tied in with what Rosa had said to me about why I would be a suitable stud. "Maybe the men have to prove intelligence, by forcing their way in."

He shrugged. "Maybe. *Fitness* doesn't mean *strength*, necessarily. It just means you fit the environment. Maybe what you, or Giuliano, need more than anything else is a certain compliance. Because your children would have to comply with life in the Crypt. One thing's for sure: men are essential for making babies, so they have to be tolerated, but they are peripheral to the Order, which is built around relationships among females. Men are just sperm machines."

"And what about Lucia's second pregnancy? She said she had only had sex once with this guy Giuliano."

He hesitated. "I'm flying another kite here. But some female ants have an organ called a spermatheca—a bag near the top of her abdomen. It's a sperm bank. The queen stores ejaculate there, and keeps sperm in a kind of suspended animation, for years if necessary. She lets them out one at a time, and they become active again and ready to fertilize more eggs . . ."

My jaw dropped. "And that's what you're saying is happening inside Lucia's body."

He looked defensive. "I'm saying it's possible."

"But ants have had a hundred million years. Peter, what I know about evolution you could write on a fingernail. But wouldn't such a major redesign of the human reproductive system need a lot of *time*?"

He shrugged. "I'm no expert. But in the fifteen centuries since Regina there has been time for sixty, seventy, eighty generations—maybe even more. A lot of it wouldn't involve particularly fundamental changes, just the timing of developments in the body. Evolution finds changes like that easy to make—a question of throwing a few switches, rather than rewiring the whole processor. Evolution can sometimes work with remarkable speed . . .

"Look at all the pieces together." Again, he ticked points off on his fingers. "You have the multiple generations sharing their resources and caring for the young. You have reproductive divisions—the sterile workers. You have nobody in control, nothing but local agents and feedback. And then if you look at its history, the Order has done what ant colonies do: it has tried to expand, it has attacked other groups. You even have 'suicides'—spectacular sacrifices, where the workers give up their lives so that their genetic legacy can continue: I told you what happened when the Crypt was broken open during the Sack of Rome. You could even argue that all the exterior 'helpers,' all the 'family' around the world, who send the Order money and recruits, they are part of the Order, too, like foraging ants—though of course they don't know it.

"And listen. Ants carry out their dead and leave them in a circle, far from the nest. I plotted the burials linked to the Order, over the centuries. There's a circle . . . I have a map."

"I don't want to see it."

"I think Regina was a kind of genius, George. An idiot savant, maybe. Of course she didn't have the vocabulary to express it, but she clearly understood emergence, and perhaps even eusociality, on some instinctive level. You can see it in her biography—the passages where she is walking around Rome, noticing how unplanned it is, but how nevertheless patterns have emerged. And she used that insight to try to protect her family. She thought she was establishing a community to protect her bloodline, a heritage of a golden past. Well, she succeeded, but not in the way she intended.

"The Order isn't a human community, George, the way we've always understood it. *The Order is a hive.* A human hive—perhaps the first of its kind." He smiled. "We used to think you would need telepathy to unite minds, to combine humans into a group organism. Well, we were wrong. All you need is people—that, and emergence."

"Peter—"

He lifted his broad face to the light from the window. "It's actually an exciting prospect we have stumbled on, George. A new kind of humanity, perhaps? A eusocial human—I call them *Coalescents* . . ."

The beer felt heavy in my belly. Suddenly I longed to get out of this smoky bar—out of the noisy, crowded city altogether—away from Peter and his crazy ideas, and the Order, which was at the center of it all.

Peter was desperate for me to understand, to believe, I saw. But I didn't want to believe; I didn't want to know. I shook my head.

"Even if you're right," I said, "what do we do about it?"

He smiled, but his smile was cold. "Well, that's the question. There's no point negotiating with Rosa, or anybody else in there, because *she isn't in control.* The organism we are dealing with is actually the collective—the Order—the hive that arises out of the interactions of the Coalescents."

"How do you negotiate with an anthill?"

"I don't know," he said. "But first we must decide what we want from it . . ."

His cell phone went off, annoyingly loud. He pulled it out of his pocket, inspected its screen, and turned white. "I'm sorry," he said.

He gathered up his gadgets and bustled out of the bar. Without breaking step he got into his car, started it up, and drove away, lurching into the dense Roman traffic. Just like that, leaving me with a bill to pay and a walk home to the hotel. I was astonished.

When I got to the hotel he wasn't there. I wouldn't see him again, in fact, for days. When I did it was in drastically different circumstances, after I received a panicky phone call from Rosa.

And it was only later that I found out it was at that moment in the café he had learned of the explosion at the lab in San Jose.

chapter 48

Rosa glared at me. "What have you done, George? *What have you done?*"

"Is this about a man called Peter McLachlan?" I'd told Rosa nothing about Peter before now; I'd had no reason to. "I haven't seen him for days, and he's not answering his calls . . ."

"He's here," Rosa hissed.

"What?"

"Inside the Crypt."

I just stared at her, disbelieving.

Rosa had met me in the Order's surface office on the Cristoforo Colombo. Compared to her sly manipulation of a few days before, there was no warmth, none of her seductive talk of family and blood, no touching. In that bright, sunlit, modern office, she was a pillar of hostility and anger.

We weren't alone. Under a wall decorated with a chrome representation of the Order's kissing-fish symbol, a salesgirl was talking an elderly couple through a brochure on the Order's genealogy services. The old folk turned and stared at us, dismayed and perhaps a little frightened. But the assistant was of the Order. She looked at me with blank smoke-gray eyes, slowly hardening to anger. I was sure she didn't know why she felt that way. I quailed nevertheless.

Rosa glanced at the customers. She said, "Come through."

I followed her to the elevator at the back, which took us down to the big modern anteroom, where cameras peered at me, insectile. The receptionist-guard behind her broad marble desk stared at me with undisguised hostility.

I asked, "If Peter's here, who let him in?"

"Nobody. He found a way down one of the old ventilation shafts."

I remembered the ancient, disused chimney; yes, I realized, if you knew what you were doing, it wouldn't be so hard to work your way in. I laughed. "Peter's a bit tubby for a pot-holer."

She stood close to me. I smelled something of the animal stink of the Crypt about her. Her fists were clenched, her body rigid, every muscle suffused with anger. "You think this is funny? Do you? *Funny?* He isn't one of us. He has nothing to do with the Order. And he's here because of *you*."

"I didn't tell him where the shaft outlets were. I don't even know myself."

"Evidently you told him enough for him to work it out. You betrayed our trust, George. You betrayed *my* trust. I took you into my home. I showed you its treasures. And you told an *outsider*. Perhaps you aren't fit to join us after all."

Her cold, angry rejection was powerful. It hurt badly to feel such exclusion, despite my ambiguous feelings about the whole setup.

"Rosa, I know Peter. Outsider or not he's an old friend who was good to Dad in his final years. He is—odd. Obsessive, eccentric. He has big ideas. But even if it's true he's broken in here he's harmless."

"Harmless. Really." Rosa walked behind the marble desk to the guard's PC. It took her a couple of minutes to find what she wanted. She swiveled the screen on its mount to show me. "This is an Interpol report. Posted by the FBI." Illustrated by small, grainy photographs, it was a report of an explosion at a university science lab in San Jose, California. The lab had been devoted to something called "geometric optics." The blast had destroyed the building and killed three people, including a cleaner and the head of the facility. The FBI appeared convinced it was some kind of sabotage. In the corner of the image the FBI had posted two photographs, of suspects they associated with the incident.

One of them was, indubitably, Peter's face.

I stood back. "Shit."

"Our face-recognition software pulled this up not five minutes after we got our first clear shot of him."

"It has to be a mistake. Peter's an eccentric, not a criminal. I can't believe he'd have anything to do with an incident like this."

Rosa briskly spun the screen back. "Tell it to the FBI. And in the meantime, this 'harmless' friend, this suspected bomber, this *murderer*, is holed up inside the Crypt—and *you* led him here."

"What do you expect me to do?"

"Come down there with me and get him out."

I hesitated. I dreaded walking deeper into this mess. But I knew I had no choice.

Rosa walked me to the high-speed elevators that would take us back into the downbelow. The doors slid open with a pneumatic sigh.

Once more I was swallowed up.

I stepped out into the now familiar crush.

Even as we hurried toward the scene of the crisis, I lifted my head and took deep breaths. The air was clammy and shallow, and my lungs pulled, trying to extract oxygen. But there was that powerful animal stink again, the musk of sweat and piss, of blood and milk, so suffocating, and yet somehow so exhilarating.

I was full of doubts about the Order, full of conflicting emotions. I had listened to Peter's extraordinary arguments about eusociality and hives and Coalescents, a new form of humanity. And above all, stuck in my head, was the image of Lucia, a fifteen-year-old tortured by the exploitation of her fecundity by—well, by *somebody* in this place, for some purpose, not her own. But for all that it was good to be back. I belonged here: walking down these dense corridors again, I seemed to feel it on some deep cellular level. However the Order was sending me signals, through body language or chimp grunts or scent or whatever the hell, it was certainly getting through.

But the Crypt felt different today.

All those ageless female faces, and a few male, all with their smoky gray eyes, peered at me uncertainly, eyes wide, mouths downturned. I was sure that few of them would know anything about what was going on, but they picked up their cues from

Rosa, and then from each other, and as we walked they all un-thinkingly flinched away from me. That silent rejection hurt.

But even through this self-pitying ache, I noticed the Crypt was *quiet*: people spoke, but softly, leaning to whisper in each others' ears. They even walked quietly, their feet padding gently on the floor. I listened for the hum of generators, the hiss and low roar of the air-conditioning systems, but could hear nothing.

"Silent running," I said to Rosa.

"What do you mean?"

"Just like a submarine, trying to evade the sonar of the surface ships. We're in a great, static, underground submarine . . ."

It struck me then that the Order, whatever its powers and wealth, being stuck immovably in this Crypt, this hole in the ground, was terribly vulnerable. No wonder Rosa had reacted so strongly to Peter's incursion. For the Crypt to be revealed was about the worst thing that could happen, because once exposed it would stay exposed. The silent running must be instinctive, I thought, a reaction bred in over generations. A great wave of fear and despondency must have rippled out through the tight-packed, touching, gossiping members of the Order, a wave of alarm but not of information, a wave that left silence and caution where it passed.

We descended to Level 2 and hurried past the great galleries of hospital wards and dormitories. Eventually we began to pass through quieter, darker corridors. I sensed we were moving out of the core of the sprawling complex, reaching areas I hadn't seen before. Perhaps the ventilation shaft Peter had used was old, long abandoned, unguarded.

At last we came to a wall, not of concrete or interior partition, but of tufa, honest, solid lava. I ran my hand along the wall. I felt oddly reassured to think that I wasn't in the middle of things anymore—that beyond my hand there were no more galleries and chambers, no more *people*, nothing but a tremendous mass of patient, silent rock.

A knot of people stood before a cleft in the rock wall, all Order members. The lighting here, coming from fluorescent lamps bolted crudely to the tufa wall, was sparse and dim, and as they watched us approach, their faces, all so similar, seemed to float, disembodied, in the gloom. I recognized none of them. There were ten of them—only one was a man—but they were all tall and hefty looking inside their smocks. They were here for physical work, I thought, perhaps to wrestle Peter to the ground.

And they were *old*, I realized with a shock; with crow's-feet eyes and sunken cheeks, they all showed far more visible signs of aging than I had seen in the Crypt before. Uneasily I remembered Peter's talk of aging ant warriors, of elderly mole rats sacrificed to the jackals; it was another unwelcome parallel.

Rosa spoke briskly to these guardians and came back to me. "He's still in there."

"Where?"

She jerked her thumb at the cleft in the rock.

I moved past her to take a look. The cleft was a crack in the tufa, barely wide enough for me to have squeezed into sideways. It looked as if it had been caused by a mild earthquake, and then widened by seeping water. The glow from the wall-mounted lamps didn't penetrate very far, and I cupped my hands over my eyes, peering into silent blackness.

Suddenly light flared in my face. I fell back, rubbing my eyes. "*Ow.* Shit."

A sardonic voice, made hollow by echoes, came drifting out of the cleft. "You took your time."

"Hello, mate. How did you get yourself in there?"

"Let's just say it wasn't easy," he said gnomically.

"What are you doing?"

"Saving the future."

"We can't get him out," Rosa said to me. "The cleft is too narrow. We haven't been able to find the way he got in—presumably from above. We might get one or two people in from the front, but they could never get behind him to bring him out. And besides, we're afraid he might harm them."

I frowned. "Harm them? Harm them how? You think he's sitting in there with a revolver?"

Rosa said heavily, "Remember San Jose."

"Look, Rosa, I don't know why he's got himself stuck in a hole in the rock. But I can't see what harm he can do you in there. I mean, all you have to do is wait a few hours, or days even, and you'll starve him out. In fact you might have to if you want him to get through that gap."

"This isn't funny, George."

"Isn't it?" I felt a little light-headed.

"Talk to him. You say he's your friend. Fine. Find out what he's doing here, what he wants, what he intends. And then find a way to resolve this situation. Because if you don't, *I will*."

I tried to read her. "Will you call the police? . . . You won't, will you? Or the FBI, or Interpol. You don't want to bring them here into the Crypt, despite the danger you perceive. *What are you planning,* Rosa?"

She said evenly, "I'm responsible for the safety of the Crypt. As is every member of the Order. I will do whatever it takes, at whatever cost, to ensure that safety. I suggest you make sure it doesn't come to that." In the gloom her face was hard, set—almost fanatical—I thought she had never looked less like me, or my parents.

I nodded, chilled. "I believe you."

I approached Peter's wall again.

"Don't listen to her," he said. "Don't let her whisper in your ear."

"Or overwhelm me with chimp pant-hoots or phero-mones? . . ."

"George, just get out of here."

"Why?"

"It doesn't concern you. Just get away—"

"Of course it concerns me. That's my sister, standing over there. But that's not why I'm staying, Peter."

"Then why?"

"For you, you arsehole."

He laughed, sardonic. "I didn't see you once in twenty years."

"But you were a good friend to my dad. Even if I didn't know about it until too late."

Silence for a while. When he spoke again, his tone was softer. "Okay, then. Do what you like. Arsehole yourself."

"Yes . . . Peter, we need to talk."

"About—"

"About San Jose."

He hesitated. "So you know about that."

"Interpol send their best. Peter, what happened over there?"

He sighed noisily. "You really want to know?"

"Tell me."

"I warn you now we will have to discuss black holes. Because that's what they were trying to build in that lab."

Even now, more spooky stuff. "Oh, for God's sake . . ."

The drones, unaware of the odd grammar of our relationship, stirred, baffled, nervous.

Peter began to describe "geometric optics." "A black hole is a space-time flaw, a hole out of which nothing can escape, not even light. Black holes suck in light through having ultrapowerful gravity fields . . ."

Black holes in nature are formed by massive collapsed stars, or by aggregates of matter at the centers of galaxies like ours—or they may have been formed in the extreme pressures of the Big Bang, the most tremendous crucible of all. It used to be thought that black holes, even microscopic ones, would be so massive and would require such immense densities that to make or manipulate them was forever beyond human reach.

But that wisdom, said George, had turned out to be false. "Light is the fastest thing in the universe—as far as we know—which is why it takes the massive gravity of a black hole to capture it. But if light were to move more slowly, then a more feeble trap might do the job."

Tense, with the gazes of the drones boring into me, I took the bait. "Fine. How can you slow down light?"

"Anytime light passes through a medium it is slowed from its vacuum speed. Even in water it is slowed by about a quarter—still bloody fast, but that's enough to give you refraction effects."

Memories of O-level physics swam into my mind. "Like the way a stick in a stream will seem bent—"

"Yes. But in the lab you can do a lot better. Pass light through a vapor of certain types of atom and you're down to a few feet per second. And if you use a Bose-Einstein condensate—"

"A what?"

He hesitated. "Supercold matter. All the atoms line up, quantum-mechanically . . . It doesn't matter. The point is, light can be slowed to *below walking pace*. I saw the trials in that lab in San Jose. It's really quite remarkable."

"And then you can make your black hole."

"You can blow your slow-moving light around—even make it move backward. Photons, thrown around like paper planes in a Texas twister. To make a black hole you set up a vortex in your medium—a whirlpool. You just pull out the plug. And if the vortex walls are moving faster than your light stream, the light gets sucked into the center and can't escape, and you have your black hole."

"That's what these Californians were doing?"

"They were getting there," Peter said. "They hit practical problems. The condensate is a quantum structure, and it doesn't respond well to being spun around . . . But all this was fixable, in principle."

"Why would anybody want to do this?"

"That's obvious. Quantum gravity," he said.

"Of course," I said. I actually had to keep from laughing. I was talking to a crack in the wall, watched by ten differently evolved hive-mind drones and my own long-lost sister. "You know, on any other day this conversation would seem bizarre."

"Pay attention, double-oh seven," he said wearily.

Quantum gravity, it seems, is the Next Big Thing in physics. The two great theories of twentieth-century physics were quantum mechanics, which describes the very small, like atomic structures, and general relativity, which describes the very large, like the universe itself. They are both successful, but they don't fit together.

"The universe today is kind of separated out," said Peter. "Large and small don't interact too much—which is why quantum mechanics and relativity work so well. You don't find many places in nature where they overlap, where you can study quantum gravity effects, the predictions of a unified theory. But the Black Hole Kit would be a tabletop gravity field. The San Jose people hoped, for instance, to explore whether space-time itself is quantized, broken into little packets, as light is, as matter is."

I said heavily, "What I don't understand is why all this should cost anybody her life. How do you justify it, Peter? Omelettes and eggs?"

"You know I don't think like that, George."

"Then tell me why that lab was destroyed."

"You already know."

"Tell me anyhow."

"Because of the future. Humankind's future. And because of the war in Heaven."

All this was so like our bullshit sessions in the park by the Forum. I could imagine his earnest face as he spoke, that big jaw, the small mouth, the beads of sweat on his brow, the half-closed eyes. But Rosa was watching me, skeptical, drawing her own conclusions, no doubt, about Peter's sanity. She twirled her finger. *Hurry it up.*

He reminded me of what he had told me, of SETI, the search for extraterrestrial life, and attempts to signal to it.

"Most of it was absurd," he whispered. "Quixotic. Like the plaques stuck on the side of Pioneer space probes. *They* will fail through sheer statistics, because the chance of any sentient being picking up such objects is minuscule. We are surrounded by that tremendous unintentional ripple of radio noise, spreading out everywhere at lightspeed—nothing we can do about that now . . . But then, most perniciously, some signaling has been intentional, and designed to succeed. Such as using the big antenna at Arecibo to throw digital signals at the nearest stars . . ."

"Pernicious?"

"George, where was the debate? Were you consulted? Did you vote to have your whereabouts blasted to the universe? What right had these people to act on your behalf?"

"I can't say it keeps me awake at night."

"It does me," he said hoarsely. "We *know* there is something out there waiting for us. The Kuiper Anomaly—long faded from the news—is still out there, orbiting silently. My seismic signals, the dark matter craft that decelerated and veered inside the Earth: more evidence. *Signaling is dangerous.* It must be. That is why the sky is so quiet. Whoever is out there has learned to keep quiet—or has been forced to be."

"Peter, I don't see what this has to do with the destruction of the black hole lab."

He sighed again. "George, there are some SETI proponents who say that our feeble attempts to signal so far are futile.

Plaques on clunky spacecraft, radio signals—all of this is laughably primitive technology. Jungle drums. It won't attract the attention of anybody advanced enough to matter."

"Right. And the kind of technology *they* will use—"

"Well, we don't know, but we can speculate. For instance, about technologies based on quantum gravity. Or even the manipulation of space-time itself. If you could do *that* there is no limit to what you could achieve. Warp drive—faster than light. Antigravity. The control of inertia—"

I began to see where this was going. "The San Jose Black Hole Kit would be a manipulation of space-time."

"That toy black hole would have stood out like a single campfire shining in the middle of a darkened landscape."

"You think the San Jose people were trying to signal to aliens?"

"Oh, they didn't *mean* to. All they were doing was trying to build a test bed for quantum gravity, just as advertised. I'm sure of that. But they wouldn't listen to our warnings—the Slan(t)ers. They would have gone on, and on, until they lit that damn campfire . . ."

And then I understood what had been done. I rubbed my eyes. "What did you use, Peter?"

"Semtex-H," he whispered. "Not difficult to get hold of if you know how. Before the fall of communism the Czechs shipped out a thousand tons of the stuff, mostly through Libya. My police background . . ."

He hadn't set the thing off, he said, but he had designed the system. It turned out to be simple. He had used electronics parts he bought from RadioShack to build a simple radar-activated sensor. It was based on dashboard detectors supposed to warn drivers of the presence of a police radar gun. If attached to a detonator, such a sensor could be used to set off a bomb, in response to a signal from a radar gun—or even from something smaller, lighter. He had learned these techniques in Northern Ireland.

"You know, Semtex is remarkable. It's brown, like putty. You can mold it to any shape. And it's safe to handle. You can hold it over a naked flame and it won't explode, not without a detonator. So easy."

I held my breath.

"You see, it's all about the future," he said softly. "That's what I've come to understand. We humans find ourselves on a curve of exponential growth, doubling in numbers and capability, and doubling again. We are wolflings now, but we are growing. We will become adults, we will become strong. Billions will flow from each of us, a torrent of minds, a great host of the future. This is our predestination. The future is ours. And *that* is what they perceive, I think."

"Who?"

"Those beyond the Earth. They see our potential. Our threat. They would want to stop it now, while we are still weak, cut down the great tree while it is still a sapling."

I tried to hold this extraordinary chain of logic in my head. "All right. I can see why you thought the San Jose lab should be stopped. But what are you doing here?"

"The hive is just as much of a threat to the future. Don't you see that yet? It is an end point to our destiny. And we have to avoid it."

I could see a glimmer of light in the rock cleft. He was holding something; it looked like a TV remote. "Peter, what's that?"

"The switch," he said. "For the bomb."

My sister stood there in her white smock, her hands clenched in fists at her sides. I didn't need to tell Rosa her worst suspicions had turned out to be accurate.

Her attendants, the beefy drones, whispered and fluttered, wide-eyed, clutching each other and walking about in little knots. Meanwhile Peter sat silently in his cave, a brooding demon.

And I was stuck in the middle, trying to find a way out for everybody.

"Peter."

"I haven't gone anywhere," he said dryly.

"Do you trust me?"

"What?"

"I've listened to your theories. I've taken your advice. I've even taken you seriously. Who else has done all that?"

He hesitated. "All right. Yes, I trust you."

"Then listen to me. There has to be a way out of this."

"You're talking about negotiation? George—you said it yourself. You can't negotiate with an anthill."

"Nevertheless we have to try," I said. "There are a lot of lives at stake."

"Nobody will be hurt. I'm not some homicidal nut, George, for God's sake. But I will open this place up. Expose it to the world."

"But maybe you won't even have to take the risk. Why not give it a try?" I fell silent and waited, forcing a response. Old management trick.

At last he replied. "All right. Since it's you."

I let out a breath I hadn't realized I was holding.

"Rosa," he hissed now. "She is the key. The rest were born here, and are beyond hope. But Rosa might understand. She has a broader perspective, a self-awareness you're not supposed to have, here in the termite mound. You might persuade her to *see* what she is. But George—you'll have to get her on her own. Get her away from the others. Otherwise you'll never jolt her out of it."

"I'll try."

I walked up to Rosa. Her eyes narrowed as she waited for me to speak. Suddenly I had power, I realized, but it wasn't a power I wanted. "He'll talk. But you have to do things my way, Rosa." I glanced at the drones, who continued to flap ineffectually behind her. "Get rid of these people."

Rosa actually quailed. I could see that the thought of being alone in a situation like this, cut off from the rest of the Order and the subtle cues of other drones, disturbed her on some deep level. But she complied. The drones went fluttering away, out of sight around the bend of the corridor.

I snapped: "And bring Lucia here."

She shook her head. "George, the doctors—"

"Just do it. *And* her baby. Otherwise I walk away."

We confronted each other. But, just as I had waited out Peter's response, I stared her down.

At last she backed off. "All right." She walked a little way down the corridor, dug a cell phone out of her pocket, and made a call.

It took a few minutes for Lucia to arrive. She was dressed in a plain smock, and she was carrying a small blanket-wrapped bundle. She was barefoot, and she walked slowly, uncertainly; I glimpsed attendants, perhaps from the chambers of the *mamme-nonne*, lingering around the bend of the corridor. When Lucia saw me she ran toward me. "Mr. Poole—oh, Mr. Poole—"

"Are you all right?"

Her face was sallow, I saw, her cheeks sunken, her eyes rheumy. Her hair was coiffed but it looked lifeless. She had lost weight; I could see her shoulder blades protrude through the smock, and her wrists and ankles were skeletal. I would never have believed she was still just fifteen. But she was smiling, and she held up her baby to me—her *second* baby, I reminded myself. She handled the child awkwardly, though. "They had to fetch her from the nurseries . . . It's the first time I've seen her since she was born. Isn't she beautiful?"

No more than a few weeks old, the baby had a small, crumpled face, and she was sleepy; but when she opened her eyes, they were mother-of-pearl gray. The baby seemed a little agitated: strange hands, my mother would have said. I felt sad for Lucia.

"Yes, she's beautiful."

She rubbed her stomach. "How is Daniel?"

"With his parents."

"I think of him often."

"What's wrong with your stomach? . . . Oh. You're pregnant again."

She shrugged and looked away.

I took her arm and found her a place to sit, on a bench carved out of the rock wall.

"Rosa, how did you get her out of the American Hospital?"

Rosa shrugged. "Do you really want the details? . . . The key was that she wanted to come out, despite everything she says. Didn't you, child?"

Lucia huddled over her baby, hiding her face.

Rosa said, "I've done what you asked, George. Can I talk to him now?"

"Go ahead."

She turned to the rock wall and raised her voice. "I don't know why you want to do this, Peter McLachlan. What harm have we done you—or anybody? We are an ancient religious order. We dedicate ourselves to the worship of God, through Mary, the mother of His son. We were founded for benevolent reasons. We educate. We store knowledge that would otherwise be lost. In times of trouble we act as a haven for vulnerable women . . . You can't deny any of this."

"Of course not," Peter said. "But you don't see yourself clearly. You can't, in fact; you're not supposed to. Rosa, even you, who were born outside, have been here too long. Your conscious purposes—the religion, your communal projects—are just by-products. No, more than that—they are glue to bind you together, dazzling concepts that distract your conscious minds. But they are not what the Order is *for*. They could be replaced by other goals—cruelty instead of benevolence, futility instead of useful purpose—and the Order would work just as well. The truth is the Order exists only for itself . . ."

In broken phrases he sketched his beliefs. The Order was an anthill, a mole rat colony, a termite mound, he told her. It was not a human society. "Your handful of *mamme-nonne*, pumping out infants. Your sterile sisters—"

Rosa frowned. "Celibacy is common in Catholic orders."

"Not celibate. *Sterile*," he hissed.

She listened to his arguments, her face working.

"And you can't argue with the reality of Lucia," he said. "Suppose she walked into a medical office in Manchester. The doctor would think Lucia was extraordinary—*and so would you,* if not for the fact that you grew up here. You have all been down in this hole for a long time. Time enough for adaptation, selection—evolution, Rosa."

Lucia looked up at me. "What's he saying? If I am not human, what am I?"

Rosa touched her hands. "Hush, child. It's all right . . ." She paced around, her heels clicking softly on the rock floor. I had no real idea what was going through her mind.

"Suppose it's true," she said suddenly. "It's hard to get my head around this nonsense—but suppose I concede that you're right. That we have formed a—a sort of self-organizing collective here. Even that, in some way, after all these centuries, we have somehow diverged from the common human stock."

"You're waking up," Peter said.

She snapped, "I don't think you are in any position to patronize *me*. Let's remember that you are the nutcase stuck in a hole in the wall with Semtex stuck up his arse."

"Go on, Rosa," I said quickly. "Suppose it's true. Then what?"

"Then—" She raised her hands, lifted her head to the levels hidden above us, the great underground city. "If this is a new way, maybe it's a better way. We have found a way to run a society, safely and healthily, with population densities *orders of magnitude* higher than anything else humans have hit on. What is the purpose of any human society? It is surely to provide a system in which as many people as possible can live out lives as long and healthy and happy and peaceful as possible. Wouldn't it be better for humankind, and this whole crowded planet, if everyone lived peaceably together as they do here?"

"Little drone, you know too much," he whispered.

She walked boldly up to the cleft. "Show your face, McLachlan."

He switched on his torch. His face, eerily underlit, hovered in the shadows, his expression unreadable.

Rosa said, "Suppose you're right. Suppose we are a new form—your word was *Coalescents*."

"Yes."

"Then shouldn't you accept us for what we are?" She spread her arms. "What have you found, here in this cave under the Appian Way? Aren't we *Homo superior*?"

He clicked off his torch; his face disappeared into the dark.

Rosa had an intense expression, almost a look of triumph.

I asked, "Did you believe all that?"

She glanced at me. "Not a word. I just want him out of there." She was formidable indeed, I realized; I felt perversely proud.

Peter whispered again, from the dark. "George, she must have already figured some of this out for herself. Even if she didn't want to face it. I just put it into words for her. *She knew it all the time.* Really, she's too smart for the hive, for her own good."

"But she's listening," I said quickly. "Maybe we should take it easy. Don't do anything destructive. We'll get the Order to

open up, bring in the health professionals, the social workers . . ."

"There's no time for that," he said.

"Why not?"

"No time . . ." He fell silent, breathing heavily.

I tiptoed away. "I think he's tiring," I said to Rosa.

"Then," she said, "before he triggers his dead man's switch
by falling asleep, I think you have a decision to make."

"*I* have a decision?"

"I can't say any more. But perhaps McLachlan will listen to
you. You can encourage him to blow us all up. You can persuade him to walk away." Of course she was right, I saw, horrified; the decision had to be mine. "Just remember," she said
coldly, "that there is a place for you here. Even now, even after
you brought this lunatic into our Crypt. This can be your
home, too. If you do anything to harm us, *then you will lose
that choice, too.*"

I seemed to smell the pounds of Semtex Peter had lodged
somewhere in the rock, sense the great weight of the subterranean city around me, the thousands of lives it contained.

Behind us Lucia sat quietly on her bench, her baby on her
lap; her gaze was fixed on its face, as if she wanted to shut us
out, a malevolent world that wanted to use and control her and
her child, even those of us motivated to save her—and I
couldn't blame her.

Now it was my turn to do some pacing. I tried to ignore the
hammering of my heart, the remote stink of the Crypt, and to
think clearly.

Did I agree with Peter?

Peter's theorizing about hives and eusociality was all very
well. But the reality of the Crypt, which I felt in my blood, was
a good deal warmer than his hostile analysis, a lot more welcoming. And I wasn't about to argue with Rosa about the
Order's history, and the work it had done over centuries. Whatever Peter said, I felt I had no more right to close that down
than to shut down the Vatican.

And then there was *Homo superior*.

I had seen for myself that Peter's "Coalescents" were not
like other humans. Perhaps they *were* a more advanced form;

perhaps Rosa was right that we would need the warm, fecund discipline of Order living to survive a difficult future on a crowded Earth. In which case, what right did I have to make decisions about their future? . . . I felt I was losing touch with the world. I drew on the thick, musty air, suddenly longing for a fresh blast of cool oxygen-rich topside atmosphere to clear my head. I was one man, flawed, vulnerable, mortal, woefully ignorant, and these issues escalated above me on every scale. How could I possibly make a decision like this?

For some reason I thought of Linda, my ex-wife. She had always had a lot more common sense than I did. What would Linda say, if she was here?

Look around you, George.

Lucia looked up at me, her eyes full of bewilderment, her body battered by childbirth, her face prematurely lined with pain.

Cut the bullshit. Remember what you said to that kid Daniel: you admired him because he had responded to this wretched child Lucia on a human level. You were as pompous as always, but you were right. Well, look at Lucia now, George; look at her with that scrap of a baby. I wouldn't trust you to adjudicate on the future of humankind. And I'm not interested in your self-pitying whinging about whether you'll die childless or not. But you are a fully functioning human being. Act that way . . .

Of course. It was obvious.

I walked up to Rosa, and said as softly as I could, "Here's the deal. I'll help you disarm Peter. But you have to open this place up. Connect with the world. I think Lucia has suffered, and if I can stop that I will."

She glared at me; her anger was taking over. "What right have you to make such pronouncements? You're a man, George, and so is that murderous fool in the rock. This is a place built by and for women. Who are you to lecture us on our humanity?"

"Take it or leave it."

Gnawing her lip, she studied my face. Then she nodded curtly.

Together, we crossed to Peter's cleft in the rock. But things didn't go as planned.

* * *

"I couldn't hear you," Peter whispered. "But I could see you. You've come to some kind of deal, haven't you, George? A deal that is bound to preserve the hive." He sighed, sounding desolate. "I suppose I knew this would happen. But I can't let you do this. I shouldn't have let you talk about negotiating at all. I'm weak, I suppose."

"Why can't we talk? . . ."

"It has to stop here, or it never will. *Because the hive is ready to break out.* Think about it. Hives need raw material—drones, lots of them, living in conditions of high population densities, and highly interconnected. Until the modern era, less than one human in thirty lived in a community of more than five thousand people. Today more than *half* the world's population lives in an urban environment. And we are more interconnected than ever before."

"What are you saying, Peter?"

"When the breakout comes it will be a phase transition—all at once—the world will transform, as water turns to ice, as a field of wildflowers suddenly blooms in the spring. In its way it will be beautiful. But it's an end point for us. There will be new gods on Earth: mindless gods, a pointless transcendence. From now on the story of the planet will not be of humanity, but of the hive . . ."

"Peter." The situation was rapidly slipping away from me. "If you'll just come out of there—"

"You know why you're prepared to betray me, to save the Order? *Because you're part of the hive, too.* George, you're just another drone—remote from the center, yes, but a drone nonetheless. Perhaps you always were. And the tragedy is, you don't even know it, do you?"

I felt as if the cave, the giant, densely peopled superstructure of the Crypt, was rotating around me. Was it possible I really had somehow been sucked into some emergent superorganism—was it possible that my decision now was being taken, not in my or Peter's or Lucia's interests, but in the mindless interests of the hive itself? If so—how could I *know*? Again I longed for oxygen.

"I can't think through that, Peter. I'm going to follow my instinct. What else can I do?"

"Nothing," he whispered. "Nothing at all. But, you see, I'm the only free mind in this whole damn place. Good-bye, George."

"Peter!"

I heard a click.

And then the floor lurched.

I clattered into one wall, an impact that knocked the wind out of me. Some of the lights failed; I heard a bulb smash with a remote tinkle. There was a remote rumbling, as if an immense truck was passing by.

There was a second's respite. I saw Lucia on the ground. She was sheltering her baby. They were both gray with dust.

Then rock fragments started hailing down from the ceiling, heavy, sharp-edged. I pushed myself away from the wall, crawled over to Lucia, and threw myself over her and the infant. I was lucky; I was hit, but by nothing large enough to hurt.

The rumbling passed. The rock bits stopped falling. Gingerly I moved away from Lucia. We were both gray with dust, and her eyes were wide—shock, perhaps—but she and the baby seemed unhurt.

I heard running footsteps, shouts. Torchlight flickered in the dimly lit corridor.

Rosa was at the cleft in the rock, pulling away rubble with her bare hands. I could see a hand, a single hand, protruding from beneath the debris. It was bloody, and gray dust clung to the dripping crimson.

I ran over. My battered legs and back were sore, my lungs and chest hurt from where I had been thrown against the wall. But I dragged at the rock. Soon my fingers were aching, the nails broken.

Rosa, meanwhile, had taken a pulse from that protruding hand. She took my arm and pulled me away. "George, forget it. There's nothing we can do."

I slowed, jerkily, as if my energy was draining. I let the last handful of rubble drop to the floor.

I took Peter's hand. It was still warm, but it was inert, and I could feel how it dangled awkwardly. I felt inexpressibly sad.

"Peter, Peter," I whispered. "You were only supposed to blow the bloody doors off."

Running footsteps closed on us. Hive workers, of course, drones, most of them women, all of them dressed in dust-covered smocks. Faces swam before me in the uncertain light, gray eyes troubled. I grabbed Lucia's hand, and she clung to me just as hard. "Go," I shouted at the drones. "Get out. There may be more falls. Take the stairs. Go, go . . ."

The drones hesitated, turned, fled, and we followed.

The long climb up stairs of cut stone and steel was a night-mare of darkness and billowing smoke. It got worse when more drones joined us, and we became part of an immense file of women, children, a few men, all clambering up those nar-row, suffocating stairwells. The power was down in some sec-tors, and by flickering emergency lights I glimpsed people running, collapsed partition walls, smashed glass. In the hos-pital areas, and in the strange chambers where the *mamme* had lived, squads of people were working busily, pushing beds and wheelchairs out of damaged rooms. But the air thickened rap-idly, and it became stiflingly hot; the ventilation systems must have failed.

I just pushed my way through the mobs of drones. My only priority was getting out of there: myself, Lucia, and the baby, for not once did I release her hand.

It was only when I got aboveground that I got a clear sense of what was happening.

Peter had placed his Semtex skillfully. He had broken open the upper carapace of the Crypt. The result was a great crater, collapsed in the middle of the Via Cristoforo Colombo, with a plume of gray-black tufa dust hanging in the air above it. Workers from the nearby offices and shops, clutching their cell phones and coffees and cigarettes, peered into the hole that had suddenly opened up in their world. There was a re-mote wail of sirens, and a lone cop was doing his best to keep the onlookers away from the hole.

And the drones simply poured out of the crater, in baffling numbers, in hundreds, thousands.

Dressed alike, with similar features, and now obscured by the dust, they looked identical. Even now there was a kind of order to them. Most of them came out over one lip of Peter's

crater, in a kind of elliptical flood. At the edge of the ellipse
were heavier, older women, some of them with their arms
linked to keep out strangers. At the center of the mass were the
younger ones, some cradling infants, and here and there I saw
hospital workers carrying the heavy chairs of the *mamme-
nonne*. Nobody was in the lead. The women at the fringe would
press forward a few paces, blinking at the staring office workers, and then turn and disappear back into the mass, to be replaced by others, who probed forward in turn. As they reached
the buildings at the sides of the road the flowing ellipse broke
up, forming ropes and tendrils and lines of people that washed
forward, breaking and recombining. They probed into doorways and alleyways, swarming, exploring. In the dusty light
they seemed to blur together into a single rippling mass, and
even in the bright air of the Roman afternoon they gave off a
musky, fetid odor.

FOUR

As the shuttle skimmed low over the surface of the frozen planet, it was the circle of the dead that first struck Abil.

Not that, in those first moments, he understood what he was seeing.

Captain Dower was piloting the shuttle herself, an effortless display of competence. The planet was far from any star, and the shuttle was a bubble, all but transparent, so that the hundred tars and their corporals flew as effortlessly as dreams over a plain of darkness. Below, Abil could see only the broad elliptical splashes of paleness picked out by the flitter's spots. The ground was mostly featureless, save for the subtle texture of ripples in the ice—the last waves of a frozen ocean—and, here and there, the glistening sheen of nitrogen slicks. Dower had said the ocean of water ice had probably frozen out within a few years, after the Target had been ripped away from its parent sun by a chance stellar collision, and then the air rained out, and then snowed.

Abil looked into the sky. This sunless world was surrounded by a great sphere of stars, hard as shards of ice themselves. In one direction he could see the great stripe that was the Galaxy. It was quite unlike the pale band seen from Earth: from here it was a broad, vibrant, complex band of light, littered with hot young stars. The Third Expansion of humankind now sprawled across tens of thousands of light-years, and had penetrated the dust clouds that shielded much of the Galaxy's true structure from Earth. When he looked back the other way, the fields of stars were unfamiliar. He wondered where Earth was—though surely Earth's sun would be invisible from here.

Once, all of humanity and all of human history had been confined to a single rocky world, a pinpoint of dust lost in the sky. But since humankind had begun to move purposefully out from the home planet, twenty thousand years had shivered across the face of the Galaxy. And now, in the direction of home, every which way he looked he was seeing stars mapped and explored and colonized by humans. It was a sky full of people.

His heart swelled with pride.

Captain Dower called, "Heads up."

Abil looked ahead. The spots splashed broad lanes across the ice, diminishing to paleness toward the horizon. But they cast enough light that Abil could see a mountain: a cone of black rock, its flanks striped by glaciers. All around it was a broad, low ridge, like a wall around a city. The diameter of the rim walls must have been many miles. There was some kind of striation on the plain of ice inside the rim wall, a series of lines that led back toward the central peak.

Dower turned. Her metallic Eyes glinted in the subtle interior lights of the shuttle. "That's our destination. First impressions—you, Abil?"

Abil shrugged inside his skinsuit. "Could be an impact crater. The rim mountains, the central peak—"

"It isn't big enough," came a voice from the darkness. "I mean, a crater that size ought to be cup-shaped, like a scoop out of the ice. You only get rim mountains and splash-back central peaks with much larger craters. And anyhow I haven't seen any other craters here. This planet is a sunless rogue. Impacts must be rare, if you wander around in interstellar space."

That had been Denh. She was in Abil's unit, and Abil needed to get back in the loop.

"So," he said, "what *do* you think it is, smart-ass?"

"That peak is tectonic," Denh said. "It's hard to tell, but it looks like granite to me."

Dower nodded. "And the rim feature?"

". . . I can't explain that, sir."

"Honesty doesn't excuse ignorance. But it helps. Let's go see."

The shuttle dropped vertiginously toward the ground.

The profile of the rim feature was—strange. It was a raised ridge of some gray-white, textured substance. It ran without a break all around that distant mountain. It had a bell-shaped profile, rising smoothly from the ice on either side, and a rounded summit. Its texture was odd—from a height it looked fibrous, or like a bank of grass, trapped in frost. Not like any rock formation Abil had ever seen.

The shuttle slowed almost to a stop now, and began to drift down toward the upper surface of the rim feature.

Abil saw that distance had fooled him. Those "fibers" were not blades of grass: they were bigger than that. They were *limbs*—arms and legs, hands and feet—and heads: human heads. The rim was a wall of the dead, a heaping of corpses huge enough to mimic a geological feature, naked and frozen into incorruptibility.

Abil was astounded. Nothing in the predrop briefings had prepared him for this.

"It's a ring cemetery," Dower said matter-of-factly. "Warren worlds are subtly different, but the template is the same, every damn time." She glanced around sharply at the hundred faces. "Everybody okay with this?"

"There are just so many of them," somebody said. "If the whole of the rim wall is like this—miles of it—there must be billions of them."

"It's an old colony," Dower said dryly.

The shuttle swam on, heading toward the central mountain.

On the edge of a lake of frozen oxygen, the shuttle landed as gently as a soap bubble. Dower ordered a skinsuit check— each trooper checked her own kit, then her buddy's—and the walls of the shuttle popped to nothingness.

Gravity was about standard. When Abil clambered off his small T-shaped chair he dropped the yard or so to the ground without any problem. He walked around, getting the feel of the ground and the gravity, listening to the whir of the exoskeletal servers built into his suit, checking telltales that hovered before him in a display of Virtual fireflies.

Around him a hundred troopers did likewise, stalking around the puddle of light cast by the shuttle's floods. Their backpacks glimmered murky green, the color of pond water.

Abil walked out to the edge of the light, where it blurred and softened to smeared-out gray. The water ice was hard under his feet, hard and unyielding. The surface of the frozen ocean was dimpled and pocked. Here and there frost glimmered, patches of crystals that returned the lights of his suit, or of the stars. The frost was not water but frozen air.

Oxygen, of course, was a relic of life. So there must have been life here—life that mightn't have been so different from Earth-origin life—long gone, crushed out of existence as the sun receded and the cold's unrelenting fist closed. Perhaps that life had spawned intelligence: perhaps this world had once had a name. Now it only had a number, generated by the great automated catalogs on Earth—a number nobody ever used, for the tars called it simply "the Target," as they called every other desolate world to which they were sent.

"Gather 'round," Dower called.

Abil joined the cluster of troopers around Dower. He found his own unit, marked by red arm stripes. He joined them, showing his command stripes of red and black.

"Look here." Dower pointed to the edge of the oxygen lake.

Footprints, on the water ice shore: human prints, made by some heavy-treaded boot in a shallow nitrogen frost, quite clear.

"The warren's bio systems are probably highly efficient recyclers, but nothing is perfect. They still need oxygen . . ."

Abil walked up to the prints. His own foot was larger, by a few sizes. Standing here, he saw that the prints led back, away from the oxygen lake, forming a path that snaked almost dead straight toward the central mountain. And when he looked the other way, beyond the lake, he saw more trails leading off toward the rim, the circular heap of corpses.

Those striations he thought he had seen on the ice, radiating inward from the rim wall, were actually ruts, he saw now, worn into water ice as hard as granite by the passage of countless feet, over countless years. All those journeys, he thought, shuddering, out to that great heaped-up pile of mummies. Year after year, generation after generation.

Dower hefted a weapon. "This is our way in. Form up."

Abil stood at the head of his unit. Briefly he surveyed their faces. There were ten of them, all friends—even Denh. They would support him now to their deaths. But his stripes were only provisional, and he knew that if he fouled up they would chew jockey to replace him for the next drop, wherever and whenever it was.

That wasn't going to happen. He grinned tightly. "Reds, forward." They formed into two rows, with Abil at the head.

They trotted along the line of the path in the ice, keeping to either side of the rut, heading steadily toward the central mountain. The going turned out to be treacherous. Even away from the main paths the ice was worn slick by the passage of human feet. There were a few stumbles, and every so often there was a silent burst of vapor as somebody stepped into an oxygen puddle. Every time one of his unit took a pratfall Abil called a halt to run fresh equipment checks.

After about a mile Dower paused. The rut had led them to a crater in the ice, maybe ten yards across—no, Abil saw, the edges of this shallow pit were too sharp for that, its circular form too regular, and the base of the pit was smooth, gunmetal gray. Dower pressed her finger to the surface, and read Virtuals that danced before her Eyes. "Metal," she said. She beckoned to Abil. "Corporal. Find a way in."

He stepped gingerly onto the metal surface. It was slick, and littered with bits of loose frost, but it was easier than walking on the ice. He sensed hollowness beneath his feet, though, a great volume, and he trod lightly, for fear of making a noise. He knelt down, pressed his palm to the metal surface, and waited. Where his knee touched the metal he could feel its cold, clawing at him through the diamond pattern of heating filaments in his skinsuit. It took a few seconds for results from his suit's sensors to be displayed, in hovering Virtuals before his face.

He was rewarded with a sketchy three-dimensional cross section. The metal plate was a couple of yards thick, and much of it was solid, fused on a base of rock. But it contained a hollow chamber, an upright cylinder. Probably some kind of low-tech backup system. The covering for the hollow was no more than a couple of yards away.

He walked that way and knelt again. His fingers, scraping over the sheer surface, quickly found a loose panel. By pressing on one side of it, he made it flip up. Beneath that was a simple handle, T-shaped. He grasped this, tugged. A lid rose up, attached by mechanical hinges.

Abil peered into the pit, using his suit lights. The pit was a little deeper than he was tall. He saw a wheel in there, a wheel set on a kind of spindle. Its purpose was obvious.

Dower came to stand beside him. She grunted. "Well done, Corporal. Okay, let's take a minute. Check your kit again." The troopers, working in pairs, complied.

Dower pointed at the mountain. "You were right—uh, Denh. The mountain's tectonic, not impact-created. We're standing over a midocean ridge: a place where the crust is cracking open, and stuff from within wells up to form new ocean floor. And where that happens, you get mountains heaping up, like this. On this planet it's still happening. The loss of the sun destroyed the surface and the air, but it made no difference to what's going on down deep. All along this ridge you will have vents, like valves, where the heat and the minerals from within the planet come bubbling up. And that heat will keep little pockets of water liquid, even now. And where there's liquid water—"

"There's life." That mumble came from a number of voices. It was a slogan from biology classes taught to five-year-olds, all across the Expansion.

"And *that* is the ecosystem that will have survived this planet's ejection from its solar system: something like bacteria colonies, or tube worms perhaps—probably anaerobic, living off the minerals and the heat that seeps out of the cracks in the ground. Radioactivity will keep the planet's core warm long after that lost sun itself has gone cold. Strange irony—life on this world will probably actually last *longer* than if it had stayed in orbit around its sun . . ."

Abil piped up: "Tell us about the warren, sir."

She began to sketch with one finger in the loose ice. "The warren is a rough toroid dug into the ice, encircling that central peak. In places it's nearly a mile deep. It's not a simple structure; it's a mess of interconnected chambers and corridors. We suspect the birthing chambers are the deepest, the closest to the mountain rock itself; that's the usual arrangement.

"Now here—" She slashed at her diagram, drawing diagonal lines that reached up from the torus and down to the face of the mountain. "Runs. Access chutes. Some of them vertical, probably the oldest, fitted with lifting equipment; the more recent ones will have stairs and ladders. You can see *these* runs provide access to the surface, for the disposal of the dead, foraging missions for oxygen, perhaps other resources. *These* lower tunnels reach down to the face of the mountain, to the pockets of liquid water and the life-forms down there. With suitable processing the colonists will be able to live off the native organic compounds." She looked up. "You need to know that it's common for colonies of this type to reprocess as much of their raw material as possible." She let that hang in the silence.

Denh said queasily, "You mean, *people*? But we saw the corpses in that great ring."

Dower shrugged. "In these wild warrens patterns vary . . . Just remember two things. First, across the Galaxy we are at war. Our alien enemy is pitiless, and cares nothing for your moral qualms, or even your nausea, Denh. We need warm bodies to be thrown into the war, and that's why we're here. We're a press gang, nothing more. And second—remember that whatever you see down there, however strange it seems to you, *these are human beings*. Not like you—a different sort—but human nevertheless. So there's nothing to fear."

"Yes, *sir*," came the ritual chorus.

"All right. Abil—"

Denh pushed herself forward. "Let me, Captain." She jumped into the pit and rubbed her hands, pretending to spit on the palms, to the soft laughter of her mates. "Clockwise, you think?" She turned the wheel.

The ground shuddered under Abil's feet. The great lid of metal and rock slid back, disappearing under the ice. Denh yelped, and jumped out of her hole.

The run was a broad, slanting tunnel cut into the ice. Crude steps had been etched into its lower surface, four, five, six parallel staircases. There was no light but the stars, and the spots of their skinsuits.

Eight of the ten teams would enter the run, leaving two on watch on the surface. Dower waved two units forward to take the lead. Abil's red team was one of them.

Abil led the way into the hole. He clambered easily down the stairs, wary, descending into deeper darkness. His hands were empty; though the weapons of his team bristled behind him, he felt naked.

Abil had descended maybe two hundred yards into the hole when suddenly the ice under his feet shook again. The lid was closing over the hole, like a great eyelid, shutting out the stars. He heard hurried, gasping breaths, the sounds of panic rising in his troopers. He tried to control his own breathing. "Red team, take it easy," he said. "Remember your briefing. We expected this."

"The corporal's right," growled Dower, somewhere above him. "This is just an air lock. Just wait, now."

For a few heartbeats they were suspended in darkness, their puddles of suit light overwhelmed by the greater dark.

There was a hiss of inrushing air. Then a coarse gray light flickered into life from fat fluorescent tubes buried in the walls. Abil looked up at the lines of troopers, weapons ready, standing on the floor of the cylindrical hall.

Dower held up her gloved hand. "You hear that?"

They listened in silence. Sound carried through the new air: muffled footsteps from beyond the walls, pattering away into the void beyond. And then more footsteps—many more, like an approaching crowd.

"They have runners," Dower whispered. "Throughout the warren. Patrolling everywhere. If one of them spots trouble, she runs off to find somebody else, and they both run back to the trouble spot, and then they split up, and run off again . . . It's a pretty efficient alarm system."

There was a noise from behind Abil, carried through the new, thick air. Only a few steps beneath him, there was another lid door, like the one they had come through from the surface. It, too, had a wheel set on an upright axle.

The wheel was turning with a scrape.

"They're coming," Dower said, hefting her weapon. "Let's have some fun."

The door slid back.

chapter 50

I like to escape from the crowds. Even in the winter, the center of Amalfi and its harbor area swarm with locals and tourists, mainly elderly British and Americans here for the winter sun.

So I climb the hills. The natural vegetation on this rich volcanic soil is woodland, but higher up the land has been terraced to make room for olive groves, vineyards, and orchards—especially lemons, the specialty of the area, though I swear I will never get used to *limoncello*; I can never get it off my teeth.

I like to think Peter would have seen the aptness of my retiring here, to Amalfi. For as it happens it was here, over a century ago, that Bedford, the protagonist of H. G. Wells's *The First Men in the Moon*, fled after his remarkable adventures in the moon, and wrote his own memoir. I keep a copy of the book, a battered old paperback, in my hotel room.

Yes, it would have pleased Peter. For what Bedford and Cavor found in the heart of the moon was, of course, the hive society of the Selenites.

I kept hold of Lucia, with her baby, all the way out of that hole in the ground.

When we could get away from the area, I found a cab and took her to my hotel. I couldn't think of anywhere else to go. We attracted some odd stares from the staff, but it did give us a chance to calm down, clean up. Then I called Daniel, whose number, on a dog-eared business card, Lucia had always kept with her.

Peter was the only fatality that day. He really had planted his bomb carefully. It wasn't hard for the forensic teams to establish his guilt, through traces of Semtex on his clothes and

under his fingernails, and to figure out the purpose of his little
remote-control radar gun. His true identity was quickly established, and he was linked with the mysterious group that had
bombed the geometric optics lab in San Jose.

But that was where the trail ran cold, happily for me. Peter
had signed into our hotel under an assumed name, and—as far
as I know—never brought any of his bomb-making equipment
there. The hotel staff hadn't seen much of him, and didn't
seem to recognize the blurred face on the news programs.

Still, I checked out—paying with cash, making sure I left no
contact address at the hotel—and fled Rome, for Amalfi.

I did bring with me all that was left of Peter's possessions. It
would surely have been a mistake for me to leave them behind.
And anyhow it didn't seem right. I burned his clothes, his
shaving gear, other junk. I kept his data, though. I copied it from
his machines to a new laptop I had bought in Rome. Then I destroyed the machines as best I could, wiping them clean,
breaking them open and smashing the chips, dumping the carcasses in the ocean.

The incident soon faded from attention: bomb attacks in
crowded cities are sadly commonplace nowadays. The authorities are still digging, of course. A common theory is that
maybe there is some kind of trail back to the usual suspects in
the Middle East. But a consensus seems to be emerging that it
must have been Peter who was primarily responsible for both
attacks, in San Jose and Rome, and that he was some kind of
lone nut with an unknowable grudge, for no other link has
been found between the geometric optics lab and the big hole
in the ground in Rome.

As for that great underground city under the Appian Way,
before the authorities were able to penetrate it fully—and I've
no idea how they did it—the swarming drones cleared it out.
There was little left to see but the infrastructure, the rooms,
the partitions, the great vents for circulating the air. The purpose of some rooms was obvious—the kitchens with their
gas supply, the dormitories where the frames of the bunk
beds have been left intact, the hospitals. Some other chambers
I could have identified, had anybody asked me, like the nurseries and the deep, musty, mysterious rooms where the

mamme-nonne had lived. They even dismantled their suite of mainframe computers.

It was obvious to everyone that some great project had been sustained down here, for a *long* time. But it was impossible to say what that project might have been. Conspiracy theories proliferated; the most popular seems to be that the Crypt was a *Doctor Strangelove* nuclear war bunker, perhaps built by Mussolini himself.

Remarkably enough, the Order itself wasn't linked with the Crypt. Somehow the surface offices closed off their links with the underground complex—they must have been prepared for an eventuality like this—so that they were able to pose as just more accidental victims of the disaster. When things calmed down they even continued to sell their genealogy services, presumably based on local copies of the Order's core data. You'd never have known anything happened.

Not all the drones from the Crypt vanished into the alley-ways. As it happened Pina, Lucia's untrustworthy friend, suffered a broken arm when she fell through a smashed ceiling, and was trapped under rubble. The drones couldn't get her out before the firefighters reached her. She was taken to one of Rome's big teaching hospitals. I conscripted Daniel's help to hack into the relevant hospital files to find out what happened.

When the doctors began to study her, and dug out the old files they had compiled when she was trapped after that similar accident years before, they were startled by Pina's "sub-adult" condition. They were able to trace the mechanism of her sterility. An impaired hypothalamic hormone secretion led to an inadequate gonadotrophic secretion, which in turn blocked ovulation ... And so on. I didn't really understand any of this, and I didn't know any medics I could trust to decode it for me. I don't suppose it mattered anyhow, for though the doctors could figure out *how* the sterility occurred, they couldn't figure out *why*. And Pina, evidently, wouldn't talk.

They kept her in hospital for two months. Strangely, by the end of that time, there were some changes in the condition of her body. It seemed that her glands were starting to secrete the complex chain of hormones that would have been necessary to trigger ovulation: it was as if she was entering puberty at last, at the much-delayed age of twenty-five. Perhaps if all the drones could be removed from the hive, they too would "recover."

But before this process was complete Pina disappeared from the hospital. She was checked out by "relatives," just as Lucia had been. I didn't hear of her again.

I did hear of Giuliano Andreoli, as it happened, having searched for his name on the Internet. Lucia's first lover was arrested for attempted rape, but committed suicide in his cell before the case could be brought to trial. I could imagine what Peter would have made of that: to the Order, Giuliano was just a sperm machine, used once and then discarded, pushed out into the glaring light of the outside world and an empty future. What he had known in the hive, that brief overwhelming moment of love and lust, must have come to seem like a dream.

As for Lucia herself, she is now living with Daniel and his family, in their bright, airy home in the hills outside Rome. Daniel's parents turned out to be decent, humane folk. And usefully enough, like many expats they don't entirely trust the competence of the Italian authorities, and were happy to get Lucia medical treatment privately and discreetly.

Lucia has had her third baby—a boy, in fact, lusty and healthy. It turned out to be a simple procedure to snip out her spermatheca, as Peter had called it, the little sac on her womb that would have continued to bleed Giuliano's seed into her for the rest of her life. Daniel's family now talk of putting her through school.

I don't know whether there will ever be love between Daniel and Lucia. Even now that the pressure of relentless childbirth is off her, nobody seems to know how her body will adjust in the future. And she is damaged. She has never heard what became of her first child, who must have been in one of those immense crèches on that fateful day. I think that is a wound that will never heal. But at least in Daniel, and his family, she has found good friends.

Sometimes, though, I wonder about Lucia's true destiny.

In all the reports about the Crypt, what was most notable for me was what was missing. The little carved *matres*, for instance, which Regina had brought from Roman Britain—the symbolic core of her family, and then of the Order. They were never mentioned, never found.

Peter told me that among some species of social insects the colonies breed by sending out a queen and a few workers, to start a colony all over again. I think I will try to keep watch on Lucia and her young family.

As for my sister, I haven't seen Rosa since I lost sight of her in the crush, deep in the Crypt. I don't think she could have gone back to the Order, though. In the end she knew too much—more than she was supposed to know—and yet she needed to know it. It must be necessary from time to time for the Order to throw up somebody like Rosa with an overview, somebody capable of perceiving greater scales, more complex threats. Peter's understanding was itself a threat to the Order—and she had to develop an equivalent understanding to beat him. But a drone isn't supposed to know she's in a hive. *Ignorance is strength.* In the end she saved the Order by sacrificing herself, as a good drone should, and knew what she was doing every step of the way.

Thus I found my sister, and lost her again.

There are other loose ends I can't resist tugging on.

I've been reading about eusocial organisms. I've learned that one characteristic of hives, just as much as the sterility of the workers and the rest, is *suicide*—the willingness of a drone to sacrifice itself for the greater good, and so for the long-term interests of its genetic heritage. You see it when a termite mound is broken open, or a predator tries to get into a mole rat colony. It's seen as proof by the biologists that the key organism is the global community, the hive, not the individual, for the individual acts completely selflessly. It was certainly true of the Order. When the Crypt was attacked, such as during the Sack of Rome, some of the members gave their lives to save the rest.

But here's the rub. In the end *Peter* committed suicide, to protect—what? He had no family. The future of humankind? But again, he had no children—and no direct connection to that future.

What he did have a connection to was the Slan(t)ers.

The Slan(t)ers have no leader; their network has no central point. Their behavior is dictated by the behavior of those "around" them in cyberspace, and governed by simple rules of online-protocol feedback. Among the Slan(t)ers—I've found—there are virtually none with children. They are too busy with Slan(t)er projects for that.

The Slan(t)ers don't have any physical connection, as did the Order. They don't even live in the same place. And their interest in the group isn't in any way genetic, as with the Order. There is no pretense that the Slan(t)ers are a family in the normal sense. But nevertheless, *I believe the Slan(t)ers are another hive*—a new, even purer form of human hive made possible by electronic interconnections—a hive of the mind, in which only ideas, not genes, are preserved.

Peter believed that everything he did was in the service of the future of humankind. But I believe that he wasn't really acting for any rational goals. The Slan(t)ers, the hive as a whole, had recognized the existence of another hive—and, like a foraging ant coming on another colony, Peter attacked.

At the crux, Peter wondered if I was a hive creature myself. Perhaps I was; perhaps I am. I am sure *he* was. And if the Order truly was a hive—and if it wasn't unique, if the Slan(t)ers are, too, a new sort altogether—then *how many others are out there*?

Anyhow, just because Peter was really following hive dictates doesn't mean he was wrong about the human future.

On his computer I found a few emails he'd been composing to send me, never finished.

"I think about the future. I believe that our greatest triumph, our greatest glory, lies ahead of us. The great events of the past—the fall of Rome, say, or the Second World War—cast long shadows, influencing generations to come. But is it possible that just as the great events of the past shape us now, so that mighty future—the peak age of humankind, the clash of cymbals—*has echoes in the present, too*? The physicists now say you have to think of the universe, and all its long, singular history, as just one page in a great book of possibilities, stacked up in higher dimensions. When those pages are slammed together, when the great book is closed, a Big Bang is generated, the page wiped clean, a new history written. And if time is circular, if future is joined to past, is it possible that messages, or even influences, could be passed around its great orbit? By reaching into the farthest future, would you at last touch the past? Are we influenced and shaped, not just by the past, but echoes of the future? . . ."

Sometimes at night I look up at the stars, and I wonder what strange future is folding down over us even now. I wish Peter was here, so we could talk this out. I can still see him leaning closer to me conspiratorially, on our bench in that dismal little park by the Forum, the sweet smell of *limoncello* on his breath.

chapter 51

Beyond the air lock door, there was a tunnel. It branched and bifurcated, and the light glowed pearl gray. It was like looking into a huge underground cathedral, shaped from the glistening ice.

And in the foreground was a mob.

There must have been a hundred people in the first rank alone, and there were more ranks behind, dimly glimpsed, more than Abil could count. They were small, squat, powerful looking. They were mostly unarmed, but some carried clubs of rusty metal. And they were naked, all of them. They looked somehow unformed, as if ill defined. The males had small, budlike genitals, and the females' breasts were small, their hips narrow. None of them seemed to have any body hair.

All this in a single glimpse. Then the Coalescents surged forward. They didn't yell, didn't threaten; the only noise was the pad of their feet on the floor, the brush of their flesh against the ice walls. Abil stood, transfixed, watching the human tide wash toward him.

Denh screamed, "Drop! Drop!"

Reflexively Abil threw himself to the ground. Laser light, cherry red, threaded the air above him, straight as a geometrical exercise.

The light sliced through the mob. Limbs were cut through and detached, intestines spilled from unzipped chest cavities, even heads came away amid unfeasibly huge founts of crimson blood. Now there was noise, screams, cries, and soft grunts.

The first wave of the mob was down, most of them dead in a heartbeat. But more came on, scrambling over the twitching carcasses of their fellows, until they, too, fell. And then a third wave came.

Abil had never confronted death on such a scale—a thousand or more dead in seconds—it was unimaginable, unreasonable. And yet they continued to come. It wasn't even murder but a kind of mass suicide. The Coalescents' only tactic seemed to be to hope that the troopers would run out of fuel and ammunition before they ran out of bodies to stand in its way. But that wouldn't happen, Abil thought sadly.

So many had been slain now that, he saw, their heaped corpses were beginning to clog the tunnel entrance. Abil tried to think like a corporal. He got to his feet, waved his arm. "Forward the throwers!"

Four of his troopers, carrying bulky backpacks, hurried forward. They launched great gouts of flame into the mounting wall of corpses, and at the defenders who continued to scramble over their fellows. Scores more Coalescents fell screaming onto the pile, their limbs alight like twigs in a bonfire. But that pile of corpses was alight, too. Soon the air was filled with smoke and grisly shards of burned bone and skin.

But the flames wouldn't hurt Abil and his men in their skinsuits. He waved again. "Go, go, go!"

He led the way into the fire. He put his arms before his faceplate as he hit the barrier of flame, and he felt the carbonized corpses crumble around him as he forced his way through them. But in seconds he was through, into the denser air of the corridor beyond the air lock.

And he faced more people—thousands of them, all eerily similar. Just for an instant the front rank held back, gazing at this man who had emerged from the lethal flames. Then they surged forward. The corridor was a great tube of people, squeezing themselves like paste toward him.

But they ran into flames. The front rank melted back like snowflakes.

After that Abil let the flamers take the lead. They just cut a corridor through the swarming crowd, and the troopers strode ahead over a carpet of burning flesh and cut bone. The crowd closed behind them, clustering like antibodies around an infection, but the troopers' disciplined and well-drilled weapons fire kept them away. It was as if they were hacking their way into some huge body, seeking its beating heart. As drones died all around him Abil began to feel numbed by it all, as the waves of faces, all so alike, crisped in the brilliant glare of the flames.

As they worked deeper, though, he began to notice a change. The assailants here were just as ferocious, but they seemed younger. That was part of the pattern he had been trained to expect. He wished he could find a way to spare the smallest, the most obviously childlike. But these young ones threw themselves on his troopers' flames as eagerly as their elders.

And then, quite suddenly, the troopers burst through a final barrier of drones, and found themselves in the birthing chamber.

It was a vast, darkened room, where ancient fluorescents glowed dimly. The troopers fanned out. They were covered in blood and bits of charred flesh, he saw, leaving bloody footprints where they passed. They looked as if they had been born, delivered through that terrible passage of death. One flamethrower still flared, but with a gesture Abil ordered it shut off.

In this chamber, people moved through the dark, as naked as those outside. Nobody came to oppose the troopers. Perhaps it was simply unthinkable for the drones that anybody should harm those who spent their lives here.

Cautiously Abil moved forward, deeper into the gloom. The air was warm and humid; his faceplate misted over.

Women, naked, nestled in shallow pits on the floor, in knots of ten or a dozen. Some of the pits were filled with milky water, and the women floated, relaxed. Attendants, young women and children, moved back and forth, carrying what looked like food and drink. In one corner there were infants, a carpet of them who crawled and toddled. Abil moved among them, a bloody pillar.

The women in the pits were all pregnant—*tremendously* pregnant, he saw, with immense bellies that must have held three, four, five infants. In one place, a woman was actually giving birth. She stood squat, supported by two helpers. A baby slid easily out from between her legs, to be caught, slapped, and cradled; but before its umbilical was cut another small head was protruding from the woman's vagina. She seemed in no pain; her expression was dreamy, abstract.

One of the breeder women looked up as he passed. She reached up a hand to him, the fingers long and feather-thin. Her limbs were etiolated, spindly; her legs could surely not have supported the weight of her immense, fecund torso. But her face was fully human.

On impulse, curious, he reached up and ran his thumbnail under his chin. His faceplate popped and swung upward. Dense air, moist and hot, pressed in on him.

The smells were extraordinary. He distinguished blood, and milk, and piss and shit, earthy human smells. There was a stink of burning that might have come from his own suit, a smell of vacuum, or of the battle he had waged in the corridors beyond this place.

And there was something else, something stronger still. Abil had never seen an animal larger than a rat. But that was how he labeled this smell: a stink like that of a huge rat's nest, pungent and overpowering.

He looked down at the woman who had reached up to him. Her face really was beautiful, he thought, narrow and delicate, with high cheekbones and large blue eyes. She smiled at him, showing a row of teeth that came to points. He felt warmed. He longed to speak to her.

An attendant leaned over her, a girl who might have been twelve. He thought the girl was kissing the pregnant woman. When the girl pulled away her jaws were opened wide, and a thin rope of some kind of paste, glistening faintly green, pulsed out of her throat, passing from her mouth into the breeder's. It was beautiful, Abil thought, overwhelmed; he had never seen such pure love as between this woman and the girl.

But he, in his clumsy, bloodstained suit, would forever be kept apart from this love. He felt tears well. He fell to his knees and reached forward with bloodstained gloves. The breeding woman screeched and thrashed backward. The attendant girl, regurgitated paste dribbling from her mouth, instantly hurled herself at him. She caught him off-balance. He fell back, and his head cracked on the ground. He struggled to get up. He had to get back to the mother, to explain.

There was an arm around his throat—a suited arm. He

struggled, but his lungs were aching. He heard Denh's voice call: "Kill the breeders. Move it!" A gloved hand passed before Abil's face, closing his faceplate, shutting out the noise of babies crying, and through its murky pane he saw fire flare once more.

The captain sat on the edge of Abil's sick bay bed. "Denh is acting corporal for now," Dower said gently.

Abil sighed. "It's no more than I deserved, sir."

Dower shook her head. "That damn curiosity of yours. You certainly made a mistake, but hardly a fatal one. But you weren't adequately briefed. In a way the fault's mine. I argue with the Commissaries before every drop. They would tell you grunts nothing if they had the chance, I think, for they believe nobody but them *needs* to know anything."

"What happened to me, sir?"

"Pheromones."

"Sir?"

"There are many ways to communicate, tar. Such as by scent. You and I are poor at smelling, you know, compared to our senses of touch, sight, hearing. We can distinguish only a few scent qualities: sweet, fetid, sour, musky, dry . . . But those Coalescent drones have been stuck in their hole in the ground for *fifteen thousand years*. Now, the human species itself is only four or five times older than that. There has been plenty of time for evolutionary divergence."

"And when I cracked my faceplate—"

"You were overwhelmed with messages you couldn't untangle." Dower leaned closer. "What was it like?"

Abil thought back. "I wanted to stay there, sir. To be with them. To be *like* them." He shuddered. "I let you down."

"There's no shame, tar. I don't think you're going to make a corporal, though; command isn't for you." Dower's metal Eyes glistened. "You weren't betrayed by fear. You were betrayed by your curiosity—perhaps imagination. You had to *know* what it was like in there, didn't you? And for that you risked your life, and the lives of your unit."

Abil tried to sit up. "Sir, I—"

"Take it easy." Dower pushed him back, gently, to his bed. "I told you, there's no shame. I've been watching you. It's one of the responsibilities of command, tar. You have to test those under you, all the time, test and assess. Because the only way the Expansion is going to prosper is if we make the best use of our resources. And I don't believe the best use of *you* is to stick you down a hole in charge of a bunch of grunts." Dower leaned closer. "Have you ever considered working for the Commission for Historical Truth?"

A vision of chill intellects and severe black robes filled Abil's mind. "The Commission, sir? *Me?*"

Dower laughed. "Just think about it . . . Ah. We're about to leave orbit."

Abil could sense the subtle inertial shift, as if he was in a huge elevator, rising from the frozen planet.

Dower snapped her fingers, and a Virtual of the Target materialized between their faces. Slowly turning, bathed in simulated light, the planet was like a toy, sparkling white, laced here and there by black ridges of true rock, stubborn mountain chains resisting the ice. Starships circled it like flies.

Dower reached out to touch one dimpled feature.

The view expanded, to reveal a broad, walled plain. Abil realized he was looking down on the warren he had visited. Around the mountain peak, great cracks had been cut into the ground. Drones were being shepherded out of the warren by the mop-up squads. The drones filed toward the bellies of freighters that had settled from space, down onto the ice, to swallow them up. The drones looked bewildered, and they milled to and fro. Here and there one or two broke lines, and even lunged at the troopers. The silent spark of weapons cut them down.

For every live drone that came walking to the surface, Abil saw, a dozen carcasses were hauled out.

Dower saw his expression. "There were probably a billion drones in that one hive alone. A *billion*. We'll be lucky to ship out more than a hundred thousand."

"A hundred thousand—is that *all*, sir?"

"The waste is terrible—yes, I know. But what does it matter? They were a billion purposeless lives, the culmination of a thousand pointless generations. And look here."

She tapped at the floating image. The deep-buried colony turned red, showing as a clear torus shape around the ice-buried mountain. And when the viewpoint pulled back, Abil saw that there were many more such red blotches scarring the planet's white face, from pole to pole, around the equator.

"There are about a thousand warrens on this one planet," Dower murmured. "Probably most of them unaware of each other. We probably won't even be able to clean them all out. I've seen this before, many times, on worlds as different from this, tar, as you can imagine—but all warrens are essentially the same. Anywhere where the living is marginal, where people are crowded in on each other, out pops the eusocial solution, over and over. I think it's a flaw in our mental processing."

In one place two of the colonies were in contact; tendrils of pale pink reached out from their red cores, and where they touched, crimson flared. Dower spoke a soft command. The simulated image's time scale accelerated, so that days, weeks passed in seconds. Abil could see how the two colonies probed toward each other, over and again, and where they came in contact crimson flared—a crimson, he realized, that showed where people were dying.

"They're fighting," he said. "It's almost as if the colonies are living things themselves, sir."

"Well, so they are," Dower said.

"But—a thousand of them. That makes um, a *trillion* people on this light-starved planet alone—all living off the scrapings from the thermal vents . . ."

"Makes you think, doesn't it? Oh, the Coalescents are efficient. But they *are* just drones. *We* own history." She waved her hands and produced a new image, a star field, crossed by a great river of light. She pointed to the Galaxy core. "Leave the Coalescents to their holes in the ground. That is where *we* are going, tar; that is where our destiny will be made—or broken."

When she had gone Abil restored the image of the slowly turning globe, its white surface pustulous with warrens.

There were no cities here, he thought, no nations. There were only the Coalescent colonies. The huge entities waged their slow and silent battles against each other, shaping and spending the lives of their human drones—drones who may have believed they were free and happy—and all without consciousness or pity. On this world the story of humankind was over, he thought. On this world, the future belonged to the hives.

But there were other worlds.

The starship leapt away with an almost imperceptible lurch. The frozen world folded over on itself and dropped into darkness.

chapter 52

One of my favorite walks is quite short. You follow the stair-cases cut into the rock, and pass through alleyways and under archways, and between the tottering houses that lean so close they almost touch. After only a few minutes, you can clamber all the way from Amalfi to Atrani, a tiny medieval town that nestles in the next bay along this indented coastline.

In the central piazza of Atrani there is an open-air café where you can sip coffee or Coke and watch the sun slide over the looming volcanic hills. It's peaceful enough, so long as you avoid the times when the schoolchildren flood through the square, or the early evenings when young men pose for the girls on their gleaming scooters and motorbikes.

Yesterday—it was a Sunday—I made the mistake of sitting there at noon. All was peaceful, just a few churchgoers, every-body remarkably smartly dressed as they strolled through the square, talking in that intense, very physical way the Italians have. The waiter had just brought me my coffee.

And somebody set off a cannon. I jumped out of my seat, my heart pounding. The waiter didn't spill a drop.

The shot turned out to be from a church set high on the hill-side, where the clergy celebrate each Sabbath with a little pyrotechnics. But in the square of Atrani the noise was deaf-ening.

It is *never* quiet in Italy.

I know I can't hide out here forever. Some time soon I'll have to reconnect with the real world.

For one thing my money won't last forever. There has been a stock market crash.

It was actually quite predictable. There's an analysis that dates back to the Great Depression that has detected cycles, called Elliott waves, in the various economic ups and downs. Why do these simple analyses work? Because they are models of the human herd instinct. The traders on the stock exchange floor don't make rational decisions based on such factors as the intrinsic value of a stock. They just see what their neighbors are doing, and copy them. Just like the rest of us.

Predictable or not, the crash has wiped out a chunk of my savings. So I must move on.

I intend to finish this account, and then . . . Well, I don't quite know what to do with it, save to send it to Claudio at the Vatican Archives. It seems right that it should be preserved. If Rosa ever gets in touch again, she will get a copy, too.

I think I should pay another visit to my sister Gina in Miami Beach. She should know what became of Rosa—she's her sister, too, whether she likes it or not. And perhaps Great-Uncle Lou will enjoy hearing of the fate of Maria Ludovica, the *mamma-nonna*, who was still producing babies like popping peas from a pod at the age of a hundred.

As for me, after that, I will go home, back to Britain. Maybe not to London, though. Somewhere without the crowds. I need a job, but I want to go freelance. I can't bear the thought of becoming enmeshed in another huge organization, a great press of people all around me.

I think I'll look up Linda. I haven't forgotten how my instinct, in those dreadful moments in the depths of the Crypt, was to turn to her memory for support. One way or another she's been there for me since we met. There's a lot to build on.

Unlike Peter, I refuse to believe the future is fixed.

I hope one day to put all this behind me. But sometimes I am overwhelmed. If I am in a crowd, sometimes I will detect a whiff of that leonine animal musk of the Coalescents, and I have to retreat to my room, or the fresh air of the empty hills above the towns. I will never be free of it. And yet a part of me, I know, will always long to be immersed again in that dense warmth, to be surrounded by smiling faces like mirrors of my own, to give myself up to the mindless, loving joy of the hive.

Don't miss the captivating sequel, *Exultant,*
coming in November 2004 from Del Rey books!

Far ahead, bathed in the light of the Galaxy's center, the
nightfighters were rising.

From his station, Pirius could see their black forms peel-
ing off the walls of their Sugar Lump carriers. They spread
graceful wings, so black they looked as if they had been cut
out of the glowing background of the Core. Some of them
were kilometers across. They were Xeelee nightfighters, but
nobody in Strike Arm called them anything but flies.

They converged on the lead human ships, and Pirius saw
cherry-red light flaring.

His fragile greenship hovered over the textured ground of
a Rock. The Rock was an asteroid, a dozen kilometers across,
charcoal gray. Trenches had been dug all over its surface, in-
terconnecting and intersecting, so that the Rock looked like
an exposed brain. Sparks of light crawled through those complex lines: soldiers, infantry, endlessly digging, digging, digging, preparing for their own collisions with destiny. It was a
good hour yet before this Rock and Pirius's own greenship
would reach the battlefield, but already men and women
were fighting and dying.

There was nothing to do but watch, and brood. There wasn't
even a sense of motion. Under the *Assimilator's Claw*'s pulsing sublight drive it was as if he were floating, here in the
crowded heart of the Galaxy. Pirius worried about the effect
of the wait on his crew.

Pirius was nineteen years old.

He was deep in the Mass, as pilots called it—the Central
Star Mass, officially, a jungle of millions of stars crammed
into a ball just thirty light-years across, a core within the
Core. Before him a veil of stars hung before a background of
turbulent, glowing gas; he could see filaments and wisps
light-years long, drawn out by the Galaxy's magnetic field.
This stellar turmoil bubbled and boiled on scales of space
and time beyond the human, as if he had been caught at the
center of a frozen explosion. The sky was *bright,* crowded
with stars and clouds, not a trace of darkness anywhere.

And through the stars he made out the Cavity, a central bubble blown clear of gas by astrophysical violence, and within *that* the Baby Spiral, a swirl of stars and molecular clouds, like a toy version of the Galaxy itself embedded fractally in the greater disc. *That* was the center of the Galaxy, a place of layered astrophysical machinery. And it was all driven by Chandra, the brooding black hole at the Galaxy's very heart.

This crowded immensity would have stunned a native of Earth—but Earth, with its patient, long-lived sun, out in the orderly stellar factory of the spiral arms, was twenty-eight thousand light-years from here. But Pirius had grown up with such visions. He was the product of a hundred generations grown in the birthing tanks of Arches Base, formally known as Base 2594, just a few light-years outside the Mass. He was human, though, with human instincts. And as he peered out at the stretching three-dimensional complexity around him he gripped the scuffed material of his seat, as if he might fall.

Everywhere Pirius looked, across this astrophysical diorama, he saw signs of war.

Pirius's ship was one of a hundred green sparks, ten whole squadrons, assigned to escort this single Rock alone. When Pirius looked up he could see more Rocks, a whole stream of them hurled in from the giant human bases that had been established around the Mass. Each of them was accompanied by its own swarm of greenships. Upstream and down, the chain of Rocks receded until kilometers-wide worldlets were reduced to pebbles lost in the glare. Hundreds of Rocks, thousands perhaps, had been committed to this one assault. It was a titanic sight, a mighty projection of human power.

But all this was dwarfed by the enemy. The Rock stream was directed at a fleet of Sugar Lumps, as those Xeelee craft were called, immense cubical ships that were themselves hundreds of kilometers across—some even bigger, some like boxes that could wrap up a whole world.

The tactic was crude. The Rocks were simply hosed in towards the Sugar Lumps, their defenders striving to protect them long enough for them to get close to the Lumps, whereupon their mighty monopole cannons would be deployed. If all went well, damage would be inflicted on the Xeelee, and the Rocks would slingshot around a suitable stellar mass and be hurled back out to the periphery, to be reequipped, re-manned, and prepared for another onslaught. If all did not go well—in that case, duty would have been done.

As the *Claw* relentlessly approached the zone of flaring action, one ship dipped out of formation, swooping down over the Rock in a series of barrel rolls. That must be Dans, one of Pirius's cadre siblings. Pirius had flown with her twice before, and each time she had shown off, demonstrating to the toiling ground troops the effortless superiority of Strike Arm, and of the Arches squadrons in particular—and in the process lifting everybody's spirits.

But it was a tiny human gesture lost in a monumental panorama.

Pirius could see his crew, in their own blisters: his navigator Cohl, a slim woman of eighteen, and his engineer, Enduring Hope, a calm, bulky young man who looked older than his years, just seventeen. While Cohl and Hope were both rookies, nineteen-year-old Pirius was a comparative veteran. Among greenship crews, the mean survival rate was one point seven missions. This was Pirius's fifth mission. He was growing a reputation as a lucky pilot, a man whose crew you wanted to be on.

"Hey," he called now. "I know how you're feeling. They always say this is the worst part of combat, the ninety-nine per cent of it that's just waiting around, the sheer bloody boredom. I should know."

Enduring Hope looked across and waved. "And if I want to throw up, lift the visor first. That's the drill, isn't it?"

Pirius forced a laugh. Not a good joke, but a joke.

Enduring Hope: defying all sorts of rules, the engineer called himself not by his properly assigned name, a random sequence of letters and syllables, but an ideological slogan. He was a Friend, as he styled it, a member of a thoroughly illegal sect that flourished in the darker corners of Arches Base, and, it was said, right across the Front, the great sphere of conflict that surrounded the Galaxy's heart. Illegal or not, right now, as the flies rose up and people started visibly to die, Hope's faith seemed to be comforting him.

But navigator Cohl, staring ahead at the combat zone, was closed in on herself.

The *Claw* was a greenship, a simple design that was the workhorse of Strike Arm; millions like it were in action all around the war zone. Its main body was a bulbous pod containing most of the ship's systems: the weapons banks, the FTL drive and two sublight drive systems. From the front of the hull projected three spars, giving the ship the look of a three-pronged claw, and at the tip of each prong was a blister, a clear bubble, containing one of the *Claw*'s three crew. For greenship crews, nobody else mattered but each other; it was just three of them lost in a dangerous sky—*Three Against the Foe,* as Strike Arm's motto went.

Pirius knew there were good reasons for the trifurcated design of the greenship. It was all to do with redundancy: the ship could lose two of its three blisters and still, in theory anyhow, fulfil its goals. But right now Pirius longed to be able to reach through these transparent walls, to touch his crewmates.

He said, "Navigator? You still with us?"

He saw Cohl glance across at him. "Trajectory's nominal, pilot."

"I wasn't asking her about the trajectory."

Cohl shrugged, as if resentfully. "What do you want me to say?"

"You saw all this in the briefing. You knew it was coming."

It was true. The whole operation had been previewed for them by the Commissaries, in full Virtual detail, down to the timetabled second. It wasn't a prediction, not just a guess, but foreknowledge: a forecast based on data that had actually leaked from the future. The officers hoped to deaden fear by making the events of the engagement familiar before it happened. But not everybody took comfort from the notion of a predetermined destiny.

Cohl was staring out through her blister wall, her lips drawn back in a cold, humorless smile. "I feel like I'm in a dream," she murmured. "A waking dream."

"It isn't set in stone," Pirius said. "The future."

"But the Commissaries—"

"No Commissary ever set foot in a greenship—none of

them is skinny enough. It isn't real until it happens. And *now* is when it happens. It's in our hands, Cohl. It's in yours. I know you'll do your duty."

"And kick ass," Enduring Hope shouted.

He saw Cohl grin at last. "Yes, *sir*!"

A green flash distracted Pirius. A ship was hurtling out of formation. One of its three struts was a stump, the blister missing. As it sailed by, Pirius recognised the gaudy, spruced-up tetrahedral sigil on its side. It was Dans's ship.

He called, "Dans? What—"

"Predestination my ass," Dans yelled on the ship-to-ship line. "Nobody saw *that* coming."

"Saw what?"

"See for yourself."

Pirius swept the crowded sky, letting Virtual feeds pour three-dimensional battlefield data into his head.

In the seconds he'd spent on his crew, everything had changed. The Xeelee hadn't stayed restricted to their source Sugar Lumps. A swarm of them speared down from above his head, from out of nowhere, heading straight for Pirius's Rock.

Pirius hadn't seen it. Sloppy, Pirius. One mistake is enough to kill you.

"This wasn't supposed to happen," Cohl said.

"Forget the projections," Pirius snapped.

There were seconds left before the flies hit the Rock. He saw swarming activity in its runs and trenches. The poor souls down there knew what was coming, too. Pirius gripped his controls, and tried to ignore the beating of his heart.

Four, three, two.

The Xeelee—pronounced *Zee-lee*—were mankind's most ancient and most powerful foe.

According to the scuttlebutt on Arches Base, in the training compounds and the vast open barracks, there were only three things you needed to know about the Xeelee.

First, their ships were better than ours. You only had to see a fly in action to realize that. Some said the Xeelee *were* their ships, which probably made them even tougher.

Second, they were smarter than us, and had a lot more resources. Xeelee operations were believed to be resourced and controlled from Chandra itself, the fat black hole at the Galaxy's very center. In fact, military planners called Chandra, a supermassive black hole, the Prime Radiant of the Xeelee. How could anything we had compete with *that*?

And third, the Xeelee knew what we would do even before we decided ourselves.

This interstellar war was fought with faster-than-light technology, on both sides. But if you flew FTL you broke the bounds of causality: an FTL ship was a time machine. And so this was a time-travel war, in which information about the future constantly leaked into the past.

But the information was never perfect. And every now and again, one side or the other was able to spring a surprise. This new maneuver of the Xeelee had *not* been in the Commissaries' careful projections.

Pirius felt his lips draw back in a fierce grin. The script had been abandoned. Today, everything really was up for grabs.

But now cherry-red light flared all around the Rock's ragged horizon.

On the loops, orders chattered from the squadron leaders. "Hold your positions. This is a new tactic and we're still trying to analyze it." "Number eight, hold your place. *Hold your place.*"

Pirius gripped his controls so tight his fingers ached.

That red glare was spreading all around the Rock's lumpy profile, a malevolent dawn. Most of the action was taking place on the far side of the Rock from his position—which was itself most unlike the Xeelee, who were usually apt to come swarming all over any Rock they attacked.

The *Claw* would be sheltered from the assault, for the first moments, anyhow. That meant Pirius was in the wrong place. He wasn't here to hide, but to fight. But he had to hold his station, until ordered otherwise.

Pirius glimpsed a fly standing off from the target. It spread night-dark wings—said to be not material but flaws in the structure of space itself—and extended a cherry-red starbreaker beam. The clean geometry of these lethal lines had a certain cold beauty, Pirius thought, even though he knew what hell was being unleashed for those unlucky enough to be caught on the exposed surface of the Rock.

Now, though, the rectilinear perfection of the starbreaker beam was blurred, as a turbulent fog rose over the Rock's horizon.

Cohl said, "What's that mist? Air? Maybe the starbreakers are cutting through to the sealed caverns."

"I don't think so," said Enduring Hope levelly. "That's rock. A mist of molten rock. They are smashing the asteroid to gas."

Molten rock, Pirius thought grimly, no doubt laced with traces of what had recently been complex organic compounds, thoroughly burned.

But still, for all the devastation they were wreaking, the Xeelee weren't coming around the horizon. They were focussing all their firepower on one side of the Rock.

Still Pirius waited for orders, but the tactical analysis took too long. Suddenly, human ships came fleeing around the curve of the Rock, sparks of Earth green bright against the dull gray of the asteroid ground. The formation had collapsed, then, despite the squadron leaders' continuing bellowed commands. And down on the Rock those little flecks of light, each a human being trapped in lethal fire, swarmed and scattered, fanning out of the trench system and over the open ground. Even from here, it looked like panic, a rout.

It got worse. All across the Rock's visible hemisphere implosions began, as if its surface was being bombarded by unseen meteorites. But the floors of these evanescent craters broke up and collapsed, and through a mist of gray dust a deeper glow was revealed, coming up from *inside* the Rock. It was as if the surface were dissolving, and pink-white light was burning its way out of this shell of stone. The Xeelee, Pirius thought: the Xeelee were burning their way right through the Rock itself.

Enduring Hope understood what was happening half a second before Pirius did. "Lethe," he said. "Get us out of here, pilot. Lift, lift!"

Cohl said weakly, "But our orders—"

But Pirius was already hauling on his controls. All around him ships were breaking from the line and pulling back.

Even as the Rock fell away, Pirius could see the endgame approaching. For a last, remarkable, instant, the Rock held together, and that inner light picked out the complex tracery of the trench network, as if the face of the Rock was covered by a map of shining threads. The asteroid's uneven horizon lifted, bulging.

And then the Rock flew apart.

Suddenly the *Claw* was surrounded by a hail of white-hot fragments that rushed upward all around it. The greenship threw itself around every axis to survive this deadly inverted storm. The motions were rapid, juddery, disconcerting; even cloaked by inertial shields, Pirius could feel a ghost of his craft's jerky motion, deep in his bones.

Everybody on the Rock must already be dead, he thought, as the ship tried to save him. It was a terrible, monstrous, thought, impossible to absorb. And the dying wasn't over yet.

Pirius's squadron leader called for discipline, for her crews to try to regroup, to take the fight to the enemy. But then she was cut off.

Cohl shrieked, "*Flies!* Here they come—"

Pirius saw them: a swarm of flies, rising out of the core of the shattered rock like insects from a corpse, their black-as-night wings unfolding. They had burned their way right through the heart of an asteroid. Some greenships were already throwing themselves back into the Xeelee fire. But the Xeelee deployed their starbreaker beams; those lethal tongues almost lovingly touched the fleeing greenships.

Pirius had no meaningful orders. So he ran. The *Claw* raced from the ruin of the Rock. The cloud of debris thinned, and the jittery motion of the *Claw* subsided. But when Pirius looked back he saw a solid black bank, a phalanx of Xeelee nightfighters.

He had no idea where he was running to, how he might evade the Xeelee. He ran anyhow.

And the Xeelee came after him.

**If you liked *Coalescent*,
you won't want to miss
Stephen Baxter's collaboration
with Sir Arthur C. Clarke,
Time's Eye.**

For eons, Earth has been under observation by the Firstborn, beings almost as old as the universe itself. The Firstborn are unknown to humankind—until they act. In an instant, Earth is carved up and reassembled like a huge jigsaw puzzle. Suddenly the planet and every living thing on it no longer exist on a single time-line. Instead, the world becomes a patchwork of eras, from prehistory to 2037, each with its own indigenous inhabitants.

Scattered across the planet are mysterious floating orbs, impervious to all weapons. The answer to their existence may lie in the ancient city of Babylon, where two groups of refugees from 2037—three cosmonauts returning to Earth from the International Space Station and three United Nations peacekeepers on a mission in Afghanistan—have detected radio signals on the planet apart from their own. Each group allies itself with one of the two most fearsome and cunning leaders of all time: Genghis Khan and Alexander the Great. As the two armies face off before the gates of Babylon, the real power watches, waiting. . . .